BOUNCE BACK

by MISAKO ROCKS!

Feiwel and Friends

New York

A FEIWEL AND FRIENDS BOOK
An imprint of Macmillan Publishing Group, LLC
120 Broadway, New York, NY 10271
mackids.com

Library of Congress Control Number: 2021907139

First edition, 2021
Book design by Sharismar Rodriguez and Cindy De la Cruz

Feiwel and Friends logo designed by Filomena Tuosto
Printed in China by RR Donnelley Asia Printing Solutions Ltd.,
Dongguan City, Guangdong Province.

ISBN 978-1-250-76845-2 (hardcover)
10 9 8 7 6 5 4 3 2 1

ISBN 978-1-250-80629-1 (paperback)
10 9 8 7 6 5 4 3 2 1

This book is dedicated to any young person
out there who is struggling to find
their place in this world.

CHAPTER 1

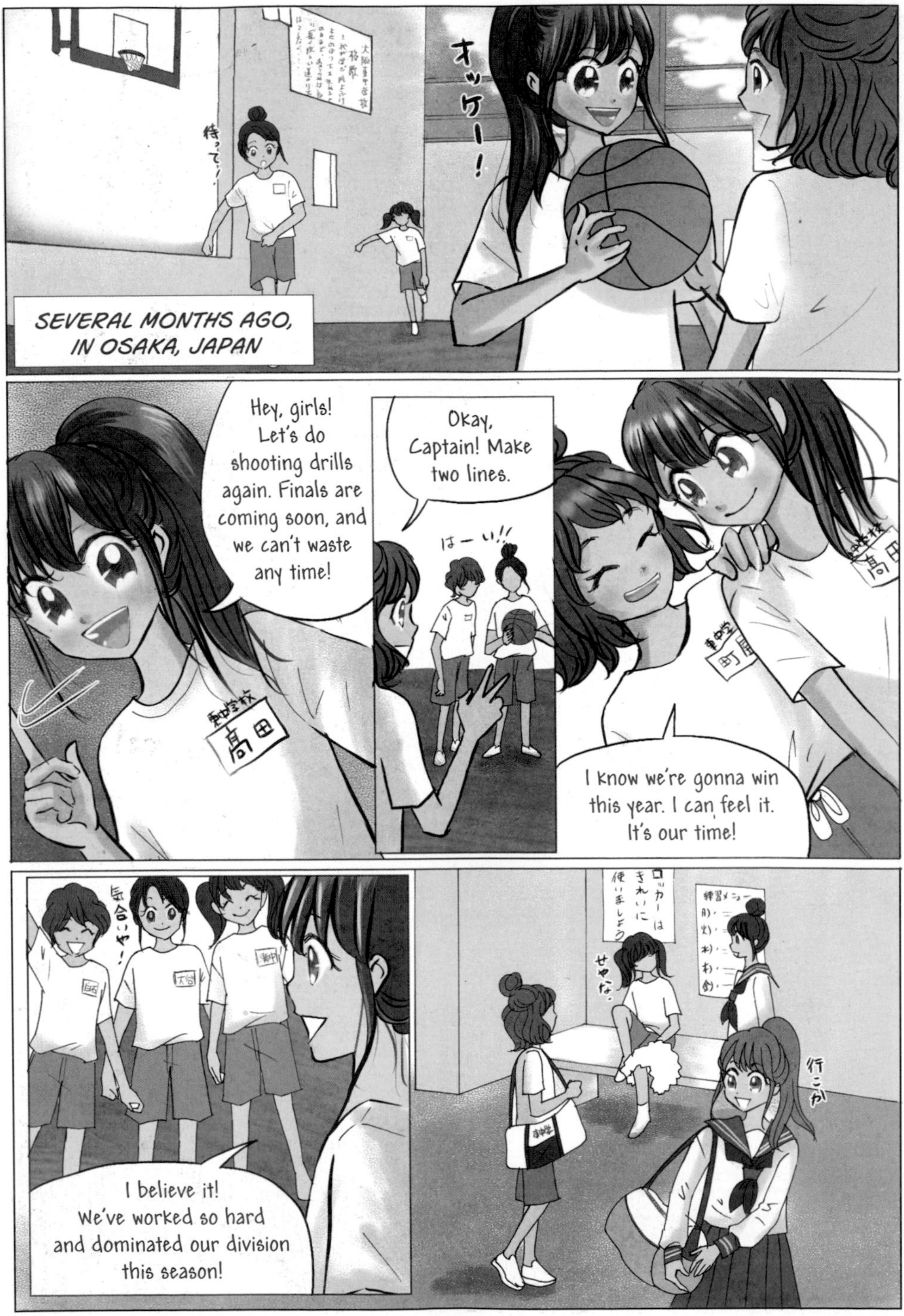

待って!
SEVERAL MONTHS AGO, IN OSAKA, JAPAN
オッケー!
Hey, girls! Let's do shooting drills again. Finals are coming soon, and we can't waste any time!
Okay, Captain! Make two lines.
はーい!!
I know we're gonna win this year. I can feel it. It's our time!
気合いや!
I believe it! We've worked so hard and dominated our division this season!
ロッカーはきれいに使いましょう
せやな。
行こか

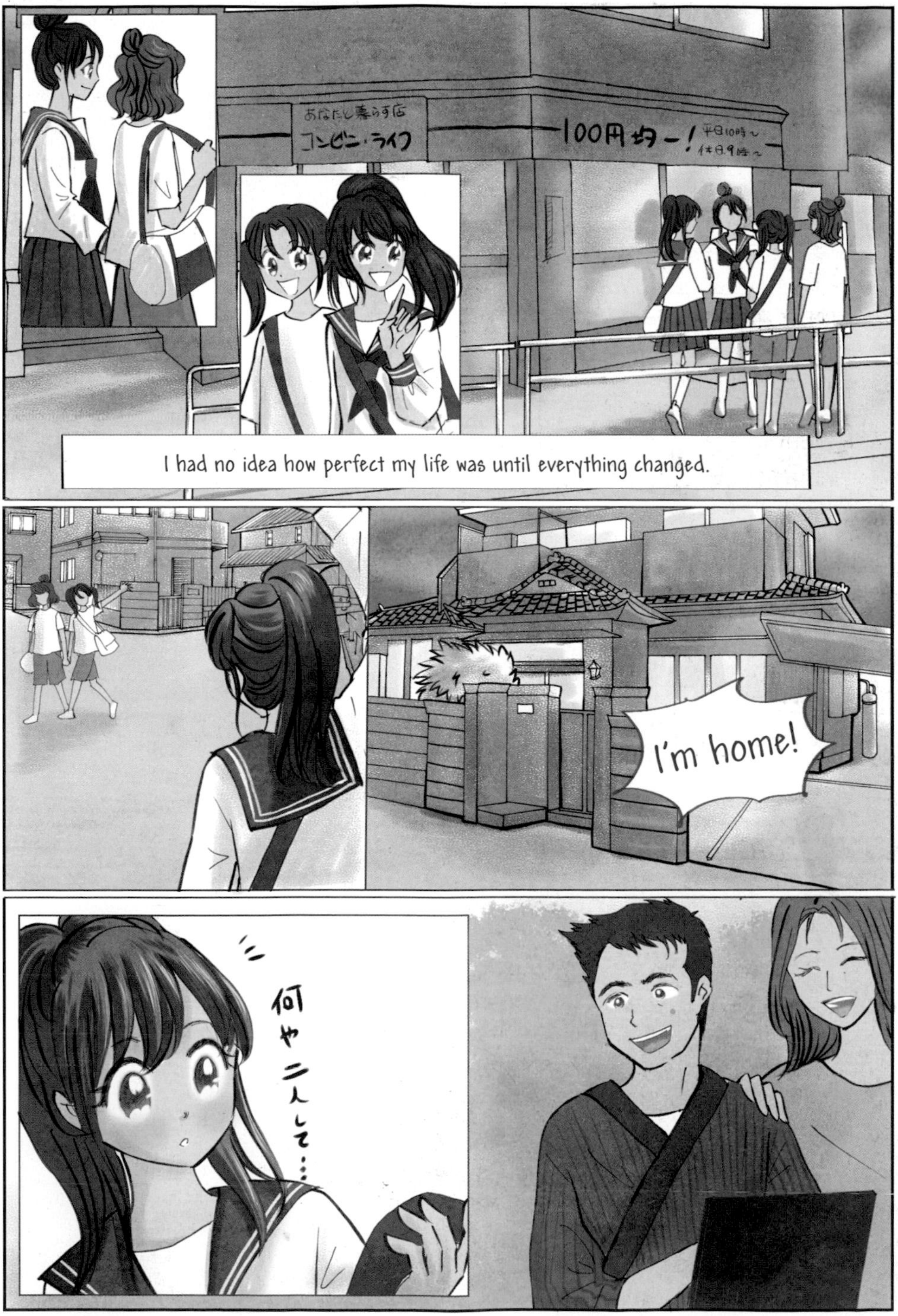
あなたと暮らす店
コンビニ・ライフ
100円均ー!
平日10時～
休日9時～
I had no idea how perfect my life was until everything changed.
I'm home!
何やニ人して…

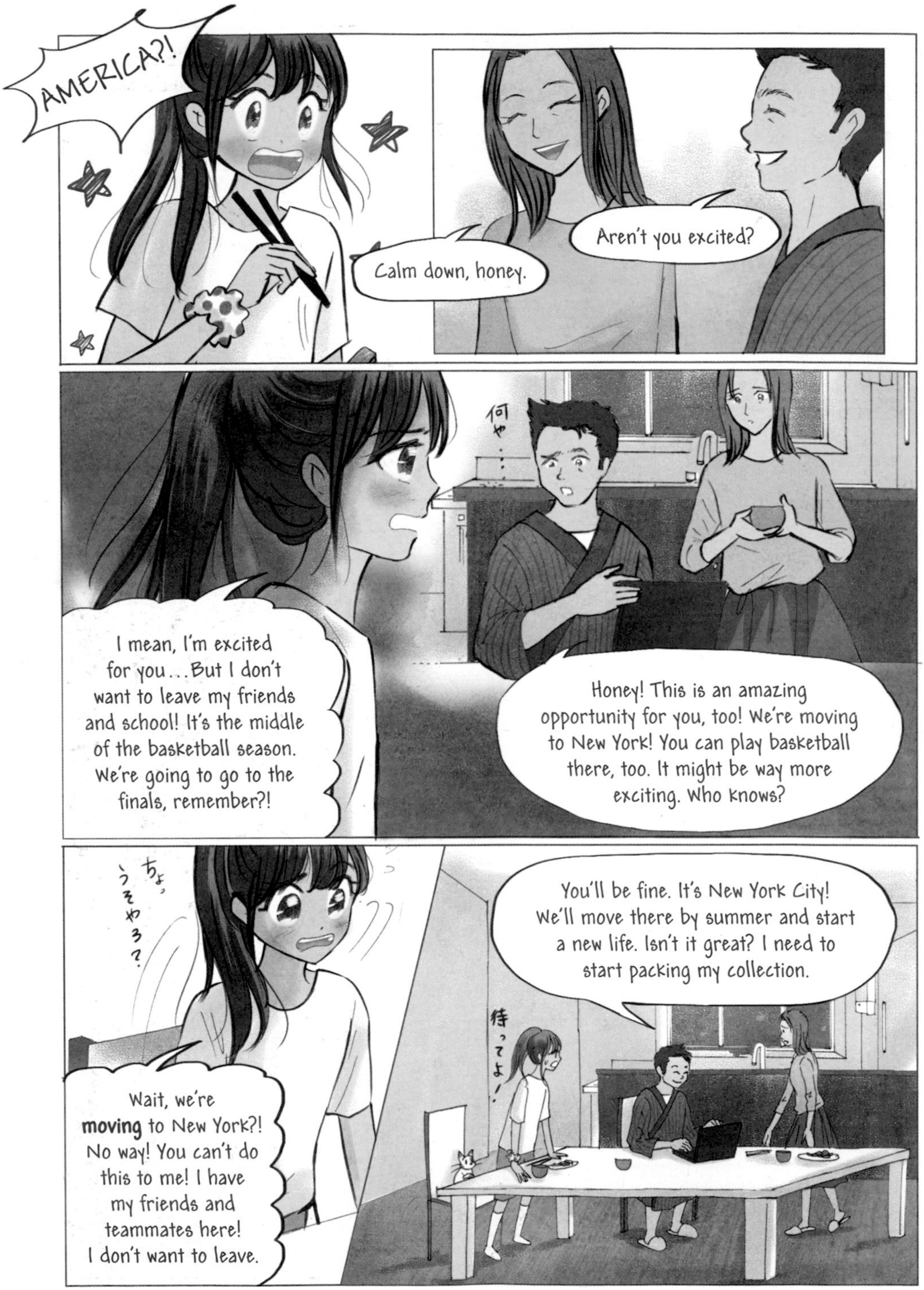
AMERICA?!
Calm down, honey.
Aren't you excited?
I mean, I'm excited for you...But I don't want to leave my friends and school! It's the middle of the basketball season. We're going to go to the finals, remember?!
何や……
Honey! This is an amazing opportunity for you, too! We're moving to New York! You can play basketball there, too. It might be way more exciting. Who knows?
ちょ、うそやろ？
Wait, we're **moving** to New York?! No way! You can't do this to me! I have my friends and teammates here! I don't want to leave.
You'll be fine. It's New York City! We'll move there by summer and start a new life. Isn't it great? I need to start packing my collection.
待ってよ！

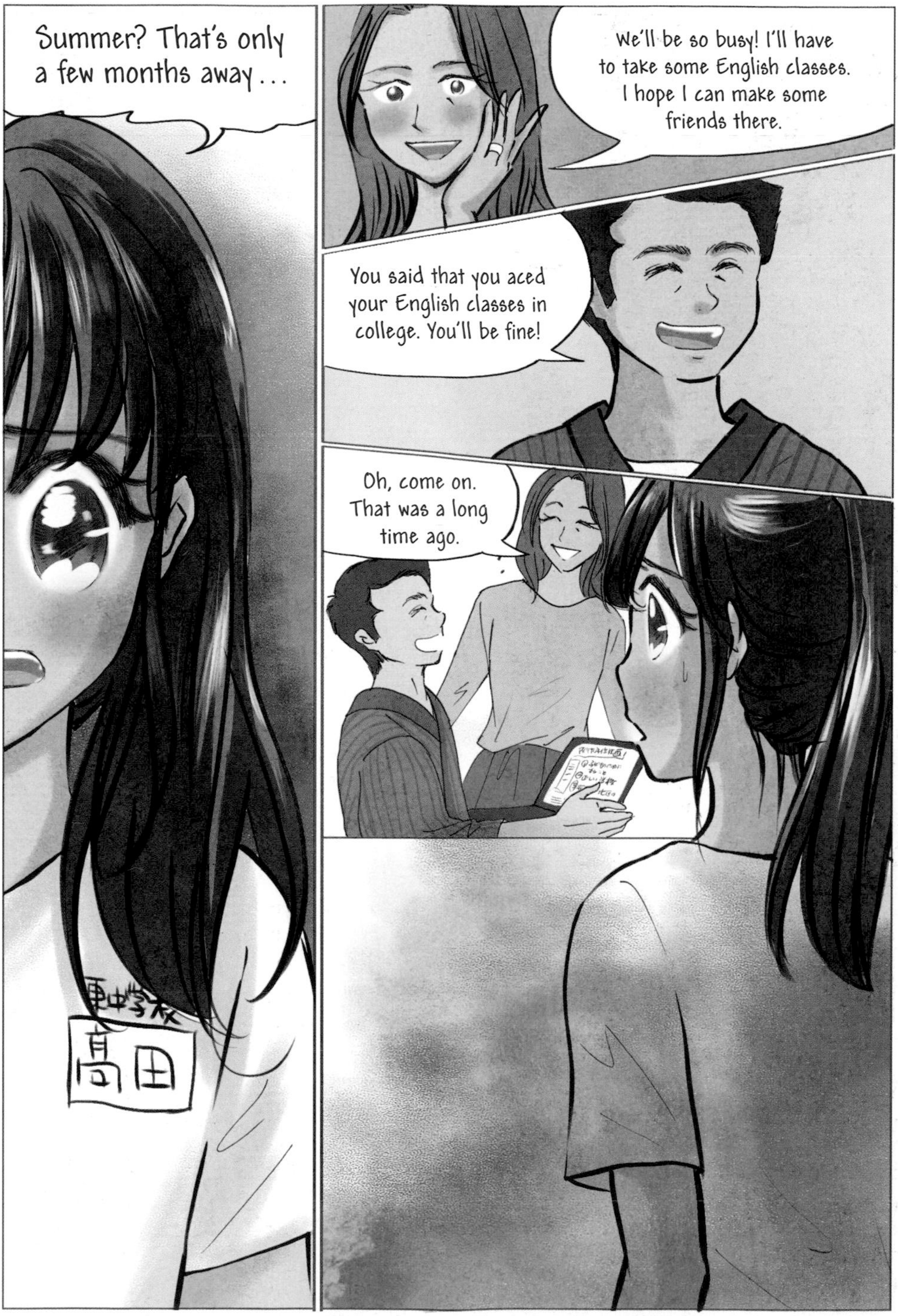
Summer? That's only a few months away...
中学校
高田
We'll be so busy! I'll have to take some English classes. I hope I can make some friends there.
You said that you aced your English classes in college. You'll be fine!
Oh, come on. That was a long time ago.

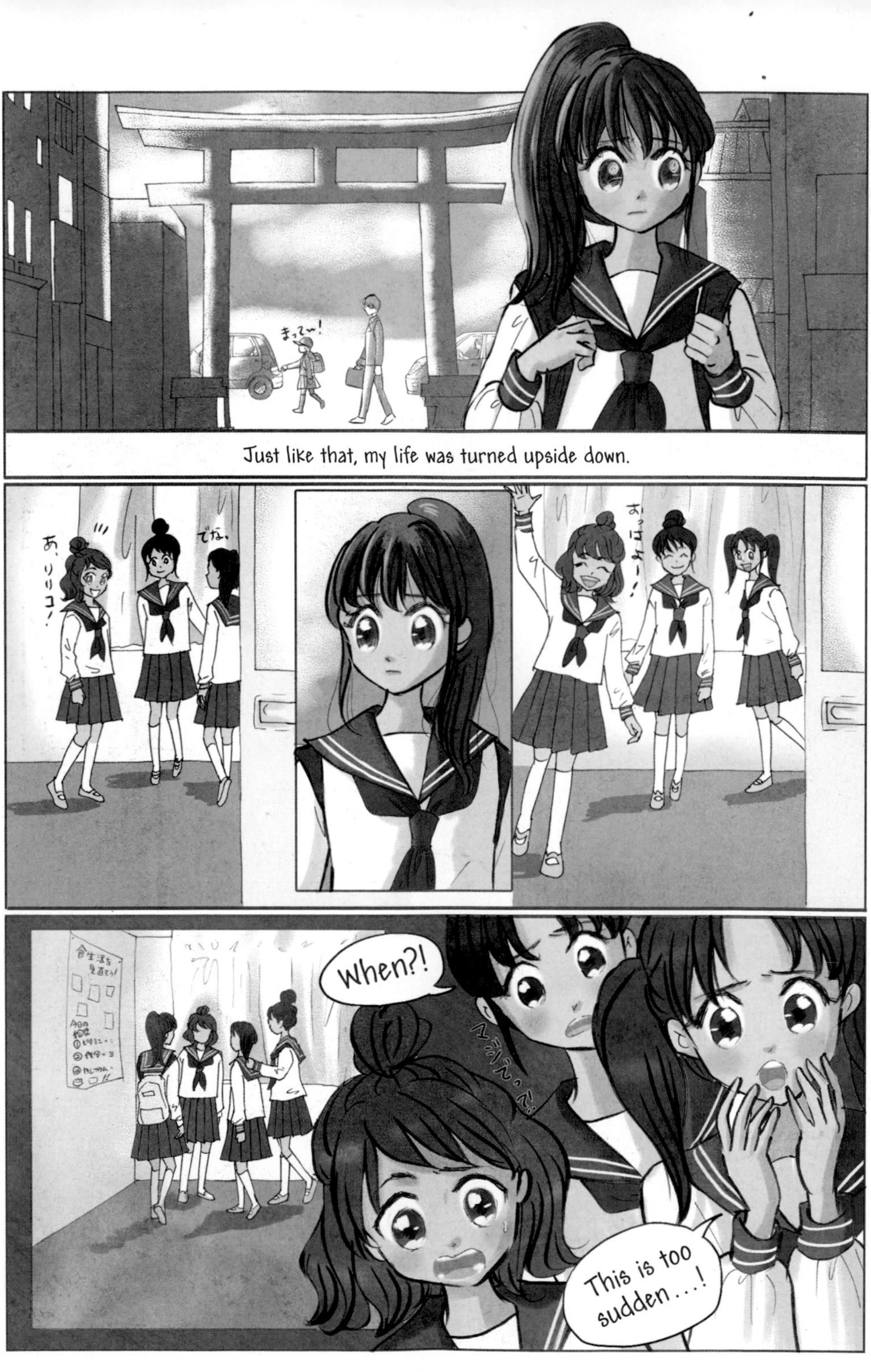
Just like that, my life was turned upside down.
When?!
This is too sudden...!

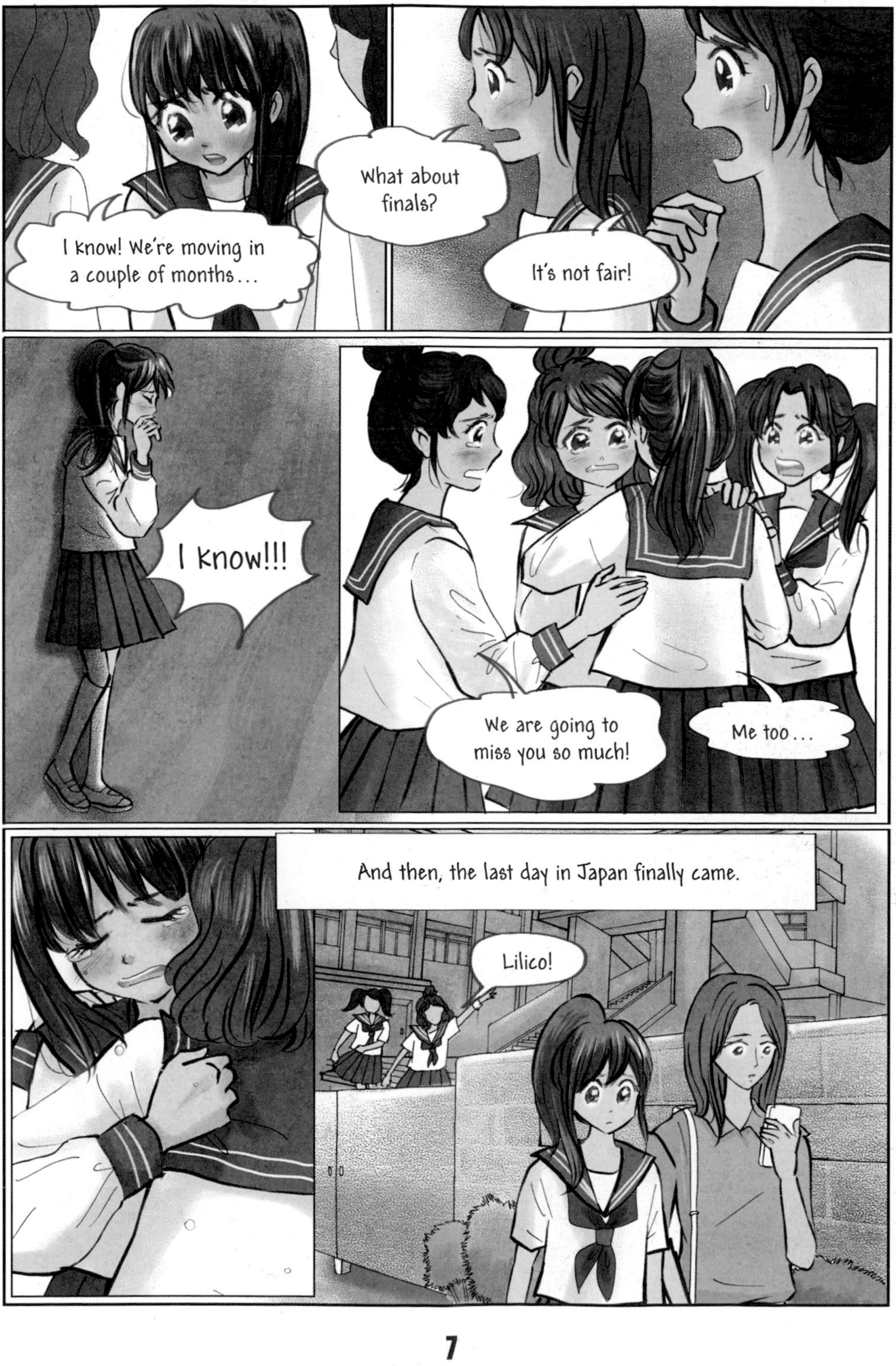
I know! We're moving in a couple of months...
What about finals?
It's not fair!
I know!!!
We are going to miss you so much!
Me too...
And then, the last day in Japan finally came.
Lilico!

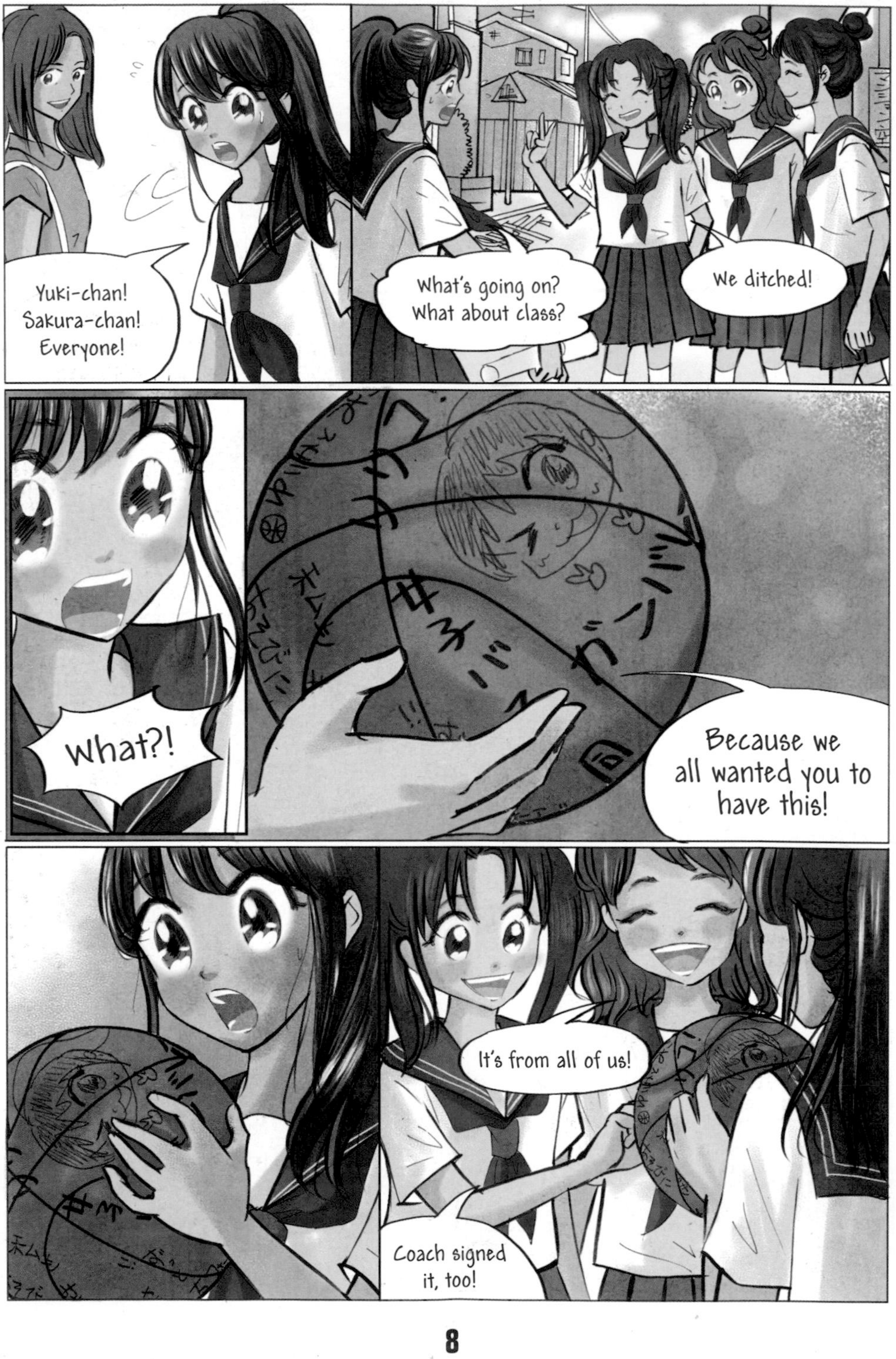
Yuki-chan! Sakura-chan! Everyone!
What's going on? What about class?
We ditched!
What?!
Because we all wanted you to have this!
It's from all of us!
Coach signed it, too!

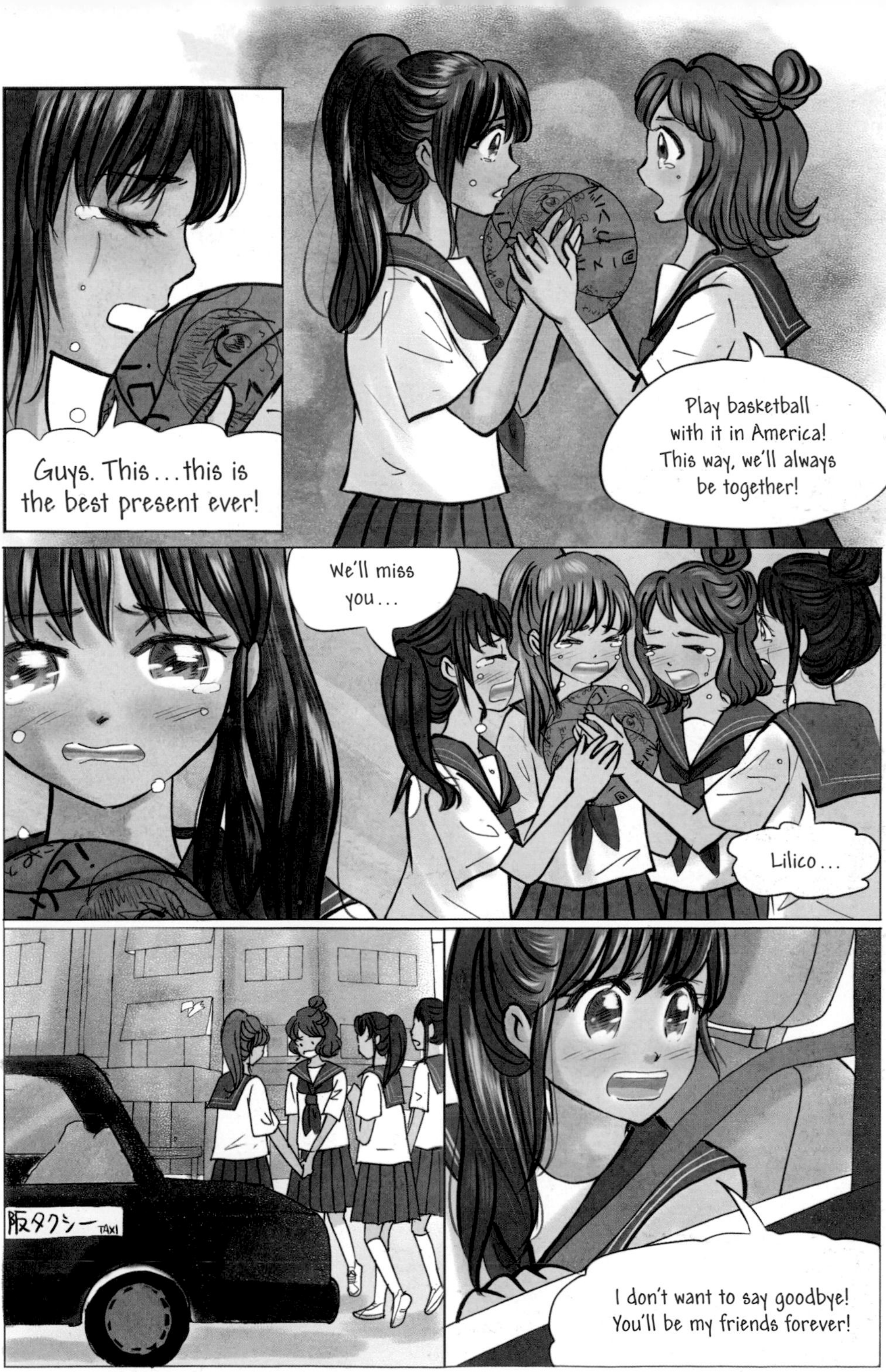
Guys. This . . . this is the best present ever!
Play basketball with it in America! This way, we'll always be together!
We'll miss you . . .
Lilico . . .
阪タクシー TAXI
I don't want to say goodbye! You'll be my friends forever!

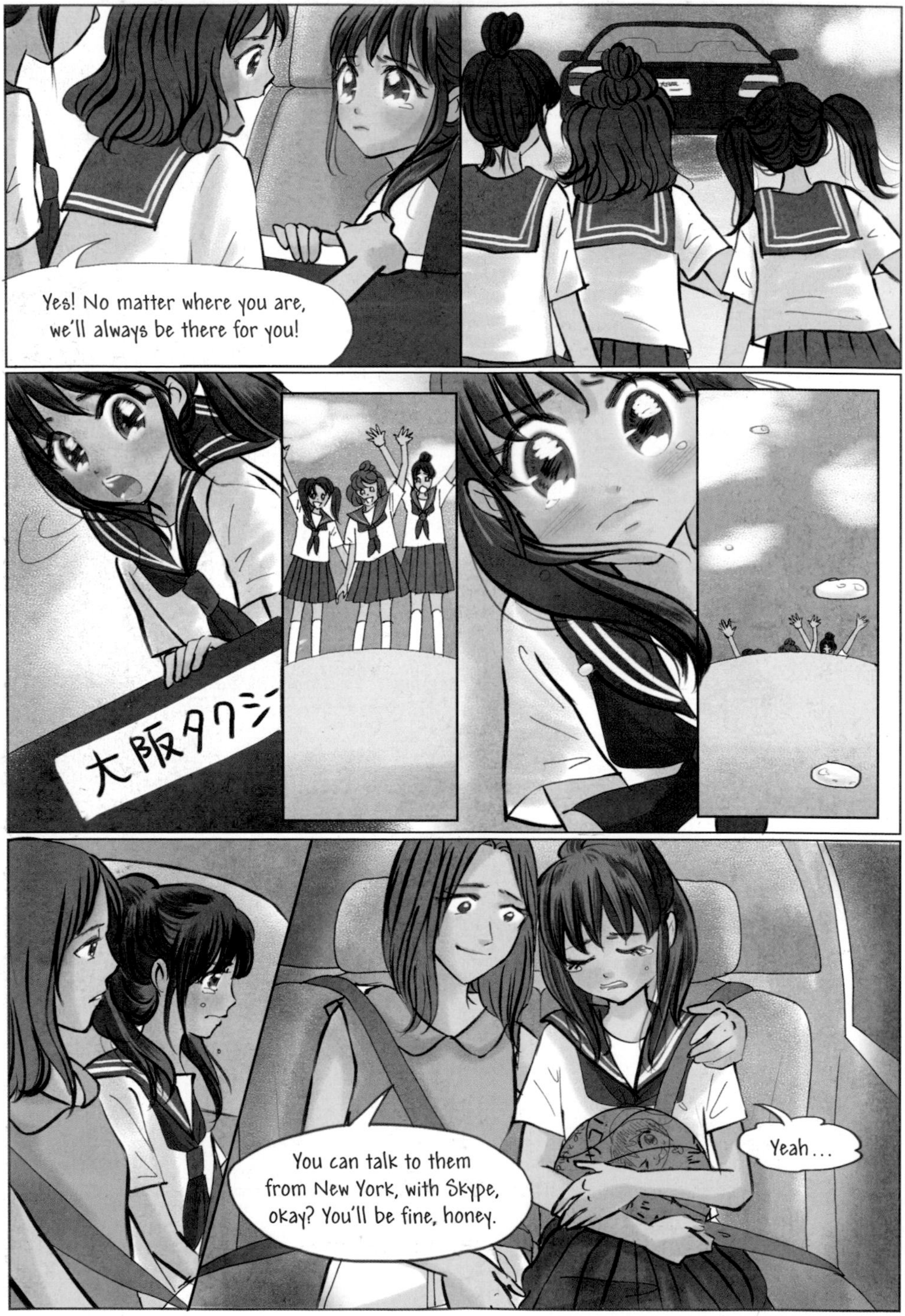
Yes! No matter where you are, we'll always be there for you!
大阪タクシ
You can talk to them from New York, with Skype, okay? You'll be fine, honey.
Yeah...

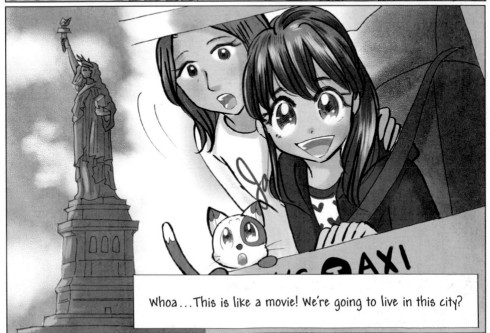

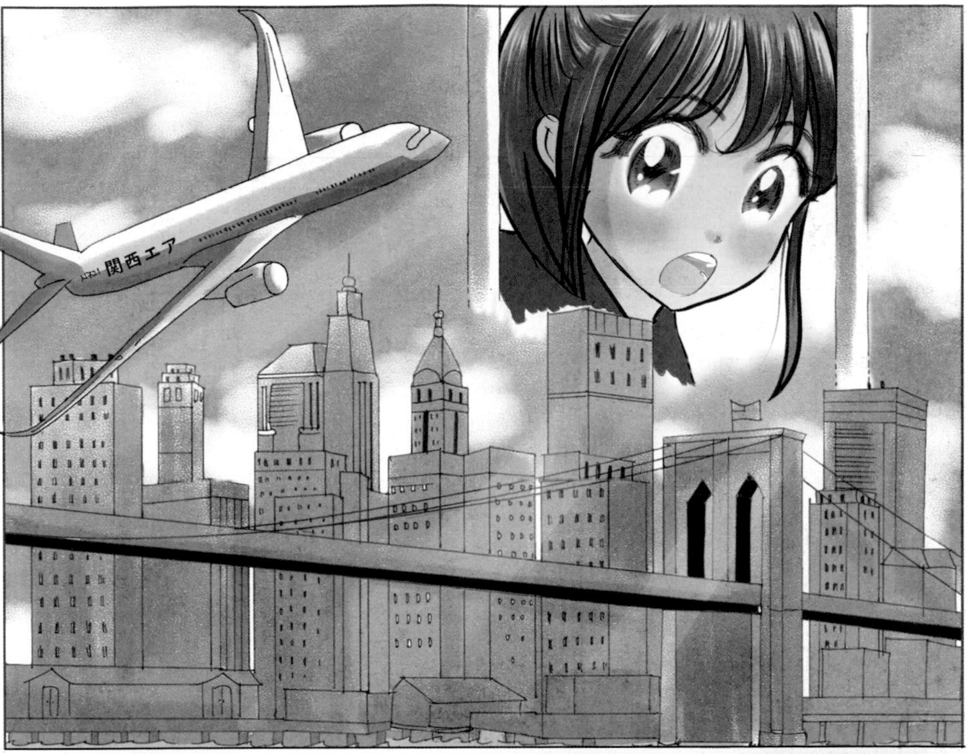
関西エア
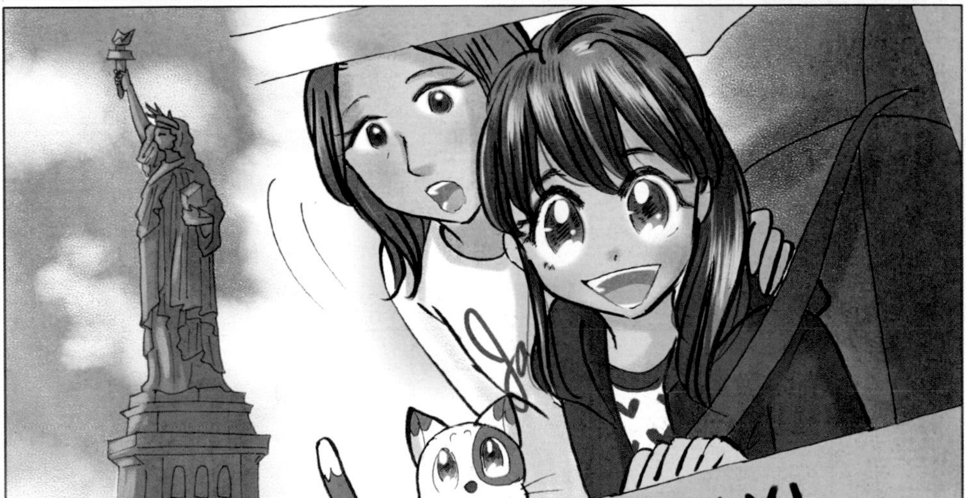
Whoa...This is like a movie! We're going to live in this city?

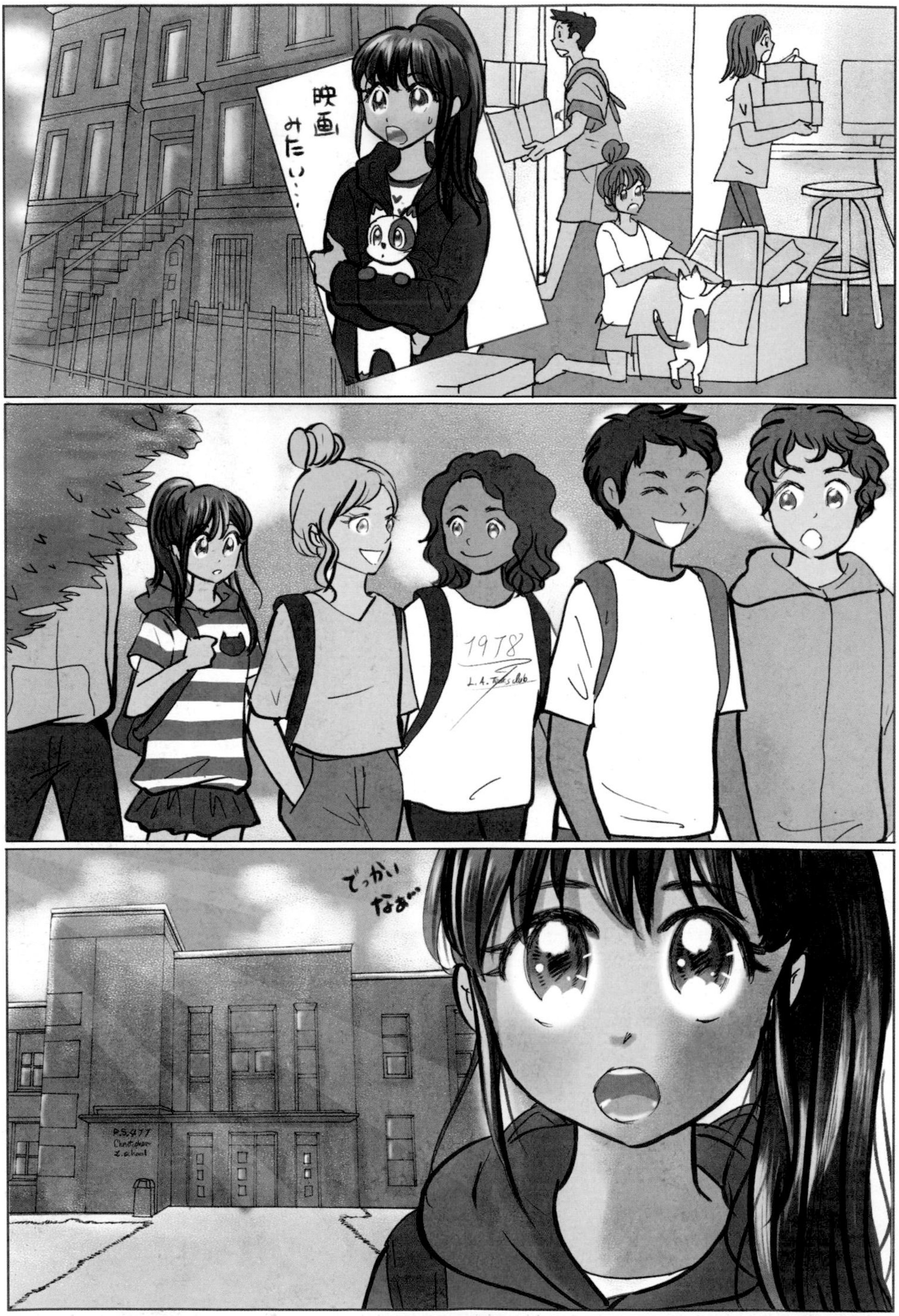
映画みたい…
1978
P.S.477
Christopher
School
でっかいなぁ

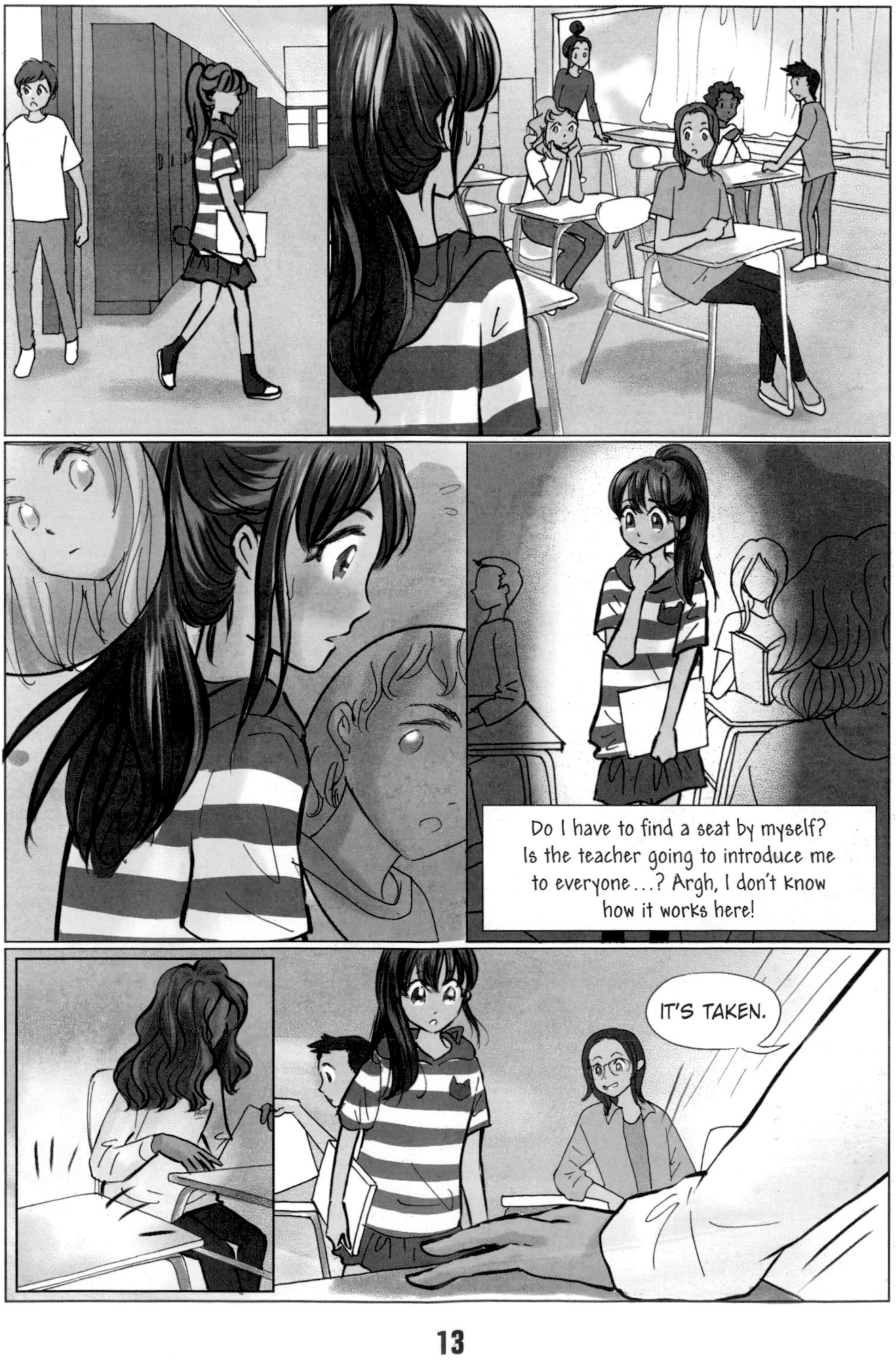
Do I have to find a seat by myself? Is the teacher going to introduce me to everyone...? Argh, I don't know how it works here!
IT'S TAKEN.

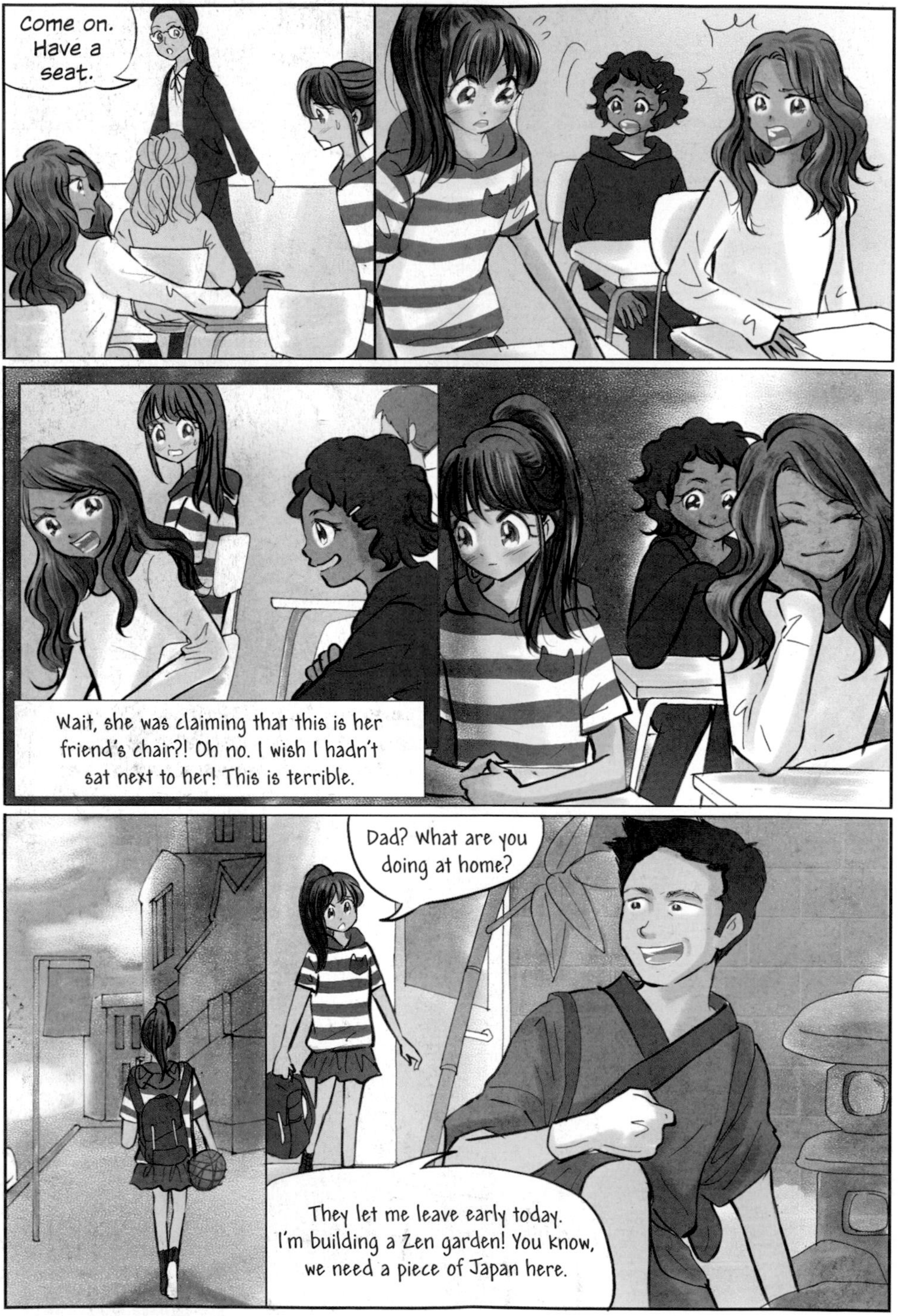
Come on. Have a seat.
Wait, she was claiming that this is her friend's chair?! Oh no. I wish I hadn't sat next to her! This is terrible.
Dad? What are you doing at home?
They let me leave early today. I'm building a Zen garden! You know, we need a piece of Japan here.

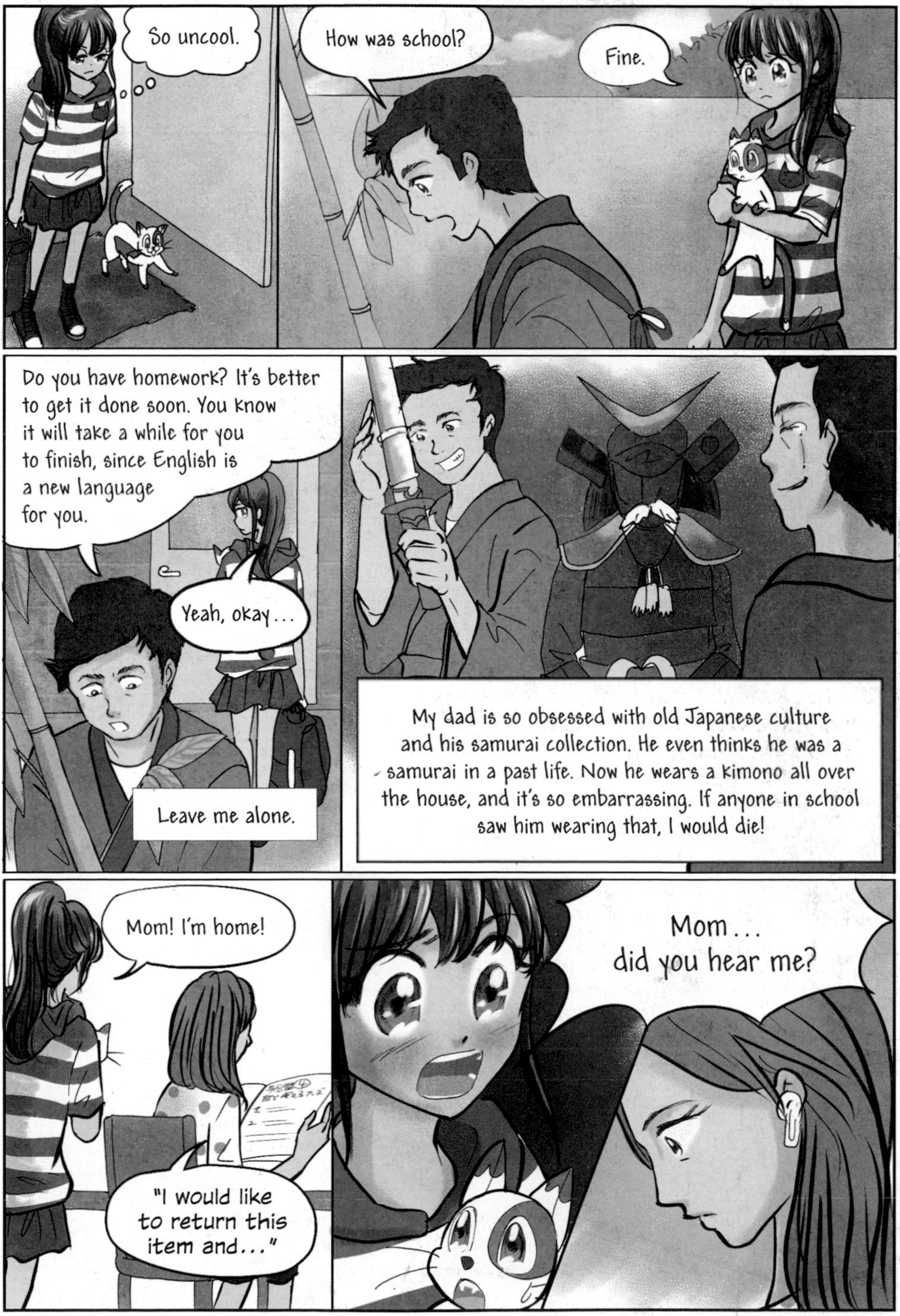
So uncool.
How was school?
Fine.
Do you have homework? It's better to get it done soon. You know it will take a while for you to finish, since English is a new language for you.
Yeah, okay...
Leave me alone.
My dad is so obsessed with old Japanese culture and his samurai collection. He even thinks he was a samurai in a past life. Now he wears a kimono all over the house, and it's so embarrassing. If anyone in school saw him wearing that, I would die!
Mom! I'm home!
"I would like to return this item and..."
Mom... did you hear me?

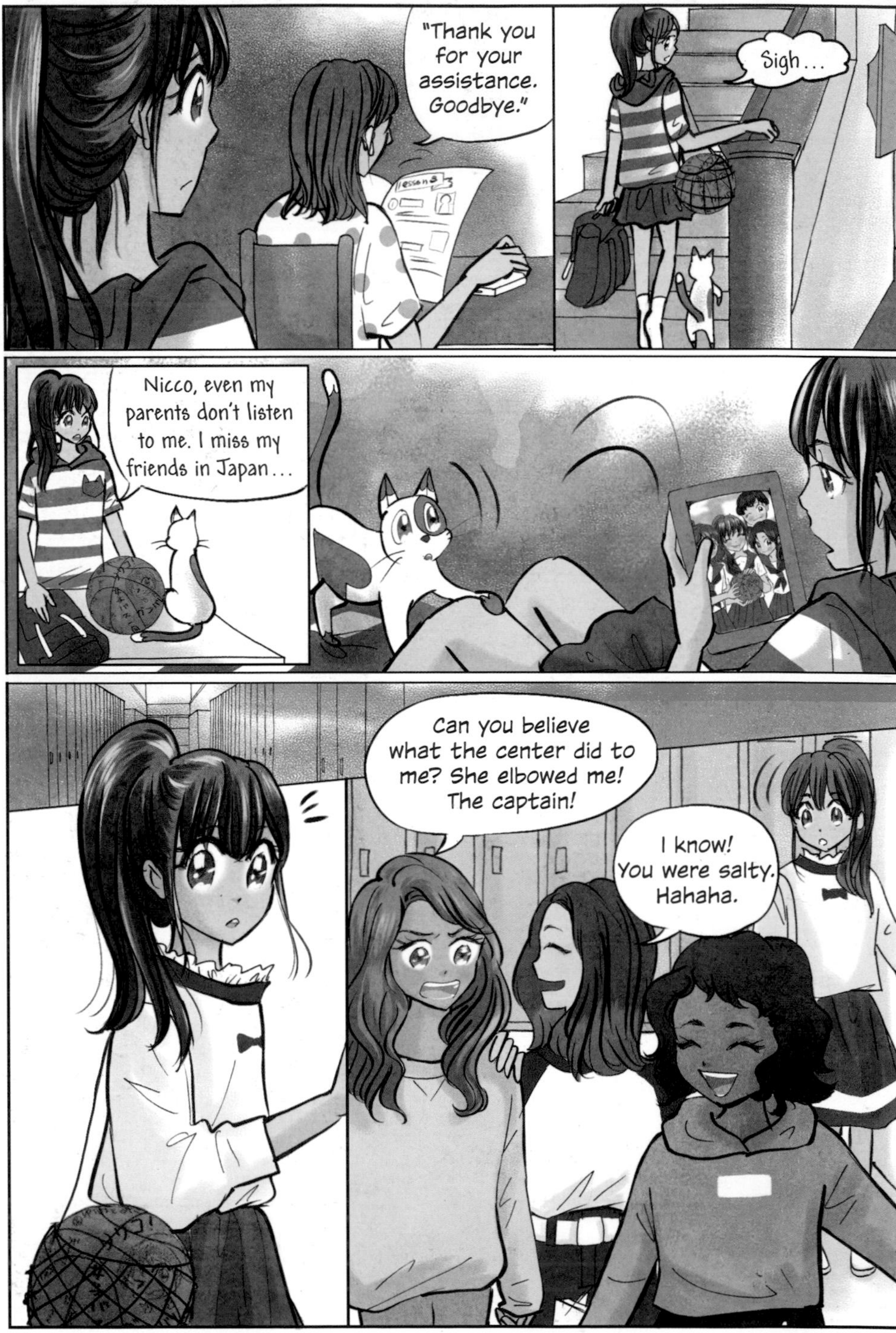
"Thank you for your assistance. Goodbye."
Sigh...
Nicco, even my parents don't listen to me. I miss my friends in Japan...
Can you believe what the center did to me? She elbowed me! The captain!
I know! You were salty. Hahaha.

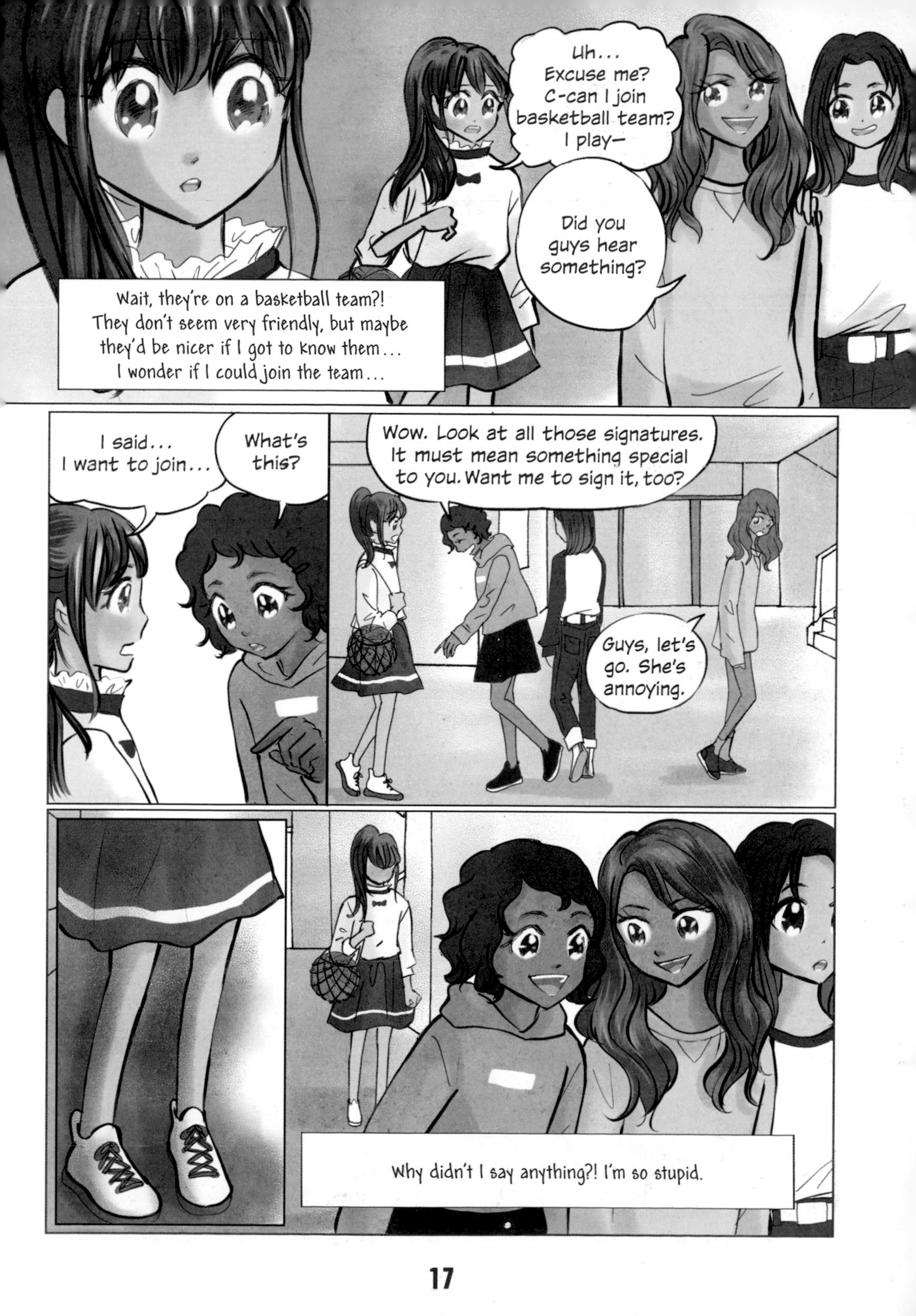
Wait, they're on a basketball team?! They don't seem very friendly, but maybe they'd be nicer if I got to know them... I wonder if I could join the team...
Uh... Excuse me? C-can I join basketball team? I play—
Did you guys hear something?
I said... I want to join...
What's this?
Wow. Look at all those signatures. It must mean something special to you. Want me to sign it, too?
Guys, let's go. She's annoying.
Why didn't I say anything?! I'm so stupid.

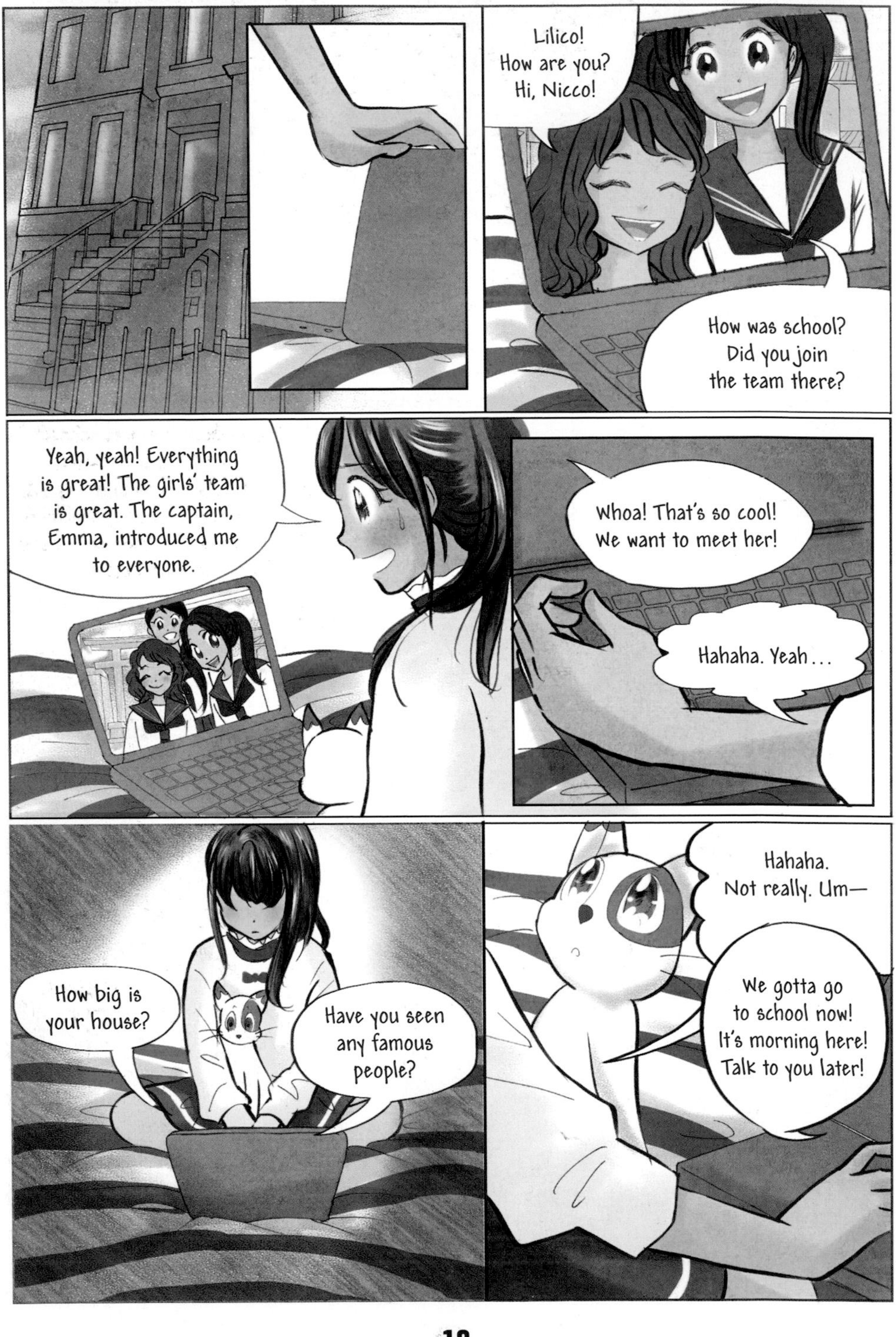
Lilico! How are you? Hi, Nicco!
How was school? Did you join the team there?
Yeah, yeah! Everything is great! The girls' team is great. The captain, Emma, introduced me to everyone.
Whoa! That's so cool! We want to meet her!
Hahaha. Yeah...
How big is your house?
Have you seen any famous people?
Hahaha. Not really. Um—
We gotta go to school now! It's morning here! Talk to you later!

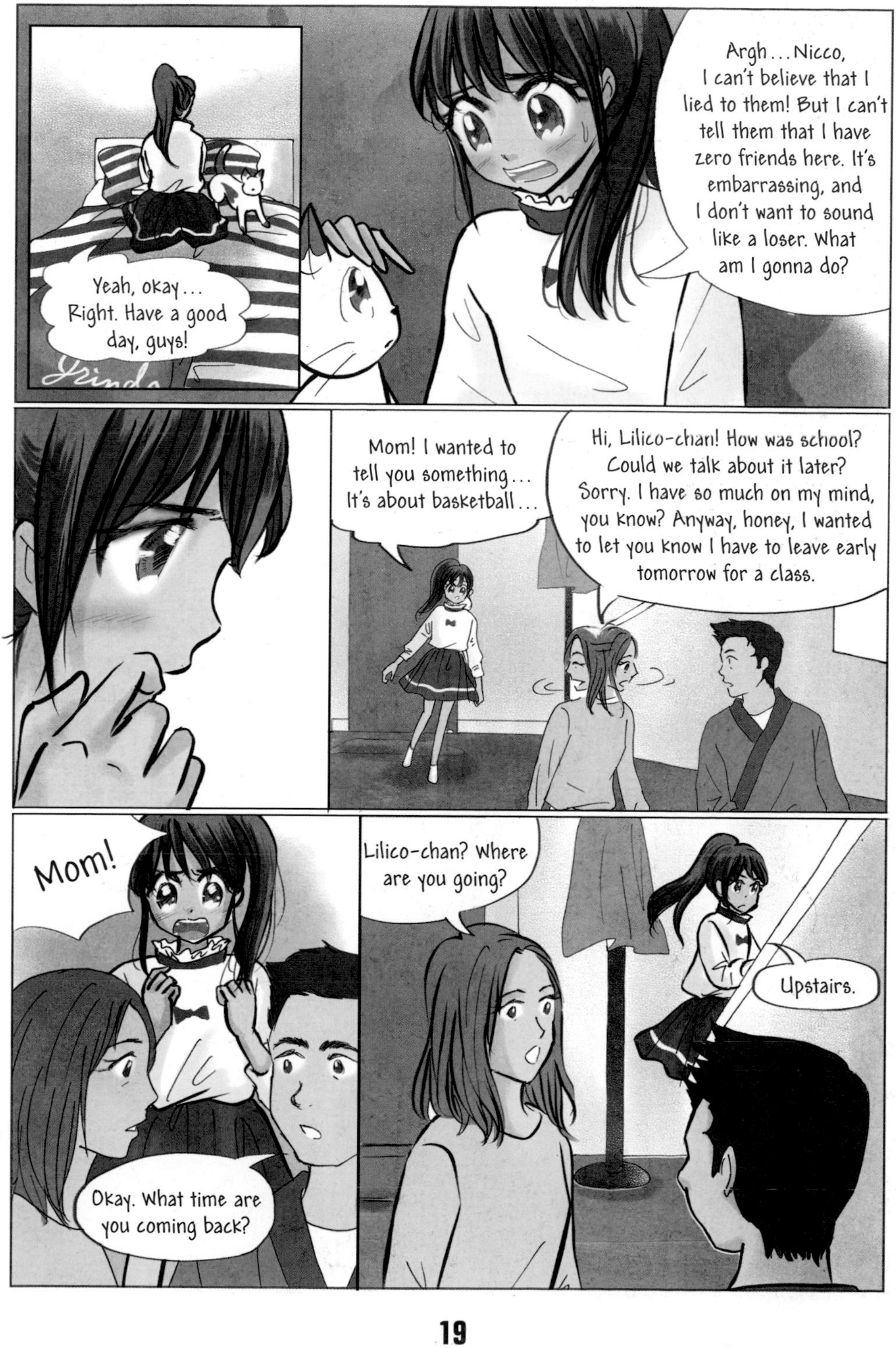
Yeah, okay… Right. Have a good day, guys!
Argh…Nicco, I can't believe that I lied to them! But I can't tell them that I have zero friends here. It's embarrassing, and I don't want to sound like a loser. What am I gonna do?
Mom! I wanted to tell you something… It's about basketball…
Hi, Lilico-chan! How was school? Could we talk about it later? Sorry. I have so much on my mind, you know? Anyway, honey, I wanted to let you know I have to leave early tomorrow for a class.
Mom!
Okay. What time are you coming back?
Lilico-chan? Where are you going?
Upstairs.

CHAPTER 2

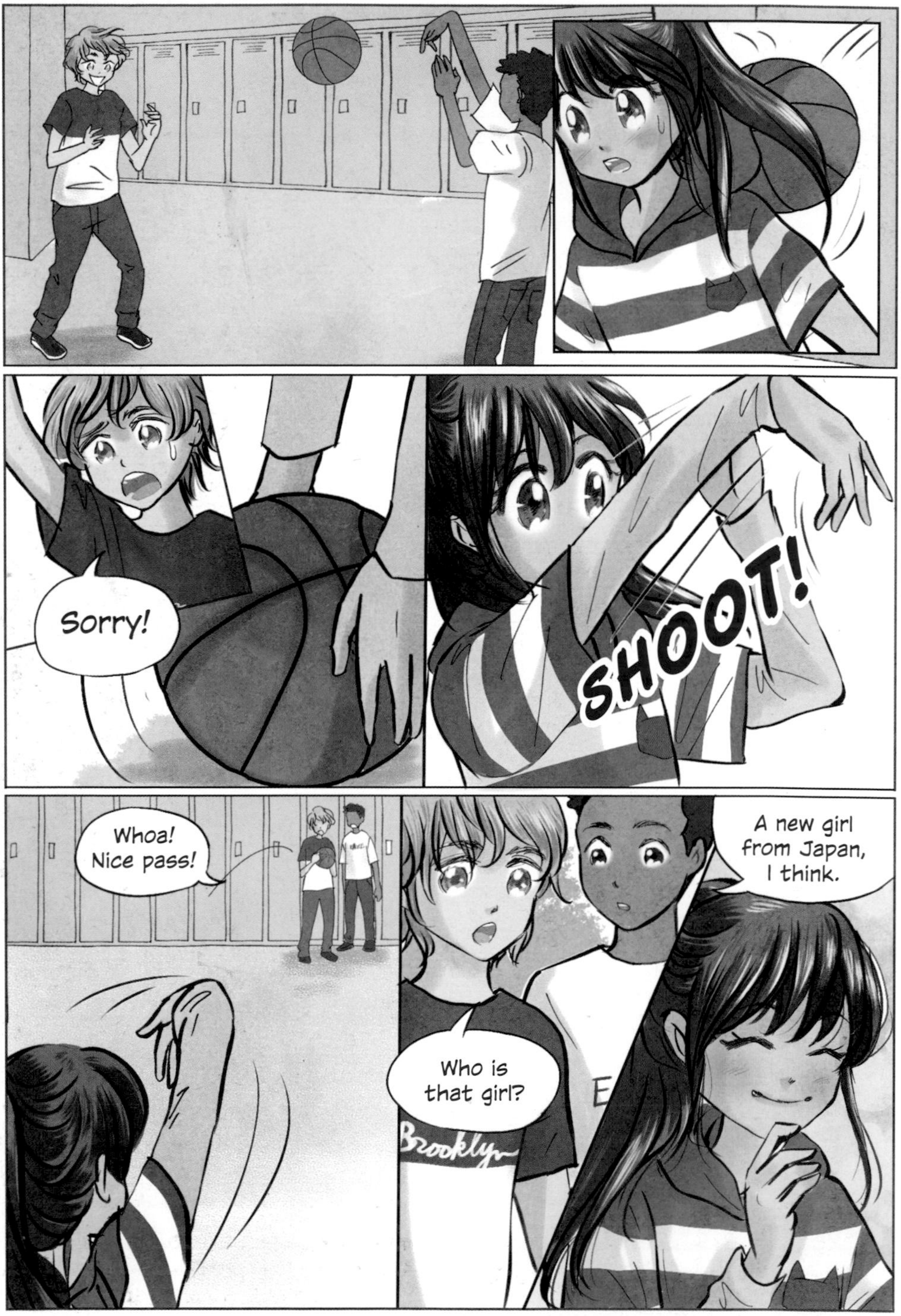
Sorry!
SHOOT!
Whoa! Nice pass!
Who is that girl?
A new girl from Japan, I think.

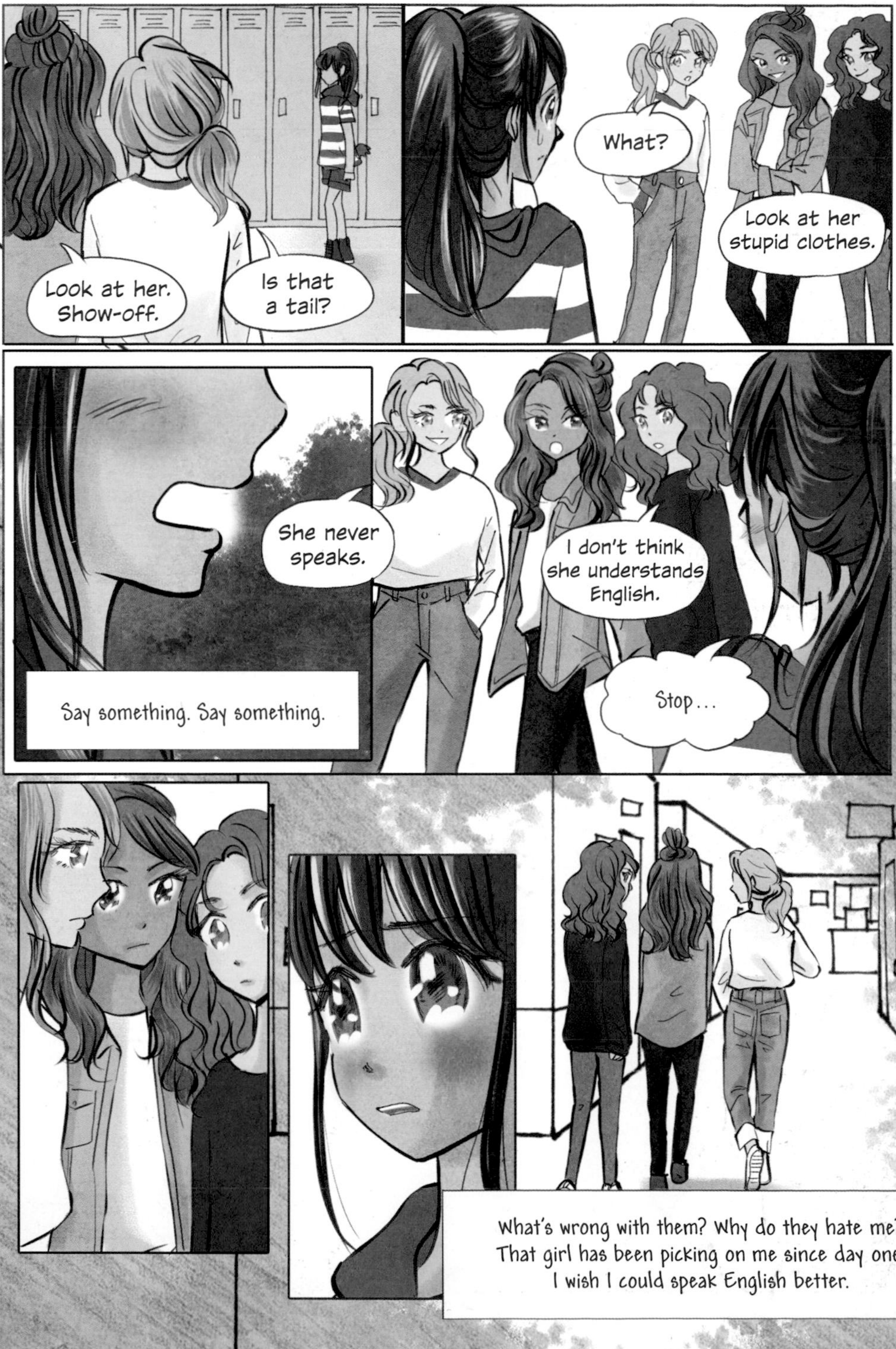
Look at her. Show-off.
Is that a tail?
What?
Look at her stupid clothes.
Say something. Say something.
She never speaks.
I don't think she understands English.
Stop...
What's wrong with them? Why do they hate me? That girl has been picking on me since day one. I wish I could speak English better.

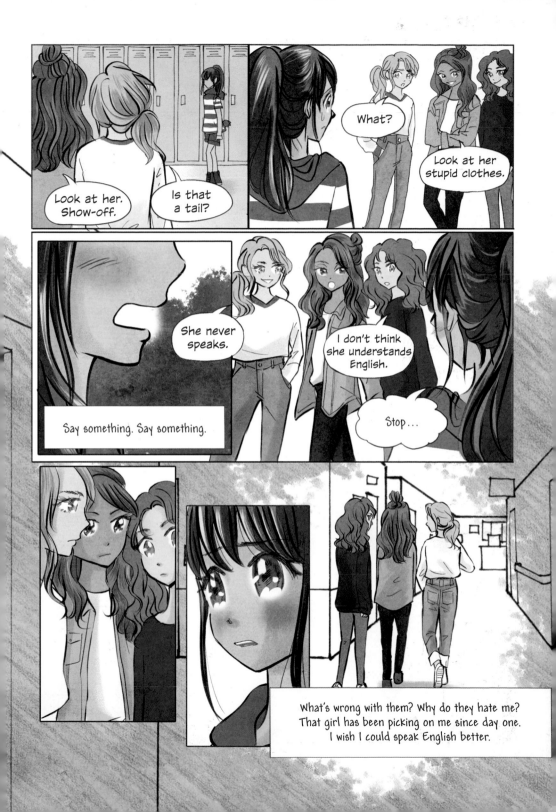

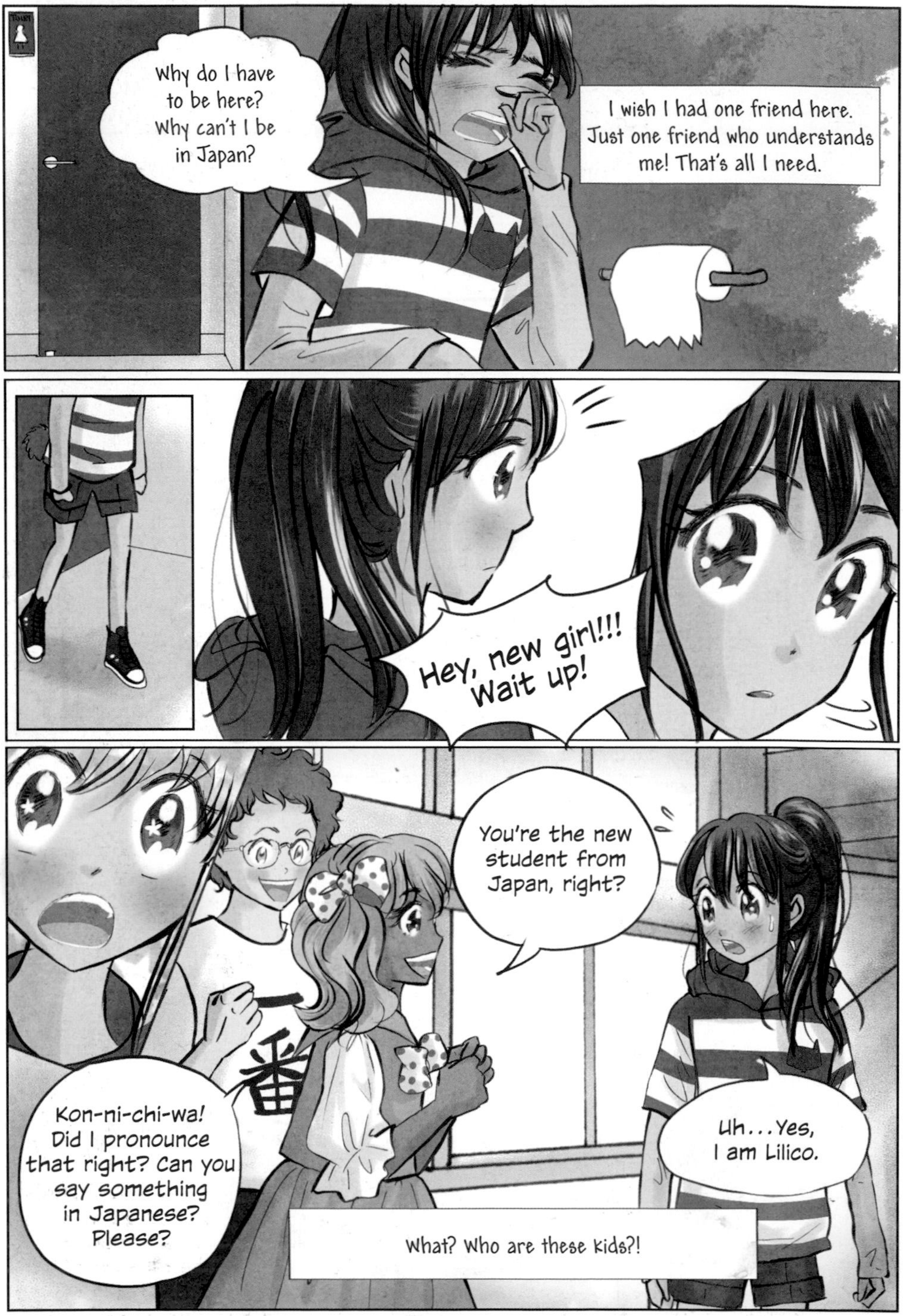
Why do I have to be here? Why can't I be in Japan?
I wish I had one friend here. Just one friend who understands me! That's all I need.
Hey, new girl!!! Wait up!
You're the new student from Japan, right?
Kon-ni-chi-wa! Did I pronounce that right? Can you say something in Japanese? Please?
Uh...Yes, I am Lilico.
What? Who are these kids?!

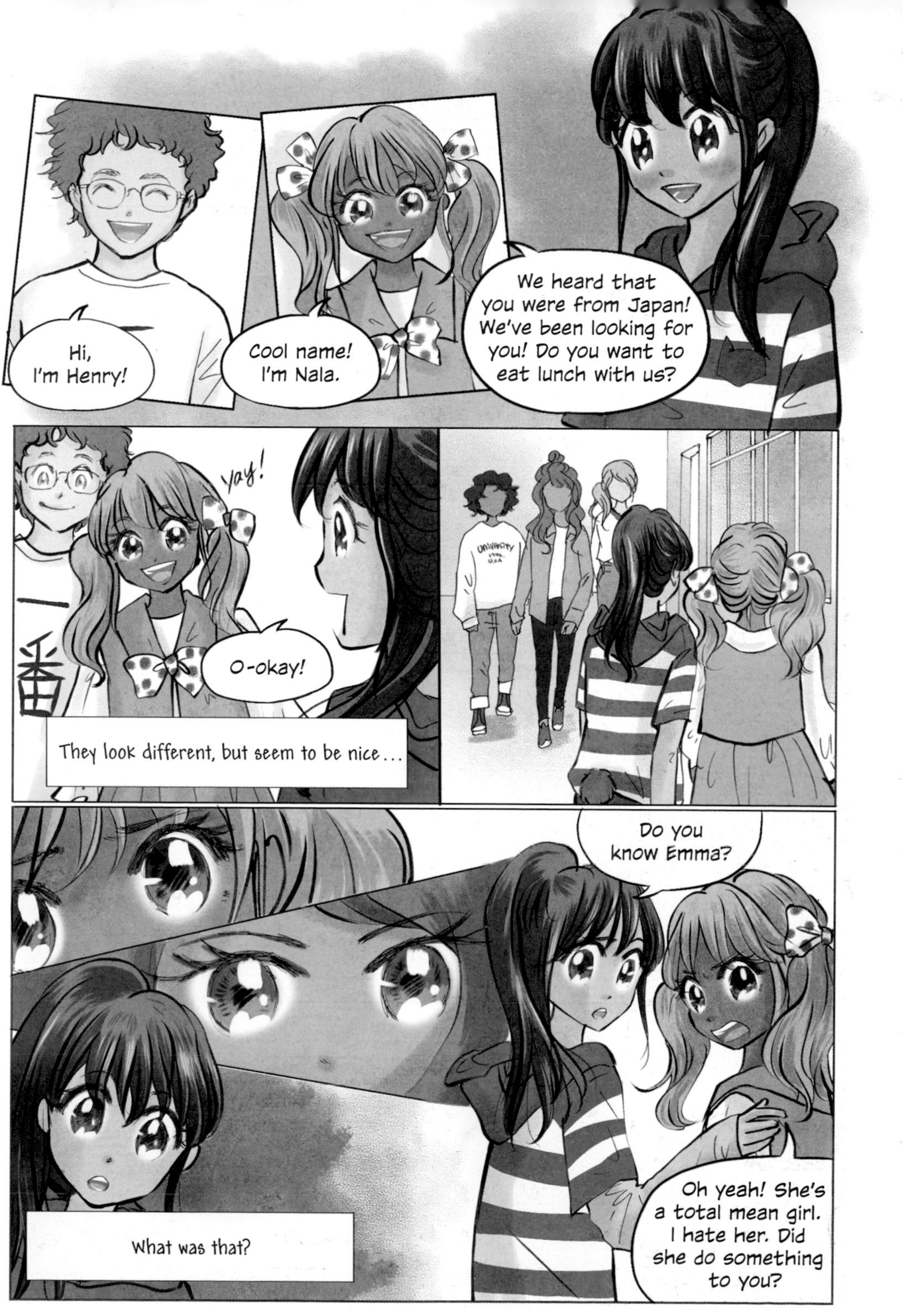
Hi,
I'm Henry!
Cool name!
I'm Nala.
We heard that you were from Japan! We've been looking for you! Do you want to eat lunch with us?
yay!
O-okay!
They look different, but seem to be nice...
Do you know Emma?
What was that?
Oh yeah! She's a total mean girl. I hate her. Did she do something to you?

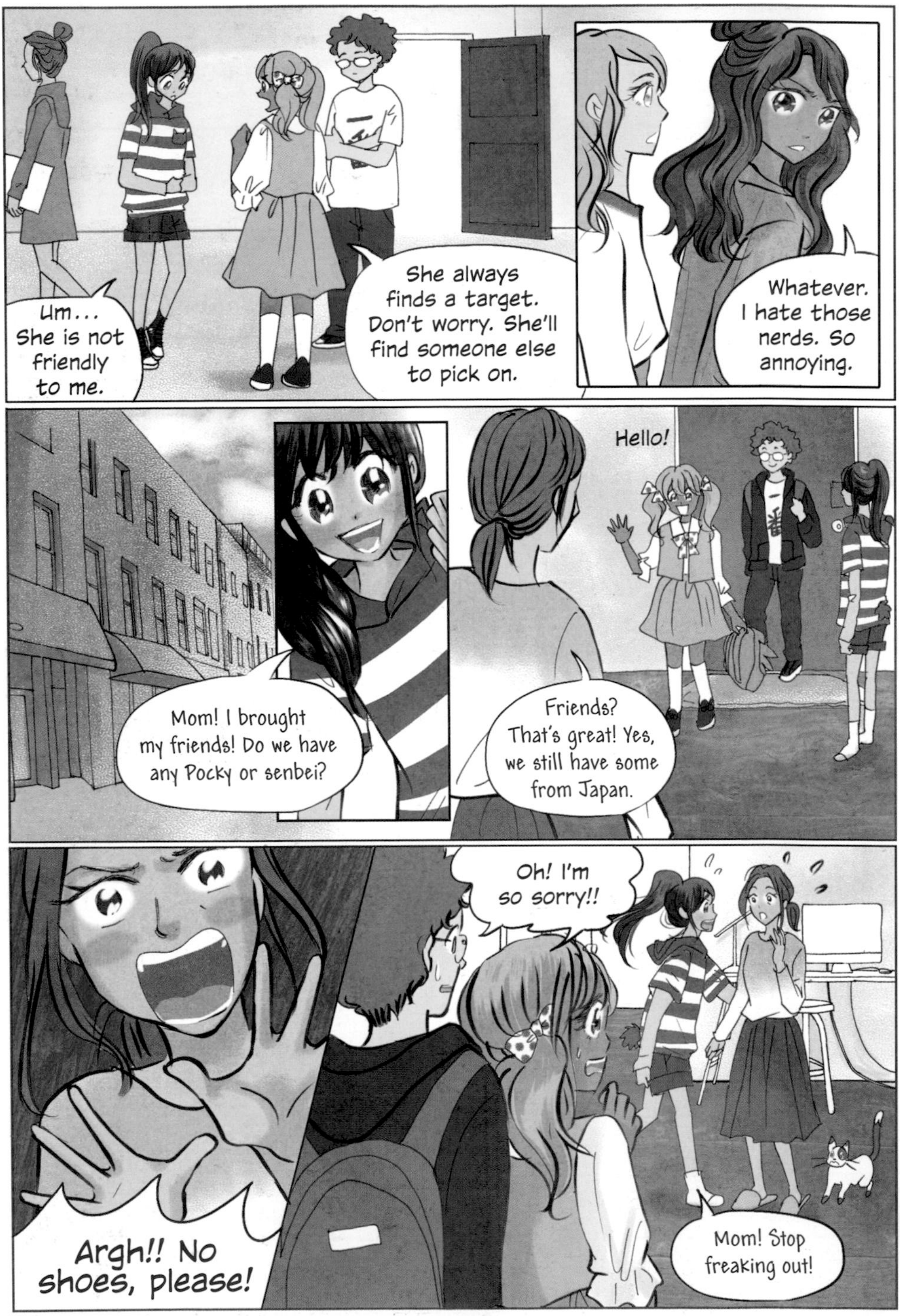
Um... She is not friendly to me.
She always finds a target. Don't worry. She'll find someone else to pick on.
Whatever. I hate those nerds. So annoying.
Mom! I brought my friends! Do we have any Pocky or senbei?
Hello!
Friends? That's great! Yes, we still have some from Japan.
Argh!! No shoes, please!
Oh! I'm so sorry!!
Mom! Stop freaking out!

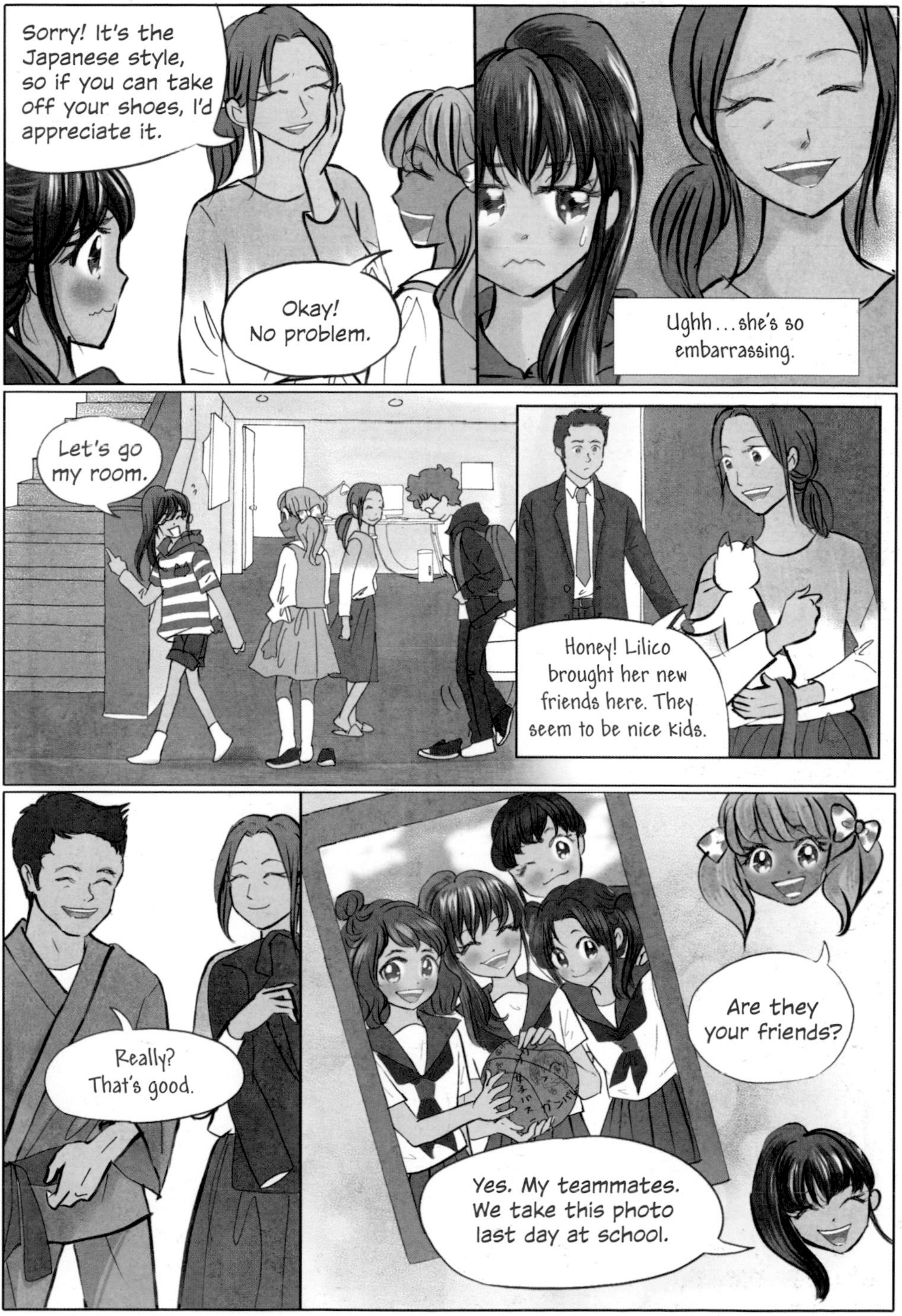
Sorry! It's the Japanese style, so if you can take off your shoes, I'd appreciate it.
Okay! No problem.
Ughh...she's so embarrassing.
Let's go my room.
Honey! Lilico brought her new friends here. They seem to be nice kids.
Really? That's good.
Are they your friends?
Yes. My teammates. We take this photo last day at school.

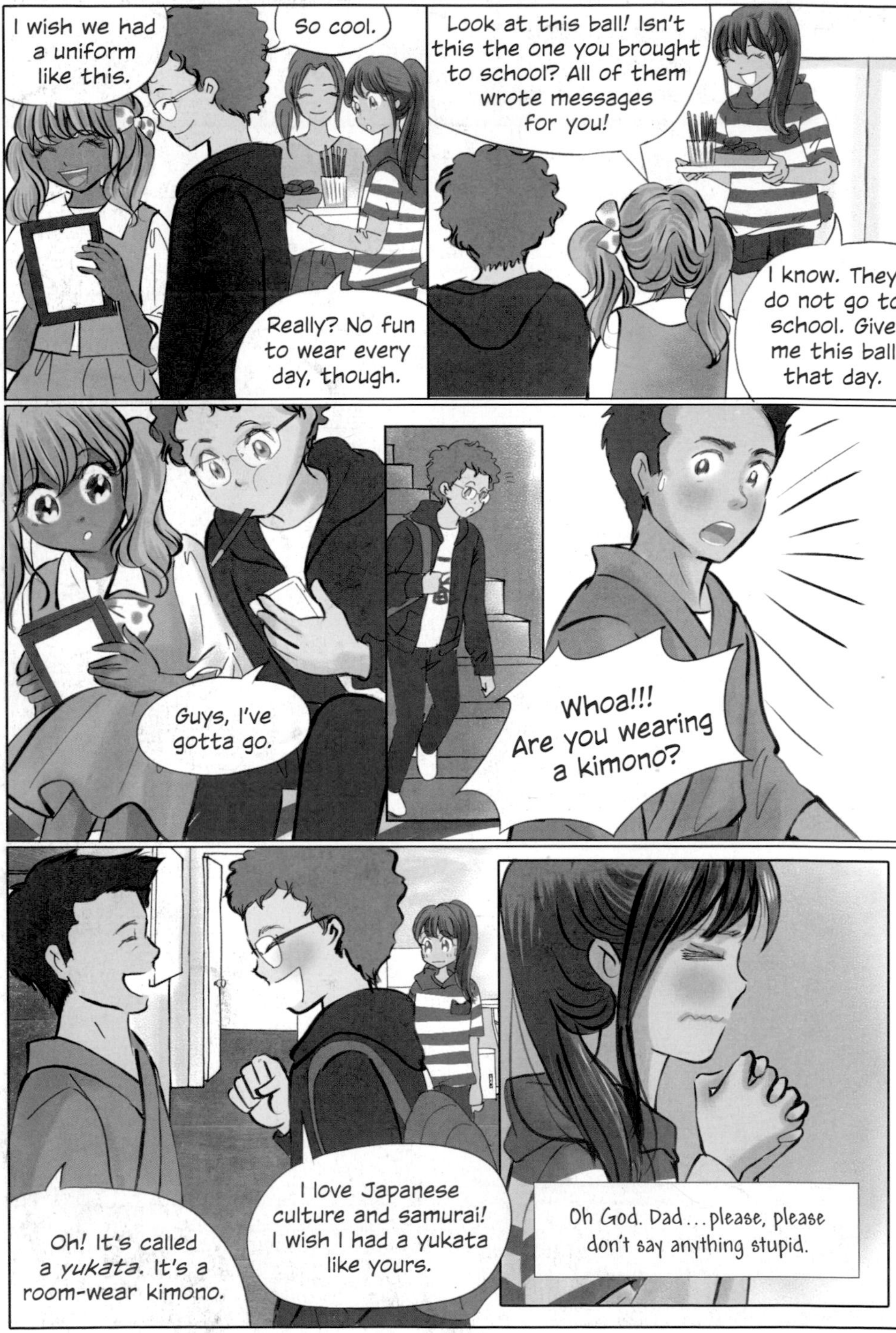
I wish we had a uniform like this.
So cool.
Really? No fun to wear every day, though.
Look at this ball! Isn't this the one you brought to school? All of them wrote messages for you!
I know. They do not go to school. Give me this ball that day.
Guys, I've gotta go.
Whoa!!! Are you wearing a kimono?
Oh! It's called a *yukata*. It's a room-wear kimono.
I love Japanese culture and samurai! I wish I had a yukata like yours.
Oh God. Dad... please, please don't say anything stupid.

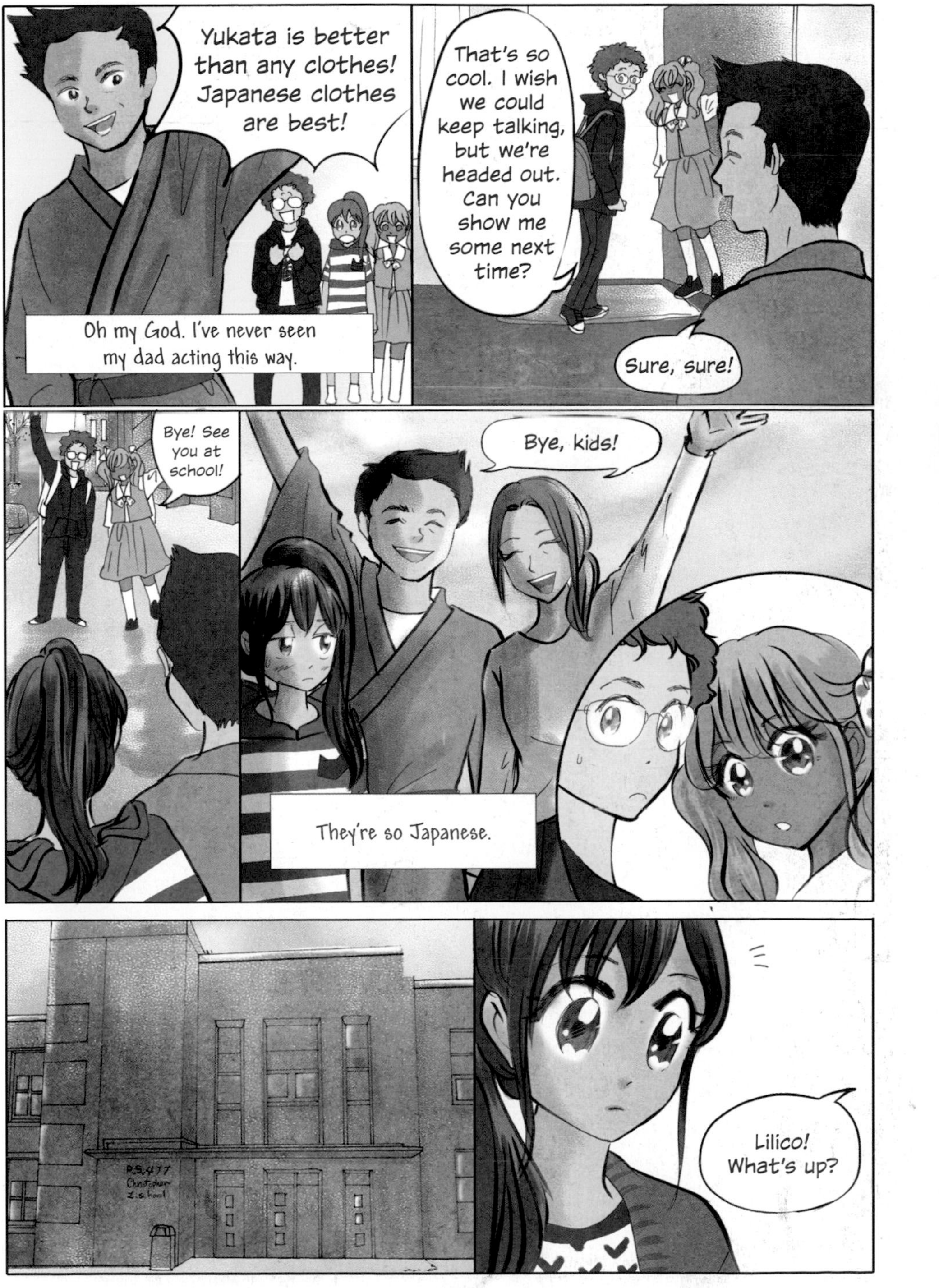
Yukata is better than any clothes! Japanese clothes are best!
Oh my God. I've never seen my dad acting this way.
That's so cool. I wish we could keep talking, but we're headed out. Can you show me some next time?
Sure, sure!
Bye! See you at school!
Bye, kids!
They're so Japanese.
Lilico! What's up?

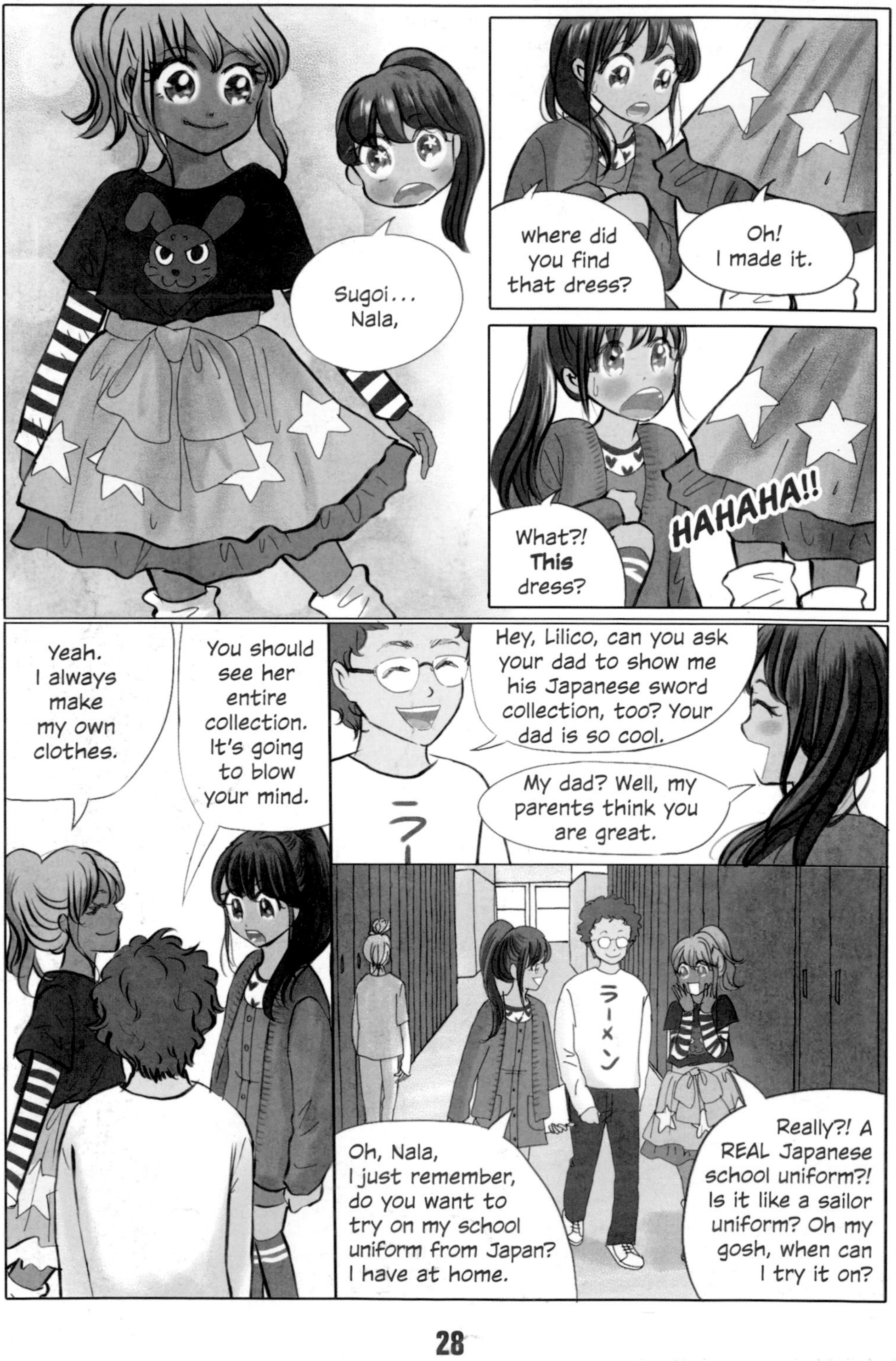
Sugoi... Nala,
where did you find that dress?
Oh! I made it.
What?! **This** dress?
HAHAHA!!
Yeah. I always make my own clothes.
You should see her entire collection. It's going to blow your mind.
Hey, Lilico, can you ask your dad to show me his Japanese sword collection, too? Your dad is so cool.
My dad? Well, my parents think you are great.
Oh, Nala, I just remember, do you want to try on my school uniform from Japan? I have at home.
Really?! A REAL Japanese school uniform?! Is it like a sailor uniform? Oh my gosh, when can I try it on?

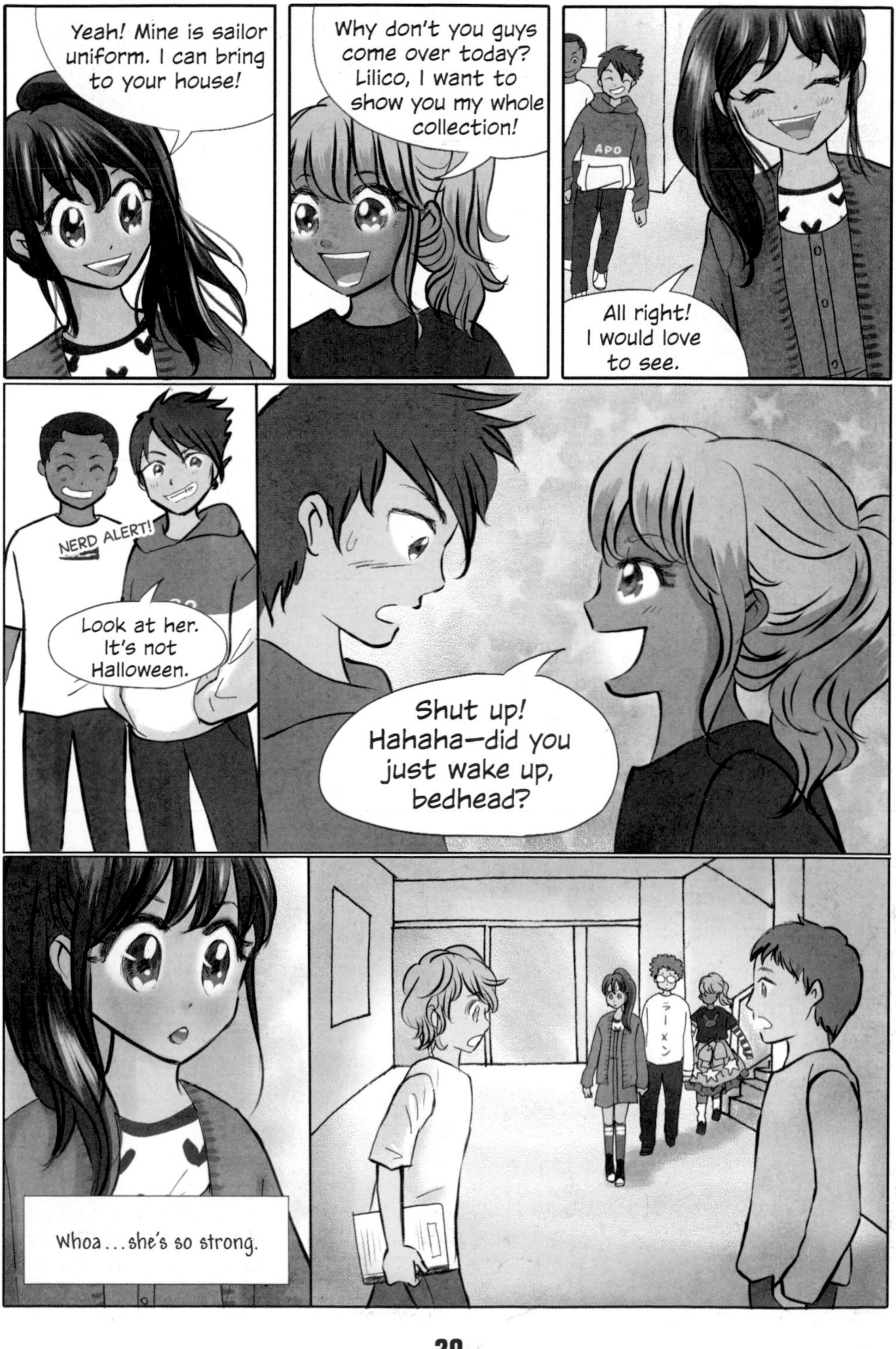
Yeah! Mine is sailor uniform. I can bring to your house!
Why don't you guys come over today? Lilico, I want to show you my whole collection!
APO
All right! I would love to see.
NERD ALERT!
Look at her. It's not Halloween.
Shut up! Hahaha—did you just wake up, bedhead?
Whoa . . . she's so strong.

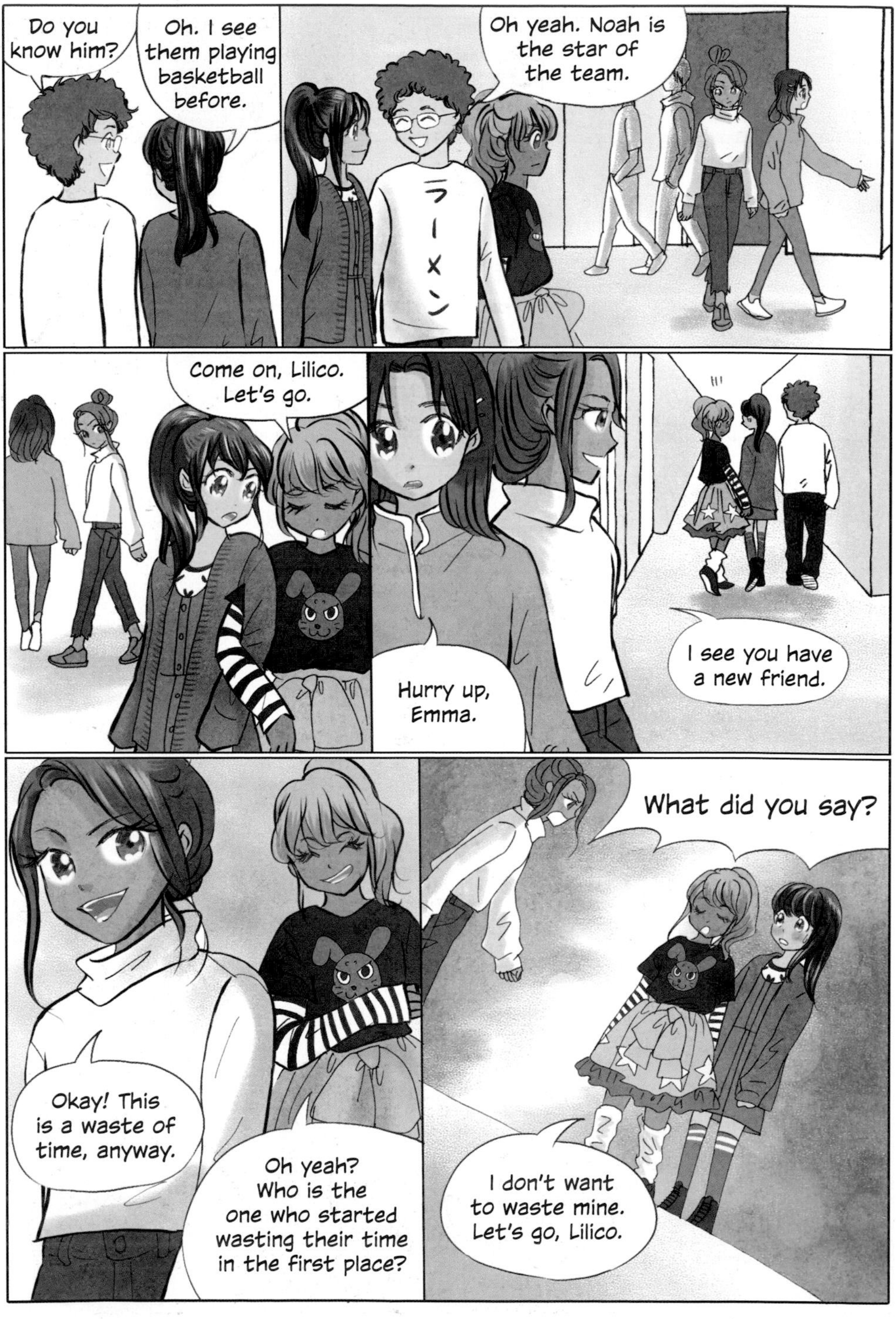
Do you know him?
Oh. I see them playing basketball before.
Oh yeah. Noah is the star of the team.
ラーメン
Come on, Lilico. Let's go.
Hurry up, Emma.
I see you have a new friend.
Okay! This is a waste of time, anyway.
Oh yeah? Who is the one who started wasting their time in the first place?
What did you say?
I don't want to waste mine. Let's go, Lilico.

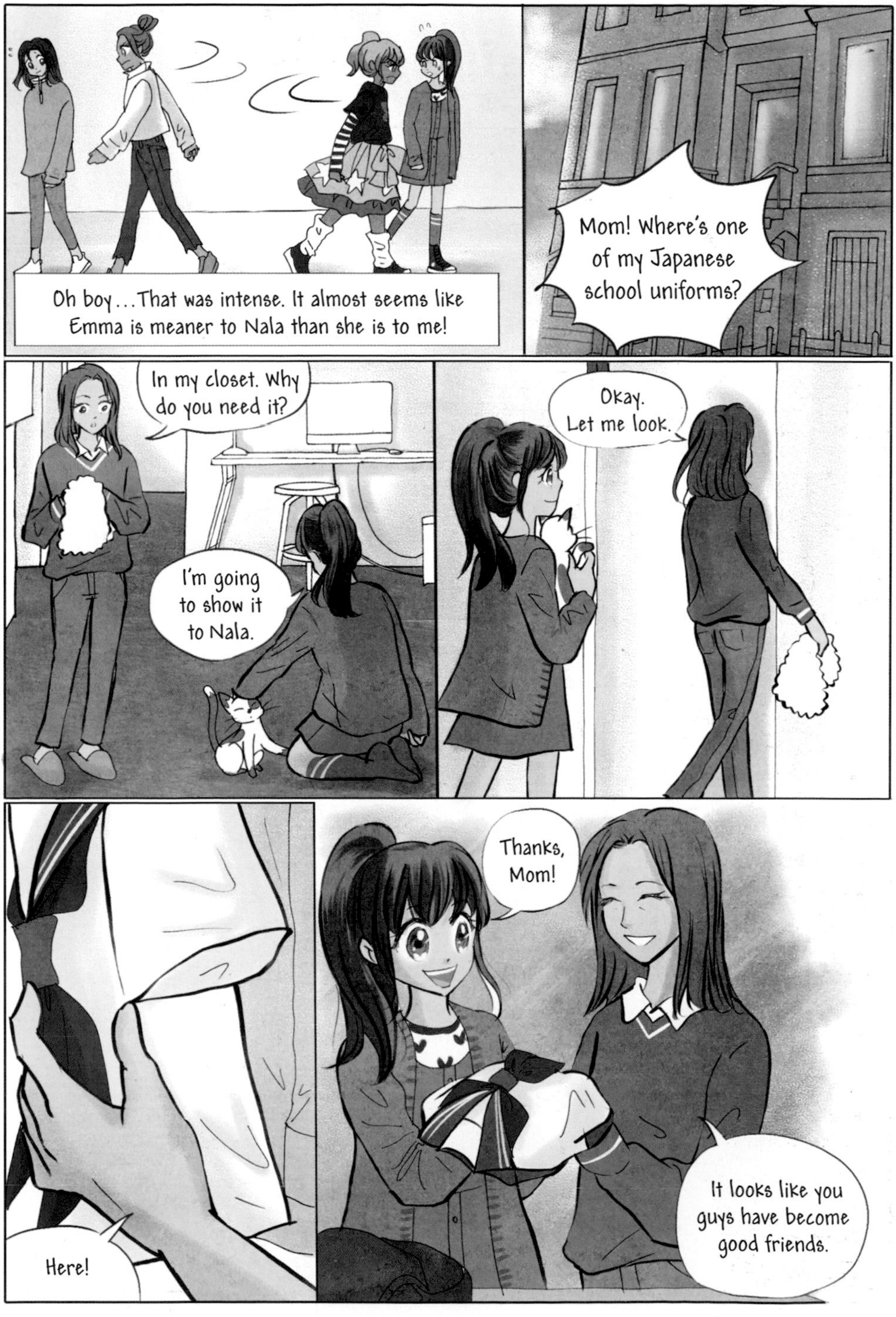
Oh boy...That was intense. It almost seems like Emma is meaner to Nala than she is to me!
Mom! Where's one of my Japanese school uniforms?
In my closet. Why do you need it?
I'm going to show it to Nala.
Okay. Let me look.
Here!
Thanks, Mom!
It looks like you guys have become good friends.

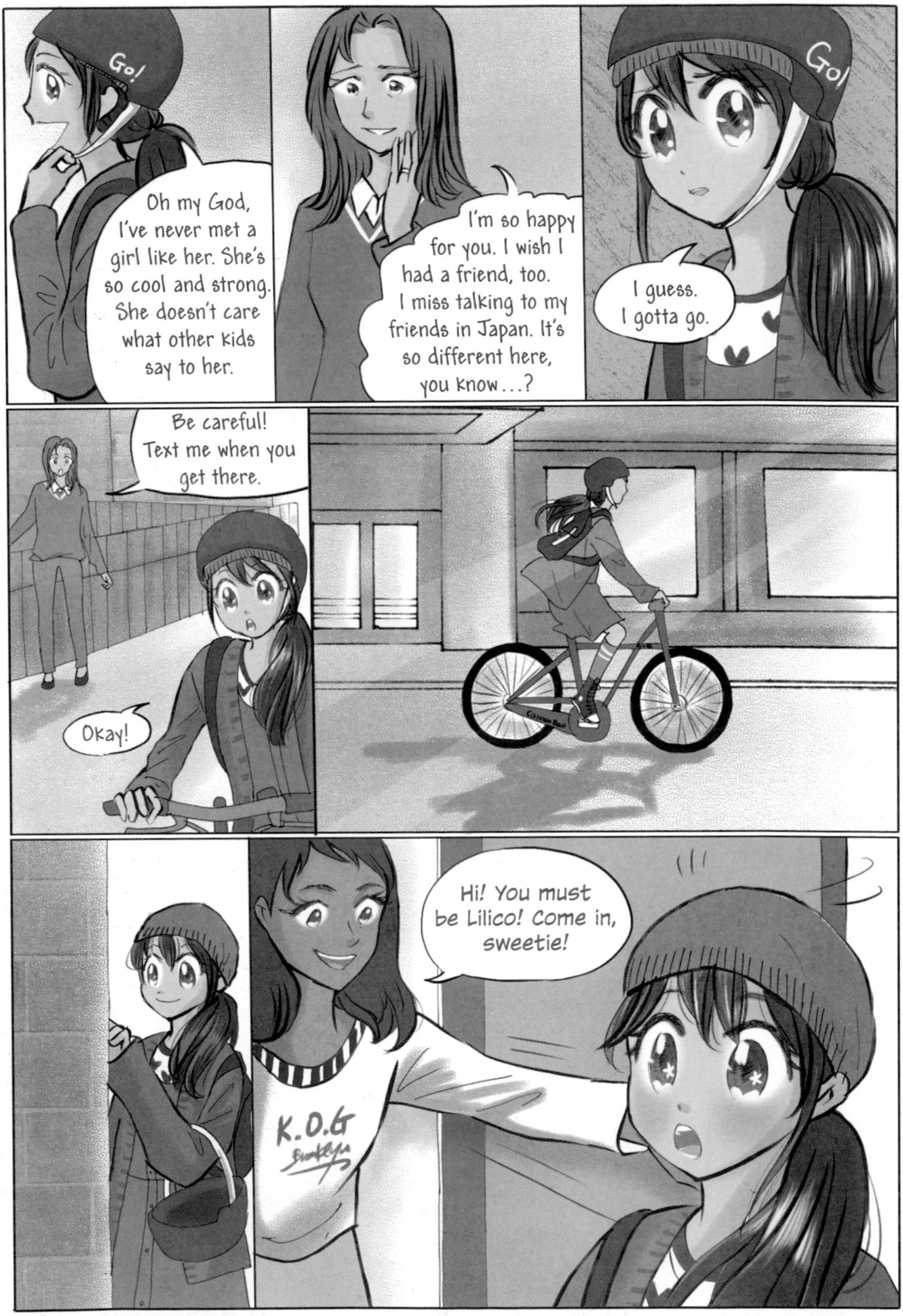
Go!
Oh my God, I've never met a girl like her. She's so cool and strong. She doesn't care what other kids say to her.
I'm so happy for you. I wish I had a friend, too. I miss talking to my friends in Japan. It's so different here, you know...?
Go!
I guess. I gotta go.
Be careful! Text me when you get there.
Okay!
Hi! You must be Lilico! Come in, sweetie!
K.O.G

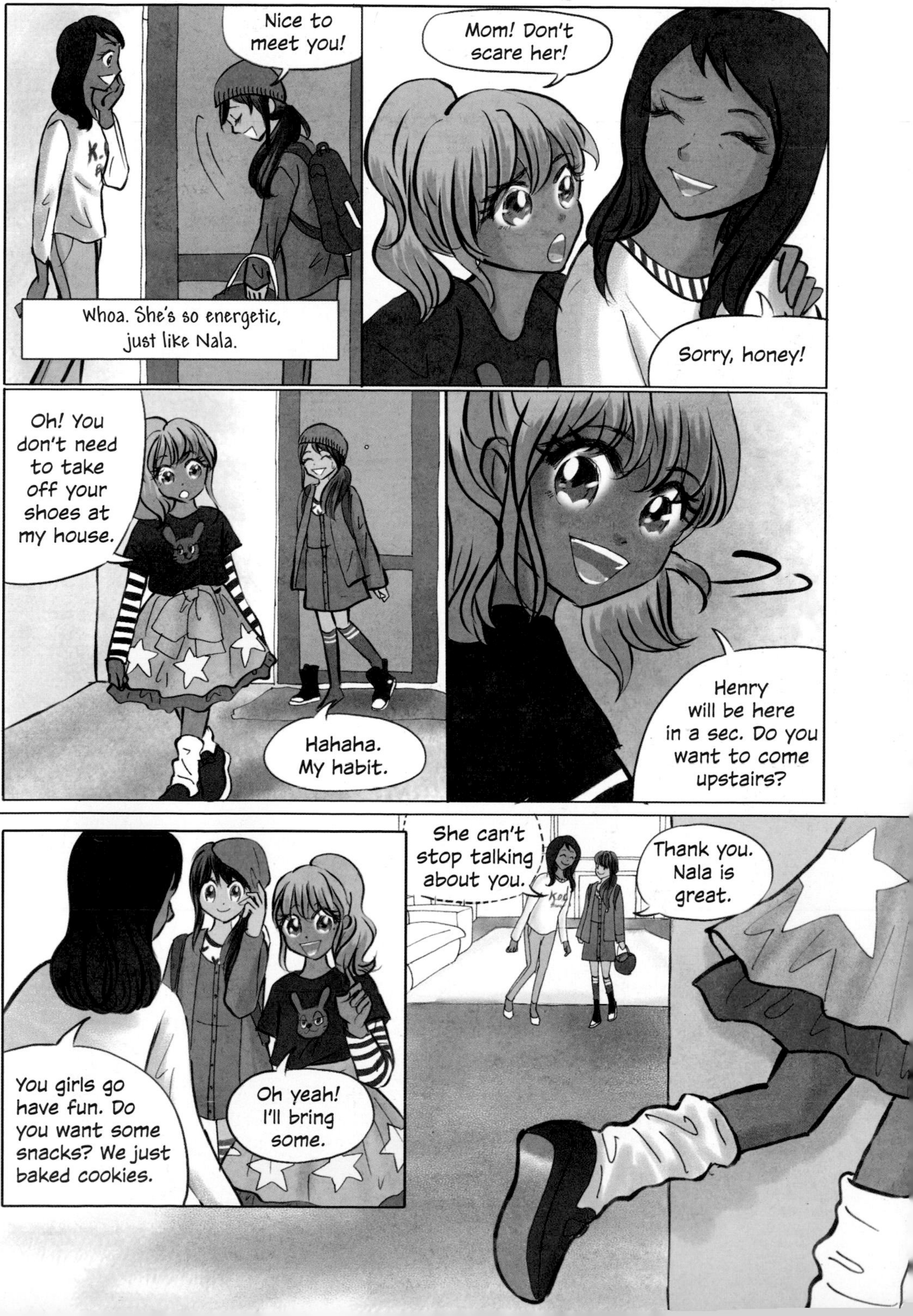
Nice to meet you!
Whoa. She's so energetic, just like Nala.
Mom! Don't scare her!
Sorry, honey!
Oh! You don't need to take off your shoes at my house.
Hahaha. My habit.
Henry will be here in a sec. Do you want to come upstairs?
You girls go have fun. Do you want some snacks? We just baked cookies.
Oh yeah! I'll bring some.
She can't stop talking about you.
Thank you. Nala is great.

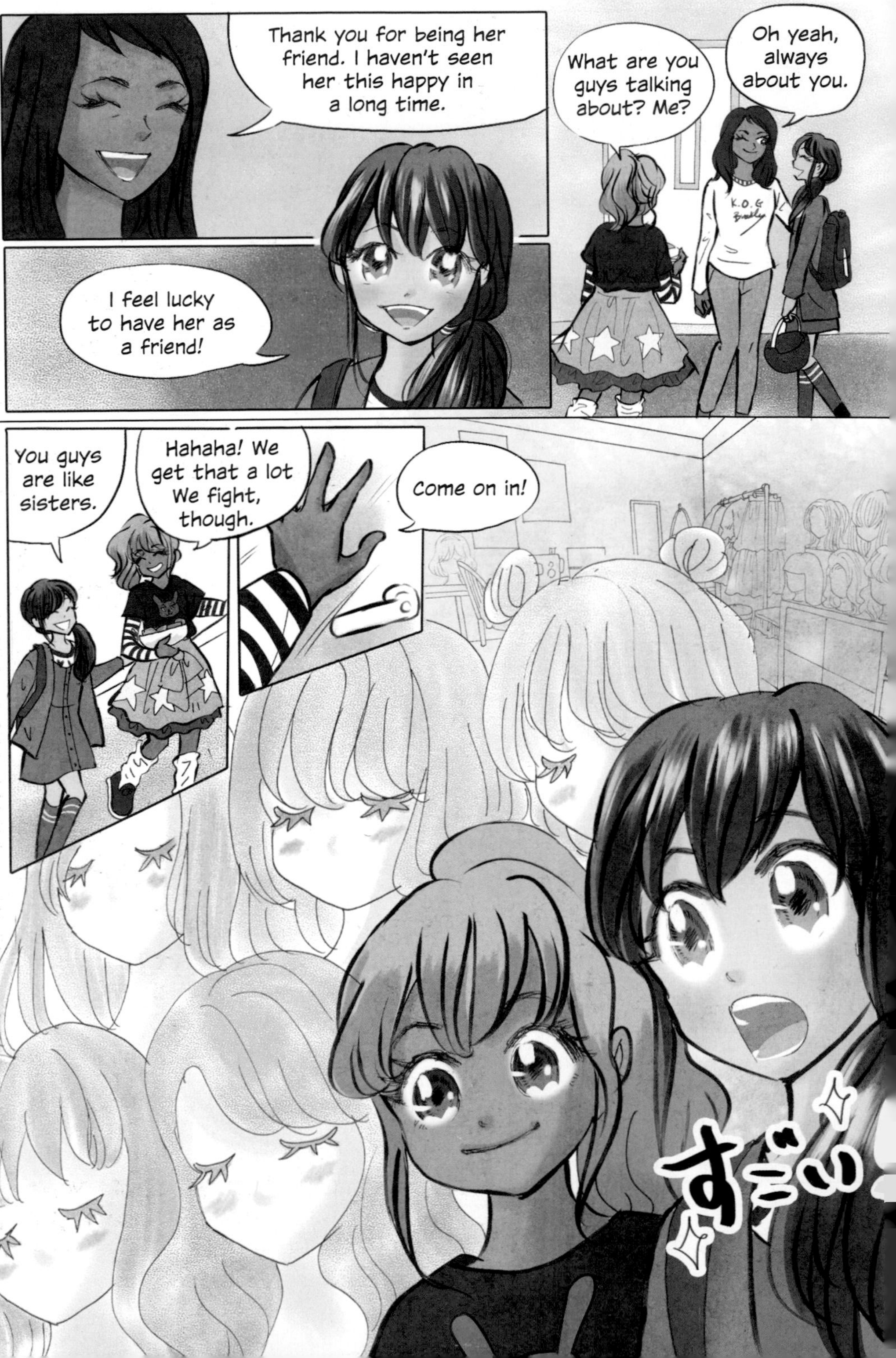
Thank you for being her friend. I haven't seen her this happy in a long time.
I feel lucky to have her as a friend!
What are you guys talking about? Me?
Oh yeah, always about you.
You guys are like sisters.
Hahaha! We get that a lot We fight, though.
Come on in!
すごい

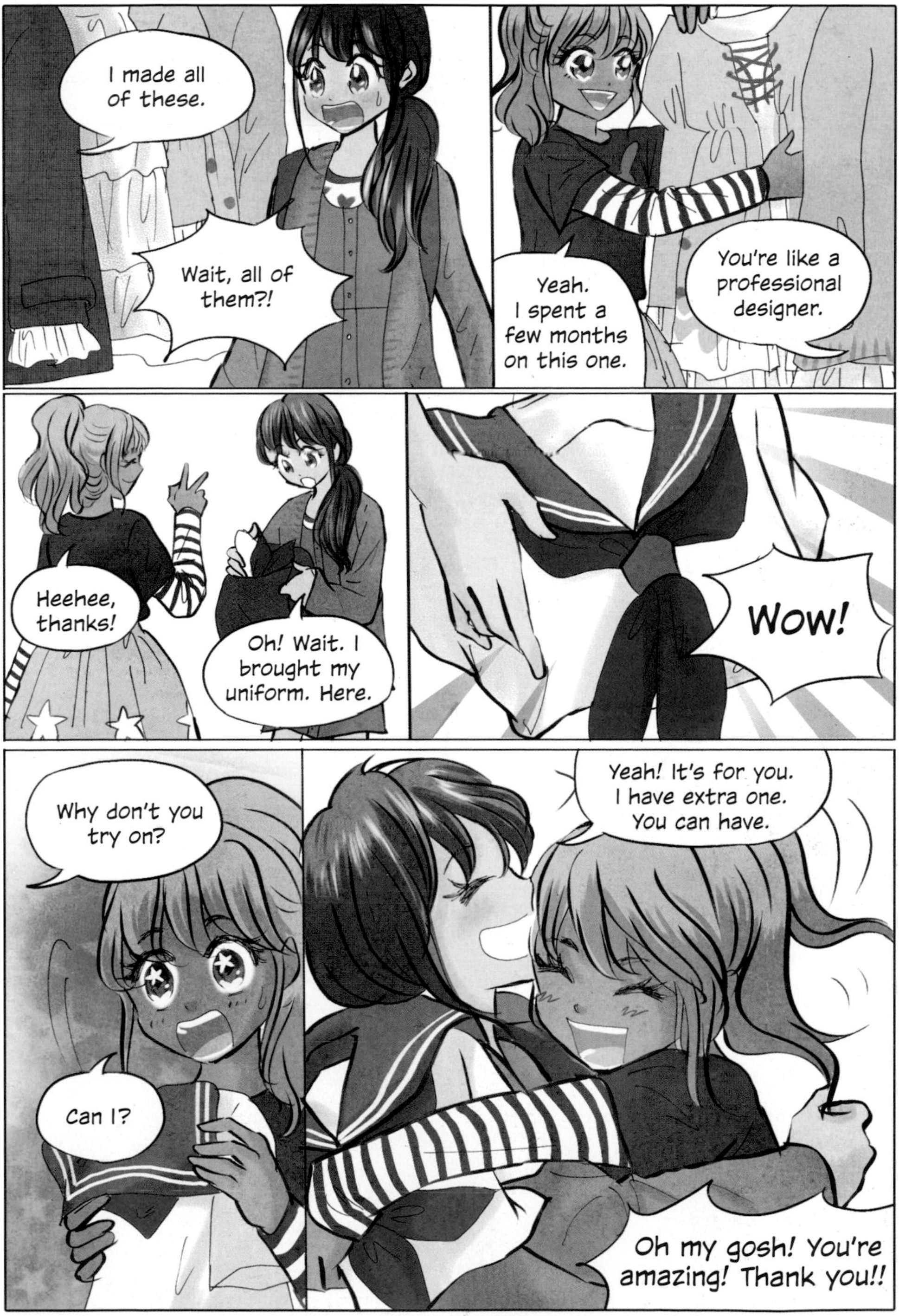

I made all of these.
Wait, all of them?!
Yeah. I spent a few months on this one.
You're like a professional designer.
Heehee, thanks!
Oh! Wait. I brought my uniform. Here.
WOW!
Why don't you try on?
Can I?
Yeah! It's for you. I have extra one. You can have.
Oh my gosh! You're amazing! Thank you!!

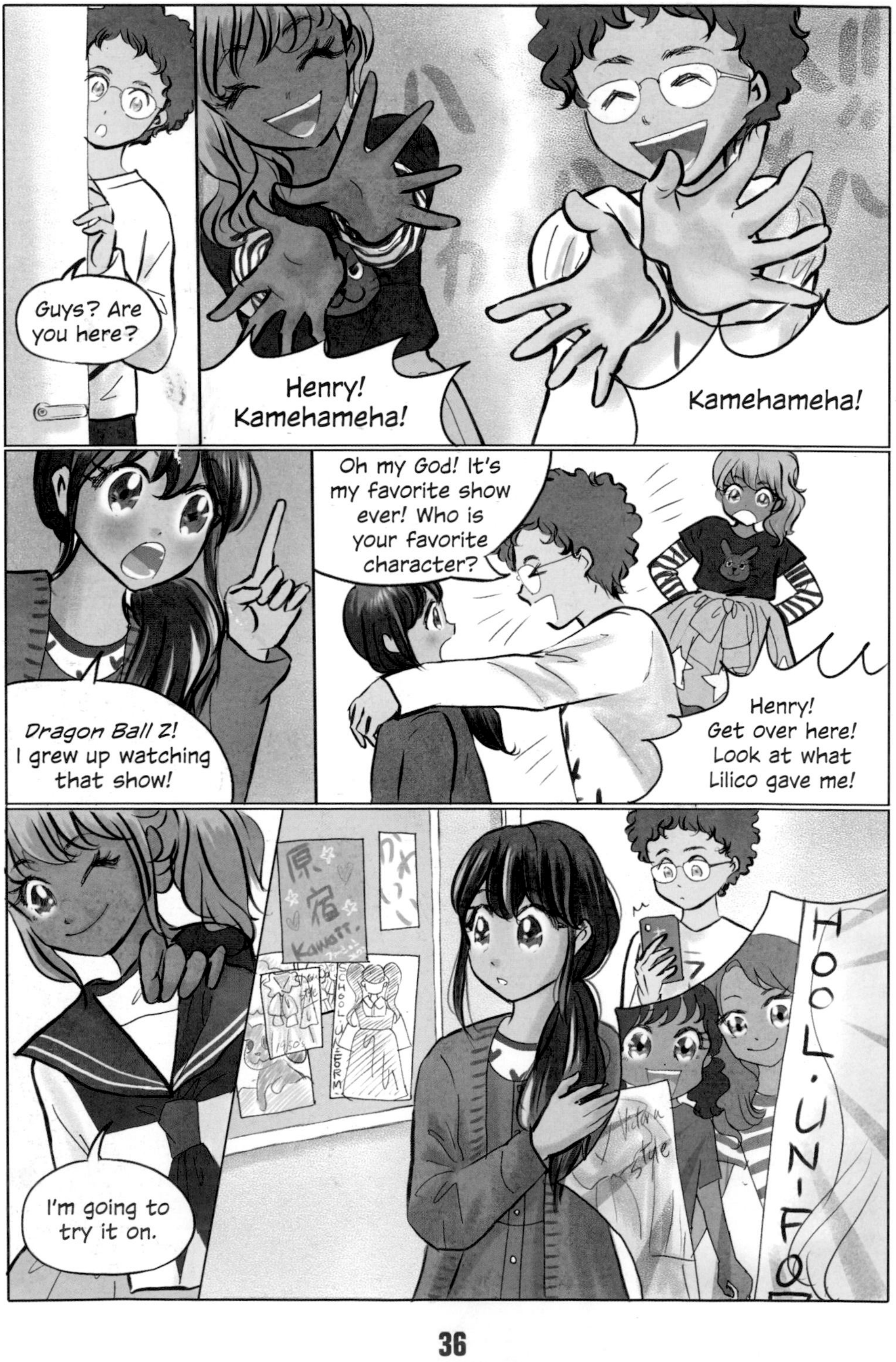
Guys? Are you here?
Henry! Kamehameha!
Kamehameha!
Dragon Ball Z! I grew up watching that show!
Oh my God! It's my favorite show ever! Who is your favorite character?
Henry! Get over here! Look at what Lilico gave me!
原宿
I'm going to try it on.

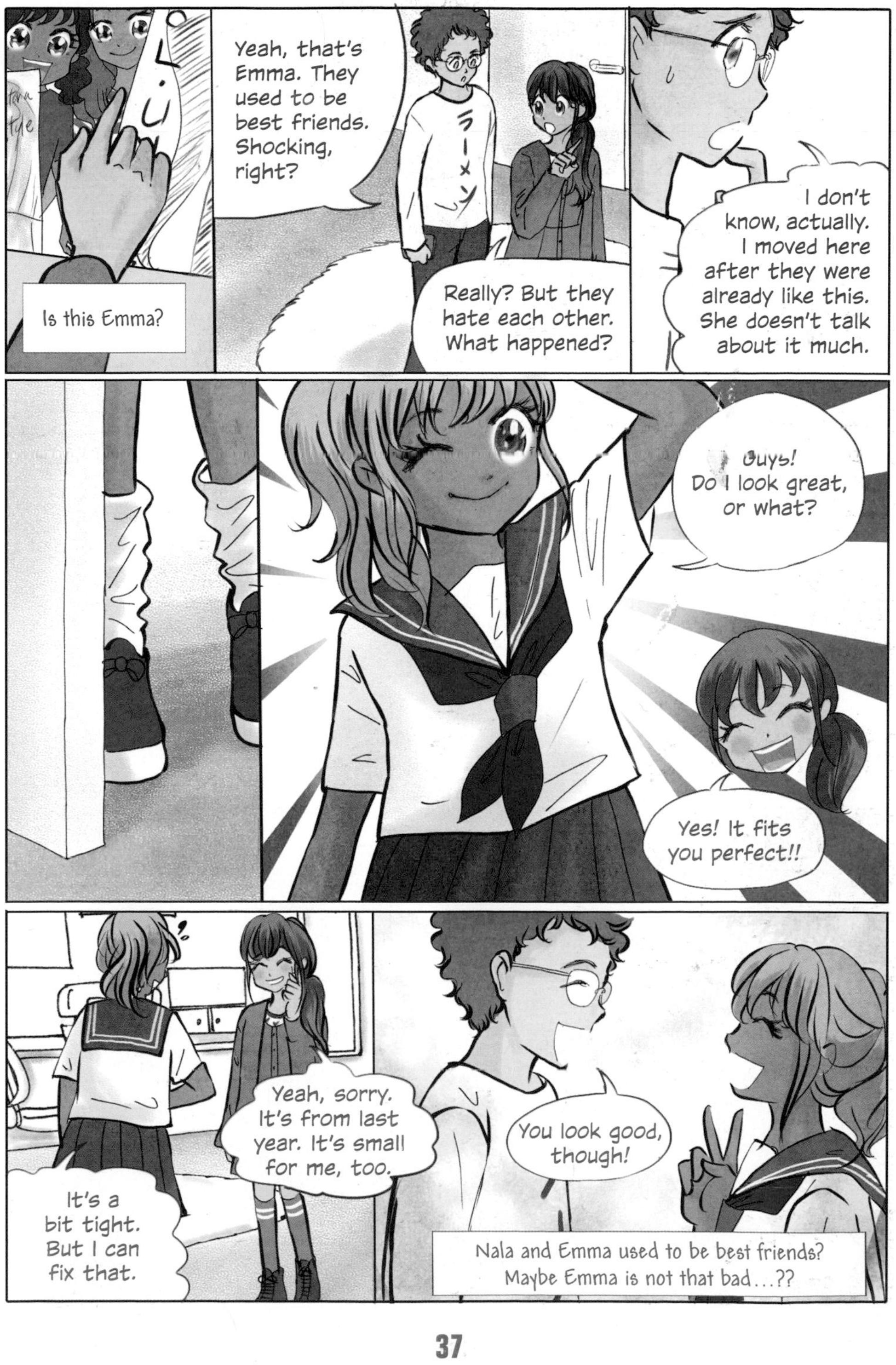
Is this Emma?
Yeah, that's Emma. They used to be best friends. Shocking, right?
ラーメン
Really? But they hate each other. What happened?
I don't know, actually. I moved here after they were already like this. She doesn't talk about it much.
Guys! Do I look great, or what?
Yes! It fits you perfect!!
It's a bit tight. But I can fix that.
Yeah, sorry. It's from last year. It's small for me, too.
You look good, though!
Nala and Emma used to be best friends? Maybe Emma is not that bad...??

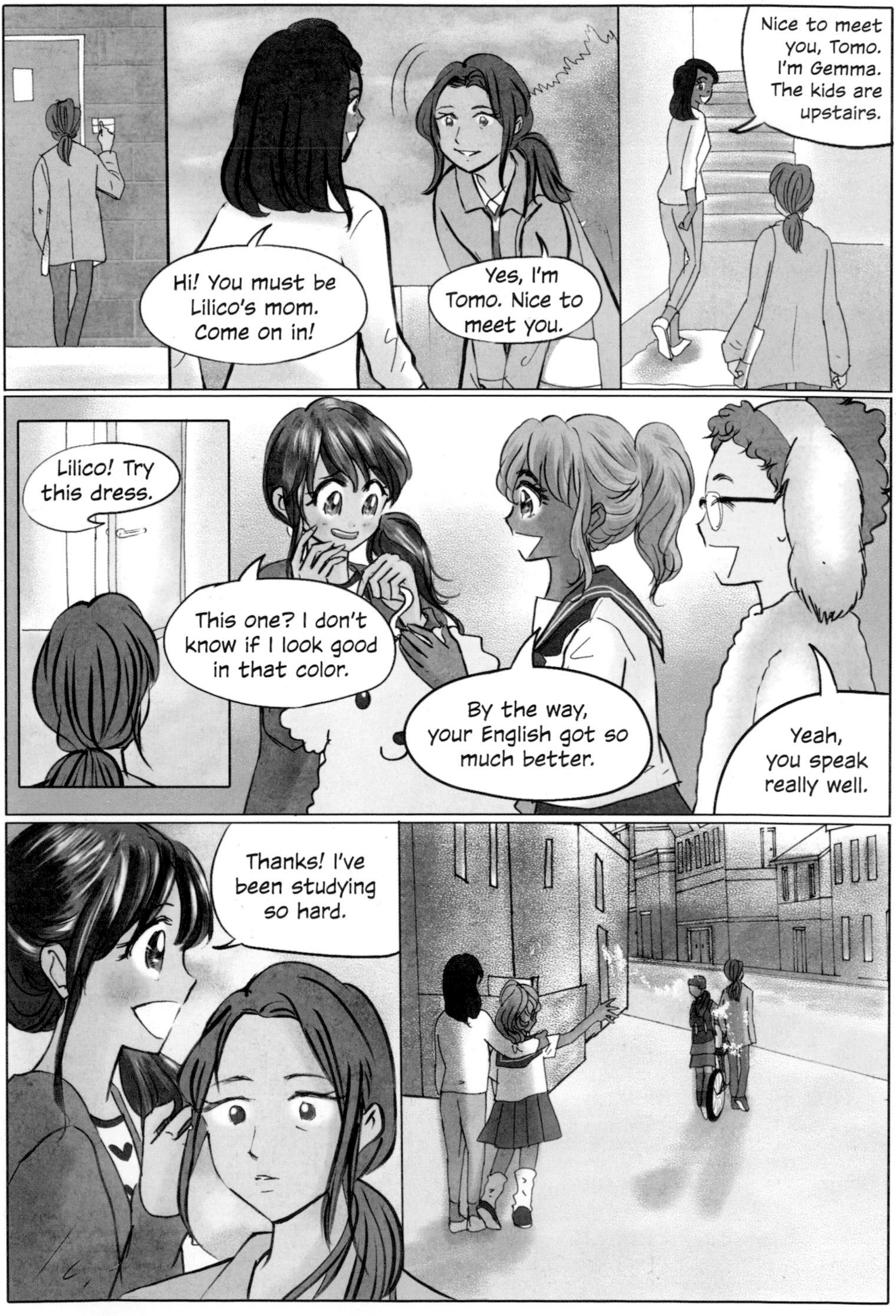
Hi! You must be Lilico's mom. Come on in!
Yes, I'm Tomo. Nice to meet you.
Nice to meet you, Tomo. I'm Gemma. The kids are upstairs.
Lilico! Try this dress.
This one? I don't know if I look good in that color.
By the way, your English got so much better.
Yeah, you speak really well.
Thanks! I've been studying so hard.

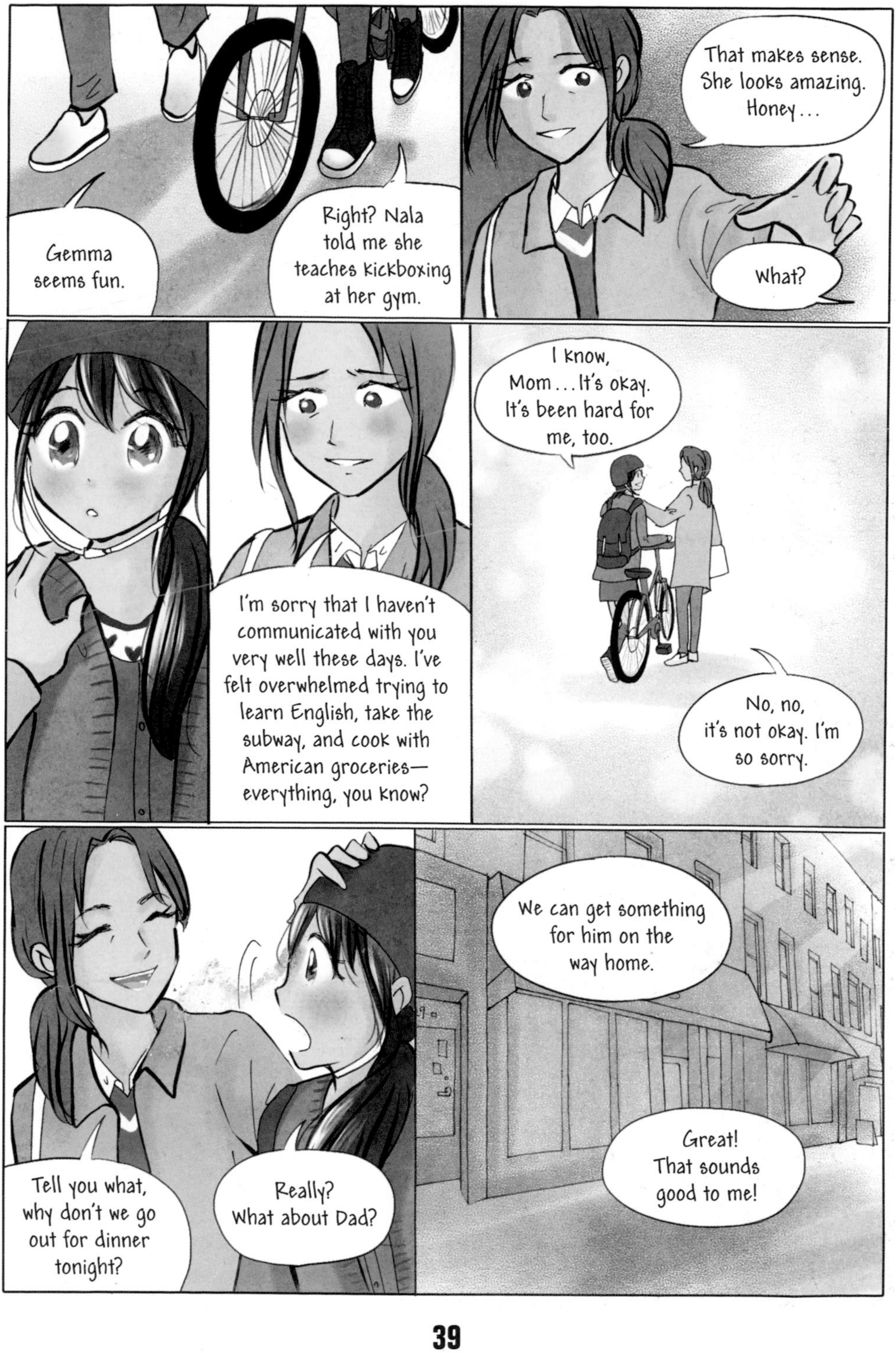
Gemma seems fun.
Right? Nala told me she teaches kickboxing at her gym.
That makes sense. She looks amazing. Honey...
What?
I'm sorry that I haven't communicated with you very well these days. I've felt overwhelmed trying to learn English, take the subway, and cook with American groceries—everything, you know?
I know, Mom... It's okay. It's been hard for me, too.
No, no, it's not okay. I'm so sorry.
Tell you what, why don't we go out for dinner tonight?
Really? What about Dad?
We can get something for him on the way home.
Great! That sounds good to me!

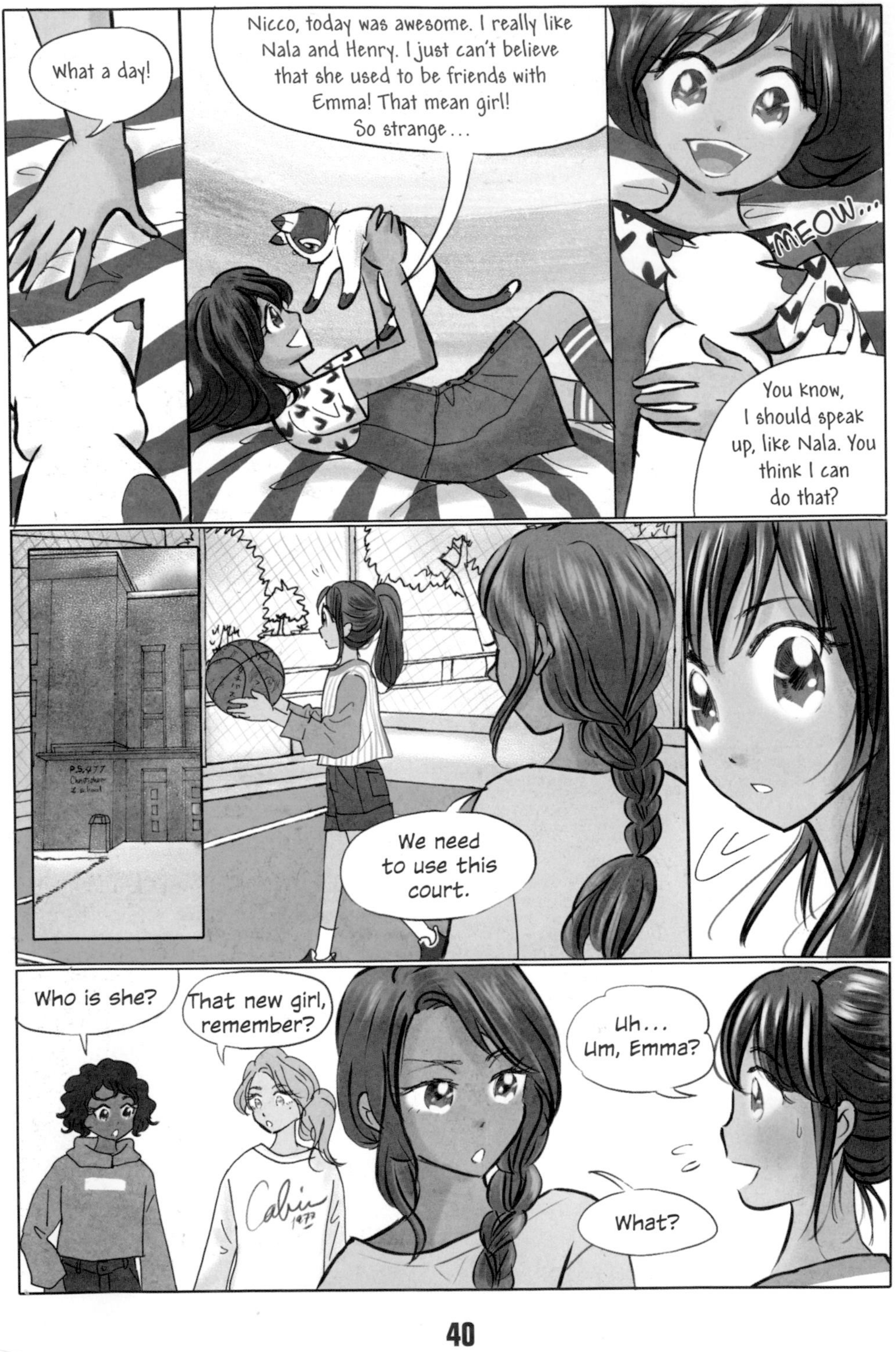
What a day!
Nicco, today was awesome. I really like Nala and Henry. I just can't believe that she used to be friends with Emma! That mean girl! So strange . . .
MEOW...
You know, I should speak up, like Nala. You think I can do that?
We need to use this court.
Who is she?
That new girl, remember?
Uh... Um, Emma?
What?

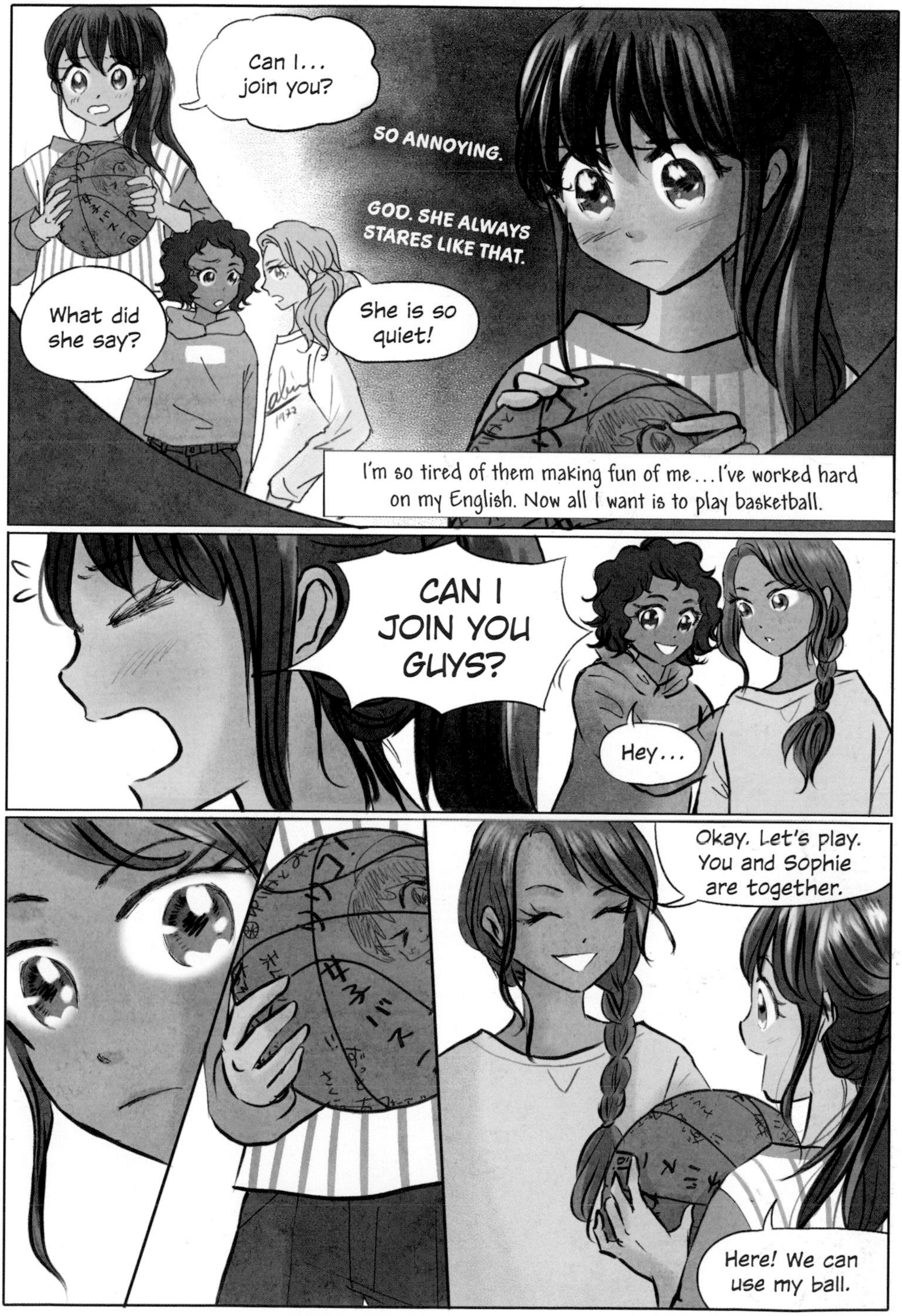
Can I...
join you?
SO ANNOYING.
GOD. SHE ALWAYS STARES LIKE THAT.
What did she say?
She is so quiet!
I'm so tired of them making fun of me... I've worked hard on my English. Now all I want is to play basketball.
CAN I JOIN YOU GUYS?
Hey...
Okay. Let's play. You and Sophie are together.
Here! We can use my ball.

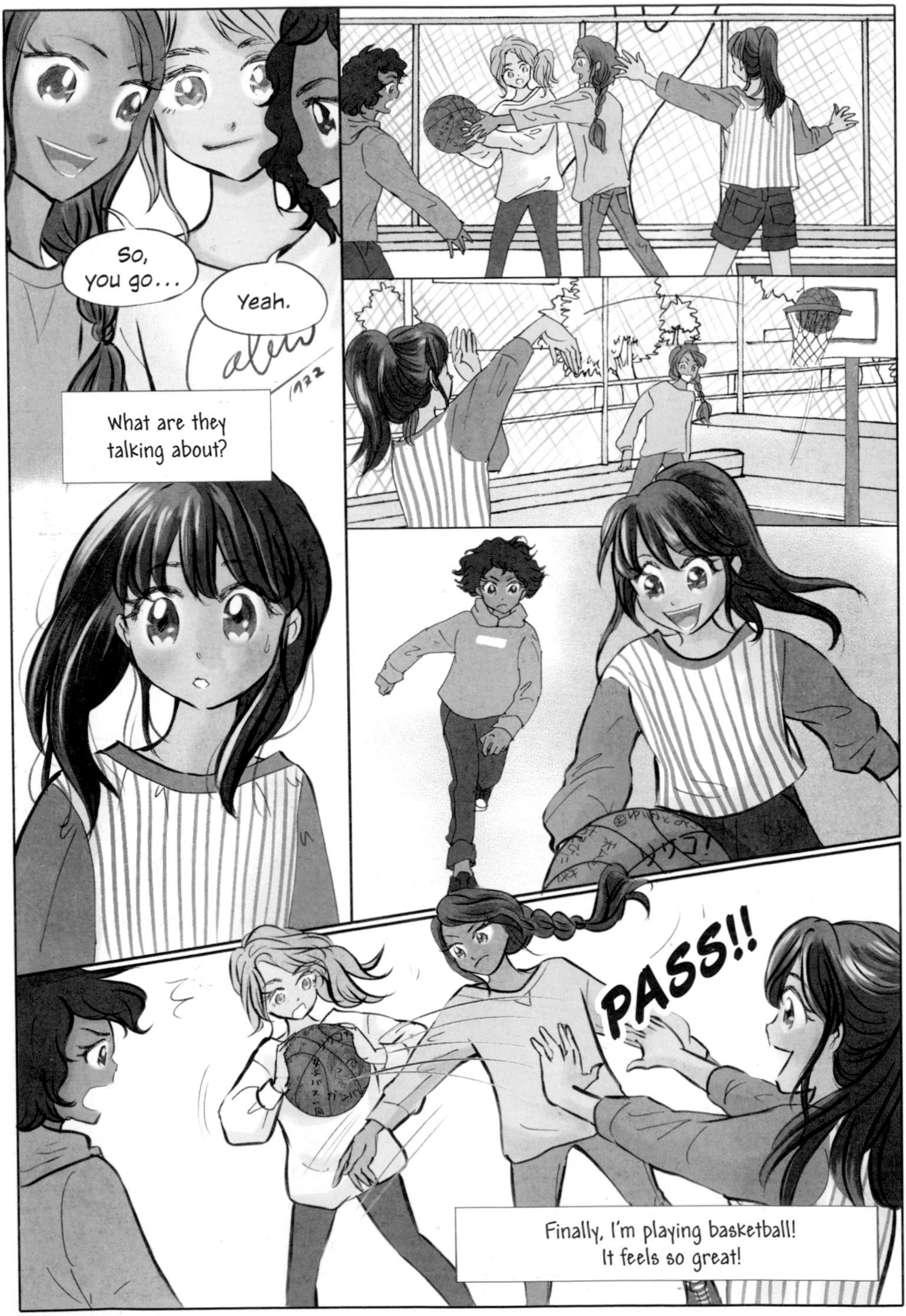

So, you go...
Yeah.
What are they talking about?
PASS!!
Finally, I'm playing basketball! It feels so great!

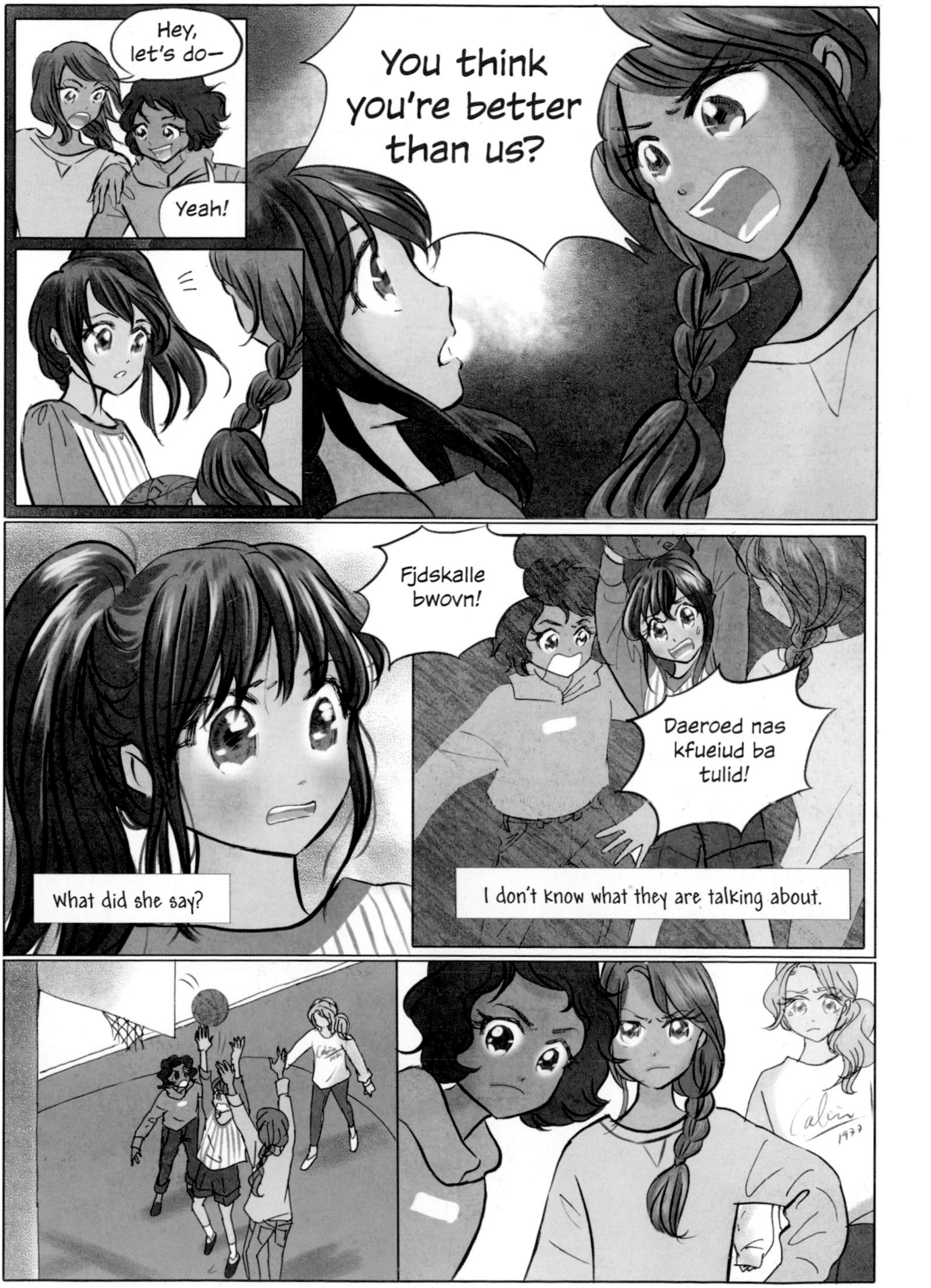
Hey, let's do—
Yeah!
You think you're better than us?
Fjdskalle bwovn!
What did she say?
Daeroed nas kfueiud ba tulid!
I don't know what they are talking about.

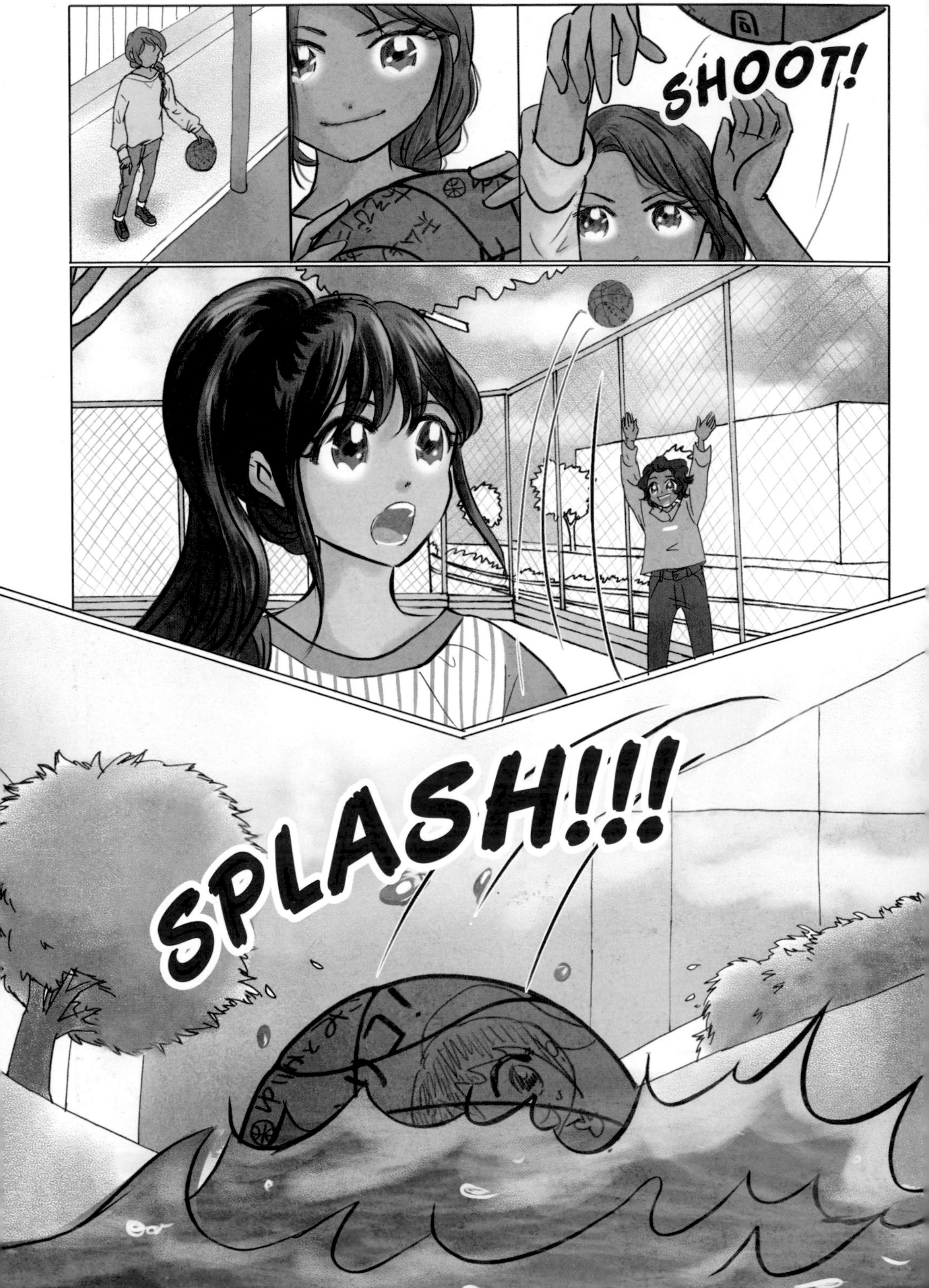
SHOOT!
SPLASH!!!

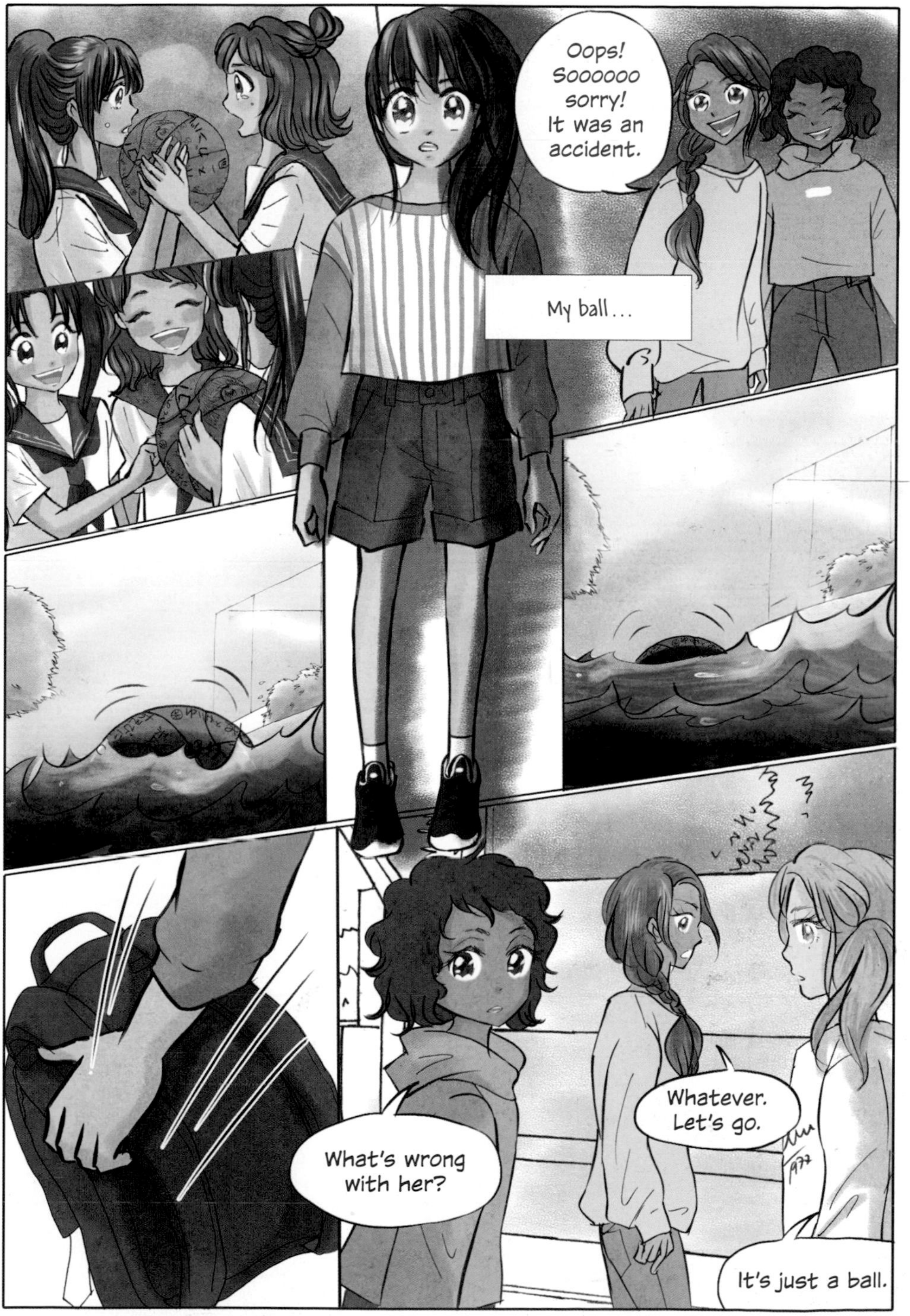
Oops! Soooooo sorry! It was an accident.
My ball...
Whatever. Let's go.
What's wrong with her?
It's just a ball.

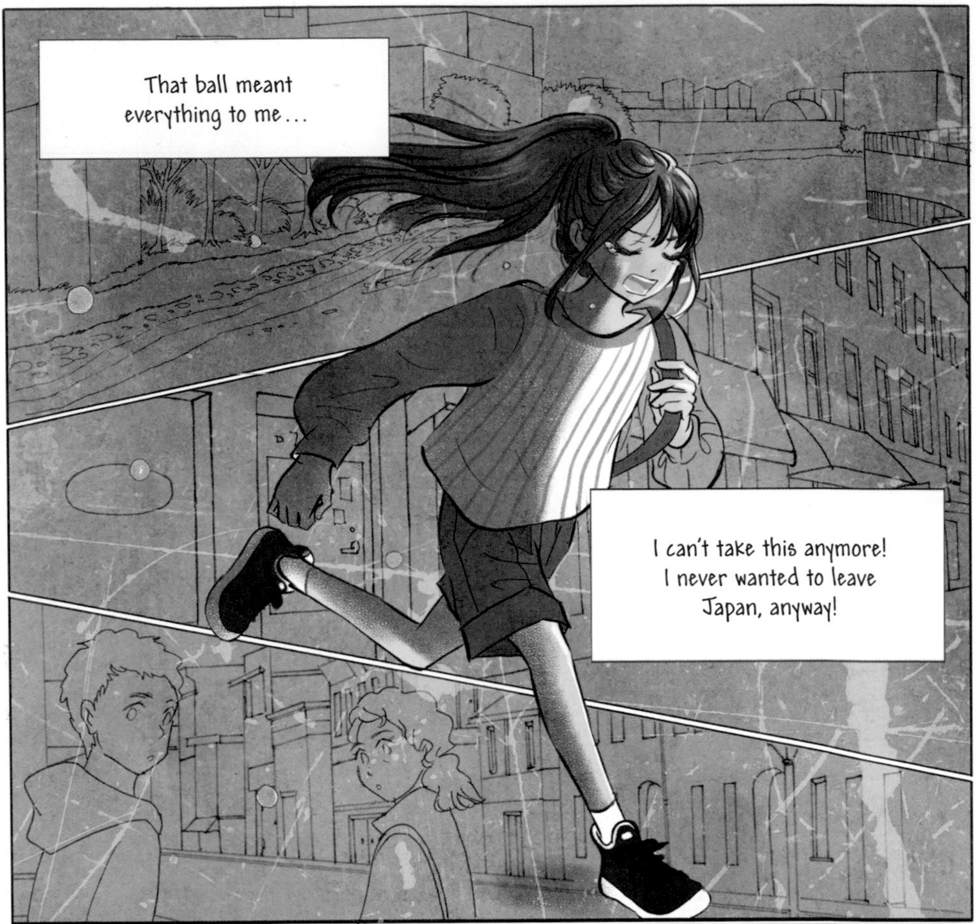
That ball meant everything to me...
I can't take this anymore! I never wanted to leave Japan, anyway!

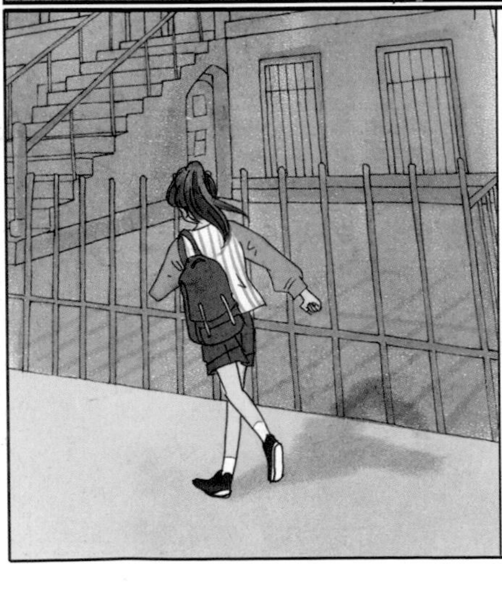

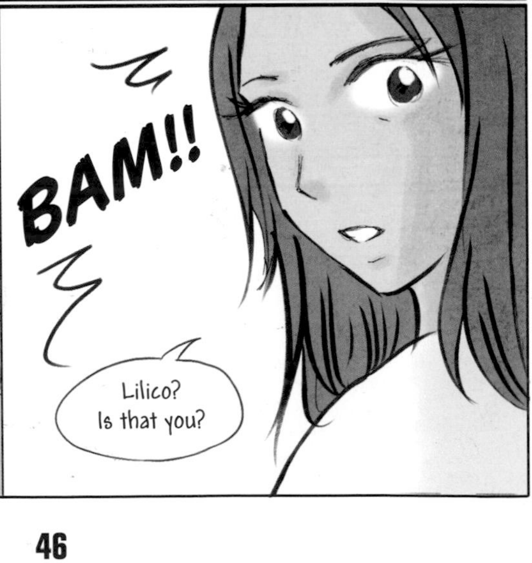
BAM!!
Lilico? Is that you?

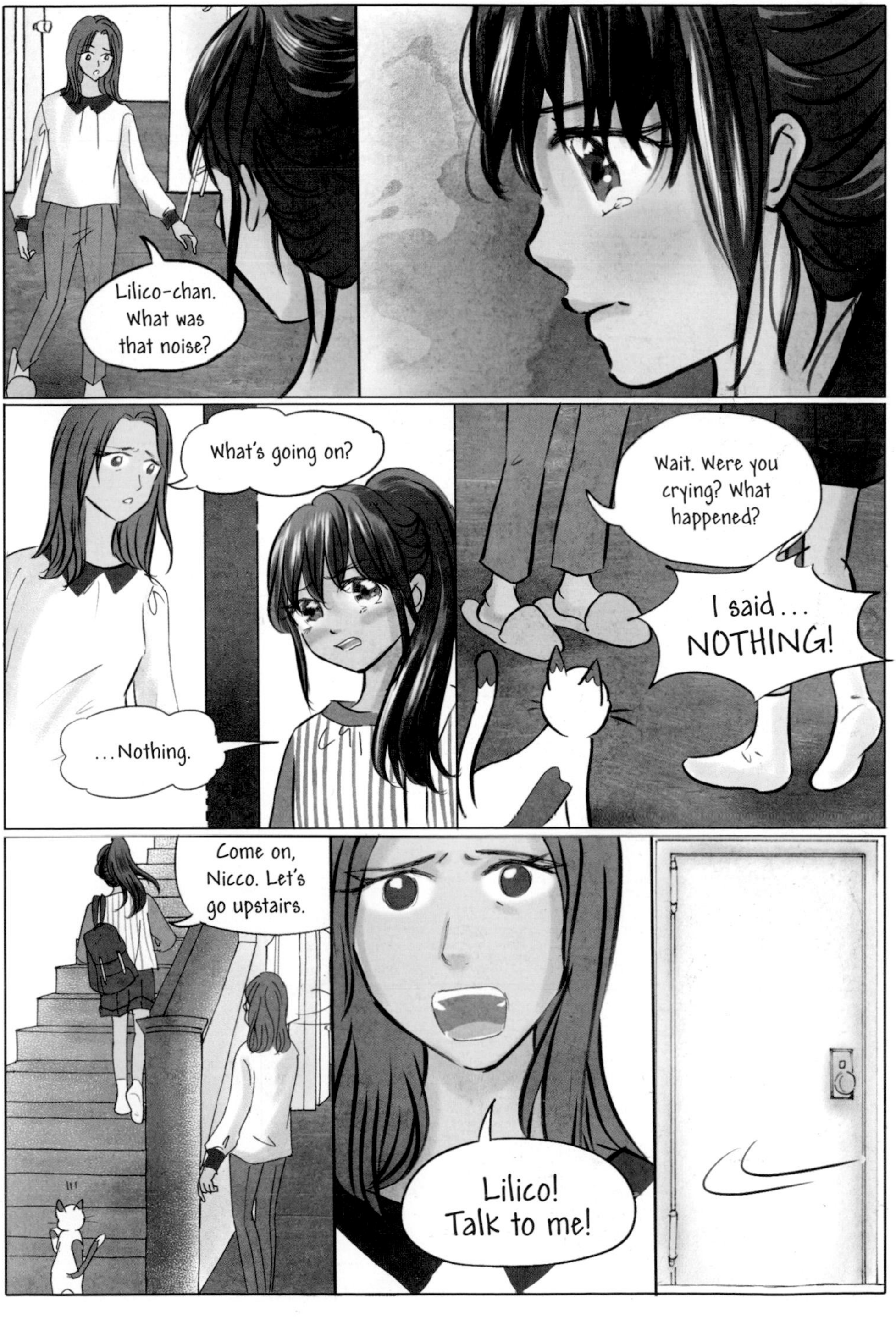
Lilico-chan. What was that noise?
What's going on?
...Nothing.
Wait. Were you crying? What happened?
I said... NOTHING!
Come on, Nicco. Let's go upstairs.
Lilico! Talk to me!

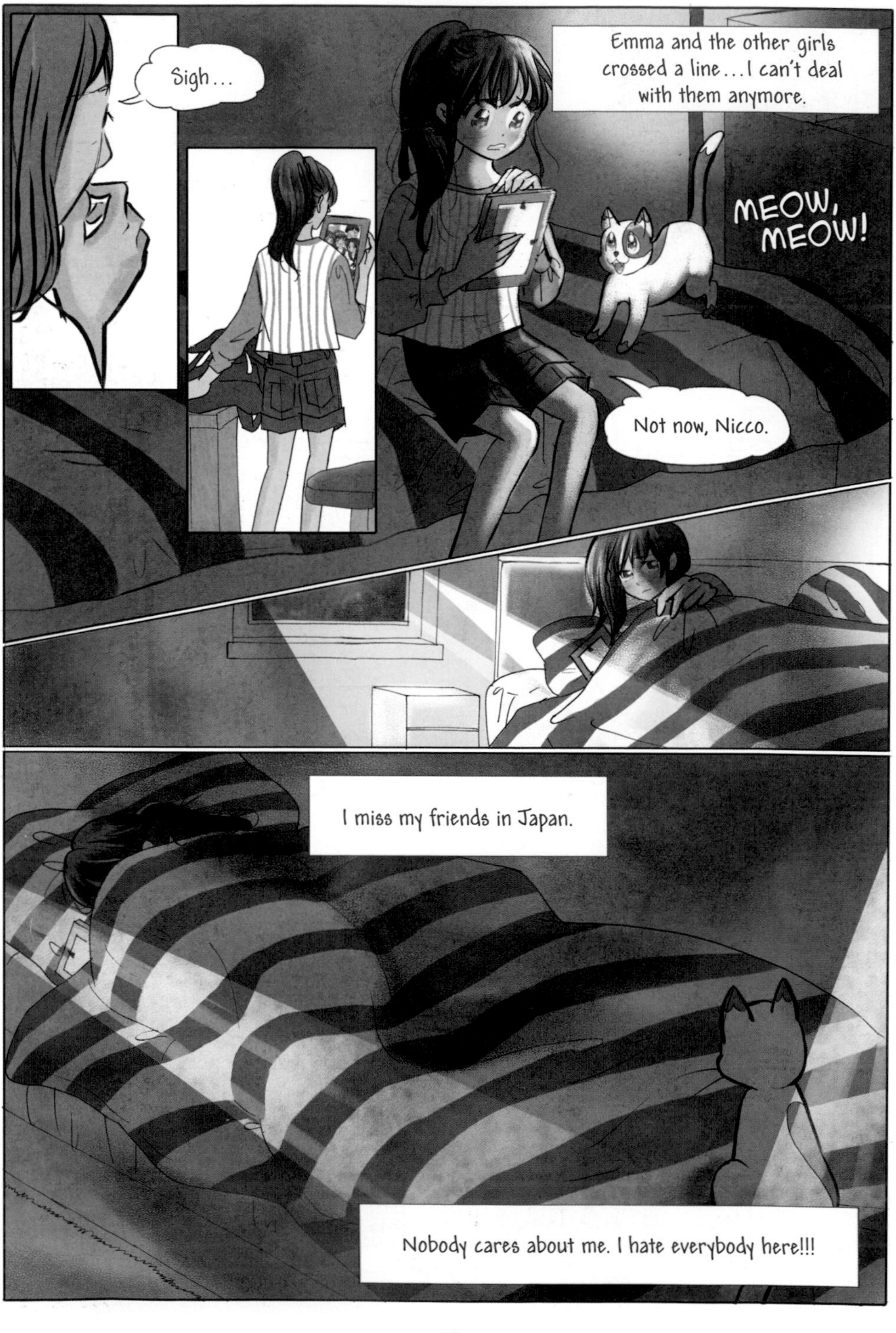
Sigh...
Emma and the other girls crossed a line... I can't deal with them anymore.
MEOW, MEOW!
Not now, Nicco.
I miss my friends in Japan.
Nobody cares about me. I hate everybody here!!!

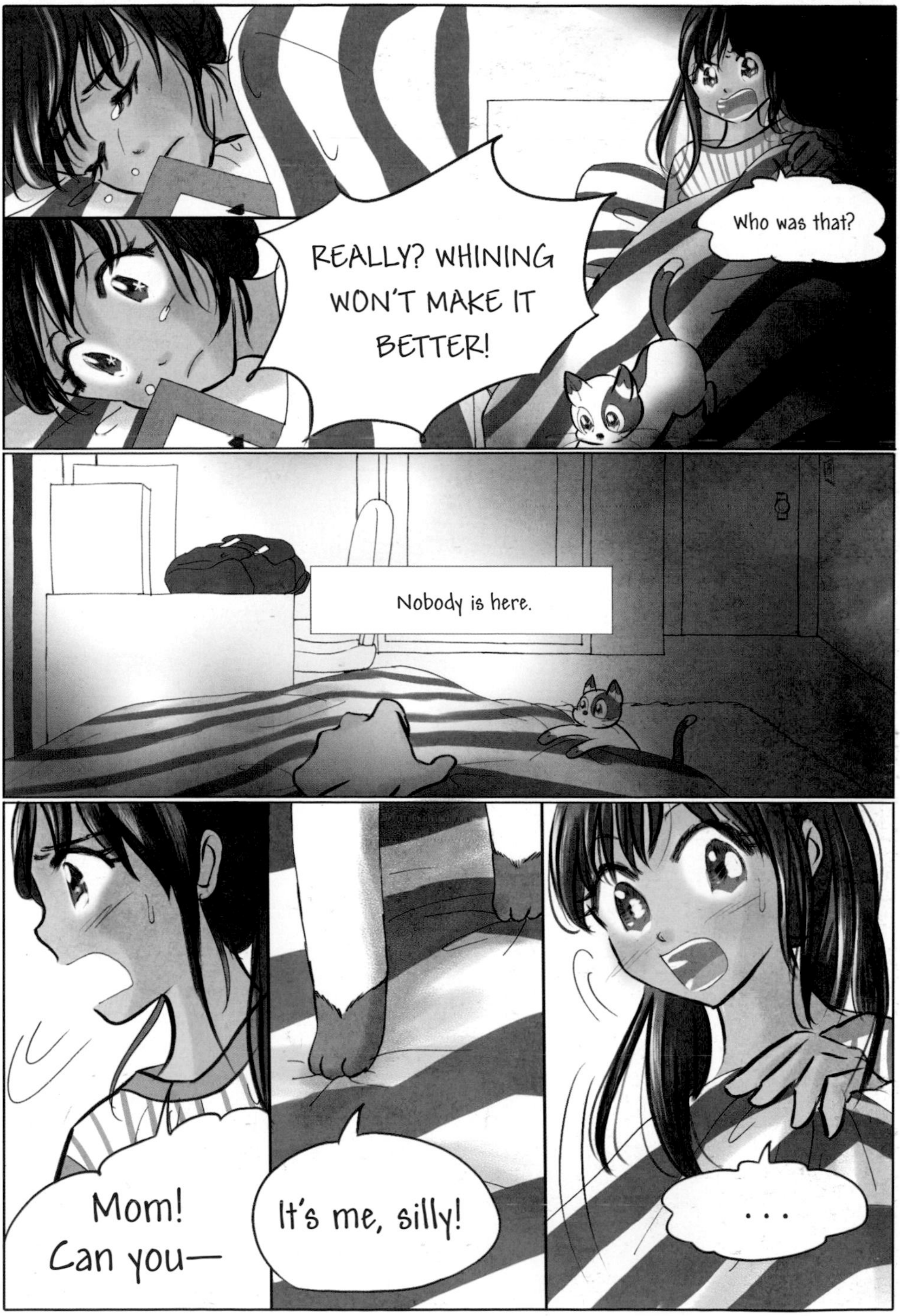
REALLY? WHINING WON'T MAKE IT BETTER!
Who was that?
Nobody is here.
Mom! Can you—
It's me, silly!
. . .

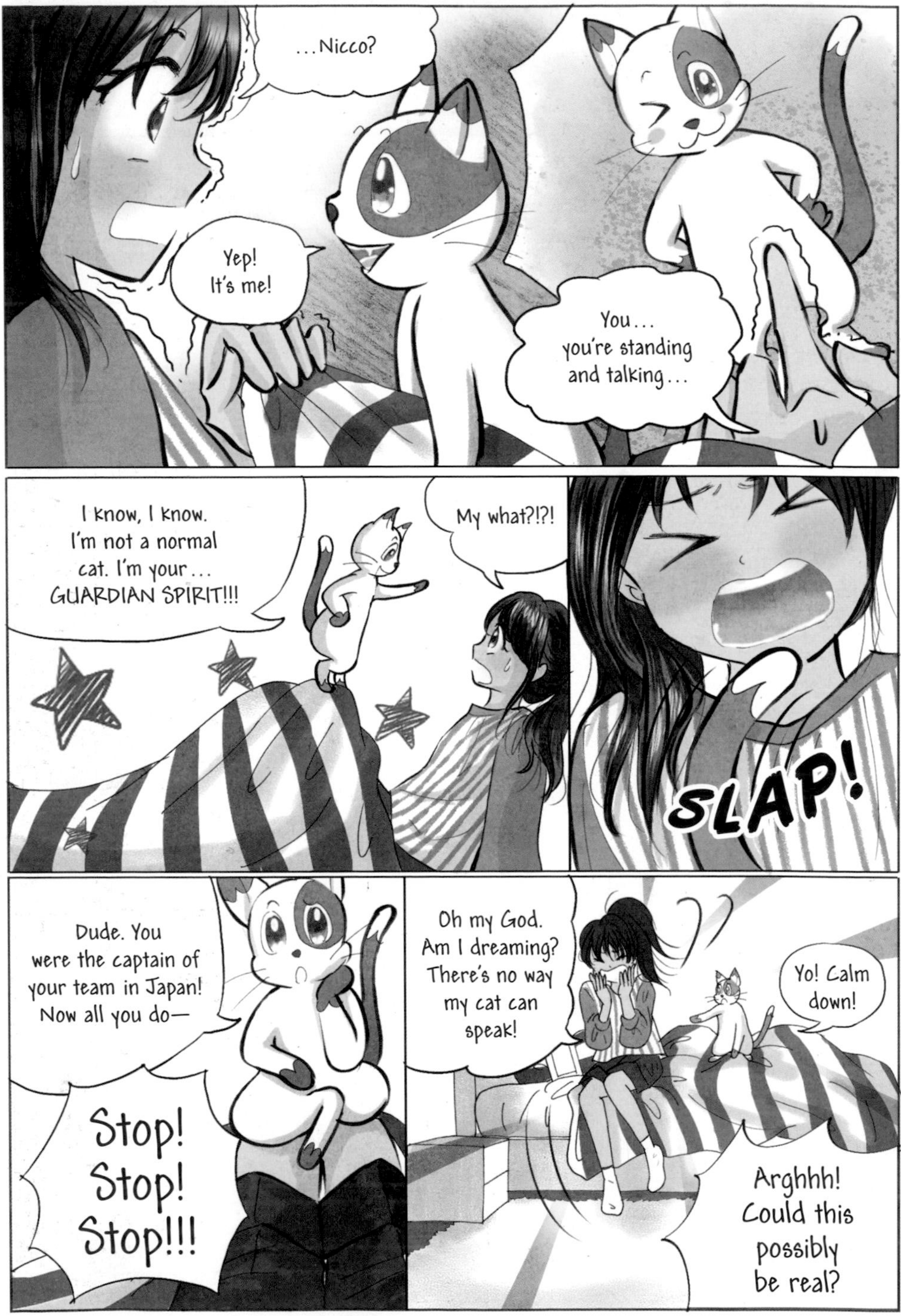
...Nicco?
Yep! It's me!
You... you're standing and talking...
I know, I know. I'm not a normal cat. I'm your... GUARDIAN SPIRIT!!!
My what?!?!
SLAP!
Dude. You were the captain of your team in Japan! Now all you do—
Stop! Stop! Stop!!!
Oh my God. Am I dreaming? There's no way my cat can speak!
Yo! Calm down!
Arghhh! Could this possibly be real?

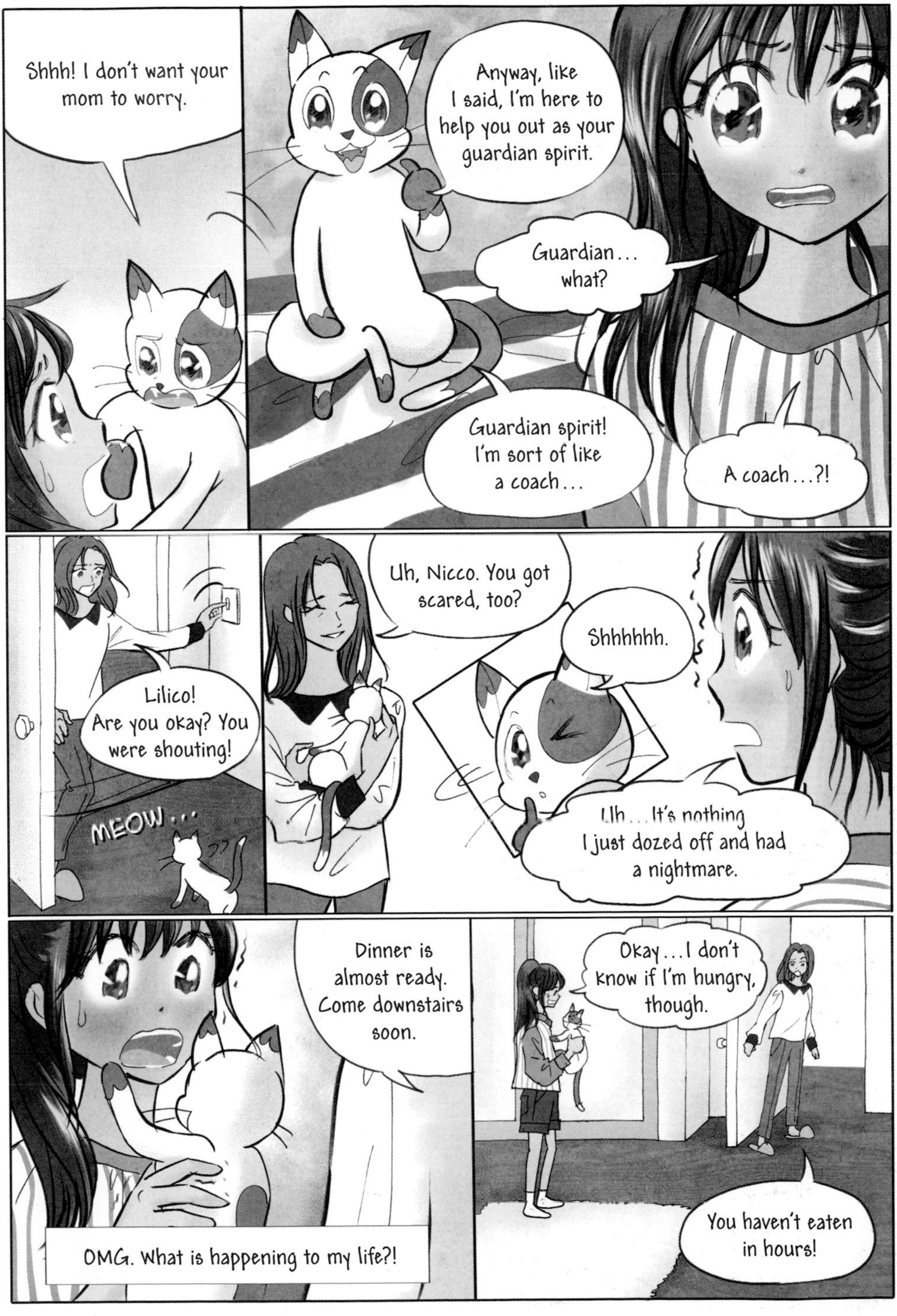
Shhh! I don't want your mom to worry.
Anyway, like I said, I'm here to help you out as your guardian spirit.
Guardian... what?
Guardian spirit! I'm sort of like a coach...
A coach...?!
Lilico! Are you okay? You were shouting!
MEOW...
??
Uh, Nicco. You got scared, too?
Shhhhhh.
Uh... It's nothing. I just dozed off and had a nightmare.
OMG. What is happening to my life?!
Dinner is almost ready. Come downstairs soon.
Okay... I don't know if I'm hungry, though.
You haven't eaten in hours!

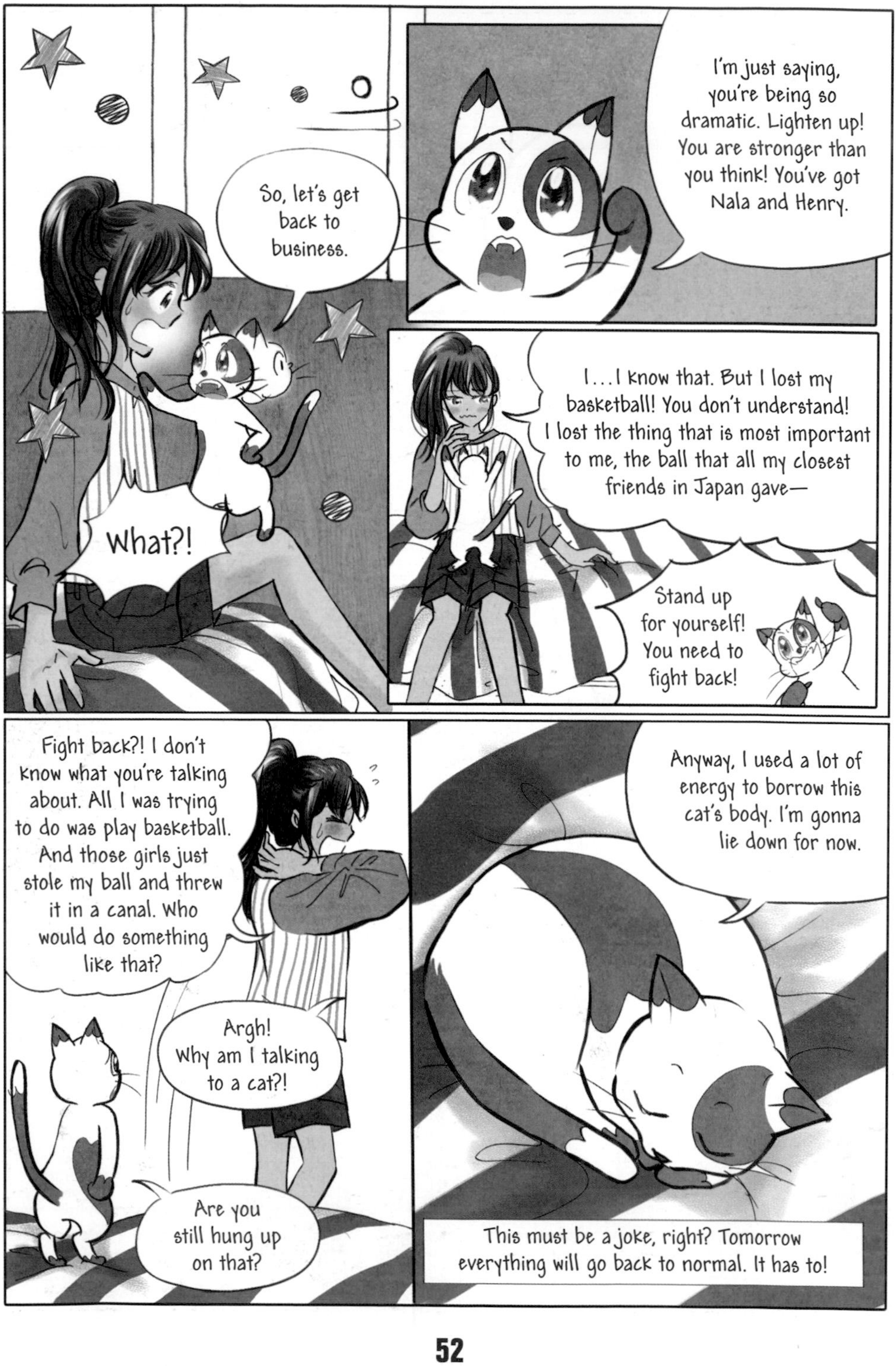
So, let's get back to business.
What?!
I'm just saying, you're being so dramatic. Lighten up! You are stronger than you think! You've got Nala and Henry.
I... I know that. But I lost my basketball! You don't understand! I lost the thing that is most important to me, the ball that all my closest friends in Japan gave—
Stand up for yourself! You need to fight back!
Fight back?! I don't know what you're talking about. All I was trying to do was play basketball. And those girls just stole my ball and threw it in a canal. Who would do something like that?
Argh! Why am I talking to a cat?!
Are you still hung up on that?
Anyway, I used a lot of energy to borrow this cat's body. I'm gonna lie down for now.
This must be a joke, right? Tomorrow everything will go back to normal. It has to!

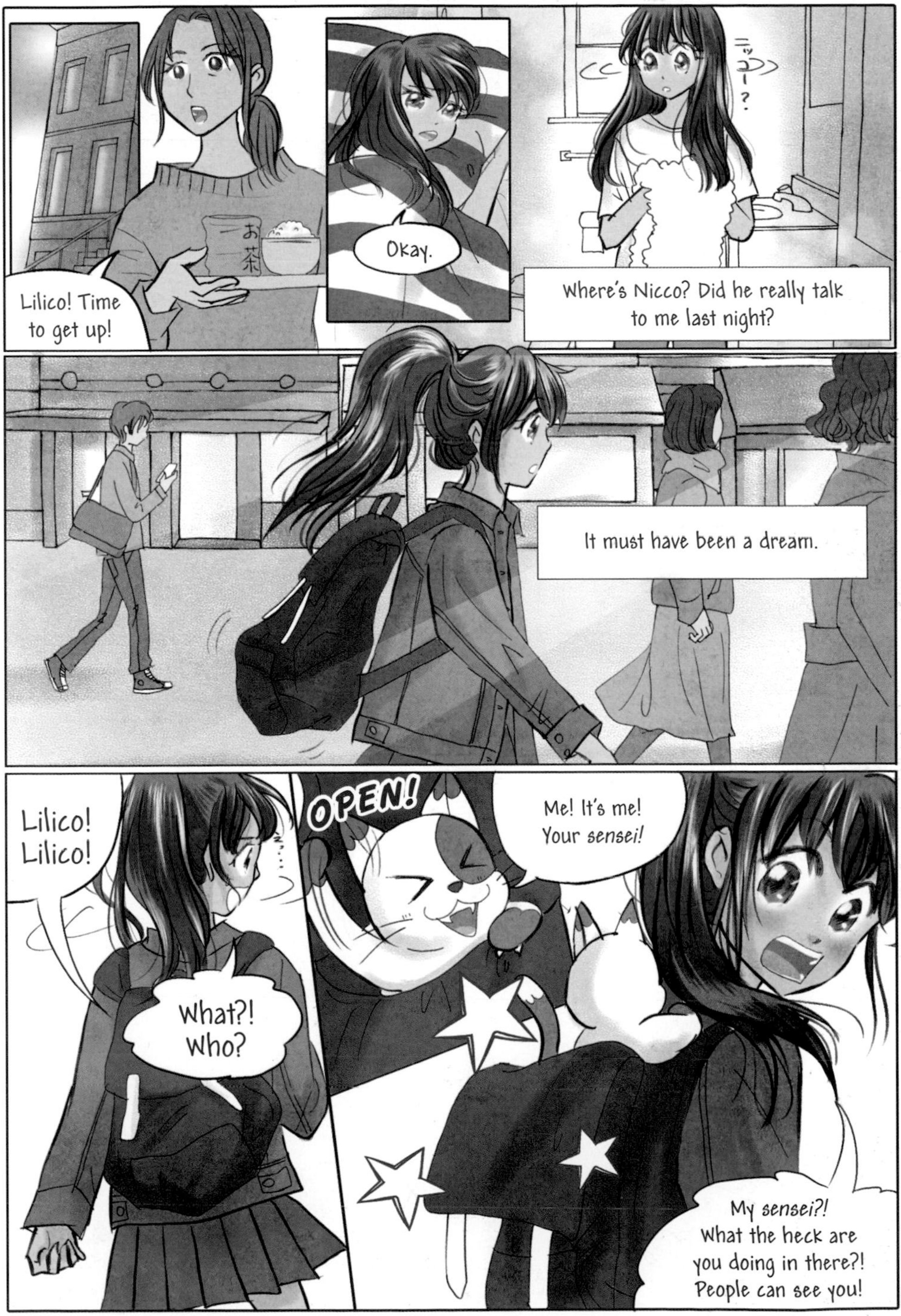
Lilico! Time to get up!
お茶
Okay.
ニッコー？
Where's Nicco? Did he really talk to me last night?
It must have been a dream.
Lilico! Lilico!
What?! Who?
OPEN!
Me! It's me! Your sensei!
My sensei?! What the heck are you doing in there?! People can see you!

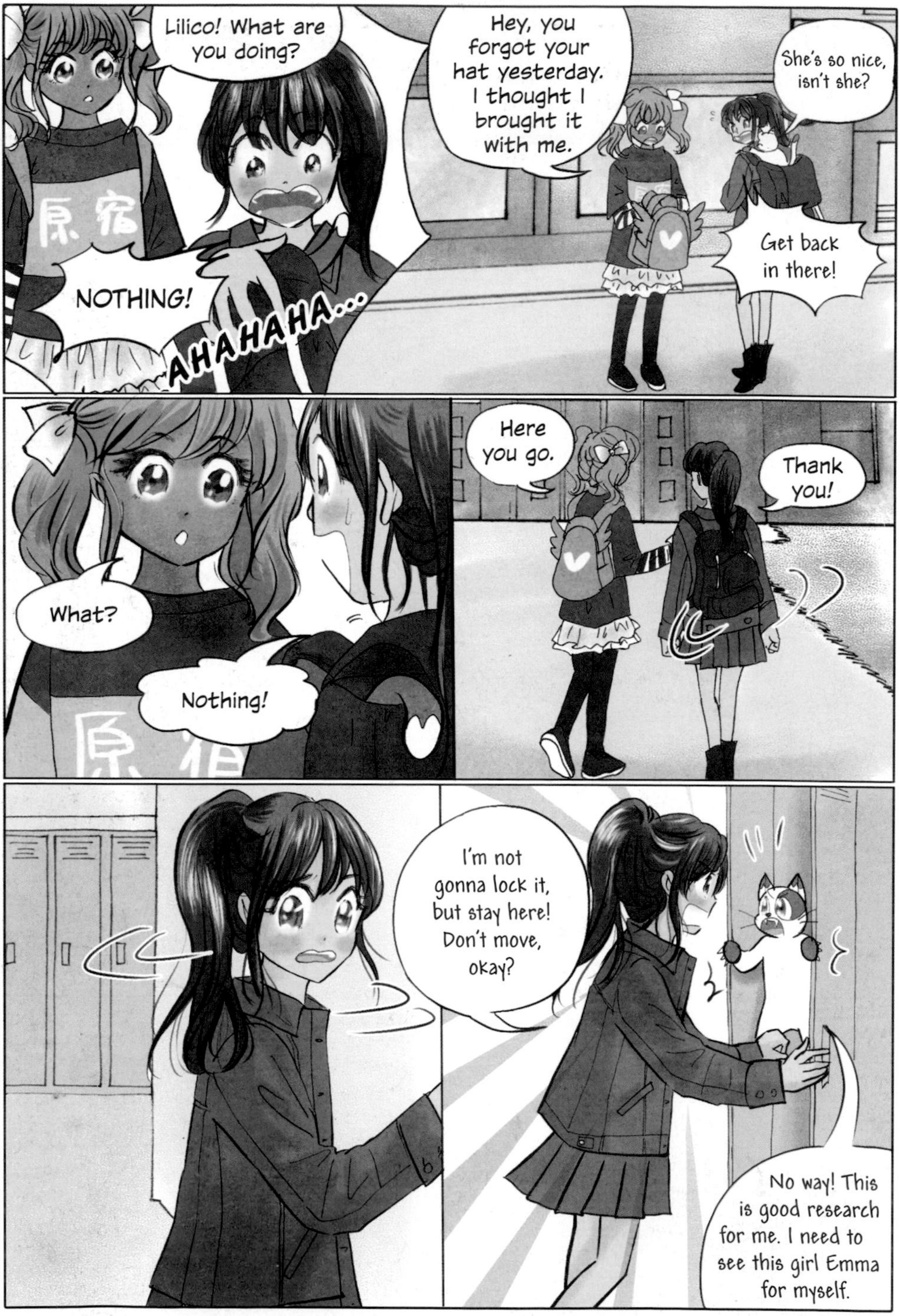
Lilico! What are you doing?
NOTHING!
AHAHAHA...
Hey, you forgot your hat yesterday. I thought I brought it with me.
She's so nice, isn't she?
Get back in there!
What?
Nothing!
Here you go.
Thank you!
I'm not gonna lock it, but stay here! Don't move, okay?
No way! This is good research for me. I need to see this girl Emma for myself.

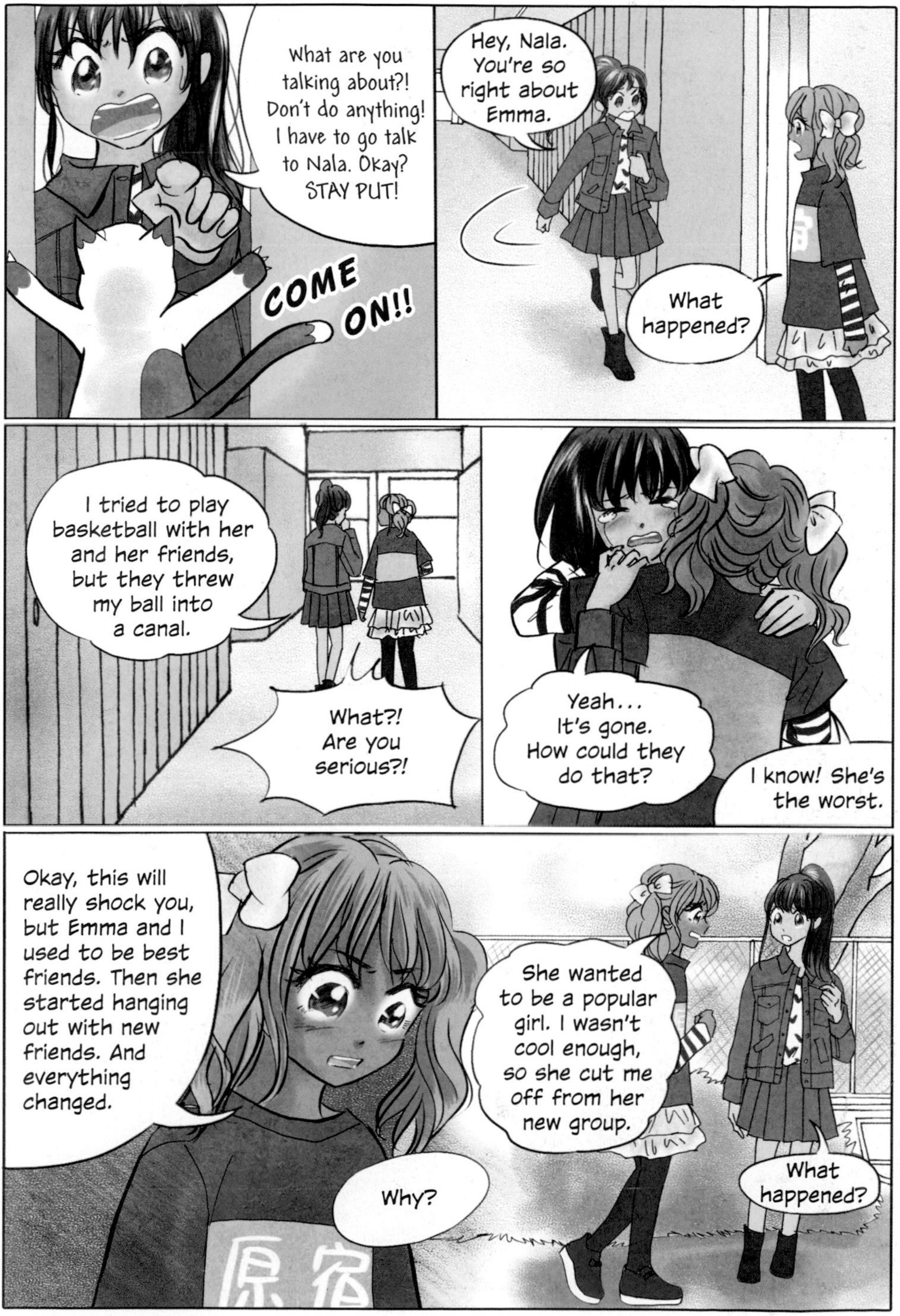
What are you talking about?! Don't do anything! I have to go talk to Nala. Okay? STAY PUT!
COME ON!!
Hey, Nala. You're so right about Emma.
What happened?
I tried to play basketball with her and her friends, but they threw my ball into a canal.
What?! Are you serious?!
Yeah... It's gone. How could they do that?
I know! She's the worst.
Okay, this will really shock you, but Emma and I used to be best friends. Then she started hanging out with new friends. And everything changed.
She wanted to be a popular girl. I wasn't cool enough, so she cut me off from her new group.
What happened?
Why?

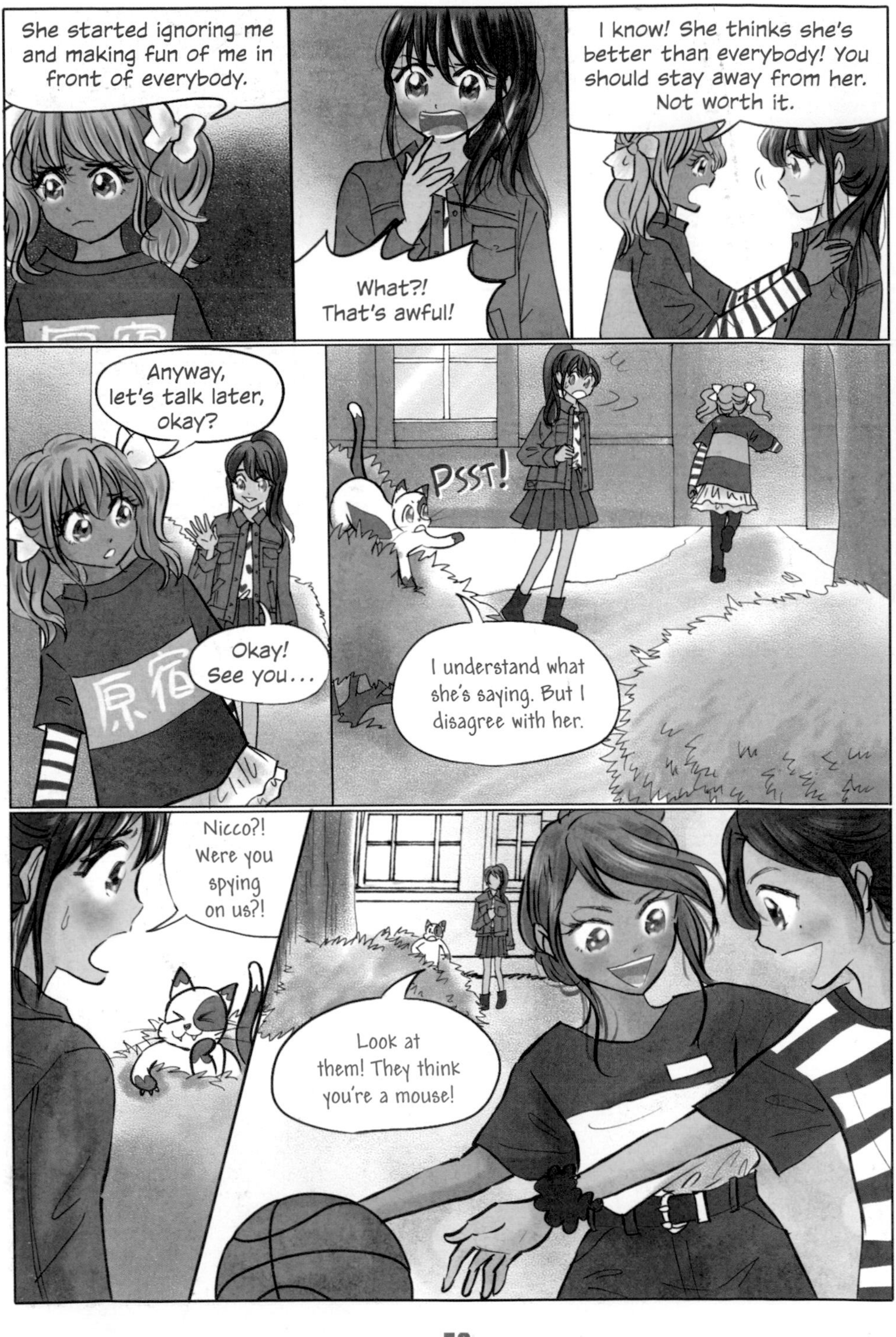
She started ignoring me and making fun of me in front of everybody.
What?! That's awful!
I know! She thinks she's better than everybody! You should stay away from her. Not worth it.
Anyway, let's talk later, okay?
Okay! See you...
PSST!
I understand what she's saying. But I disagree with her.
Nicco?! Were you spying on us?!
Look at them! They think you're a mouse!

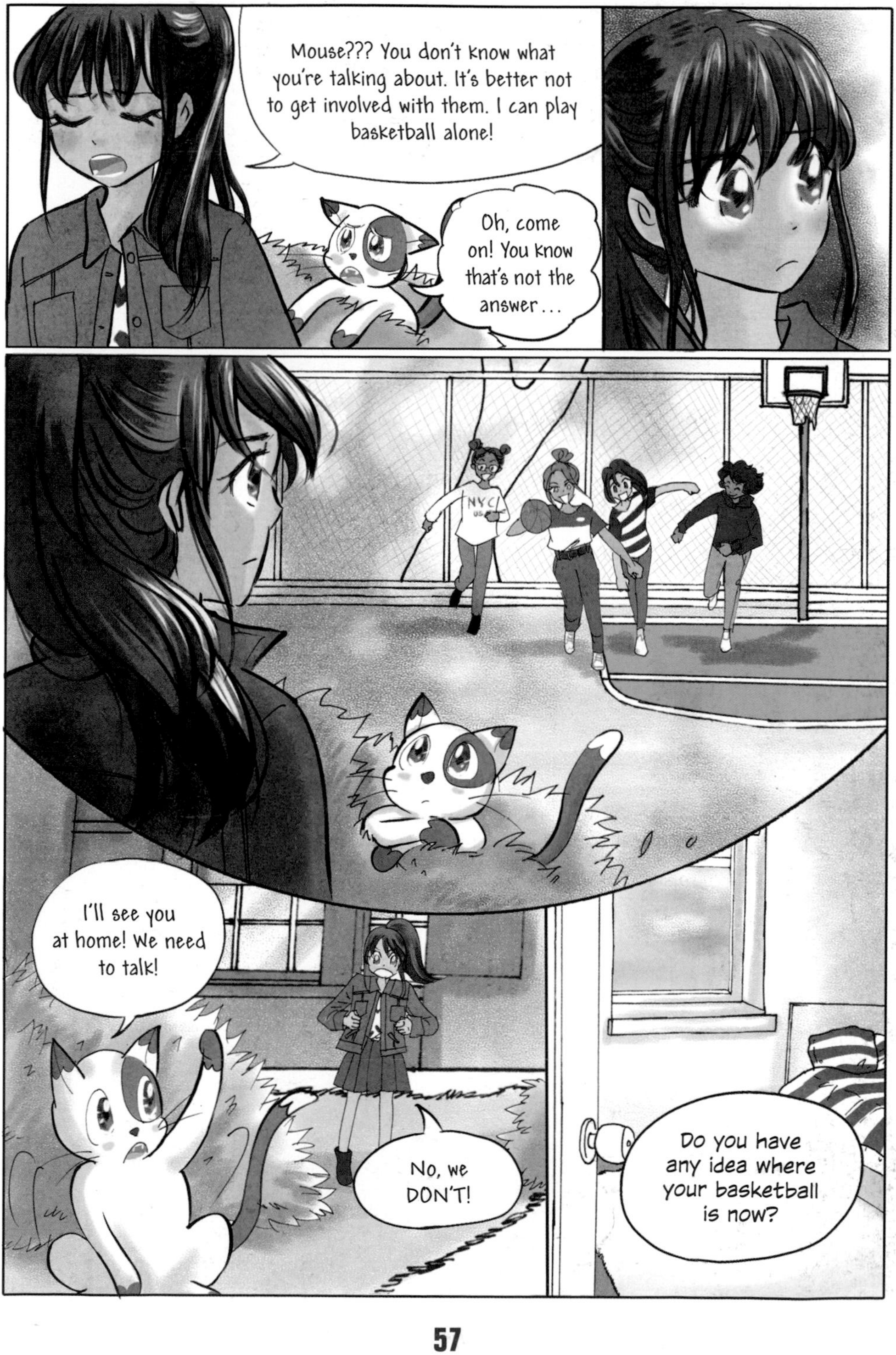
Mouse??? You don't know what you're talking about. It's better not to get involved with them. I can play basketball alone!
Oh, come on! You know that's not the answer...
I'll see you at home! We need to talk!
No, we DON'T!
Do you have any idea where your basketball is now?

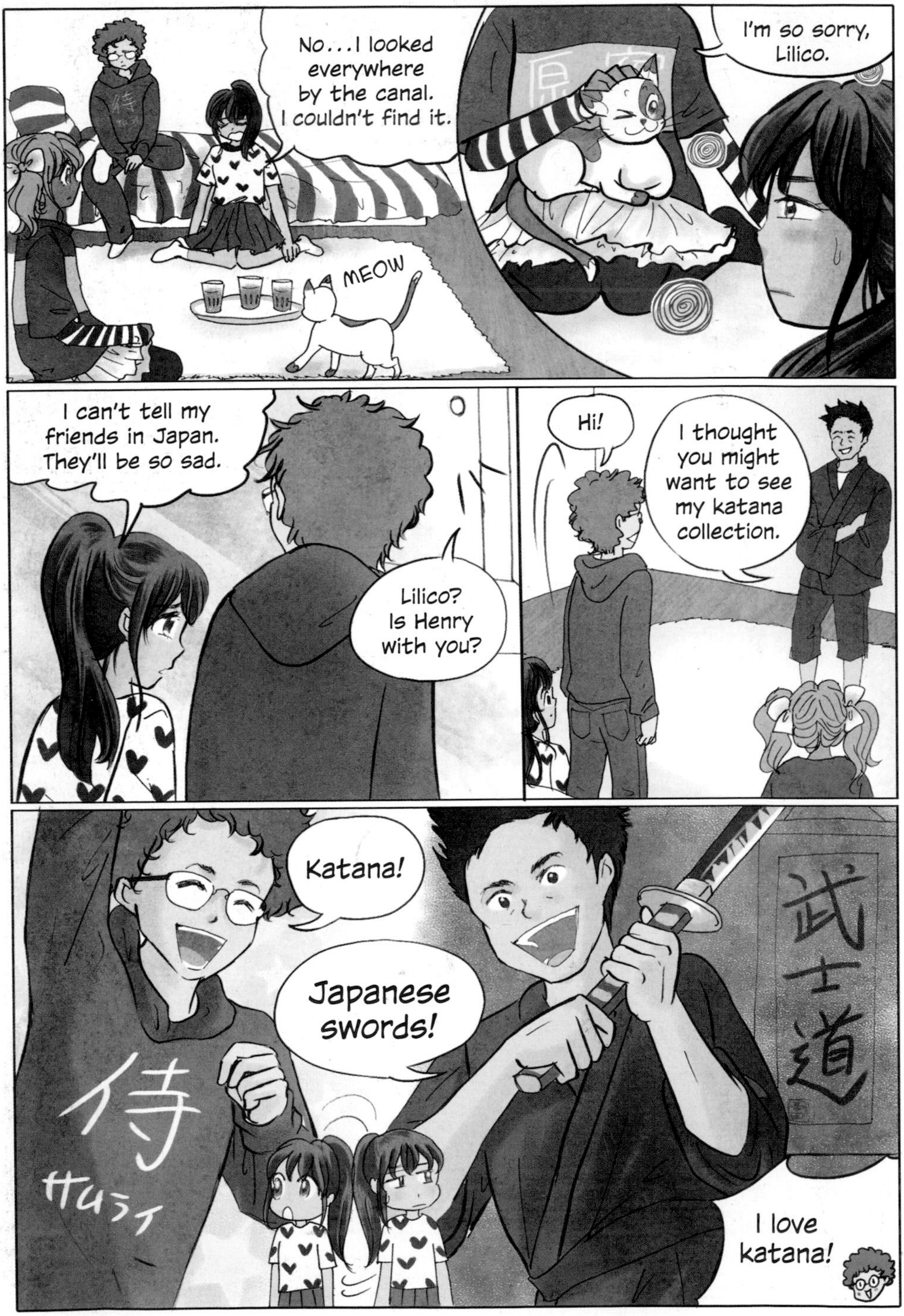

No . . . I looked everywhere by the canal. I couldn't find it.
MEOW
I'm so sorry, Lilico.
I can't tell my friends in Japan. They'll be so sad.
Lilico? Is Henry with you?
Hi!
I thought you might want to see my katana collection.
Katana!
Japanese swords!
侍
サムライ
武士道
I love katana!

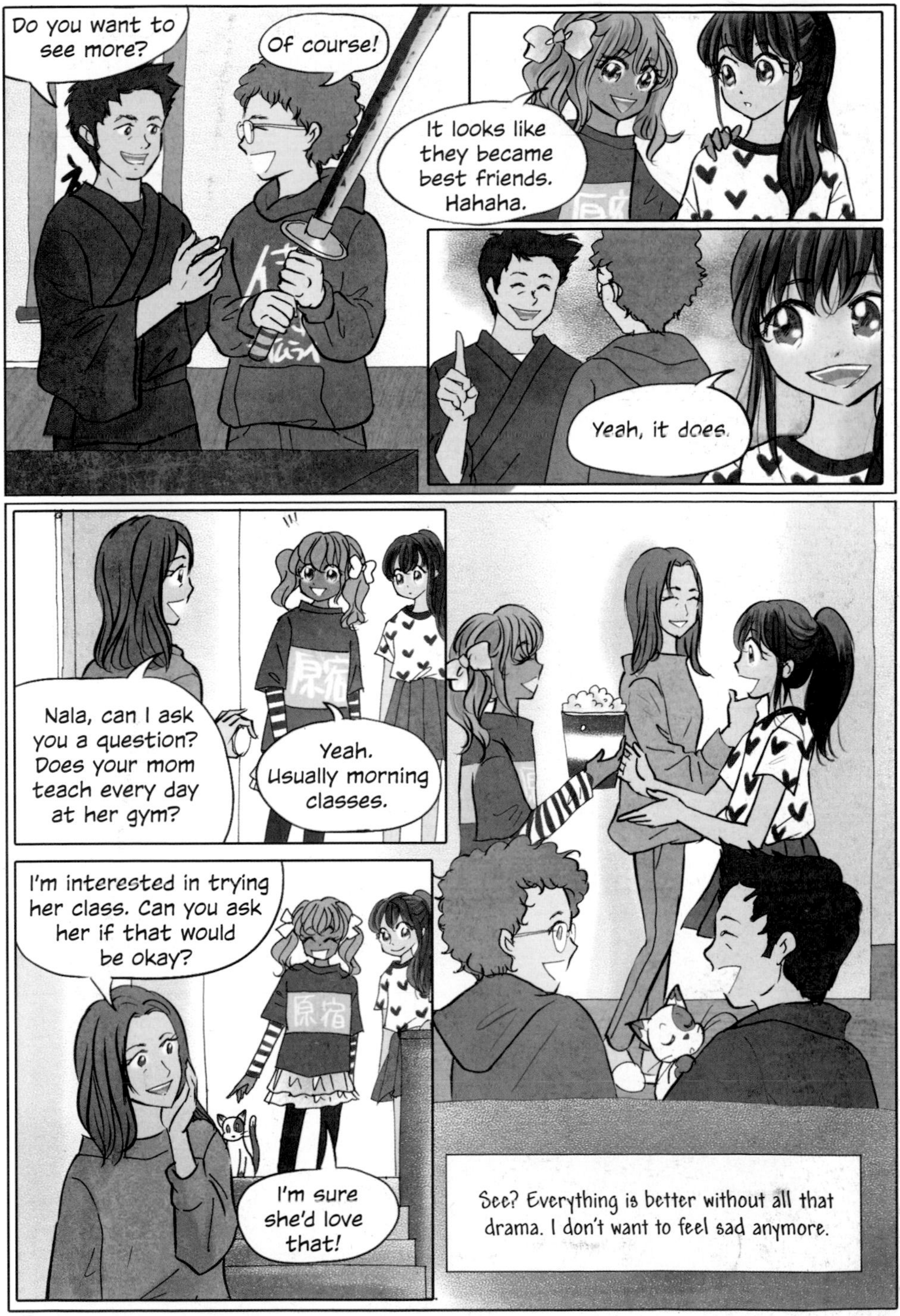
Do you want to see more?
Of course!
It looks like they became best friends. Hahaha.
Yeah, it does.
Nala, can I ask you a question? Does your mom teach every day at her gym?
Yeah. Usually morning classes.
I'm interested in trying her class. Can you ask her if that would be okay?
I'm sure she'd love that!
See? Everything is better without all that drama. I don't want to feel sad anymore.

CHAPTER 3

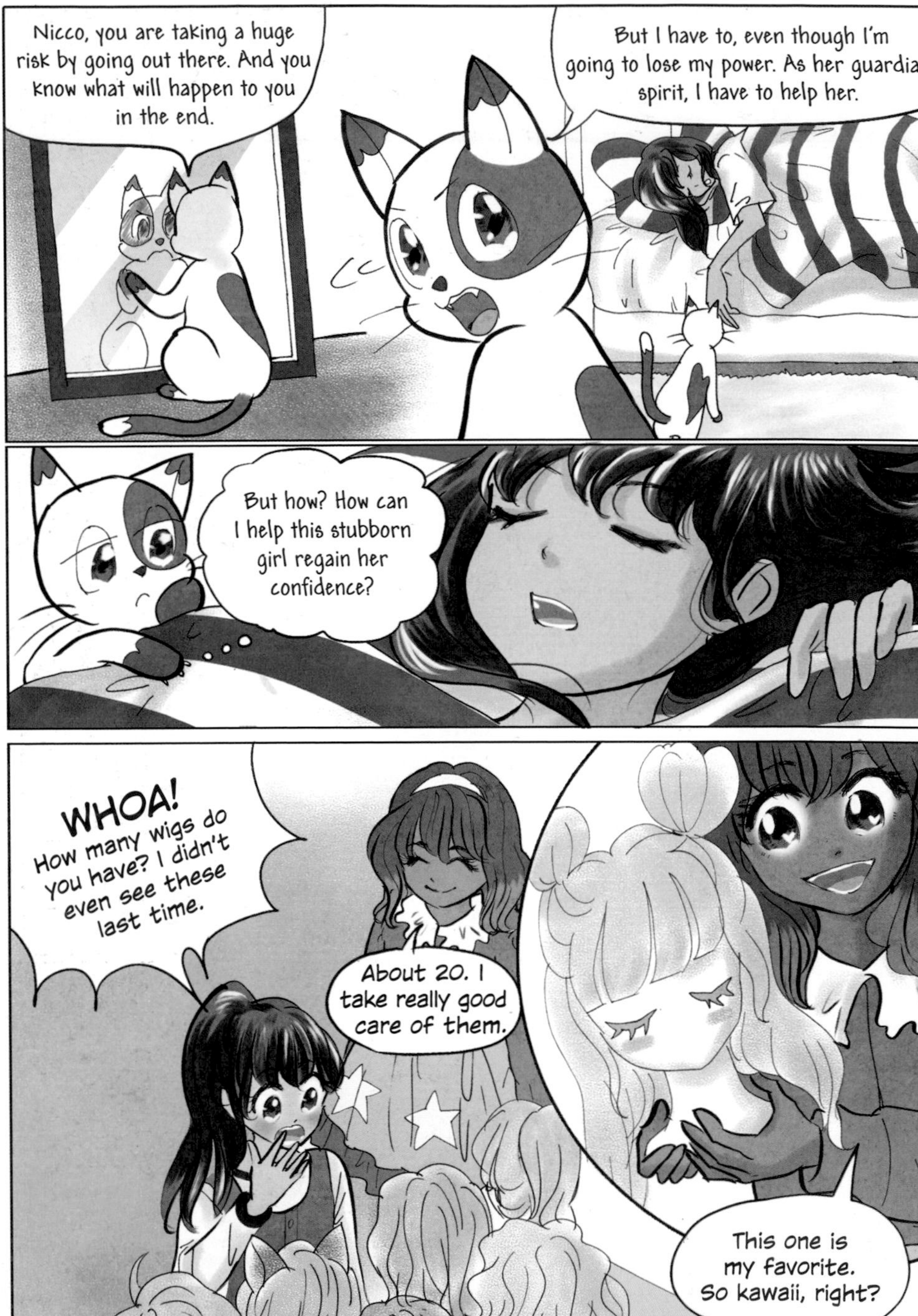
Nicco, you are taking a huge risk by going out there. And you know what will happen to you in the end.
But I have to, even though I'm going to lose my power. As her guardian spirit, I have to help her.
But how? How can I help this stubborn girl regain her confidence?
WHOA! How many wigs do you have? I didn't even see these last time.
About 20. I take really good care of them.
This one is my favorite. So kawaii, right?

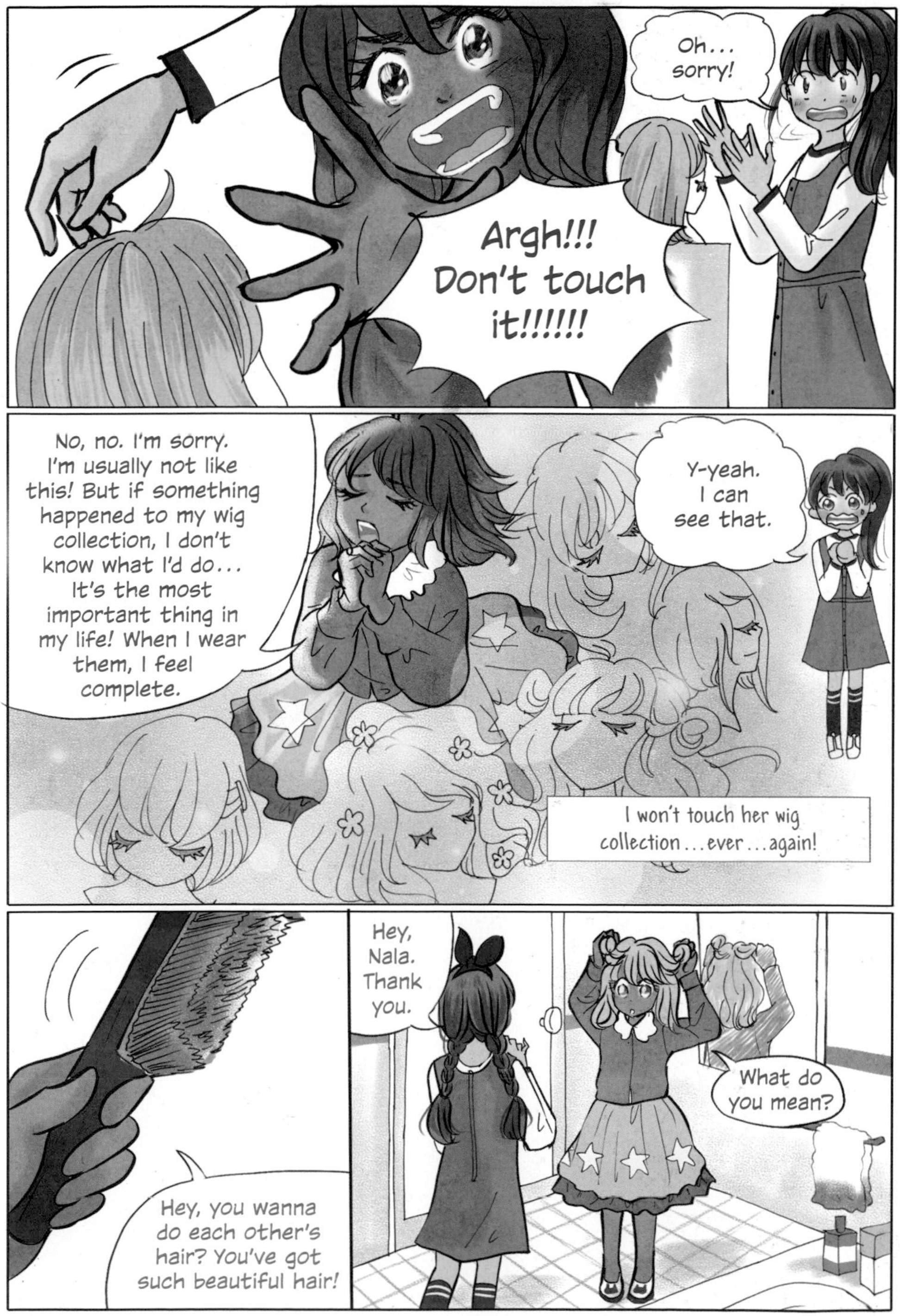
Argh!!! Don't touch it!!!!!!
Oh... sorry!
No, no. I'm sorry. I'm usually not like this! But if something happened to my wig collection, I don't know what I'd do... It's the most important thing in my life! When I wear them, I feel complete.
Y-yeah. I can see that.
I won't touch her wig collection...ever...again!
Hey, you wanna do each other's hair? You've got such beautiful hair!
Hey, Nala. Thank you.
What do you mean?

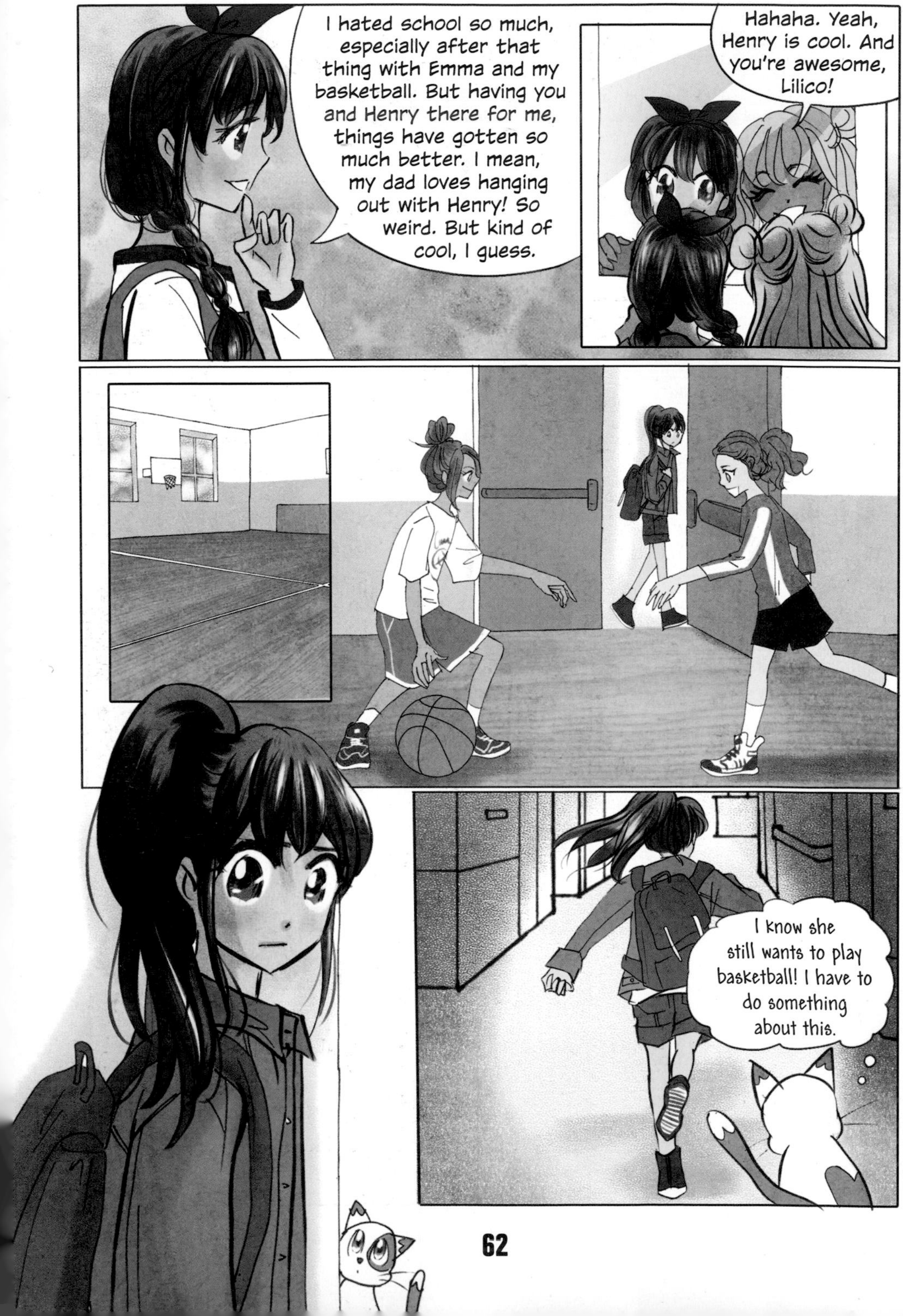
I hated school so much, especially after that thing with Emma and my basketball. But having you and Henry there for me, things have gotten so much better. I mean, my dad loves hanging out with Henry! So weird. But kind of cool, I guess.
Hahaha. Yeah, Henry is cool. And you're awesome, Lilico!
I know she still wants to play basketball! I have to do something about this.

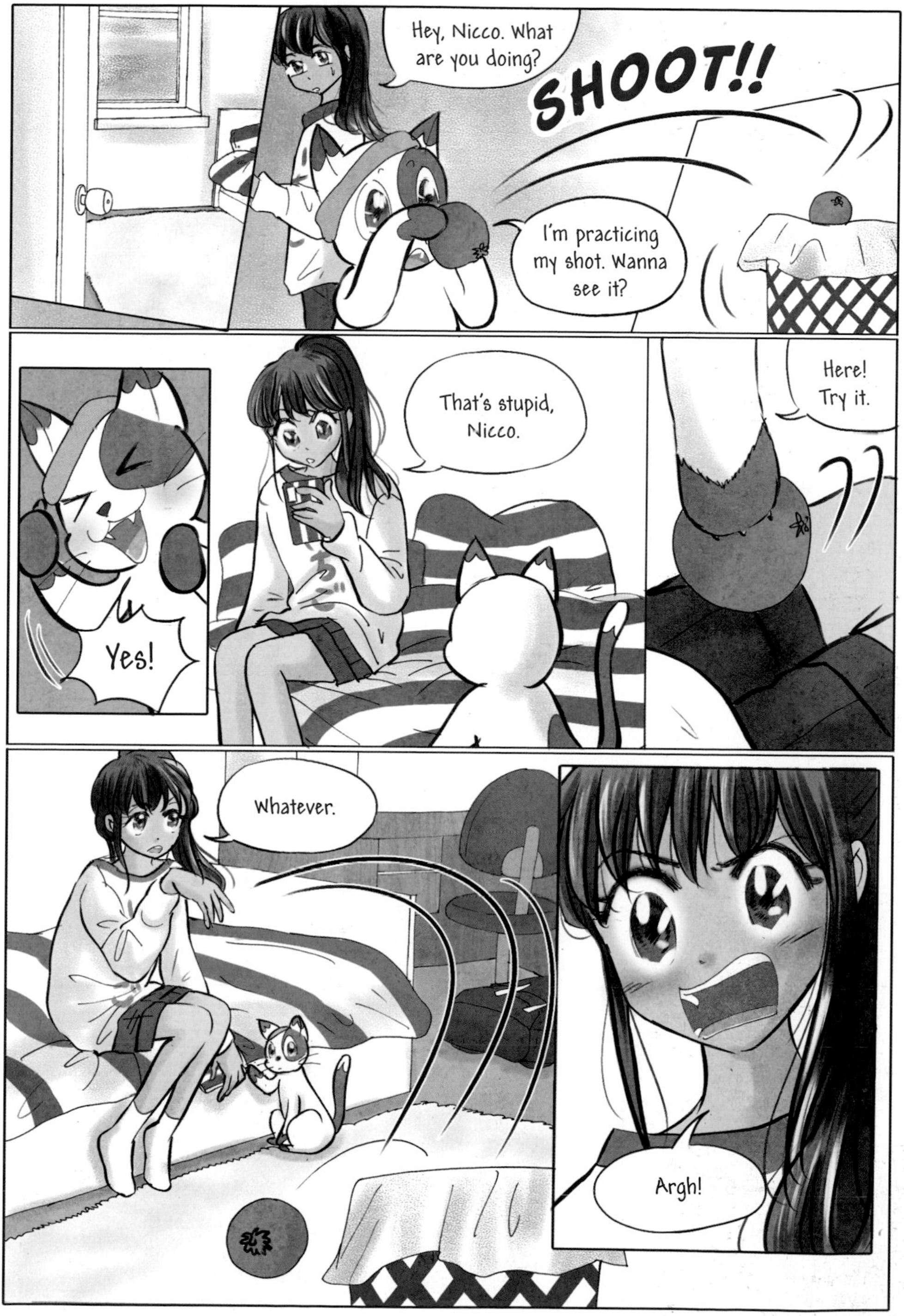
Hey, Nicco. What are you doing?
SHOOT!!
I'm practicing my shot. Wanna see it?
Yes!
That's stupid, Nicco.
Here! Try it.
Whatever.
Argh!

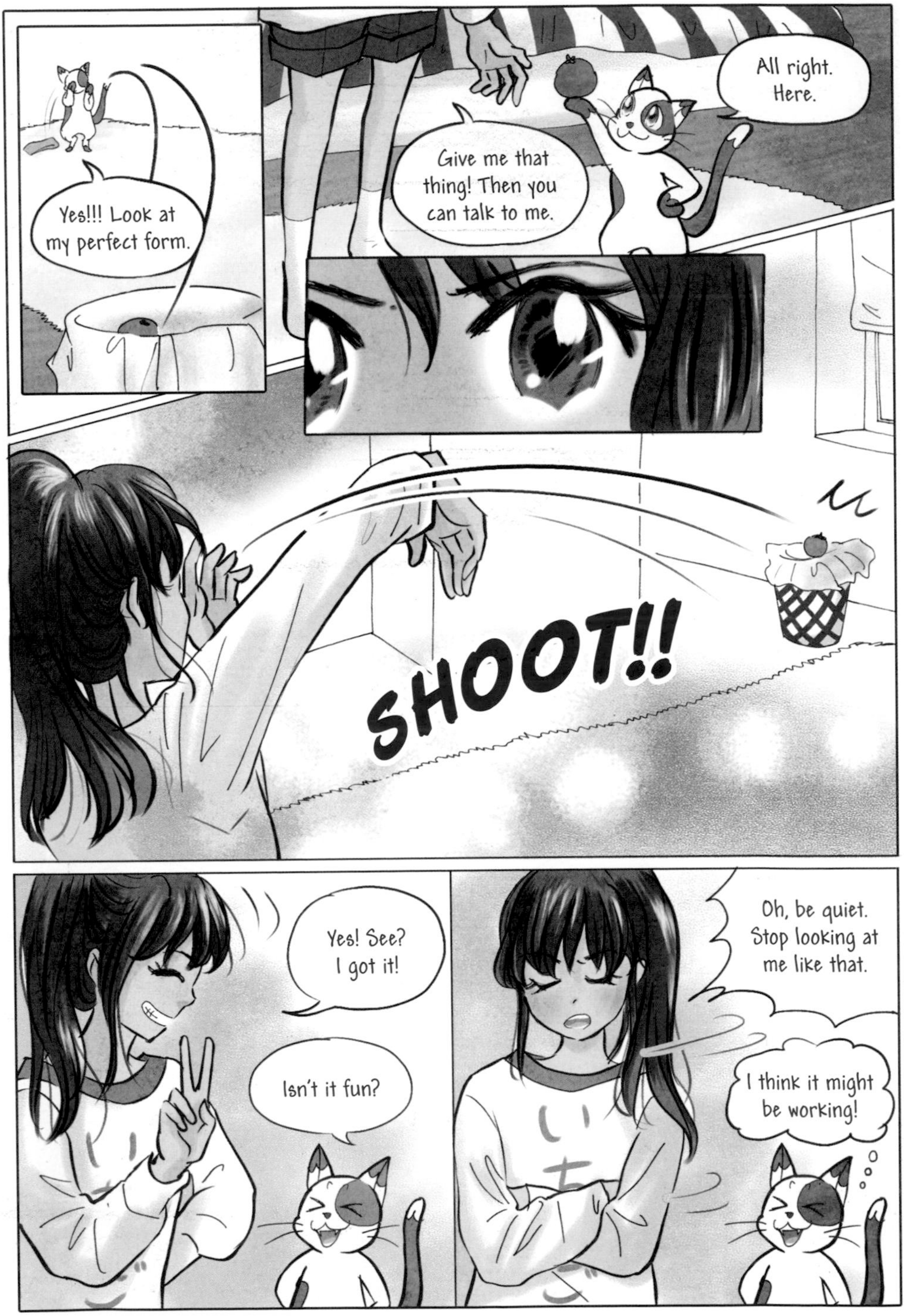
Yes!!! Look at my perfect form.
Give me that thing! Then you can talk to me.
All right. Here.
SHOOT!!
Yes! See? I got it!
Isn't it fun?
Oh, be quiet. Stop looking at me like that.
I think it might be working!

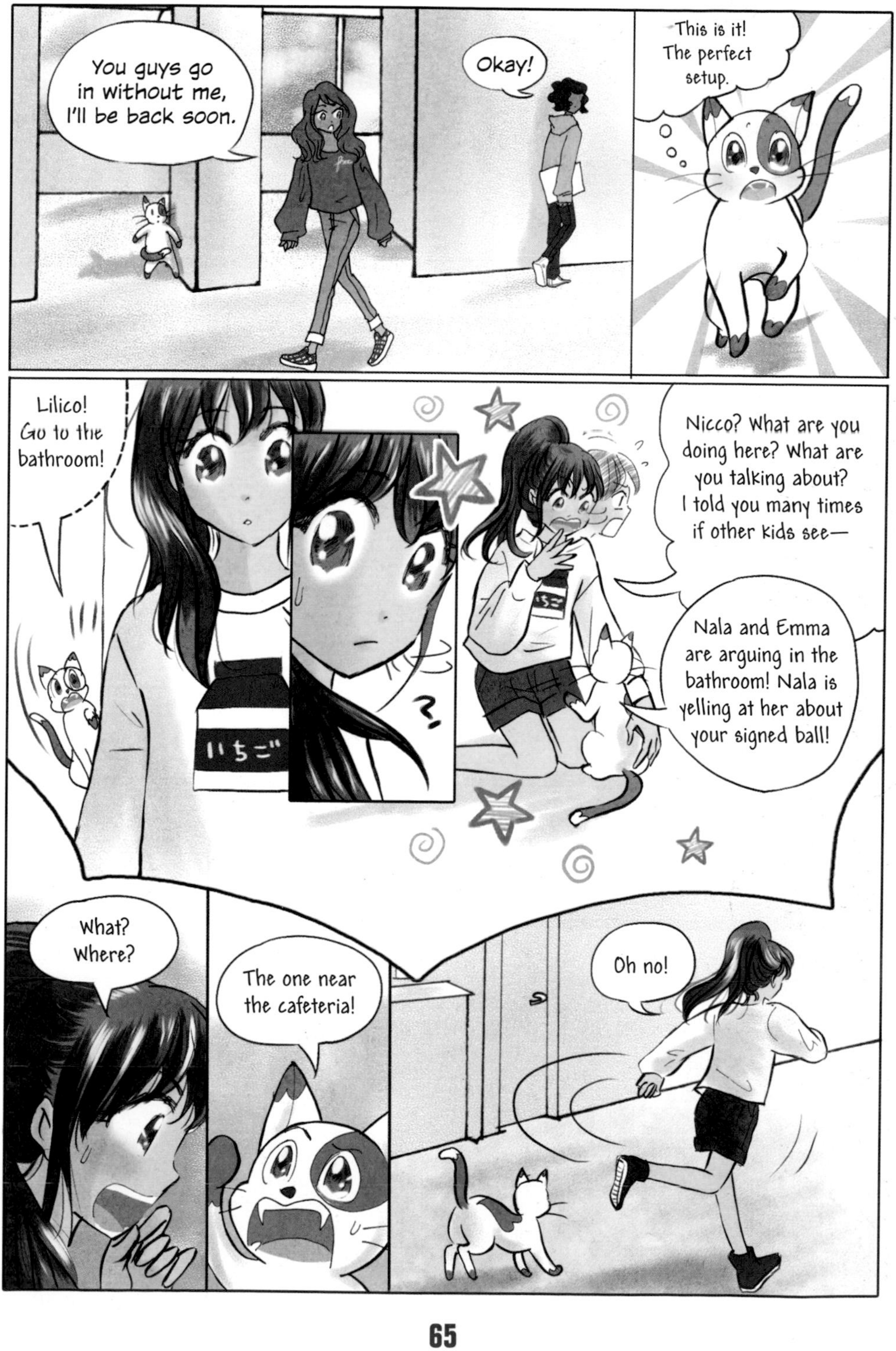
You guys go in without me, I'll be back soon.
Okay!
This is it! The perfect setup.
Lilico! Go to the bathroom!
Nicco? What are you doing here? What are you talking about? I told you many times if other kids see—
Nala and Emma are arguing in the bathroom! Nala is yelling at her about your signed ball!
いちご
What? Where?
The one near the cafeteria!
Oh no!

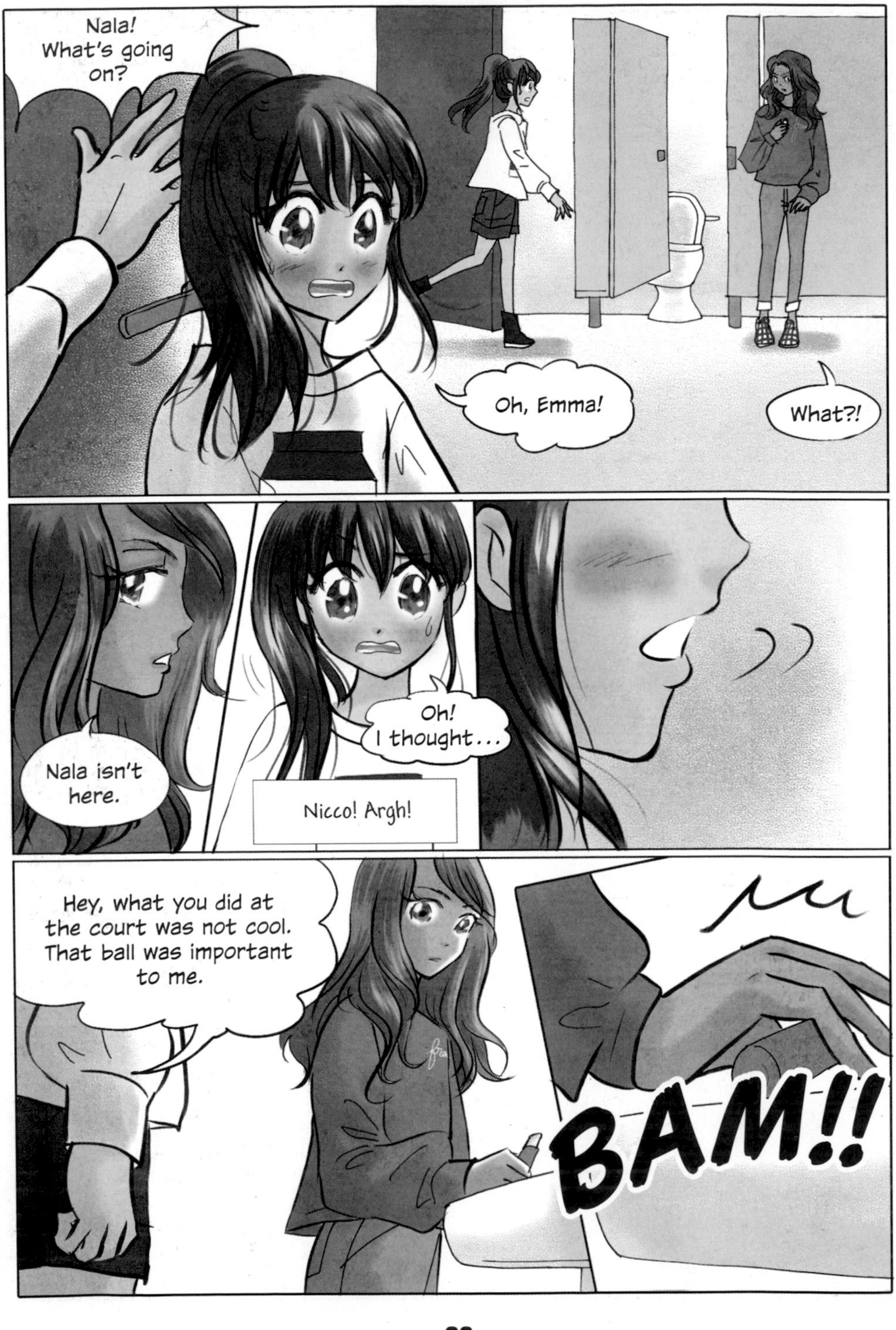
Nala! What's going on?
Oh, Emma!
What?!
Nala isn't here.
Oh! I thought...
Nicco! Argh!
Hey, what you did at the court was not cool. That ball was important to me.
BAM!!

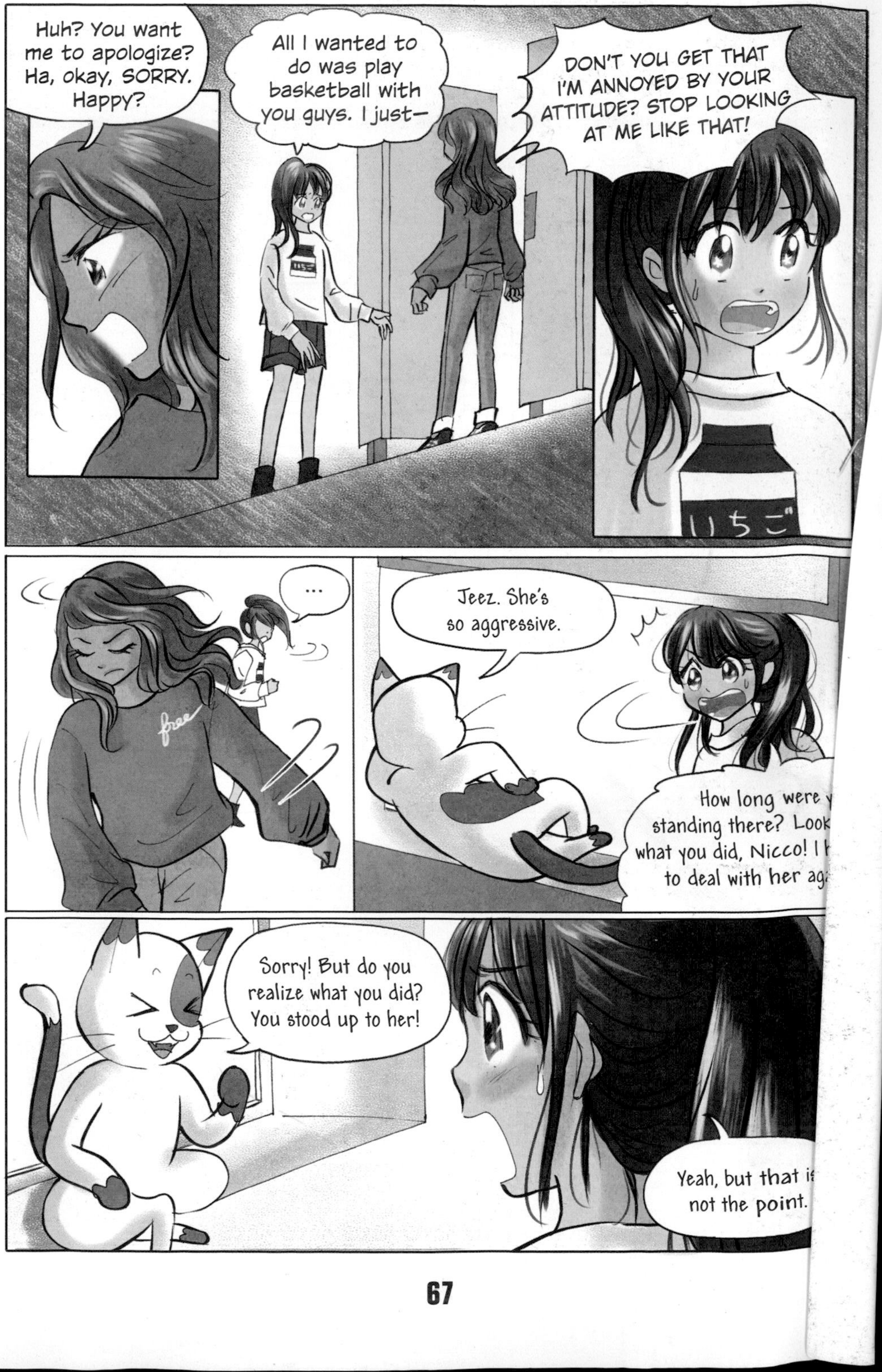

Huh? You want me to apologize? Ha, okay, SORRY. Happy?
All I wanted to do was play basketball with you guys. I just—
DON'T YOU GET THAT I'M ANNOYED BY YOUR ATTITUDE? STOP LOOKING AT ME LIKE THAT!
いちご
free
...
Jeez. She's so aggressive.
How long were y standing there? Look what you did, Nicco! I h to deal with her ag
Sorry! But do you realize what you did? You stood up to her!
Yeah, but that i not the point.

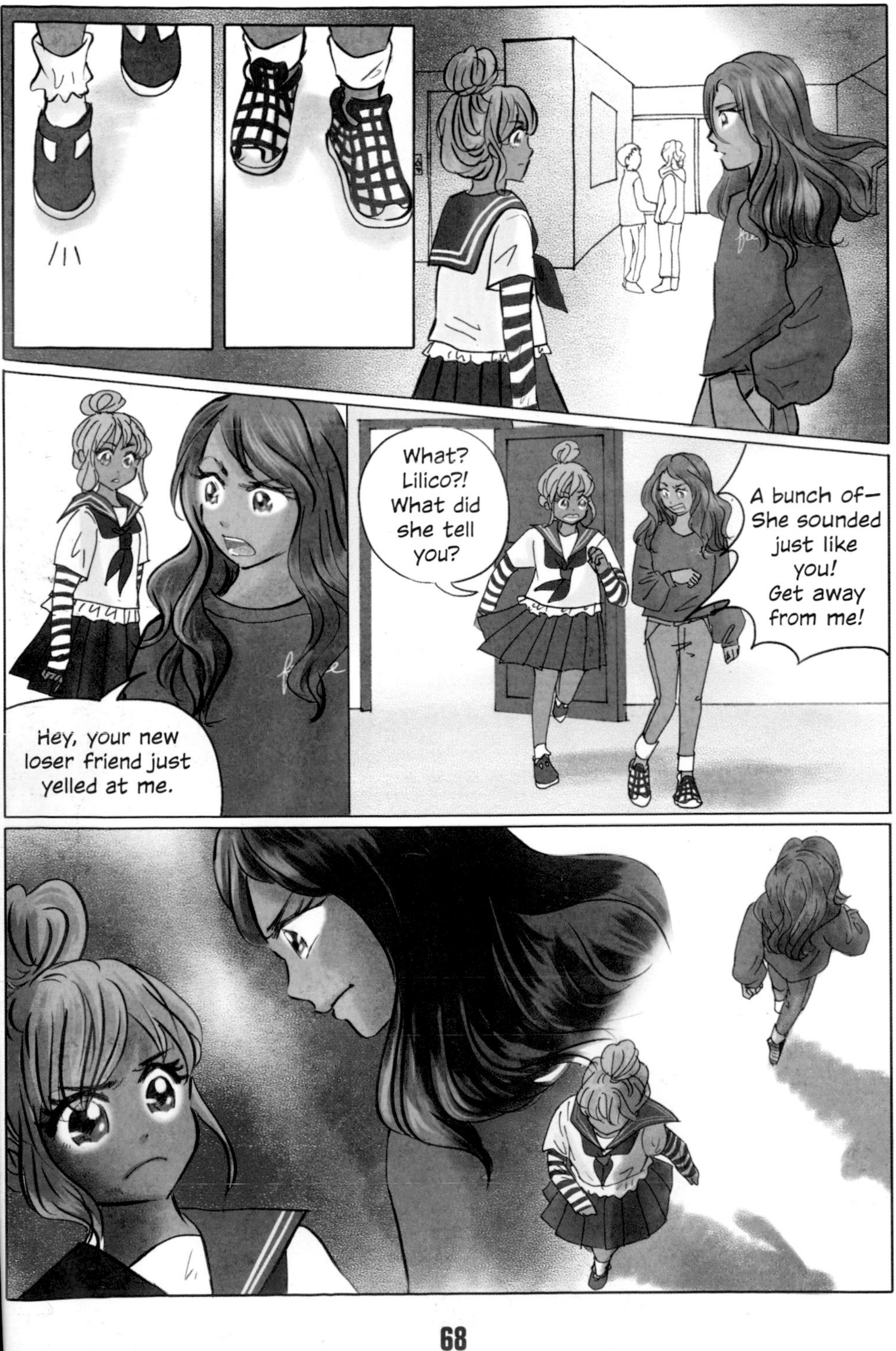
Hey, your new loser friend just yelled at me.
What? Lilico?! What did she tell you?
A bunch of— She sounded just like you! Get away from me!

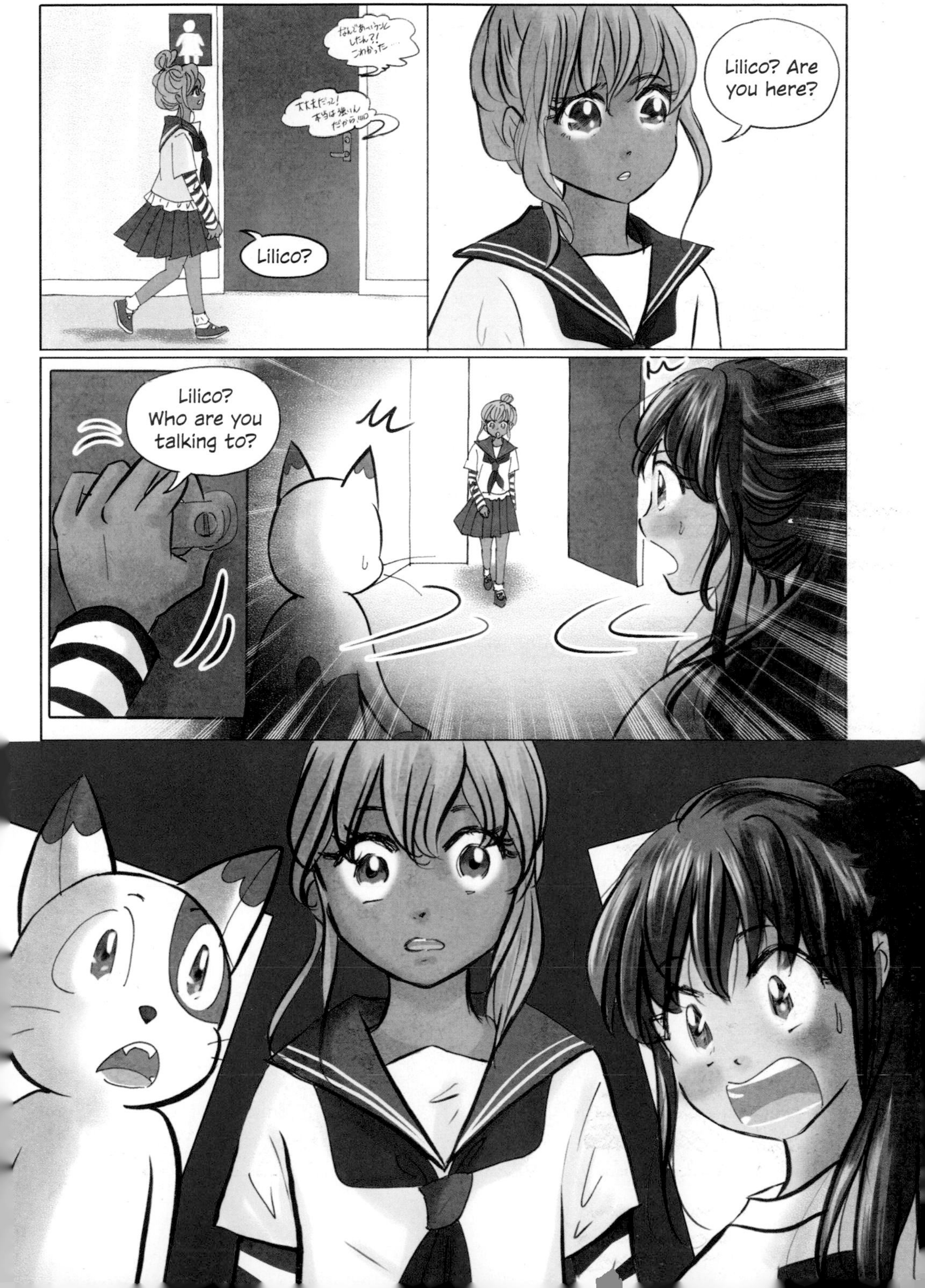
なんであーいうことしたん?! こわかった……
大丈夫だって! 本当は強いんだから!!!
Lilico?
Lilico? Are you here?
Lilico? Who are you talking to?

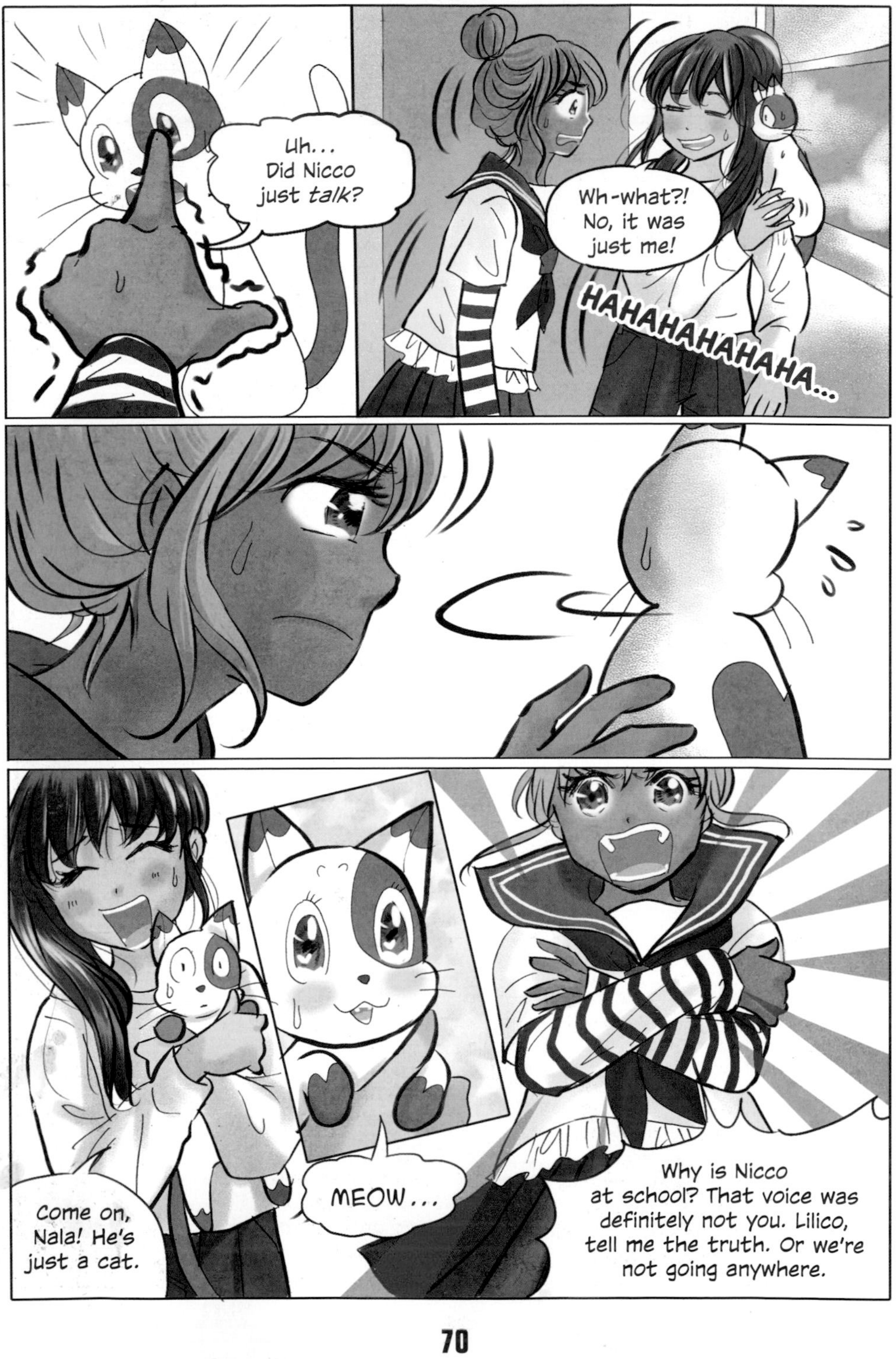
Uh...
Did Nicco
just *talk*?
Wh-what?!
No, it was
just me!
HAHAHAHAHAHAHA...
Come on,
Nala! He's
just a cat.
MEOW...
Why is Nicco
at school? That voice was
definitely not you. Lilico,
tell me the truth. Or we're
not going anywhere.

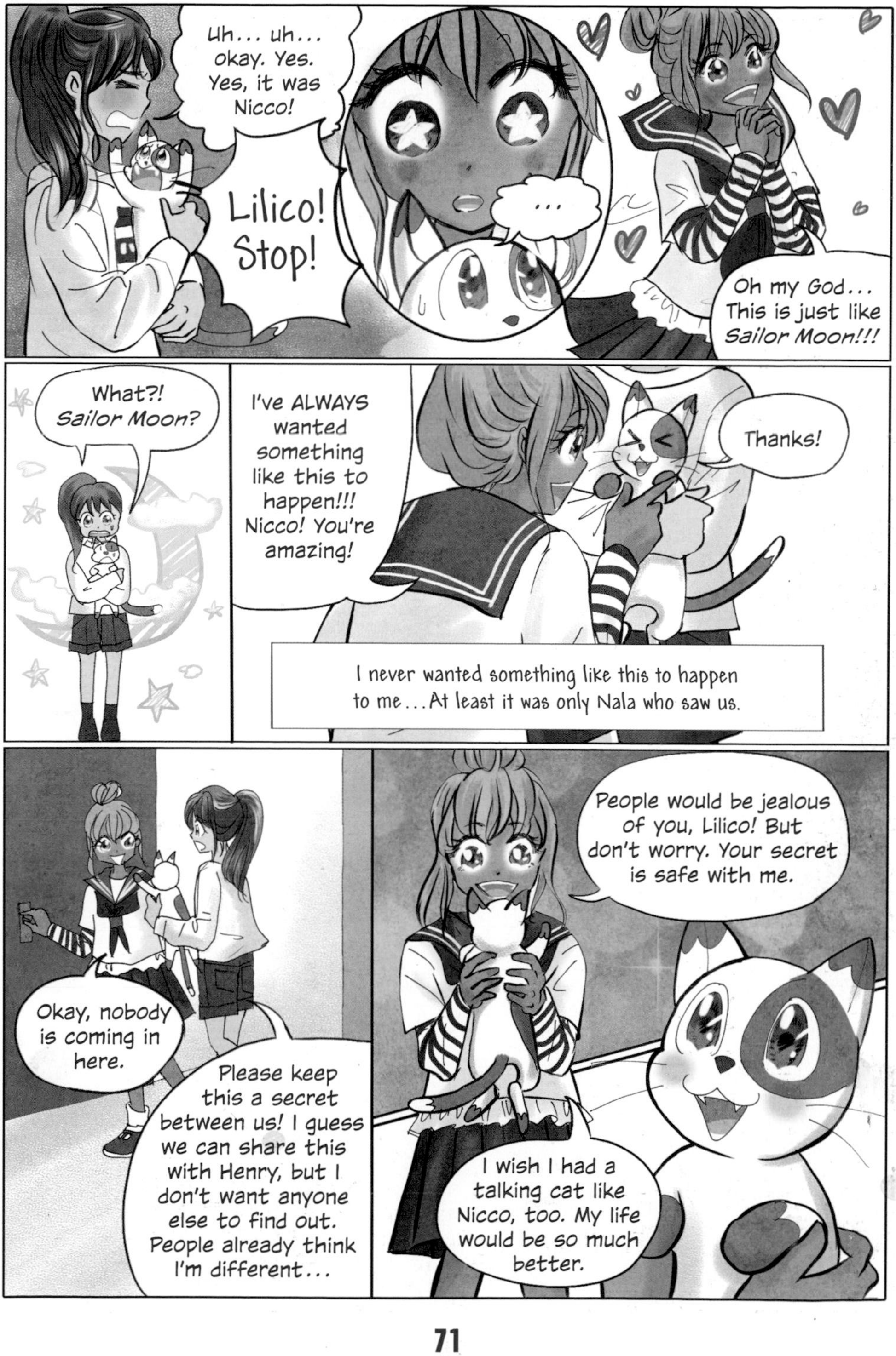
Uh... uh... okay. Yes. Yes, it was Nicco!
Lilico! Stop!
...
Oh my God... This is just like *Sailor Moon*!!!
What?! *Sailor Moon*?
I've ALWAYS wanted something like this to happen!!! Nicco! You're amazing!
Thanks!
I never wanted something like this to happen to me... At least it was only Nala who saw us.
Okay, nobody is coming in here.
Please keep this a secret between us! I guess we can share this with Henry, but I don't want anyone else to find out. People already think I'm different...
People would be jealous of you, Lilico! But don't worry. Your secret is safe with me.
I wish I had a talking cat like Nicco, too. My life would be so much better.

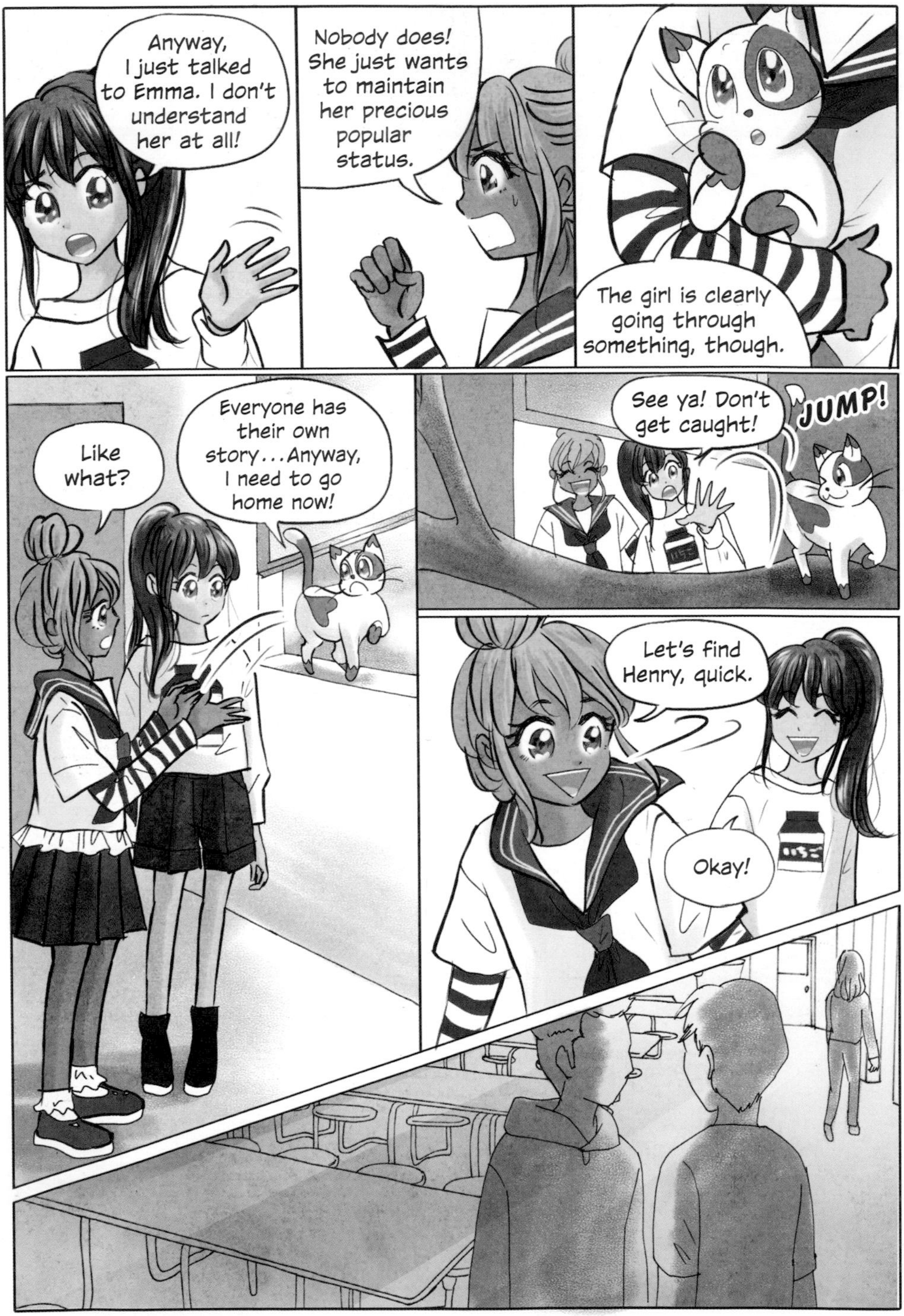

Anyway, I just talked to Emma. I don't understand her at all!
Nobody does! She just wants to maintain her precious popular status.
The girl is clearly going through something, though.
Like what?
Everyone has their own story...Anyway, I need to go home now!
See ya! Don't get caught!
JUMP!
Let's find Henry, quick.
Okay!

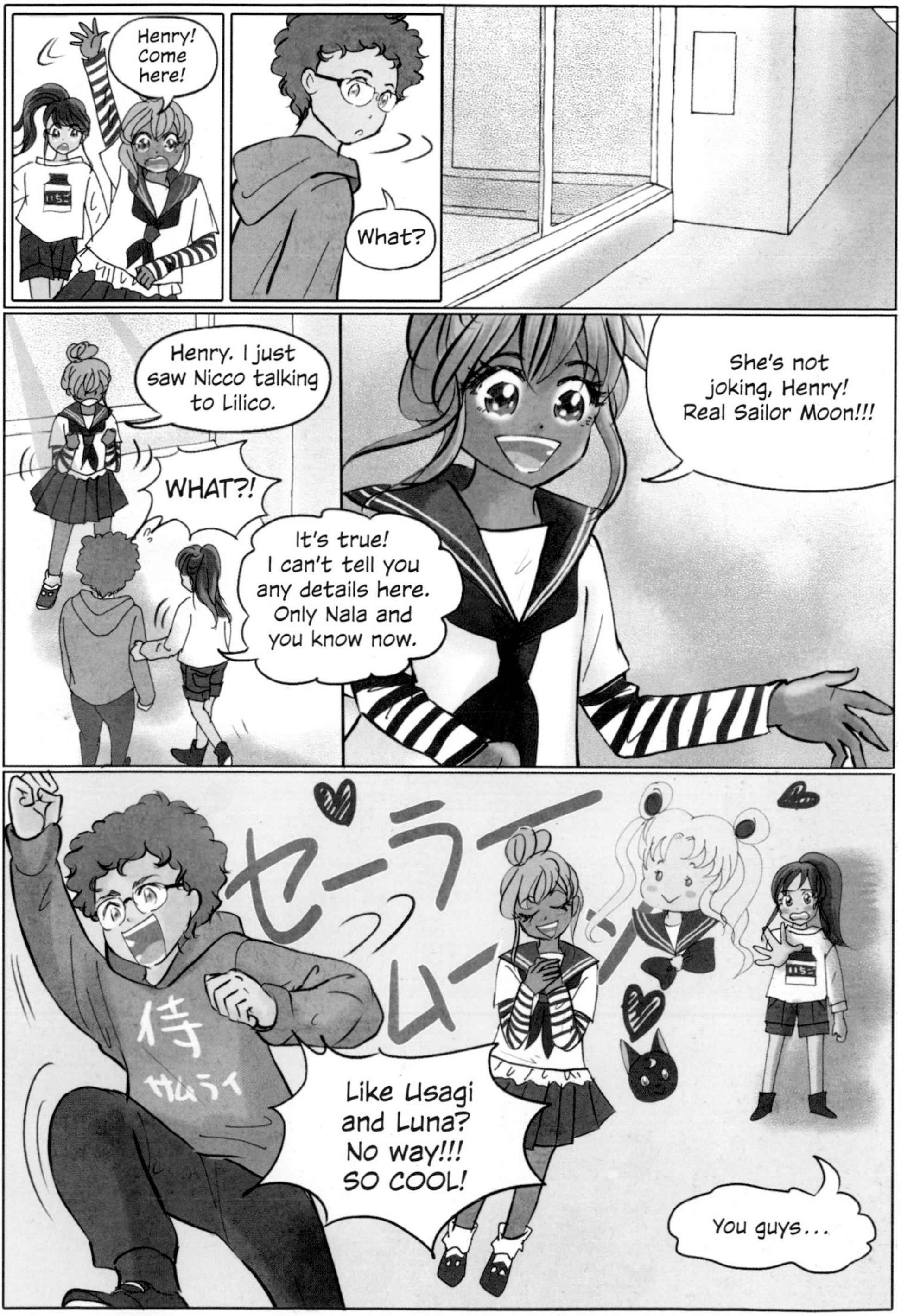
Henry! Come here!
What?
Henry. I just saw Nicco talking to Lilico.
WHAT?!
It's true! I can't tell you any details here. Only Nala and you know now.
She's not joking, Henry! Real Sailor Moon!!!
侍 サムライ
セーラームーン
Like Usagi and Luna? No way!!! SO COOL!
You guys...

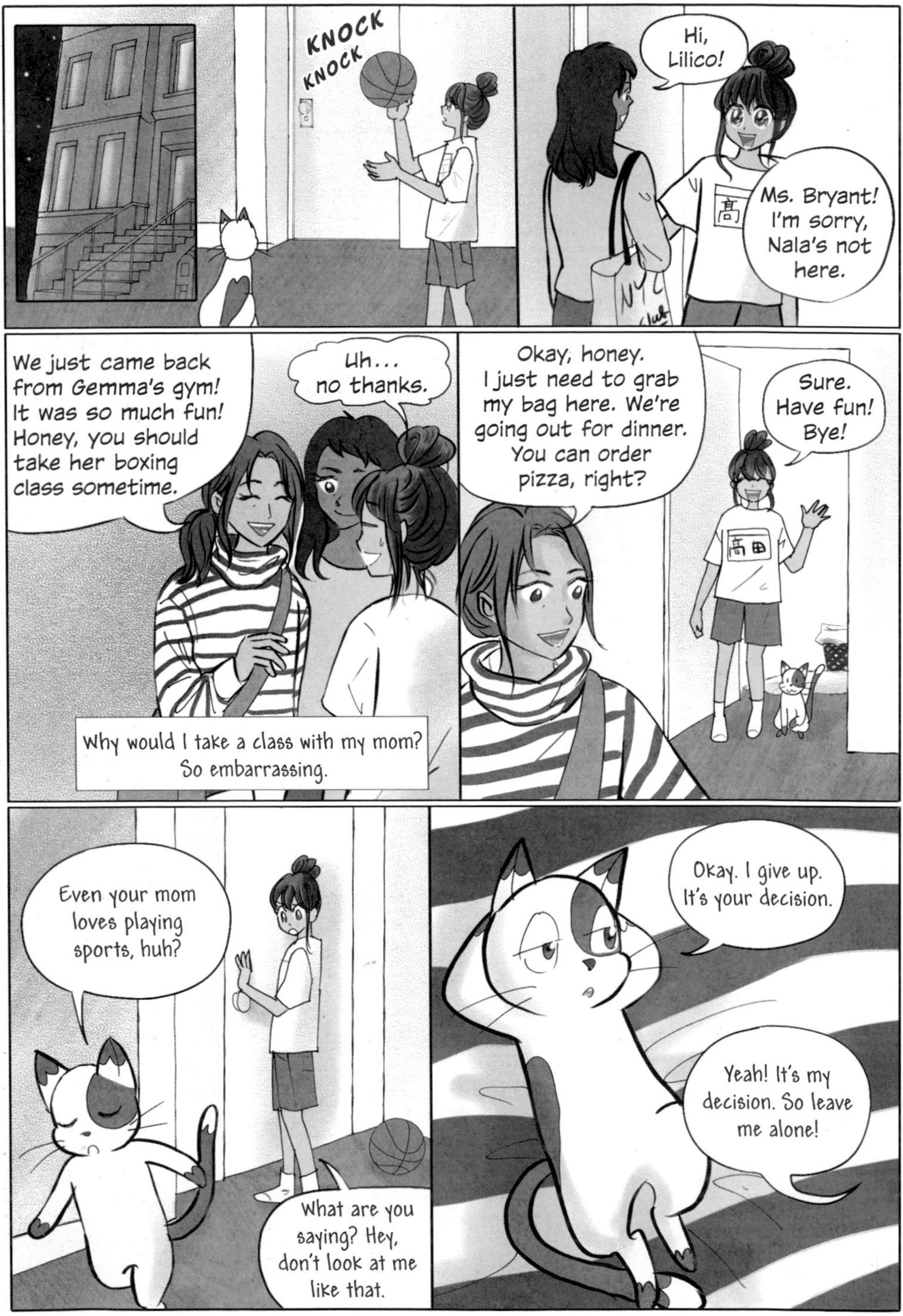
KNOCK
KNOCK
Hi, Lilico!
Ms. Bryant! I'm sorry, Nala's not here.
We just came back from Gemma's gym! It was so much fun! Honey, you should take her boxing class sometime.
Uh... no thanks.
Why would I take a class with my mom? So embarrassing.
Okay, honey. I just need to grab my bag here. We're going out for dinner. You can order pizza, right?
Sure. Have fun! Bye!
Even your mom loves playing sports, huh?
What are you saying? Hey, don't look at me like that.
Okay. I give up. It's your decision.
Yeah! It's my decision. So leave me alone!

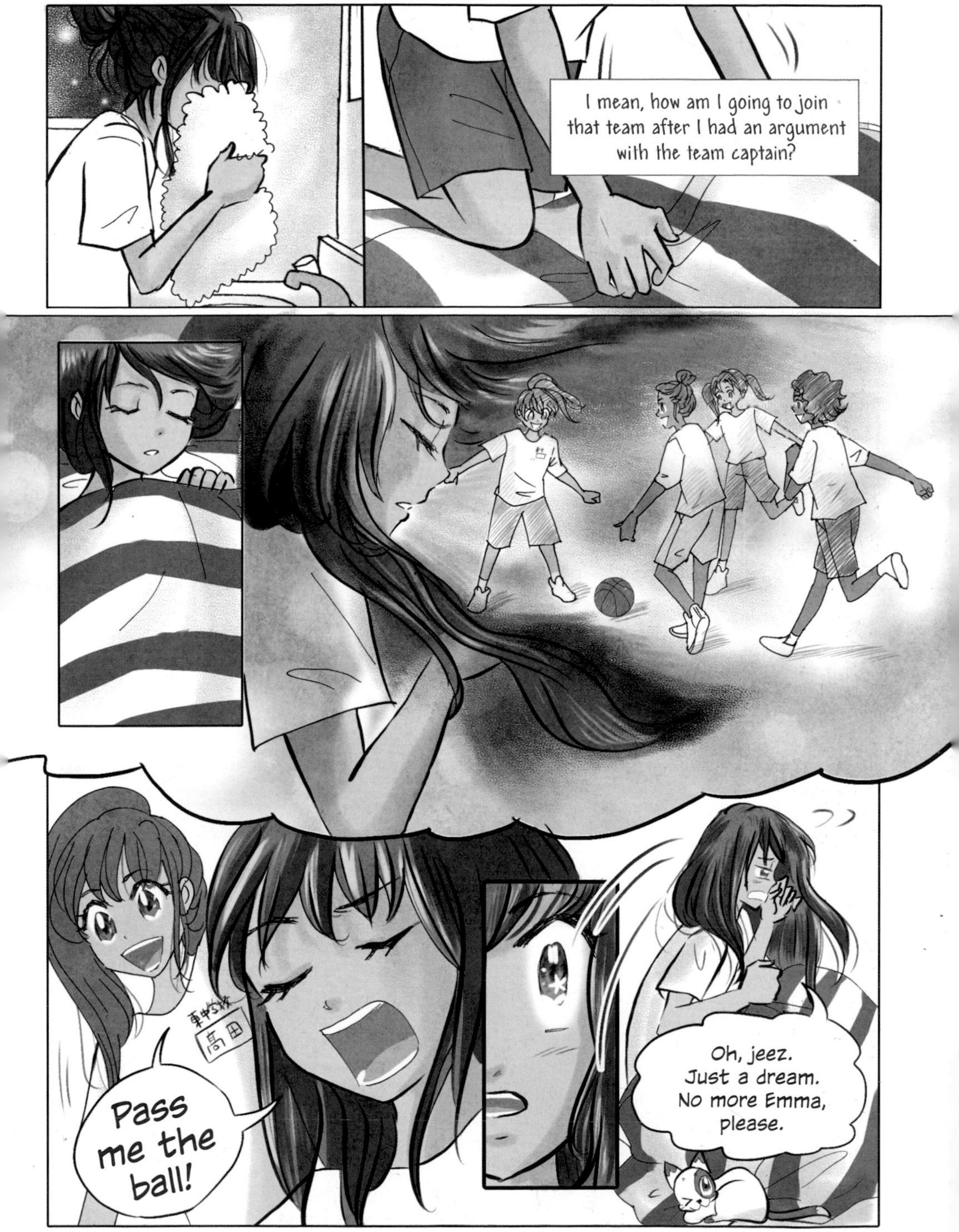
I mean, how am I going to join that team after I had an argument with the team captain?
東中学校
高田
Pass me the ball!
Oh, jeez. Just a dream. No more Emma, please.

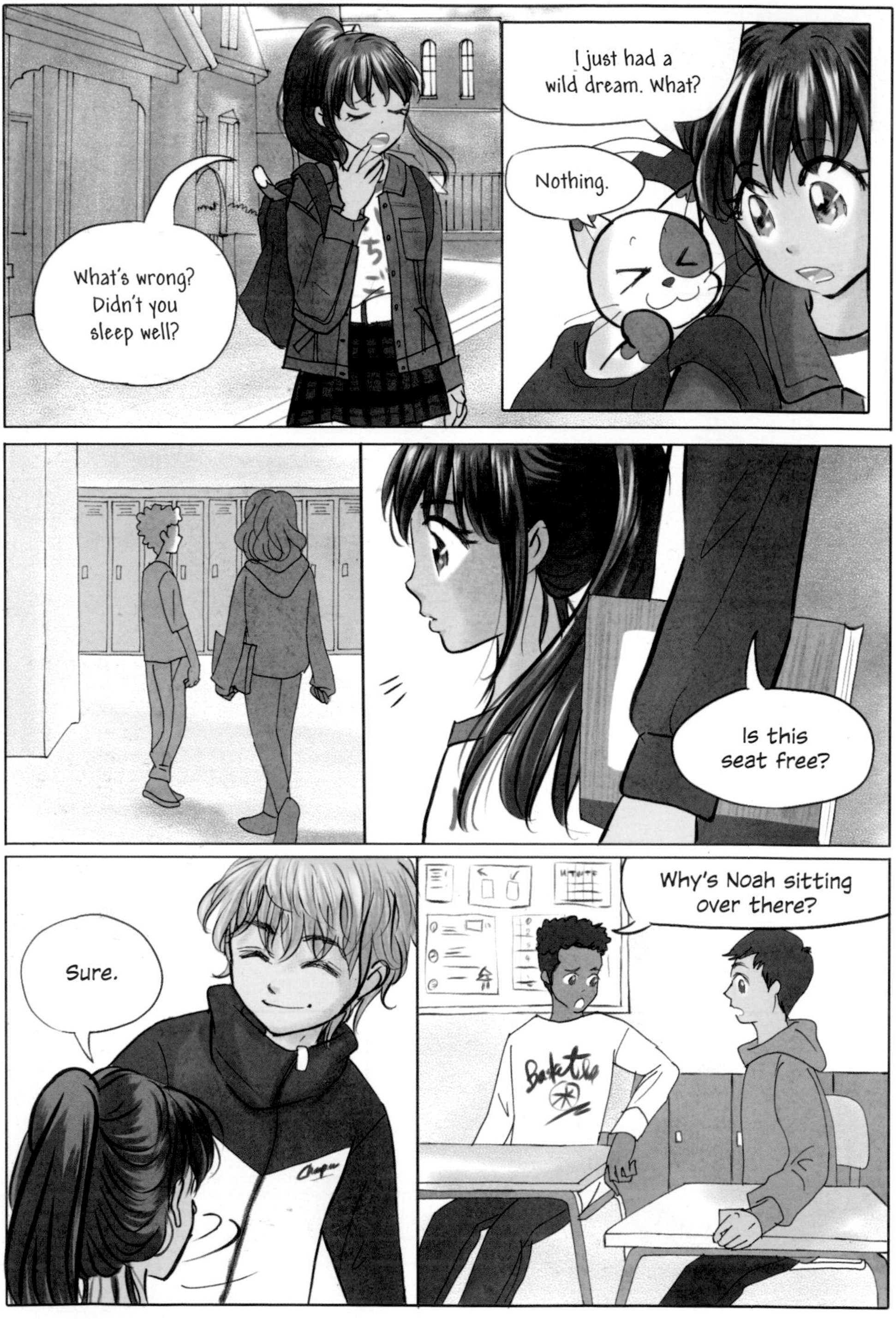
What's wrong?
Didn't you sleep well?
I just had a wild dream. What?
Nothing.
Is this seat free?
Sure.
Why's Noah sitting over there?

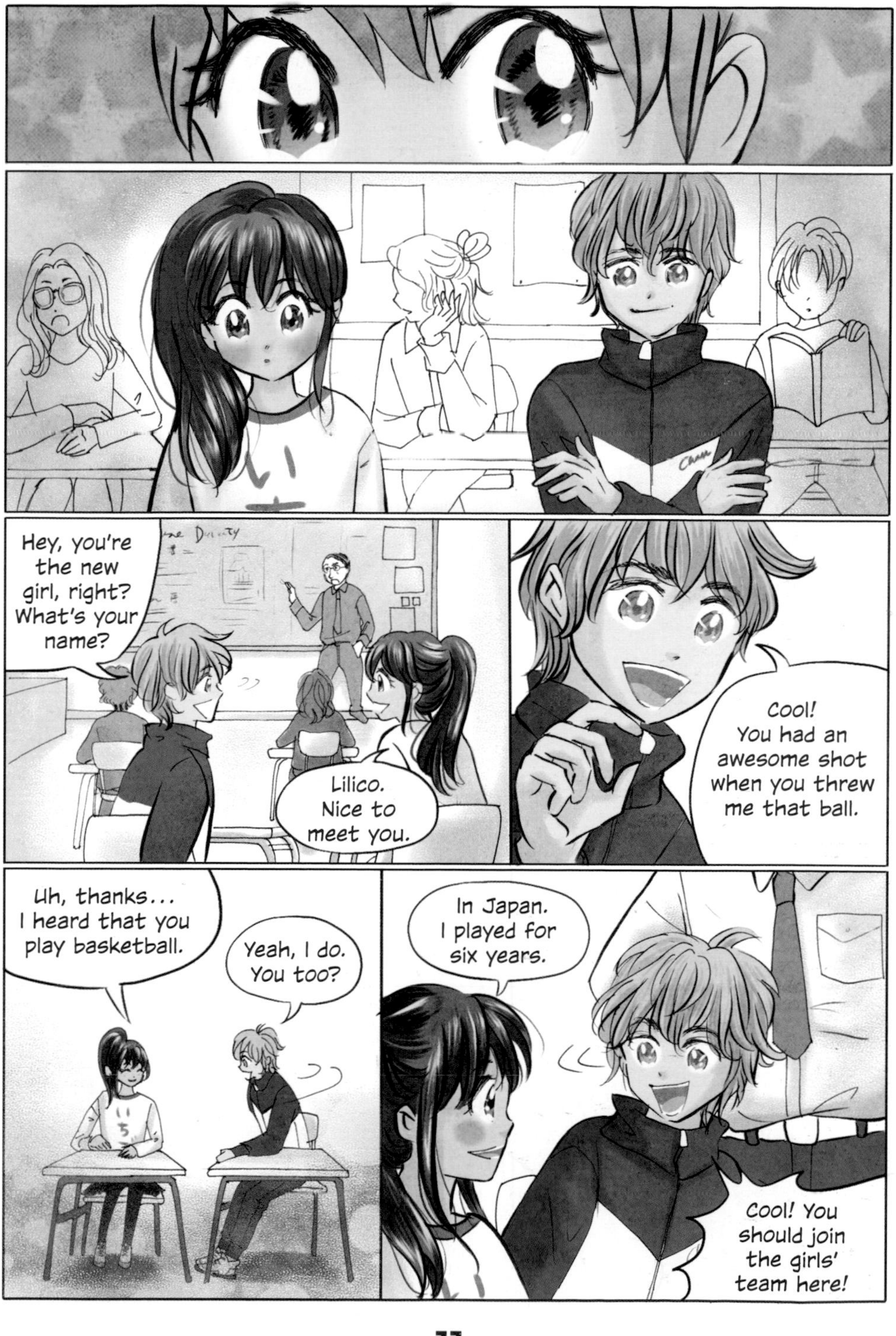
Hey, you're the new girl, right? What's your name?
Lilico. Nice to meet you.
Cool! You had an awesome shot when you threw me that ball.
Uh, thanks... I heard that you play basketball.
Yeah, I do. You too?
In Japan. I played for six years.
Cool! You should join the girls' team here!

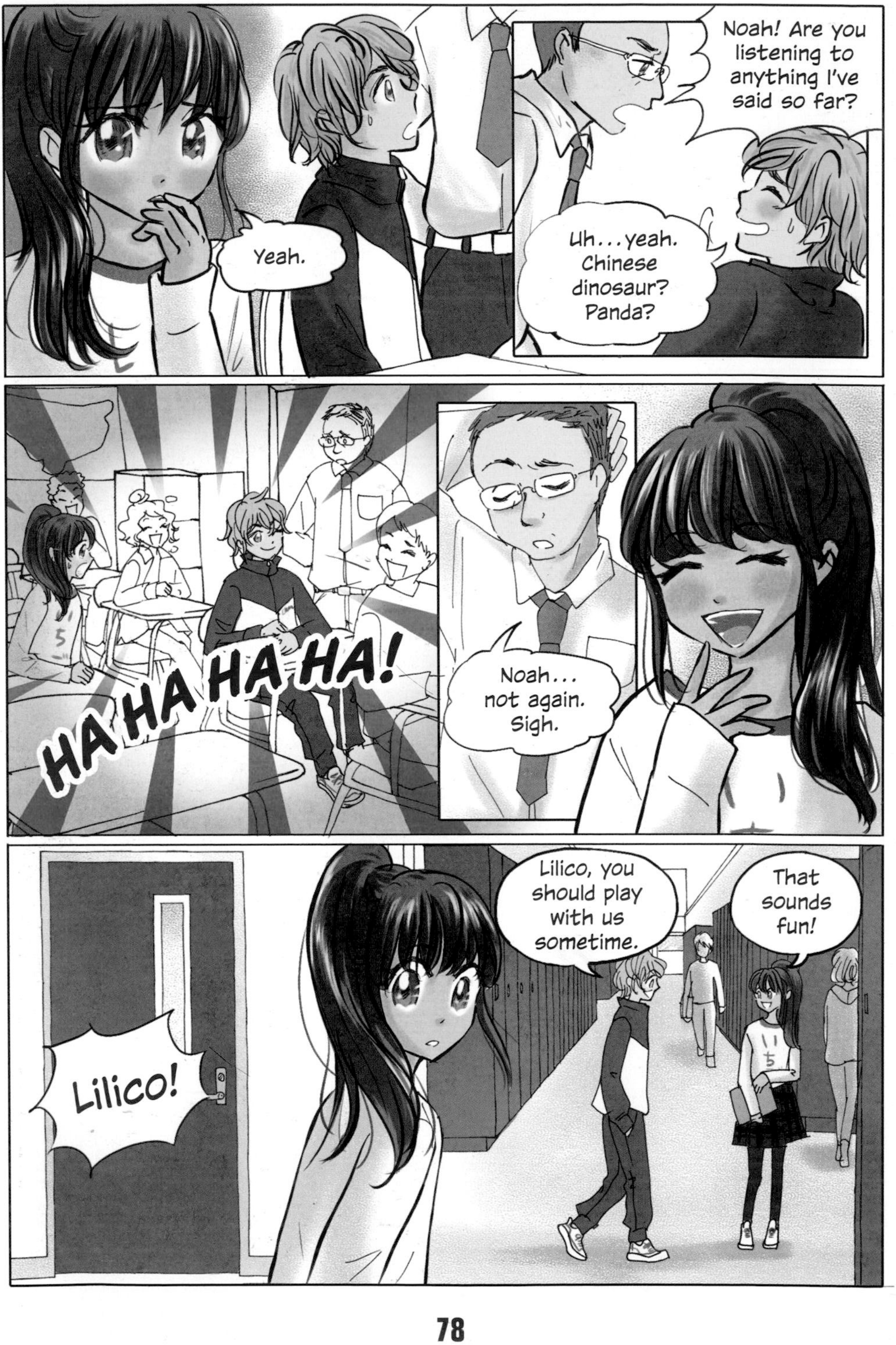
Yeah.
Noah! Are you listening to anything I've said so far?
Uh...yeah. Chinese dinosaur? Panda?
HA HA HA HA!
Noah... not again. Sigh.
Lilico!
Lilico, you should play with us sometime.
That sounds fun!

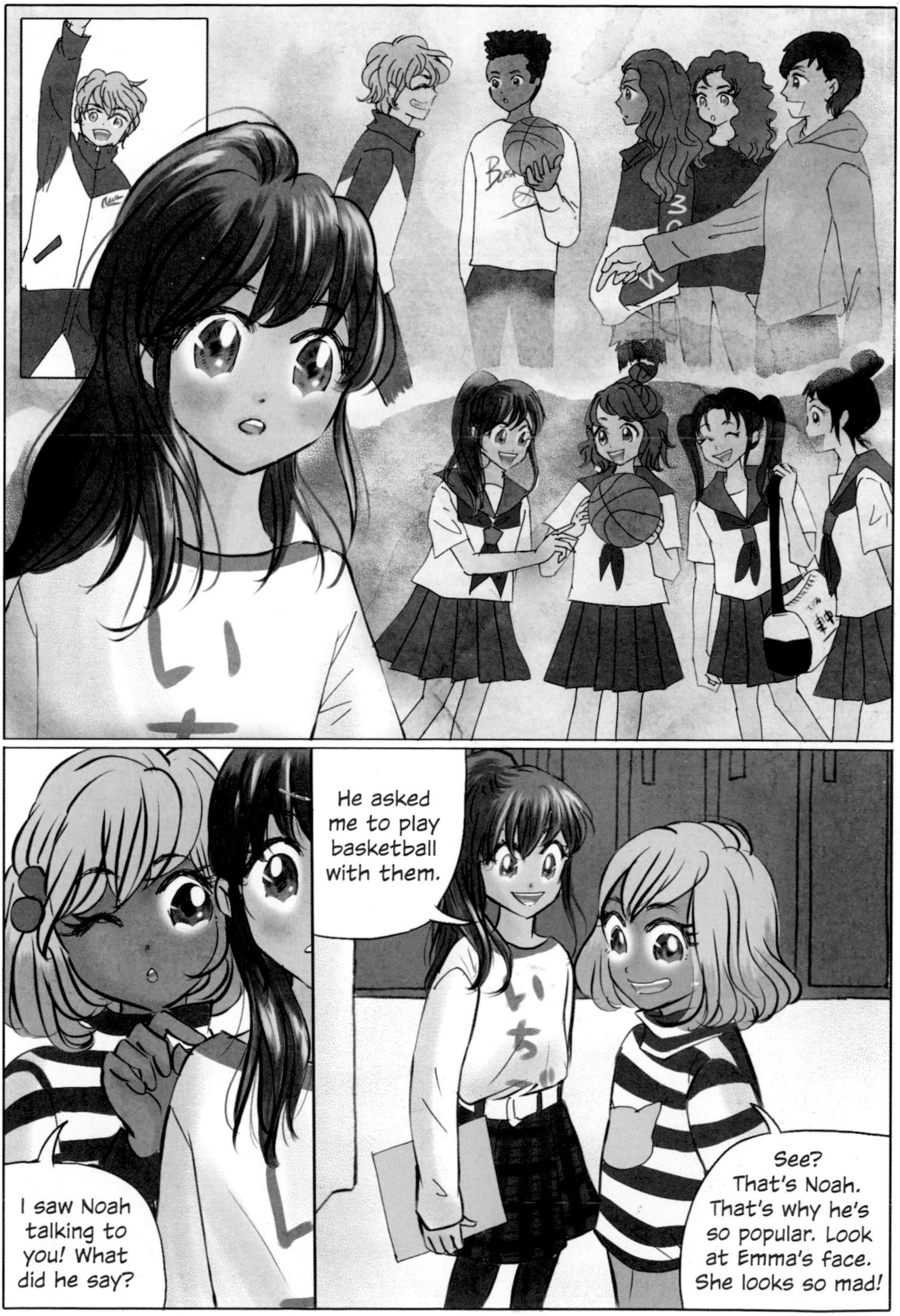
I saw Noah talking to you! What did he say?
He asked me to play basketball with them.
See? That's Noah. That's why he's so popular. Look at Emma's face. She looks so mad!

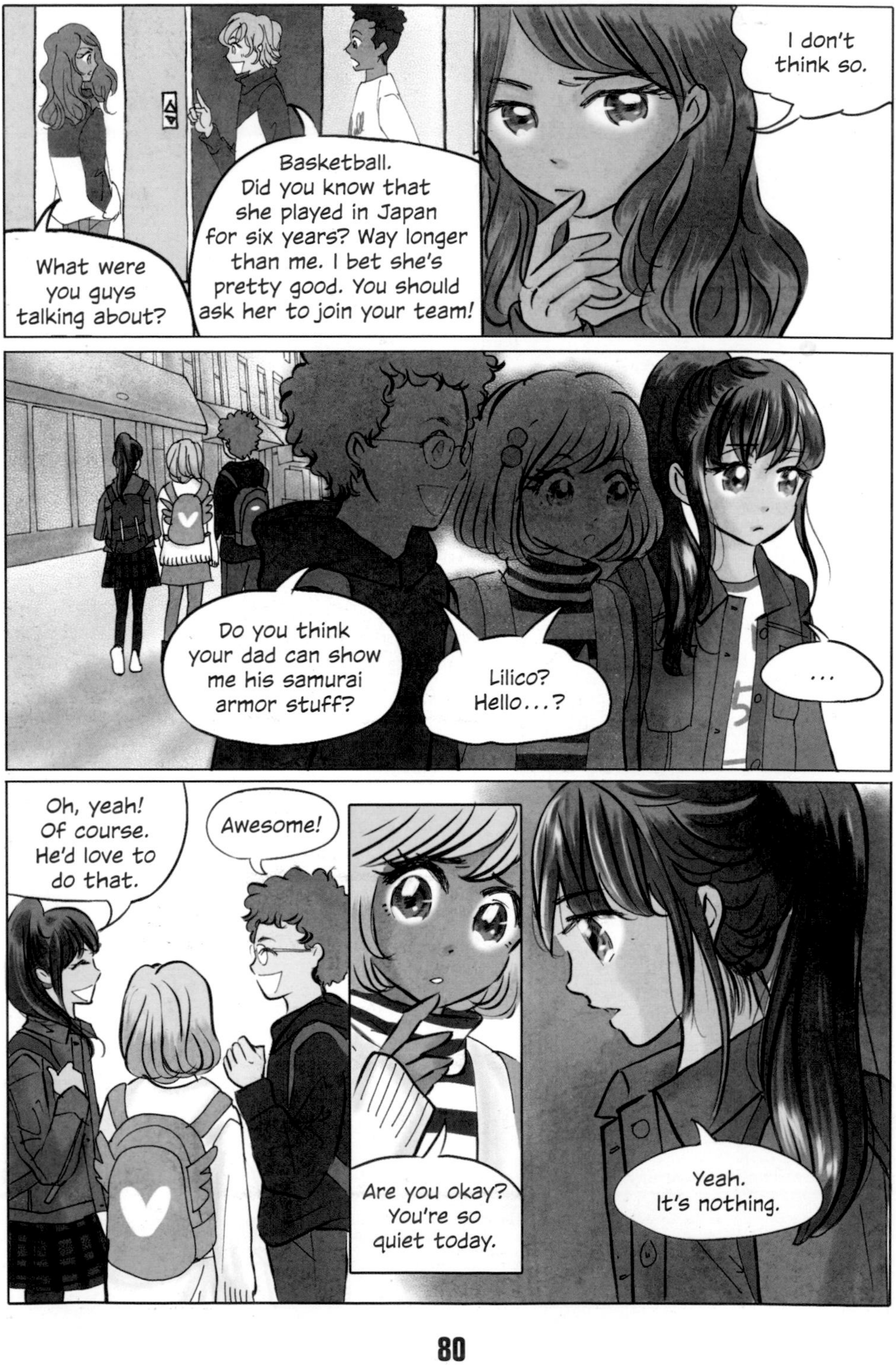
What were you guys talking about?
Basketball. Did you know that she played in Japan for six years? Way longer than me. I bet she's pretty good. You should ask her to join your team!
I don't think so.
Do you think your dad can show me his samurai armor stuff?
Lilico? Hello...?
...
Oh, yeah! Of course. He'd love to do that.
Awesome!
Are you okay? You're so quiet today.
Yeah. It's nothing.

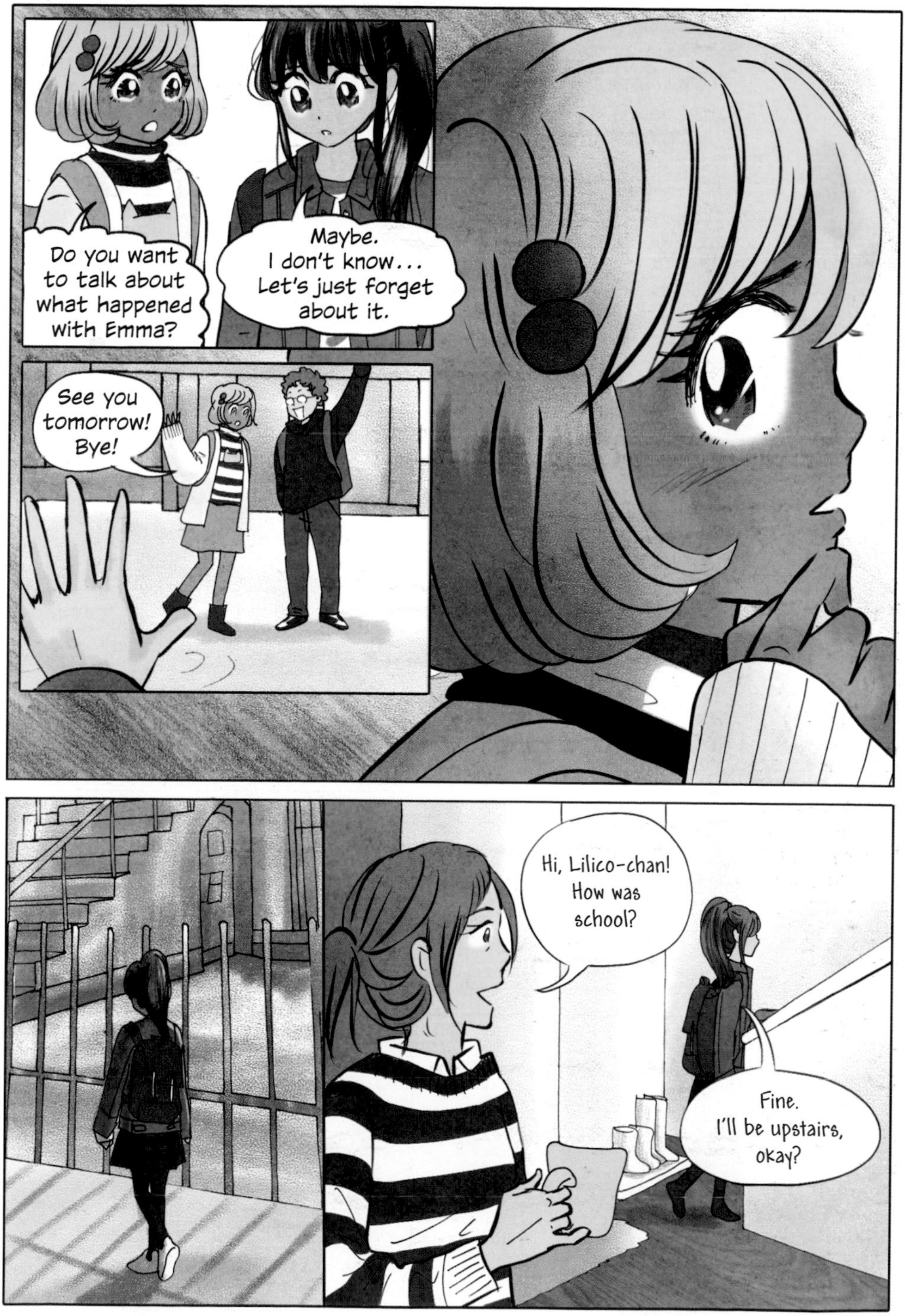

Do you want to talk about what happened with Emma?
Maybe. I don't know... Let's just forget about it.
See you tomorrow! Bye!
Hi, Lilico-chan! How was school?
Fine. I'll be upstairs, okay?

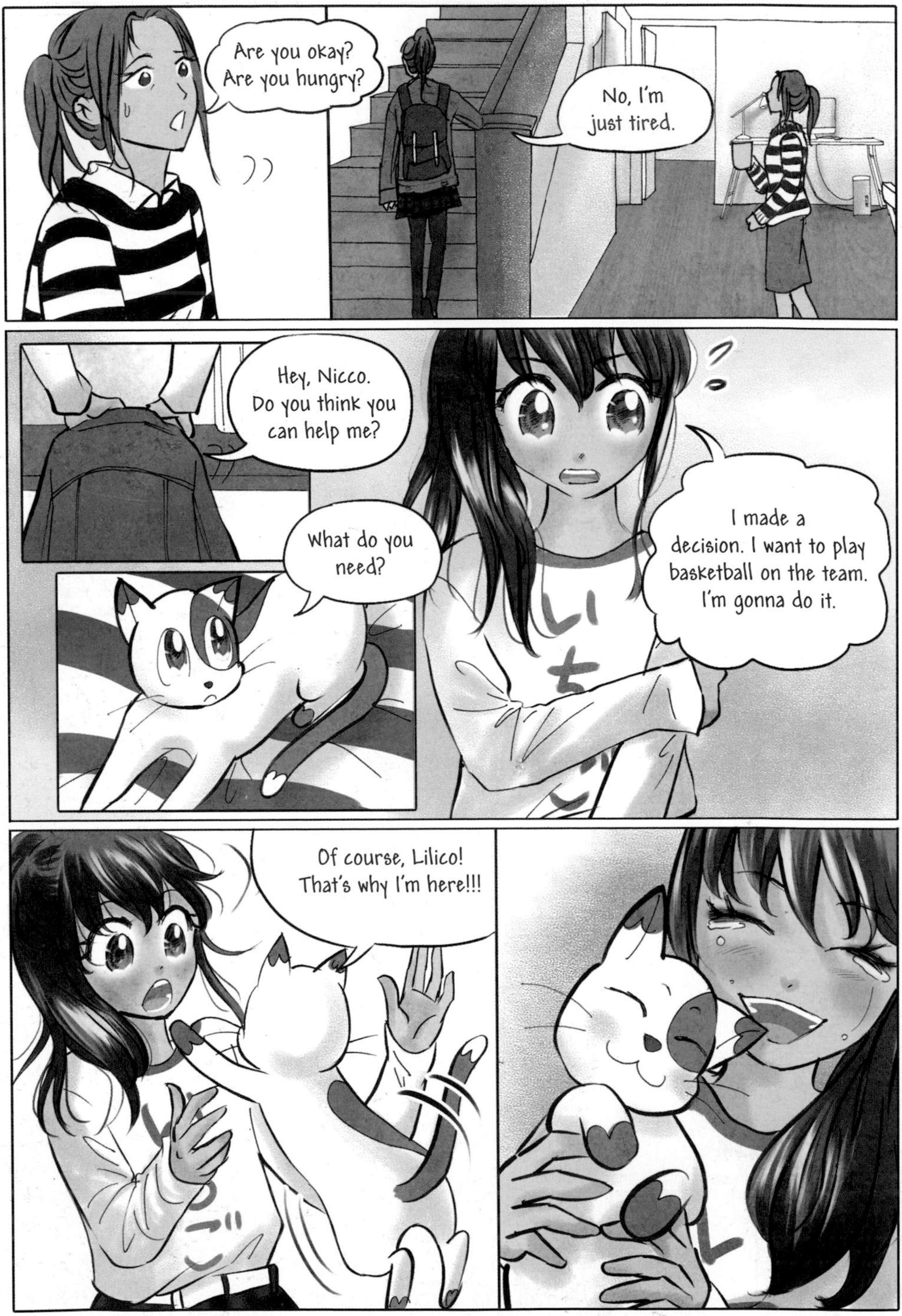
Are you okay? Are you hungry?
No, I'm just tired.
Hey, Nicco. Do you think you can help me?
What do you need?
I made a decision. I want to play basketball on the team. I'm gonna do it.
Of course, Lilico! That's why I'm here!!!

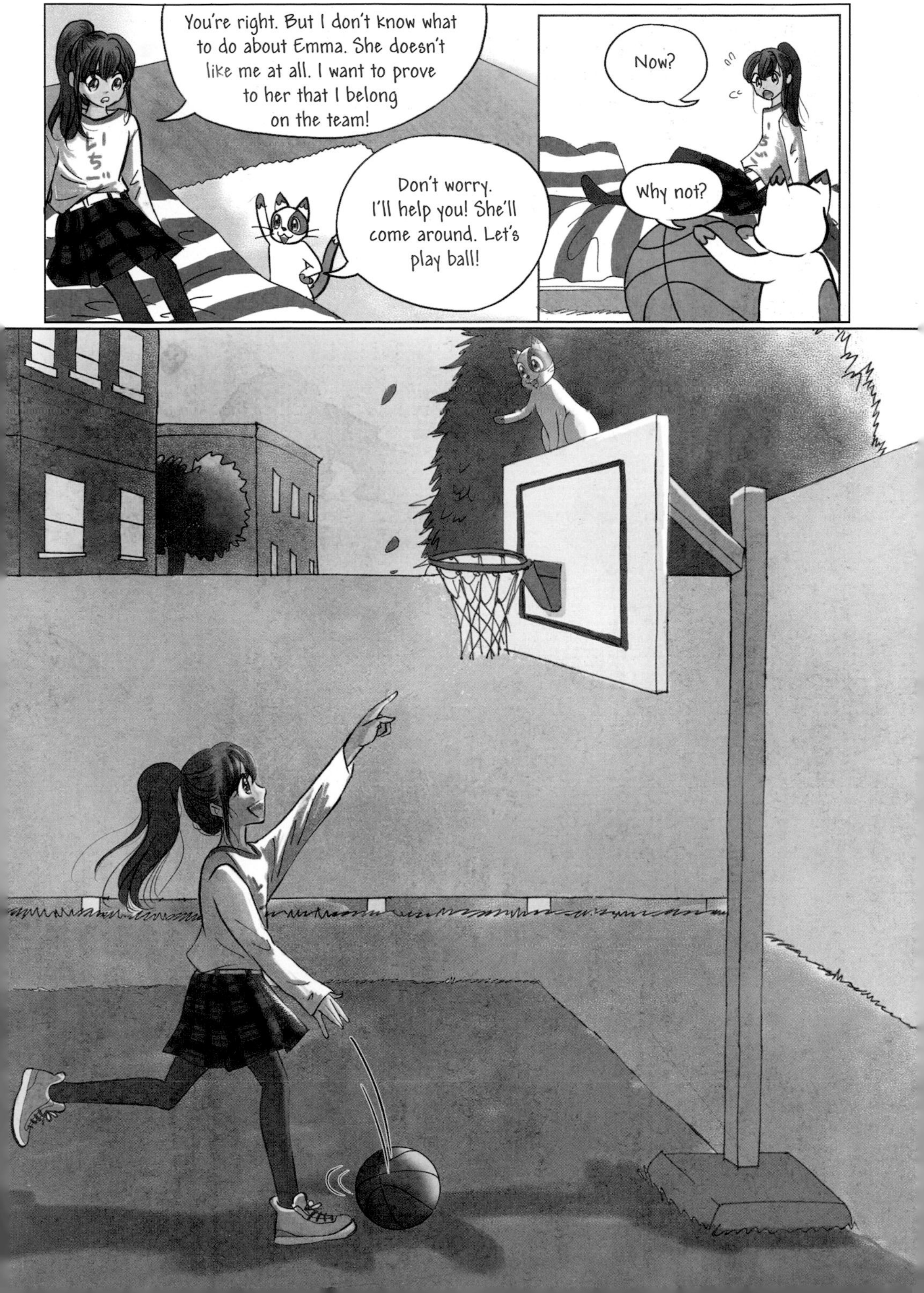
You're right. But I don't know what to do about Emma. She doesn't like me at all. I want to prove to her that I belong on the team!
Don't worry. I'll help you! She'll come around. Let's play ball!
Now?
Why not?

CHAPTER 4

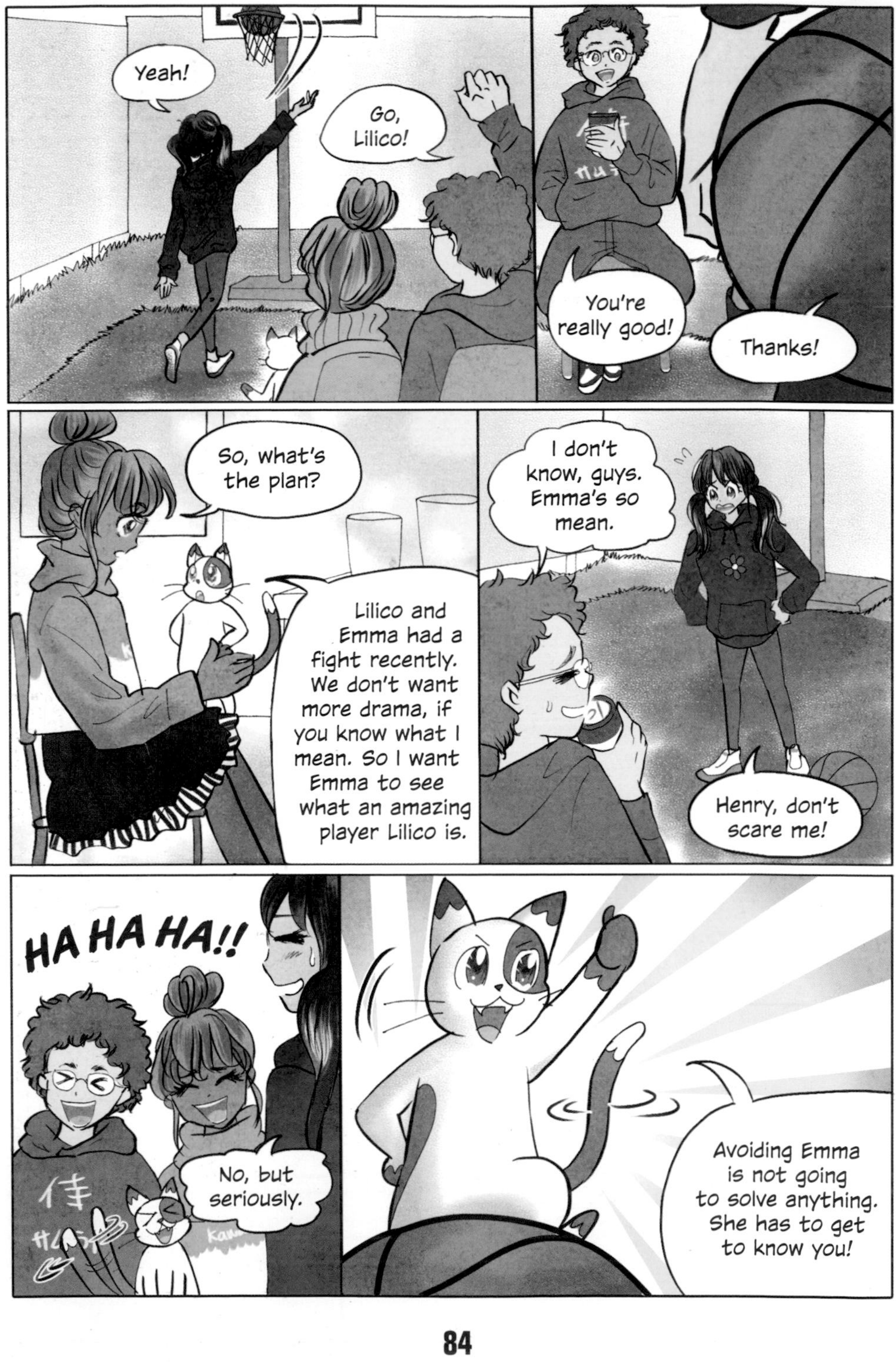

Yeah!
Go, Lilico!
You're really good!
Thanks!
So, what's the plan?
Lilico and Emma had a fight recently. We don't want more drama, if you know what I mean. So I want Emma to see what an amazing player Lilico is.
I don't know, guys. Emma's so mean.
Henry, don't scare me!
HA HA HA!!
No, but seriously.
Avoiding Emma is not going to solve anything. She has to get to know you!

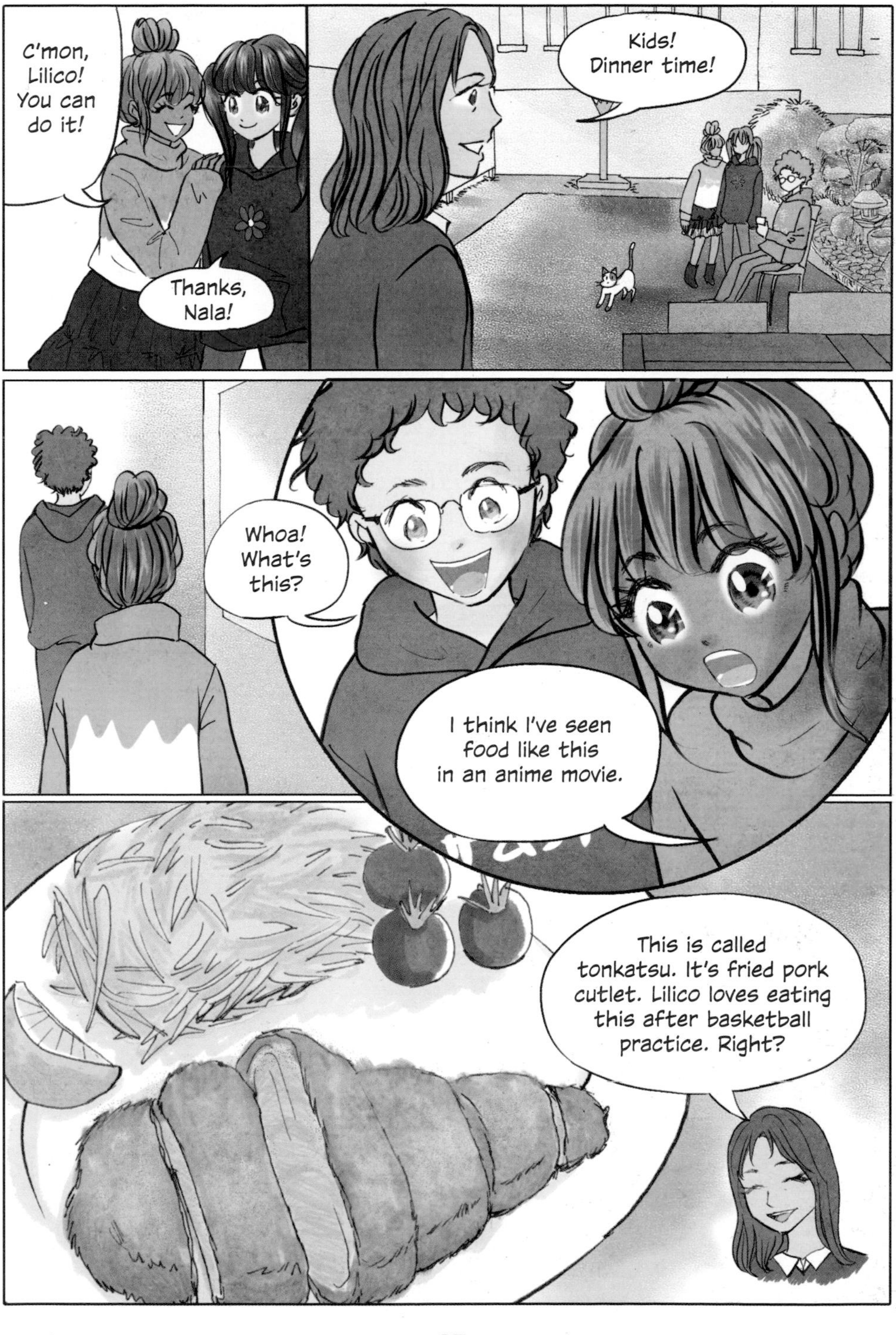
C'mon, Lilico! You can do it!
Thanks, Nala!
Kids! Dinner time!
Whoa! What's this?
I think I've seen food like this in an anime movie.
This is called tonkatsu. It's fried pork cutlet. Lilico loves eating this after basketball practice. Right?

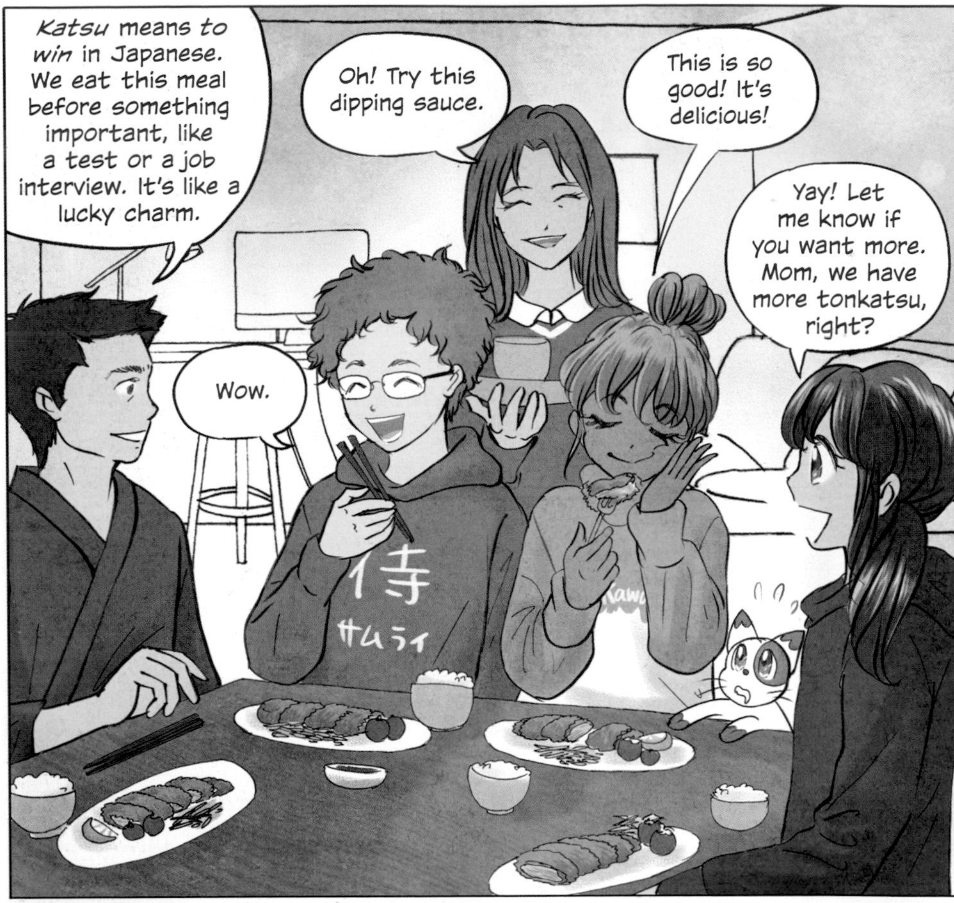
Katsu means to *win* in Japanese. We eat this meal before something important, like a test or a job interview. It's like a lucky charm.
Oh! Try this dipping sauce.
This is so good! It's delicious!
Yay! Let me know if you want more. Mom, we have more tonkatsu, right?
Wow.
侍
サムライ

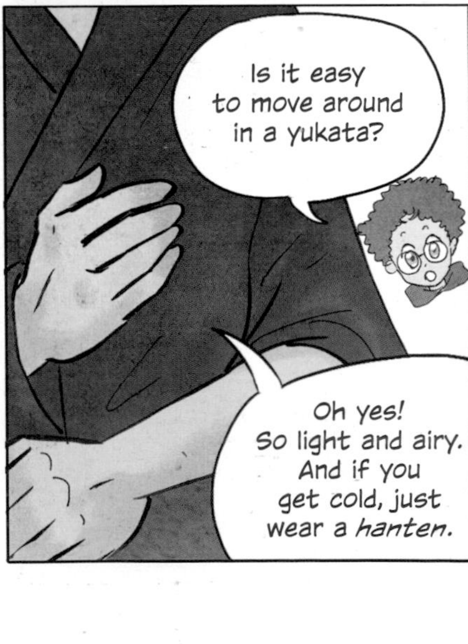
Is it easy to move around in a yukata?
Oh yes! So light and airy. And if you get cold, just wear a *hanten*.

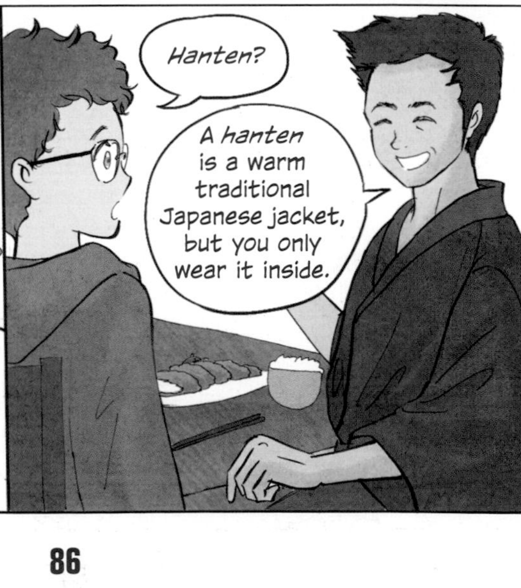
Hanten?
A *hanten* is a warm traditional Japanese jacket, but you only wear it inside.

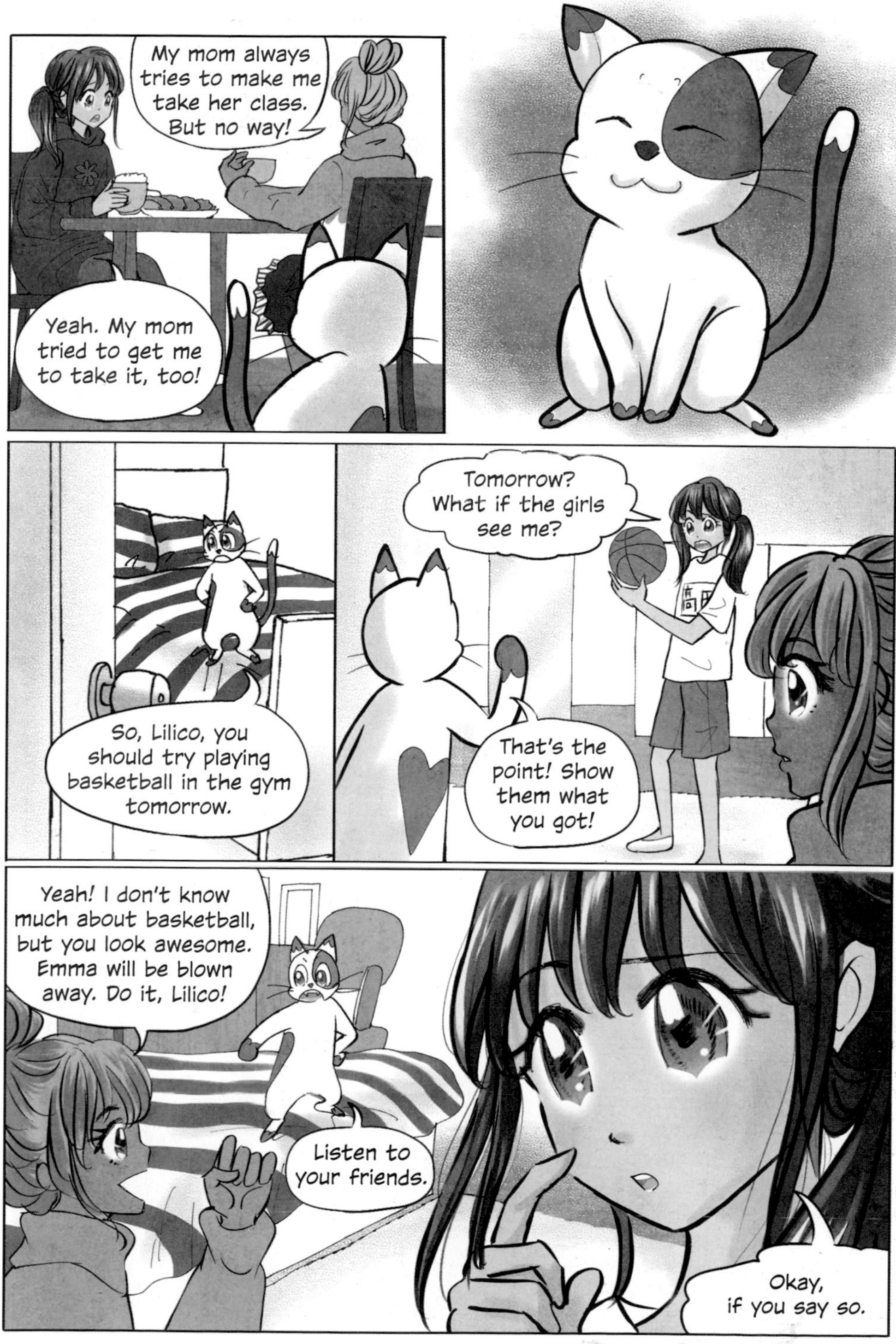
My mom always tries to make me take her class. But no way!
Yeah. My mom tried to get me to take it, too!
So, Lilico, you should try playing basketball in the gym tomorrow.
Tomorrow? What if the girls see me?
That's the point! Show them what you got!
Yeah! I don't know much about basketball, but you look awesome. Emma will be blown away. Do it, Lilico!
Listen to your friends.
Okay, if you say so.

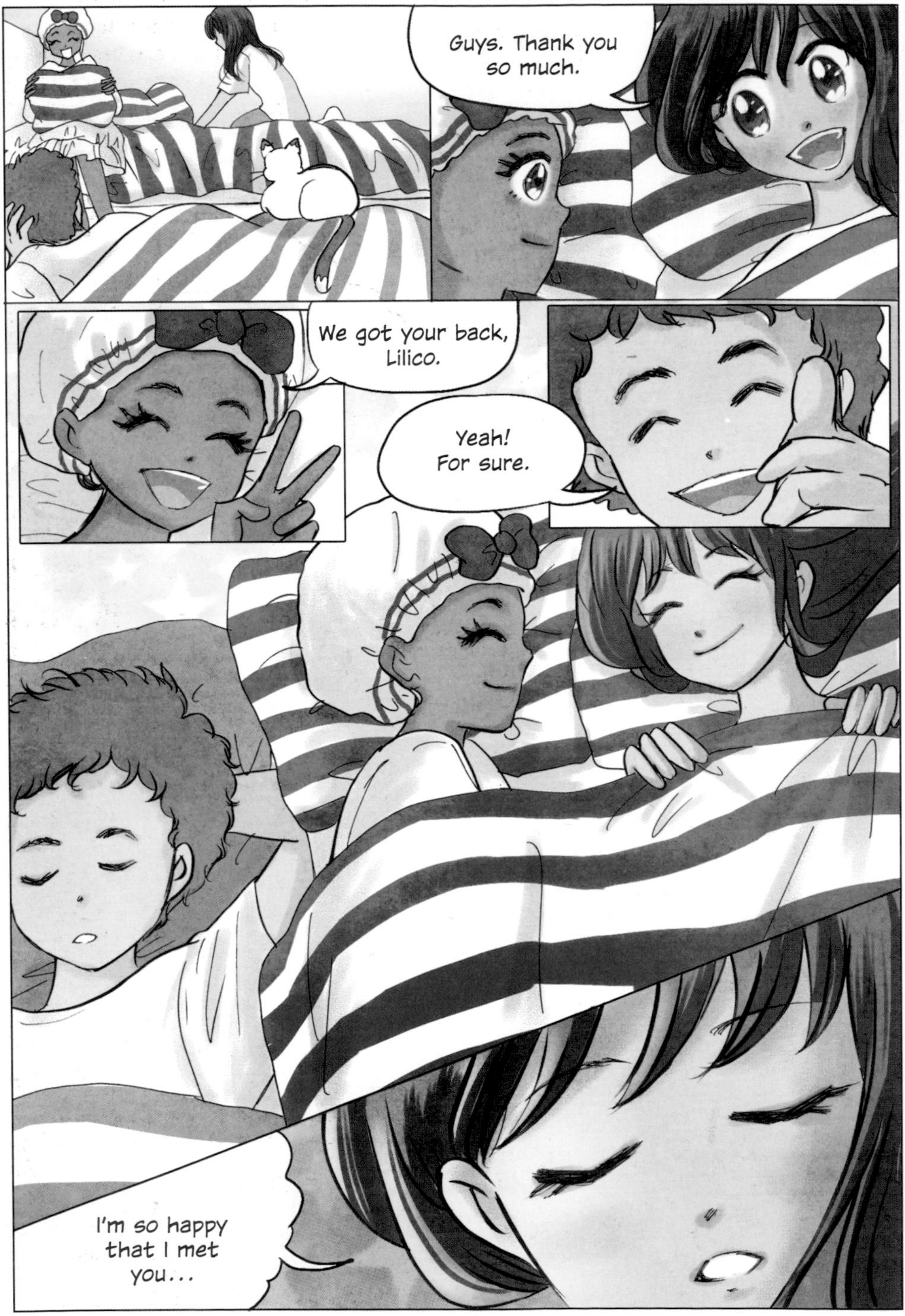
Guys. Thank you so much.
We got your back, Lilico.
Yeah! For sure.
I'm so happy that I met you...

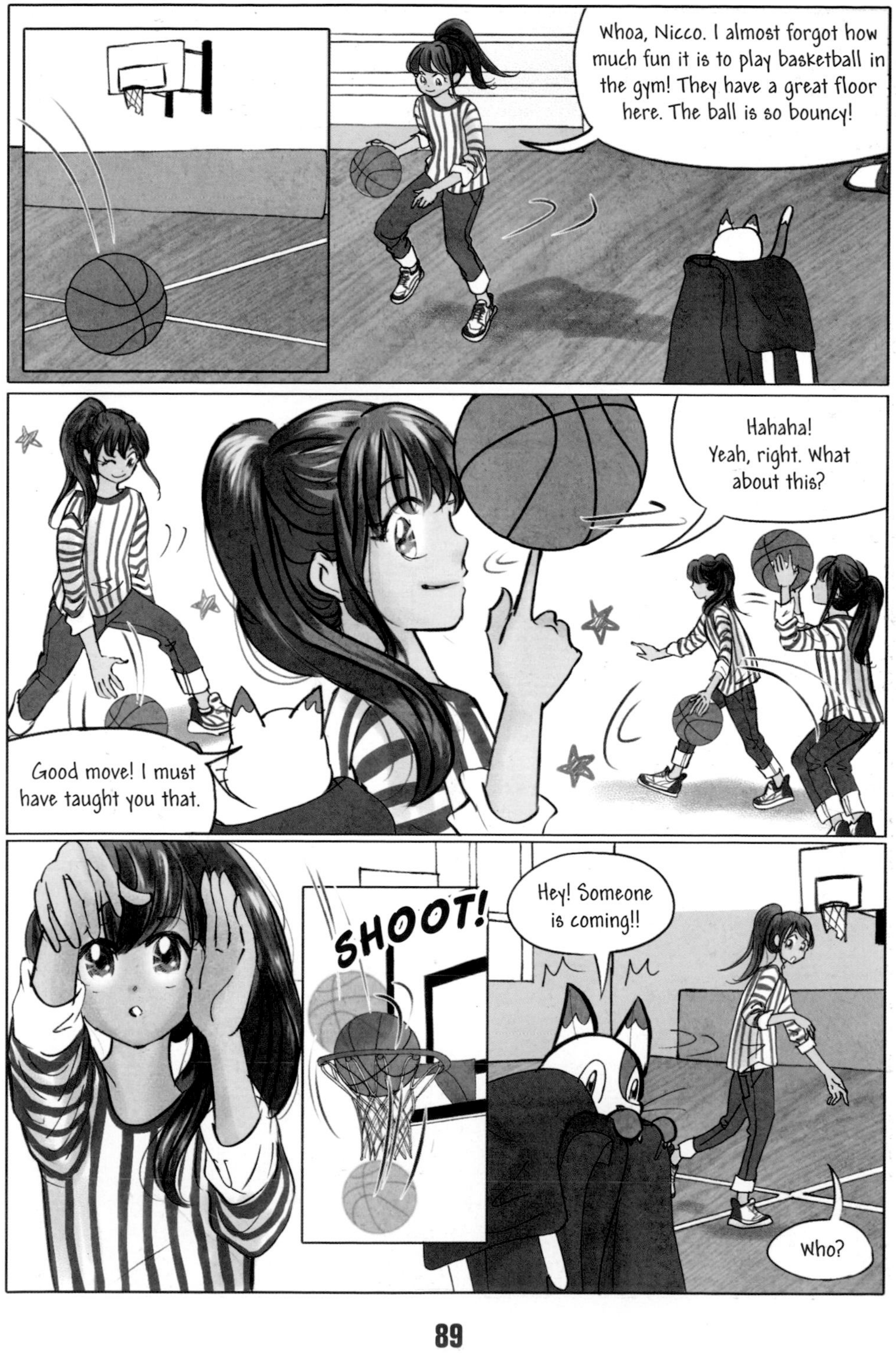
Whoa, Nicco. I almost forgot how much fun it is to play basketball in the gym! They have a great floor here. The ball is so bouncy!
Good move! I must have taught you that.
Hahaha! Yeah, right. What about this?
SHOOT!
Hey! Someone is coming!!
Who?

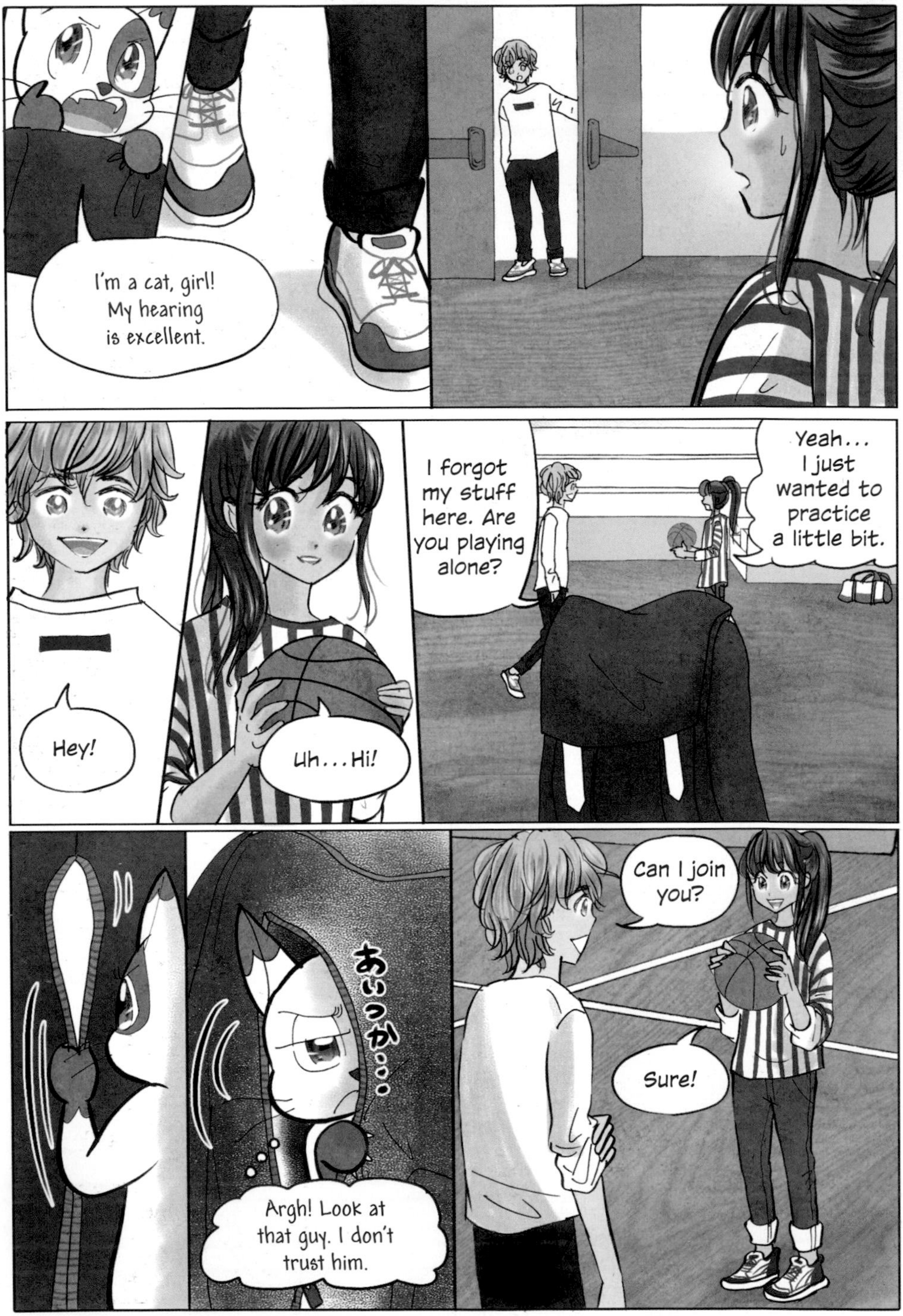
I'm a cat, girl! My hearing is excellent.
Hey!
Uh...Hi!
I forgot my stuff here. Are you playing alone?
Yeah... I just wanted to practice a little bit.
あいつか…
Argh! Look at that guy. I don't trust him.
Can I join you?
Sure!

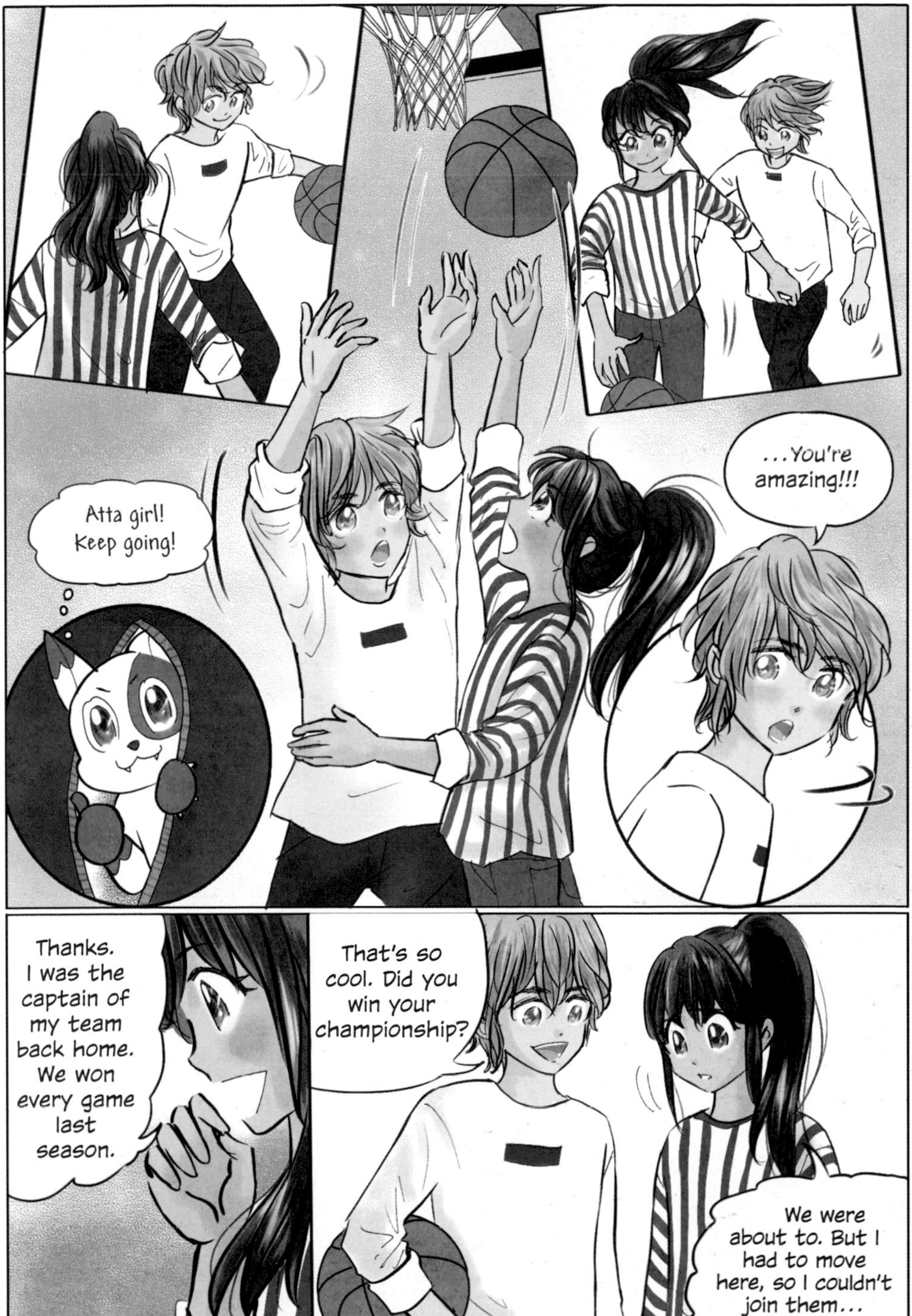
Atta girl! Keep going!
...You're amazing!!!
Thanks. I was the captain of my team back home. We won every game last season.
That's so cool. Did you win your championship?
We were about to. But I had to move here, so I couldn't join them...

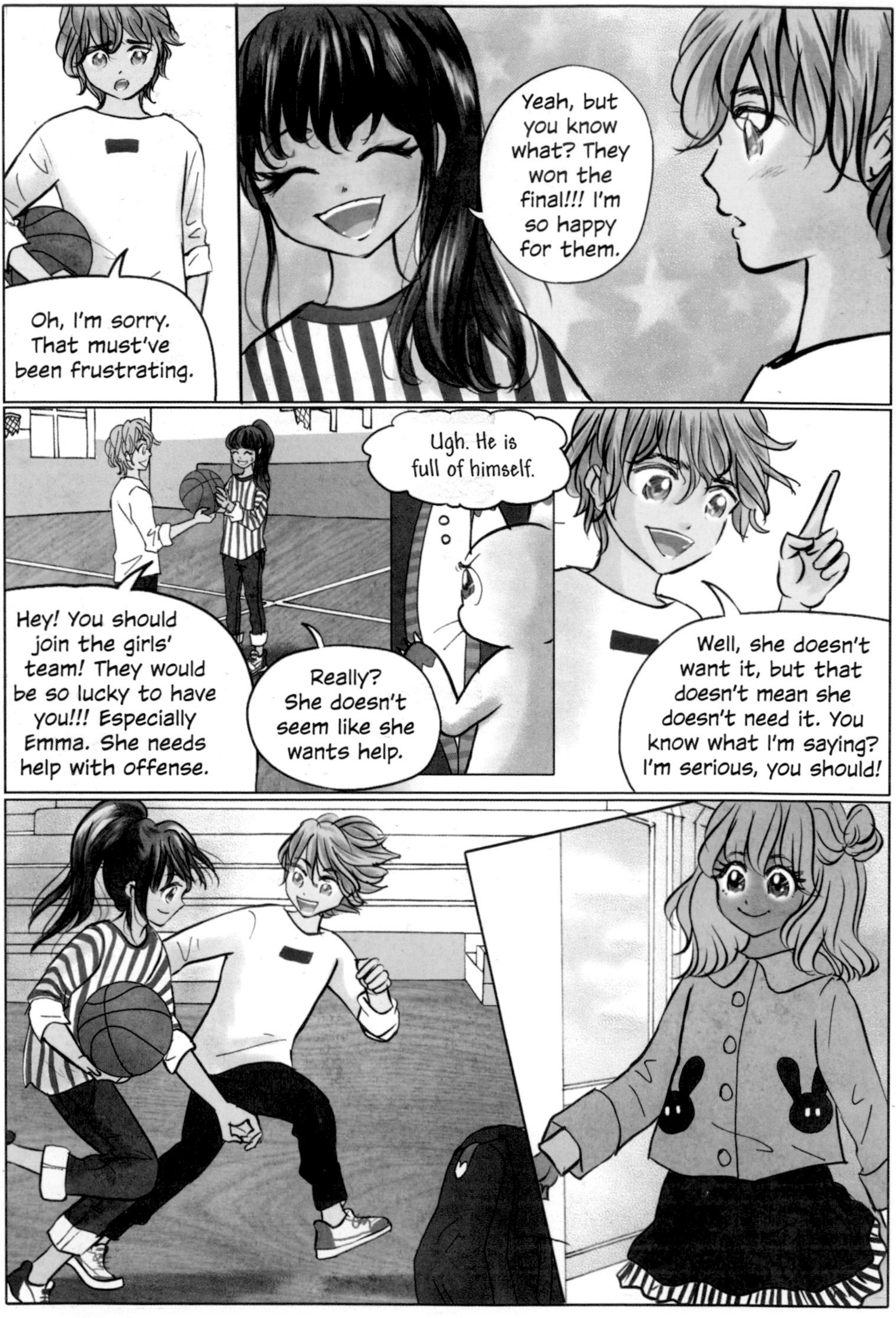

Oh, I'm sorry. That must've been frustrating.
Yeah, but you know what? They won the final!!! I'm so happy for them.
Hey! You should join the girls' team! They would be so lucky to have you!!! Especially Emma. She needs help with offense.
Ugh. He is full of himself.
Really? She doesn't seem like she wants help.
Well, she doesn't want it, but that doesn't mean she doesn't need it. You know what I'm saying? I'm serious, you should!

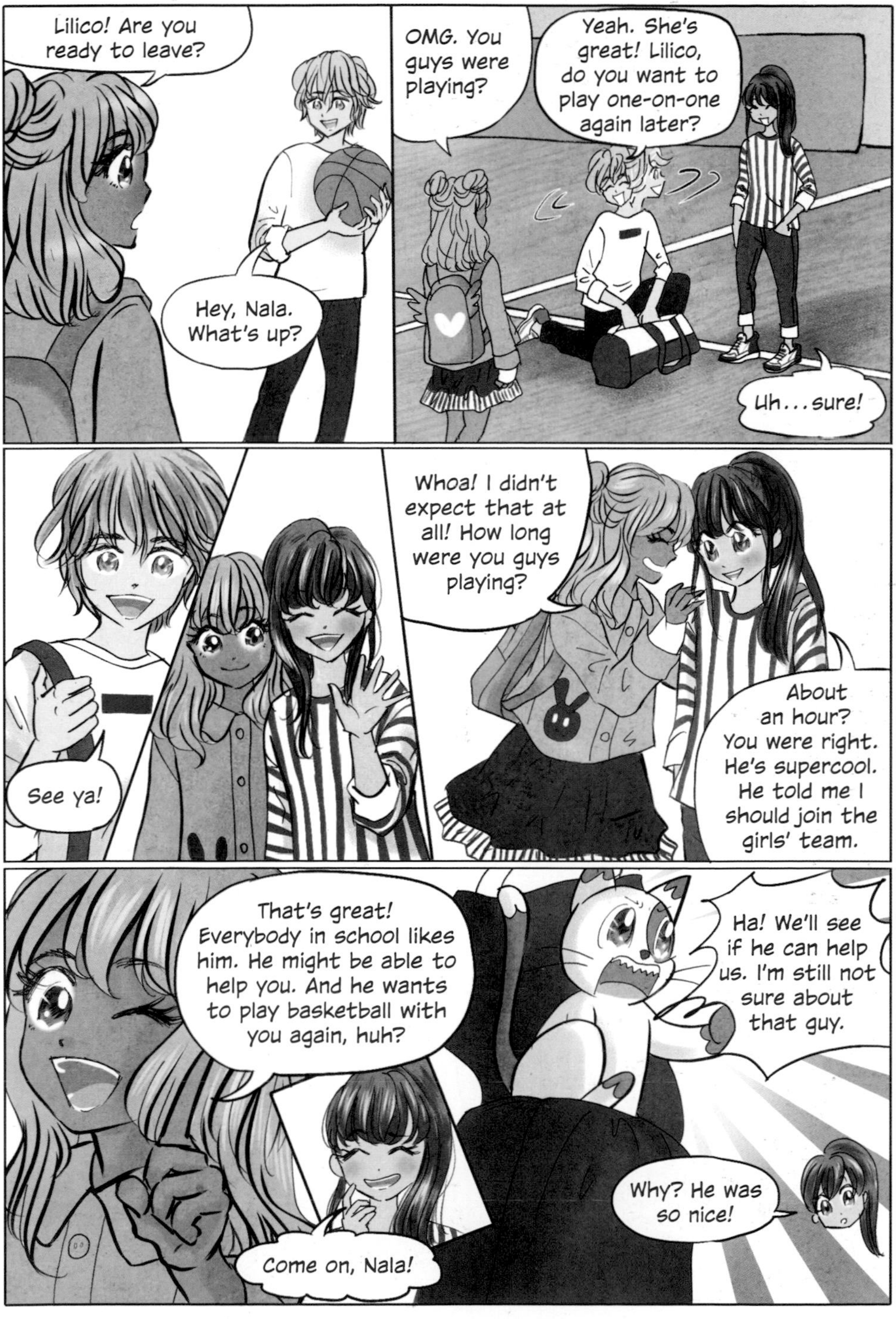
Lilico! Are you ready to leave?
Hey, Nala. What's up?
OMG. You guys were playing?
Yeah. She's great! Lilico, do you want to play one-on-one again later?
Uh...sure!
See ya!
Whoa! I didn't expect that at all! How long were you guys playing?
About an hour? You were right. He's supercool. He told me I should join the girls' team.
That's great! Everybody in school likes him. He might be able to help you. And he wants to play basketball with you again, huh?
Come on, Nala!
Ha! We'll see if he can help us. I'm still not sure about that guy.
Why? He was so nice!

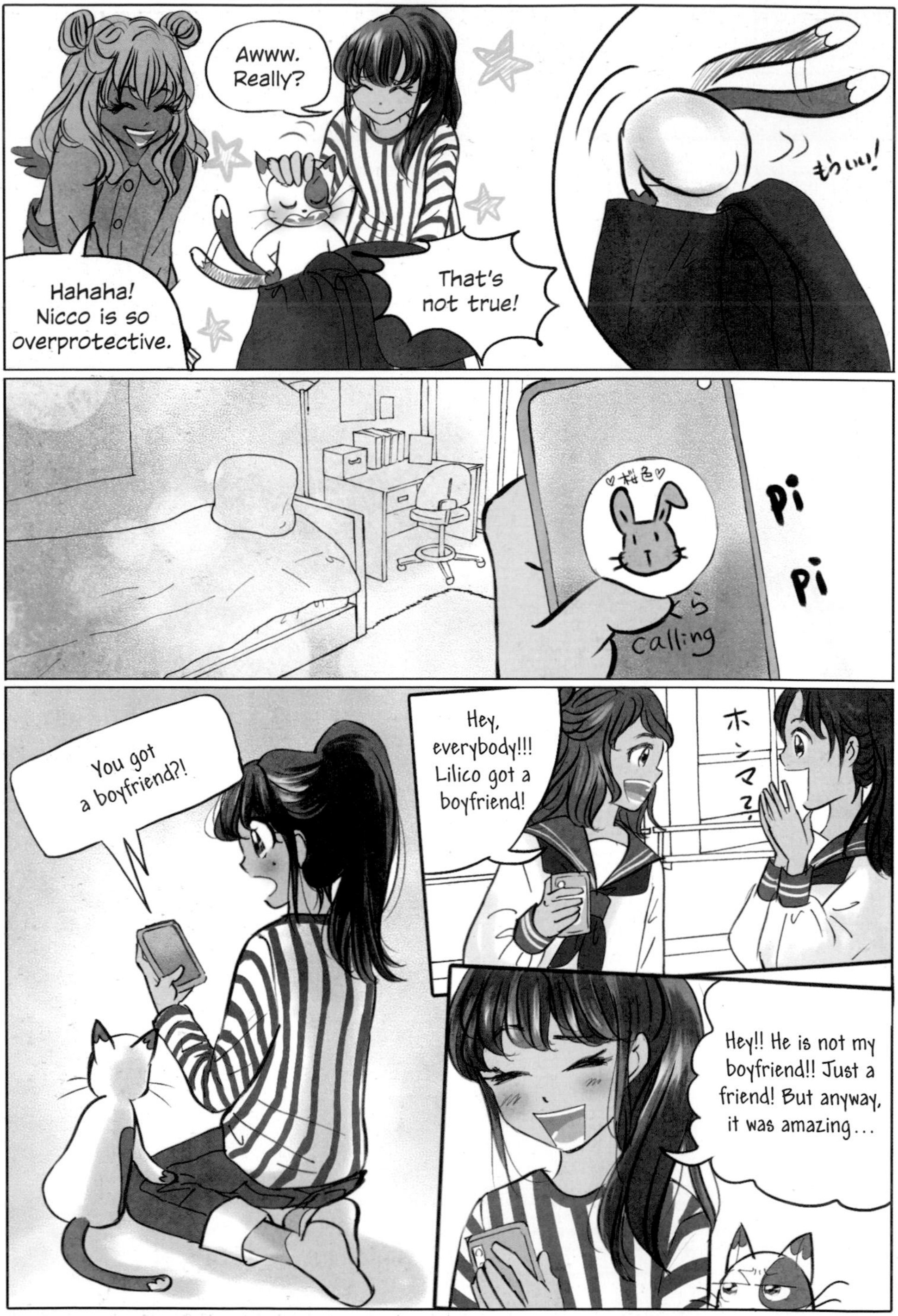

Awww. Really?
Hahaha! Nicco is so overprotective.
That's not true!
もういい!
♡桜色♡
calling
Pi
Pi
You got a boyfriend?!
Hey, everybody!!! Lilico got a boyfriend!
ホンマ?
Hey!! He is not my boyfriend!! Just a friend! But anyway, it was amazing…

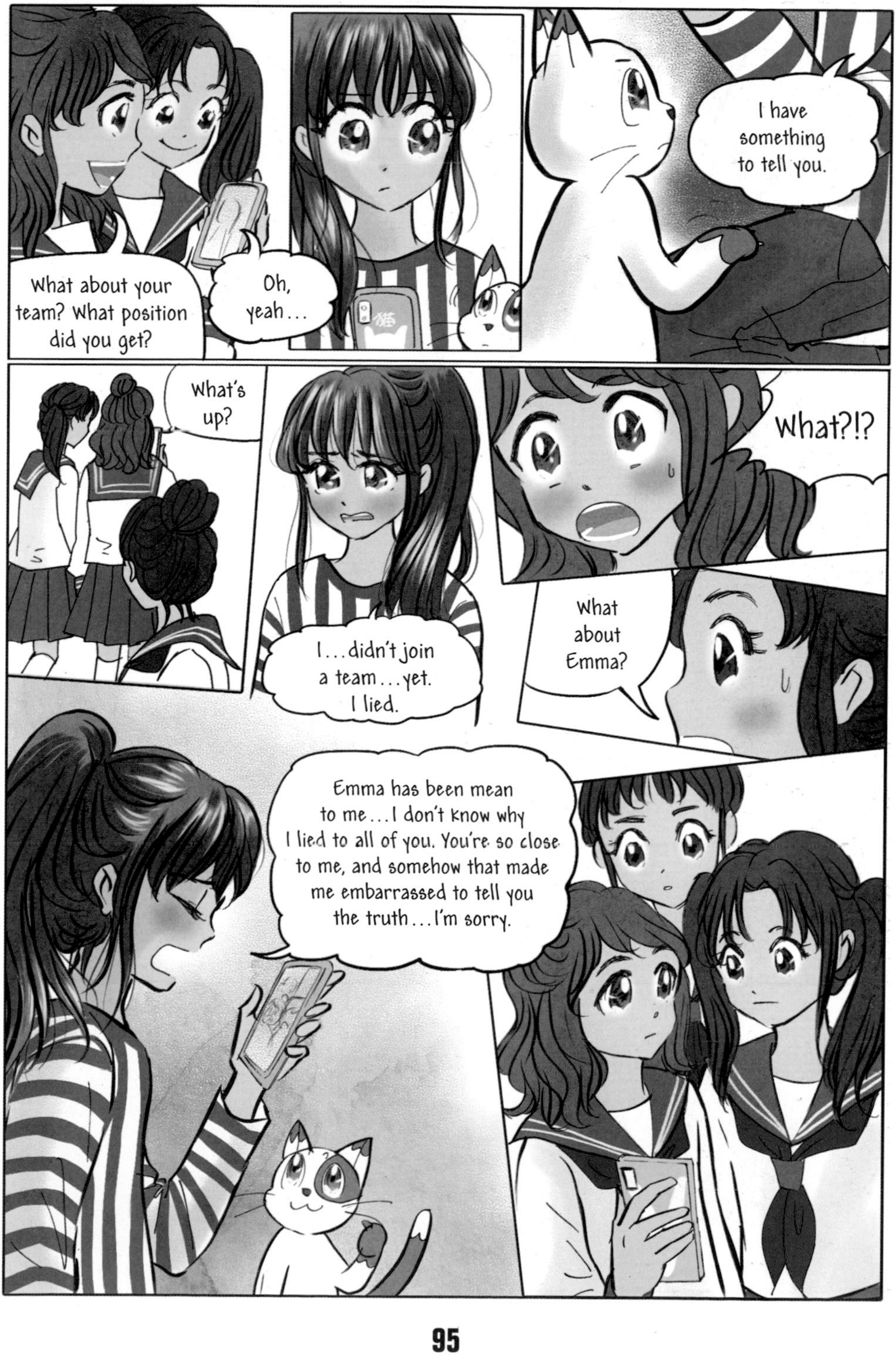
What about your team? What position did you get?
Oh, yeah...
I have something to tell you.
What's up?
I...didn't join a team...yet. I lied.
What?!?
What about Emma?
Emma has been mean to me...I don't know why I lied to all of you. You're so close to me, and somehow that made me embarrassed to tell you the truth...I'm sorry.

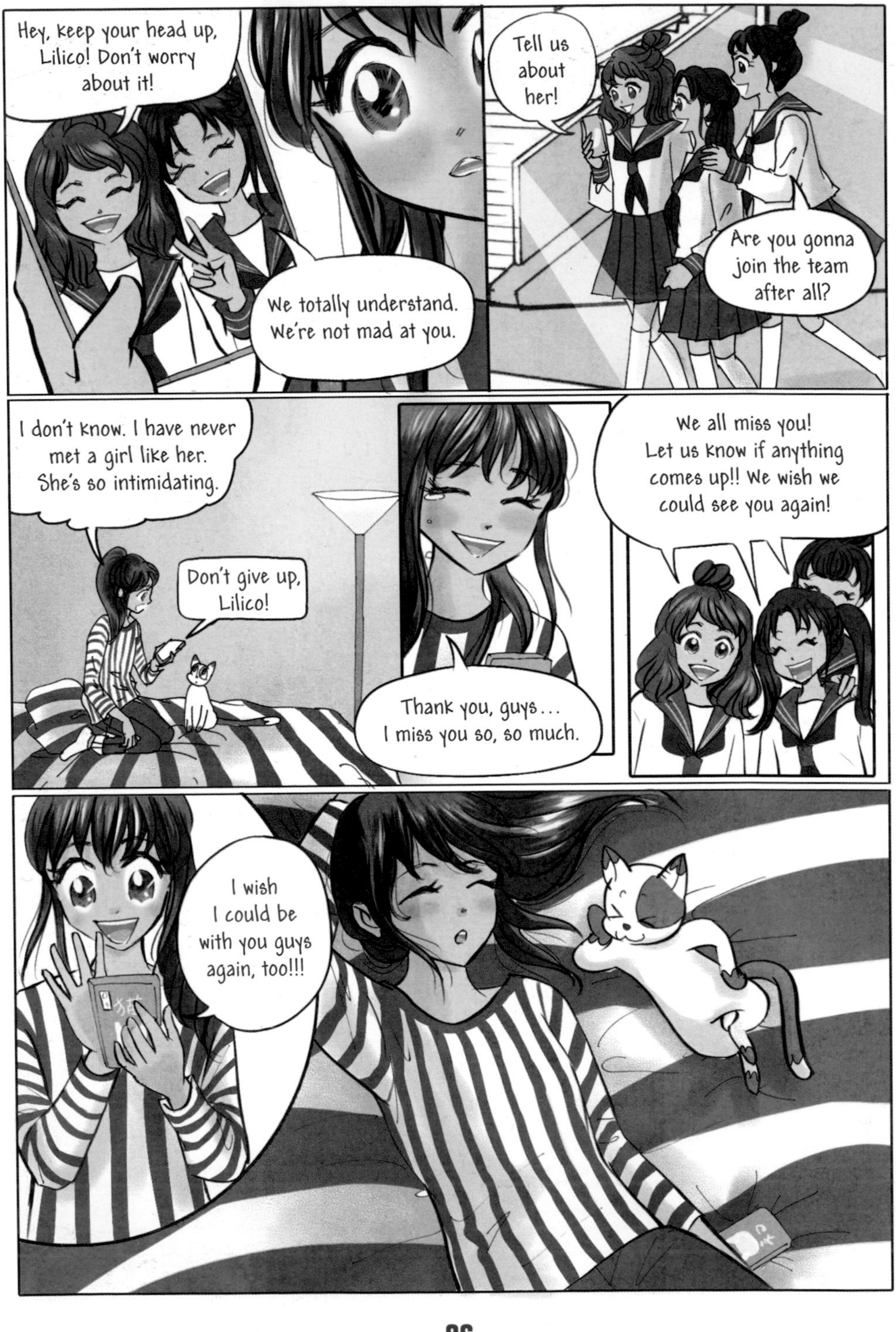

Hey, keep your head up, Lilico! Don't worry about it!
We totally understand. We're not mad at you.
Tell us about her!
Are you gonna join the team after all?
I don't know. I have never met a girl like her. She's so intimidating.
Don't give up, Lilico!
Thank you, guys... I miss you so, so much.
We all miss you! Let us know if anything comes up!! We wish we could see you again!
I wish I could be with you guys again, too!!!

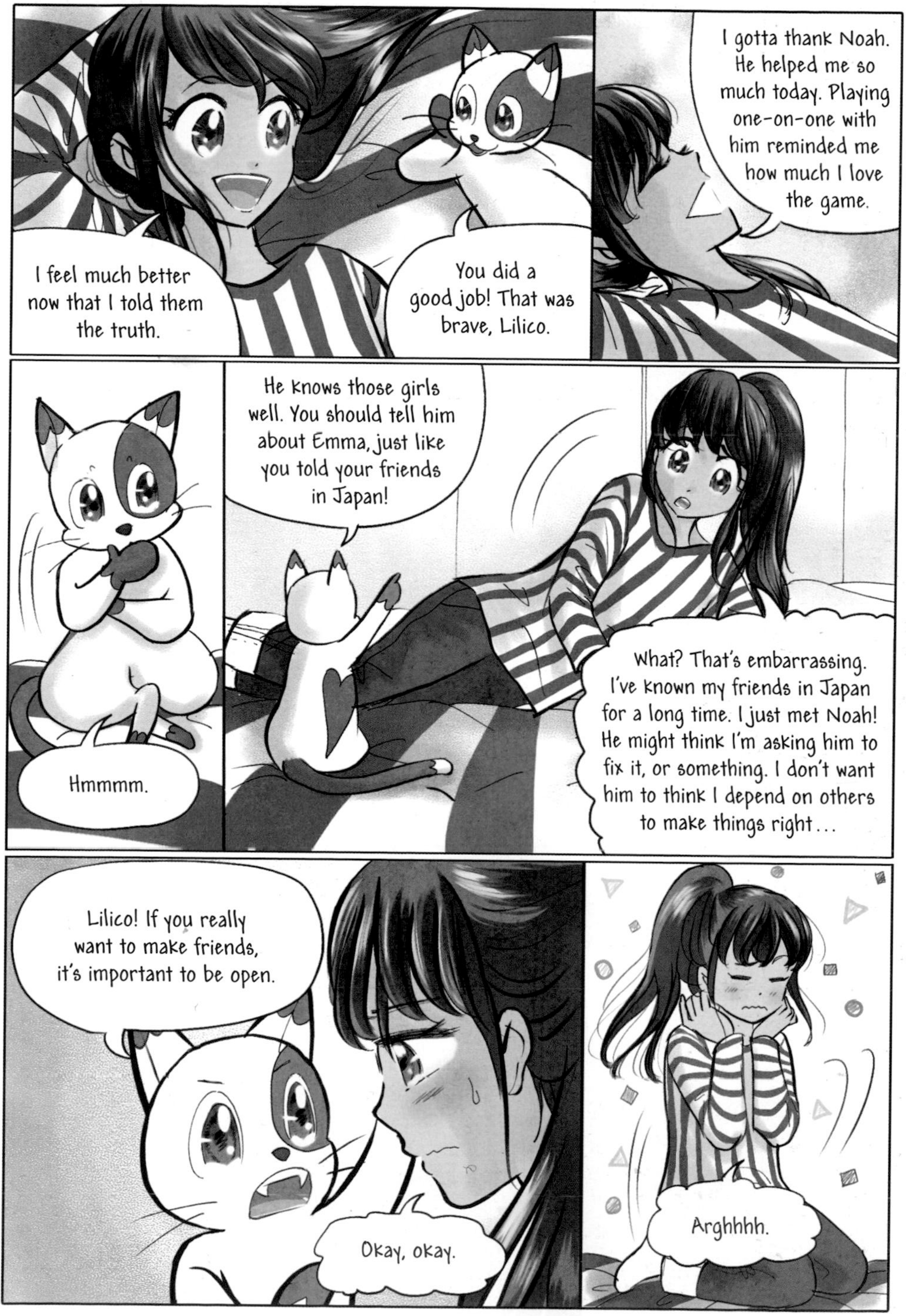
I feel much better now that I told them the truth.
You did a good job! That was brave, Lilico.
I gotta thank Noah. He helped me so much today. Playing one-on-one with him reminded me how much I love the game.
Hmmmm.
He knows those girls well. You should tell him about Emma, just like you told your friends in Japan!
What? That's embarrassing. I've known my friends in Japan for a long time. I just met Noah! He might think I'm asking him to fix it, or something. I don't want him to think I depend on others to make things right...
Lilico! If you really want to make friends, it's important to be open.
Okay, okay.
Arghhhh.

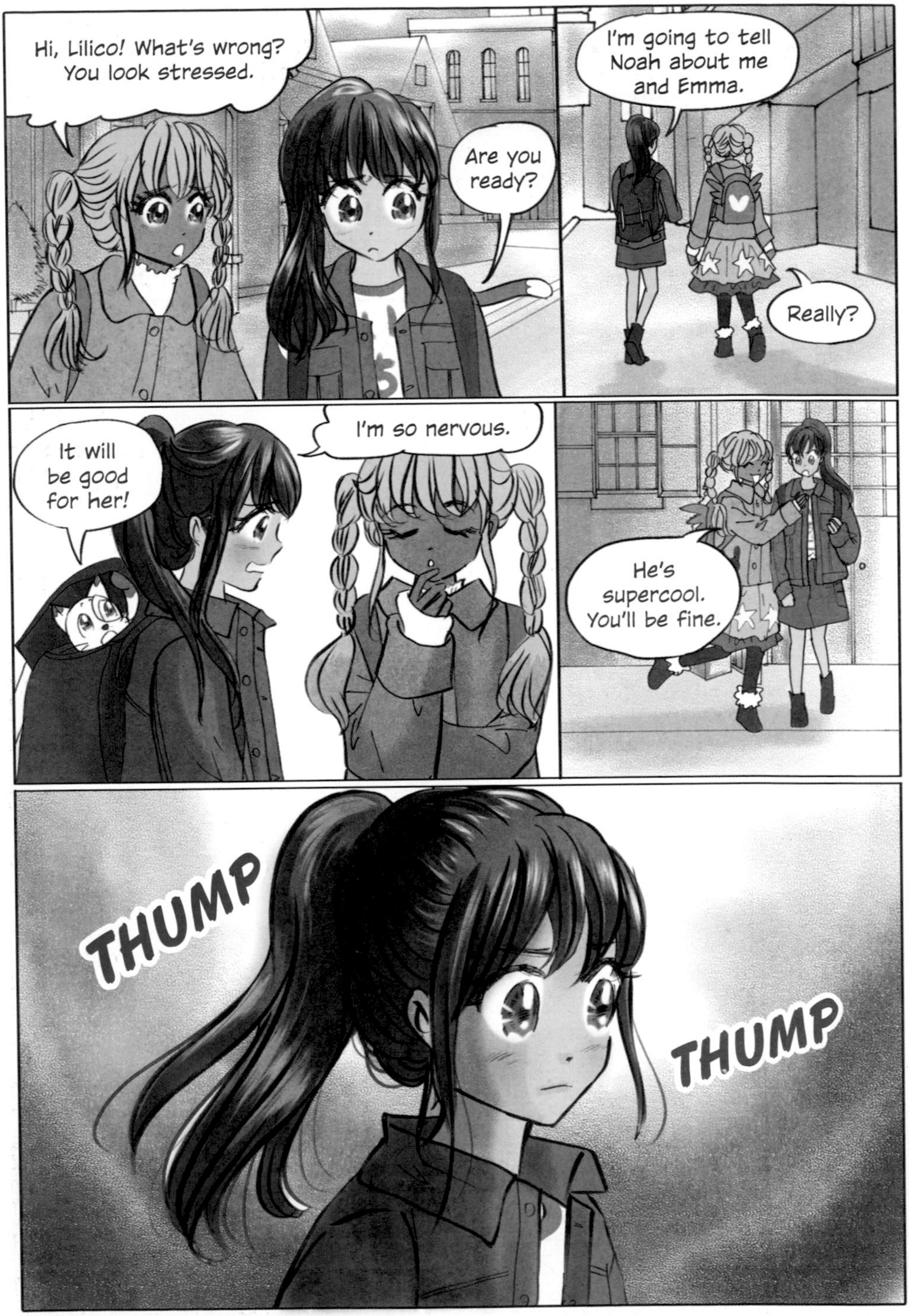
Hi, Lilico! What's wrong? You look stressed.
Are you ready?
I'm going to tell Noah about me and Emma.
Really?
It will be good for her!
I'm so nervous.
He's supercool. You'll be fine.
THUMP
THUMP

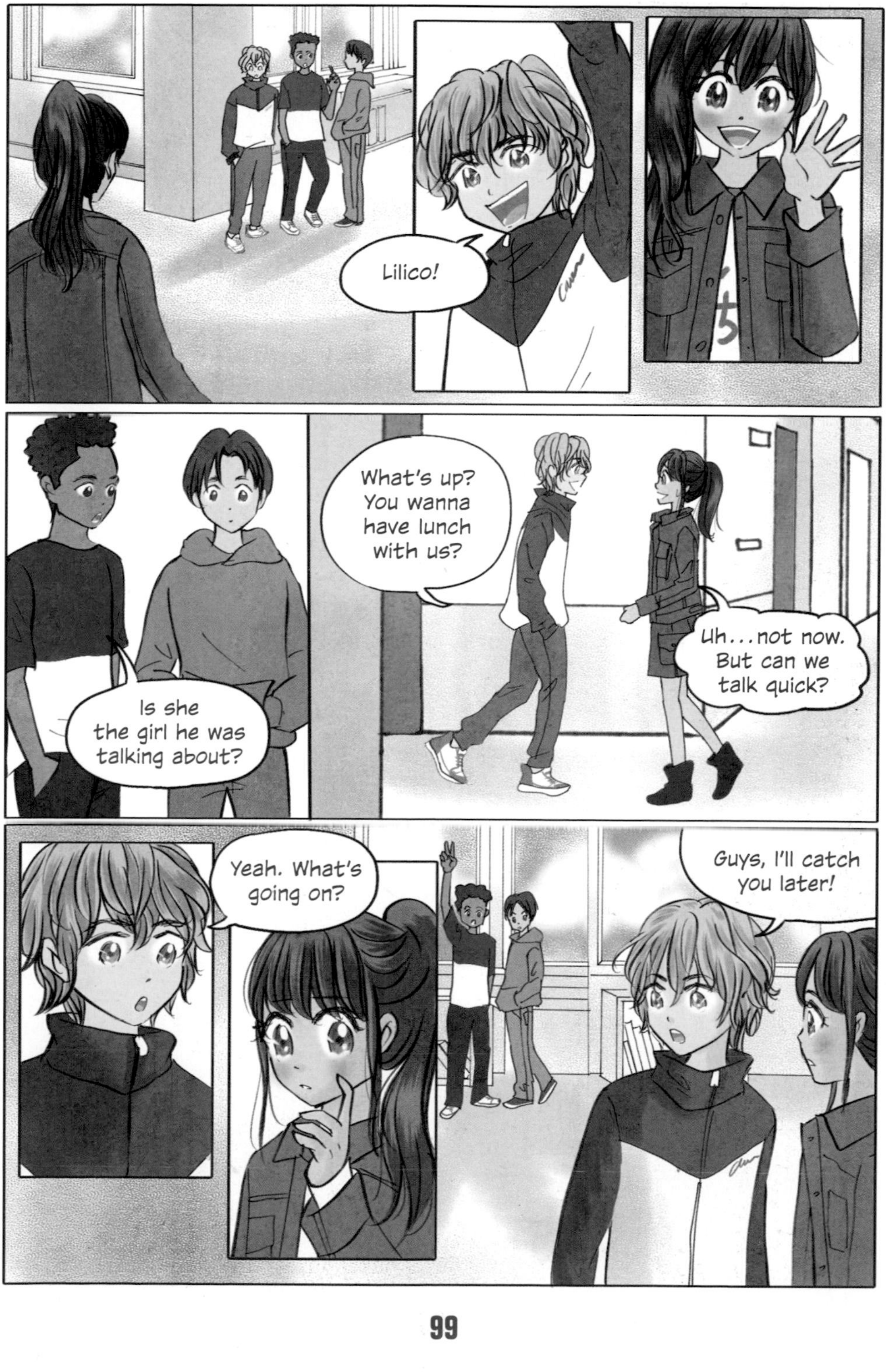
Lilico!
Is she the girl he was talking about?
What's up? You wanna have lunch with us?
Uh...not now. But can we talk quick?
Yeah. What's going on?
Guys, I'll catch you later!

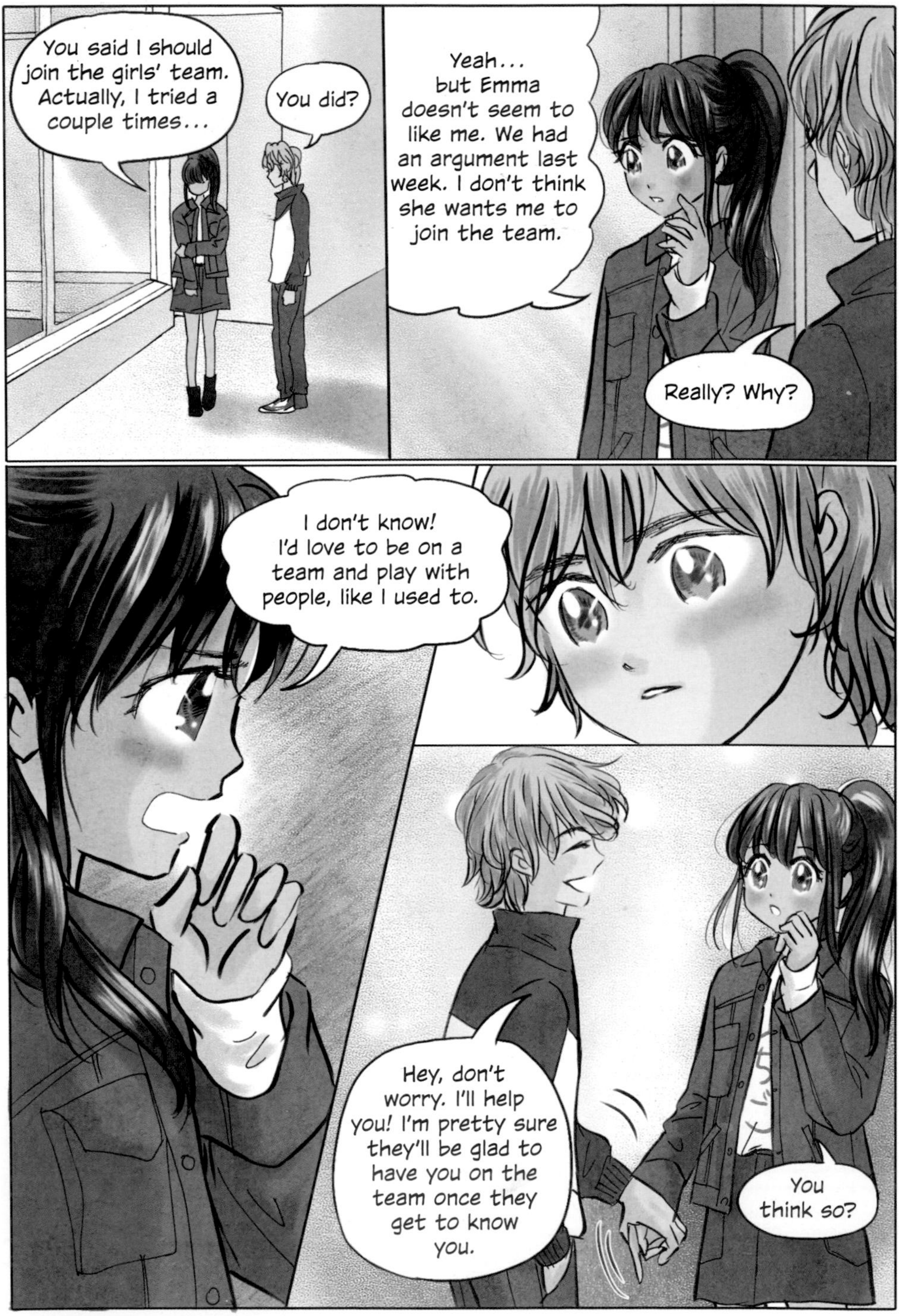

You said I should join the girls' team. Actually, I tried a couple times...
You did?
Yeah... but Emma doesn't seem to like me. We had an argument last week. I don't think she wants me to join the team.
Really? Why?
I don't know! I'd love to be on a team and play with people, like I used to.
Hey, don't worry. I'll help you! I'm pretty sure they'll be glad to have you on the team once they get to know you.
You think so?

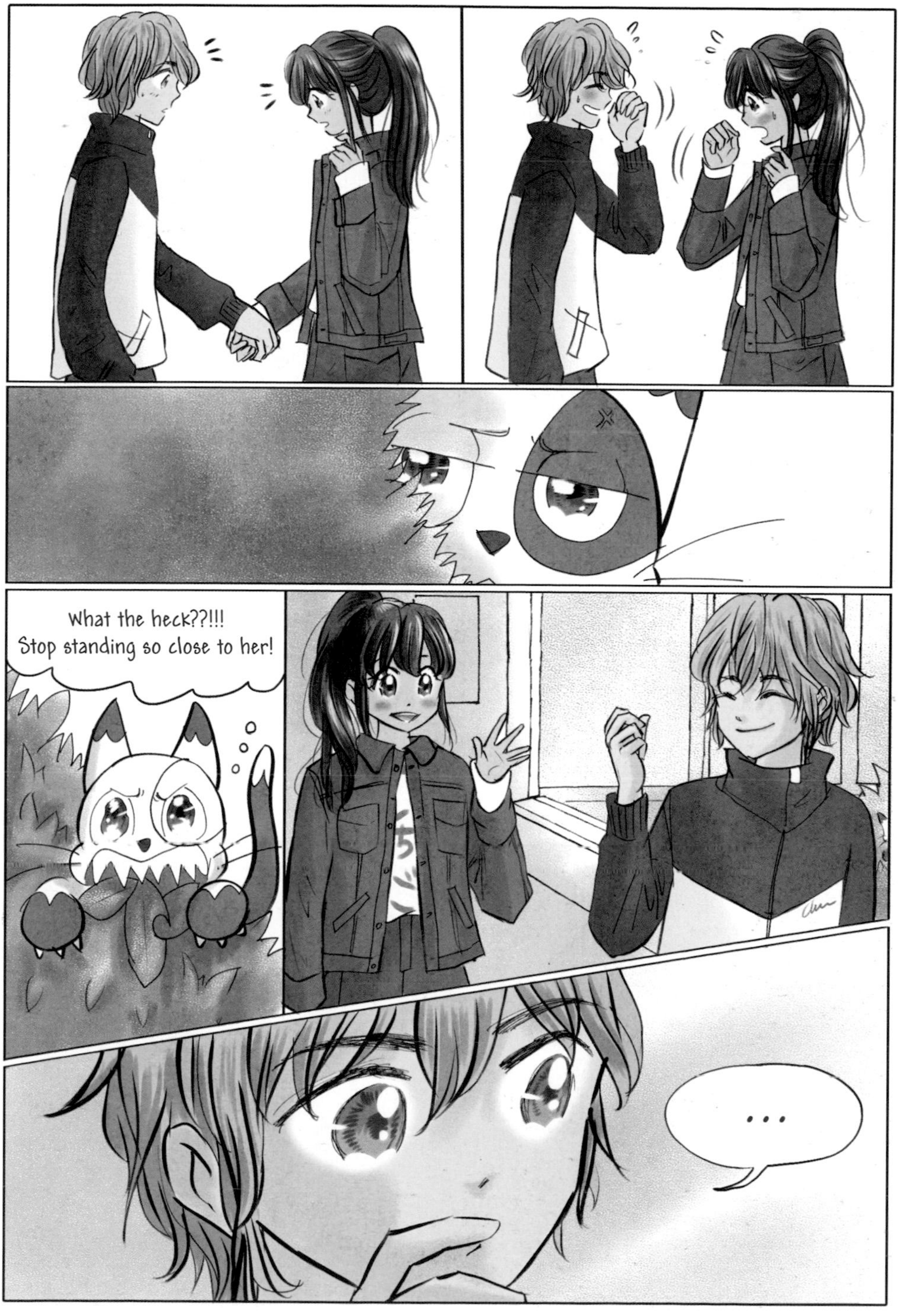
What the heck??!!!
Stop standing so close to her!
...

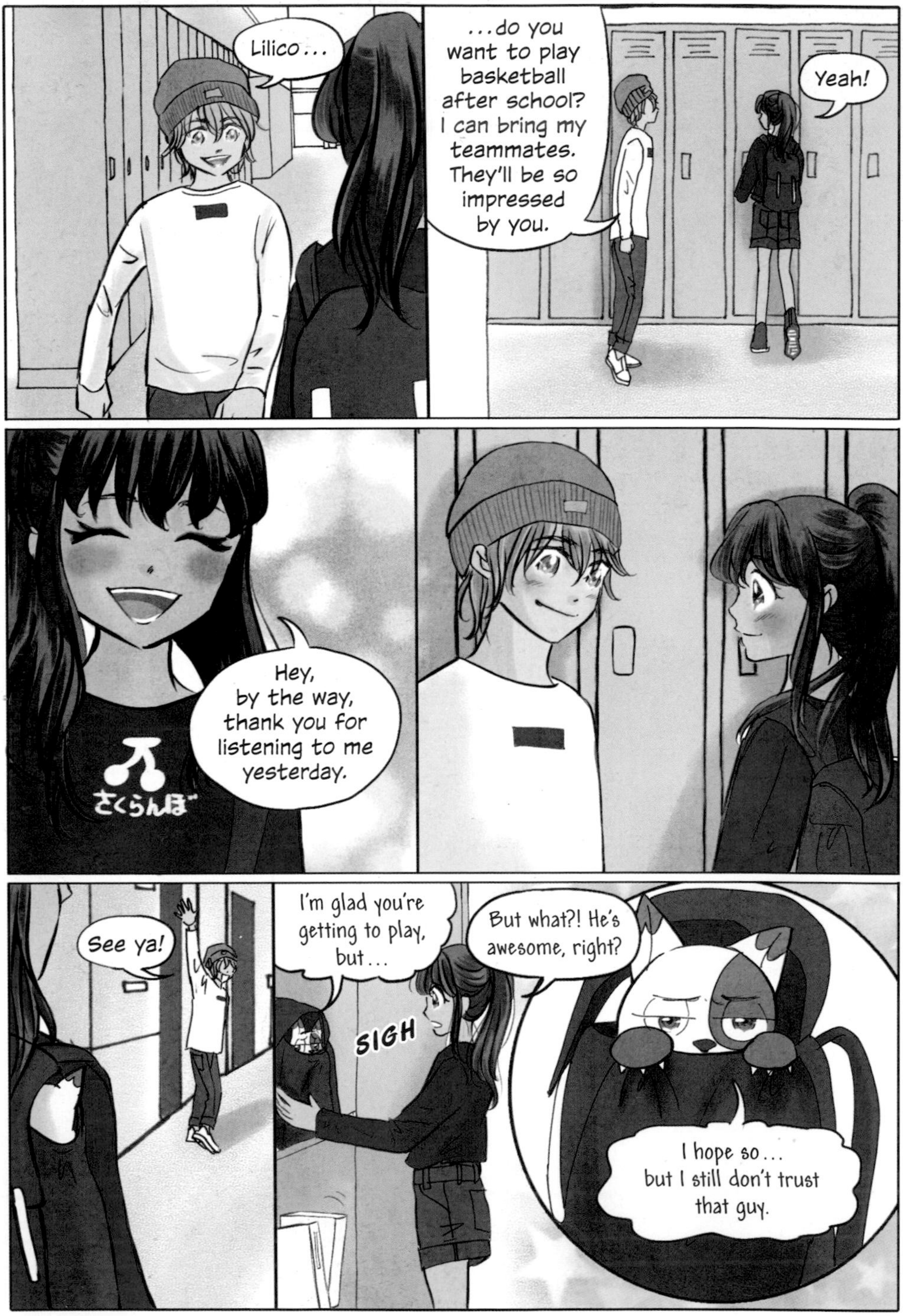
Lilico...
...do you want to play basketball after school? I can bring my teammates. They'll be so impressed by you.
Yeah!
さくらんぼ
Hey, by the way, thank you for listening to me yesterday.
See ya!
I'm glad you're getting to play, but...
SIGH
But what?! He's awesome, right?
I hope so... but I still don't trust that guy.

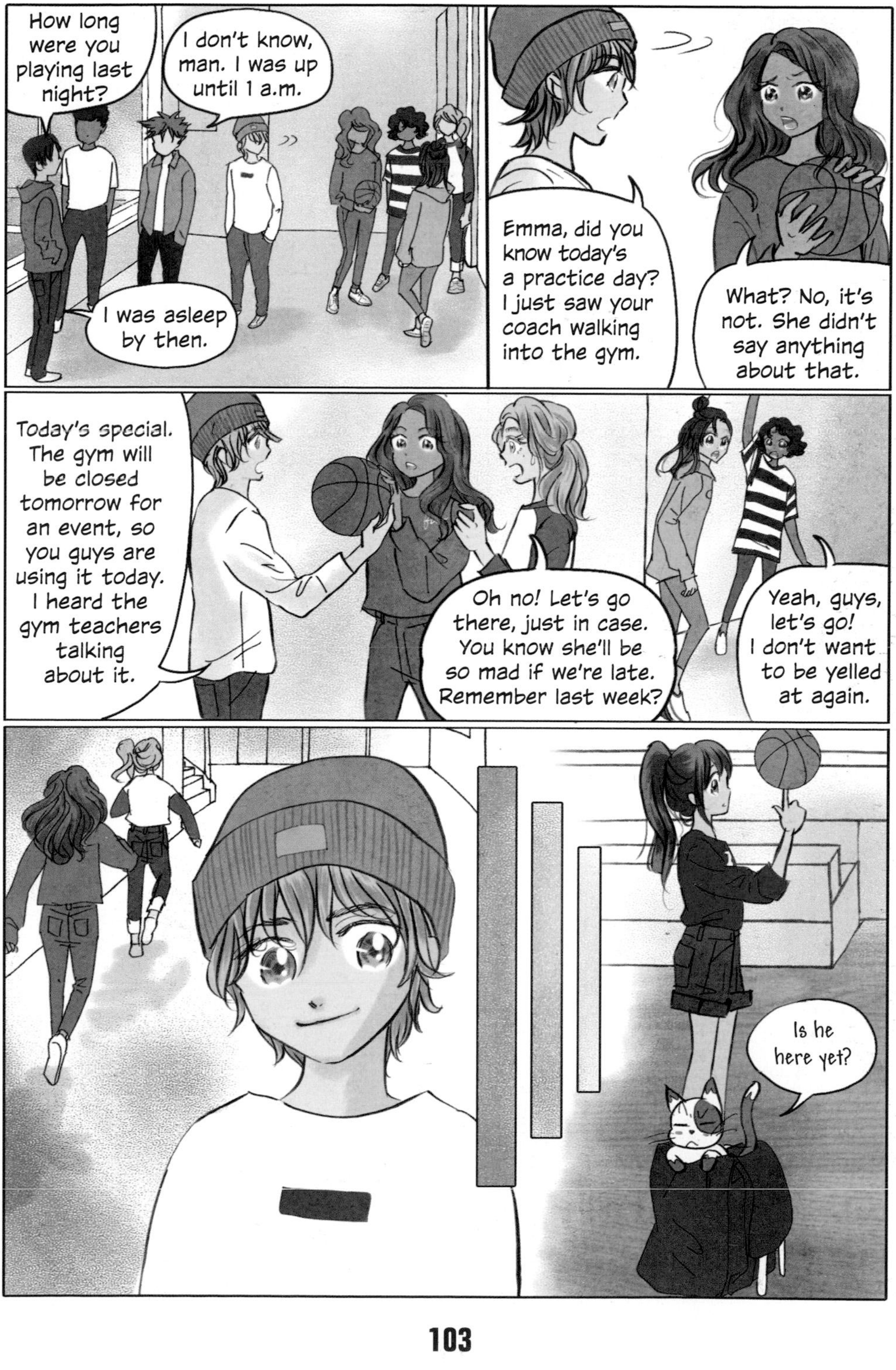
How long were you playing last night?
I don't know, man. I was up until 1 a.m.
I was asleep by then.
Emma, did you know today's a practice day? I just saw your coach walking into the gym.
What? No, it's not. She didn't say anything about that.
Today's special. The gym will be closed tomorrow for an event, so you guys are using it today. I heard the gym teachers talking about it.
Oh no! Let's go there, just in case. You know she'll be so mad if we're late. Remember last week?
Yeah, guys, let's go! I don't want to be yelled at again.
Is he here yet?

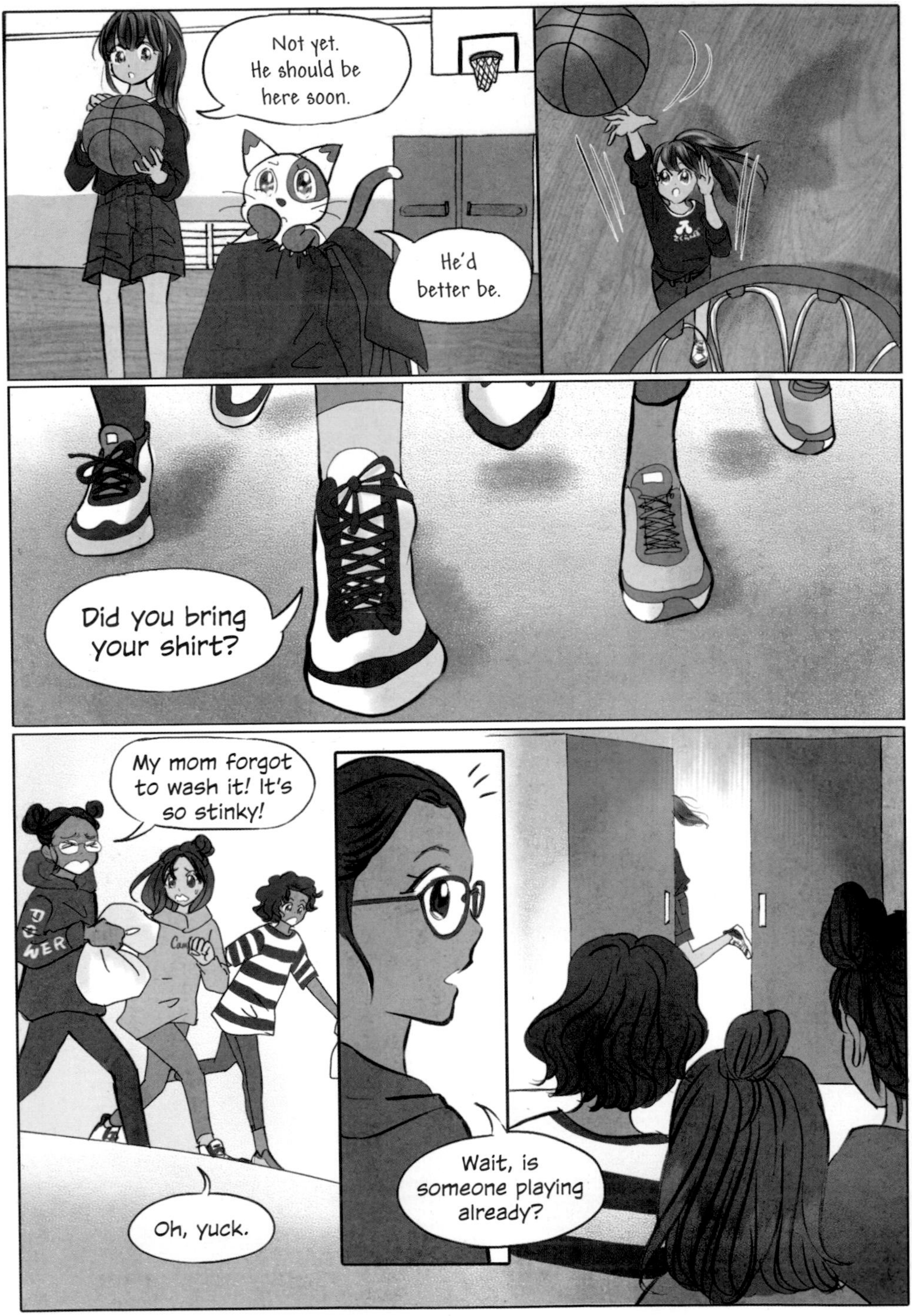
Not yet. He should be here soon.
He'd better be.
Did you bring your shirt?
My mom forgot to wash it! It's so stinky!
POWER
Oh, yuck.
Wait, is someone playing already?

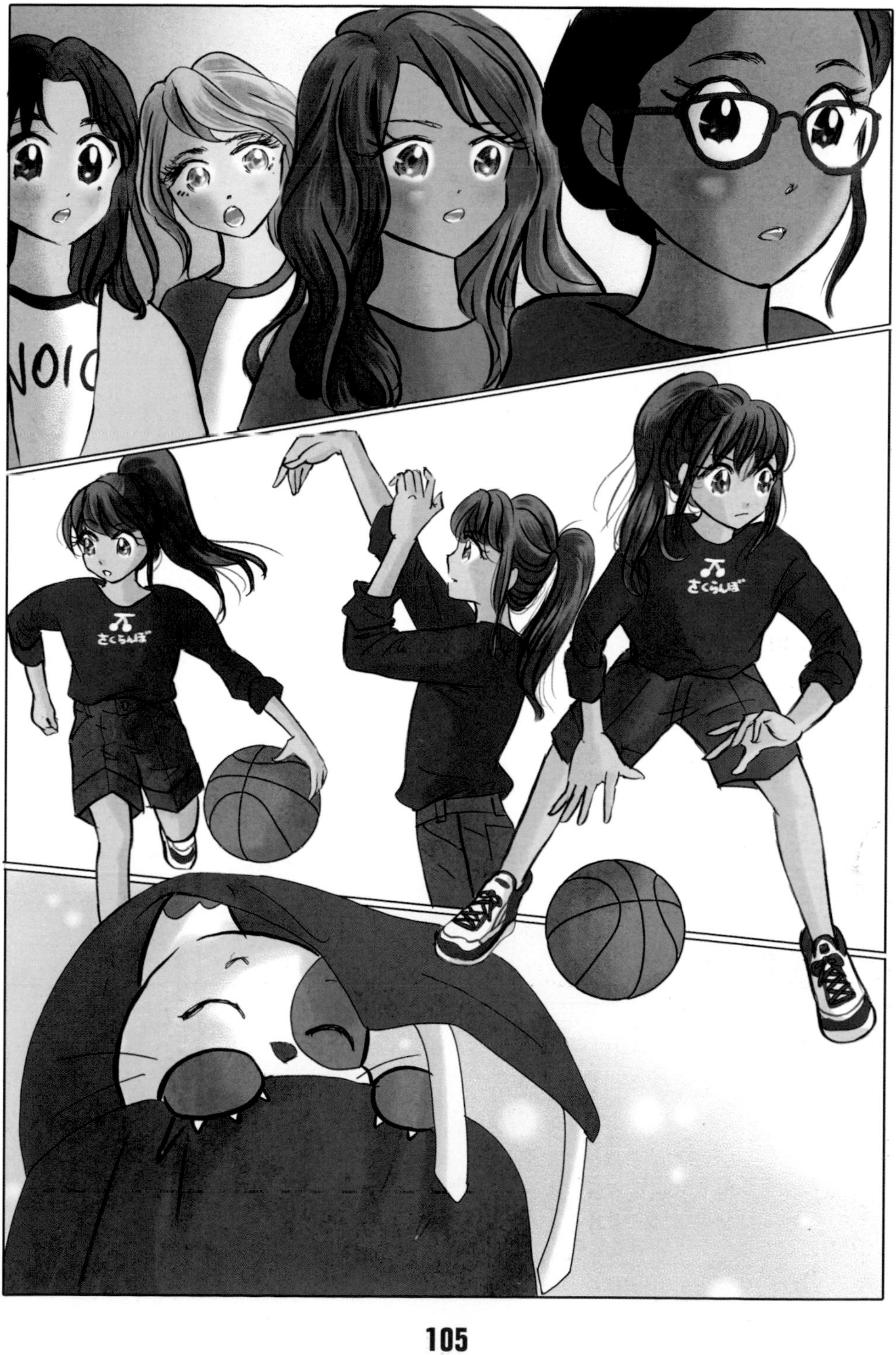
さくらんぼ
さくらんぼ

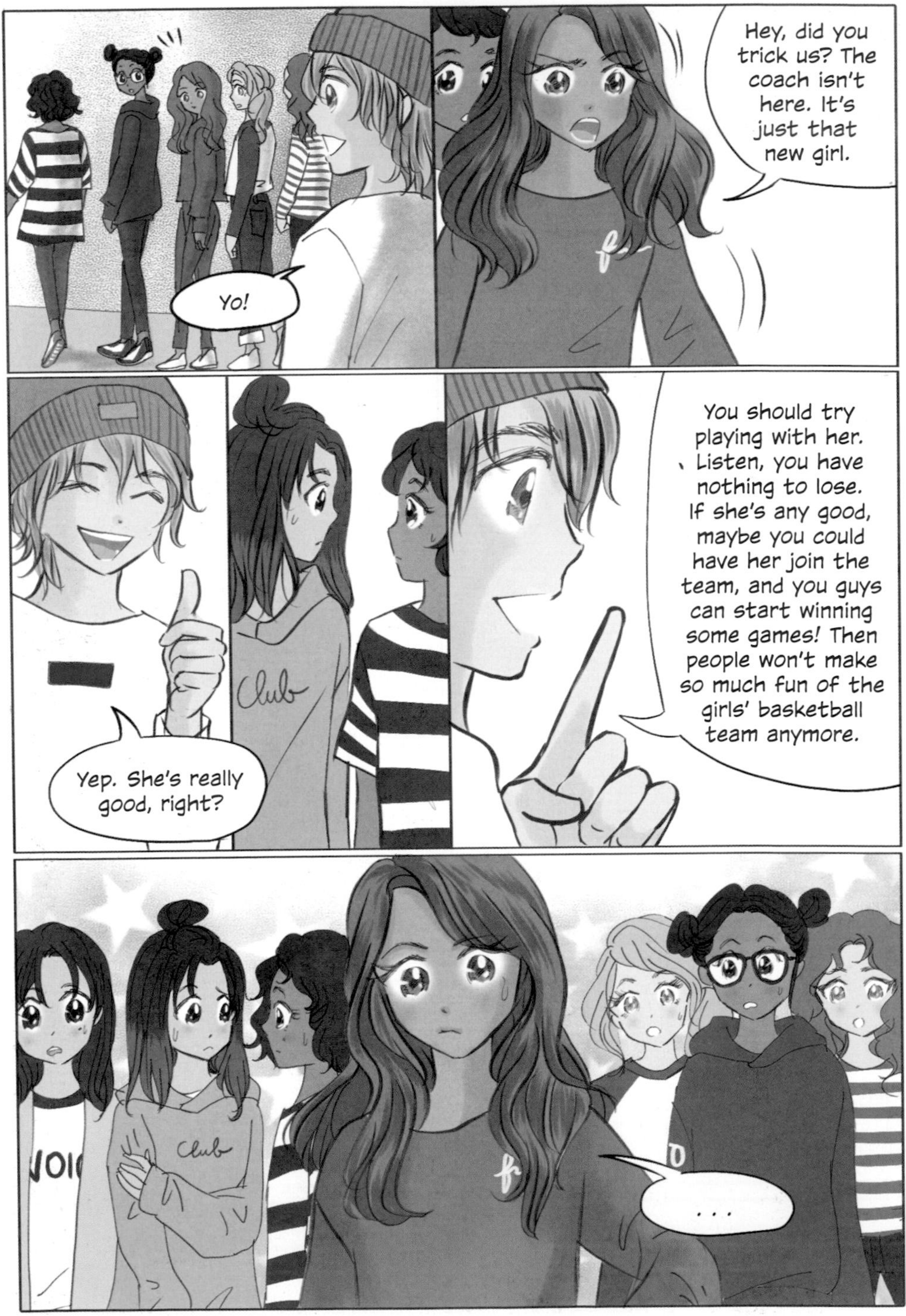
Yo!
Hey, did you trick us? The coach isn't here. It's just that new girl.
Yep. She's really good, right?
You should try playing with her. Listen, you have nothing to lose. If she's any good, maybe you could have her join the team, and you guys can start winning some games! Then people won't make so much fun of the girls' basketball team anymore.
. . .

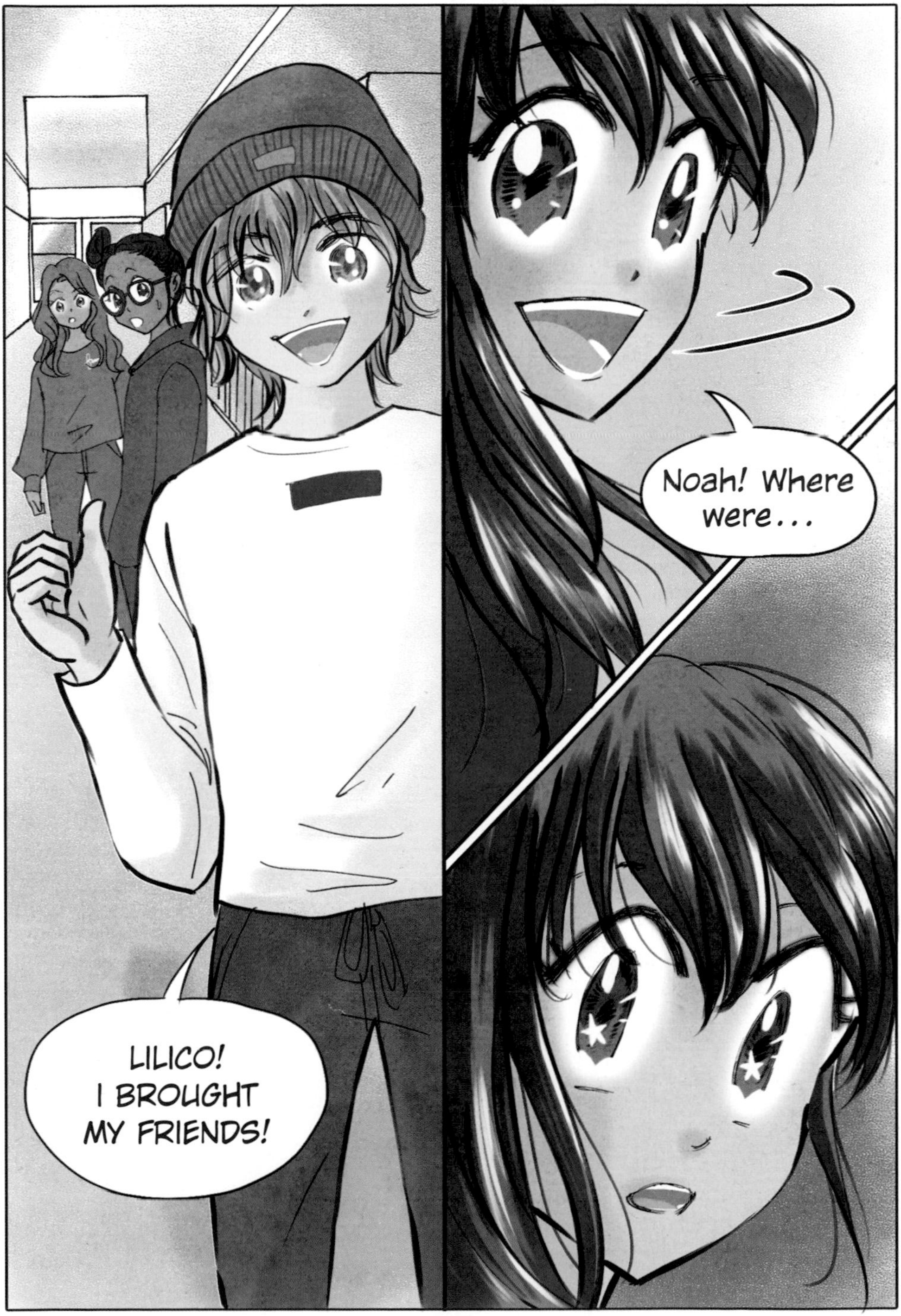
LILICO! I BROUGHT MY FRIENDS!
Noah! Where were...

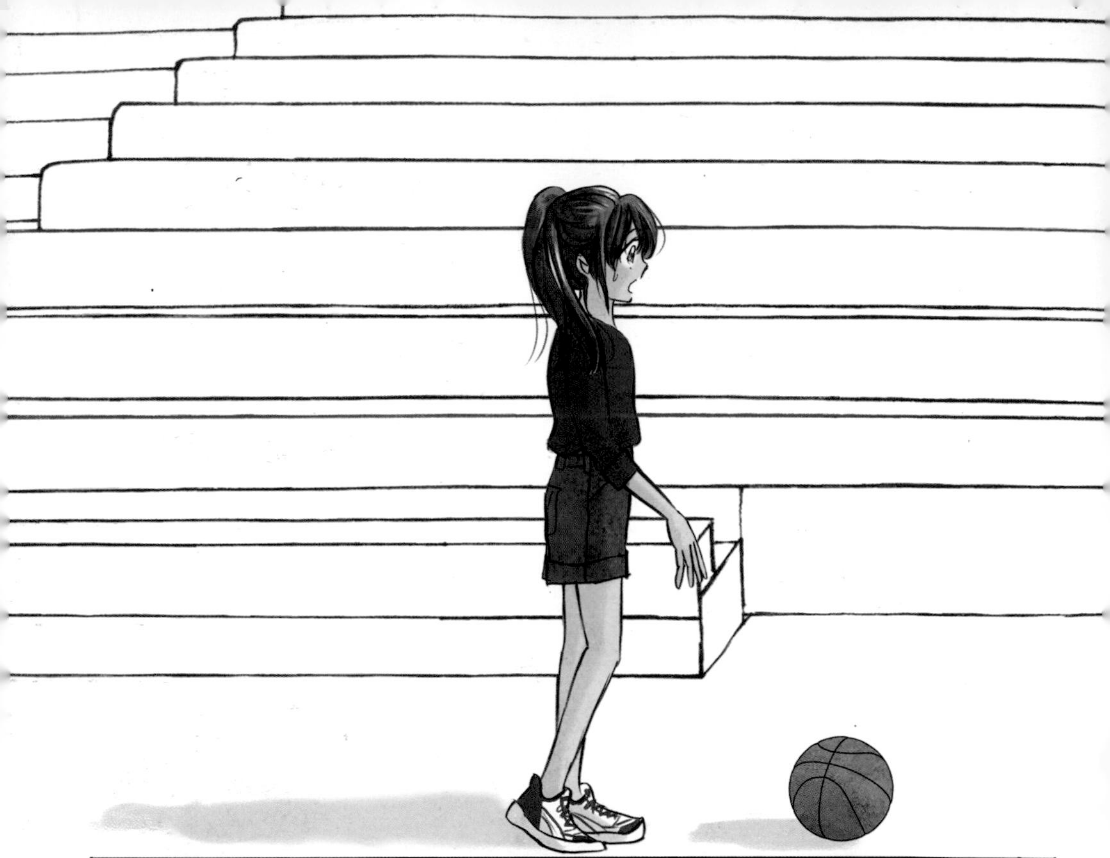

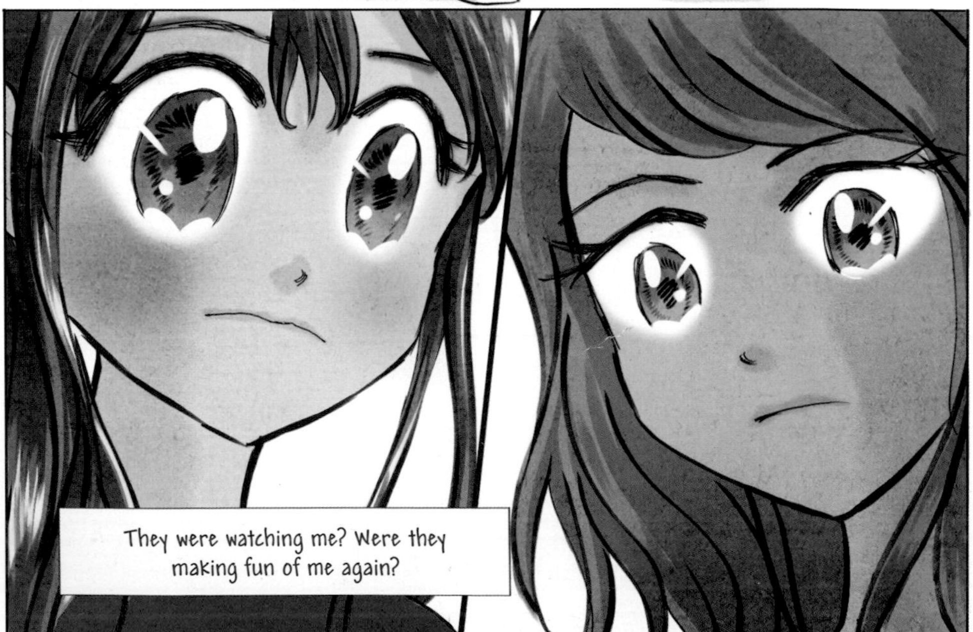
They were watching me? Were they making fun of me again?

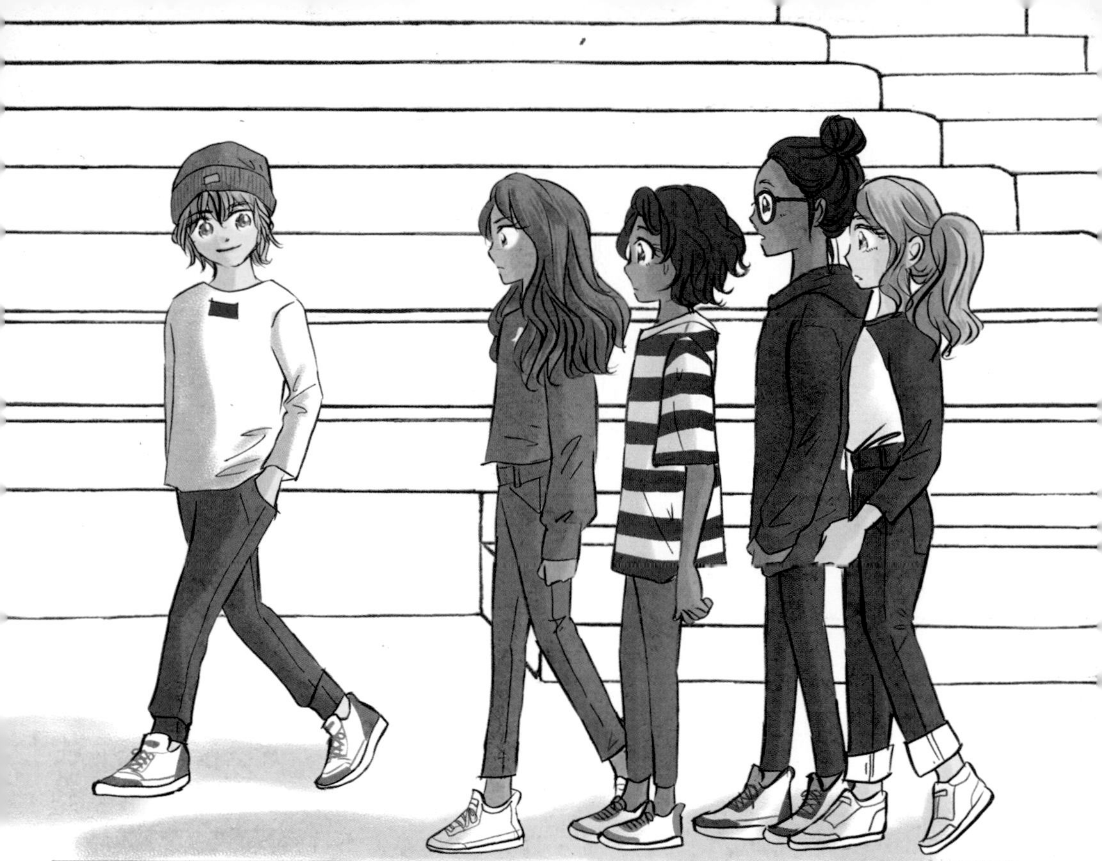

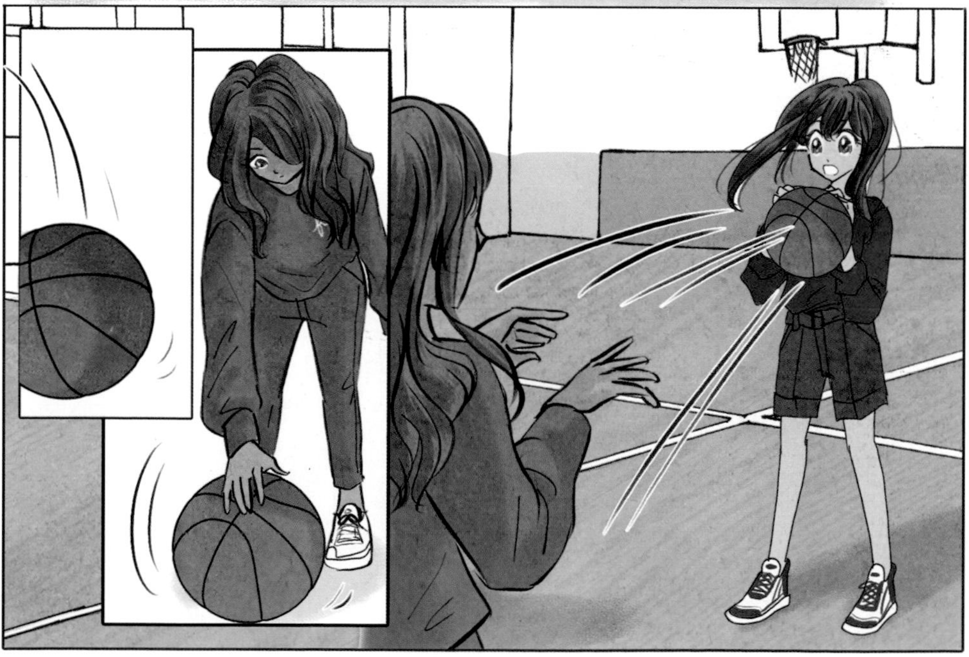

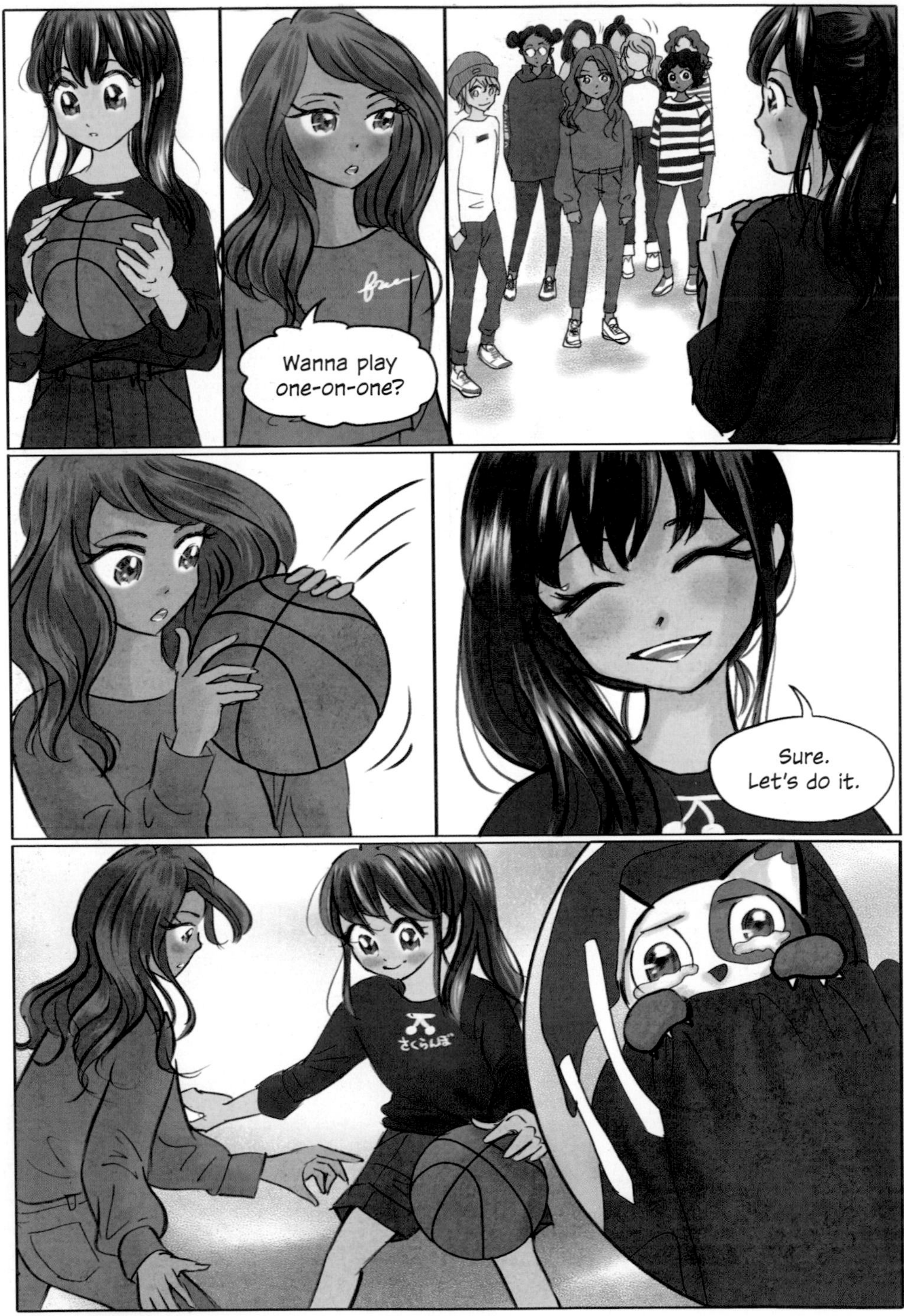
Wanna play one-on-one?
Sure. Let's do it.
さくらんぼ

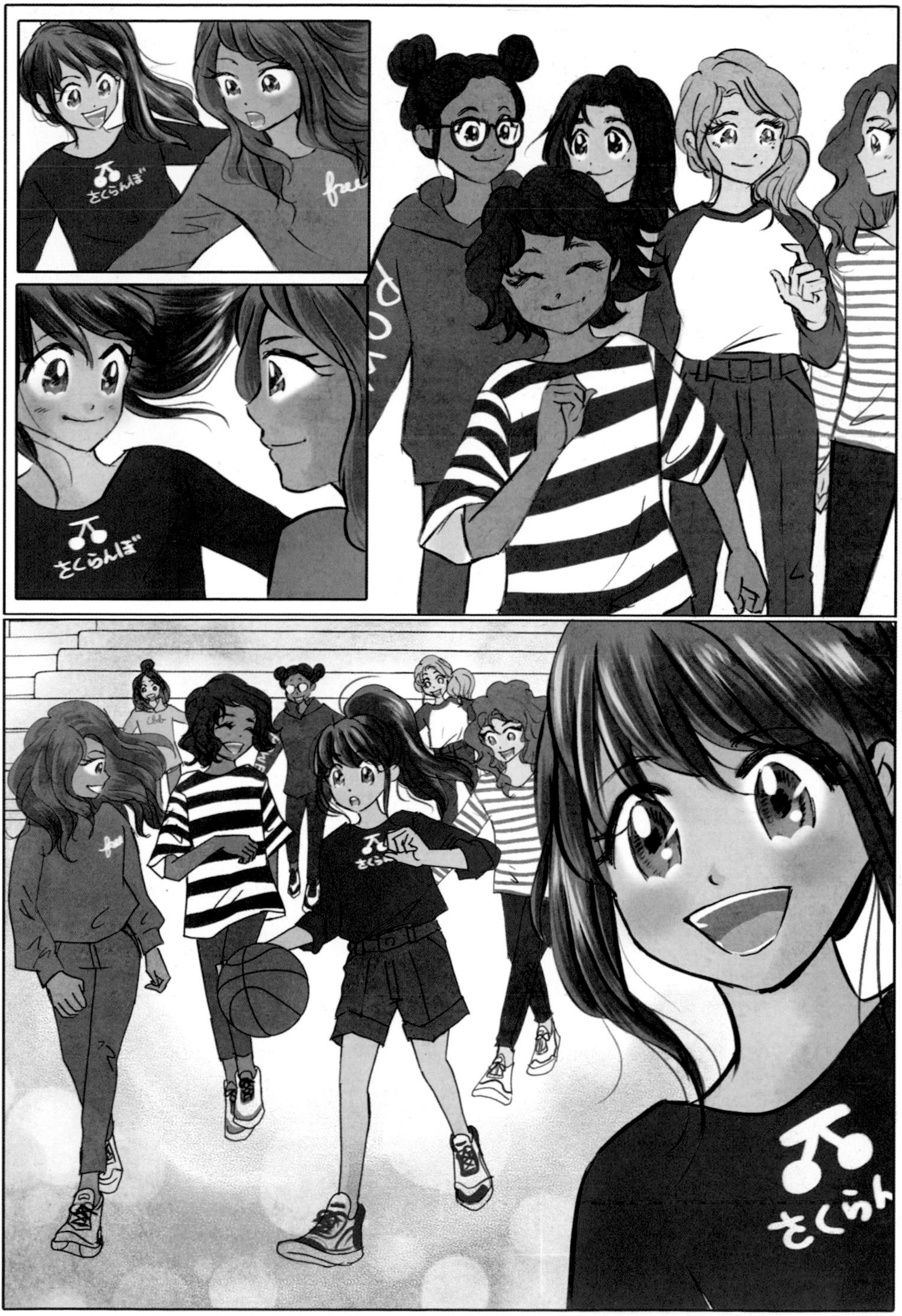
さくらんぼ
free
さくらんぼ

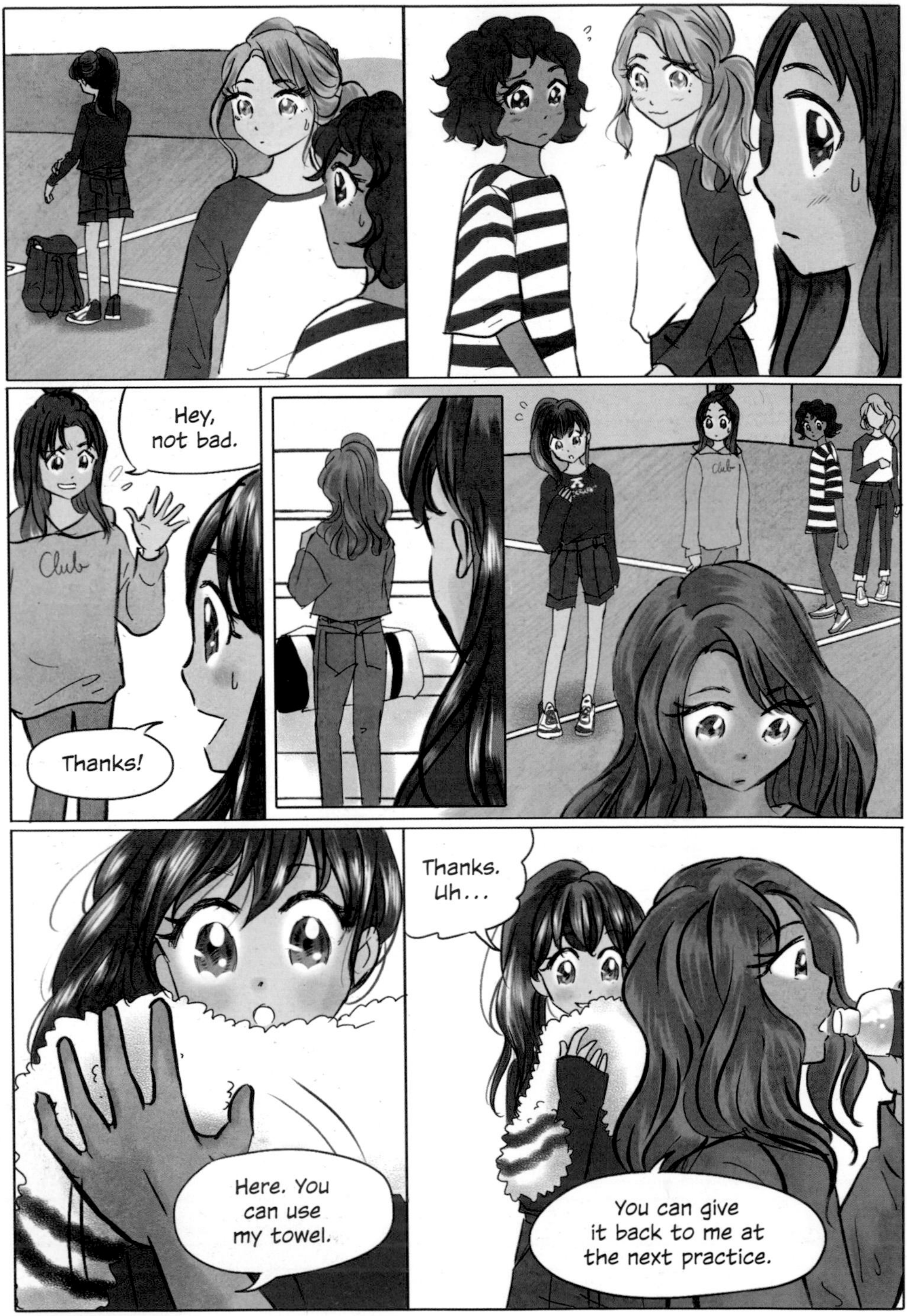
Hey, not bad.
Thanks!
Here. You can use my towel.
Thanks. Uh...
You can give it back to me at the next practice.

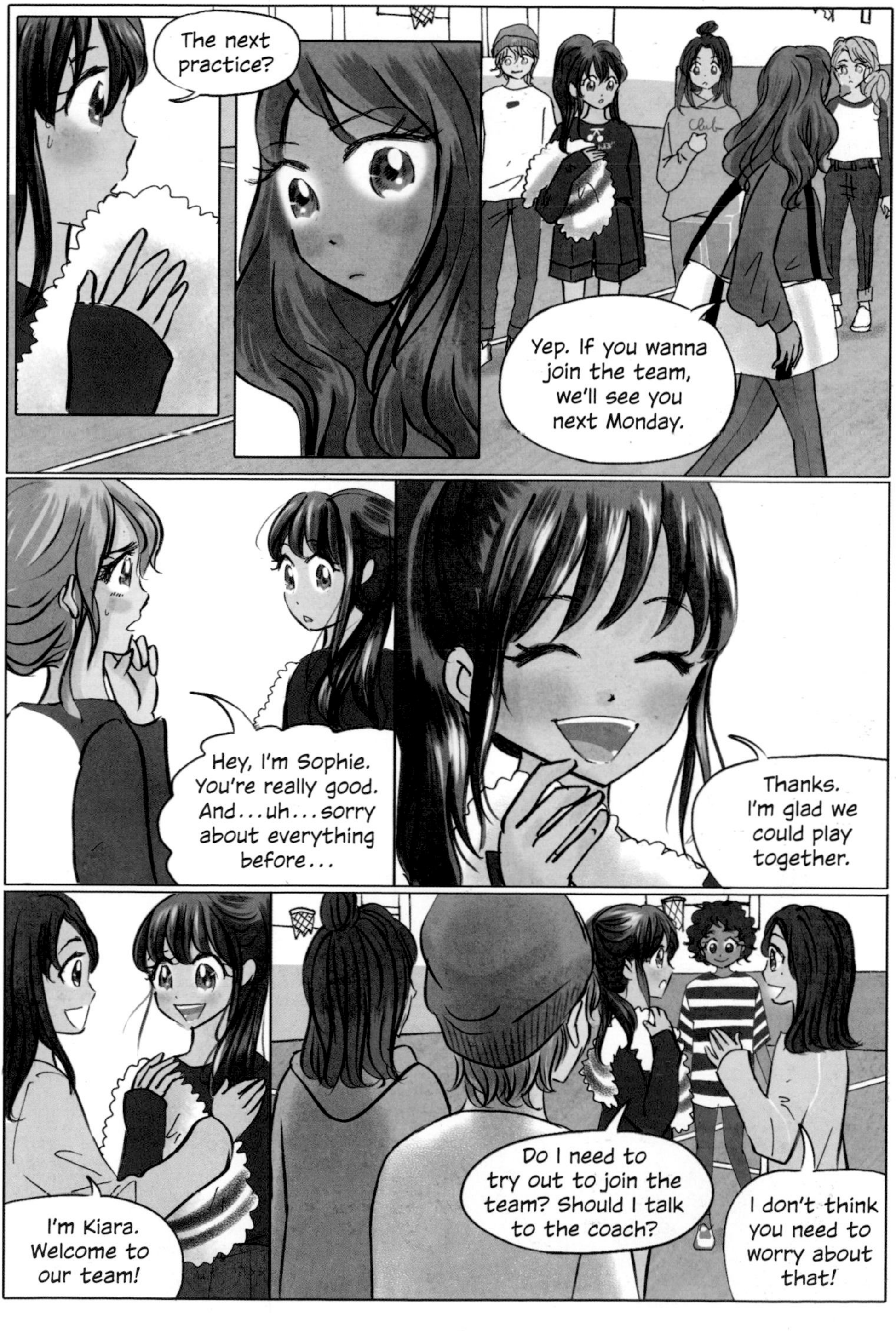

The next practice?
Yep. If you wanna join the team, we'll see you next Monday.
Hey, I'm Sophie. You're really good. And...uh...sorry about everything before...
Thanks. I'm glad we could play together.
I'm Kiara. Welcome to our team!
Do I need to try out to join the team? Should I talk to the coach?
I don't think you need to worry about that!

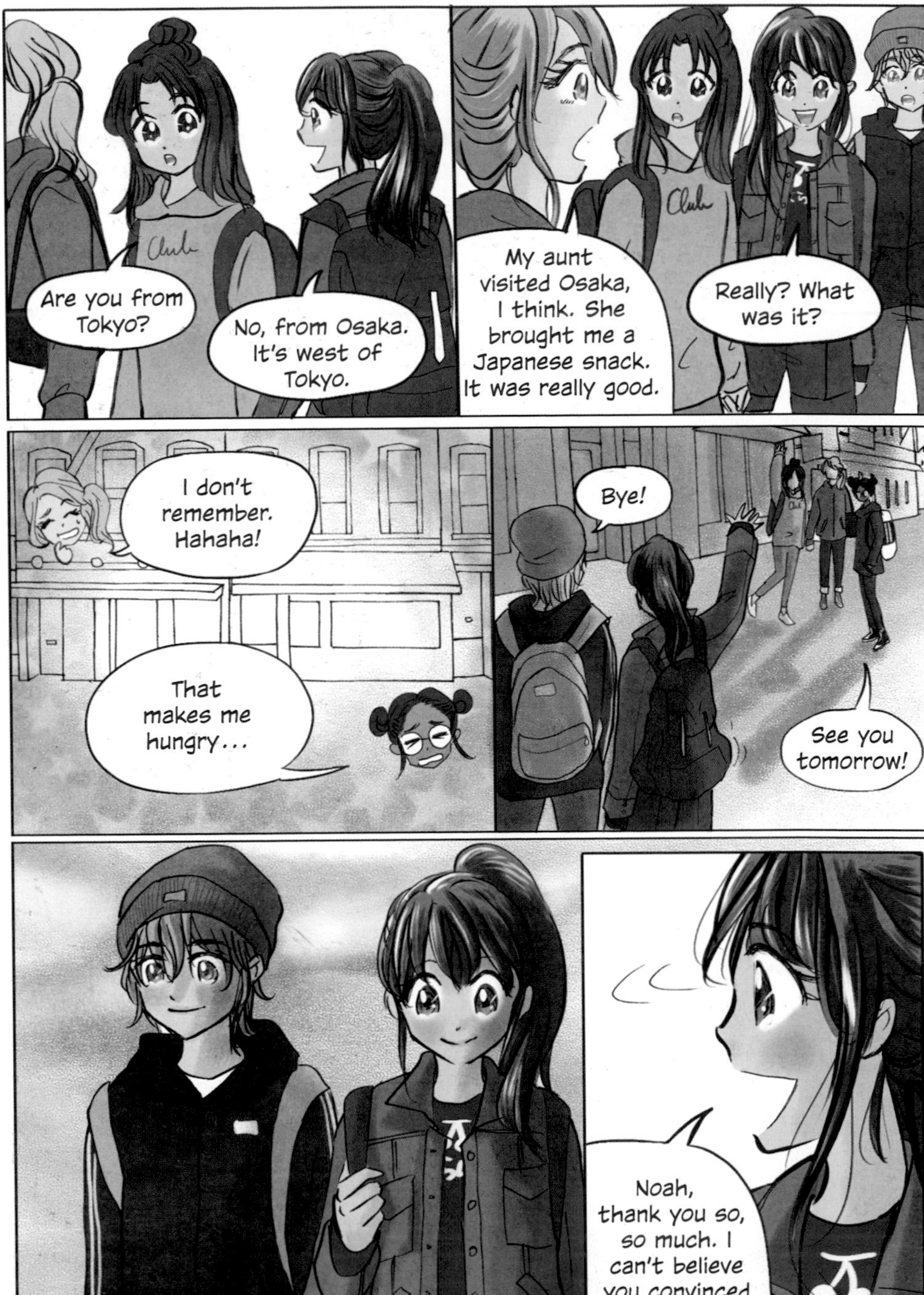
Are you from Tokyo?
No, from Osaka. It's west of Tokyo.
My aunt visited Osaka, I think. She brought me a Japanese snack. It was really good.
Really? What was it?
I don't remember. Hahaha!
That makes me hungry...
Bye!
See you tomorrow!
Noah, thank you so, so much. I can't believe you convinced them to come.

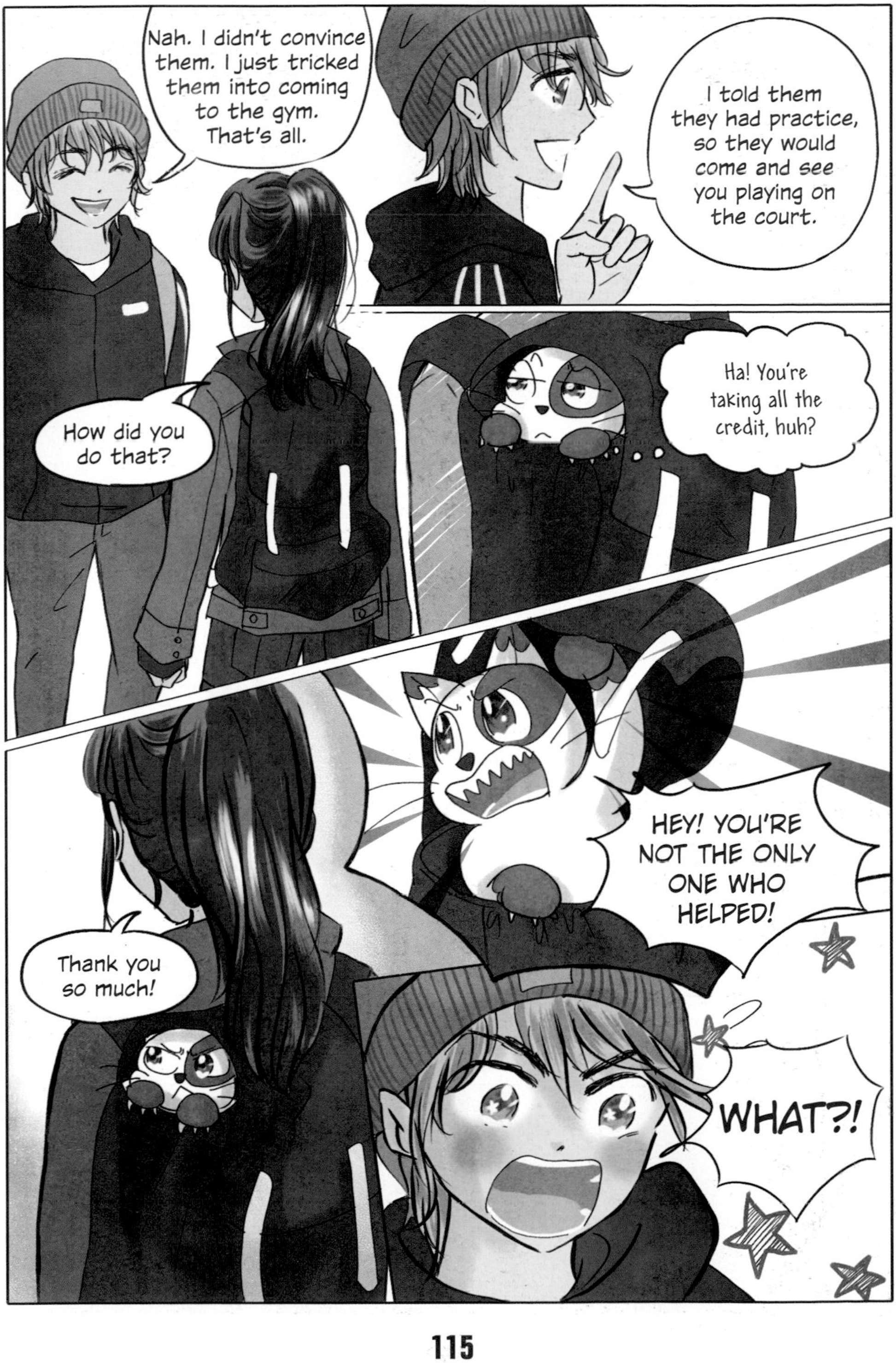
Nah. I didn't convince them. I just tricked them into coming to the gym. That's all.
I told them they had practice, so they would come and see you playing on the court.
How did you do that?
Ha! You're taking all the credit, huh?
HEY! YOU'RE NOT THE ONLY ONE WHO HELPED!
Thank you so much!
WHAT?!

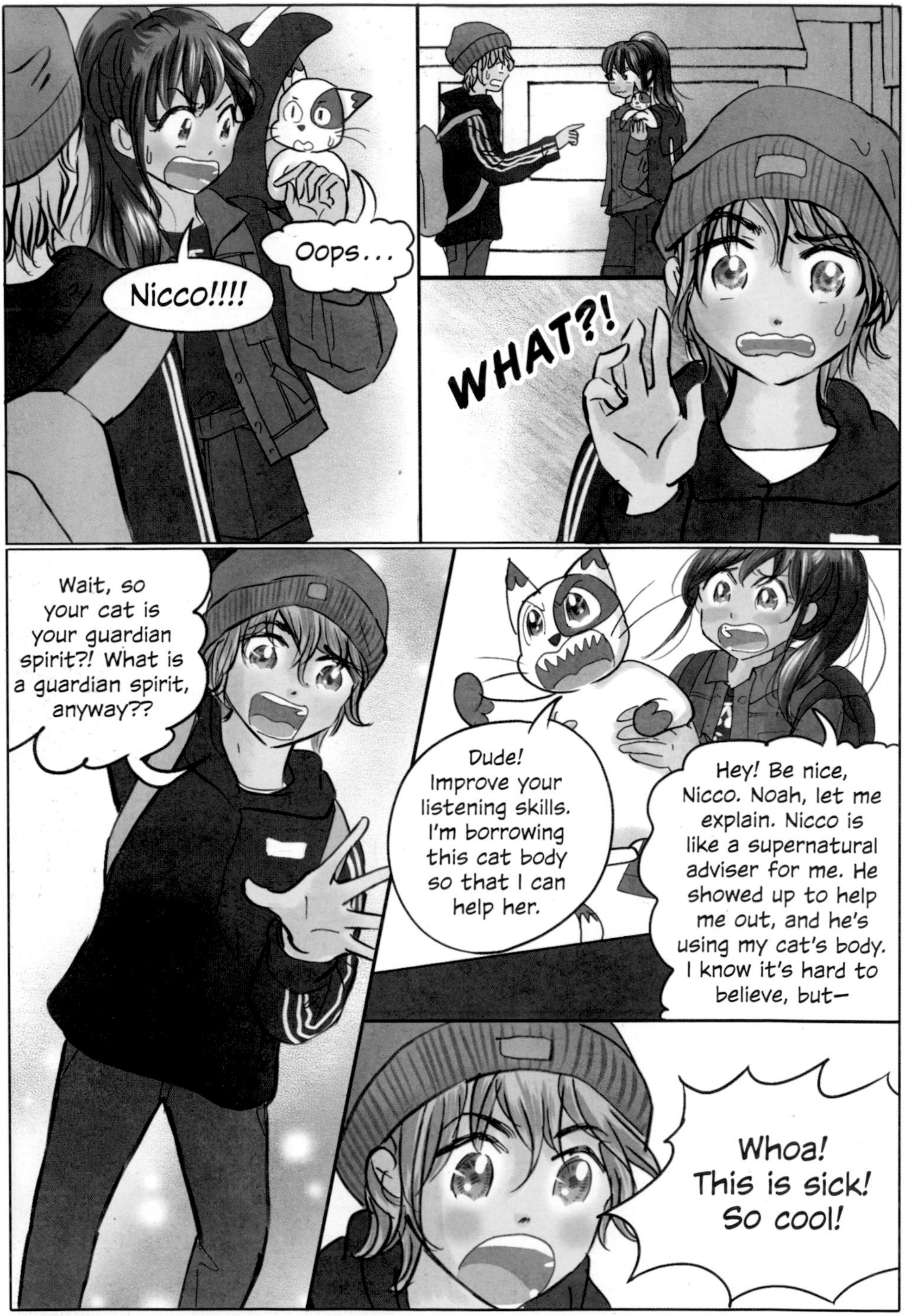
Nicco!!!!
Oops...
WHAT?!
Wait, so your cat is your guardian spirit?! What is a guardian spirit, anyway??
Dude! Improve your listening skills. I'm borrowing this cat body so that I can help her.
Hey! Be nice, Nicco. Noah, let me explain. Nicco is like a supernatural adviser for me. He showed up to help me out, and he's using my cat's body. I know it's hard to believe, but—
Whoa! This is sick! So cool!

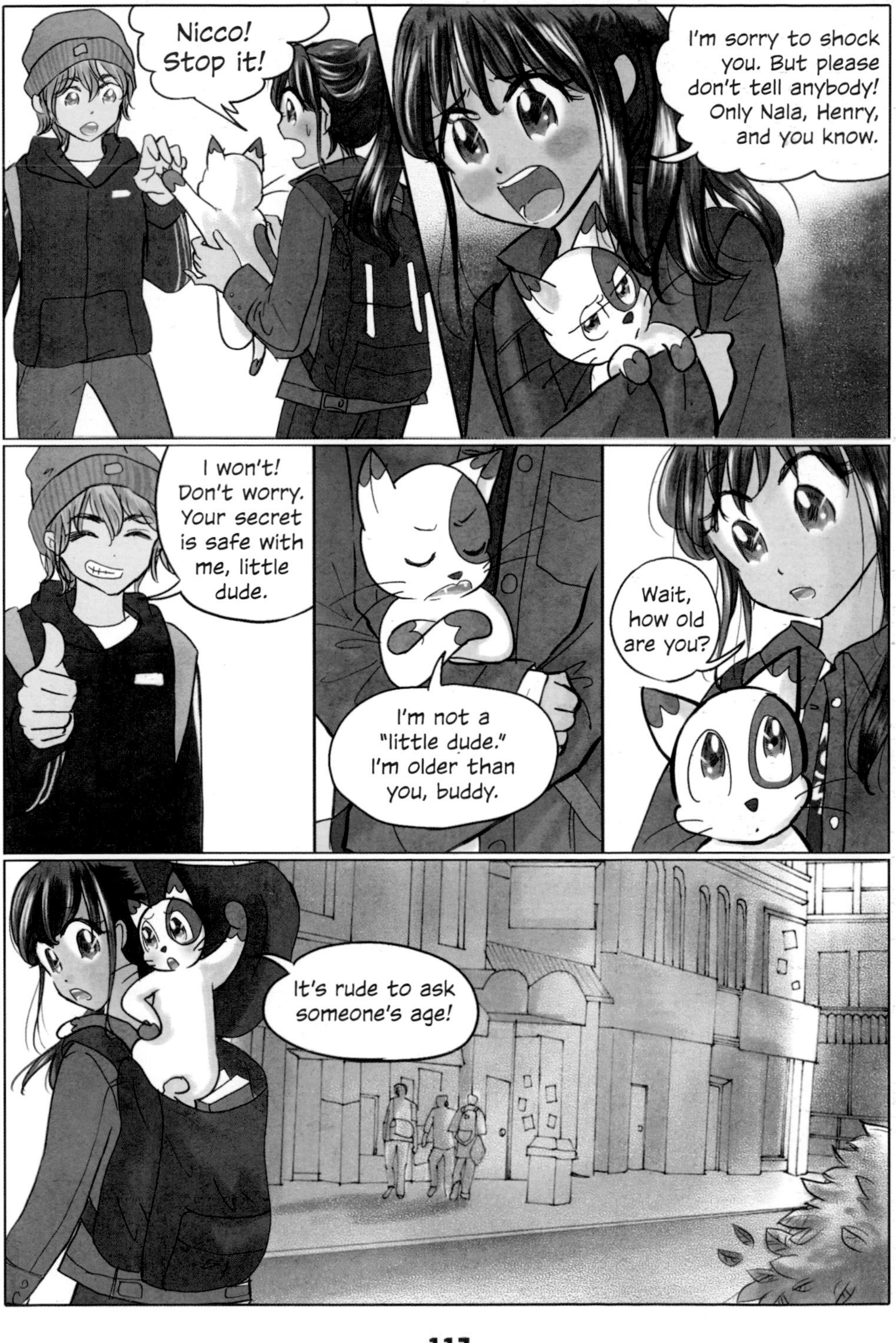

Nicco! Stop it!
I'm sorry to shock you. But please don't tell anybody! Only Nala, Henry, and you know.
I won't! Don't worry. Your secret is safe with me, little dude.
I'm not a "little dude." I'm older than you, buddy.
Wait, how old are you?
It's rude to ask someone's age!

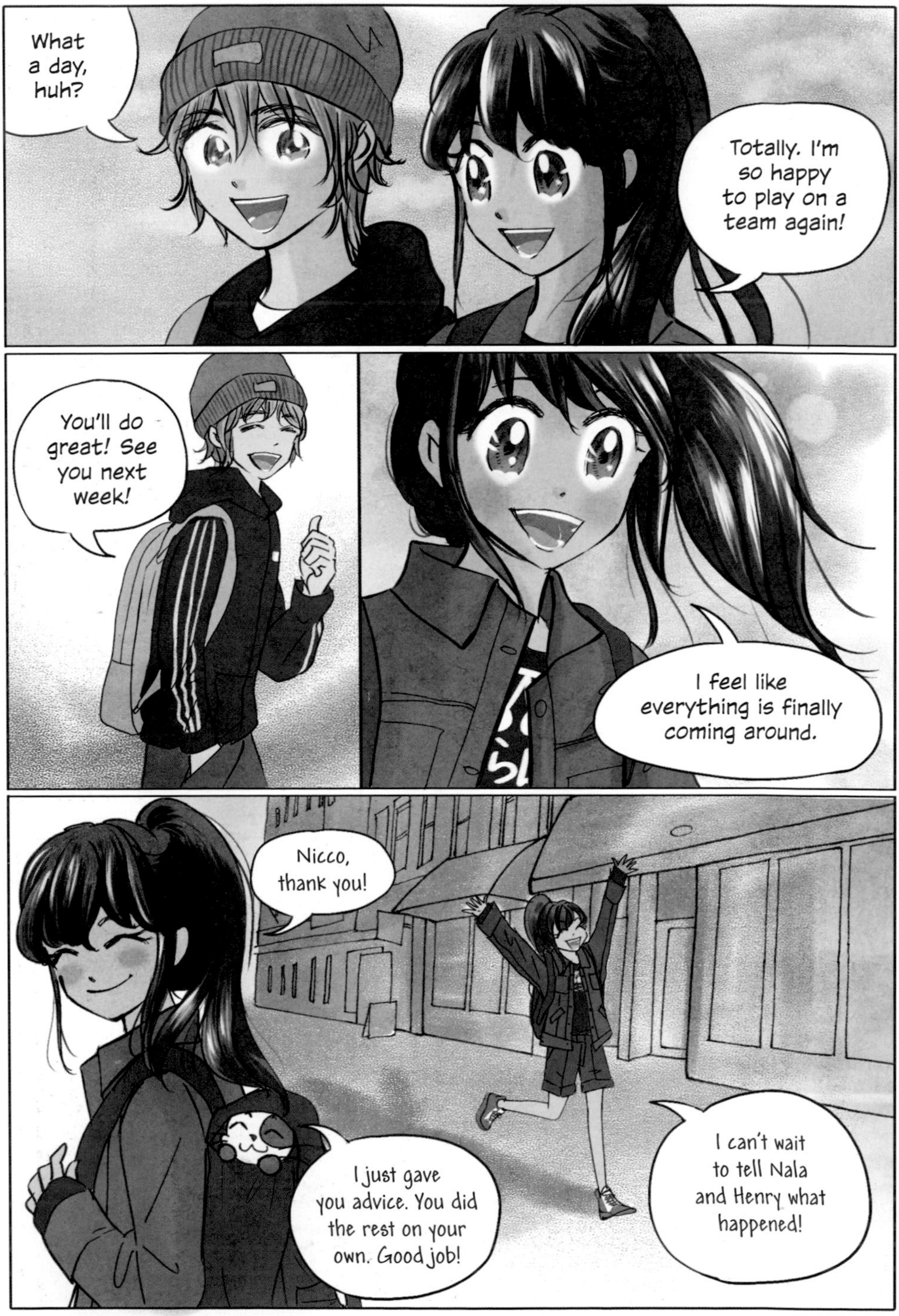
What a day, huh?
Totally. I'm so happy to play on a team again!
You'll do great! See you next week!
I feel like everything is finally coming around.
Nicco, thank you!
I just gave you advice. You did the rest on your own. Good job!
I can't wait to tell Nala and Henry what happened!

CHAPTER 5

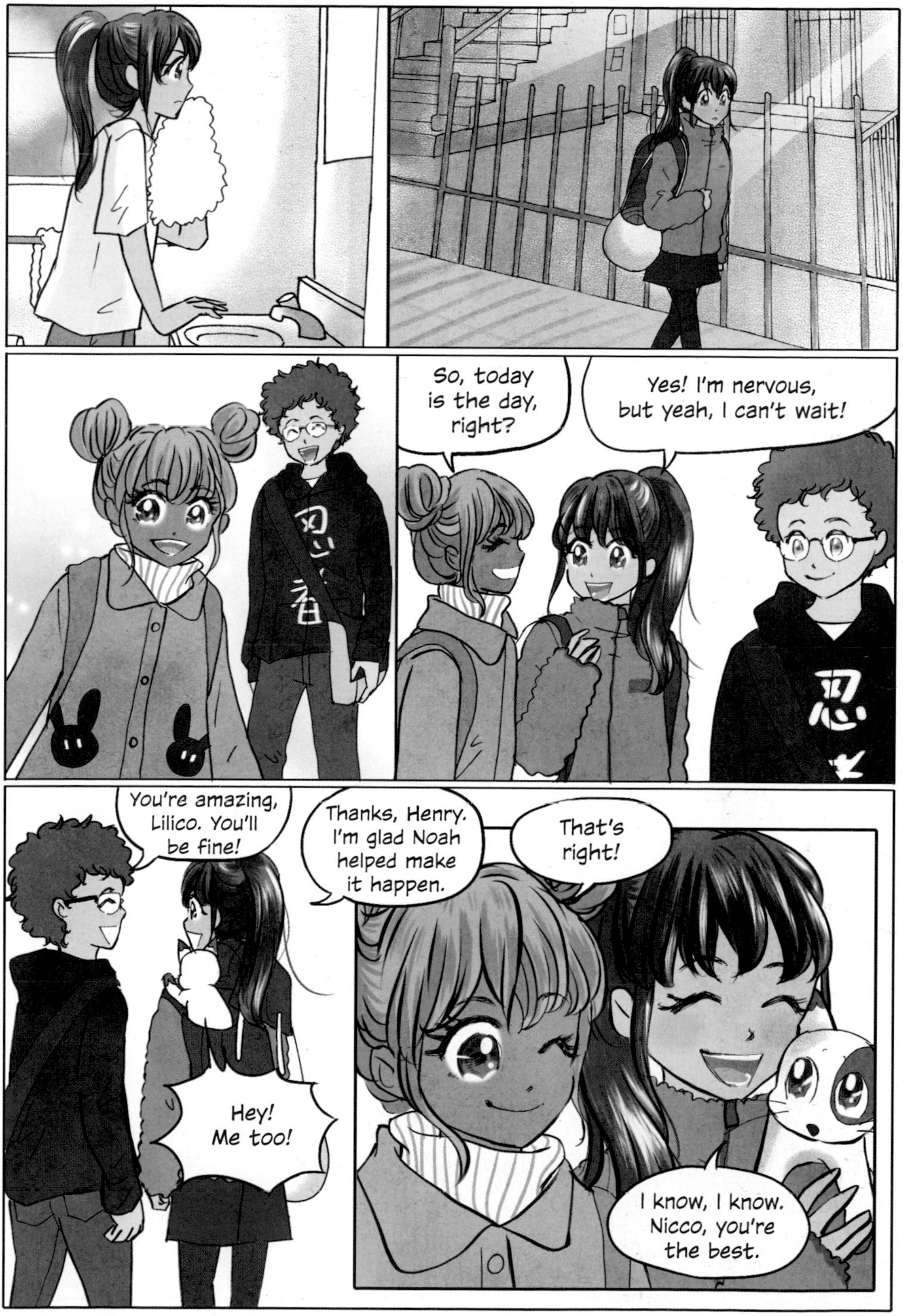
So, today is the day, right?
Yes! I'm nervous, but yeah, I can't wait!
You're amazing, Lilico. You'll be fine!
Thanks, Henry. I'm glad Noah helped make it happen.
Hey! Me too!
That's right!
I know, I know. Nicco, you're the best.

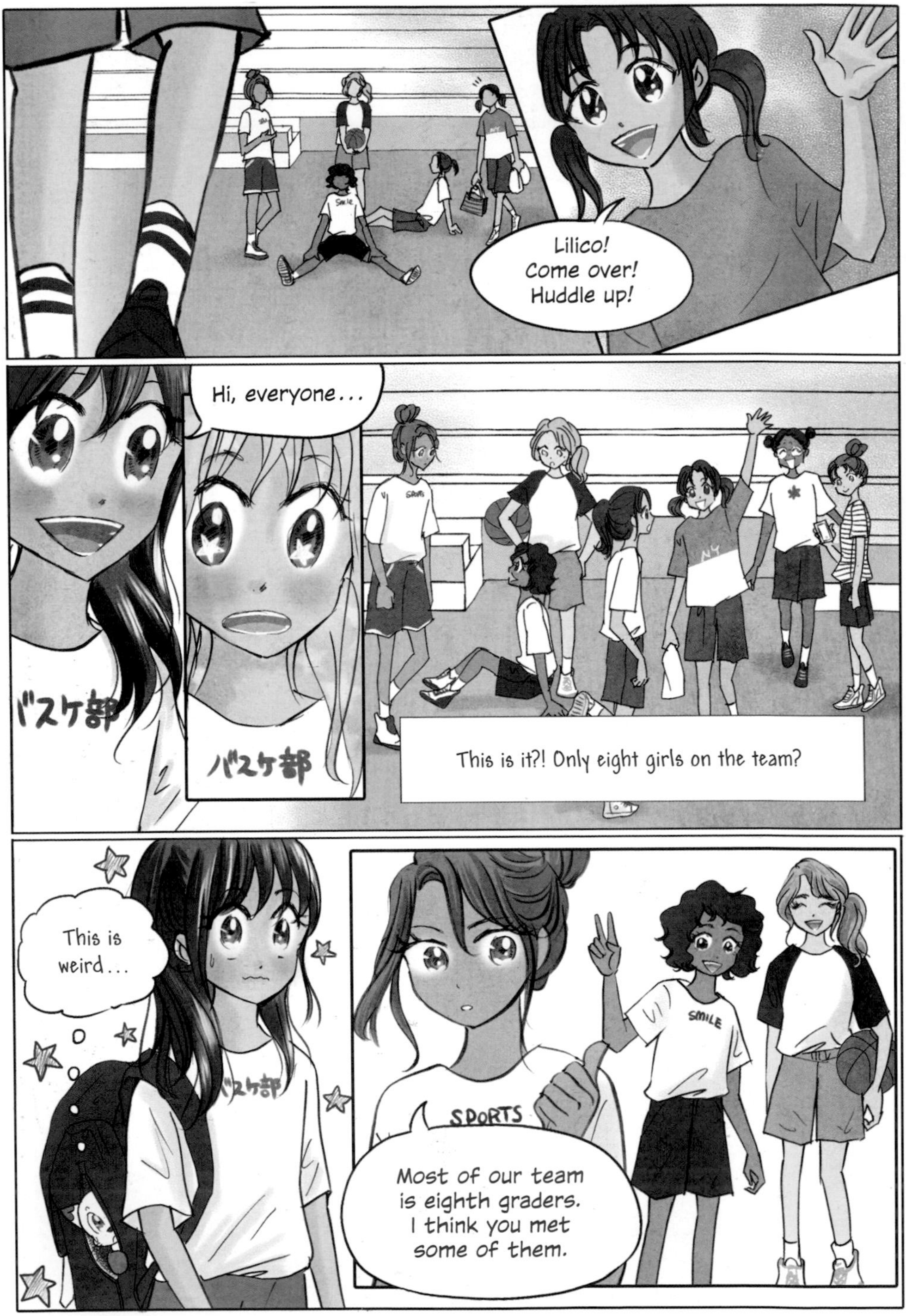
Lilico!
Come over!
Huddle up!
Hi, everyone...
バスケ部
バスケ部
This is it?! Only eight girls on the team?
This is weird...
バスケ部
SPORTS
SMILE
Most of our team is eighth graders. I think you met some of them.

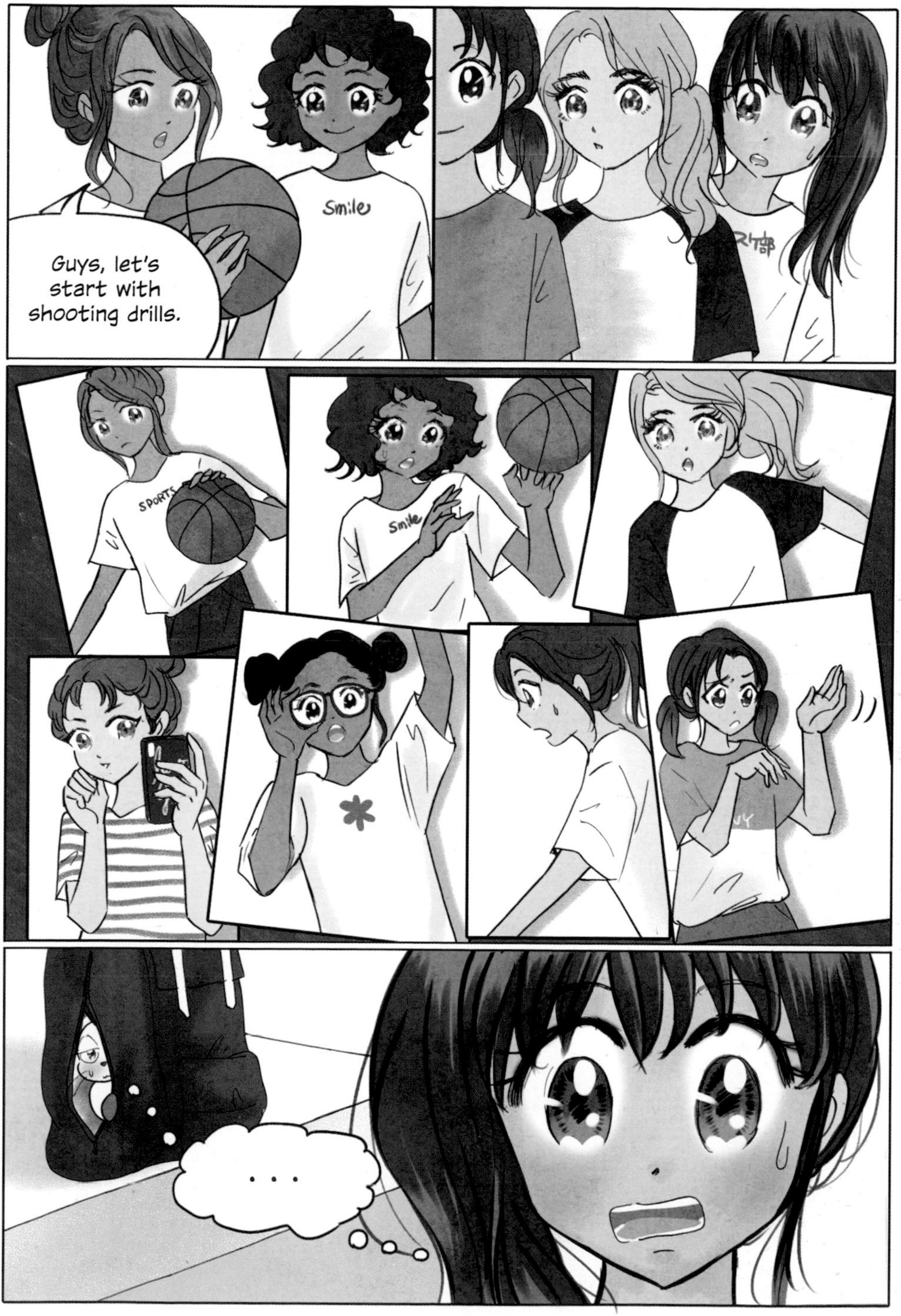
Guys, let's start with shooting drills.
...

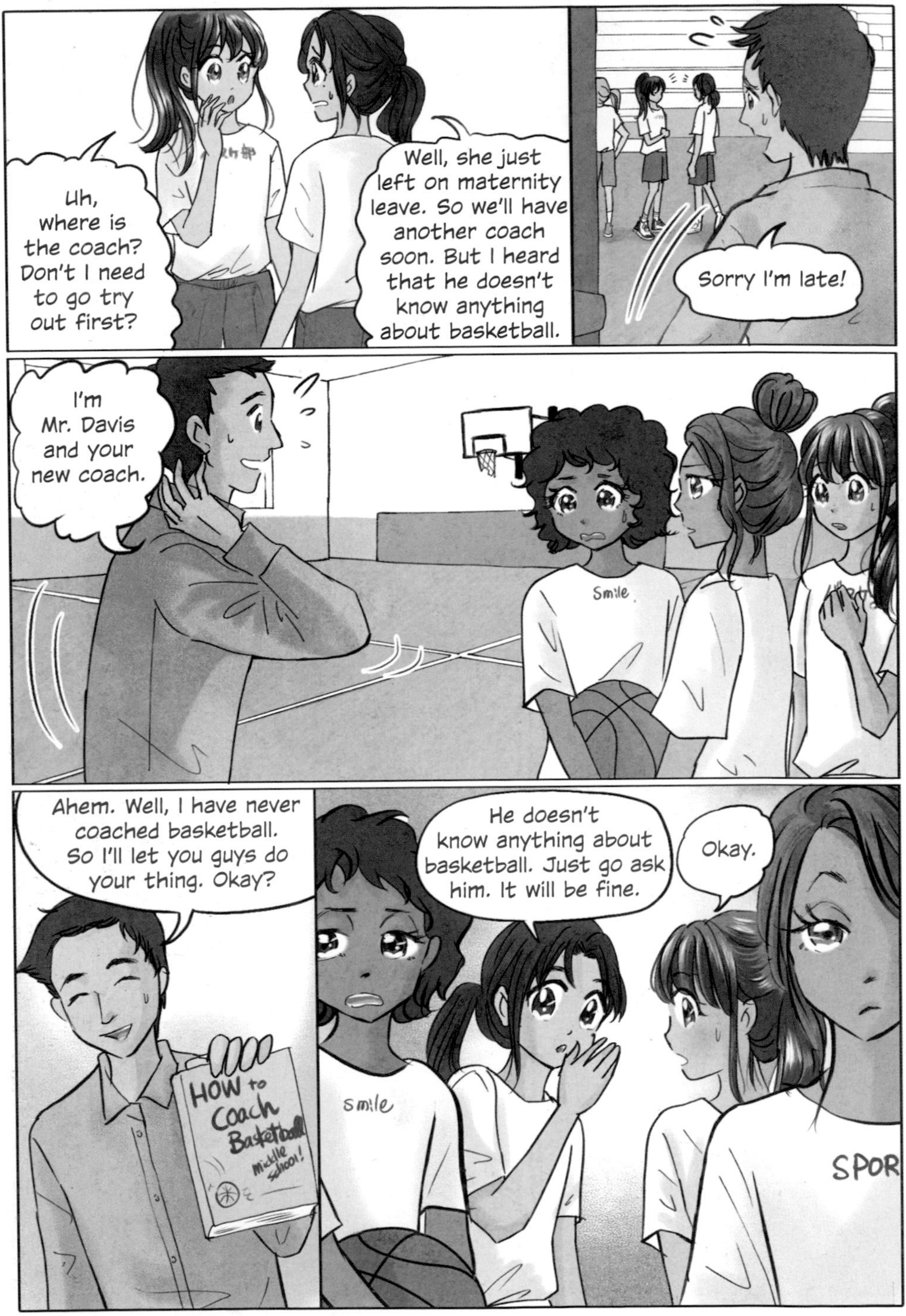
Uh, where is the coach? Don't I need to go try out first?
Well, she just left on maternity leave. So we'll have another coach soon. But I heard that he doesn't know anything about basketball.
Sorry I'm late!
I'm Mr. Davis and your new coach.
Smile
Ahem. Well, I have never coached basketball. So I'll let you guys do your thing. Okay?
HOW to Coach Basketball middle school!
He doesn't know anything about basketball. Just go ask him. It will be fine.
Okay.
smile
SPOR

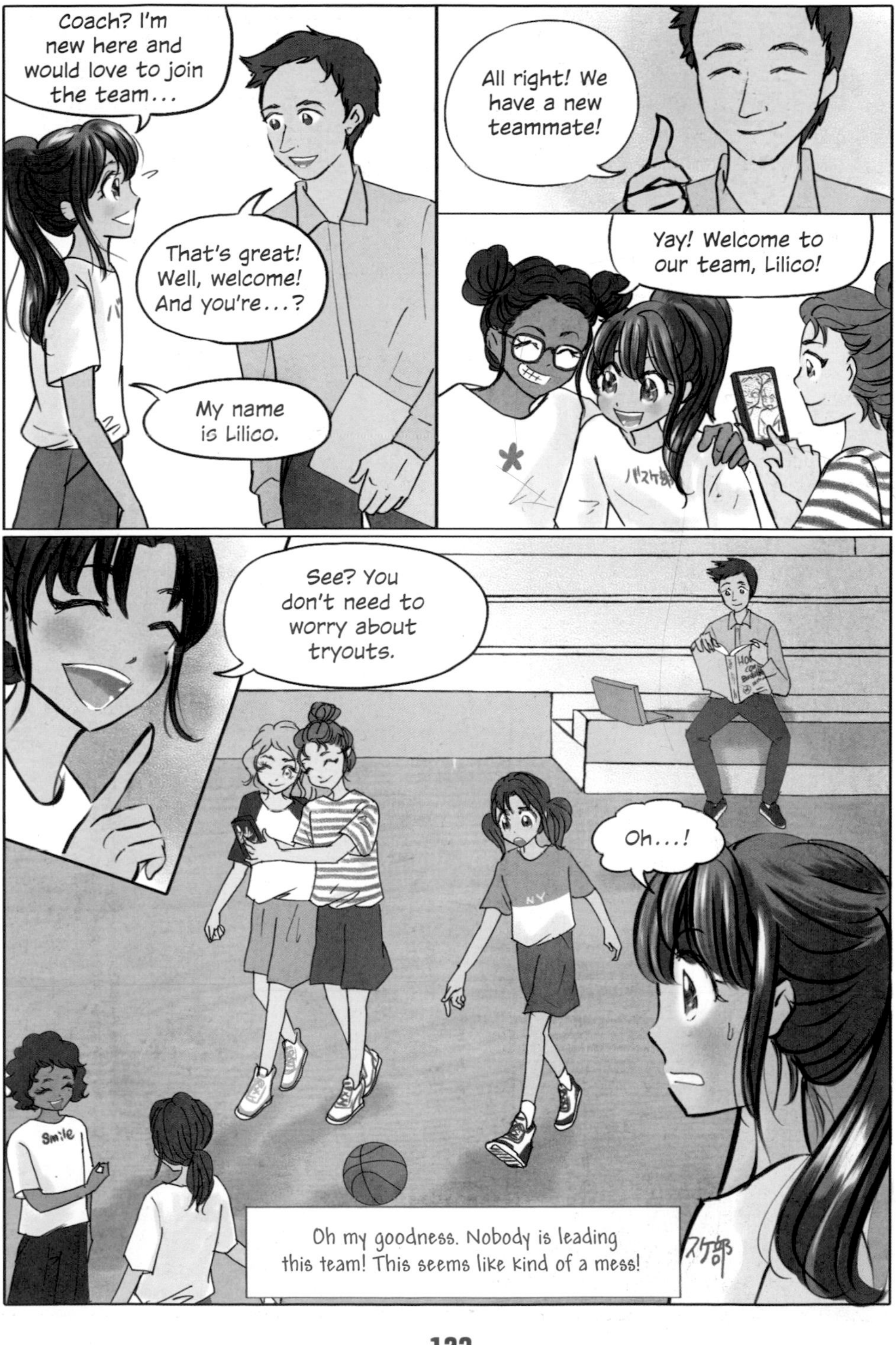
Coach? I'm new here and would love to join the team...
That's great! Well, welcome! And you're...?
My name is Lilico.
All right! We have a new teammate!
Yay! Welcome to our team, Lilico!
See? You don't need to worry about tryouts.
Oh...!
Oh my goodness. Nobody is leading this team! This seems like kind of a mess!

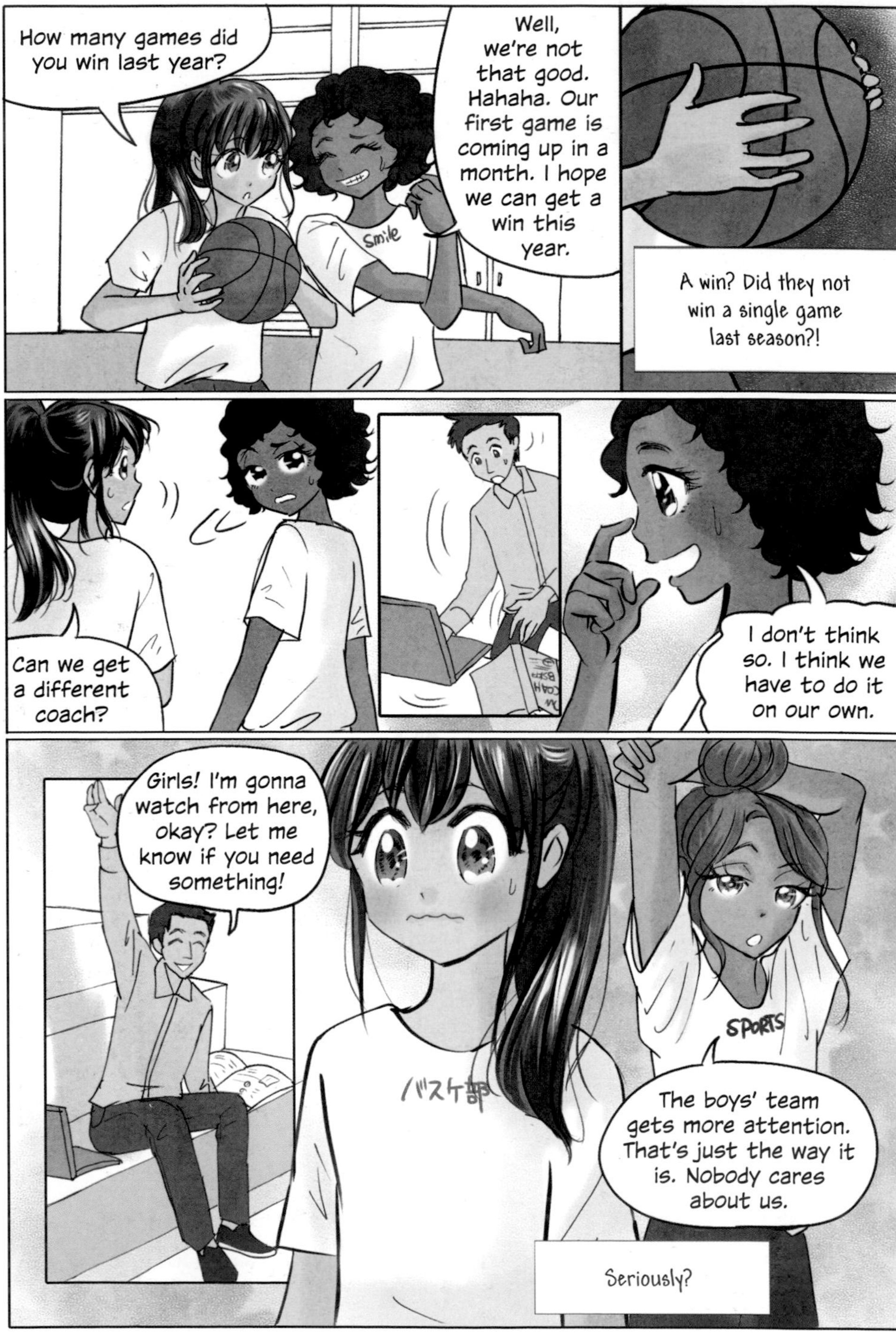
How many games did you win last year?
Well, we're not that good. Hahaha. Our first game is coming up in a month. I hope we can get a win this year.
Smile
A win? Did they not win a single game last season?!
Can we get a different coach?
I don't think so. I think we have to do it on our own.
Girls! I'm gonna watch from here, okay? Let me know if you need something!
バスケ部
SPORTS
The boys' team gets more attention. That's just the way it is. Nobody cares about us.
Seriously?

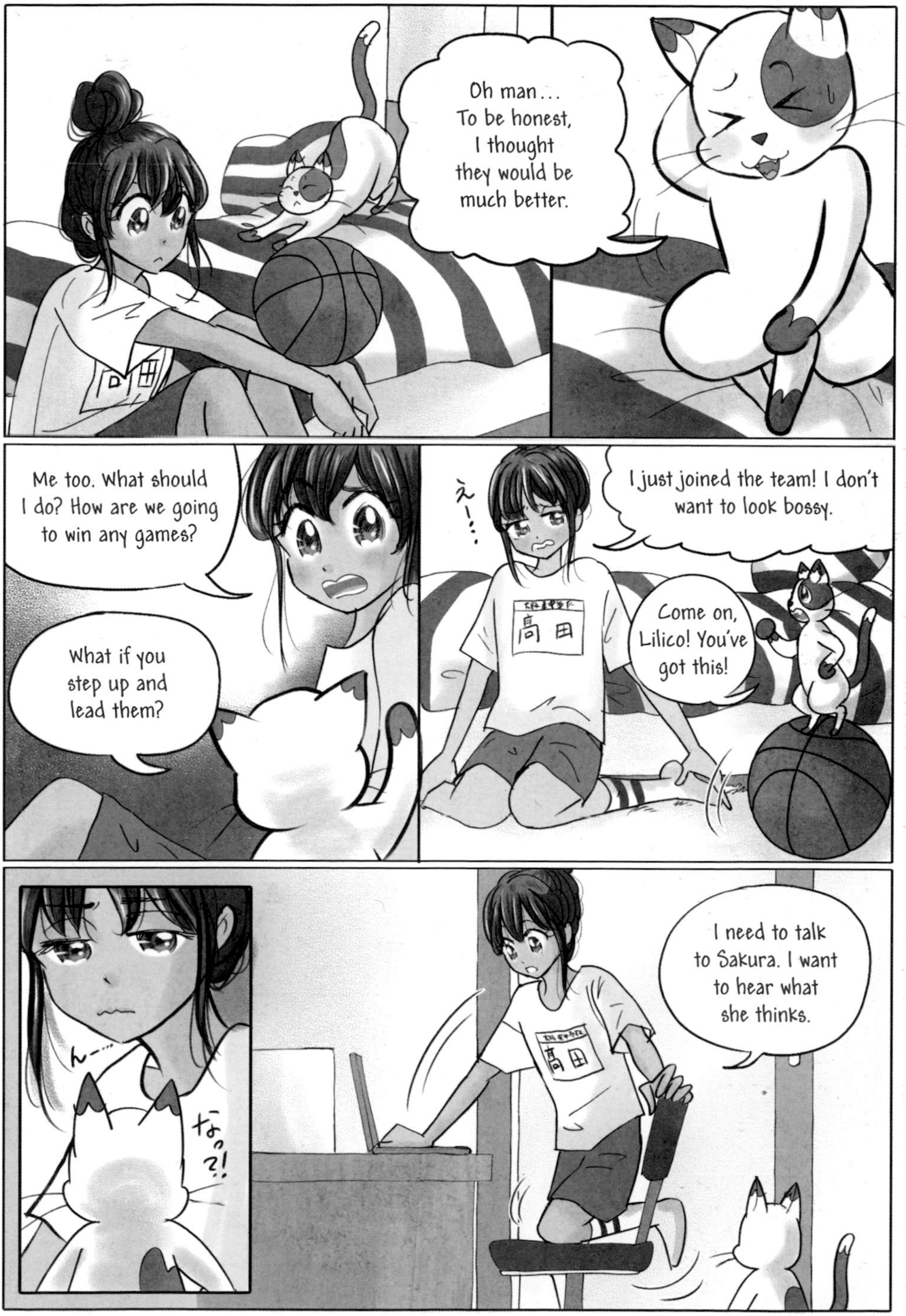
Oh man... To be honest, I thought they would be much better.
Me too. What should I do? How are we going to win any games?
What if you step up and lead them?
えー…
I just joined the team! I don't want to look bossy.
Come on, Lilico! You've got this!
高田
ん…
なっ?!
I need to talk to Sakura. I want to hear what she thinks.
高田

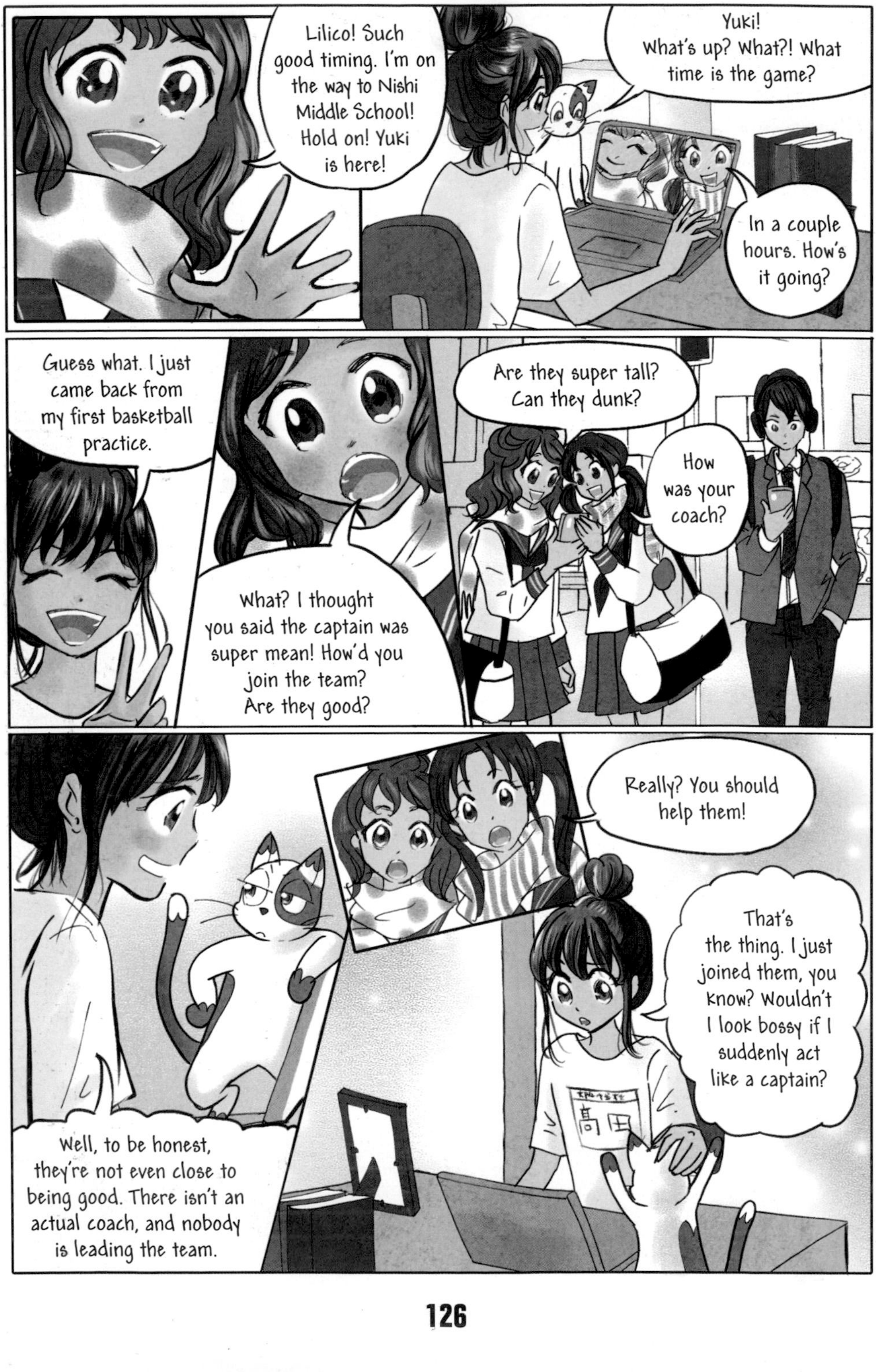
Lilico! Such good timing. I'm on the way to Nishi Middle School! Hold on! Yuki is here!
Yuki! What's up? What?! What time is the game?
In a couple hours. How's it going?
Guess what. I just came back from my first basketball practice.
What? I thought you said the captain was super mean! How'd you join the team? Are they good?
Are they super tall? Can they dunk?
How was your coach?
Well, to be honest, they're not even close to being good. There isn't an actual coach, and nobody is leading the team.
Really? You should help them!
That's the thing. I just joined them, you know? Wouldn't I look bossy if I suddenly act like a captain?

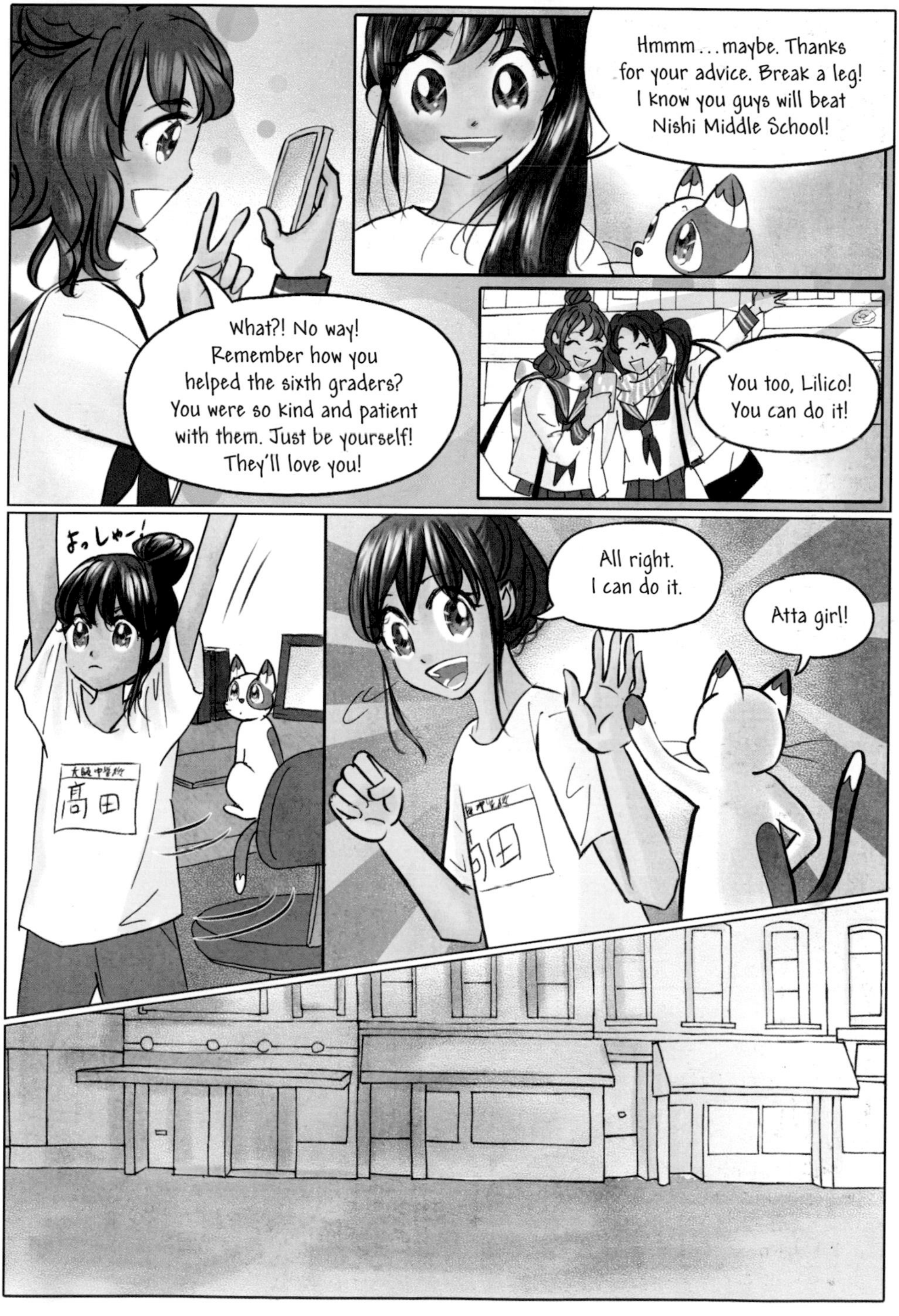
What?! No way! Remember how you helped the sixth graders? You were so kind and patient with them. Just be yourself! They'll love you!
Hmmm . . . maybe. Thanks for your advice. Break a leg! I know you guys will beat Nishi Middle School!
You too, Lilico! You can do it!
よっしゃー!
All right. I can do it.
Atta girl!

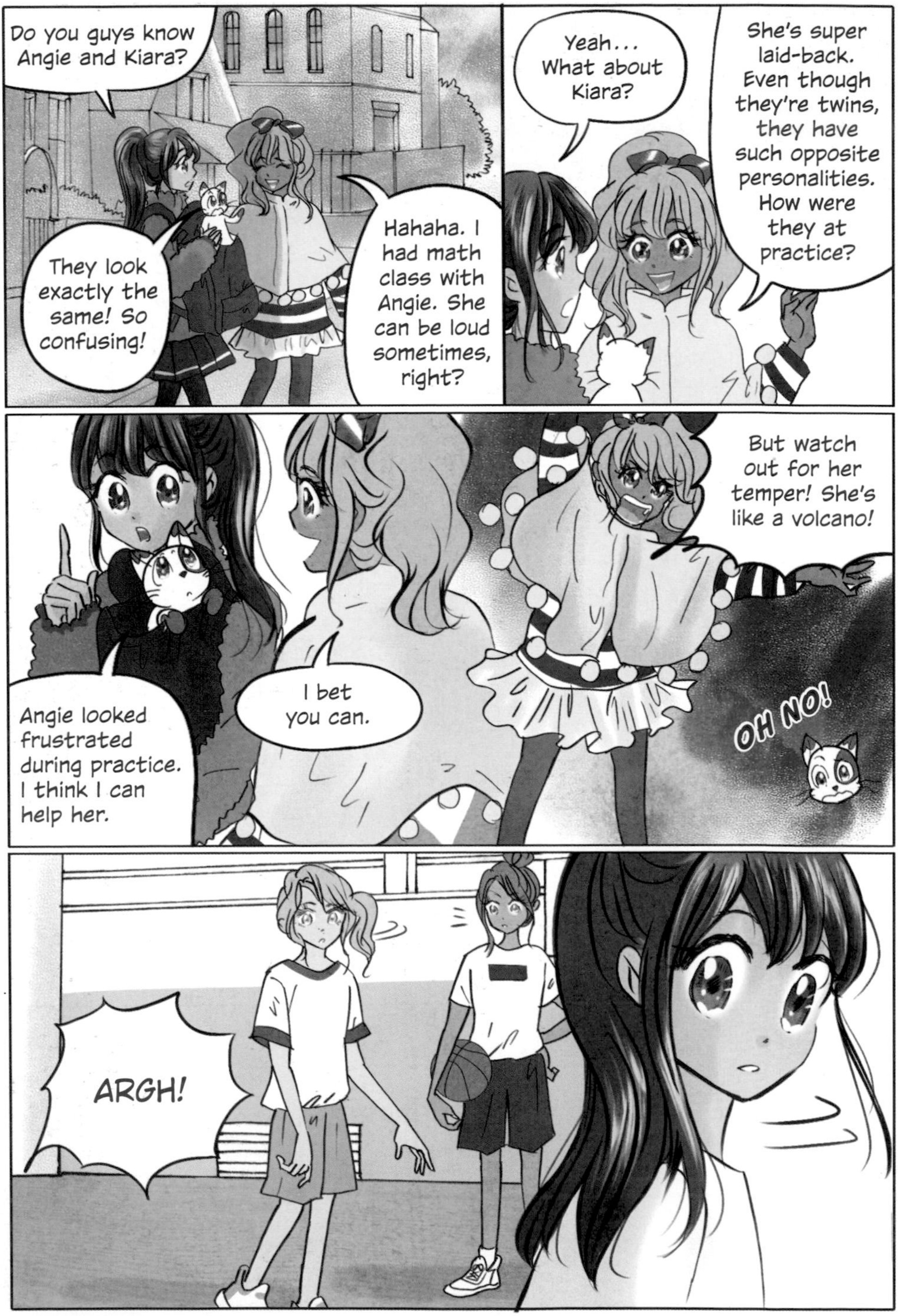
Do you guys know Angie and Kiara?
They look exactly the same! So confusing!
Hahaha. I had math class with Angie. She can be loud sometimes, right?
Yeah... What about Kiara?
She's super laid-back. Even though they're twins, they have such opposite personalities. How were they at practice?
Angie looked frustrated during practice. I think I can help her.
I bet you can.
But watch out for her temper! She's like a volcano!
OH NO!
ARGH!

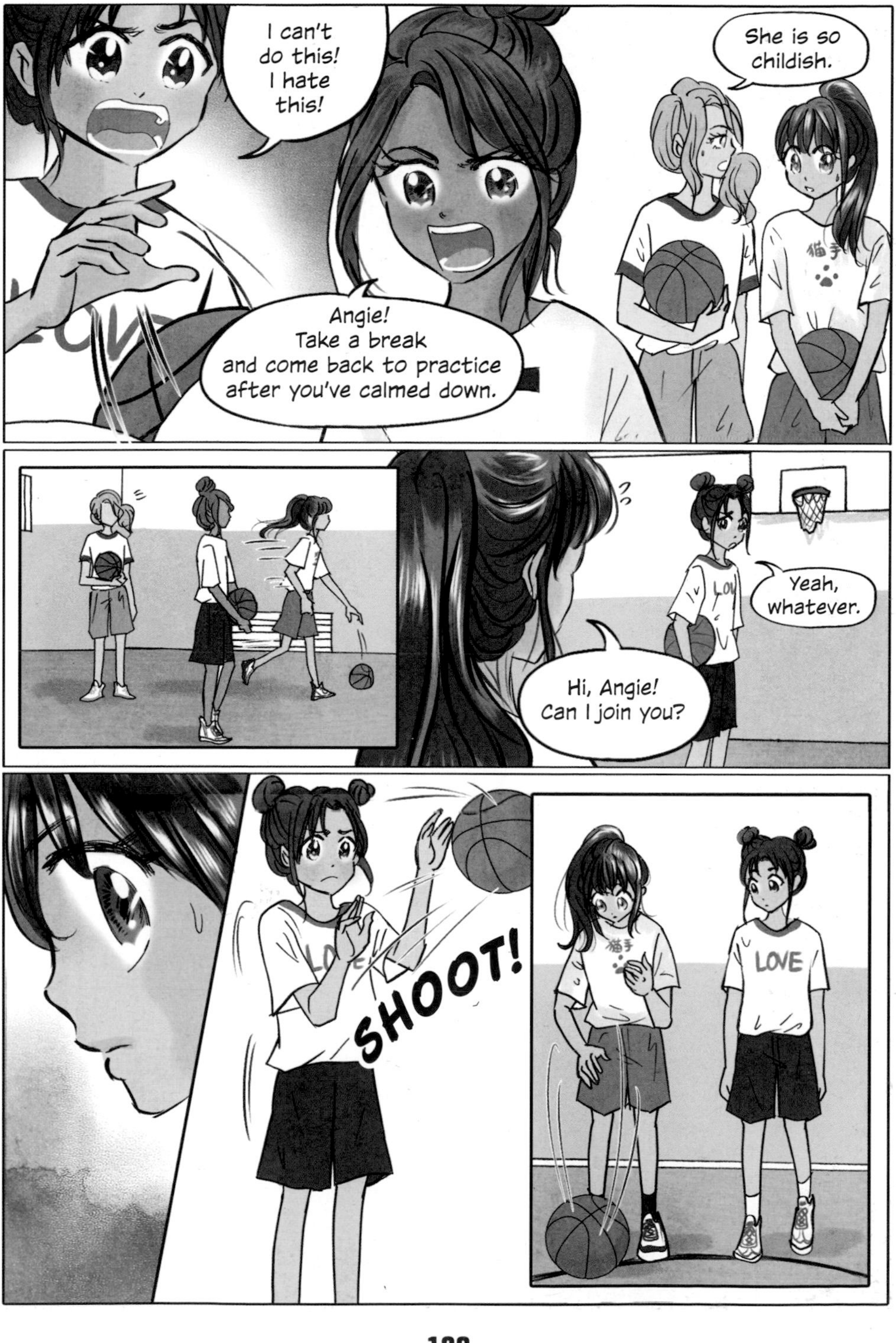

I can't do this! I hate this!
Angie! Take a break and come back to practice after you've calmed down.
She is so childish.
Hi, Angie! Can I join you?
Yeah, whatever.
LOVE
SHOOT!
猫手
LOVE

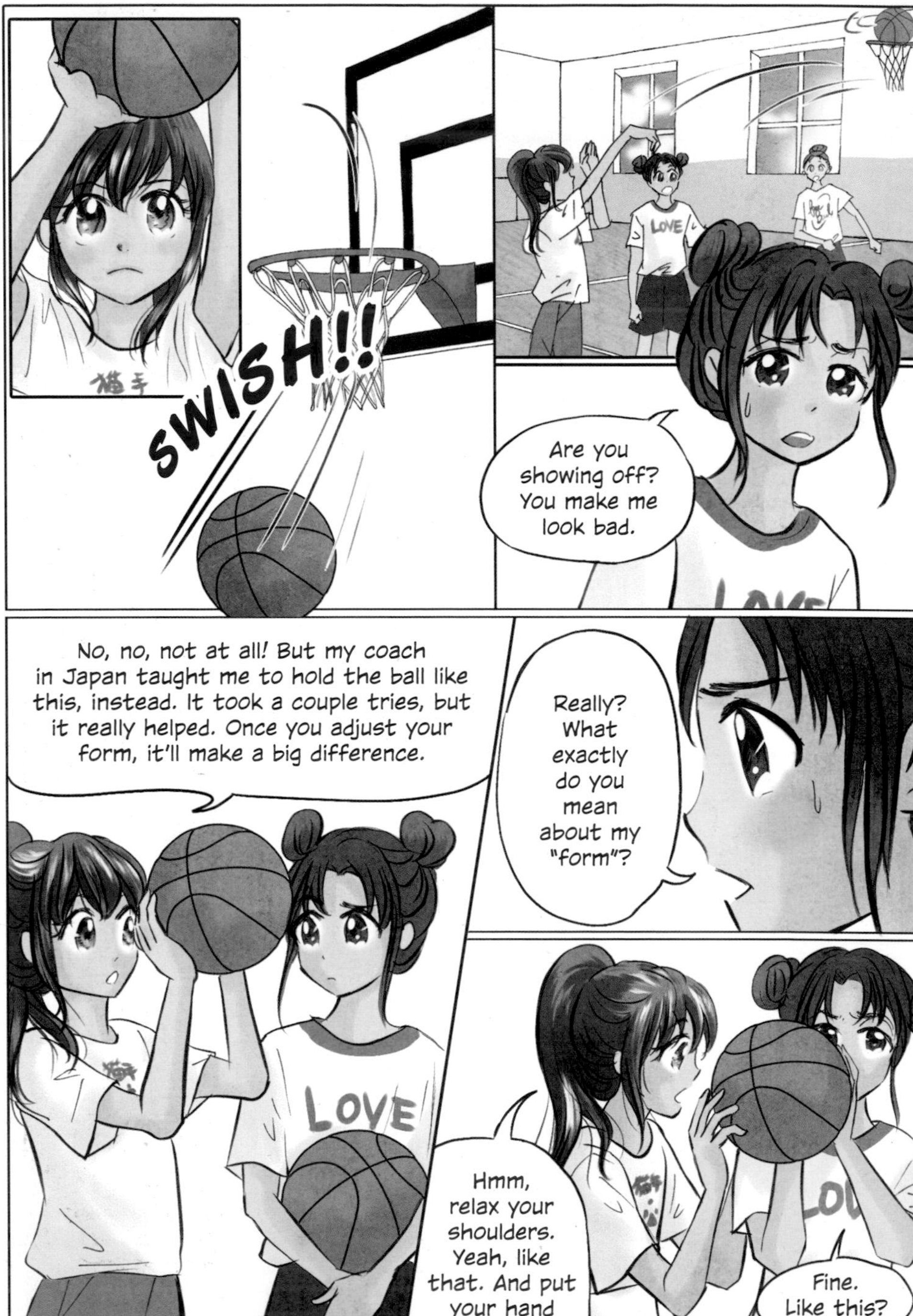
SWISH!!
Are you showing off? You make me look bad.
No, no, not at all! But my coach in Japan taught me to hold the ball like this, instead. It took a couple tries, but it really helped. Once you adjust your form, it'll make a big difference.
Really? What exactly do you mean about my "form"?
Hmm, relax your shoulders. Yeah, like that. And put your hand here.
Fine. Like this?

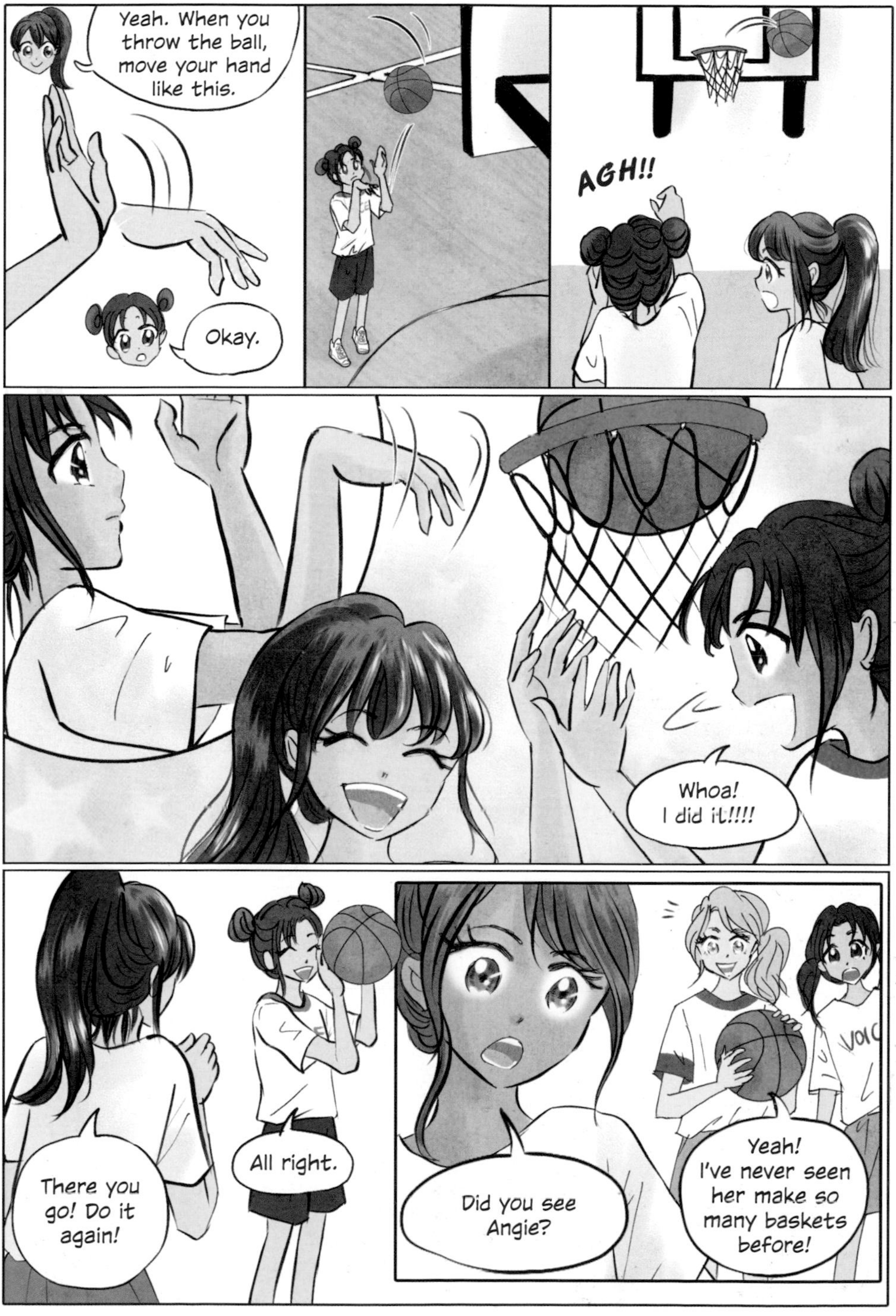
Yeah. When you throw the ball, move your hand like this.
Okay.
AGH!!
Whoa! I did it!!!!
There you go! Do it again!
All right.
Did you see Angie?
Yeah! I've never seen her make so many baskets before!

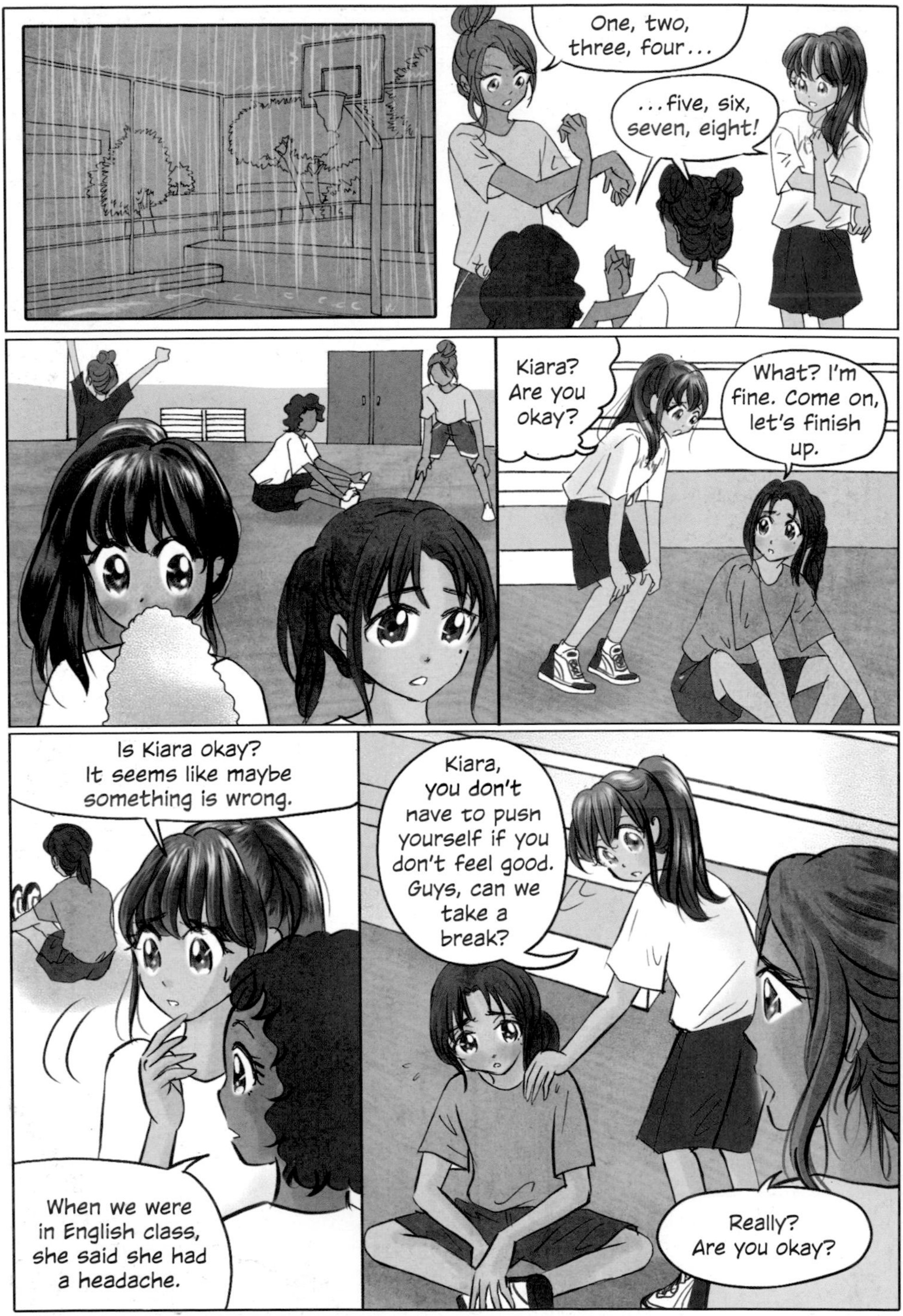
One, two, three, four...
...five, six, seven, eight!
Kiara? Are you okay?
What? I'm fine. Come on, let's finish up.
Is Kiara okay? It seems like maybe something is wrong.
When we were in English class, she said she had a headache.
Kiara, you don't have to push yourself if you don't feel good. Guys, can we take a break?
Really? Are you okay?

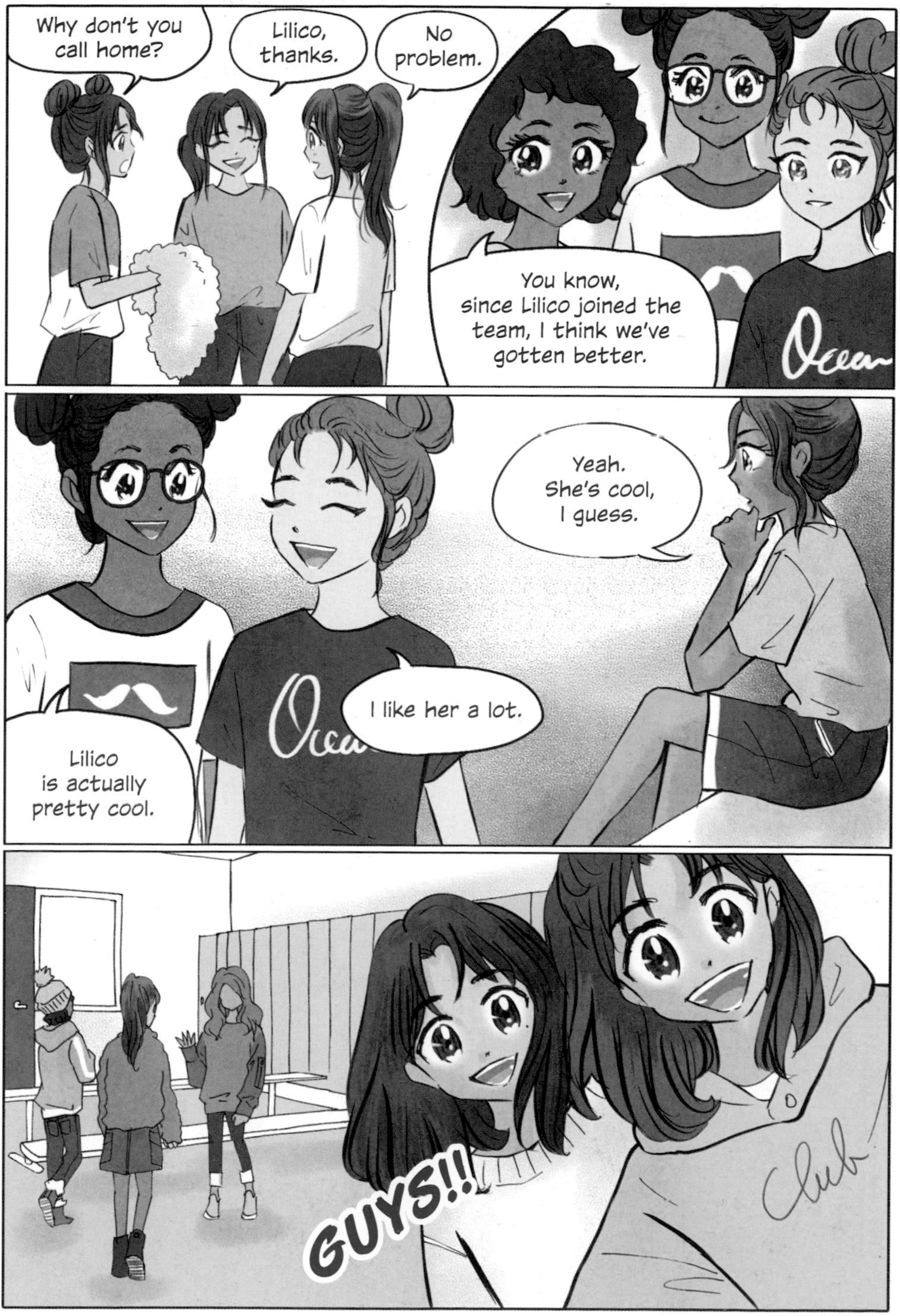

Why don't you call home?
Lilico, thanks.
No problem.
You know, since Lilico joined the team, I think we've gotten better.
Yeah. She's cool, I guess.
I like her a lot.
Lilico is actually pretty cool.
GUYS!!

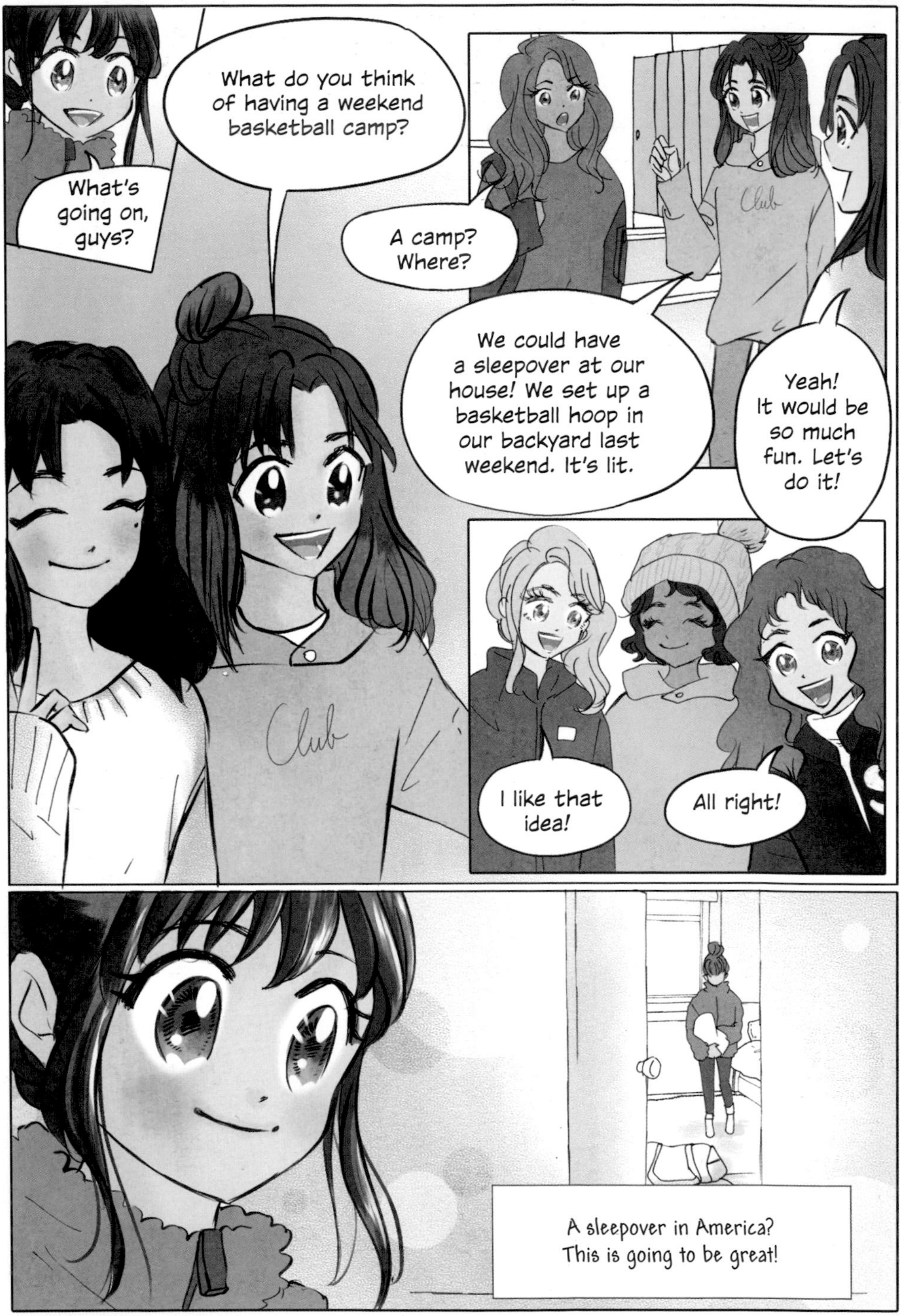
What's going on, guys?
What do you think of having a weekend basketball camp?
A camp? Where?
We could have a sleepover at our house! We set up a basketball hoop in our backyard last weekend. It's lit.
Yeah! It would be so much fun. Let's do it!
I like that idea!
All right!
A sleepover in America? This is going to be great!

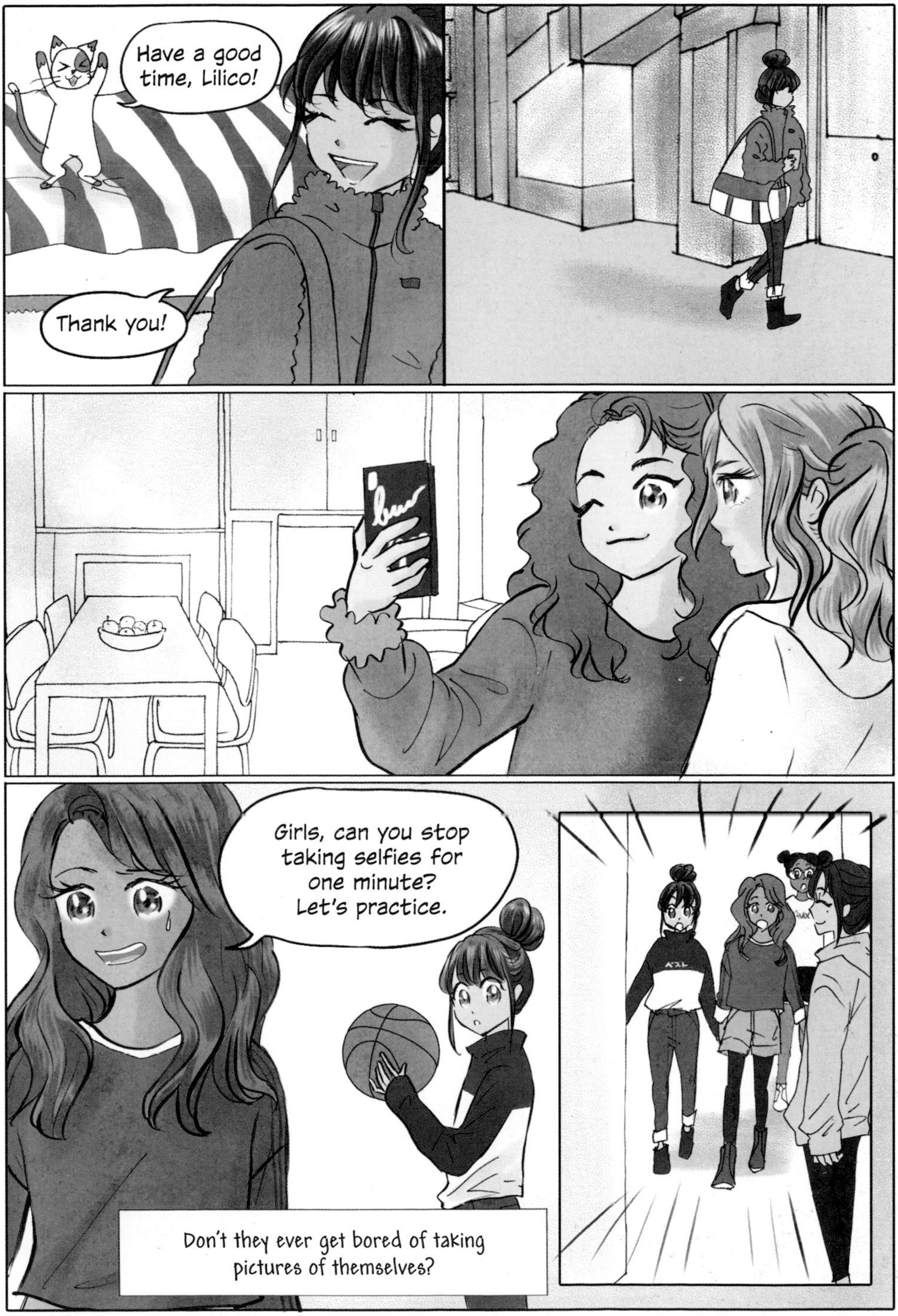

Have a good time, Lilico!
Thank you!
Girls, can you stop taking selfies for one minute? Let's practice.
Don't they ever get bored of taking pictures of themselves?

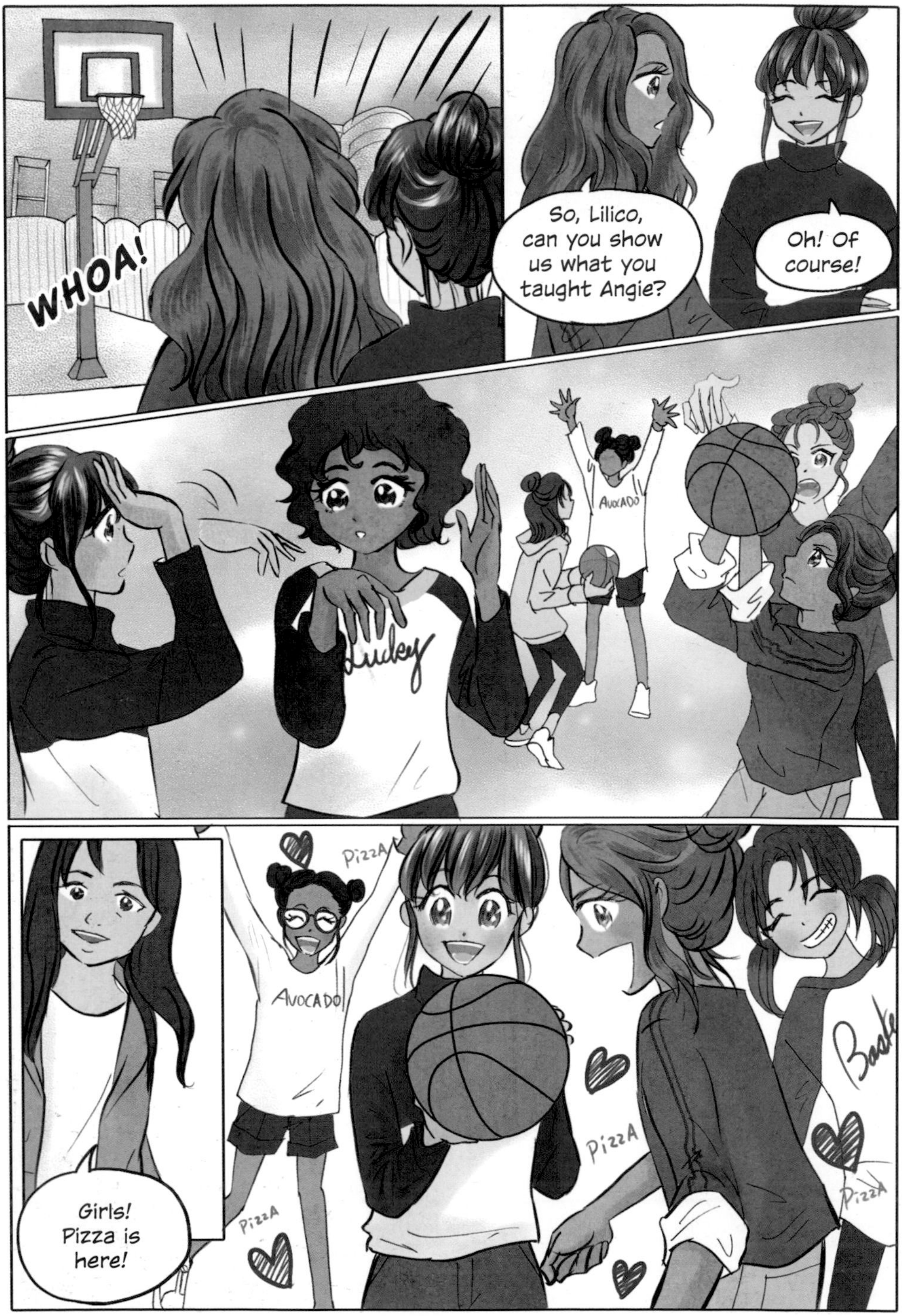
WHOA!
So, Lilico, can you show us what you taught Angie?
Oh! Of course!
AVOCADO
PizzA
AVOCADO
PizzA
PizzA
PizzA
Girls! Pizza is here!

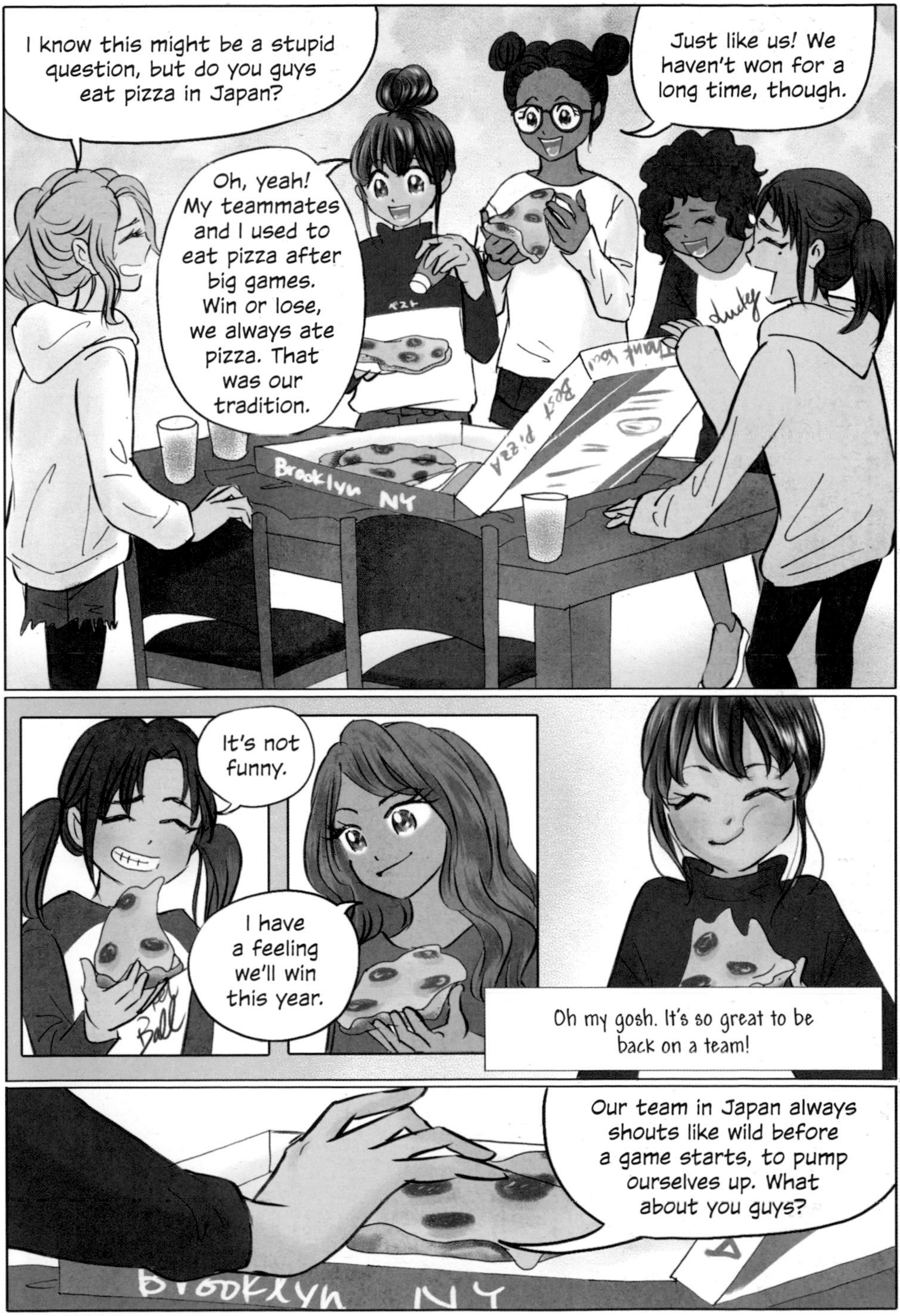
I know this might be a stupid question, but do you guys eat pizza in Japan?
Oh, yeah! My teammates and I used to eat pizza after big games. Win or lose, we always ate pizza. That was our tradition.
Just like us! We haven't won for a long time, though.
Brooklyn NY
Best Pizza
It's not funny.
I have a feeling we'll win this year.
Oh my gosh. It's so great to be back on a team!
Our team in Japan always shouts like wild before a game starts, to pump ourselves up. What about you guys?

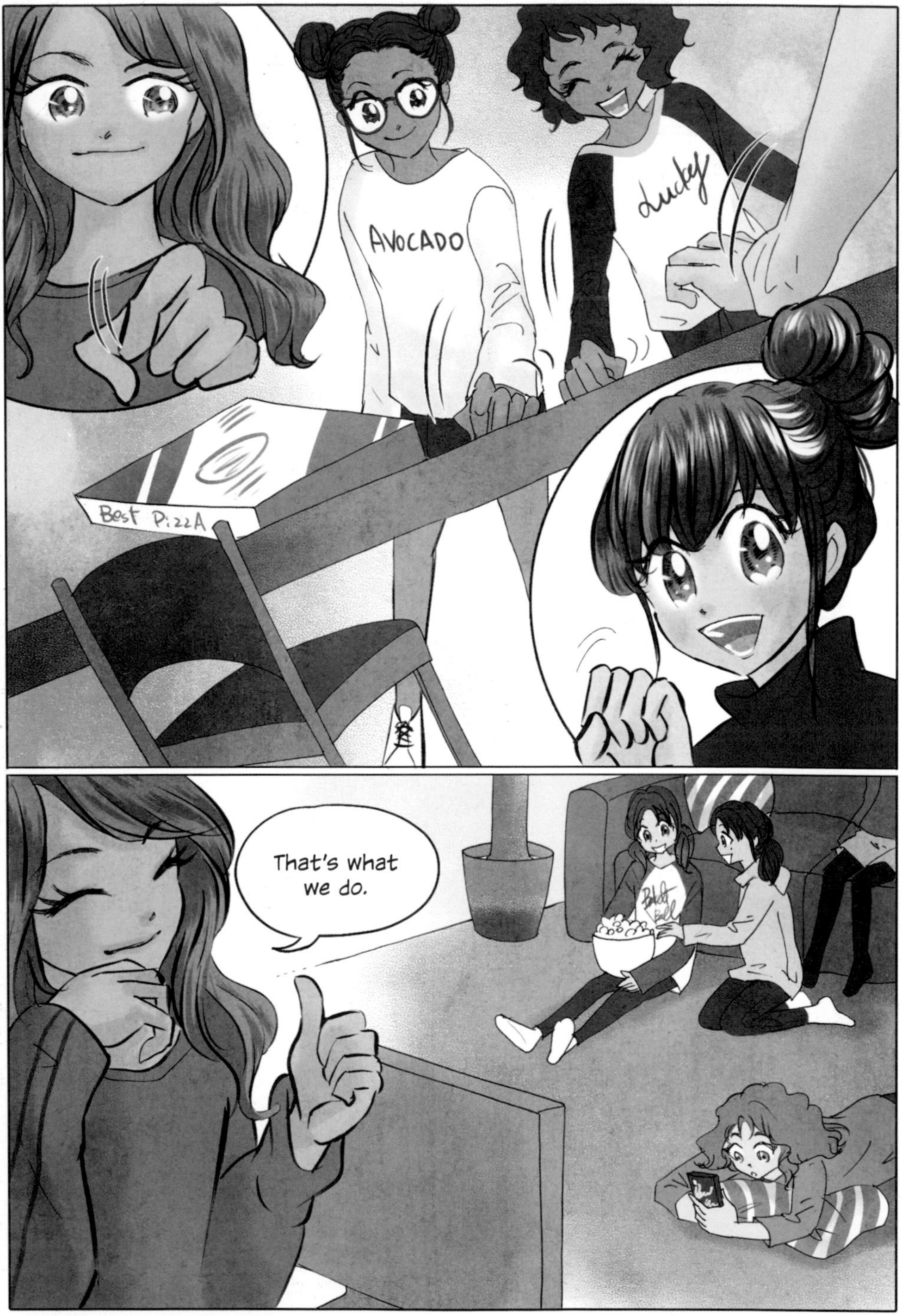
AVOCADO
Lucky
Best PizzA
That's what we do.

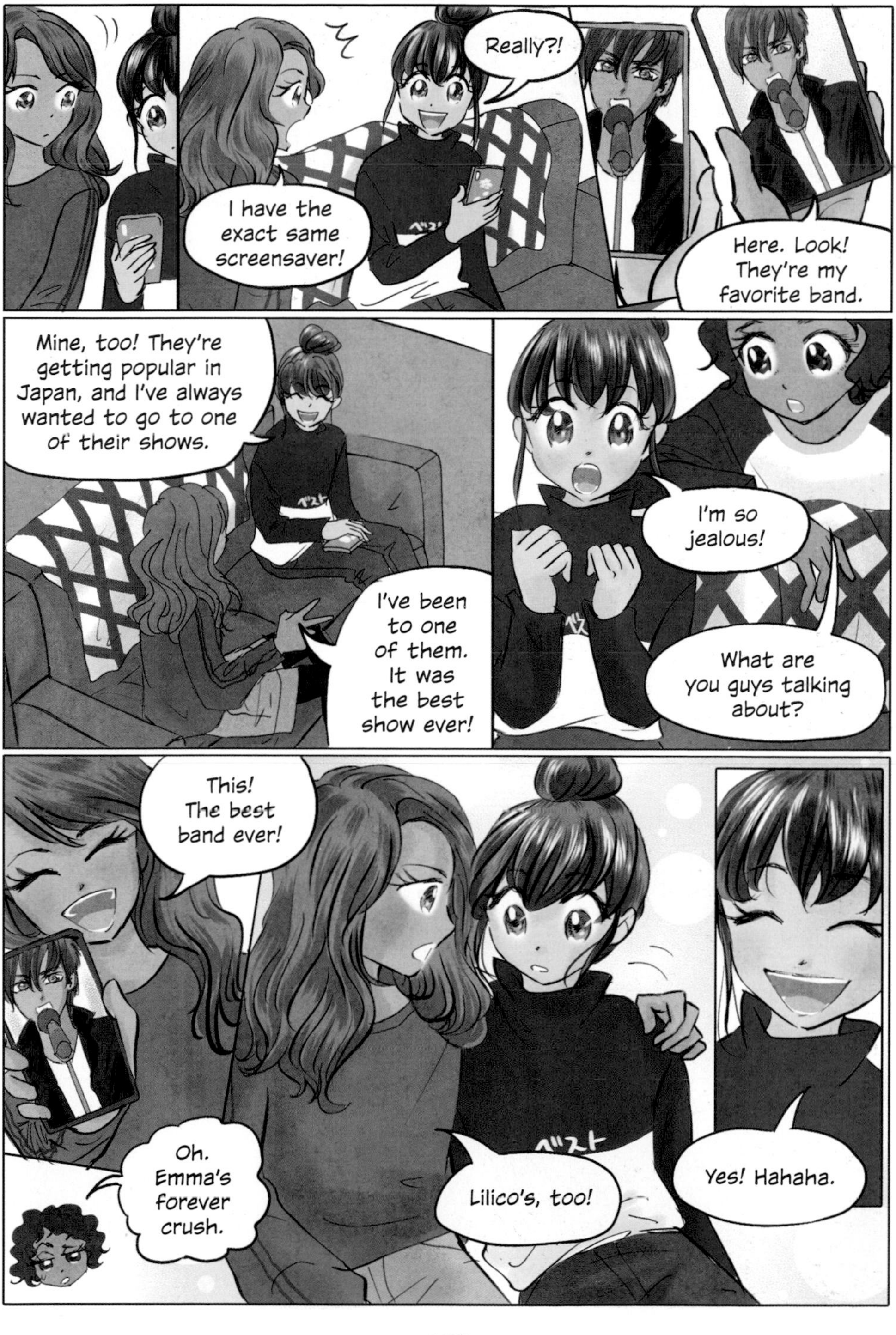
Really?!
I have the exact same screensaver!
Here. Look! They're my favorite band.
Mine, too! They're getting popular in Japan, and I've always wanted to go to one of their shows.
I've been to one of them. It was the best show ever!
I'm so jealous!
What are you guys talking about?
This! The best band ever!
Oh. Emma's forever crush.
Lilico's, too!
Yes! Hahaha.

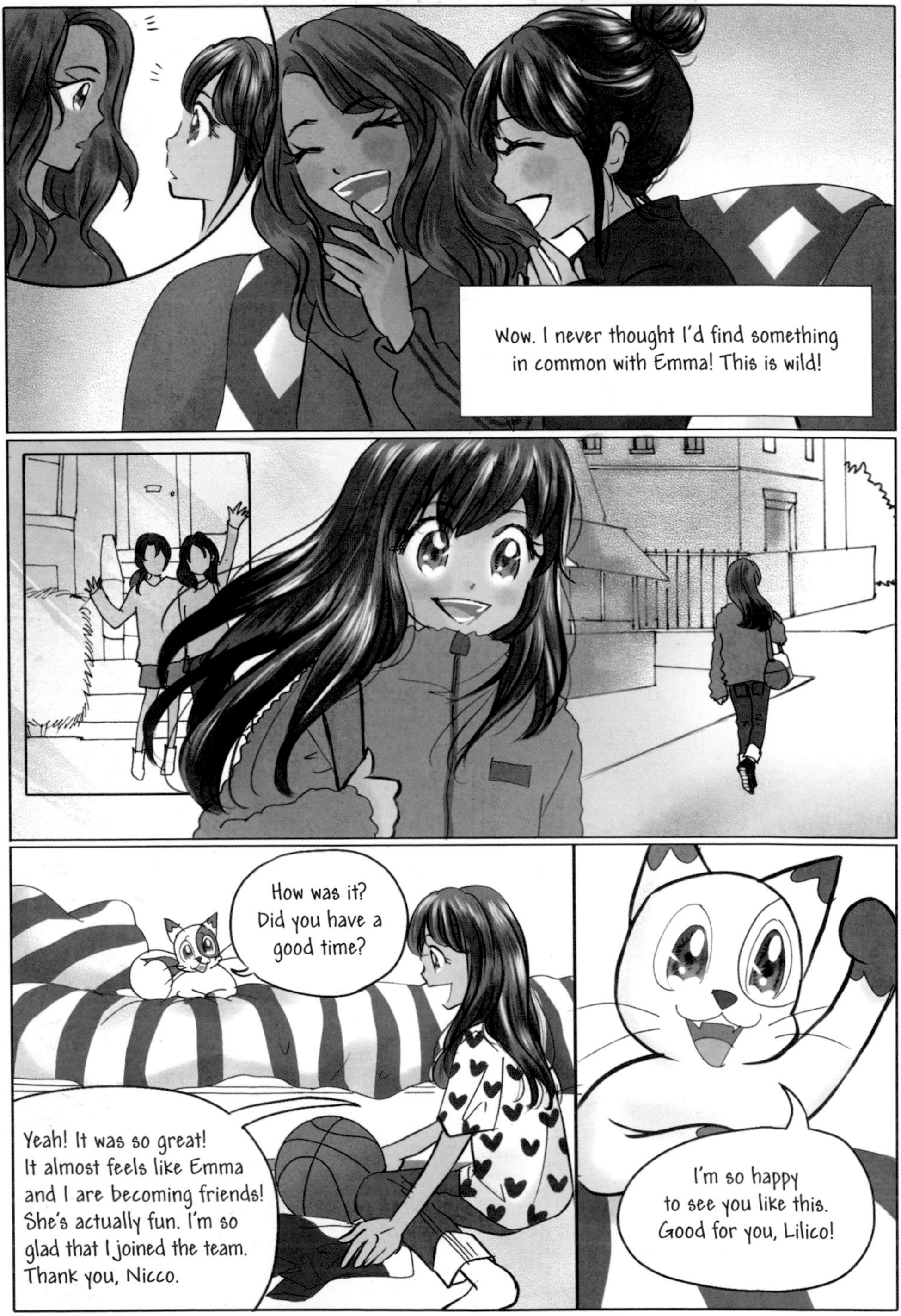
Wow. I never thought I'd find something in common with Emma! This is wild!
How was it? Did you have a good time?
Yeah! It was so great! It almost feels like Emma and I are becoming friends! She's actually fun. I'm so glad that I joined the team. Thank you, Nicco.
I'm so happy to see you like this. Good for you, Lilico!

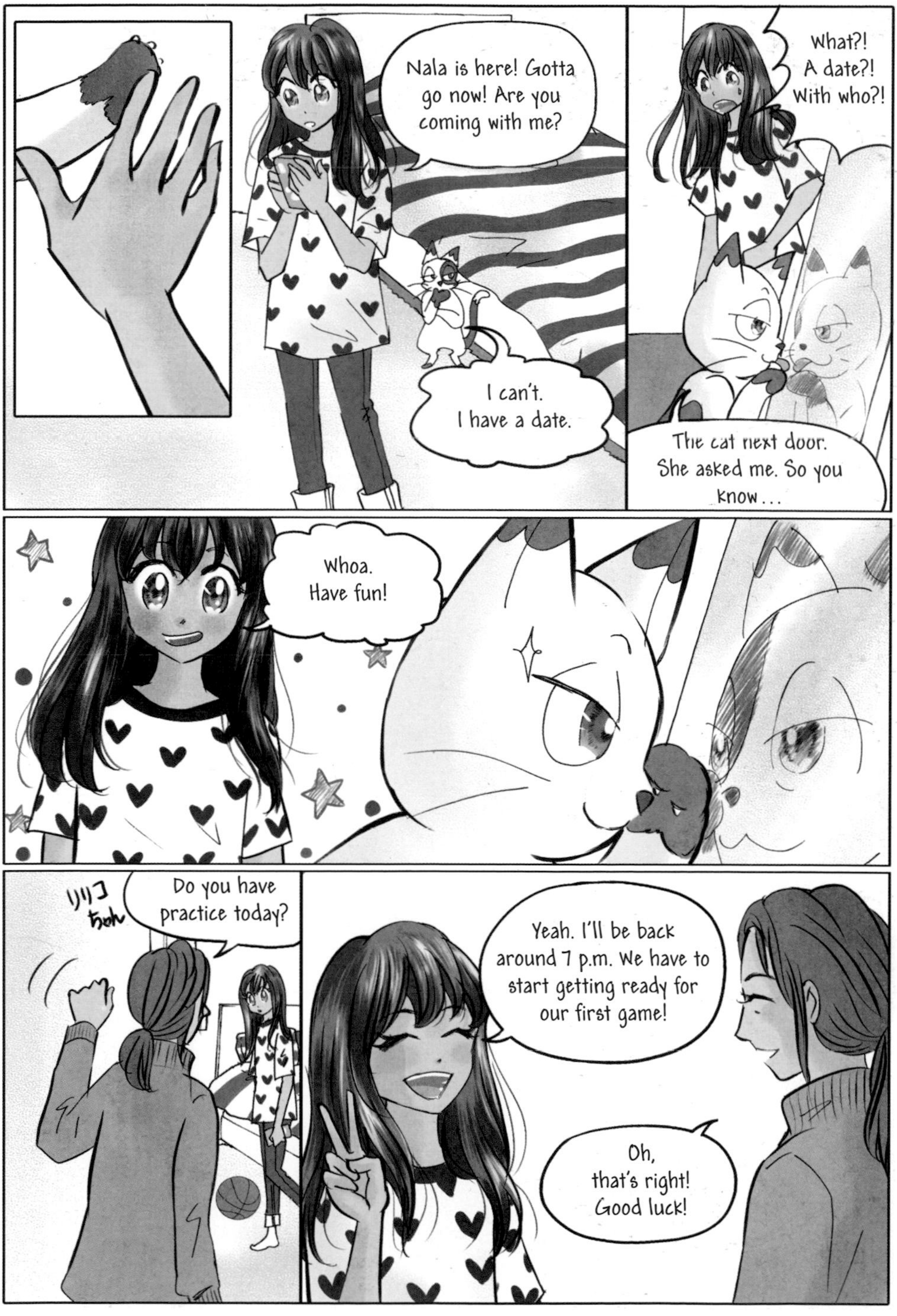
Nala is here! Gotta go now! Are you coming with me?
I can't. I have a date.
What?! A date?! With who?!
The cat next door. She asked me. So you know...
Whoa. Have fun!
リリコちゃん
Do you have practice today?
Yeah. I'll be back around 7 p.m. We have to start getting ready for our first game!
Oh, that's right! Good luck!

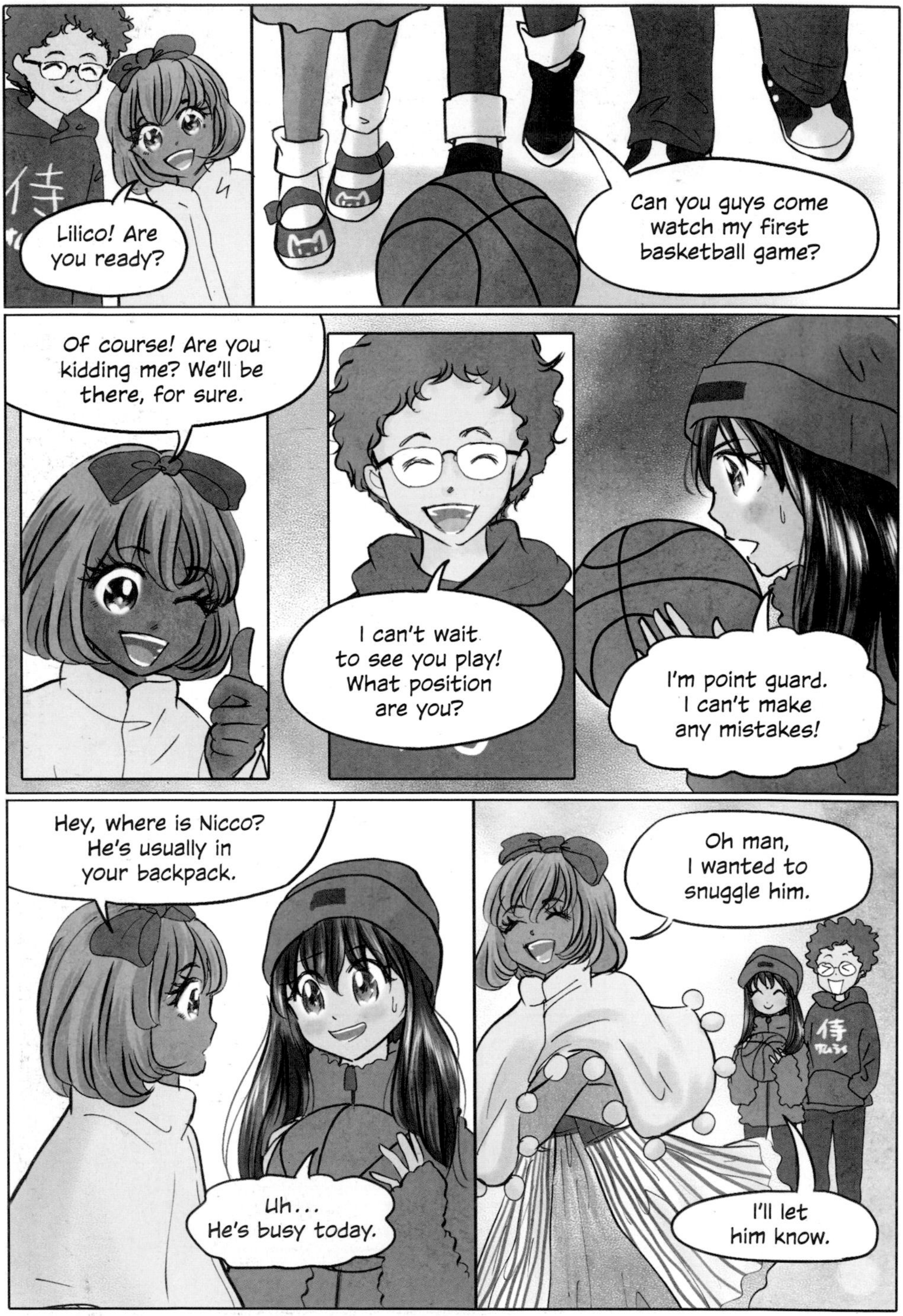
Lilico! Are you ready?
Can you guys come watch my first basketball game?
Of course! Are you kidding me? We'll be there, for sure.
I can't wait to see you play! What position are you?
I'm point guard. I can't make any mistakes!
Hey, where is Nicco? He's usually in your backpack.
Uh... He's busy today.
Oh man, I wanted to snuggle him.
I'll let him know.

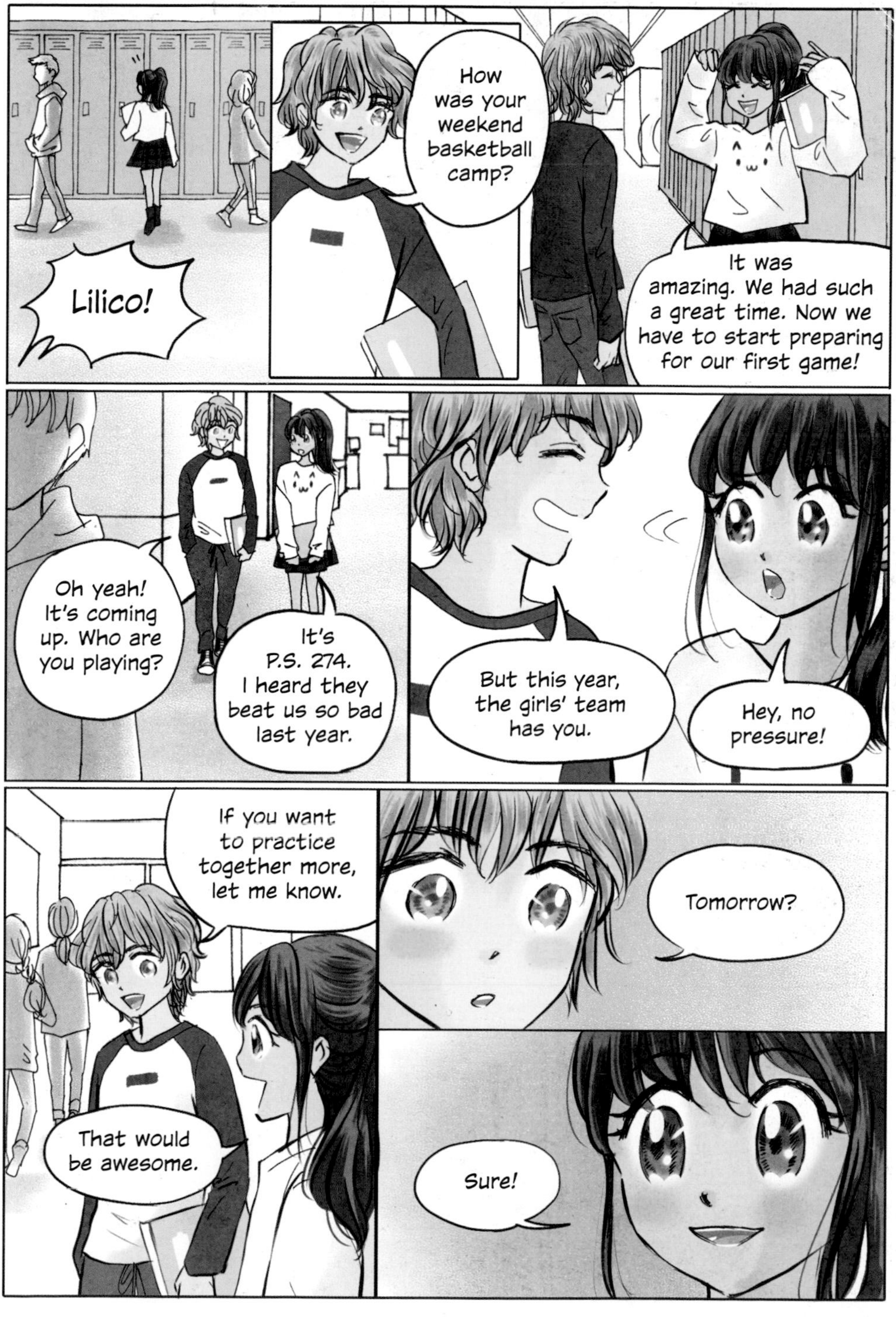
Lilico!
How was your weekend basketball camp?
It was amazing. We had such a great time. Now we have to start preparing for our first game!
Oh yeah! It's coming up. Who are you playing?
It's P.S. 274. I heard they beat us so bad last year.
But this year, the girls' team has you.
Hey, no pressure!
If you want to practice together more, let me know.
That would be awesome.
Tomorrow?
Sure!

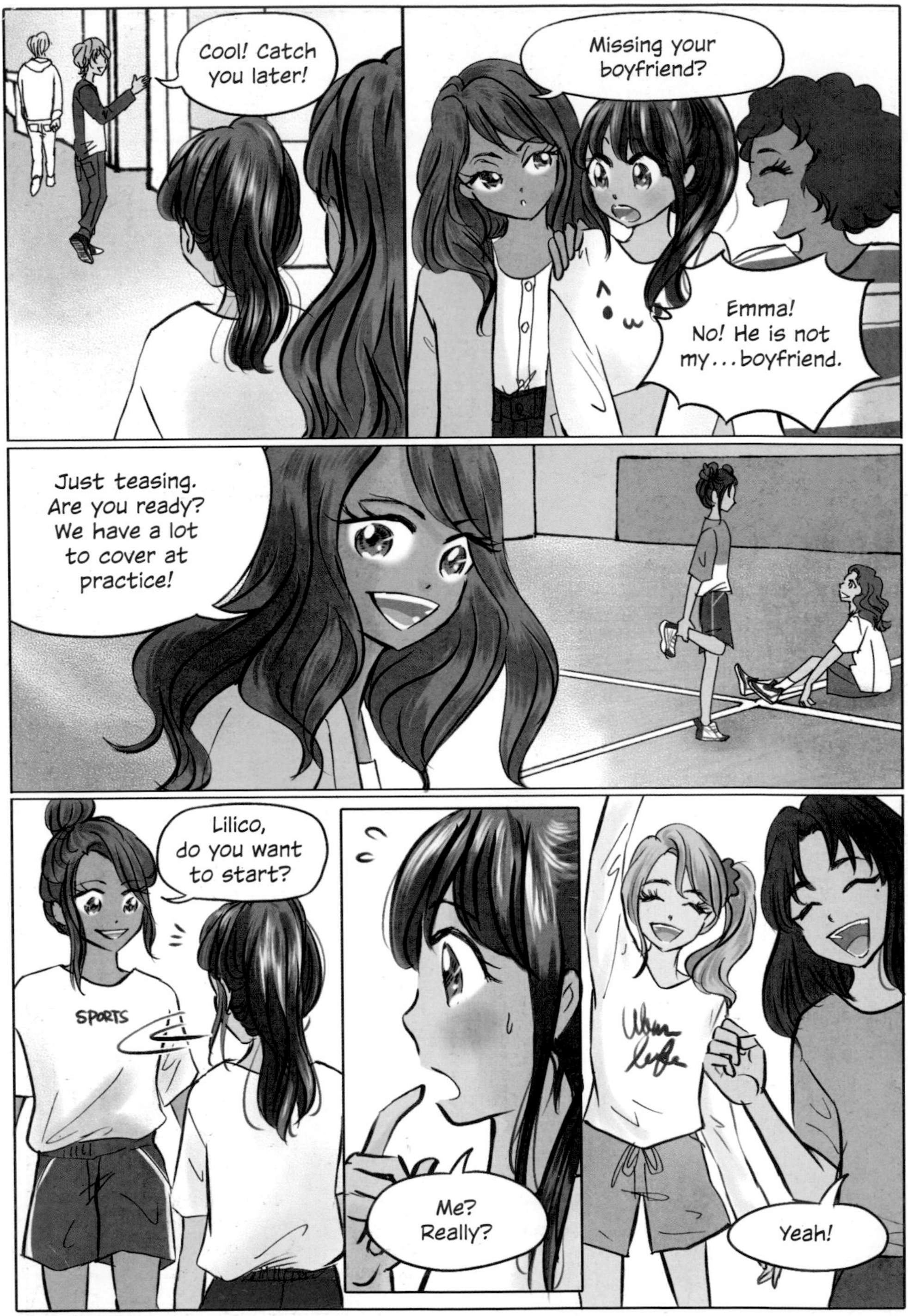
Cool! Catch you later!
Missing your boyfriend?
Emma! No! He is not my...boyfriend.
Just teasing. Are you ready? We have a lot to cover at practice!
Lilico, do you want to start?
SPORTS
Me? Really?
Yeah!

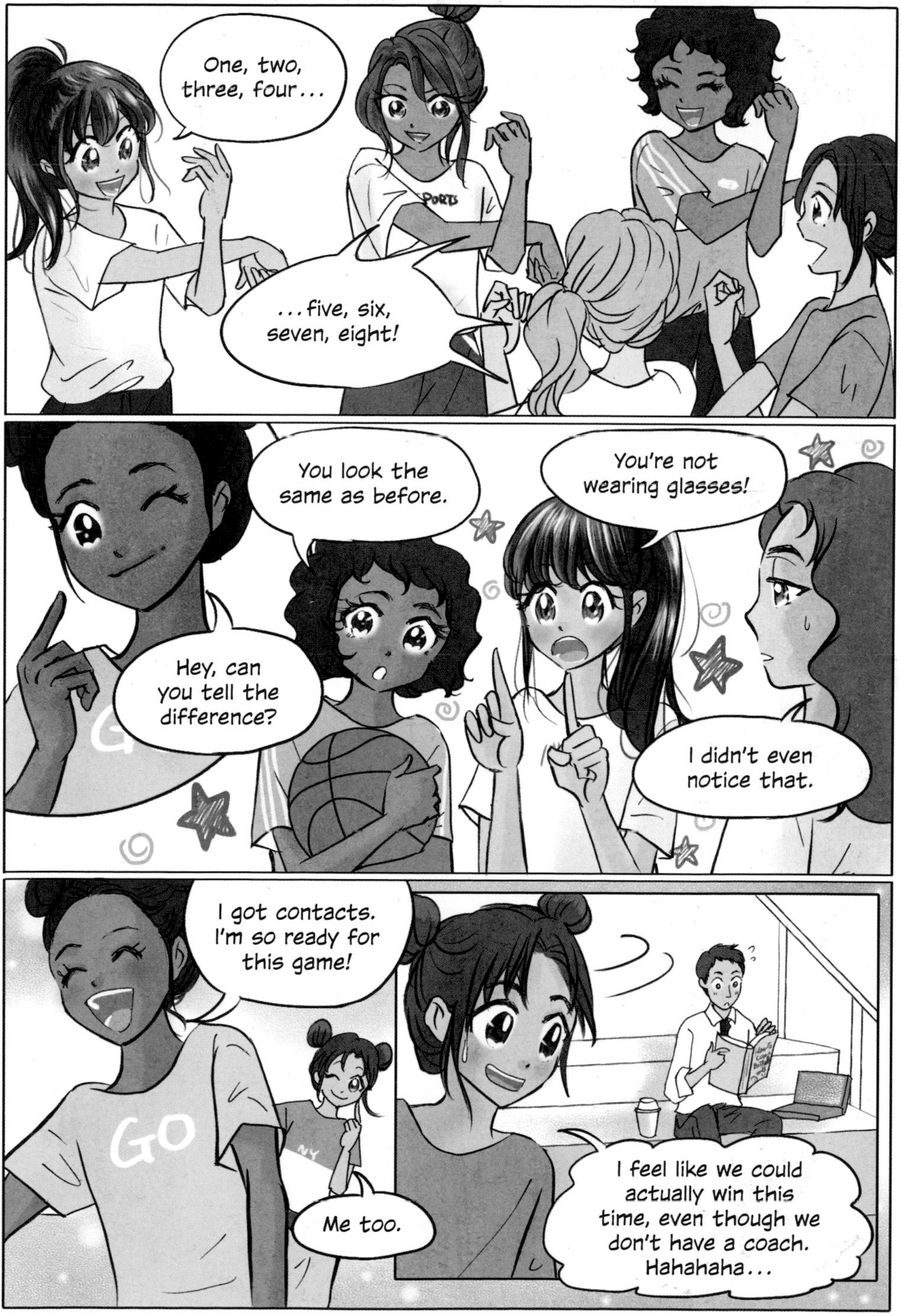
One, two, three, four...
...five, six, seven, eight!
Hey, can you tell the difference?
You look the same as before.
You're not wearing glasses!
I didn't even notice that.
I got contacts. I'm so ready for this game!
Me too.
I feel like we could actually win this time, even though we don't have a coach. Hahahaha...

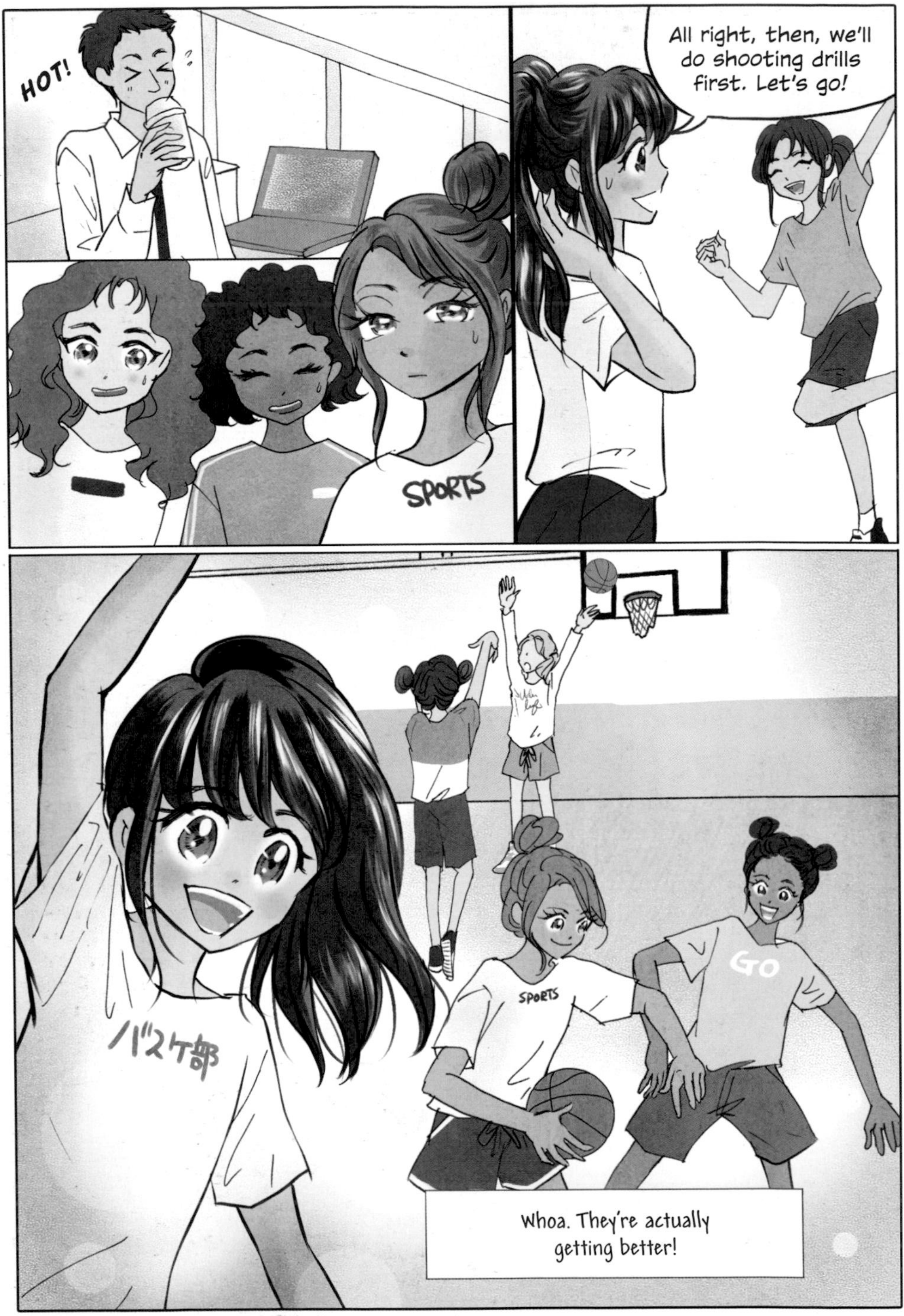
HOT!
SPORTS
All right, then, we'll do shooting drills first. Let's go!
バスケ部
SPORTS
GO
Whoa. They're actually getting better!

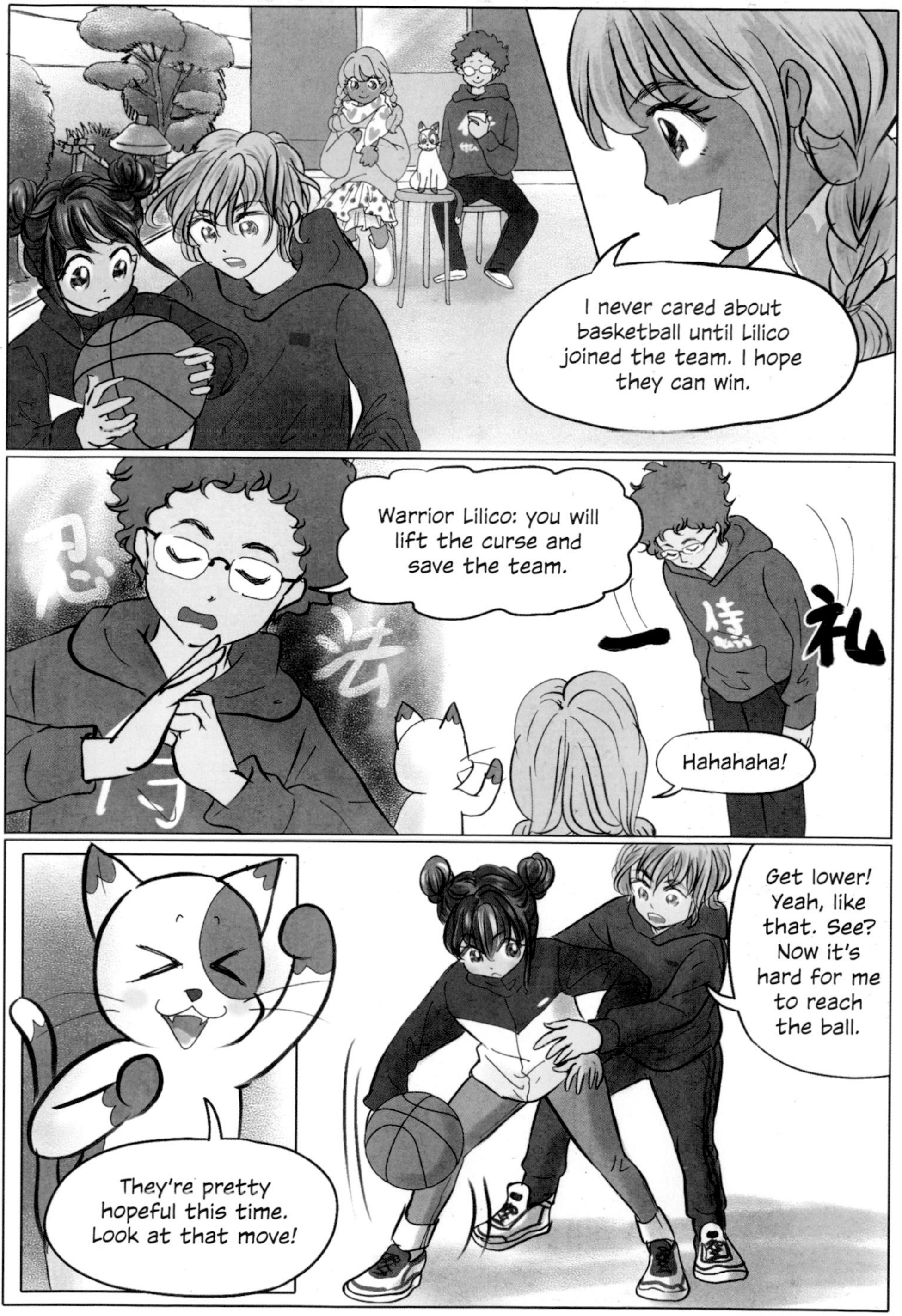
I never cared about basketball until Lilico joined the team. I hope they can win.
Warrior Lilico: you will lift the curse and save the team.
一礼
Hahahaha!
They're pretty hopeful this time. Look at that move!
Get lower! Yeah, like that. See? Now it's hard for me to reach the ball.

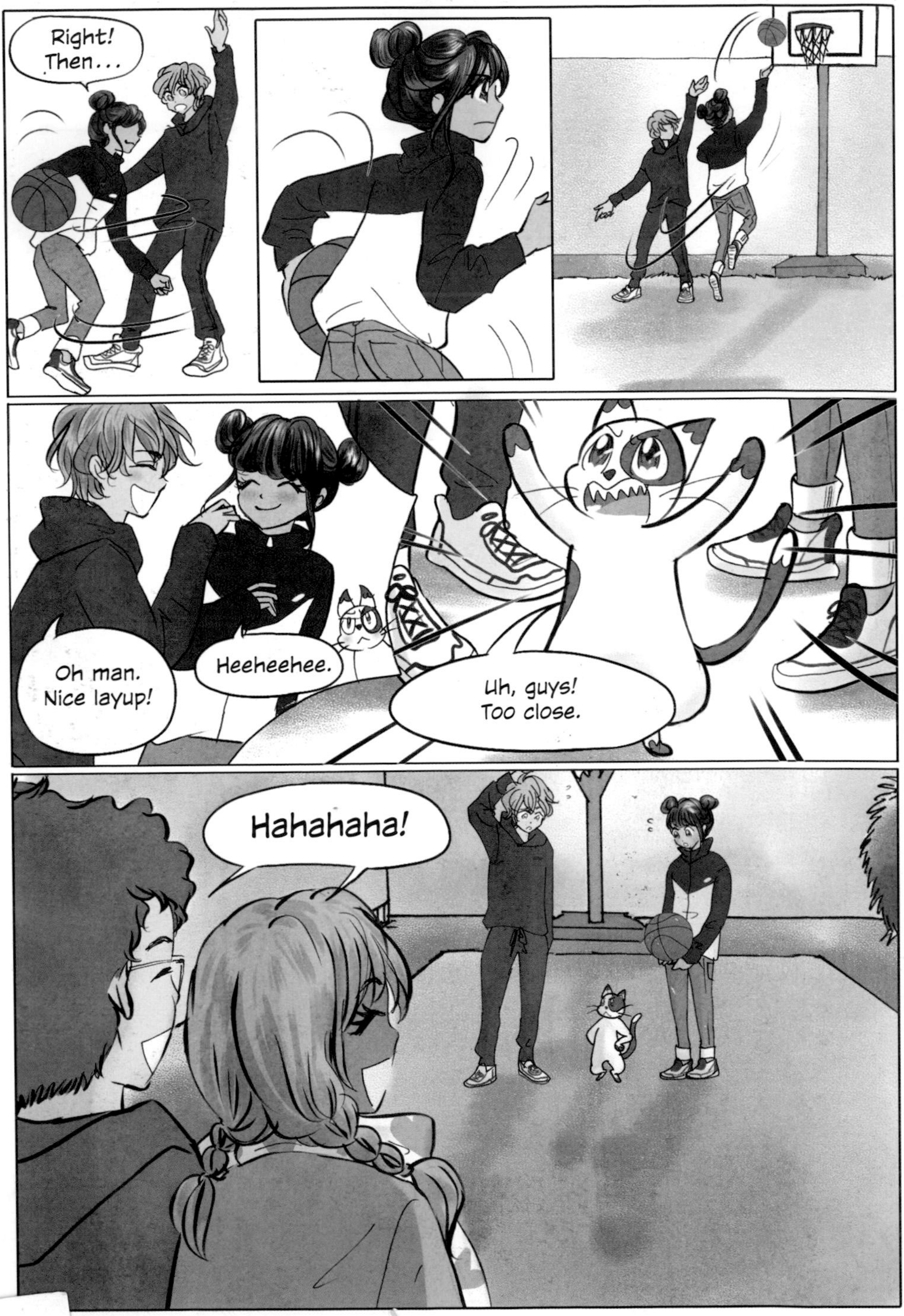
Right! Then...
Oh man. Nice layup!
Heeheehee.
Uh, guys! Too close.
Hahahaha!

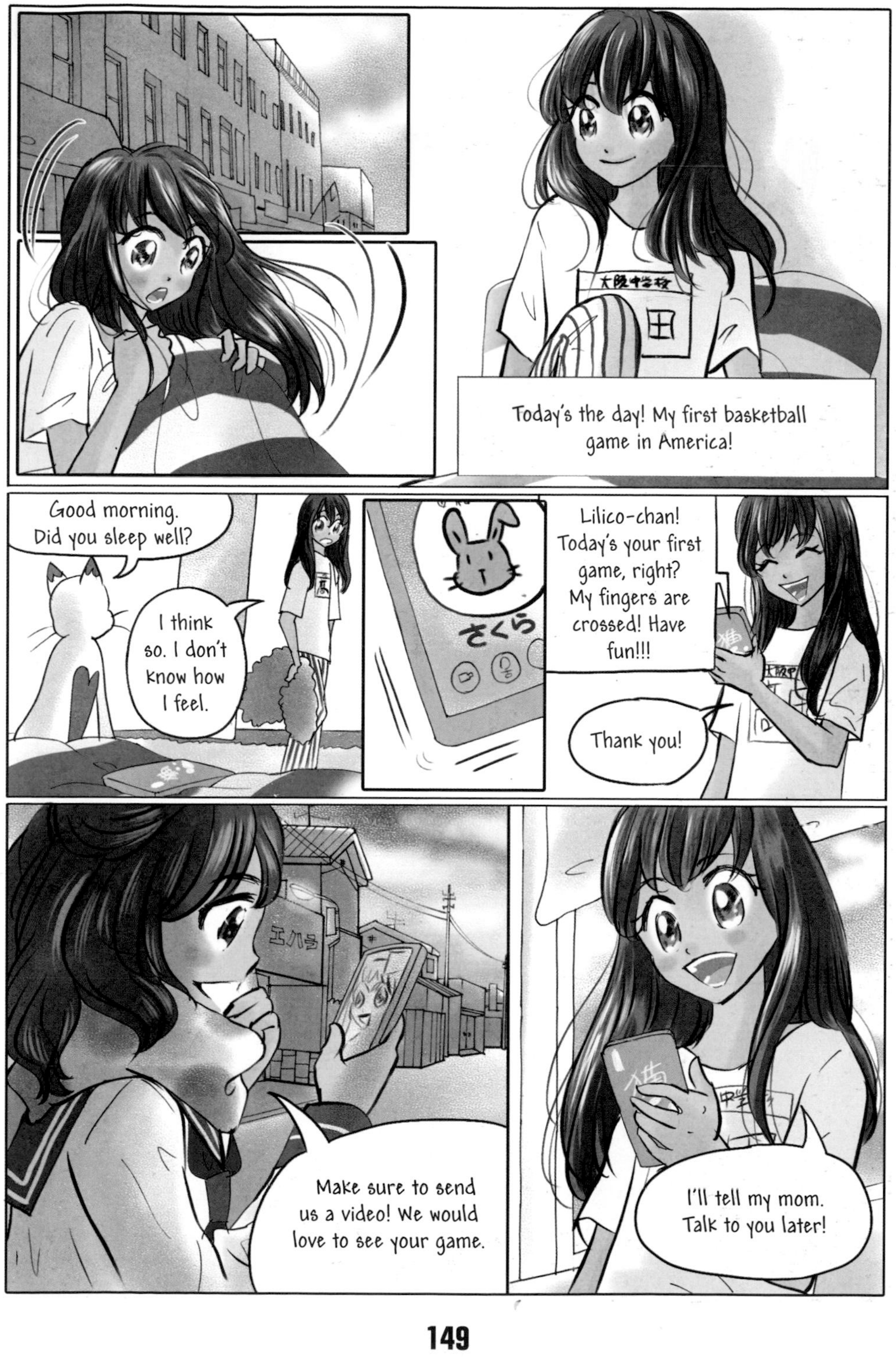
Today's the day! My first basketball game in America!
Good morning. Did you sleep well?
I think so. I don't know how I feel.
さくら
Lilico-chan! Today's your first game, right? My fingers are crossed! Have fun!!!
Thank you!
Make sure to send us a video! We would love to see your game.
I'll tell my mom. Talk to you later!

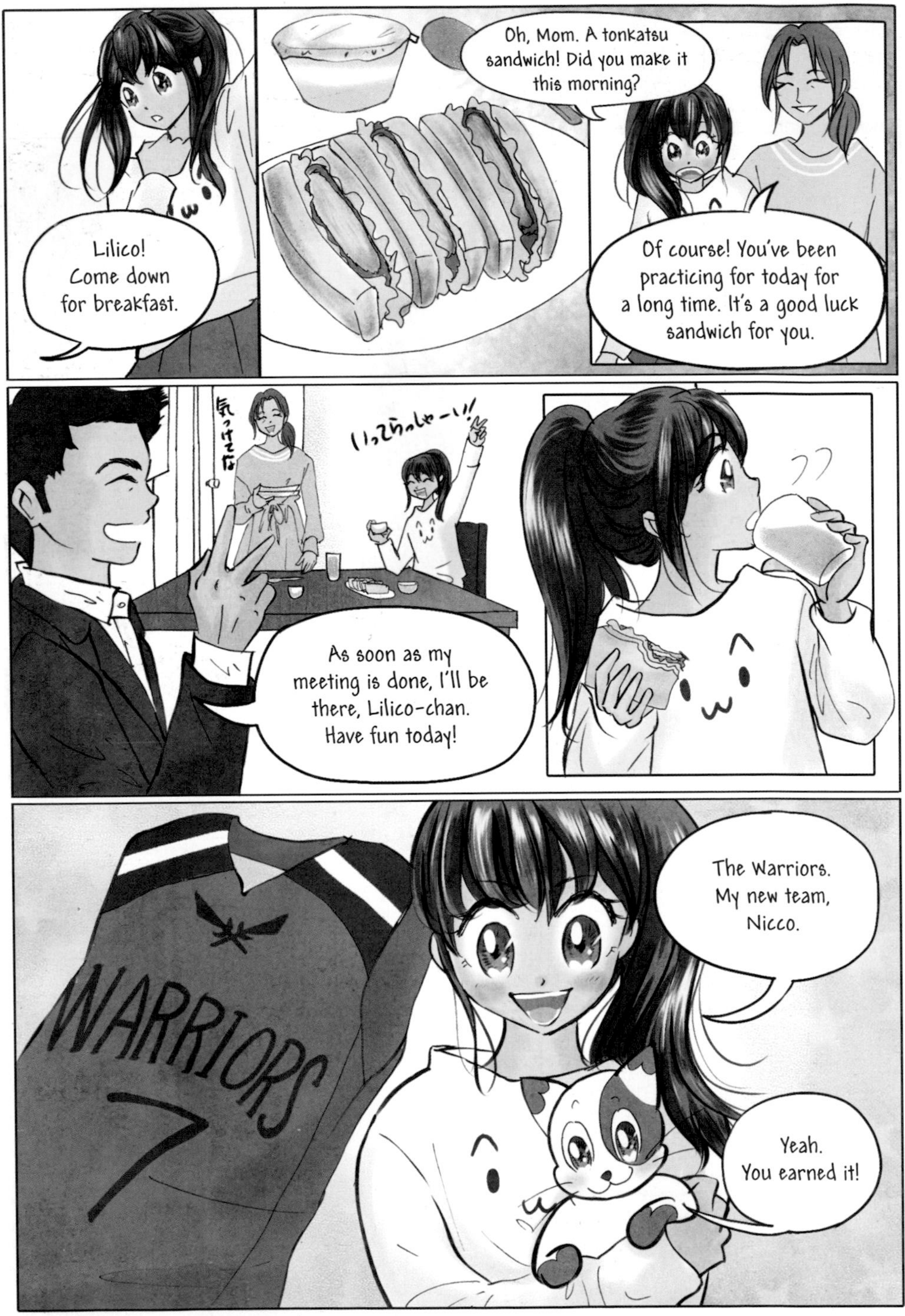
Lilico! Come down for breakfast.
Oh, Mom. A tonkatsu sandwich! Did you make it this morning?
Of course! You've been practicing for today for a long time. It's a good luck sandwich for you.
気っけてな
いってらっしゃーい!!
As soon as my meeting is done, I'll be there, Lilico-chan. Have fun today!
WARRIORS
7
The Warriors. My new team, Nicco.
Yeah. You earned it!

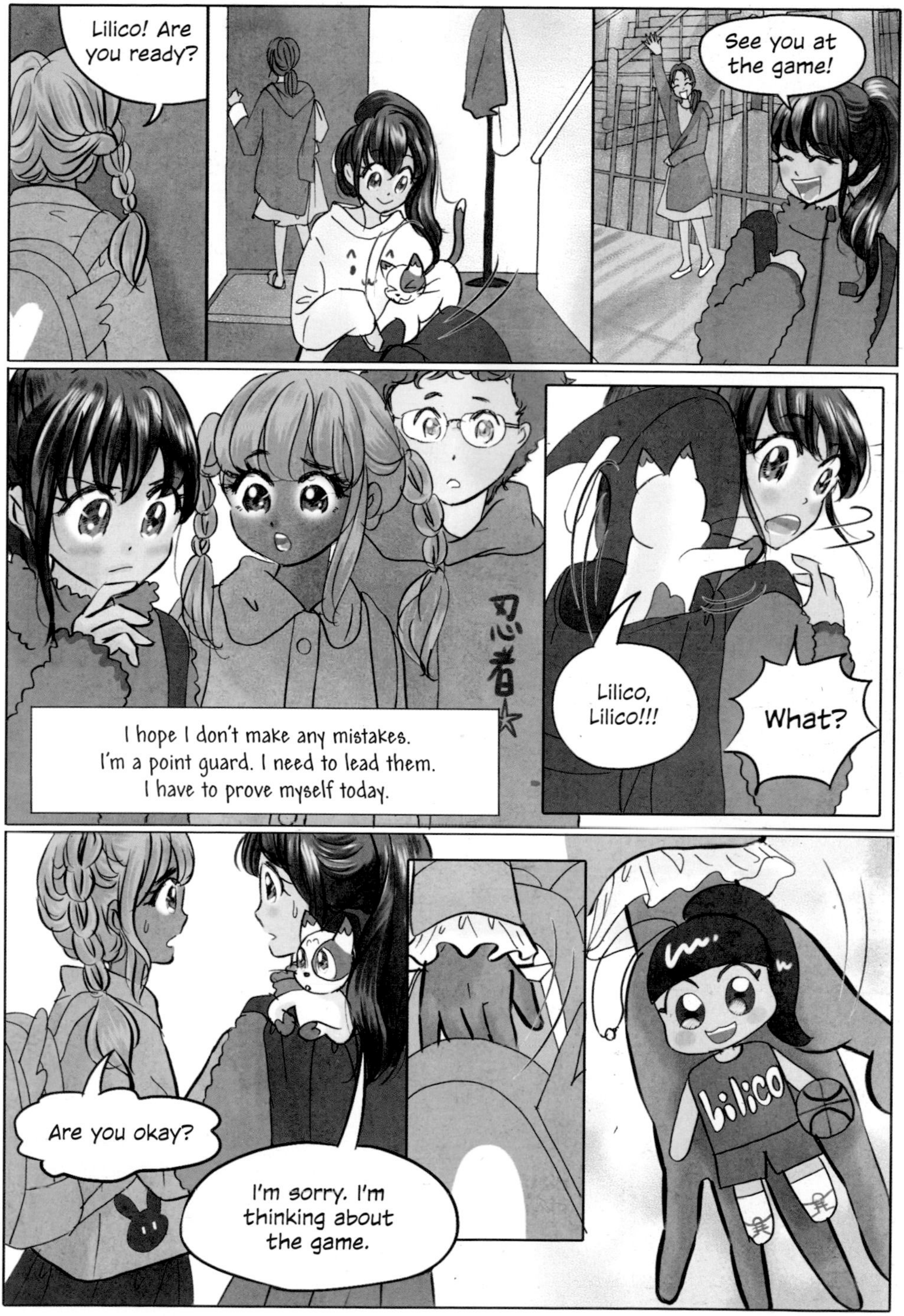

Lilico! Are you ready?
See you at the game!
忍者
I hope I don't make any mistakes. I'm a point guard. I need to lead them. I have to prove myself today.
Lilico, Lilico!!!
What?
Are you okay?
I'm sorry. I'm thinking about the game.
Lilico

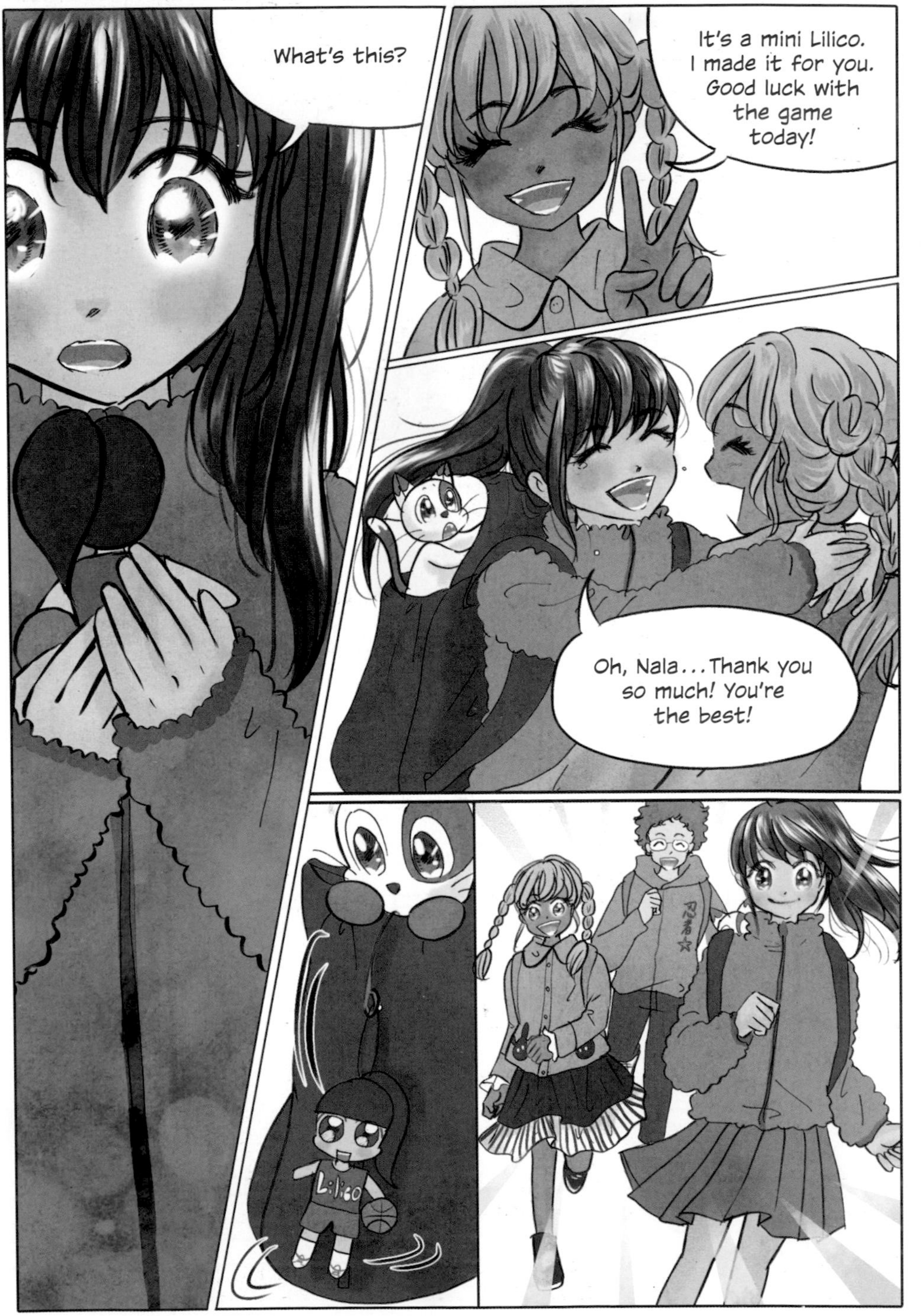
What's this?
It's a mini Lilico. I made it for you. Good luck with the game today!
Oh, Nala...Thank you so much! You're the best!

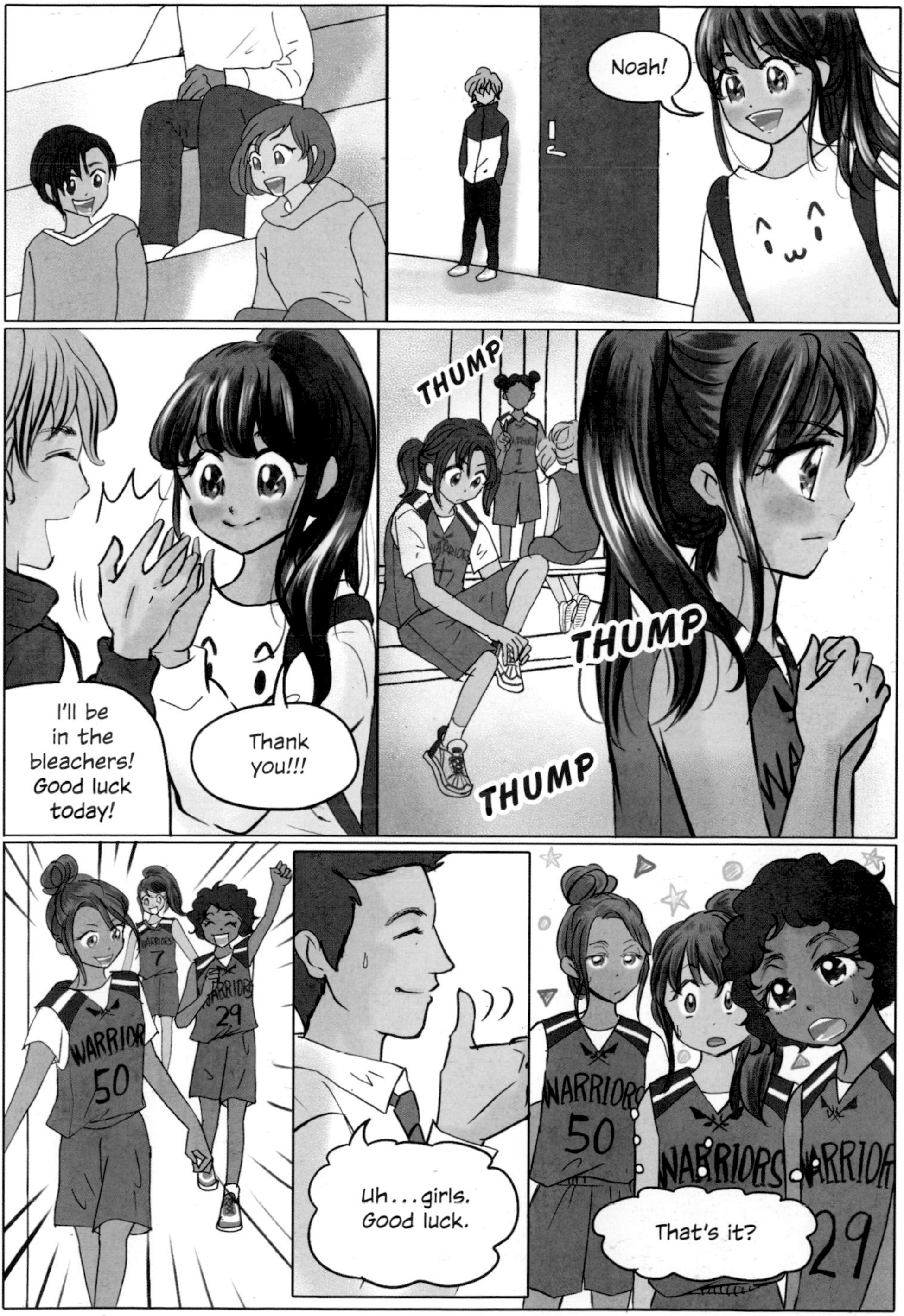
Noah!
I'll be in the bleachers! Good luck today!
Thank you!!!
THUMP
THUMP
THUMP
Uh...girls. Good luck.
That's it?

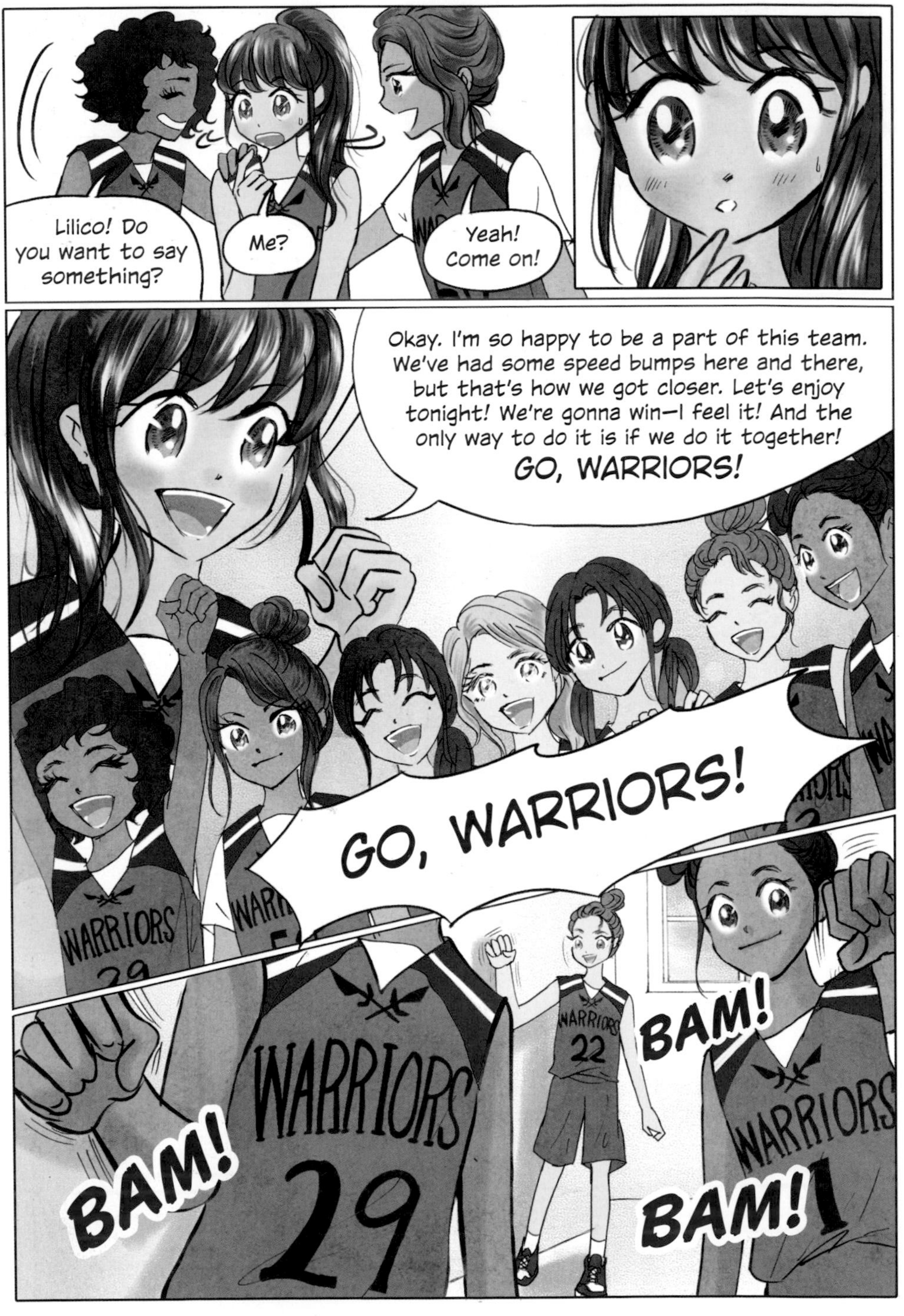
Lilico! Do you want to say something?
Me?
Yeah! Come on!
Okay. I'm so happy to be a part of this team. We've had some speed bumps here and there, but that's how we got closer. Let's enjoy tonight! We're gonna win—I feel it! And the only way to do it is if we do it together!
GO, WARRIORS!
GO, WARRIORS!
WARRIORS
29
BAM!
WARRIORS
22
BAM!
WARRIORS
BAM!

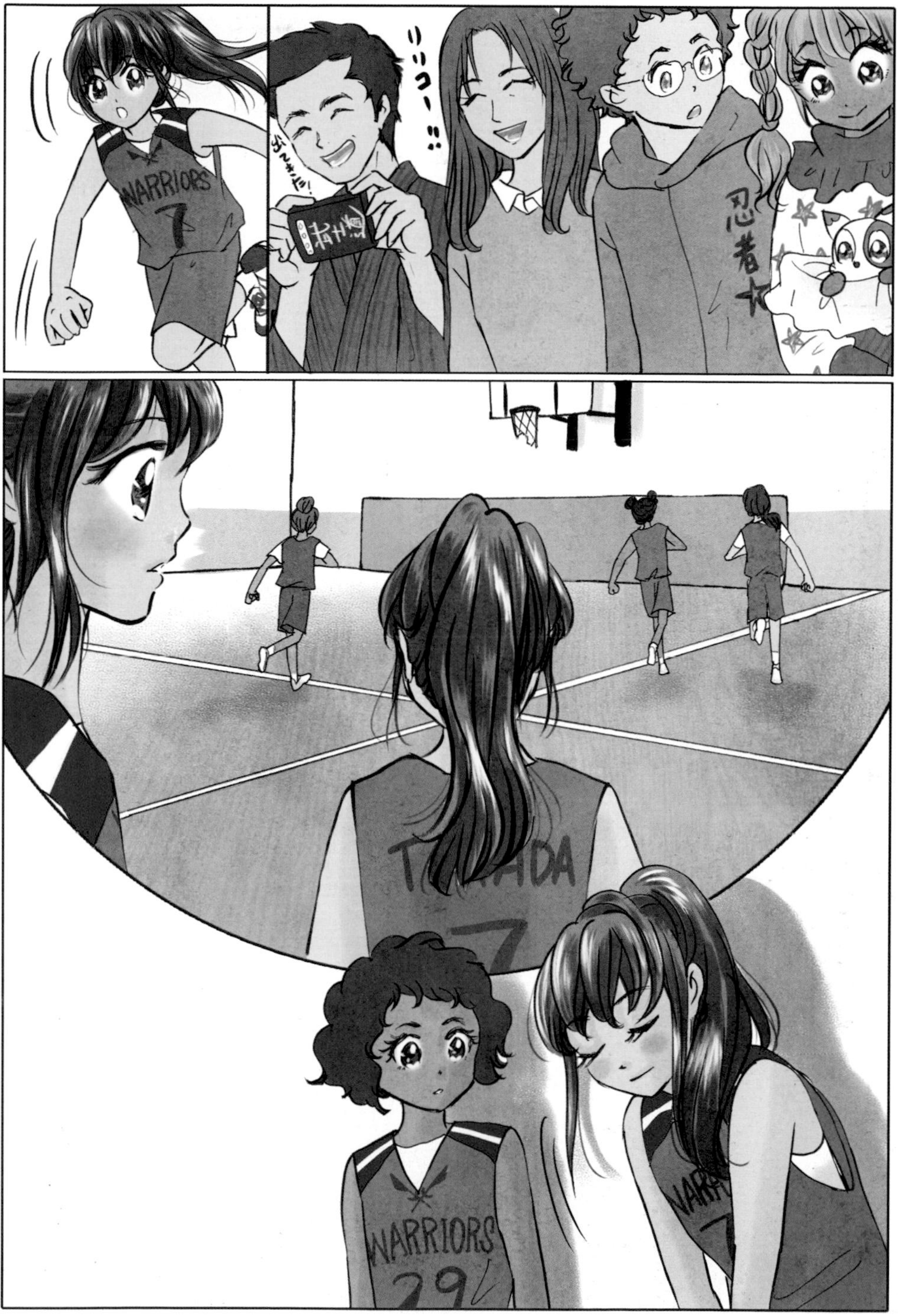
WARRIORS 7
リリコー!!
忍者☆
WARRIORS 29

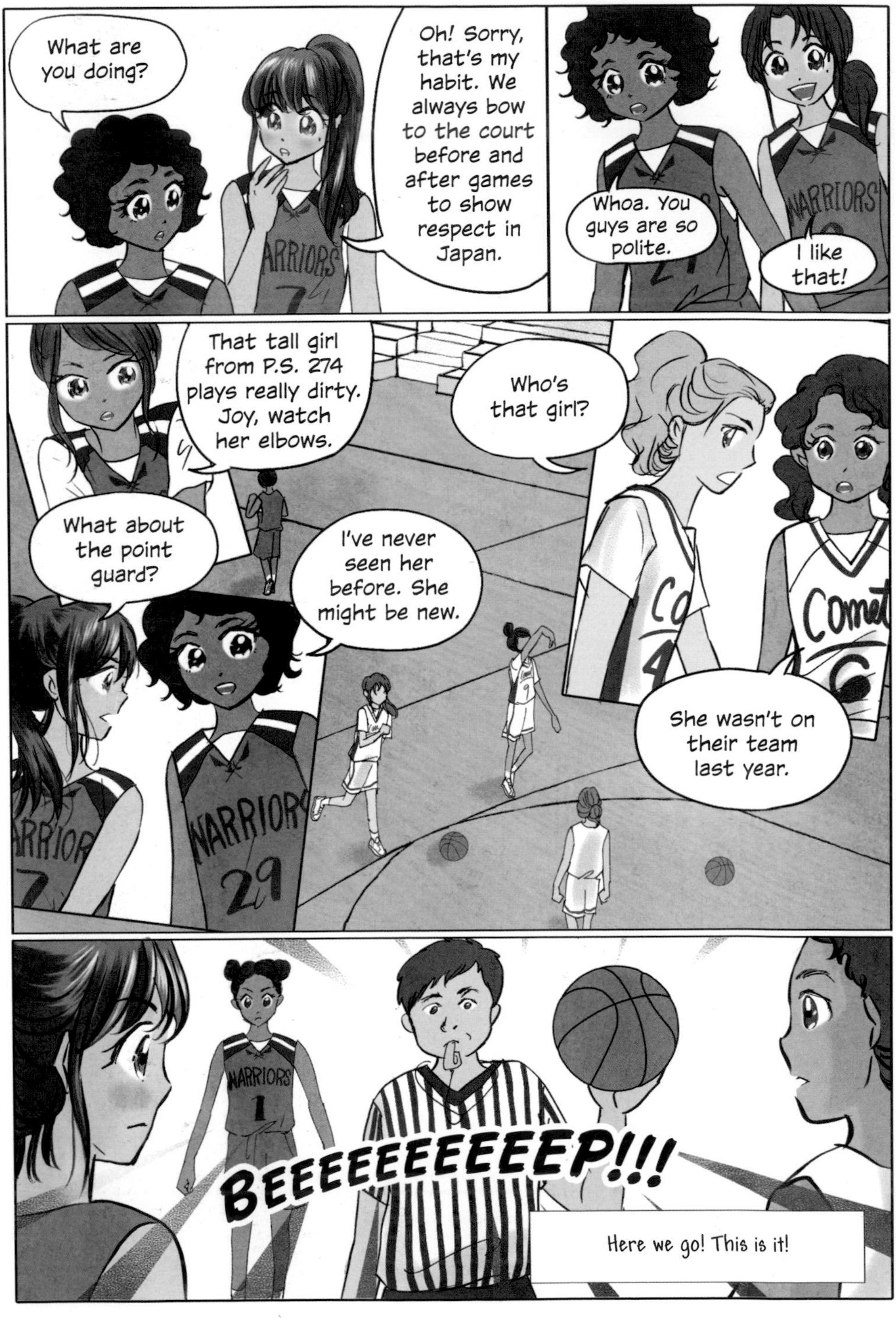
What are you doing?
Oh! Sorry, that's my habit. We always bow to the court before and after games to show respect in Japan.
Whoa. You guys are so polite.
I like that!
That tall girl from P.S. 274 plays really dirty. Joy, watch her elbows.
What about the point guard?
I've never seen her before. She might be new.
Who's that girl?
She wasn't on their team last year.
BEEEEEEEEEEEP!!!
Here we go! This is it!

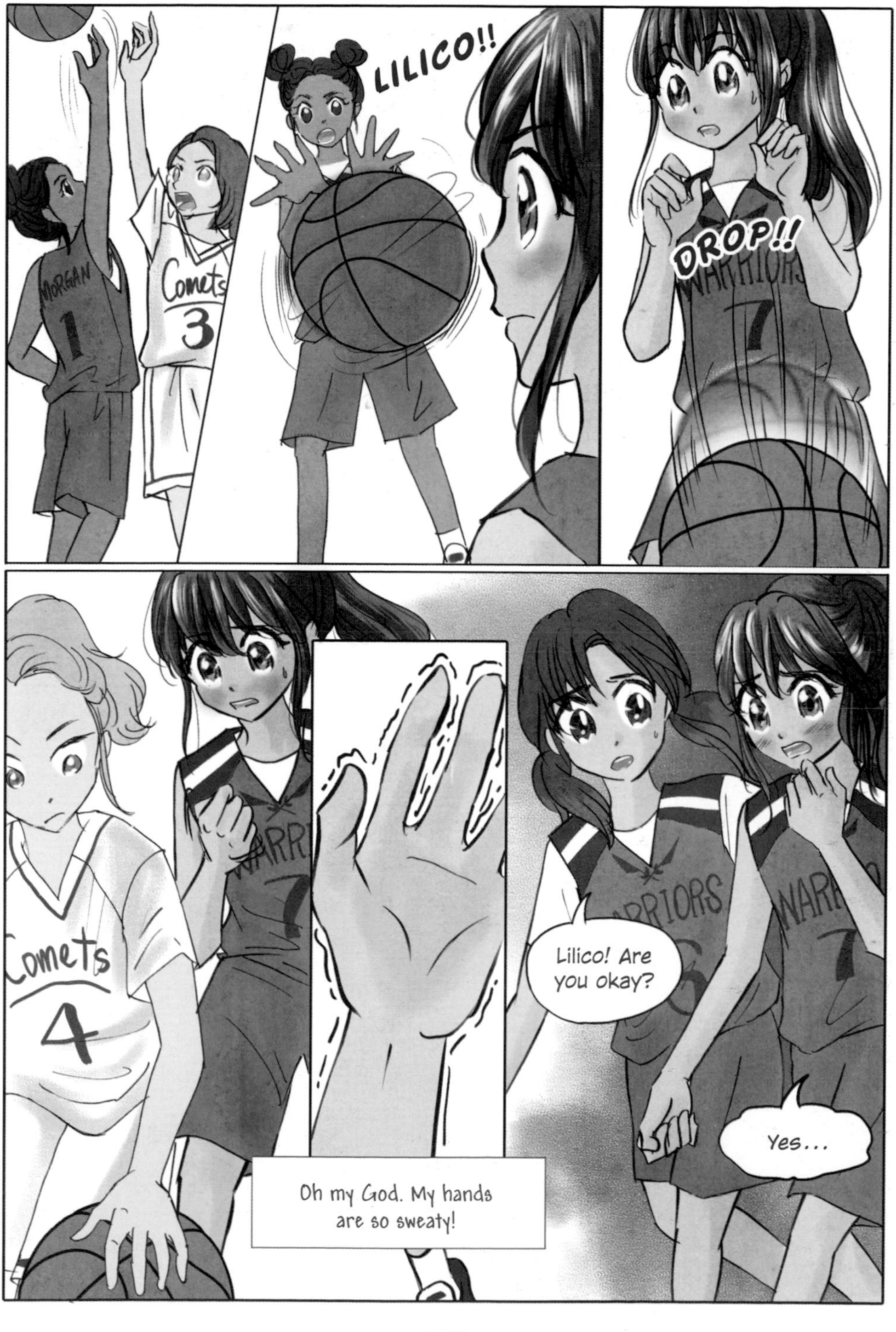
MORGAN
1
Comets
3
LILICO!!
DROP!!
WARRIORS
7
Comets
4
WARRI
7
Oh my God. My hands are so sweaty!
WARRIORS
Lilico! Are you okay?
WARRI
7
Yes...

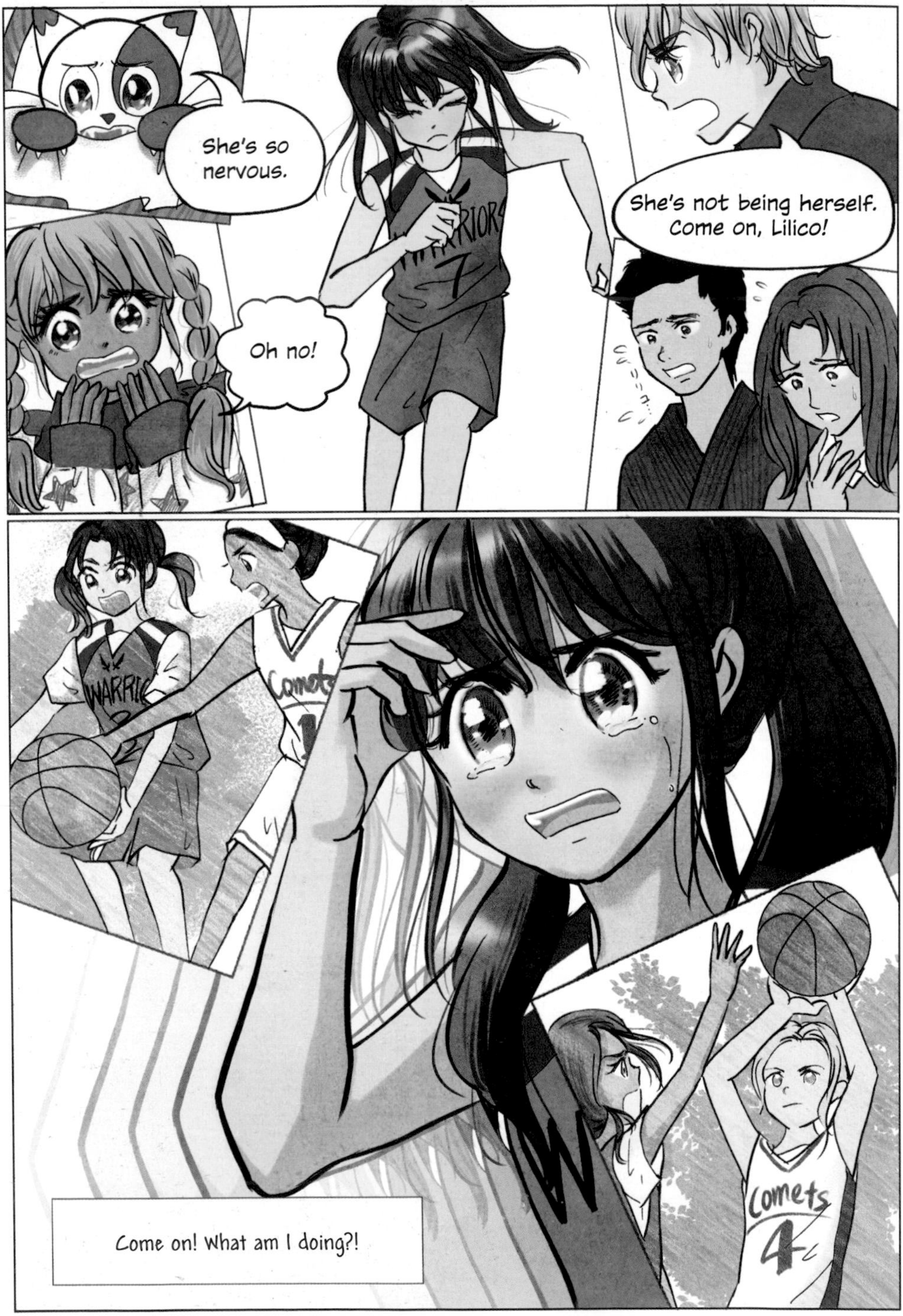
She's so nervous.
Oh no!
She's not being herself. Come on, Lilico!
WARRIORS
7
WARRIO
Comets
Come on! What am I doing?!
Comets
4

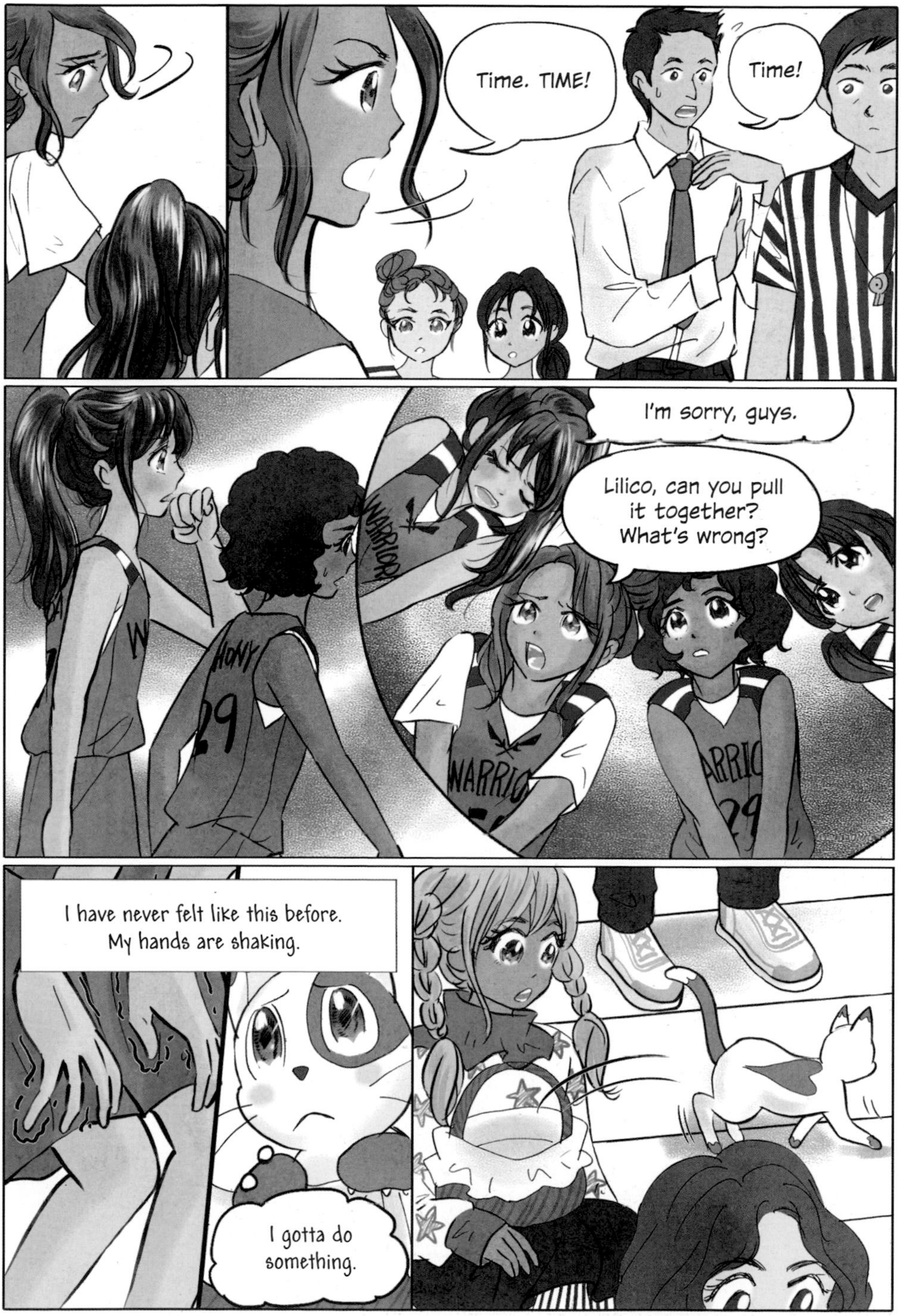
Time. TIME!
Time!
I'm sorry, guys.
Lilico, can you pull it together? What's wrong?
I have never felt like this before. My hands are shaking.
I gotta do something.

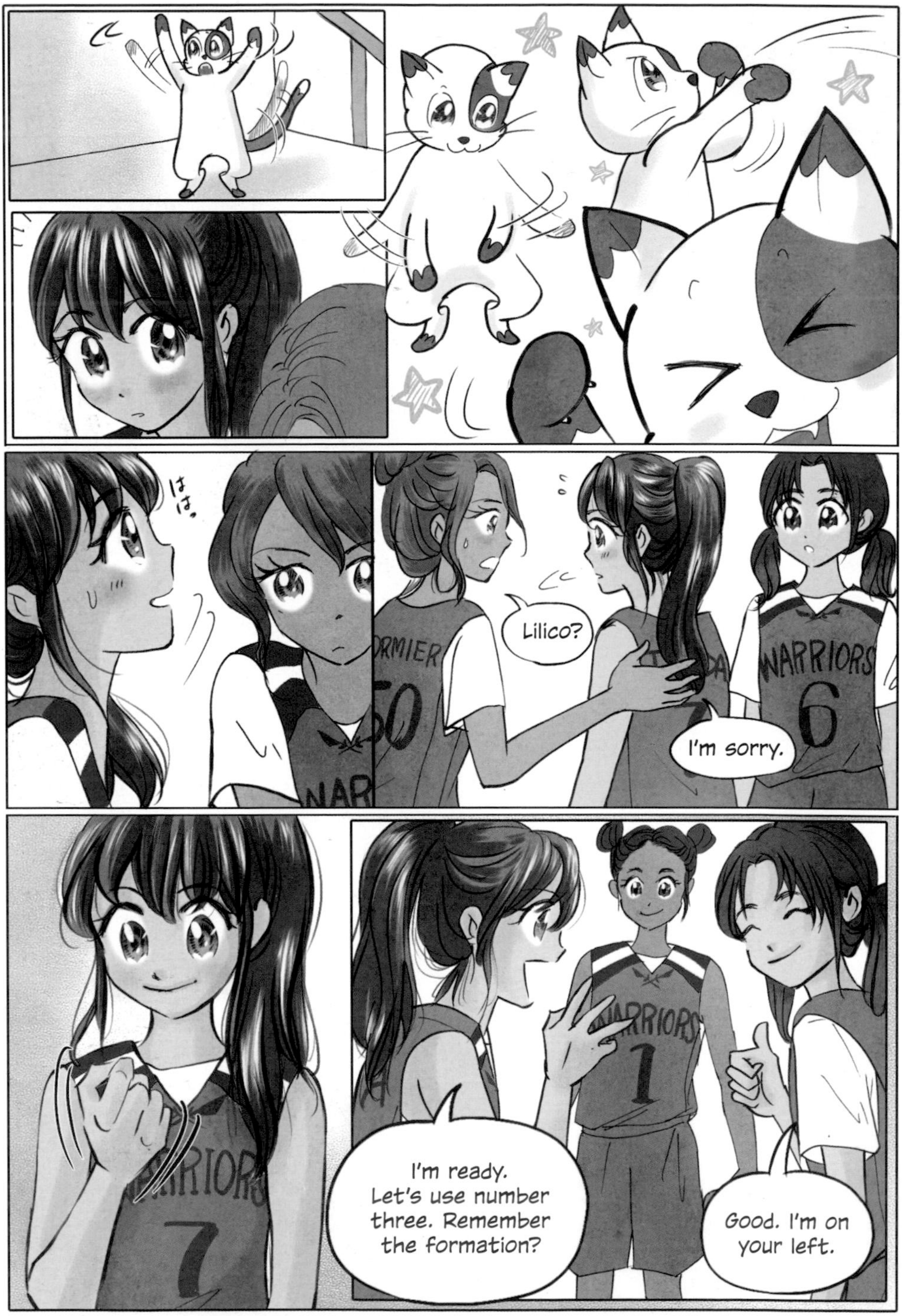
はは。
Lilico?
I'm sorry.
I'm ready. Let's use number three. Remember the formation?
Good. I'm on your left.

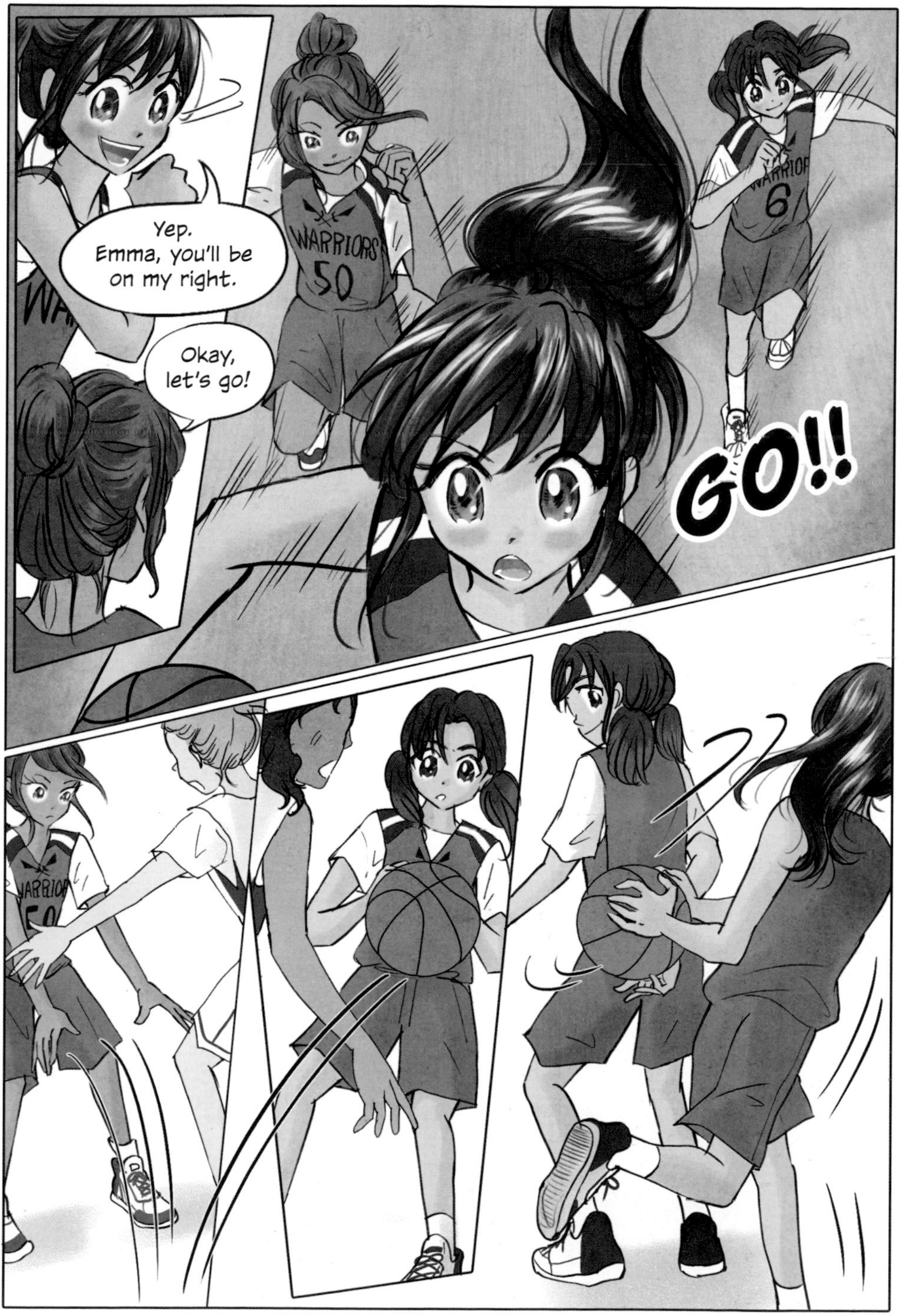
WARRIORS
50
WARRIOR
6
Yep. Emma, you'll be on my right.
Okay, let's go!
GO!!
WARRIORS
50

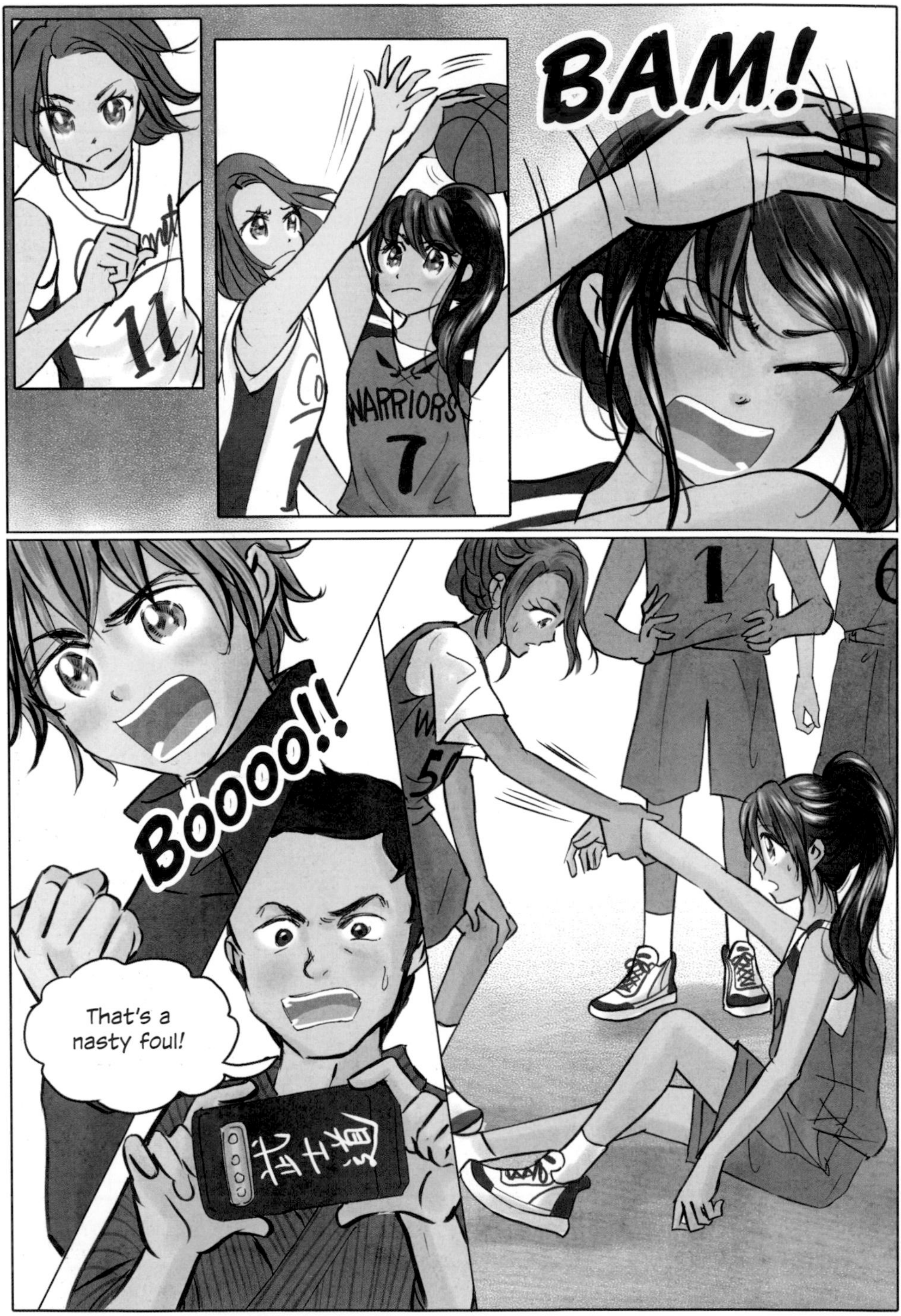
BAM!
WARRIORS
7
11
Boooo!!
That's a nasty foul!

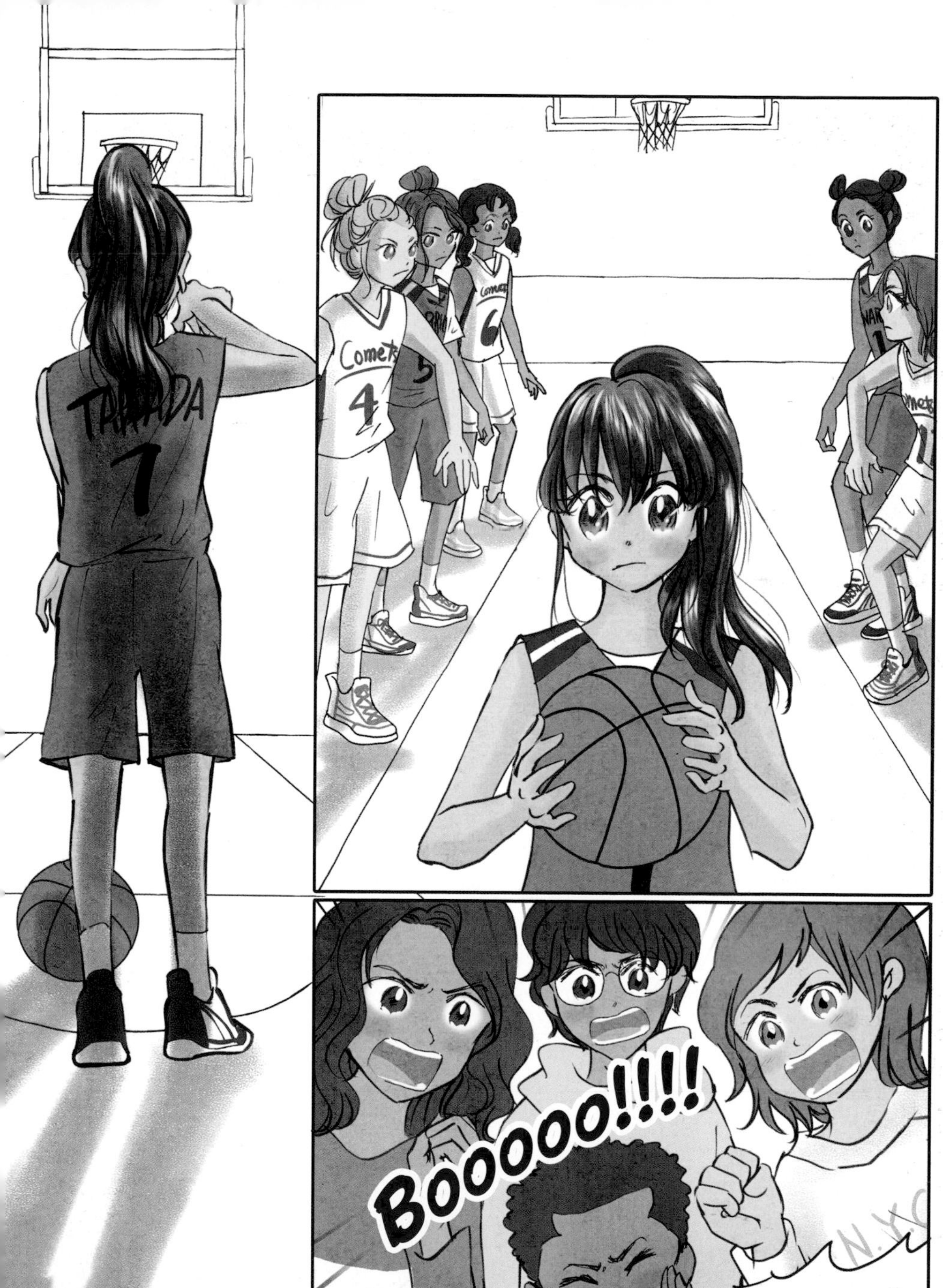
Booooo!!!!
Miss! Miss!
Miss! Miss!!!!

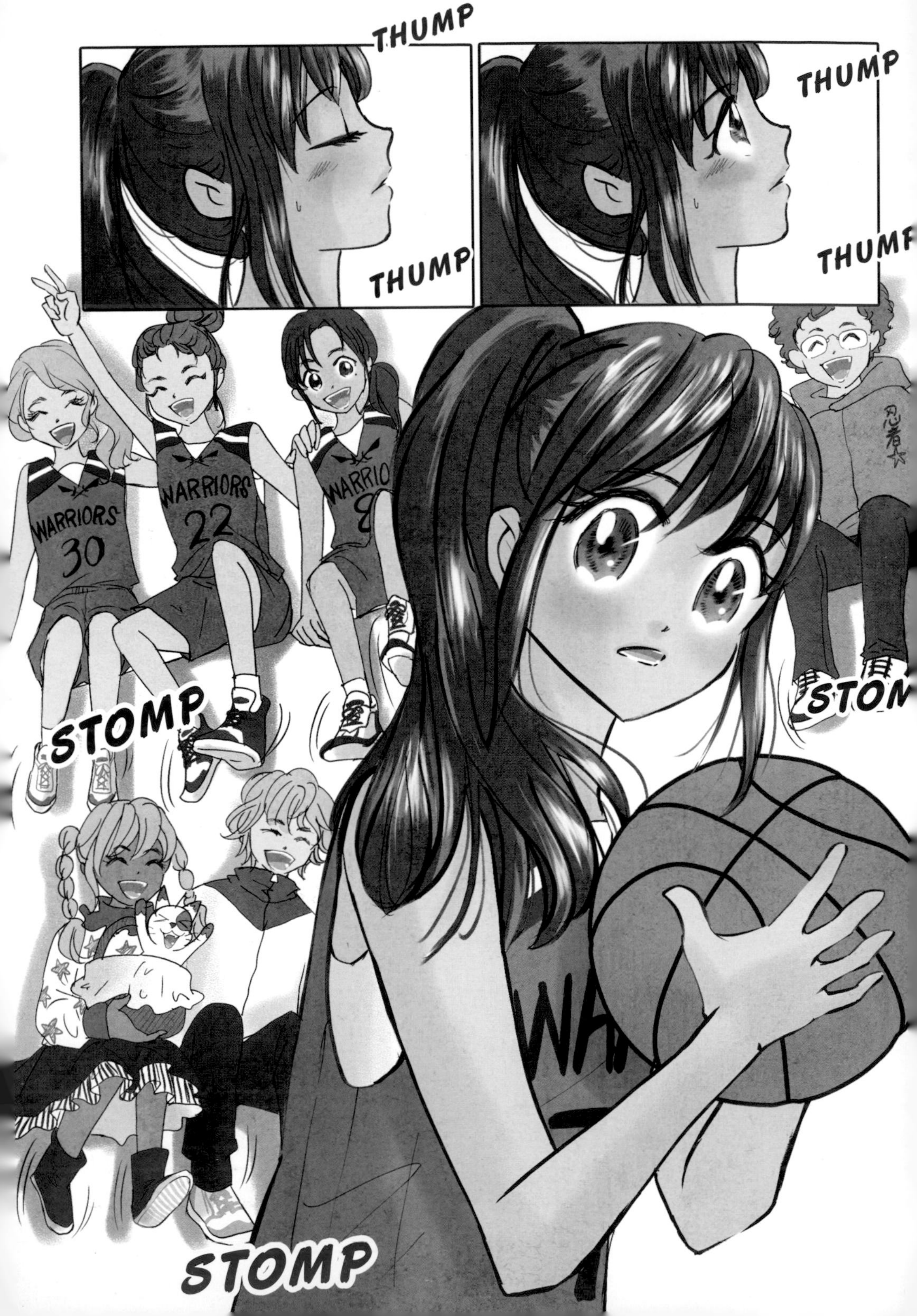
THUMP
THUMP
THUMP
WARRIORS
30
WARRIORS
22
STOMP
STOMP

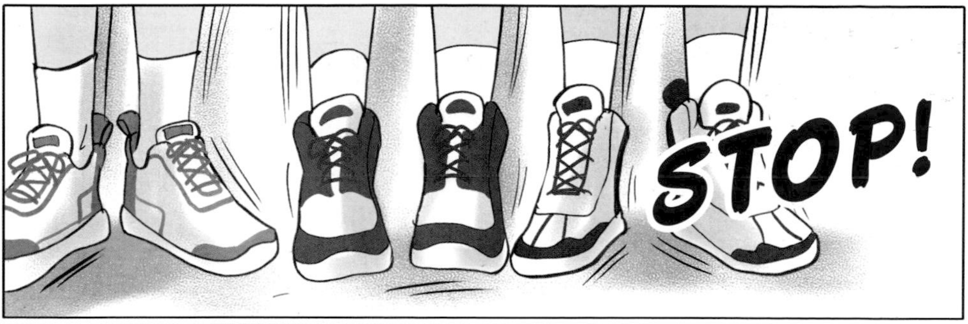
STOP!

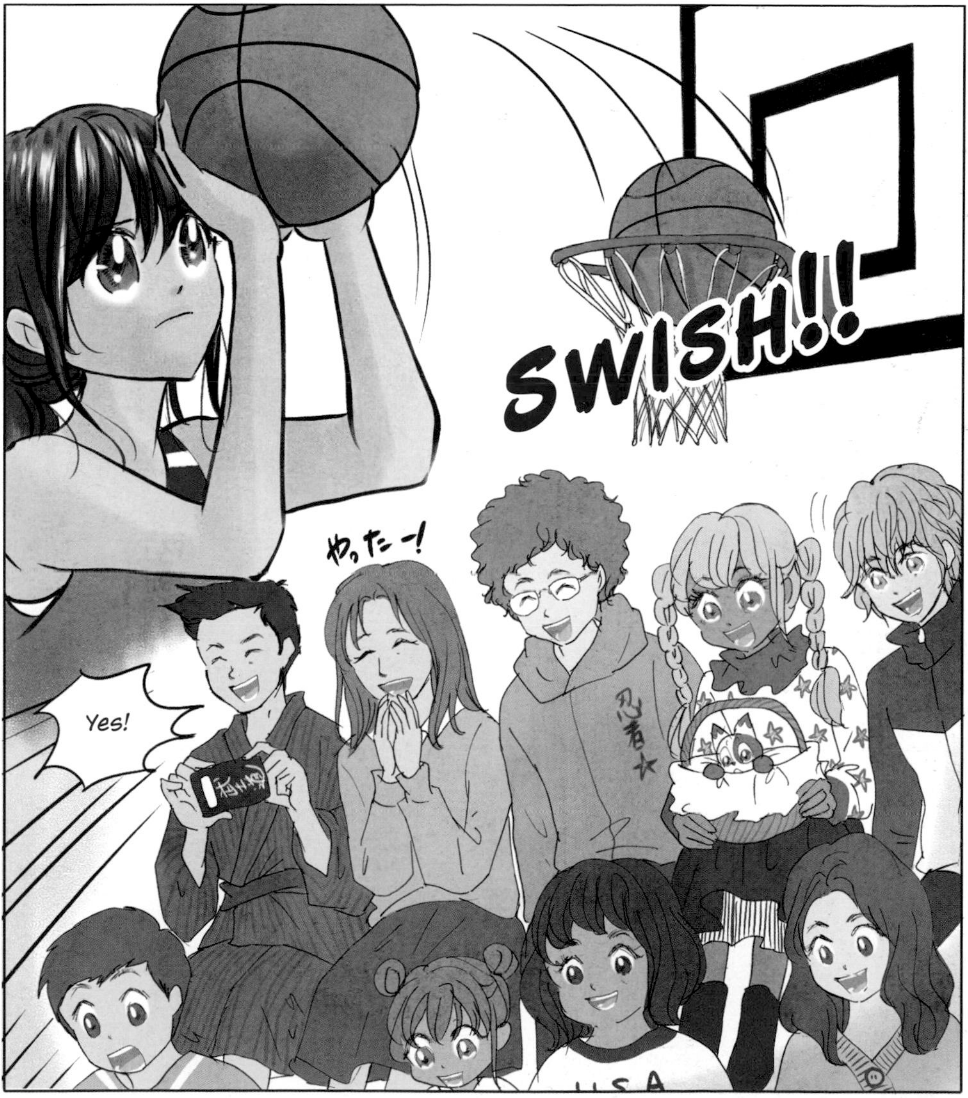
SWISH!!
やったー!
Yes!

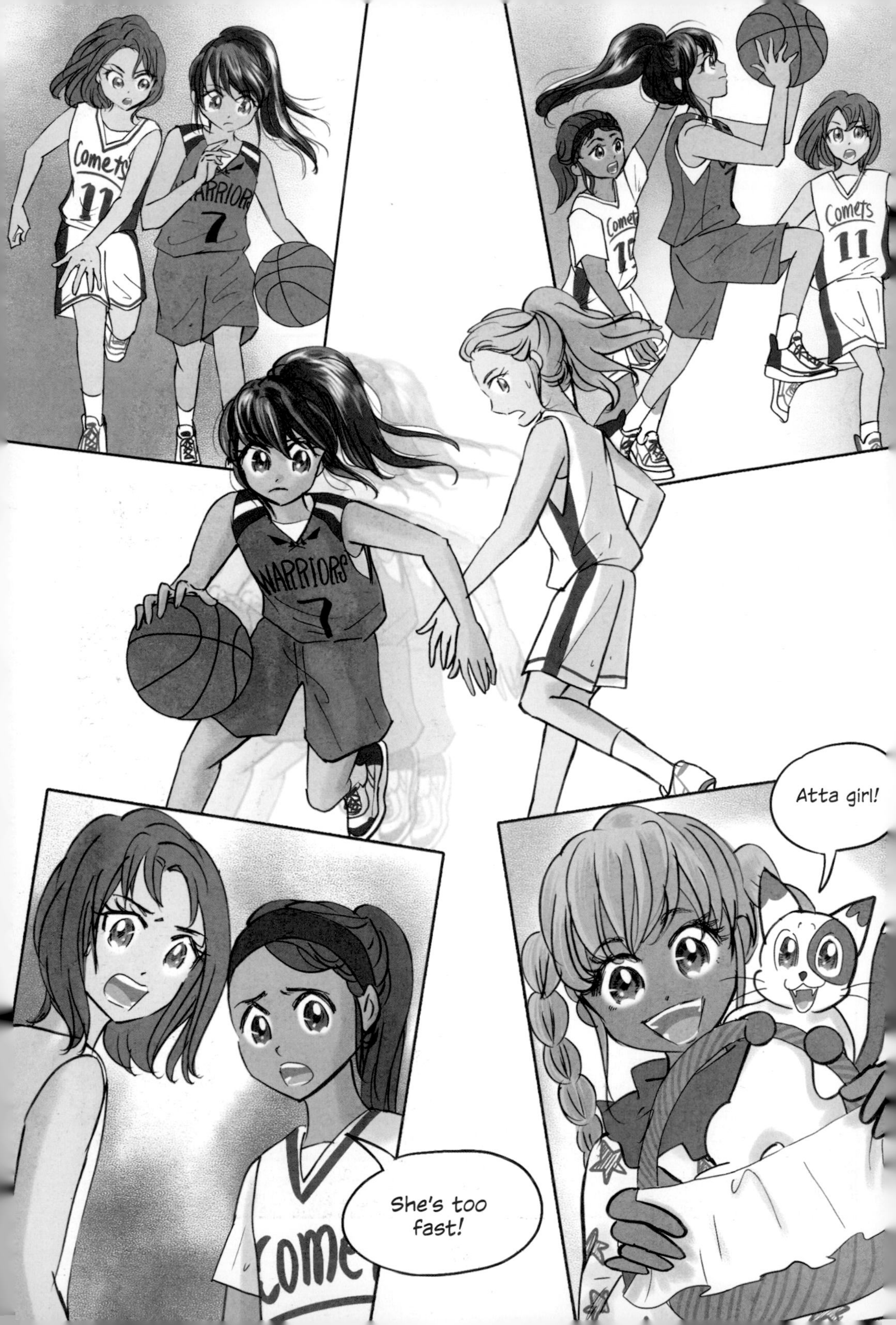
She's too fast!
Atta girl!

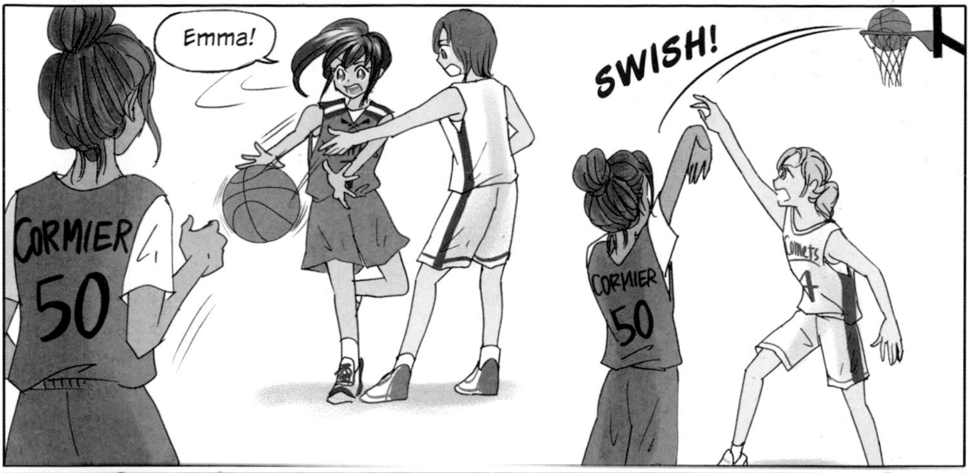
Emma!
SWISH!
CORMIER
50
CORMIER
50
Comets

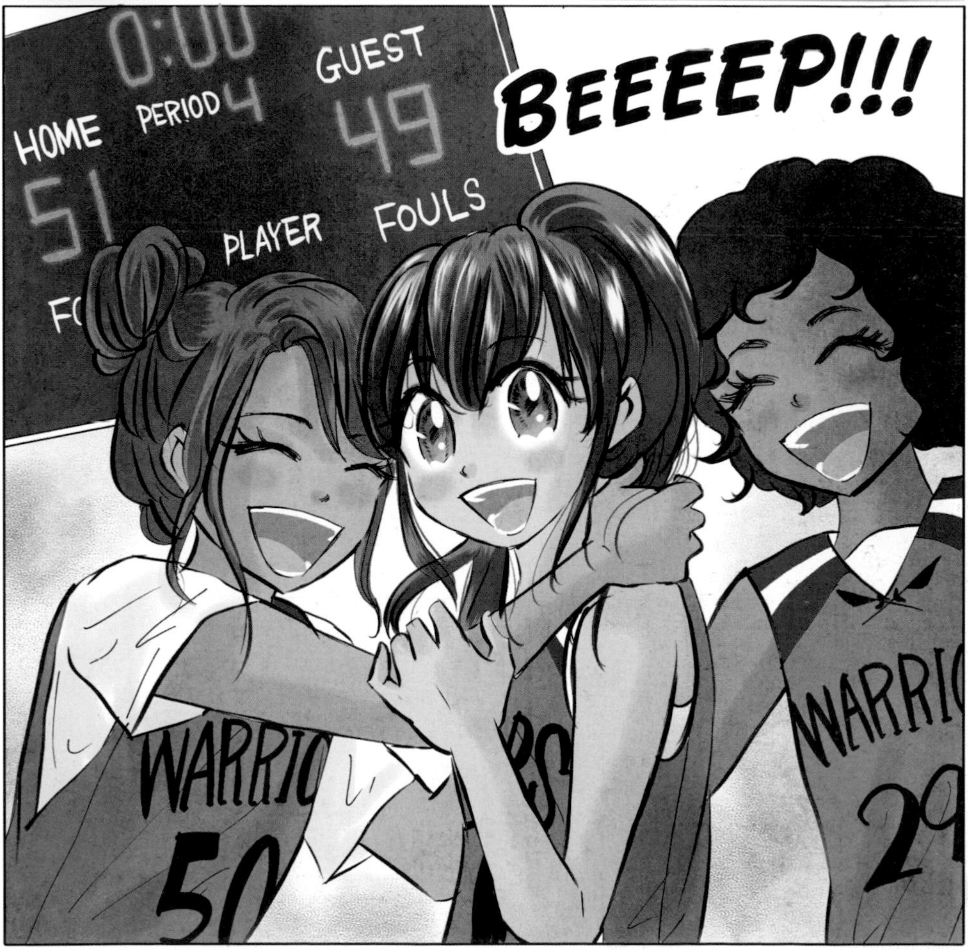
0:00
GUEST
HOME PERIOD 4
49
51
PLAYER FOULS
BEEEEP!!!
WARRIO
50
WARRIO
29

CHAPTER 6

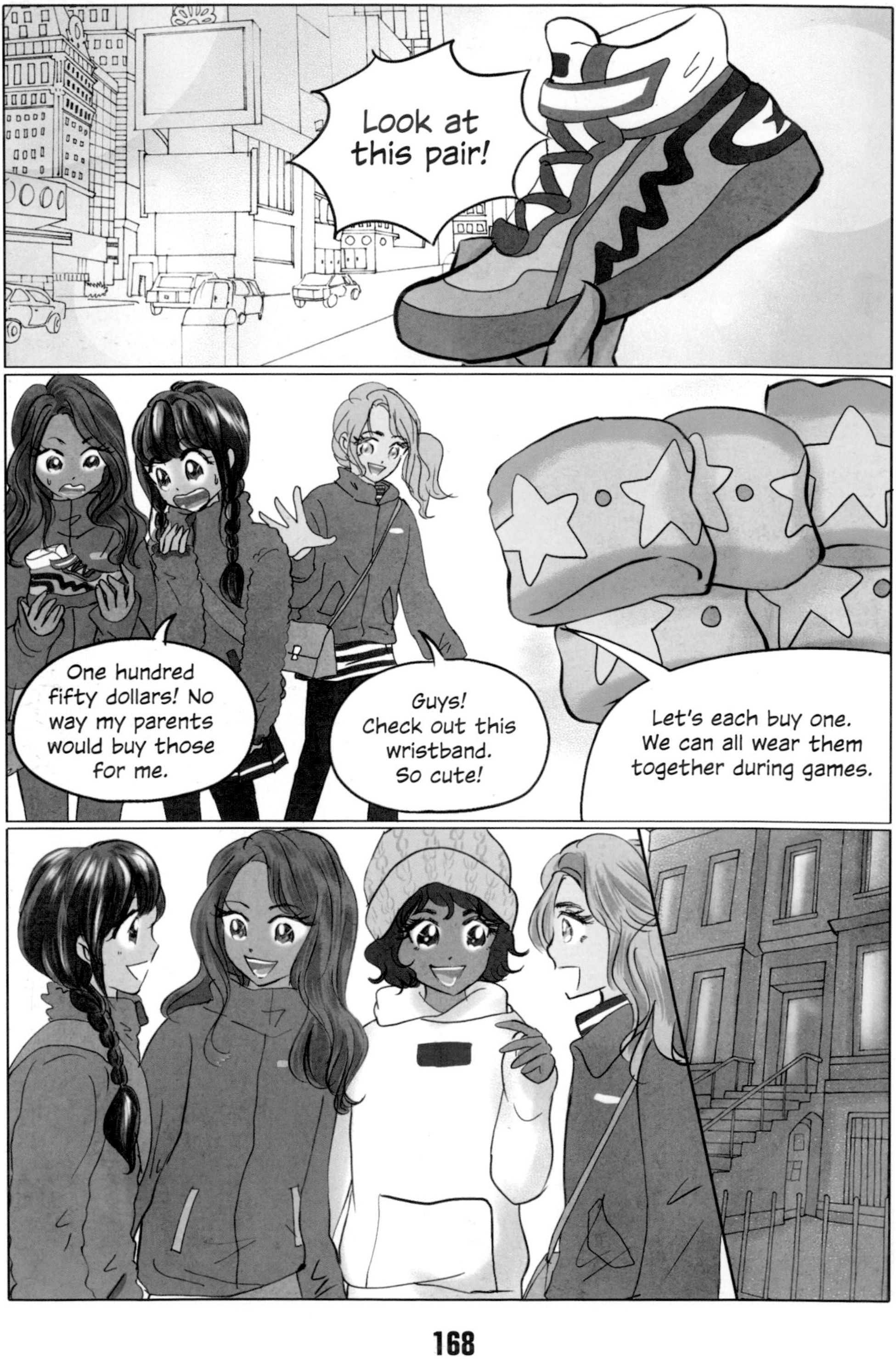
Look at this pair!
One hundred fifty dollars! No way my parents would buy those for me.
Guys! Check out this wristband. So cute!
Let's each buy one. We can all wear them together during games.

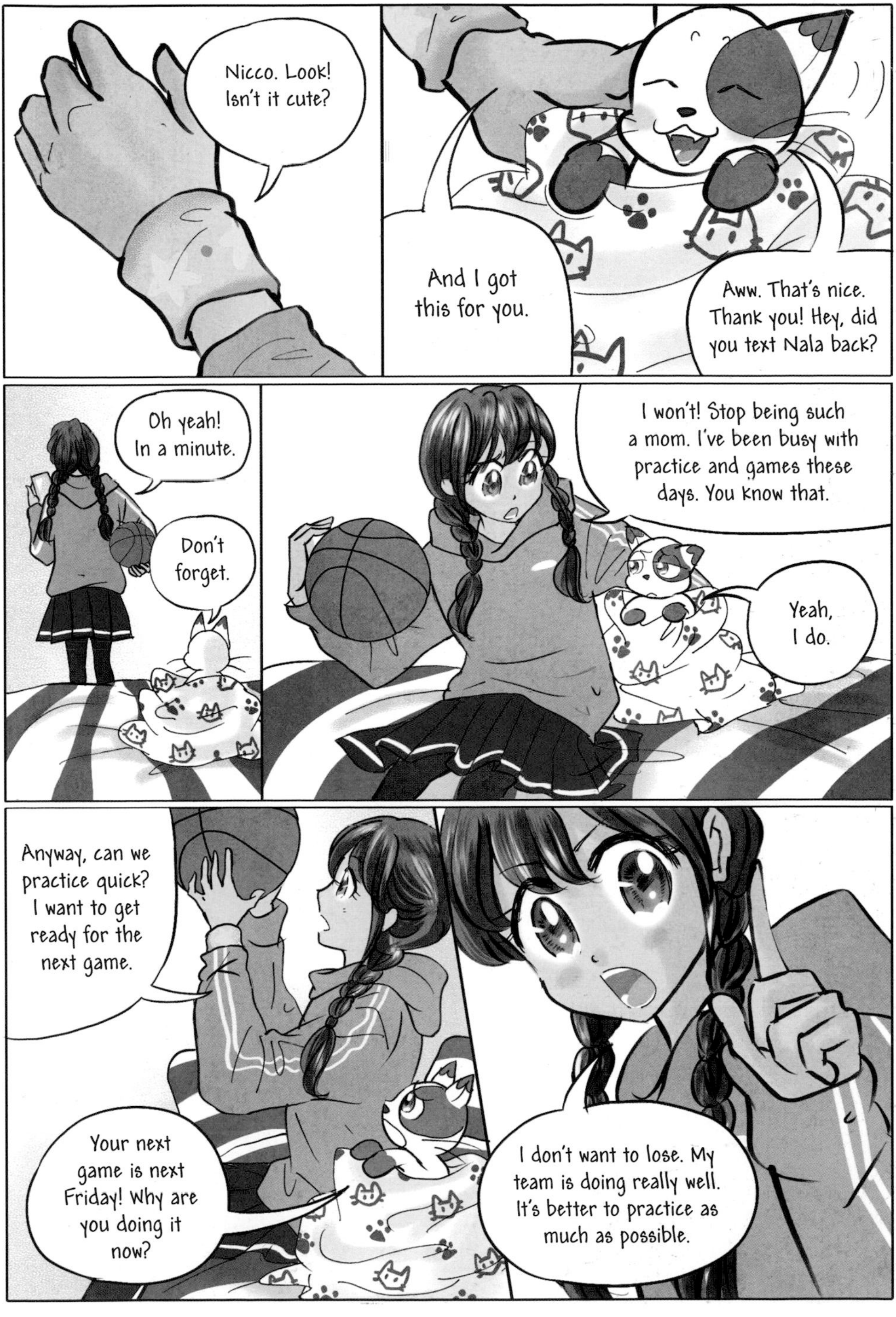
Nicco. Look! Isn't it cute?
And I got this for you.
Aww. That's nice. Thank you! Hey, did you text Nala back?
Oh yeah! In a minute.
Don't forget.
I won't! Stop being such a mom. I've been busy with practice and games these days. You know that.
Yeah, I do.
Anyway, can we practice quick? I want to get ready for the next game.
Your next game is next Friday! Why are you doing it now?
I don't want to lose. My team is doing really well. It's better to practice as much as possible.

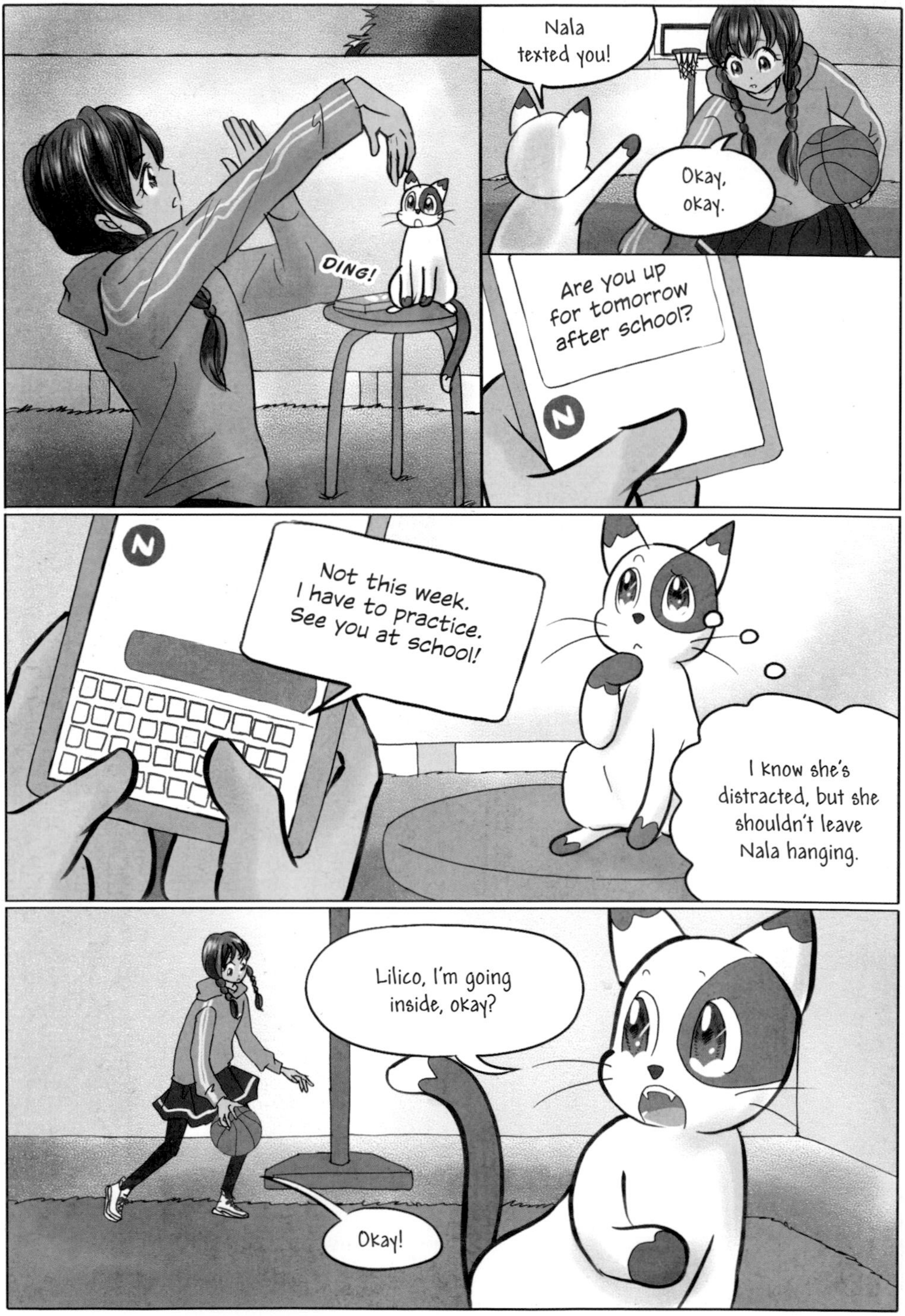
DING!
Nala texted you!
Okay, okay.
Are you up for tomorrow after school?
N
N
Not this week. I have to practice. See you at school!
I know she's distracted, but she shouldn't leave Nala hanging.
Lilico, I'm going inside, okay?
Okay!

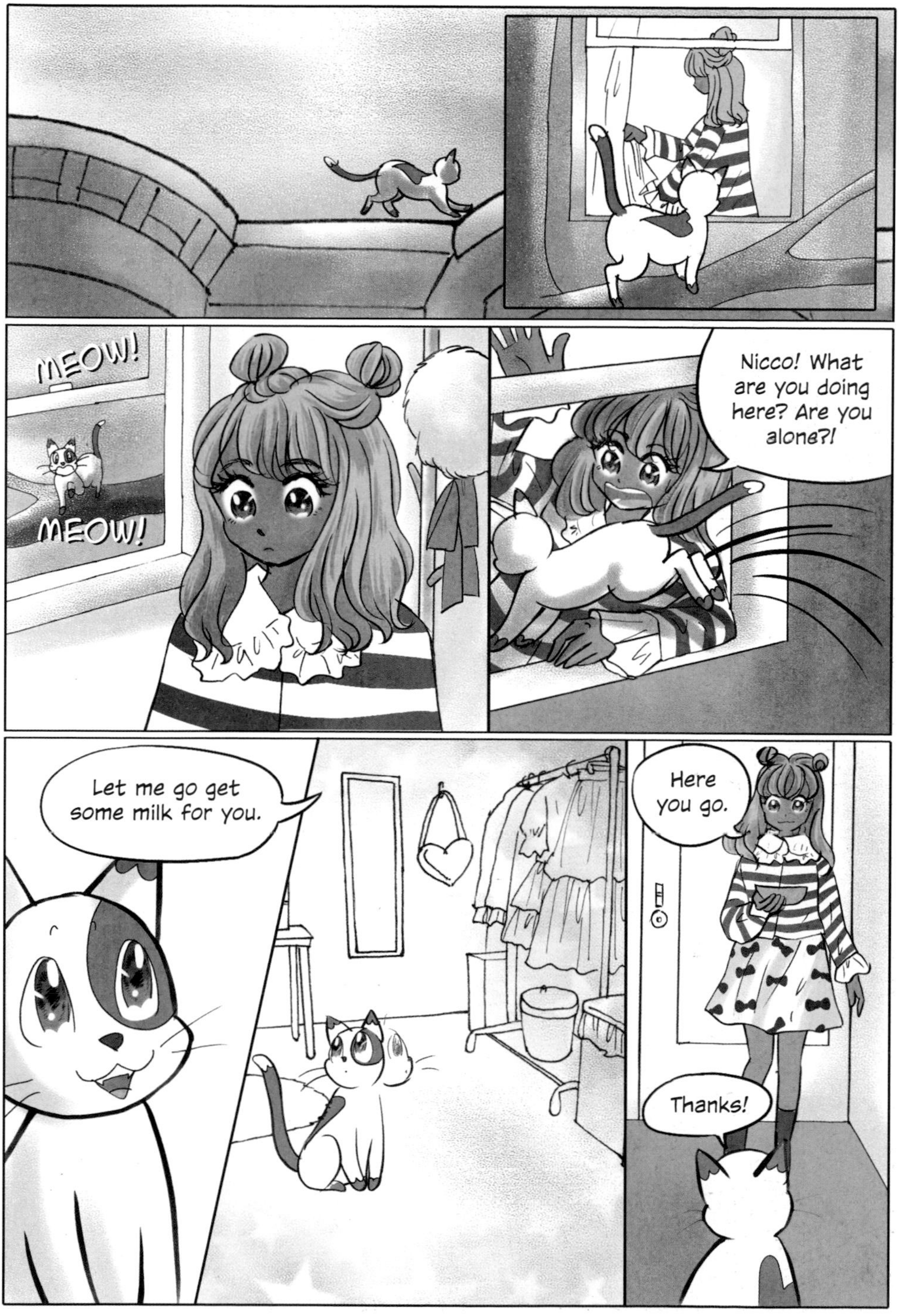
MEOW!
MEOW!
Nicco! What are you doing here? Are you alone?!
Let me go get some milk for you.
Here you go.
Thanks!

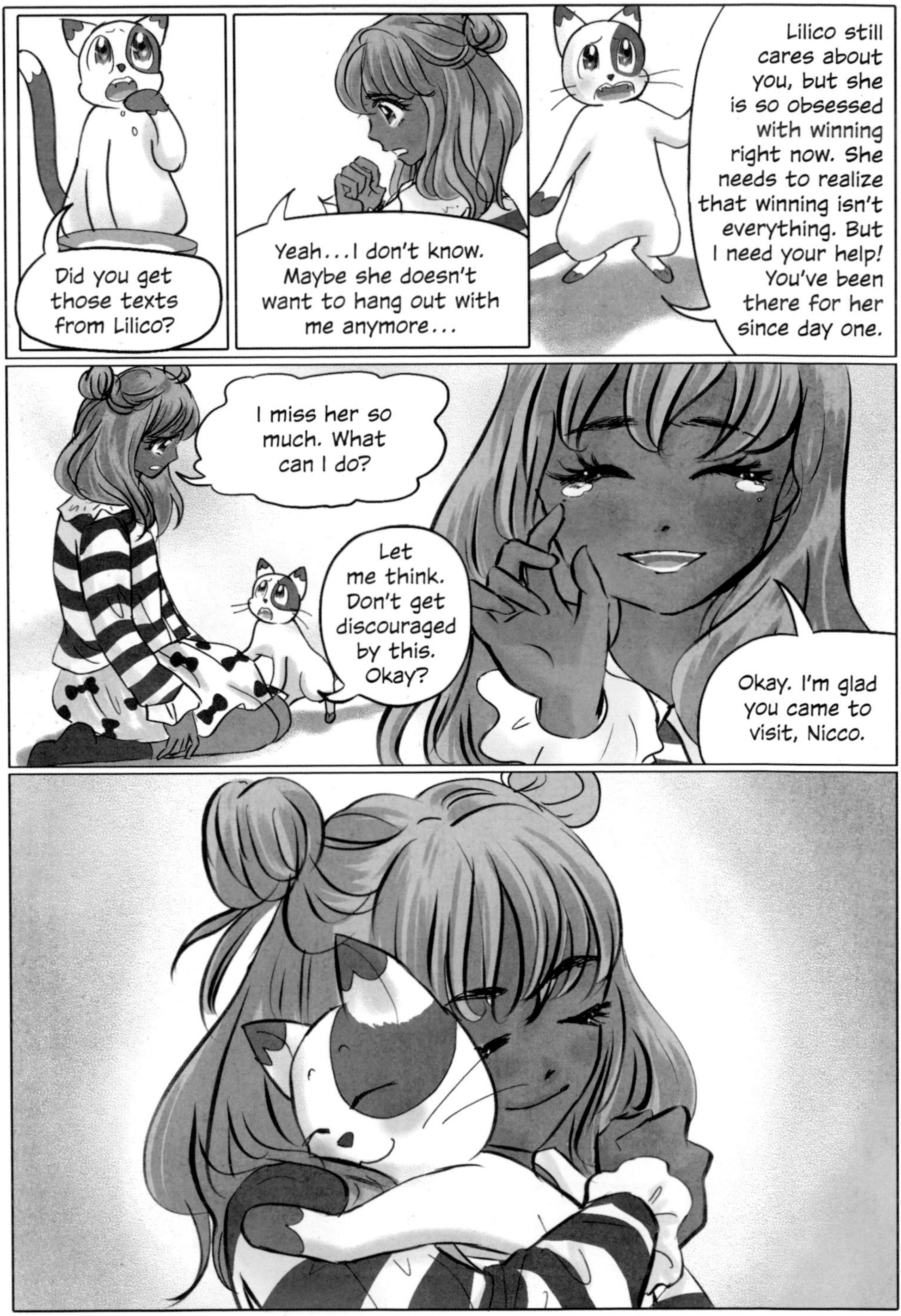
Did you get those texts from Lilico?
Yeah... I don't know. Maybe she doesn't want to hang out with me anymore...
Lilico still cares about you, but she is so obsessed with winning right now. She needs to realize that winning isn't everything. But I need your help! You've been there for her since day one.
I miss her so much. What can I do?
Let me think. Don't get discouraged by this. Okay?
Okay. I'm glad you came to visit, Nicco.

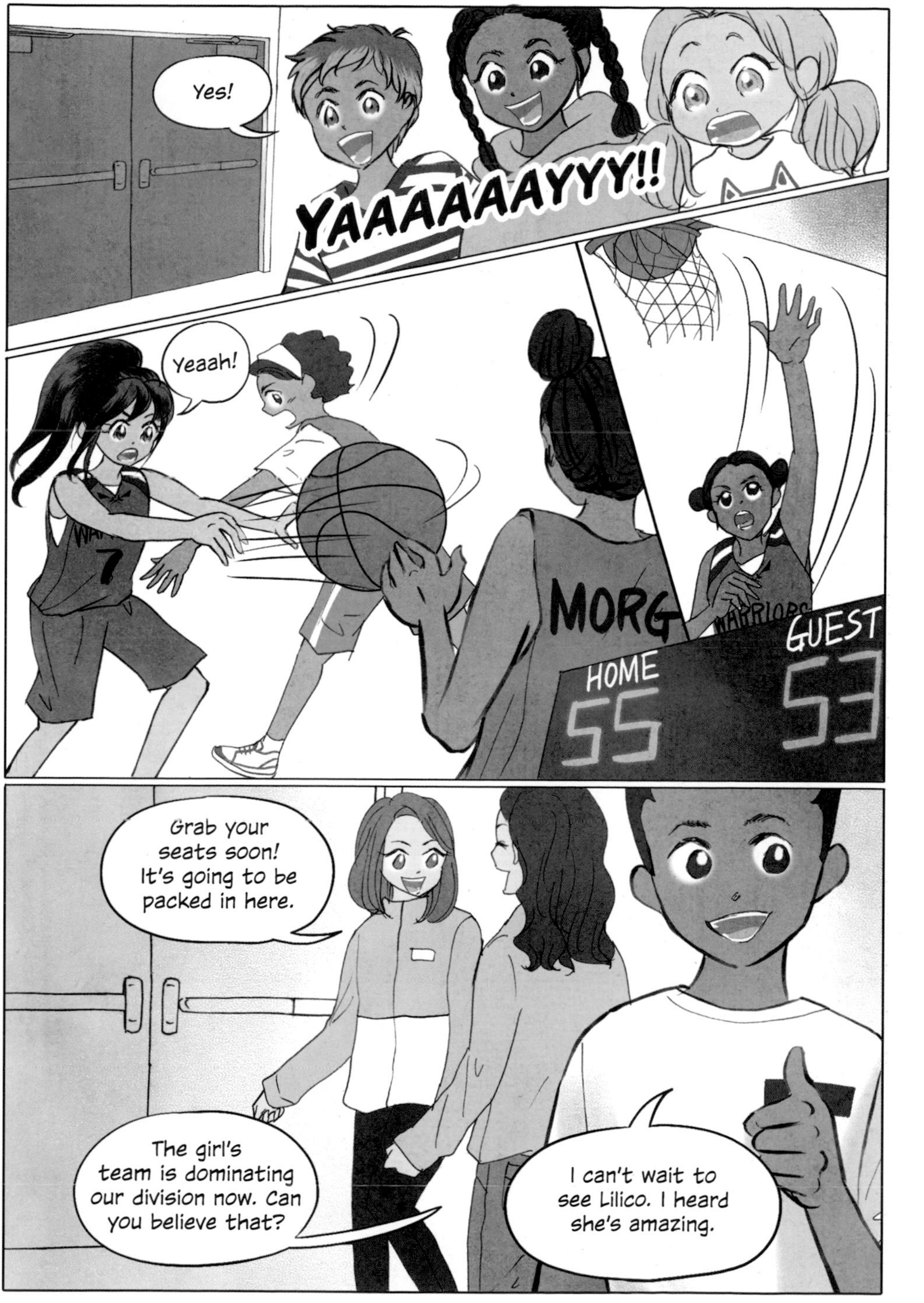
Yes!
YAAAAAAYYY!!
Yeaah!
MORG
GUEST
HOME
55
53
Grab your seats soon! It's going to be packed in here.
The girl's team is dominating our division now. Can you believe that?
I can't wait to see Lilico. I heard she's amazing.

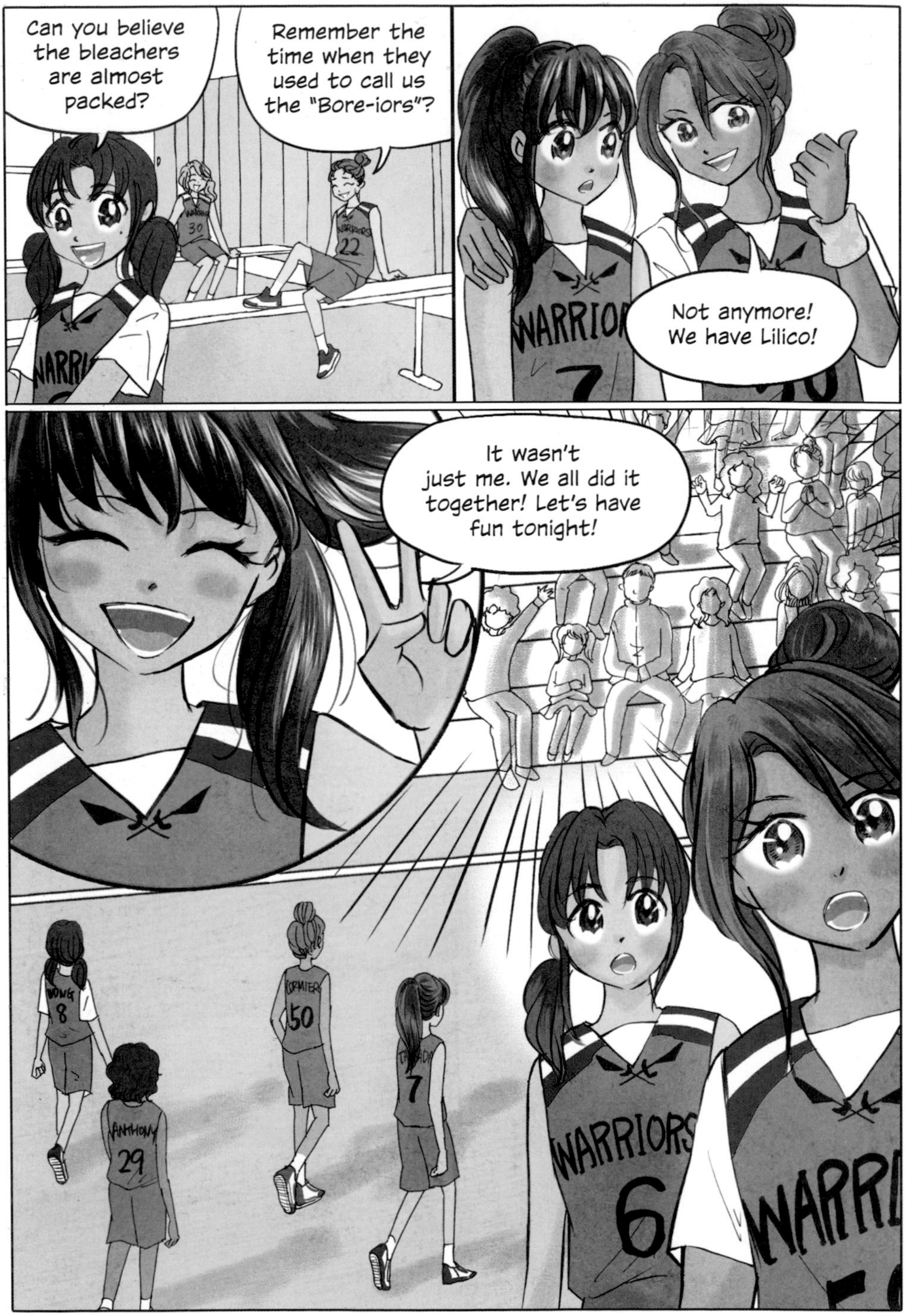
Can you believe the bleachers are almost packed?
Remember the time when they used to call us the "Bore-iors"?
Not anymore! We have Lilico!
It wasn't just me. We all did it together! Let's have fun tonight!

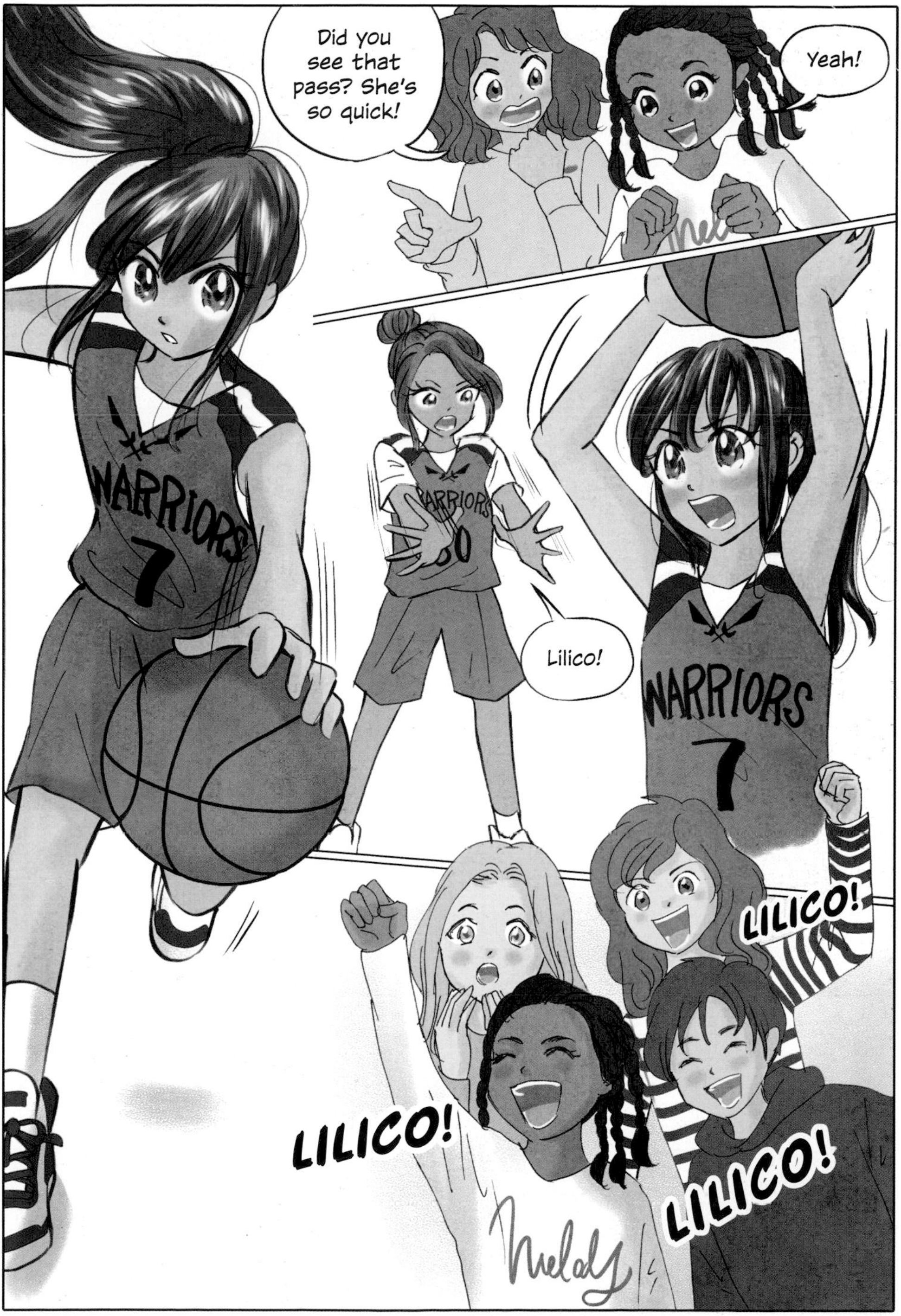
Did you see that pass? She's so quick!
Yeah!
Lilico!
LILICO!
LILICO!
LILICO!

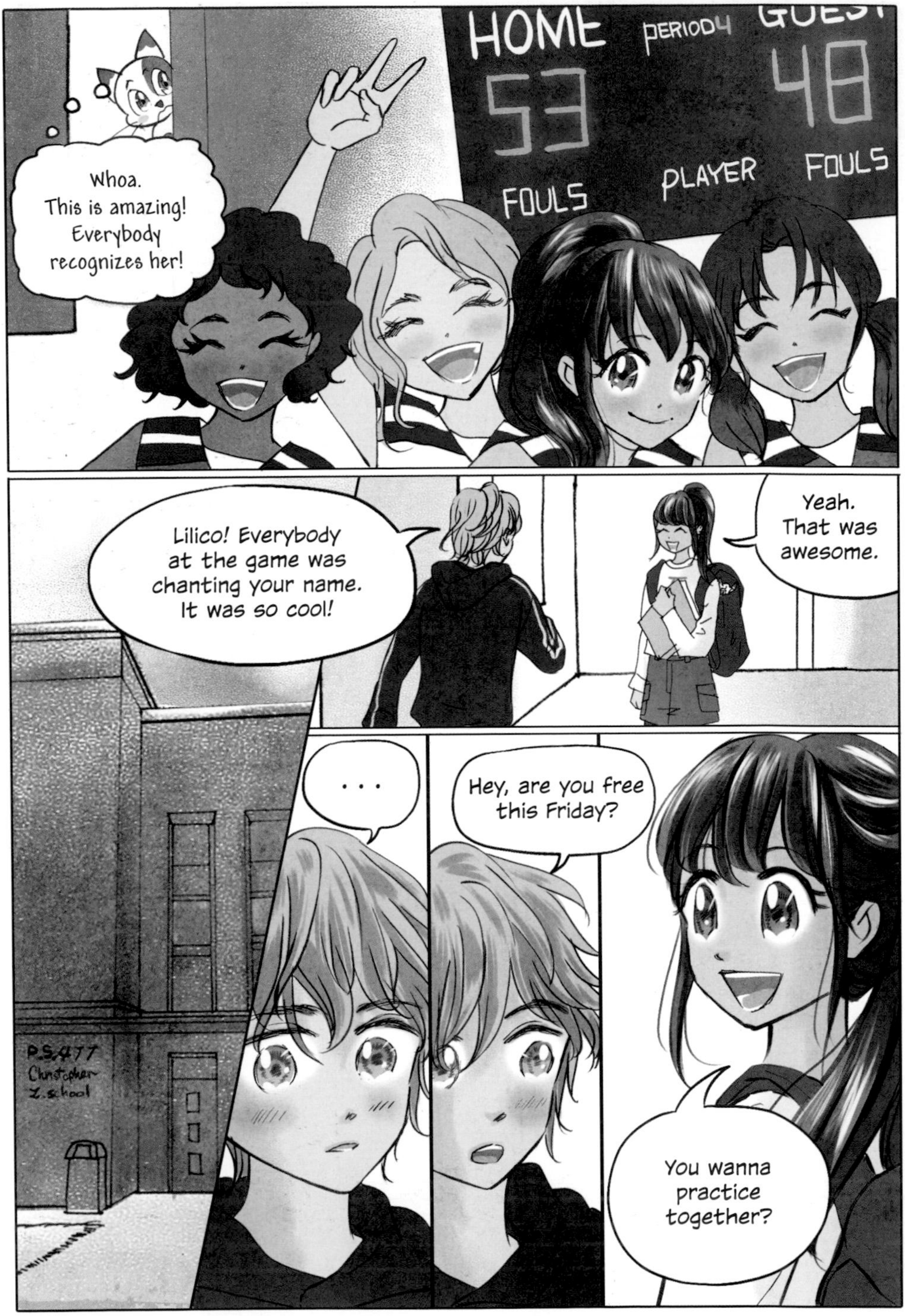
HOME
PERIOD 4
GUEST
53
48
PLAYER
FOULS
FOULS
Whoa. This is amazing! Everybody recognizes her!
Lilico! Everybody at the game was chanting your name. It was so cool!
Yeah. That was awesome.
P.S. 477 Christopher Z. school
. . .
Hey, are you free this Friday?
You wanna practice together?

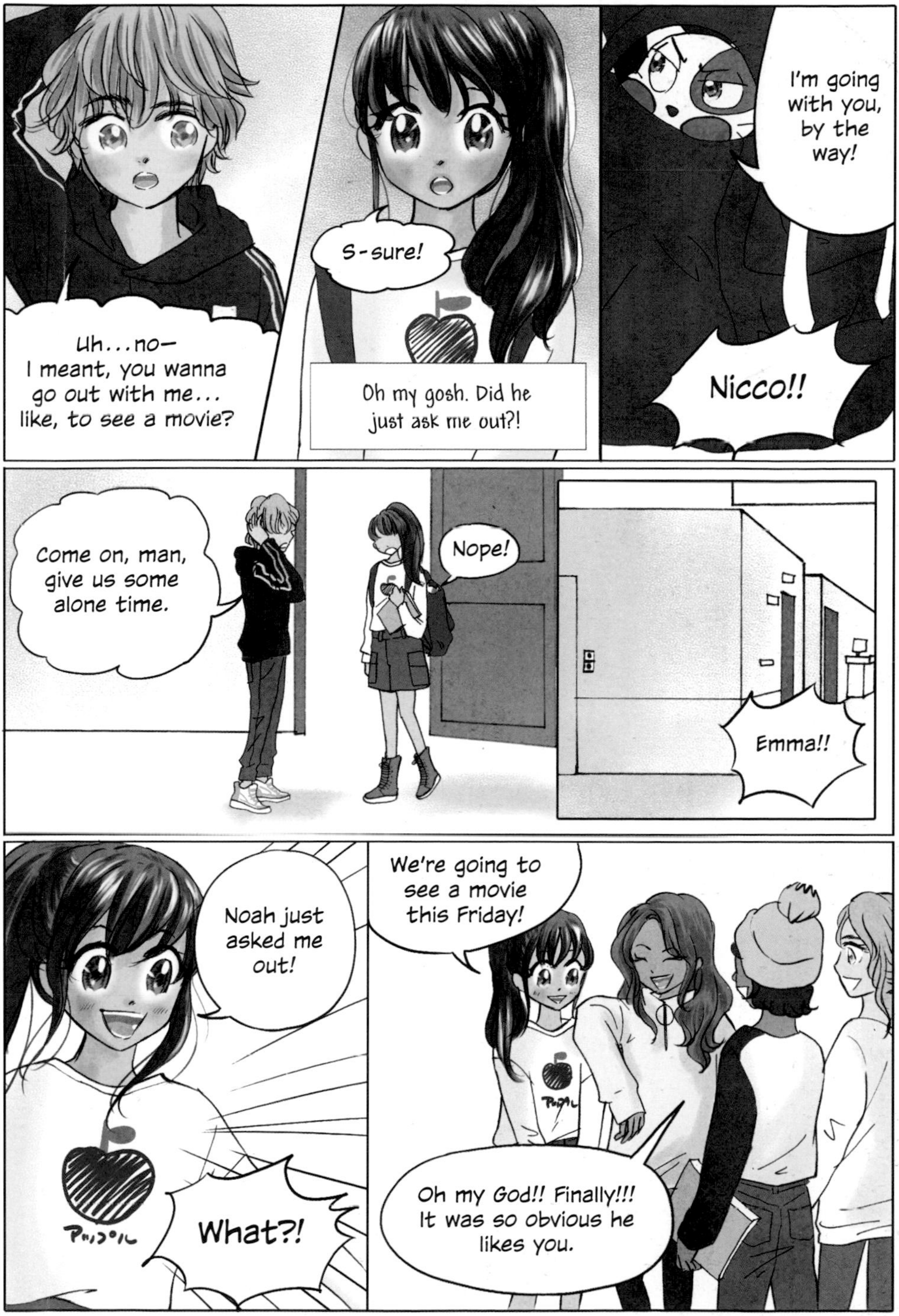
Uh...no—
I meant, you wanna go out with me... like, to see a movie?
S-sure!
Oh my gosh. Did he just ask me out?!
I'm going with you, by the way!
Nicco!!
Come on, man, give us some alone time.
Nope!
Emma!!
Noah just asked me out!
What?!
We're going to see a movie this Friday!
Oh my God!! Finally!!! It was so obvious he likes you.

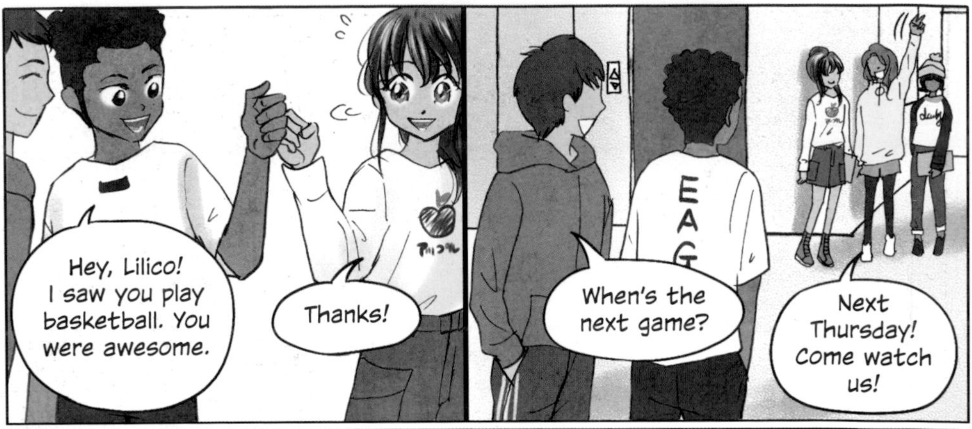
Hey, Lilico! I saw you play basketball. You were awesome.
Thanks!
When's the next game?
Next Thursday! Come watch us!

Wow, everybody knows me! I can't believe I was the new girl only a couple of months ago.

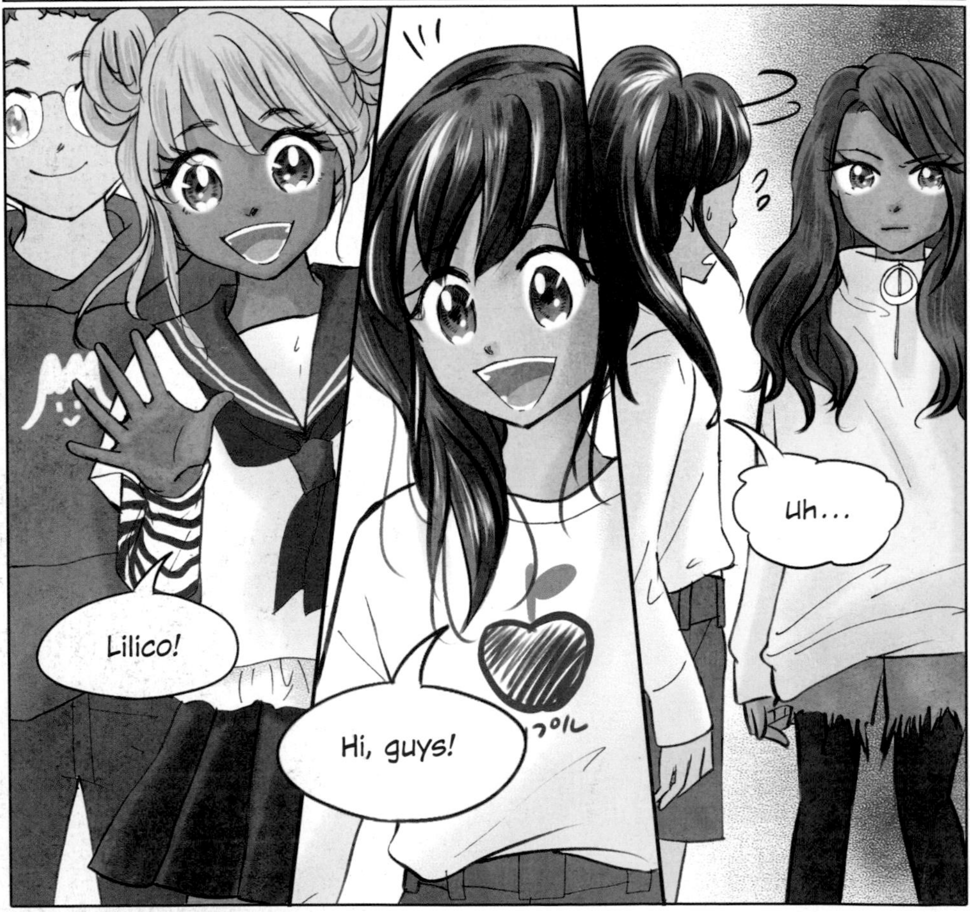
Lilico!
Hi, guys!
Uh...

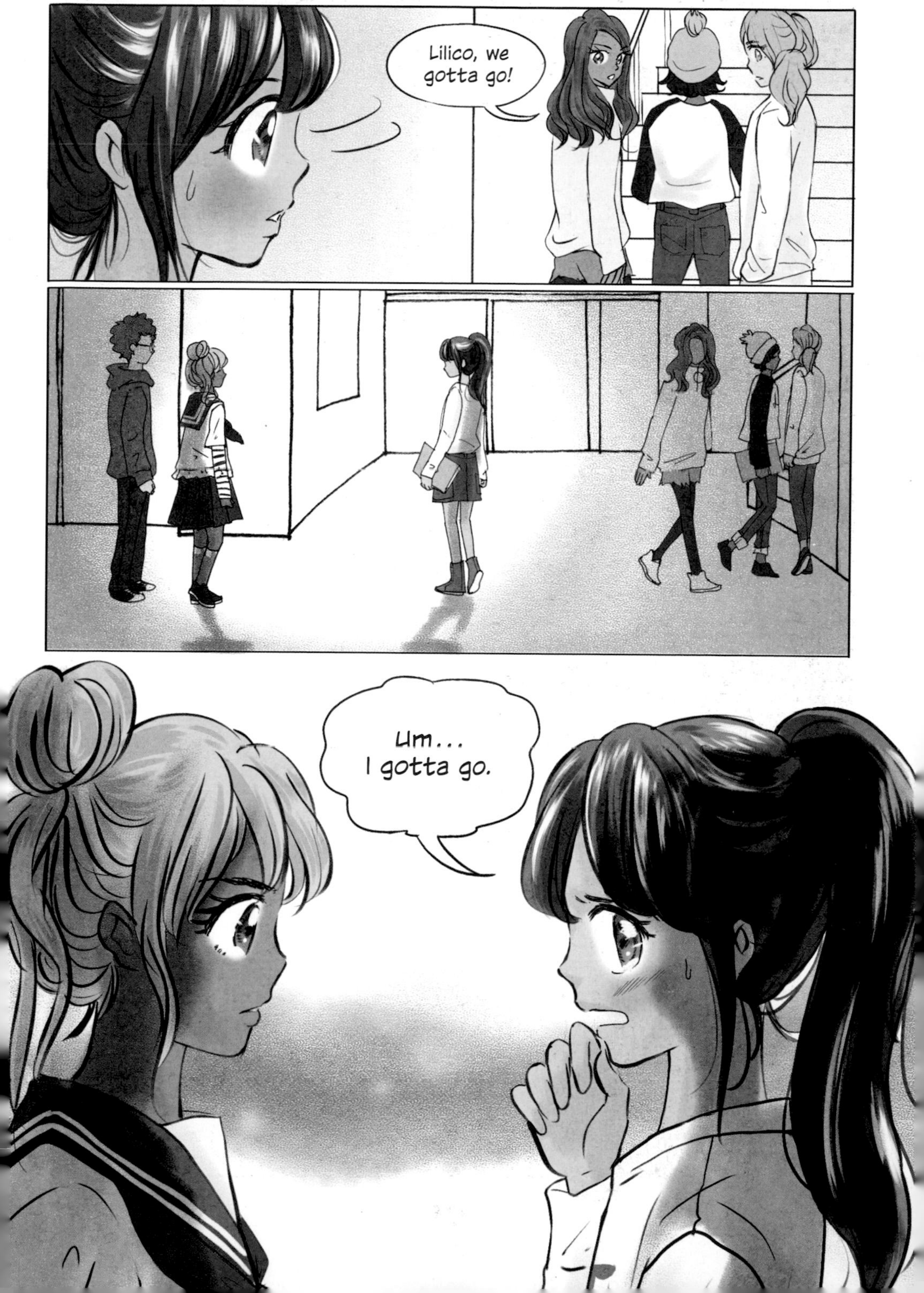
Lilico, we gotta go!
Um... I gotta go.

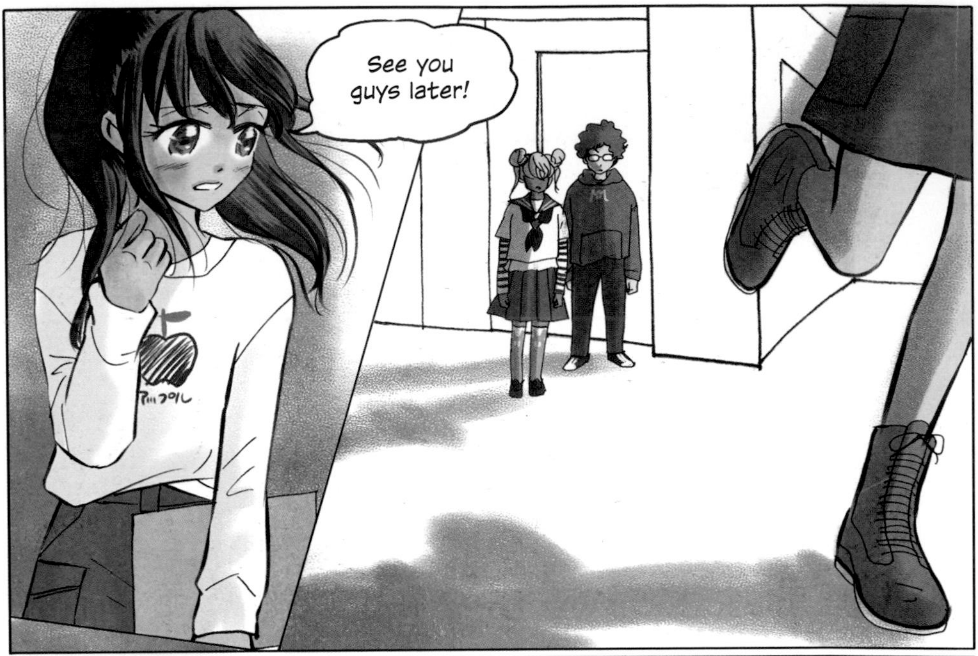
See you guys later!

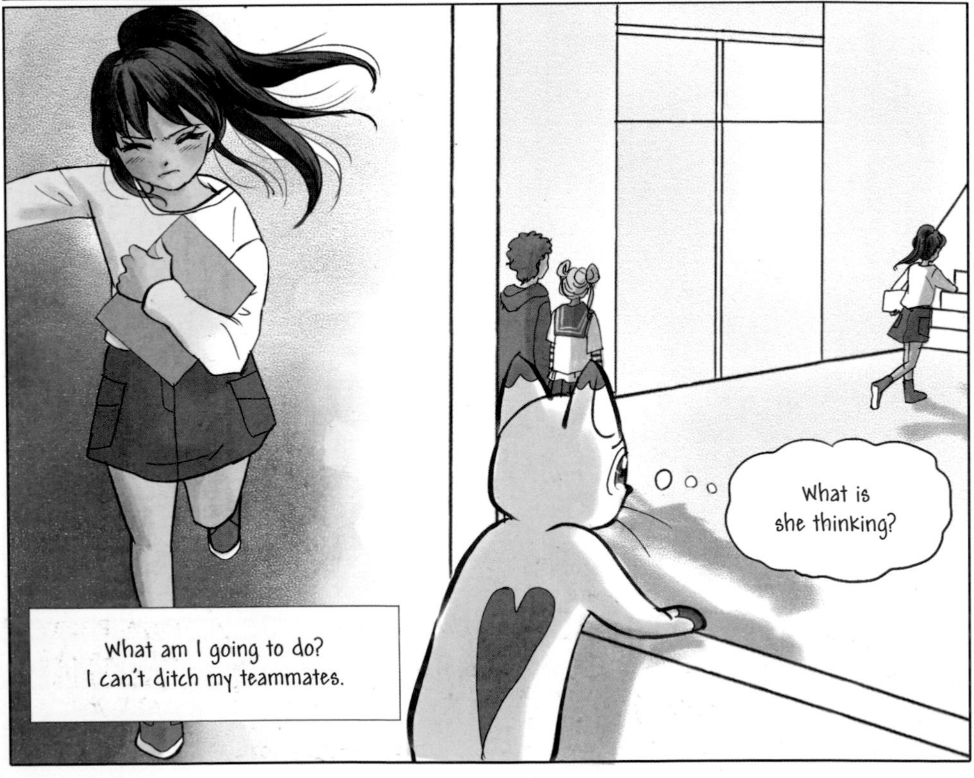
What am I going to do?
I can't ditch my teammates.
What is she thinking?

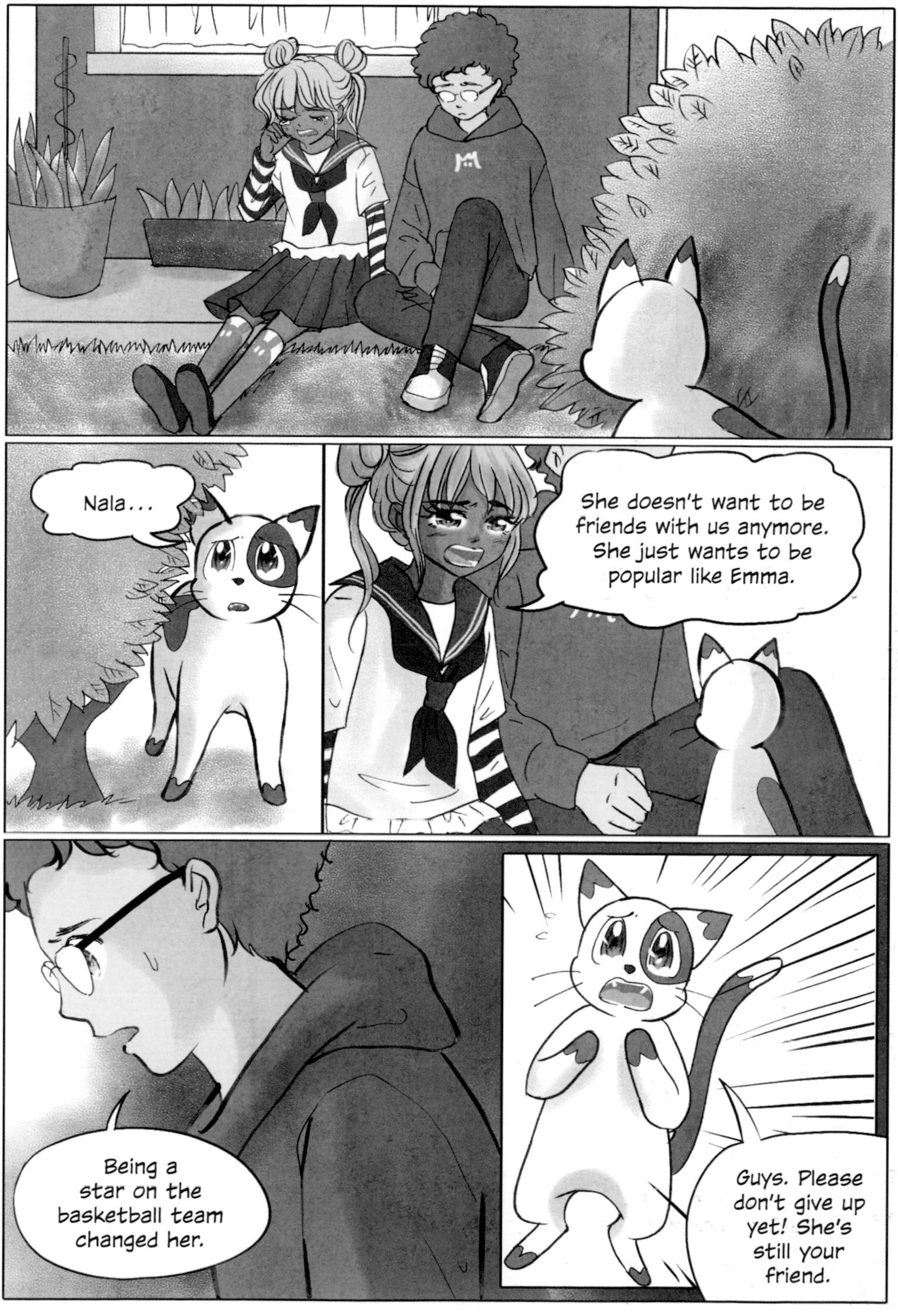
Nala...
She doesn't want to be friends with us anymore. She just wants to be popular like Emma.
Being a star on the basketball team changed her.
Guys. Please don't give up yet! She's still your friend.

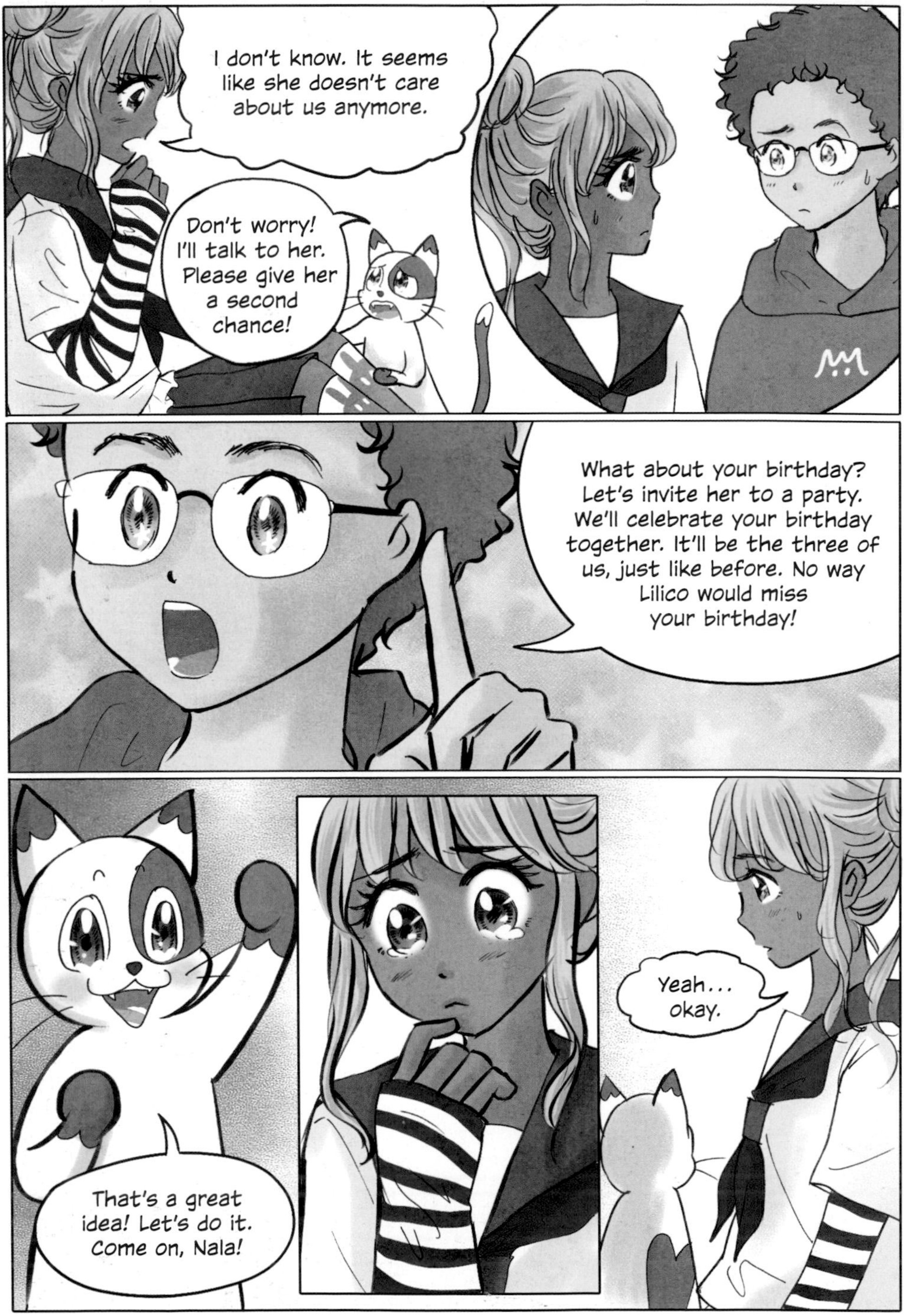
I don't know. It seems like she doesn't care about us anymore.
Don't worry! I'll talk to her. Please give her a second chance!
What about your birthday? Let's invite her to a party. We'll celebrate your birthday together. It'll be the three of us, just like before. No way Lilico would miss your birthday!
That's a great idea! Let's do it. Come on, Nala!
Yeah... okay.

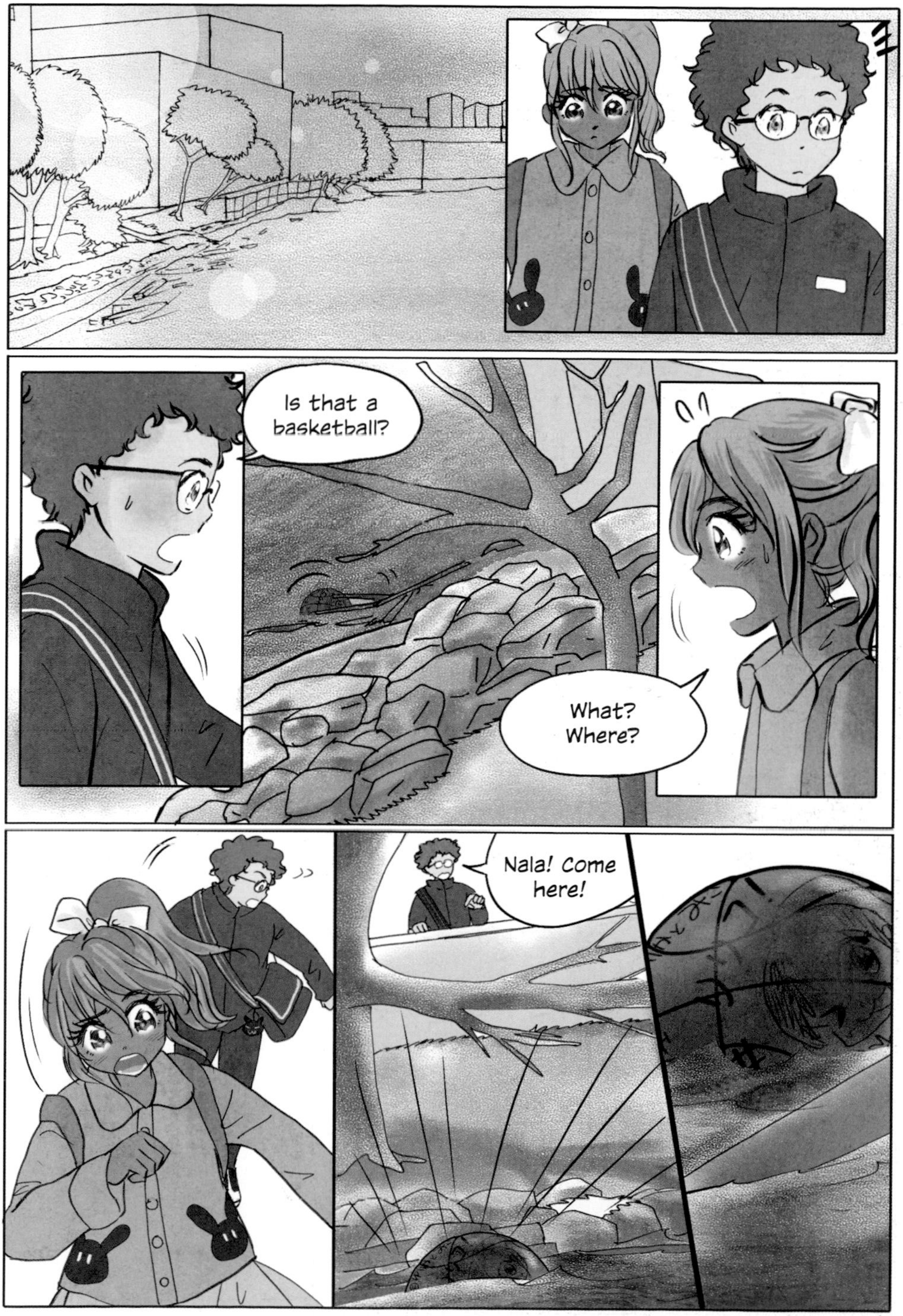
Is that a basketball?
What? Where?
Nala! Come here!

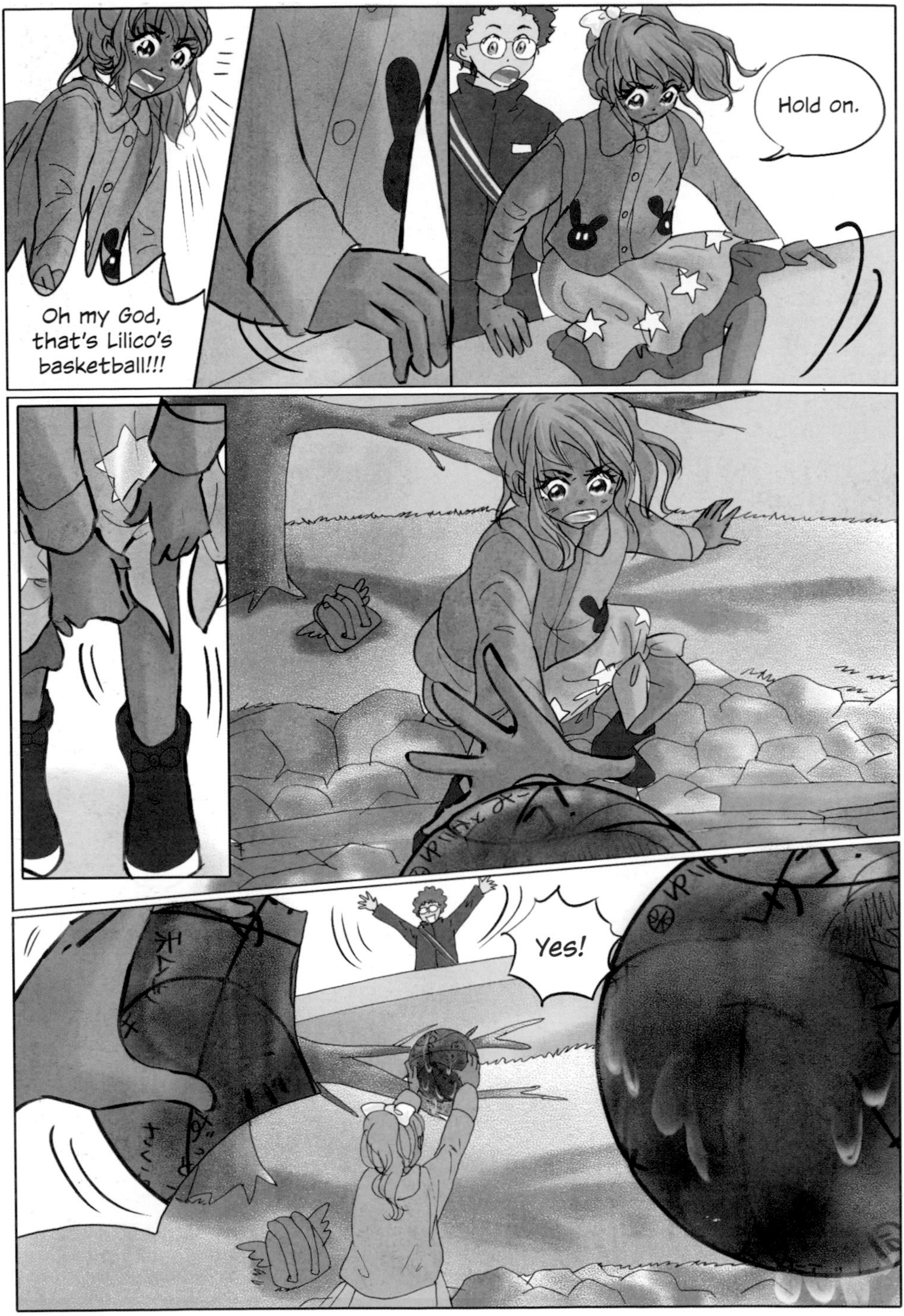
Oh my God, that's Lilico's basketball!!!
Hold on.
Yes!

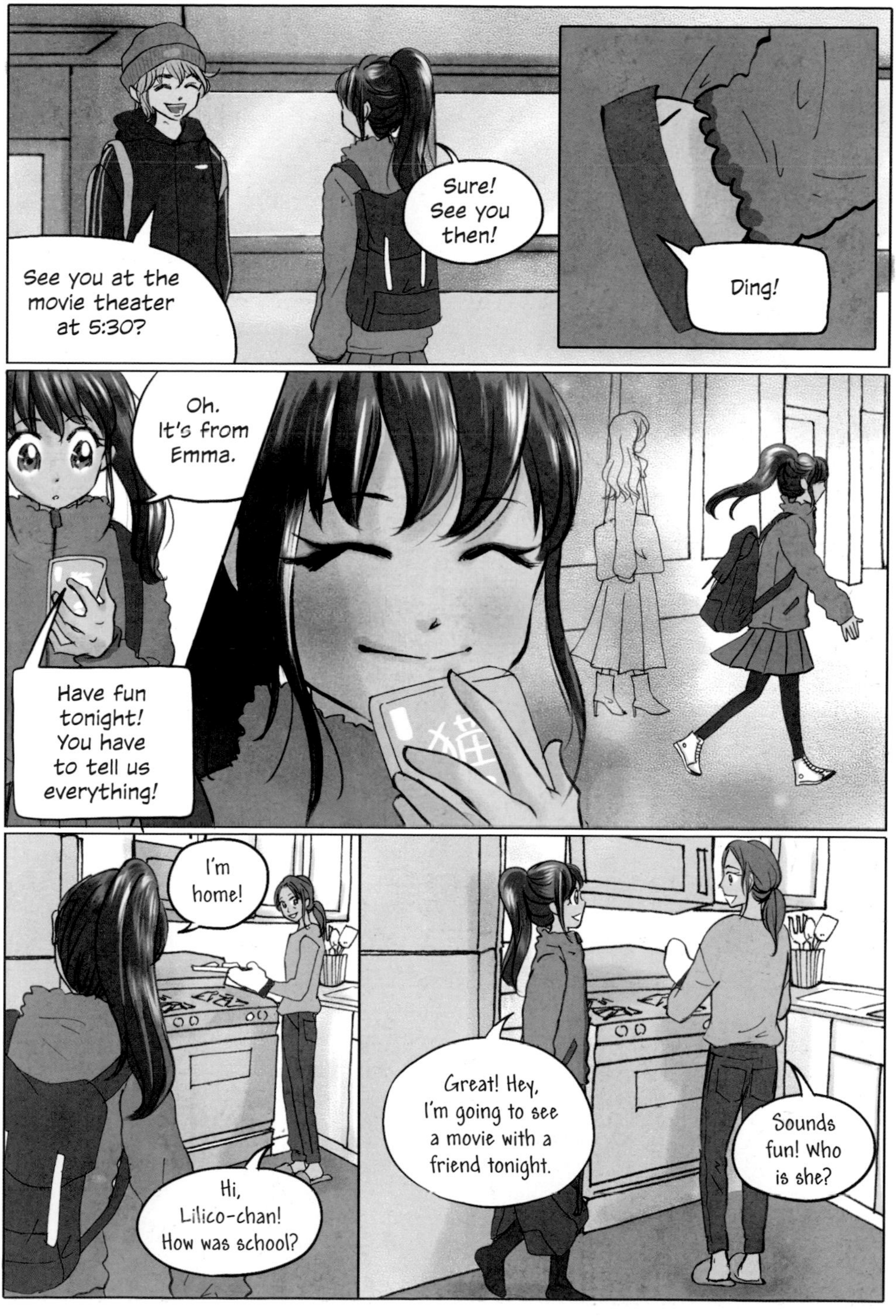
See you at the movie theater at 5:30?
Sure! See you then!
Ding!
Oh. It's from Emma.
Have fun tonight! You have to tell us everything!
I'm home!
Hi, Lilico-chan! How was school?
Great! Hey, I'm going to see a movie with a friend tonight.
Sounds fun! Who is she?

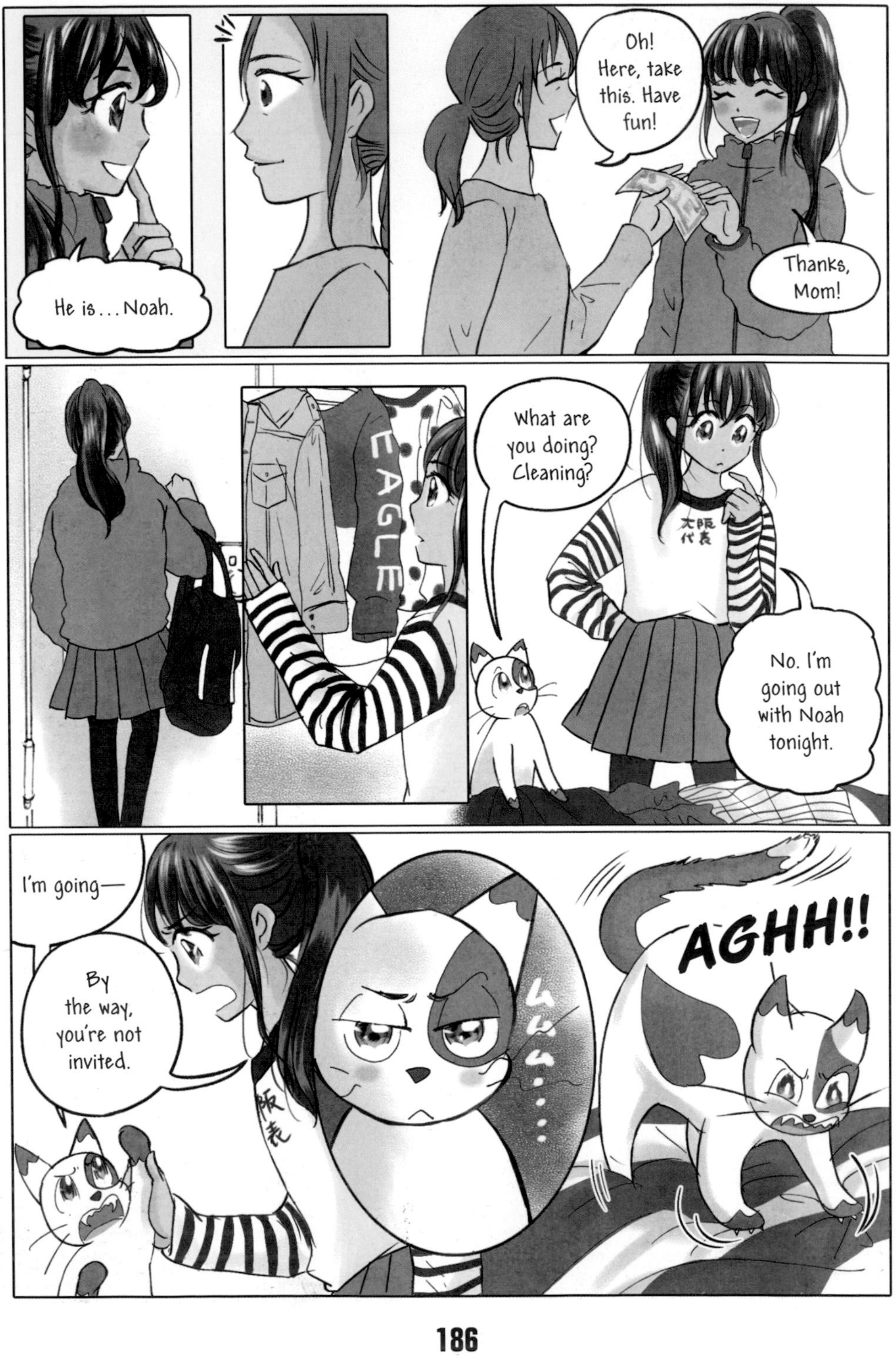
He is . . . Noah.
Oh! Here, take this. Have fun!
Thanks, Mom!
EAGLE
What are you doing? Cleaning?
大阪代表
No. I'm going out with Noah tonight.
I'm going—
By the way, you're not invited.
ムム…
AGHH!!

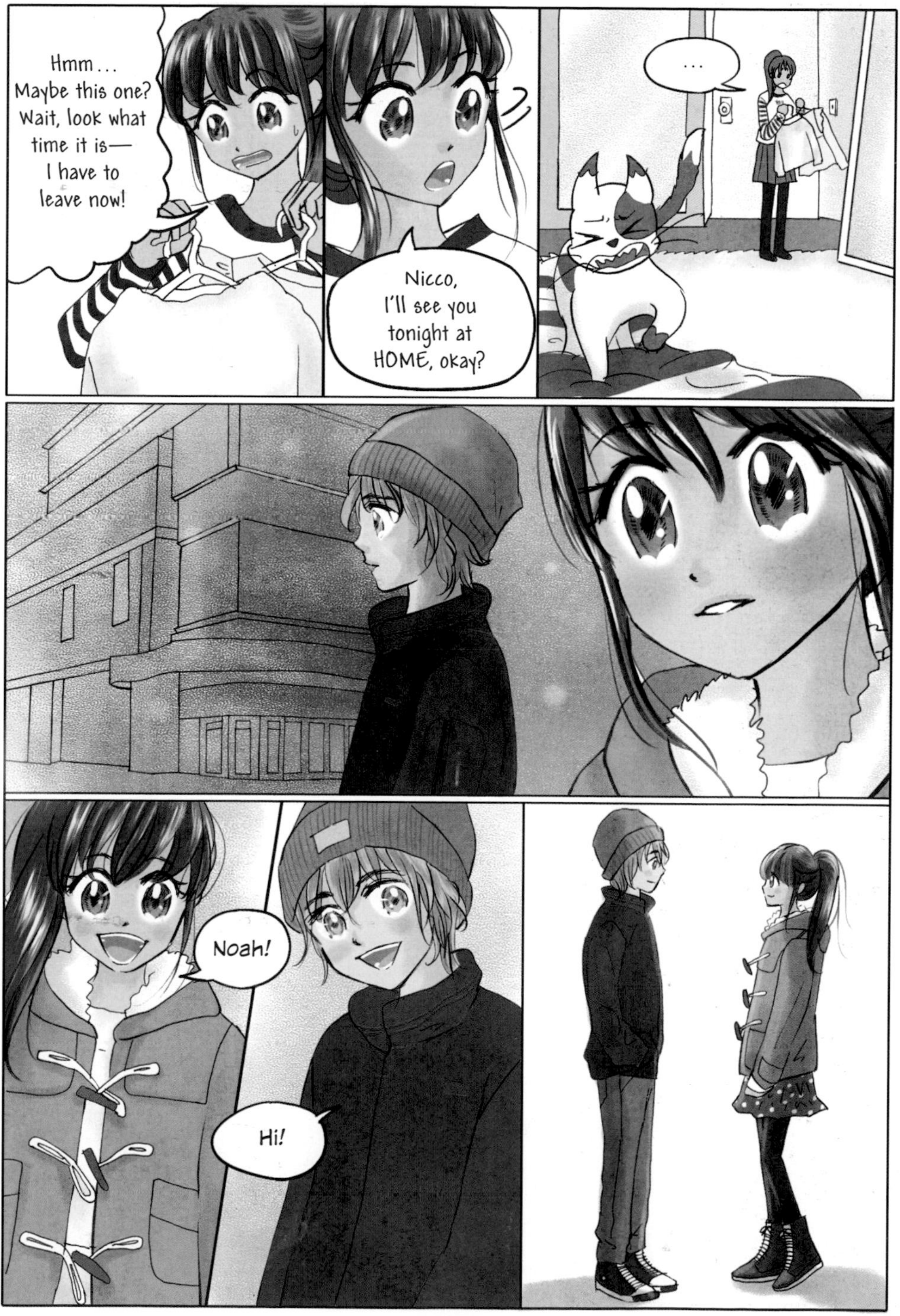
Hmm... Maybe this one? Wait, look what time it is— I have to leave now!
Nicco, I'll see you tonight at HOME, okay?
...
Noah!
Hi!

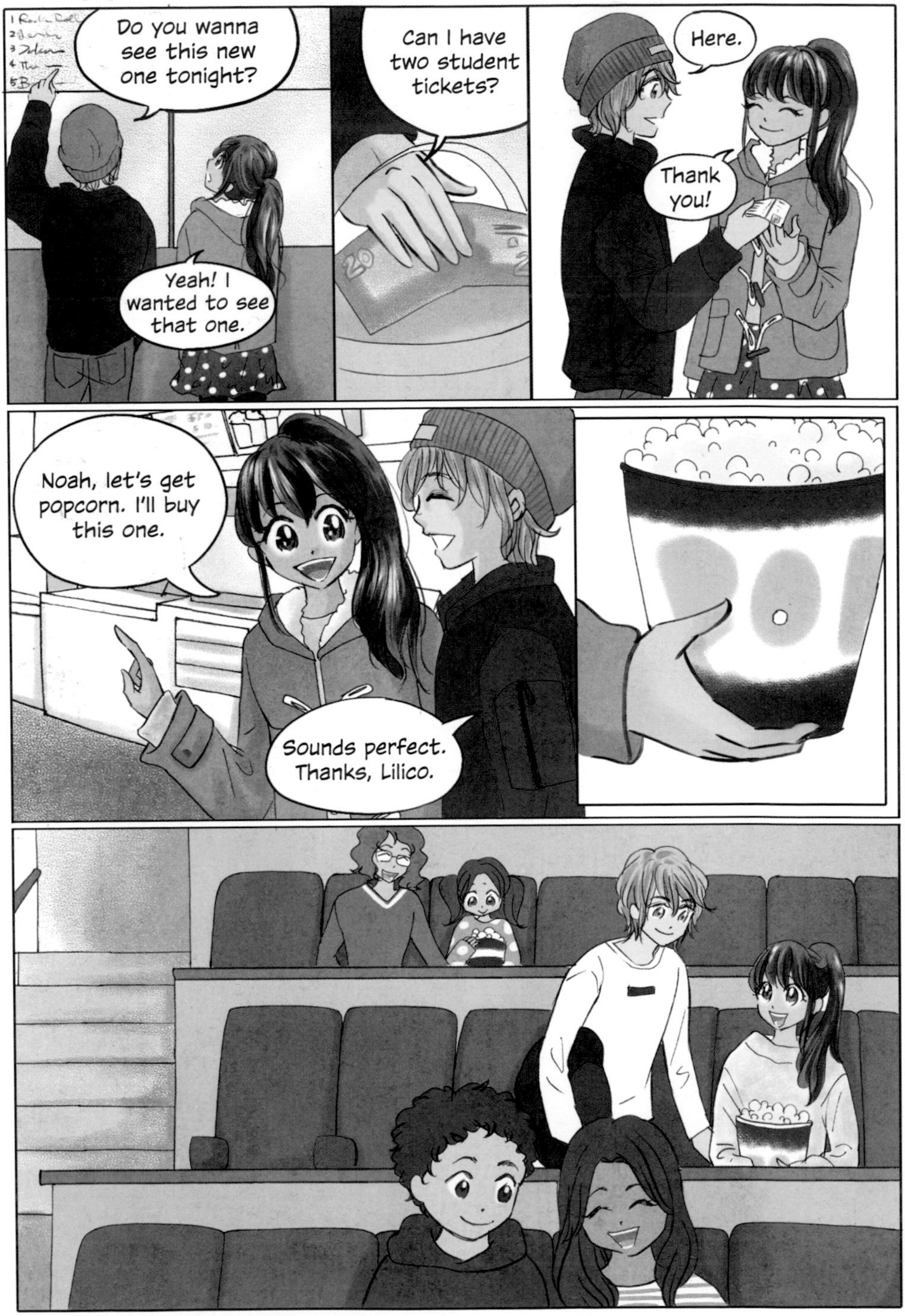
Do you wanna see this new one tonight?
Yeah! I wanted to see that one.
Can I have two student tickets?
Here.
Thank you!
Noah, let's get popcorn. I'll buy this one.
Sounds perfect. Thanks, Lilico.

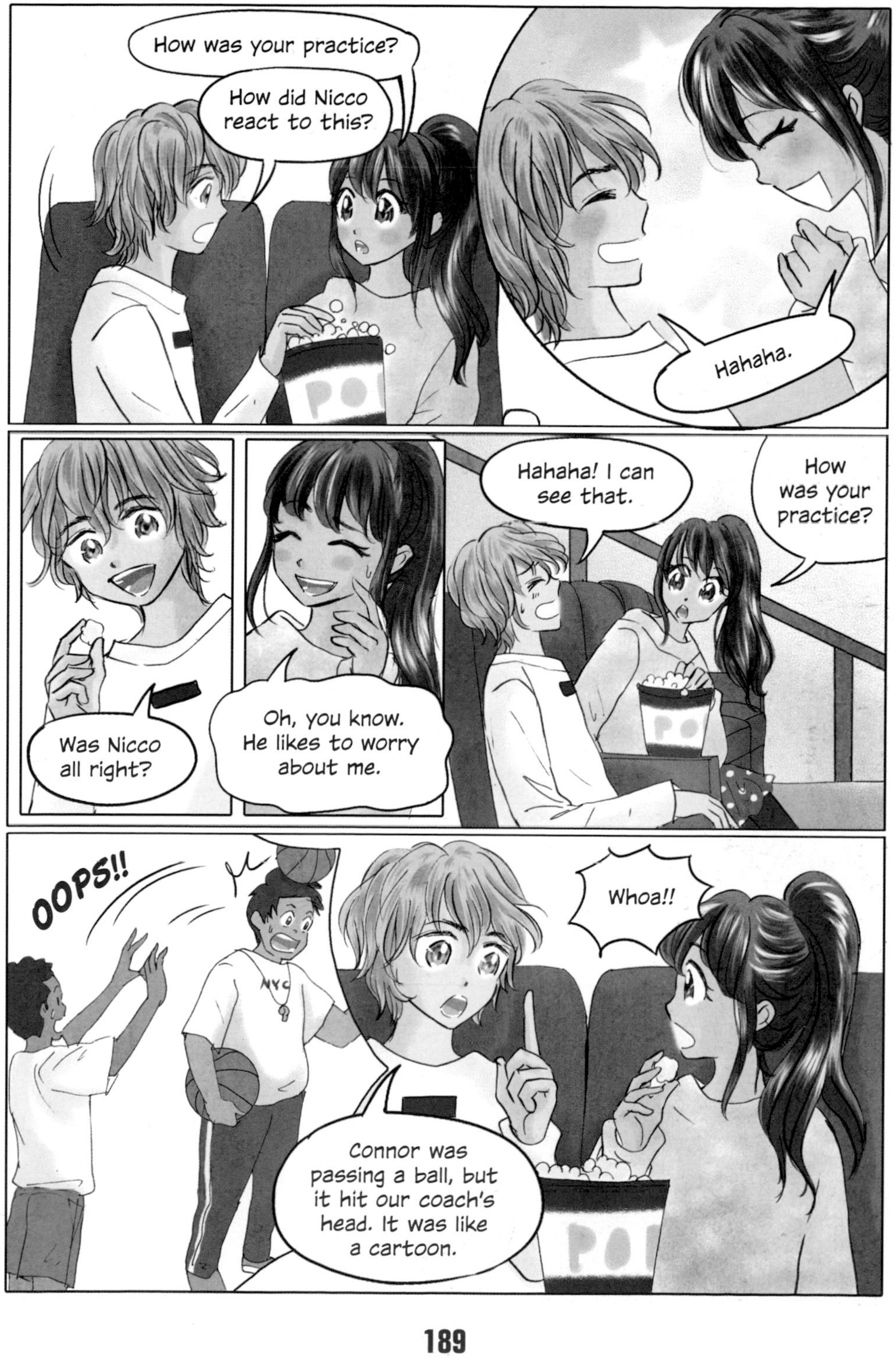
How was your practice?
How did Nicco react to this?
Hahaha.
Was Nicco all right?
Oh, you know. He likes to worry about me.
Hahaha! I can see that.
How was your practice?
OOPS!!
Whoa!!
Connor was passing a ball, but it hit our coach's head. It was like a cartoon.

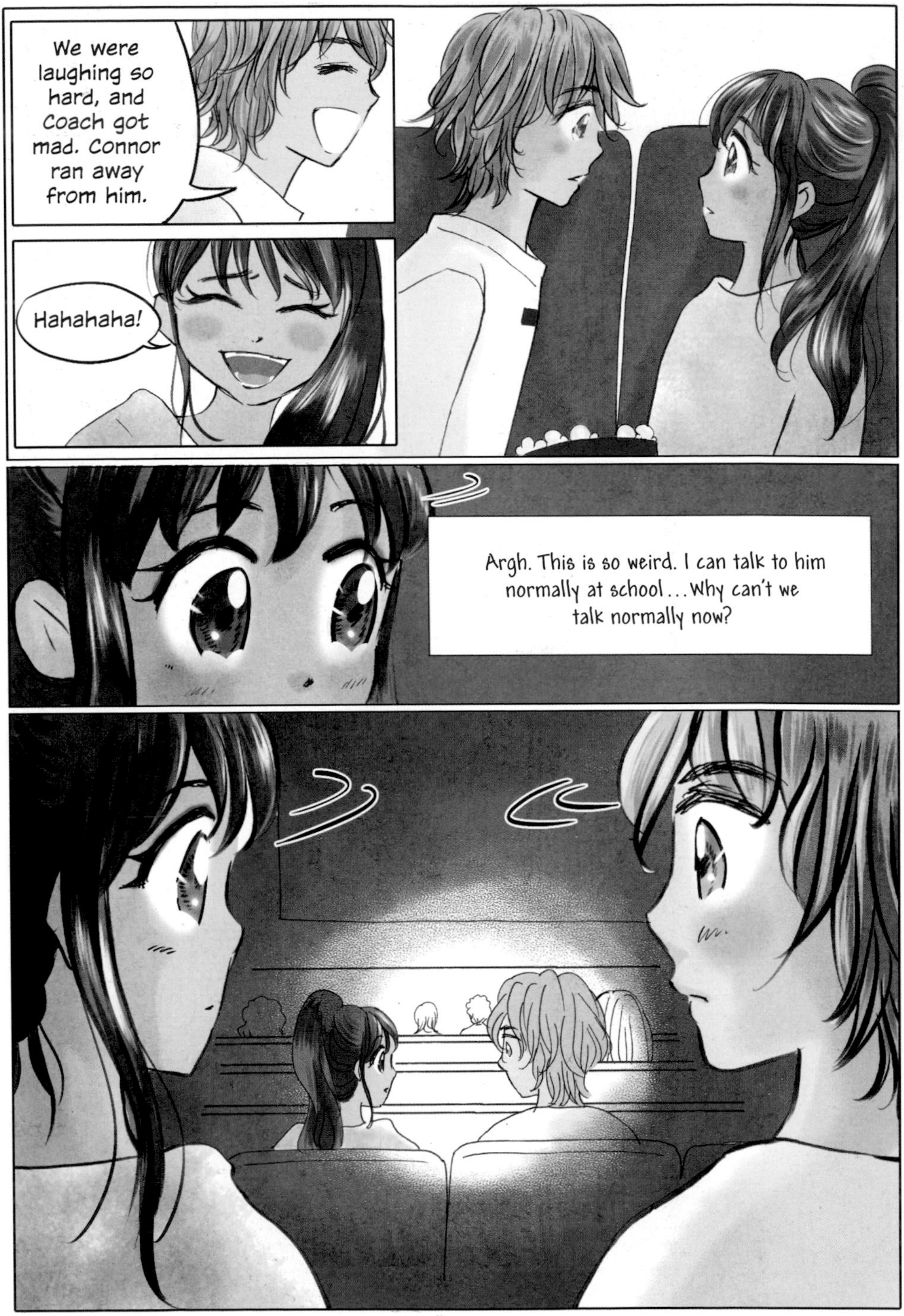
We were laughing so hard, and Coach got mad. Connor ran away from him.
Hahahaha!
Argh. This is so weird. I can talk to him normally at school...Why can't we talk normally now?

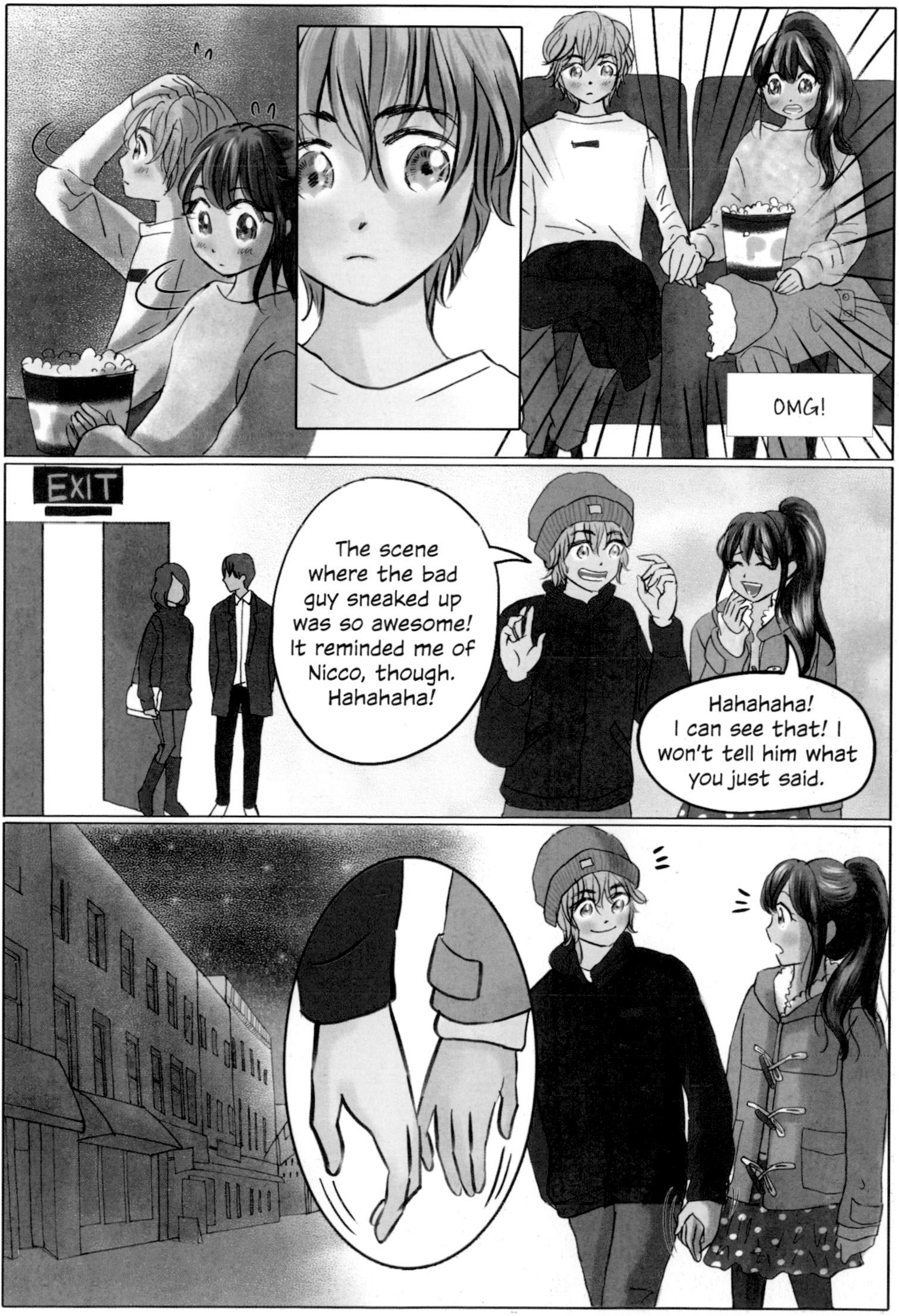
OMG!
EXIT
The scene where the bad guy sneaked up was so awesome! It reminded me of Nicco, though. Hahahaha!
Hahahaha! I can see that! I won't tell him what you just said.

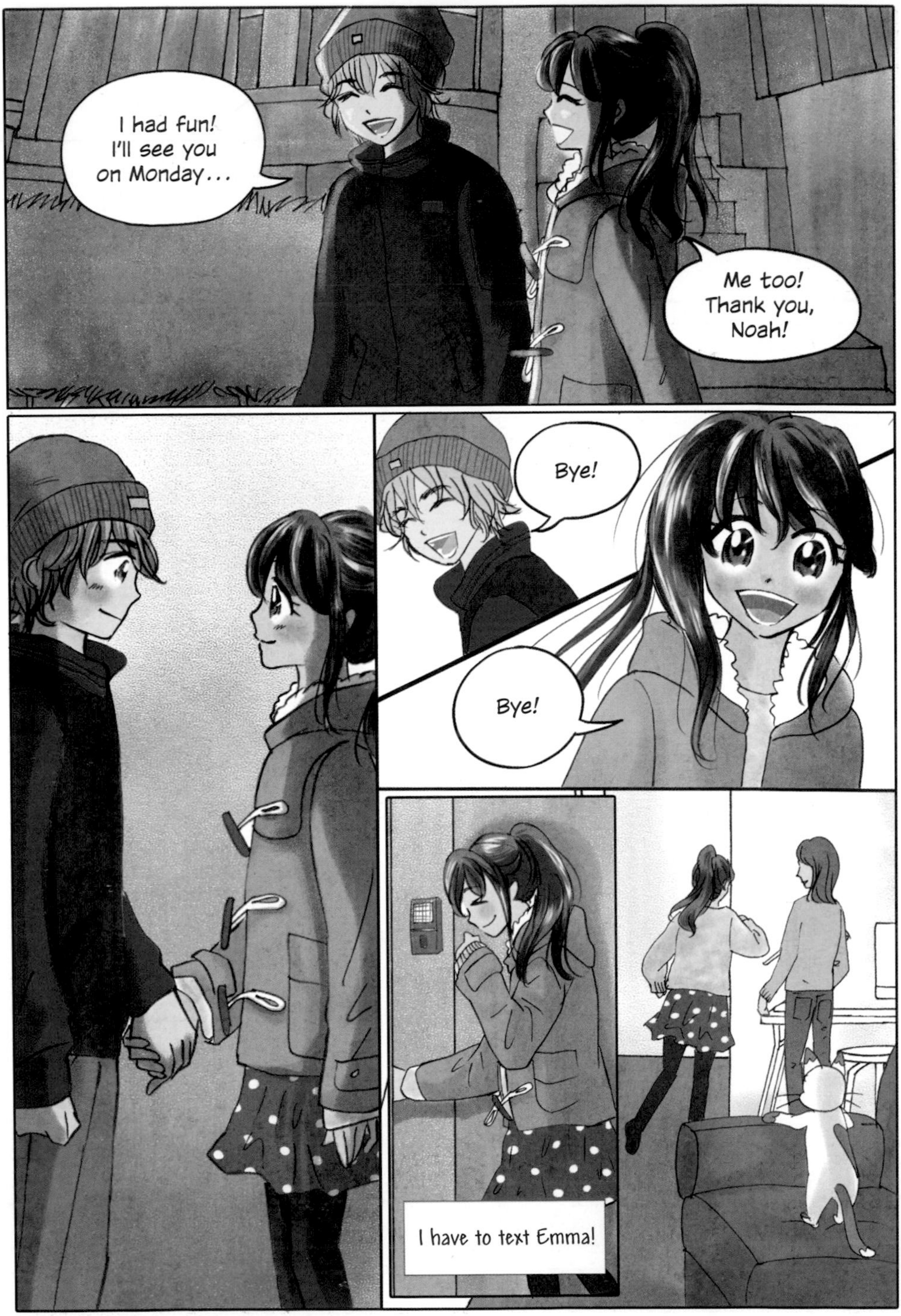
I had fun! I'll see you on Monday...
Me too! Thank you, Noah!
Bye!
Bye!
I have to text Emma!

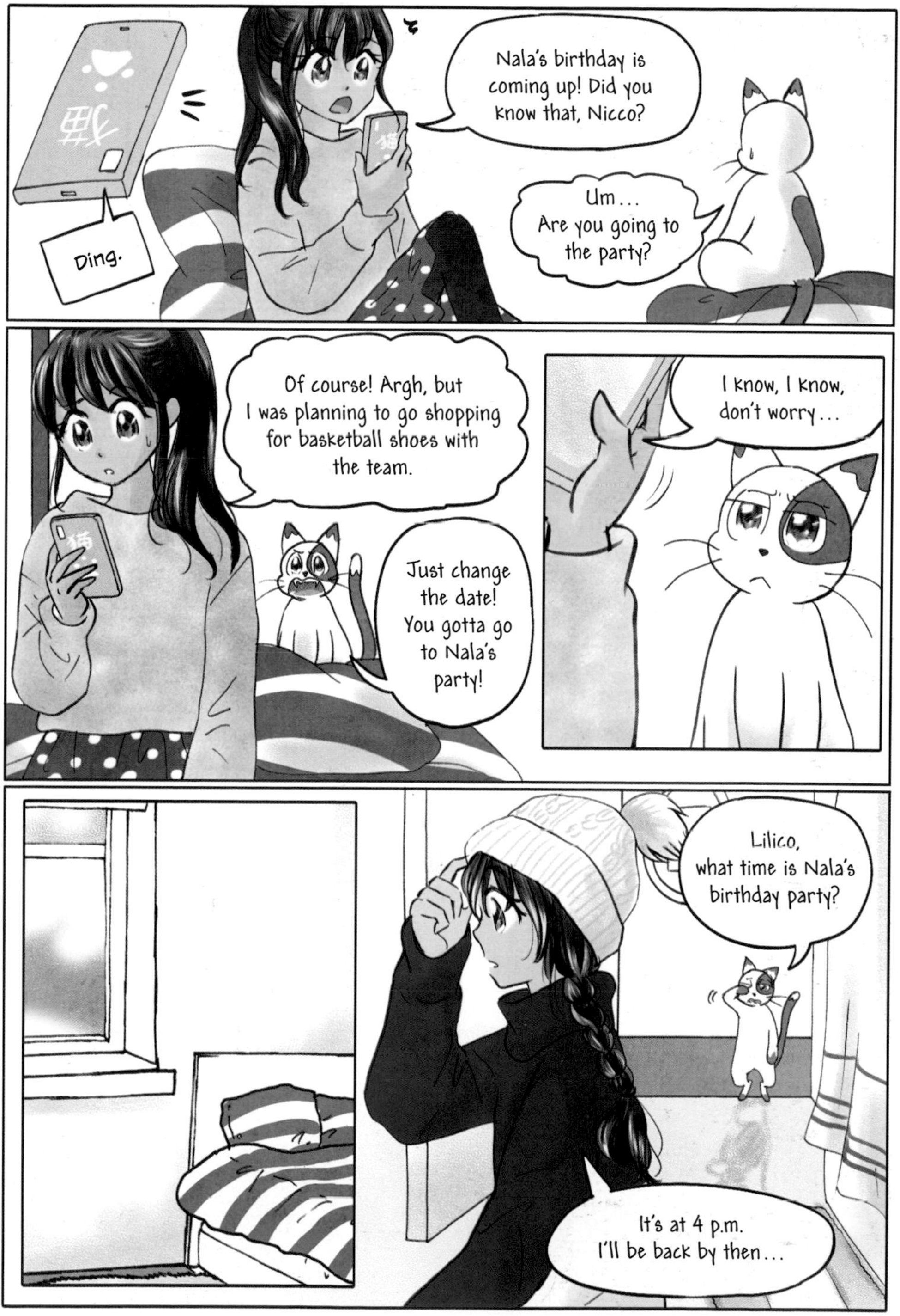
Ding.
Nala's birthday is coming up! Did you know that, Nicco?
Um… Are you going to the party?
Of course! Argh, but I was planning to go shopping for basketball shoes with the team.
Just change the date! You gotta go to Nala's party!
I know, I know, don't worry…
Lilico, what time is Nala's birthday party?
It's at 4 p.m. I'll be back by then…

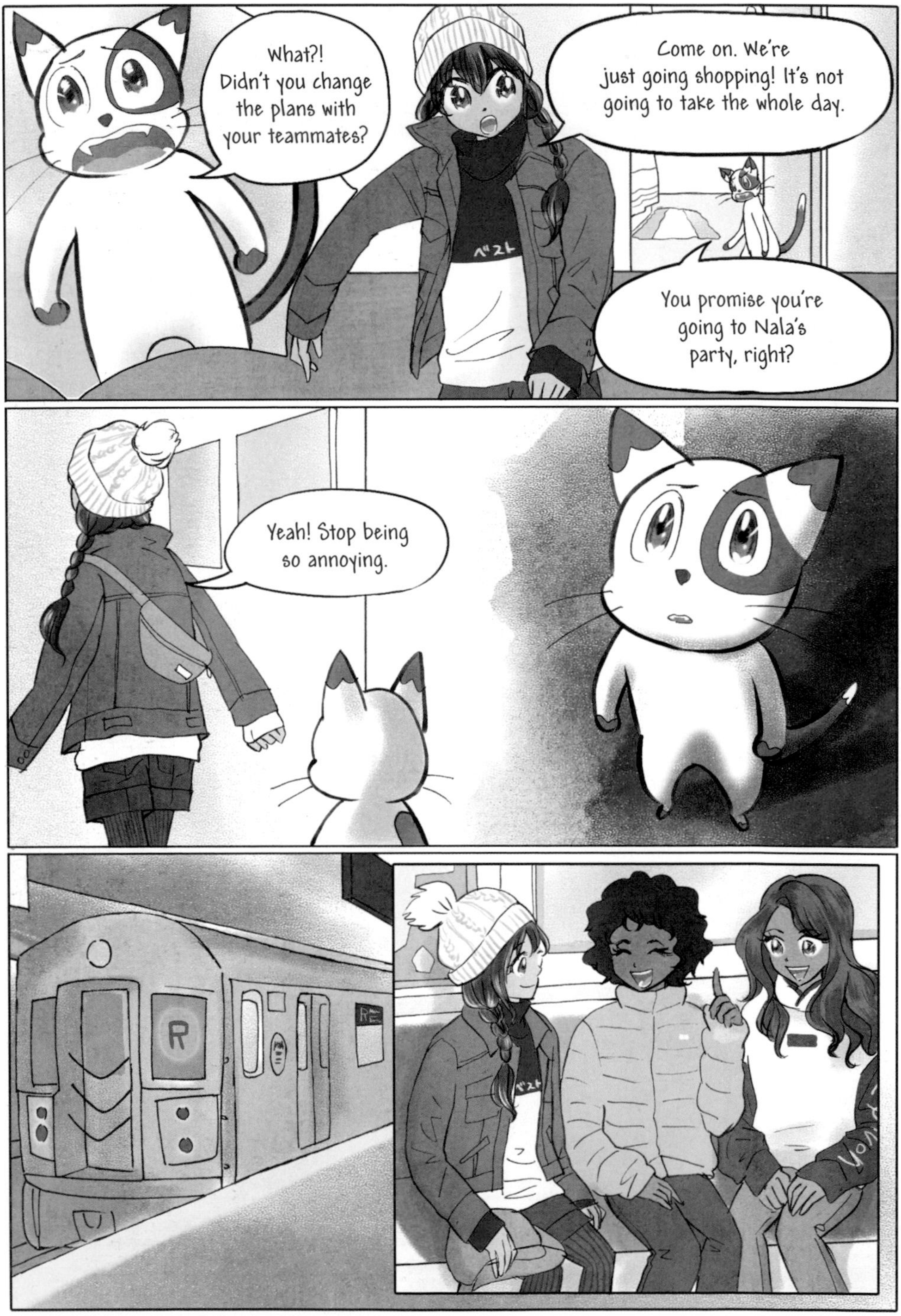
What?! Didn't you change the plans with your teammates?
Come on. We're just going shopping! It's not going to take the whole day.
You promise you're going to Nala's party, right?
Yeah! Stop being so annoying.
R

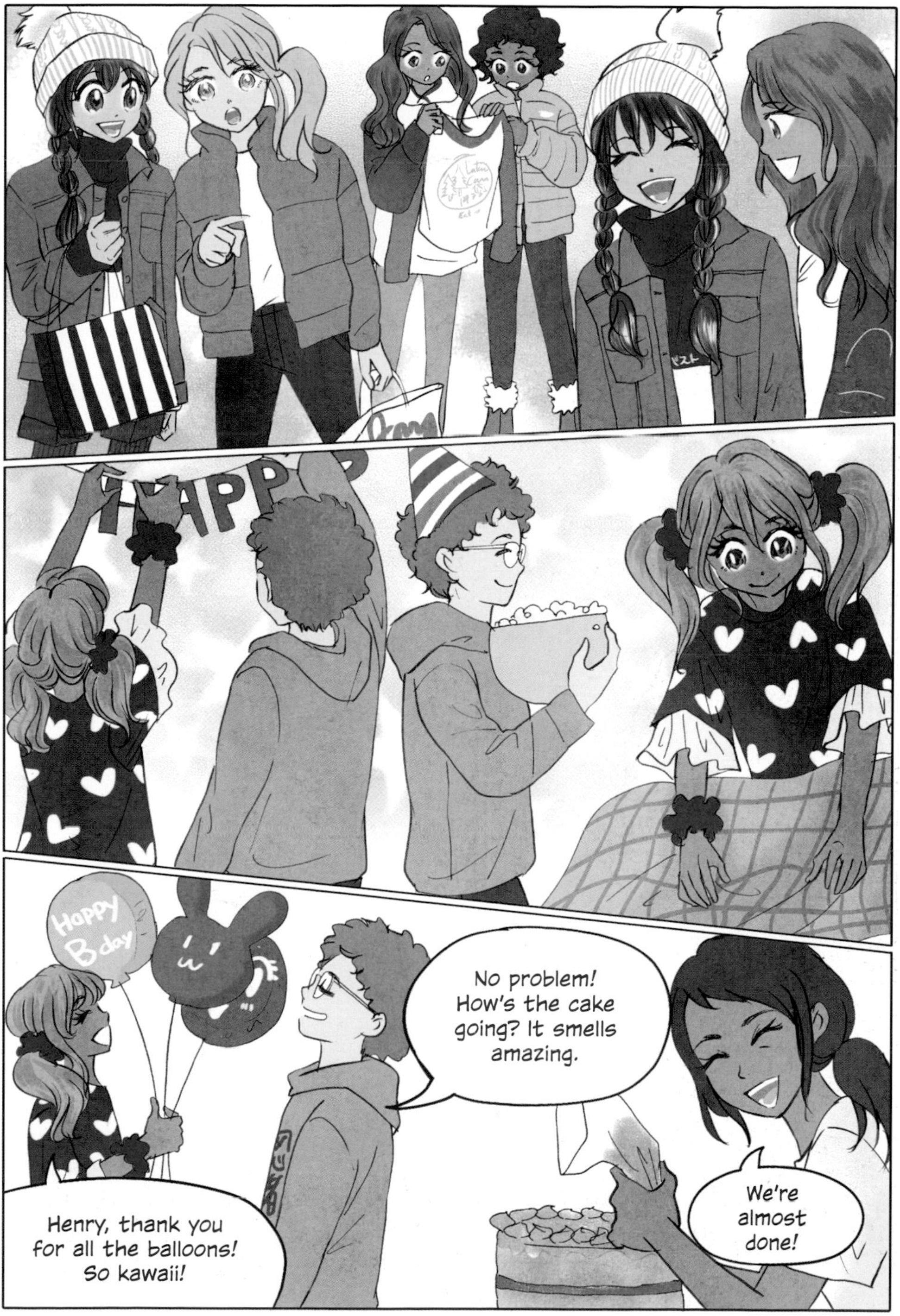
Happy B day
Henry, thank you for all the balloons! So kawaii!
No problem! How's the cake going? It smells amazing.
We're almost done!

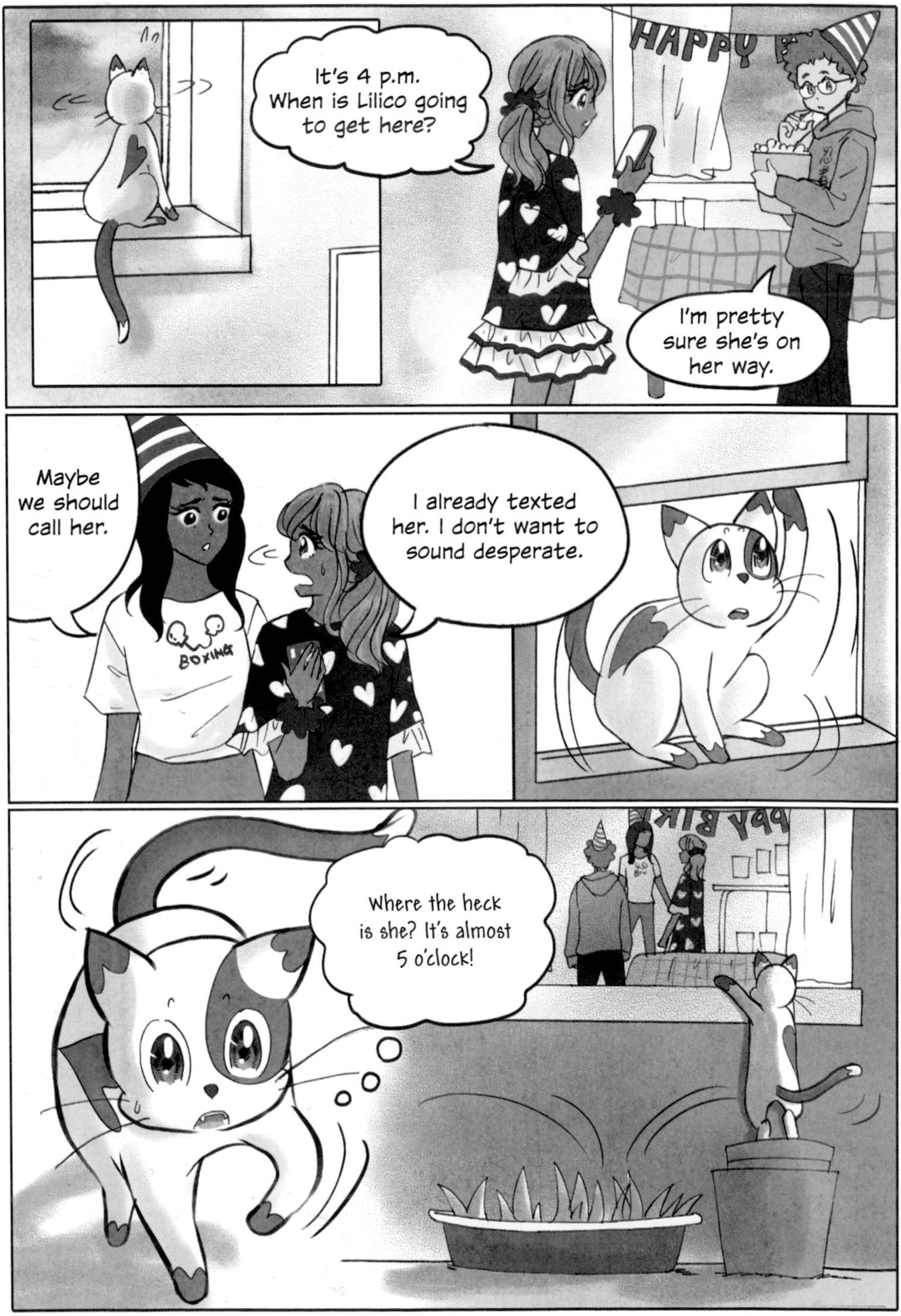
It's 4 p.m. When is Lilico going to get here?
HAPPY
I'm pretty sure she's on her way.
Maybe we should call her.
BOXING
I already texted her. I don't want to sound desperate.
Where the heck is she? It's almost 5 o'clock!

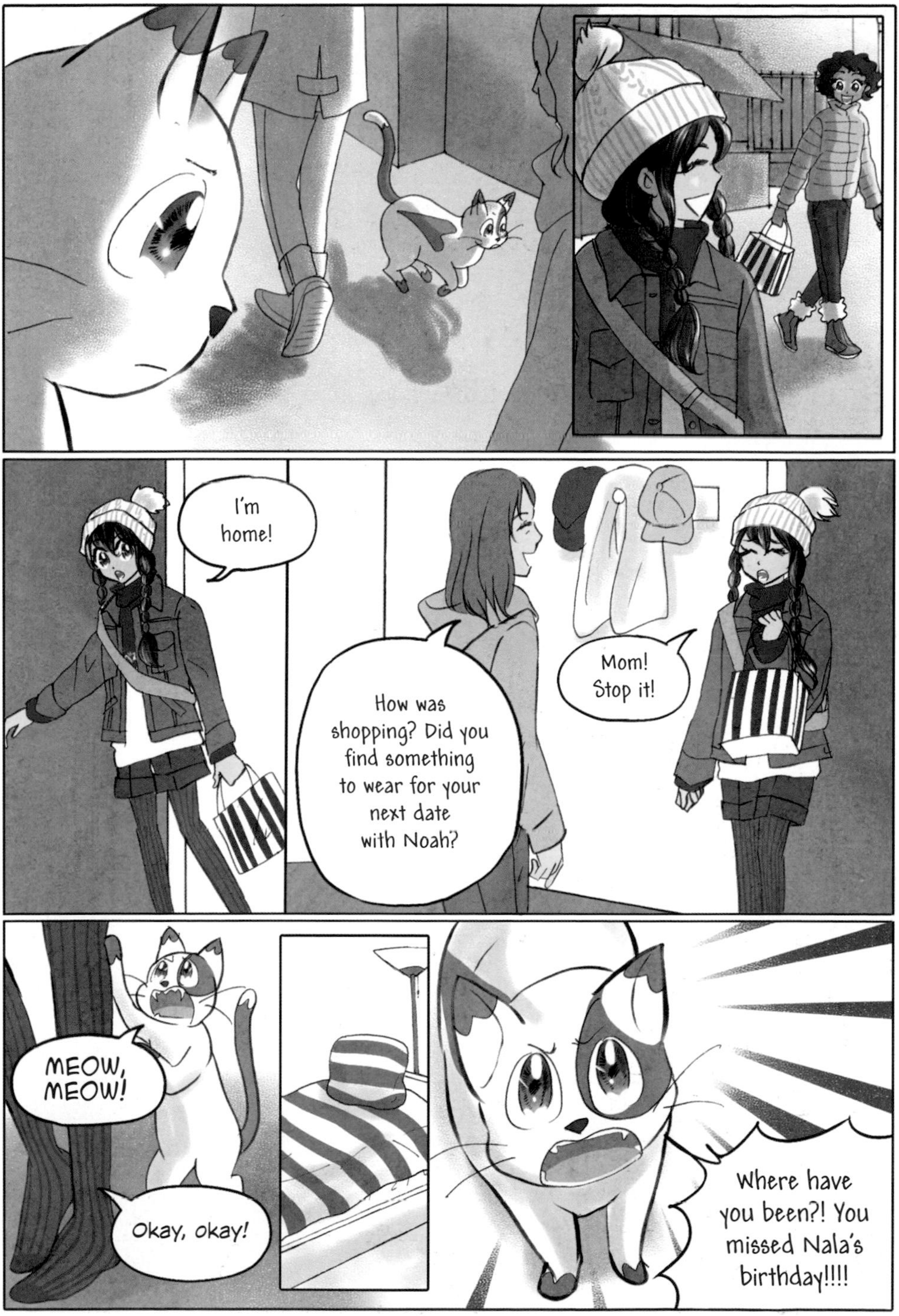
I'm home!
How was shopping? Did you find something to wear for your next date with Noah?
Mom! Stop it!
MEOW, MEOW!
Okay, okay!
Where have you been?! You missed Nala's birthday!!!!

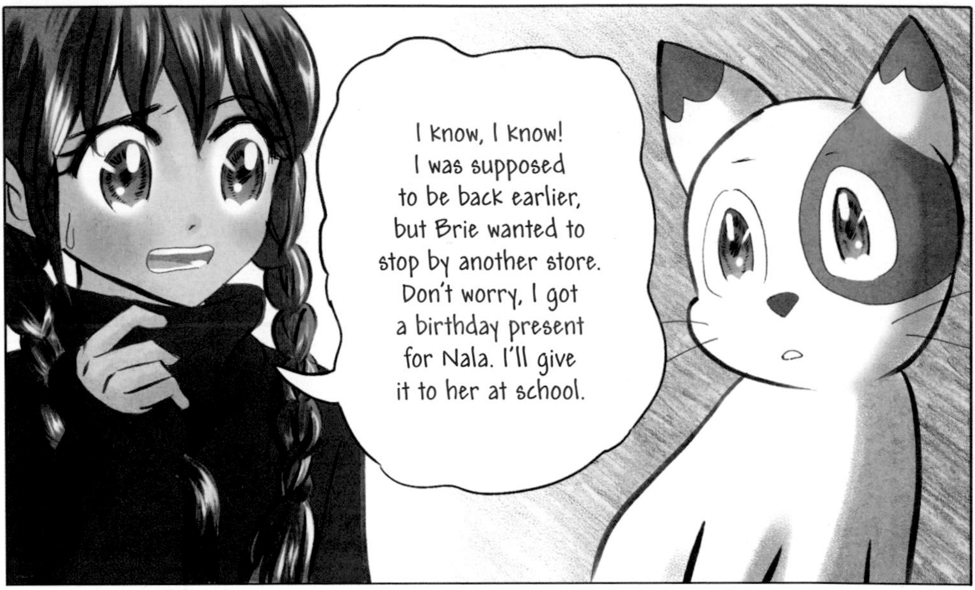
I know, I know! I was supposed to be back earlier, but Brie wanted to stop by another store. Don't worry, I got a birthday present for Nala. I'll give it to her at school.

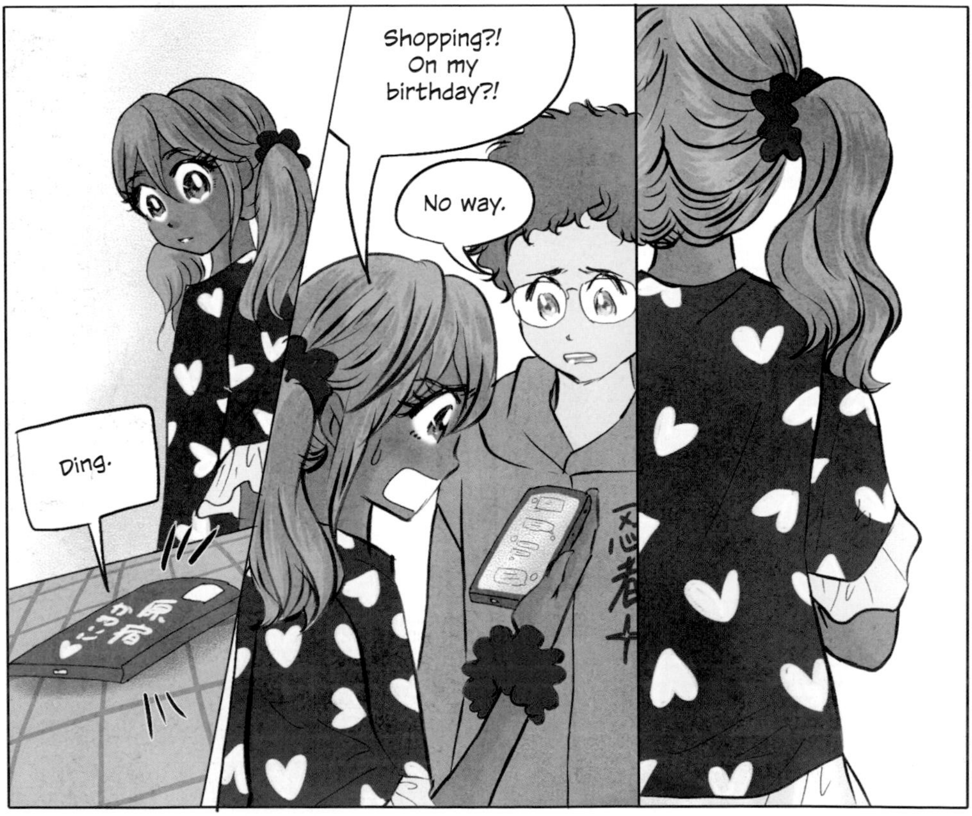
Ding.
Shopping?! On my birthday?!
No way.

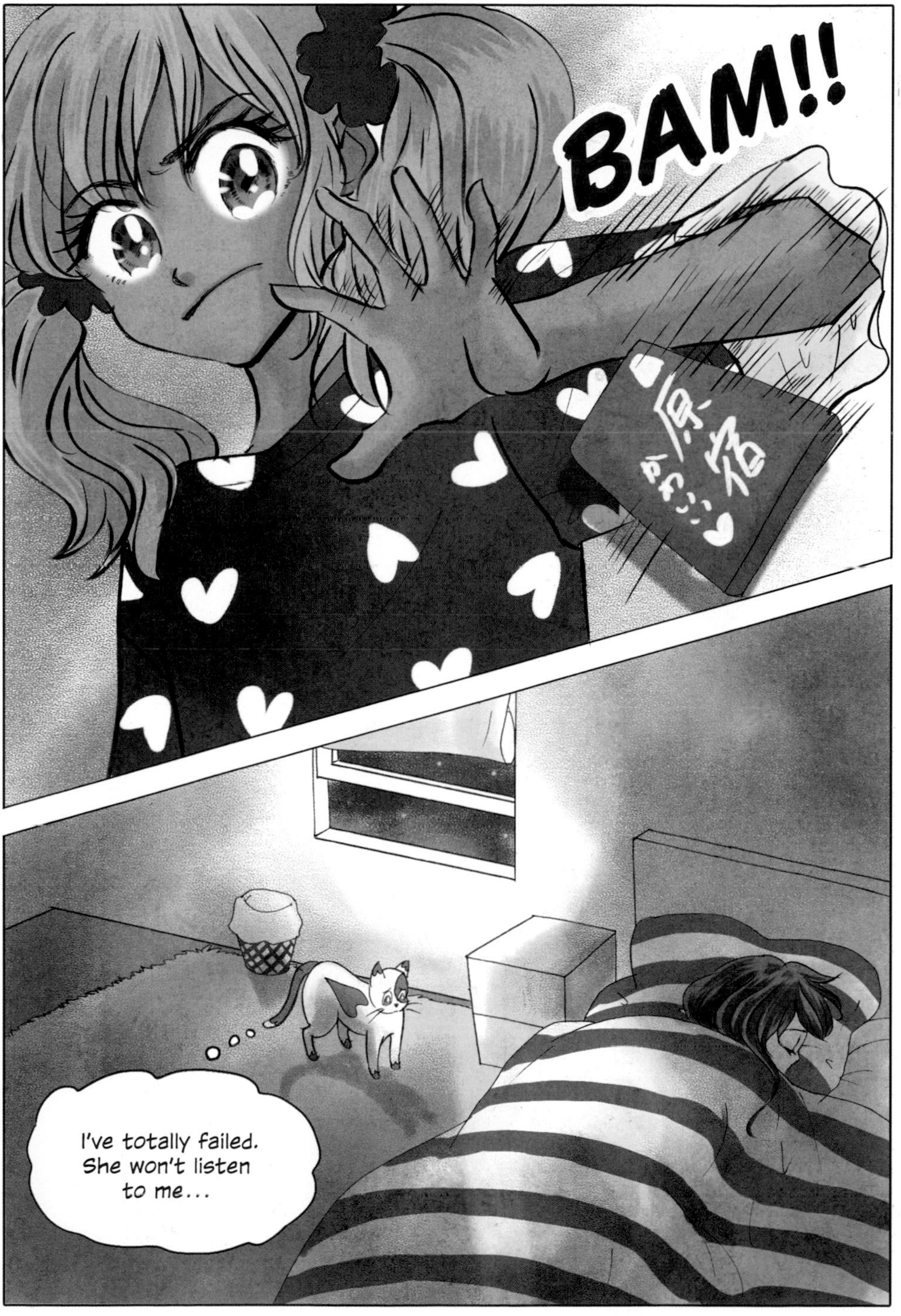
BAM!!
I've totally failed. She won't listen to me...

CHAPTER 7

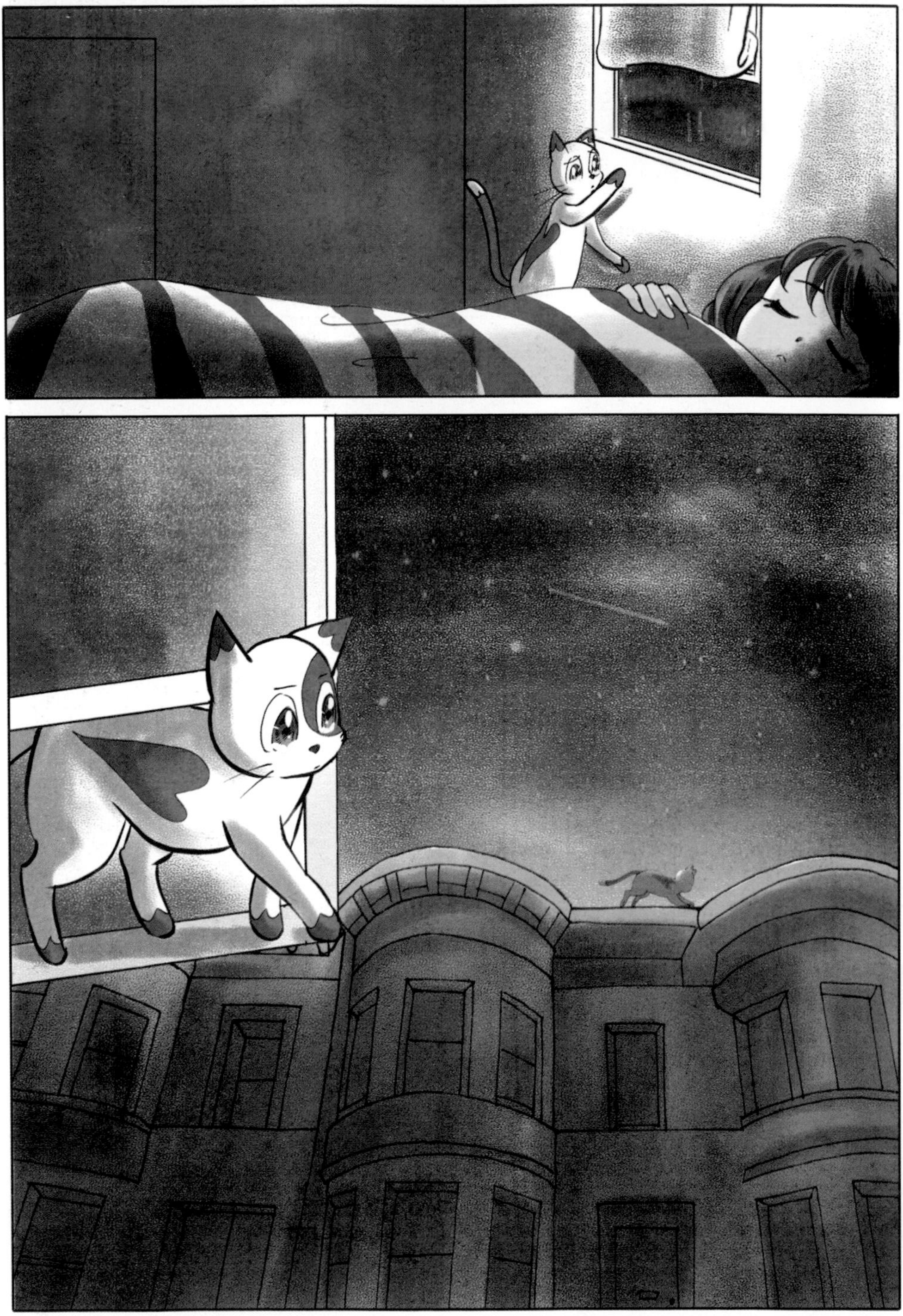

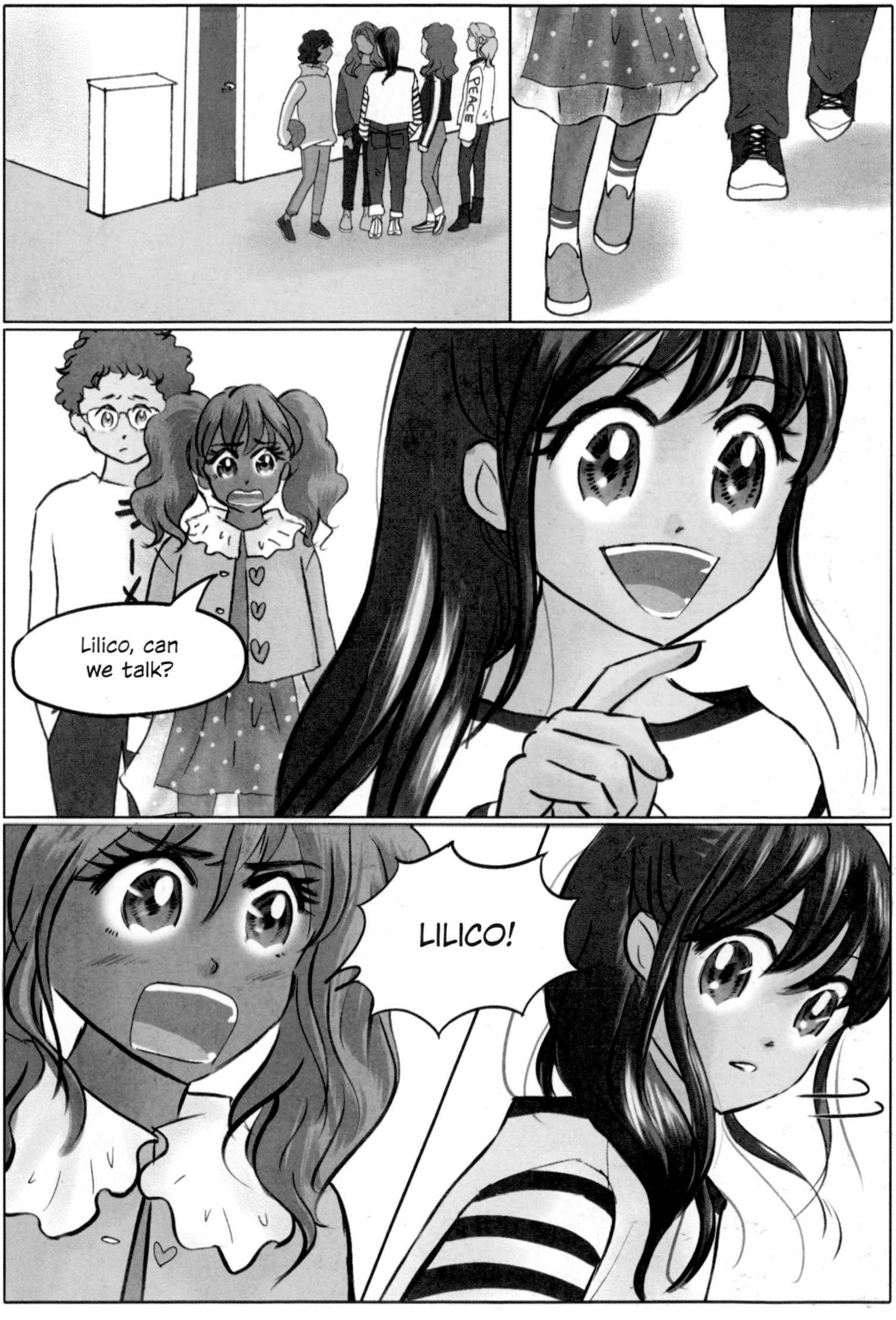
PEACE
Lilico, can we talk?
LILICO!

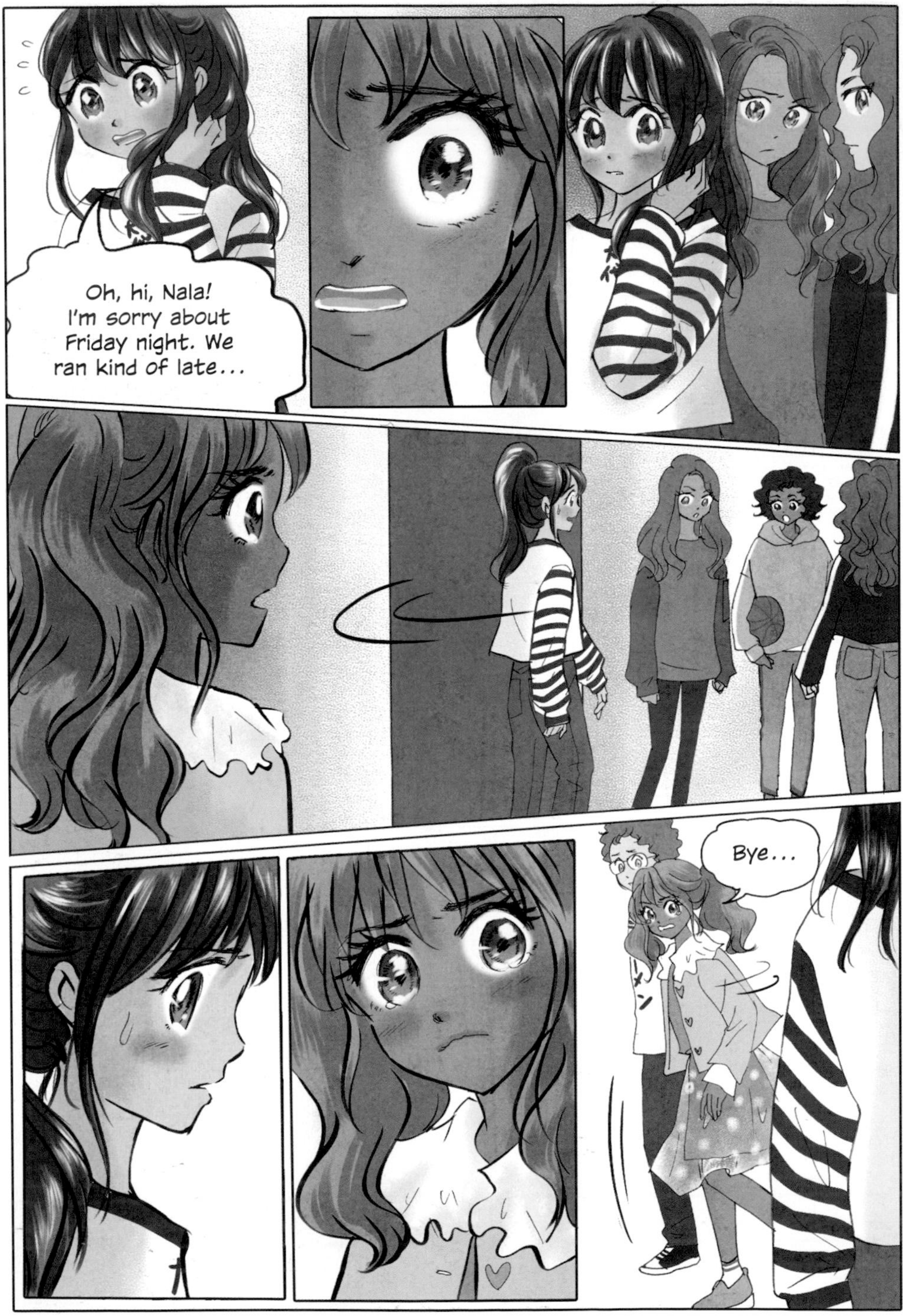
Oh, hi, Nala! I'm sorry about Friday night. We ran kind of late...
Bye...

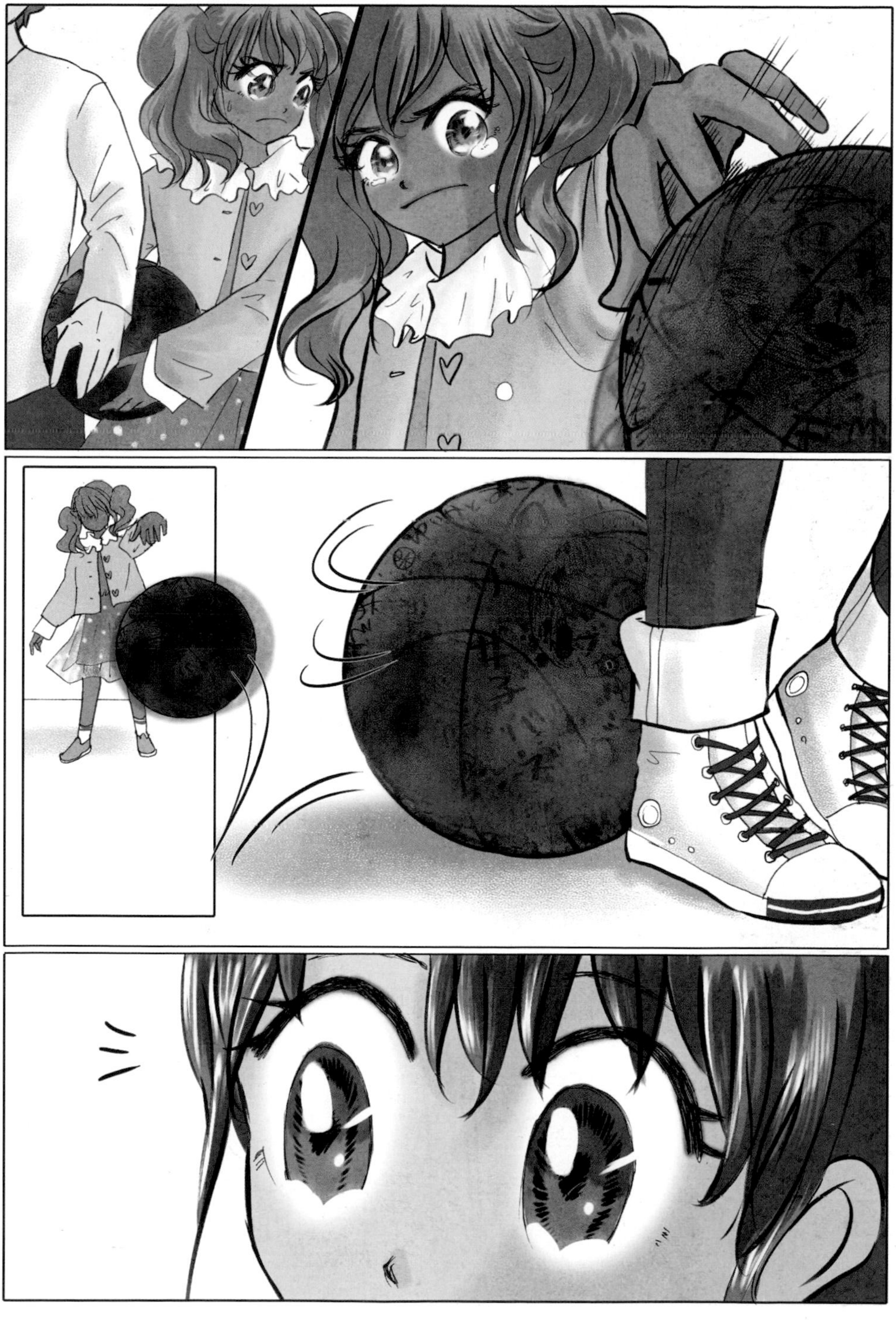

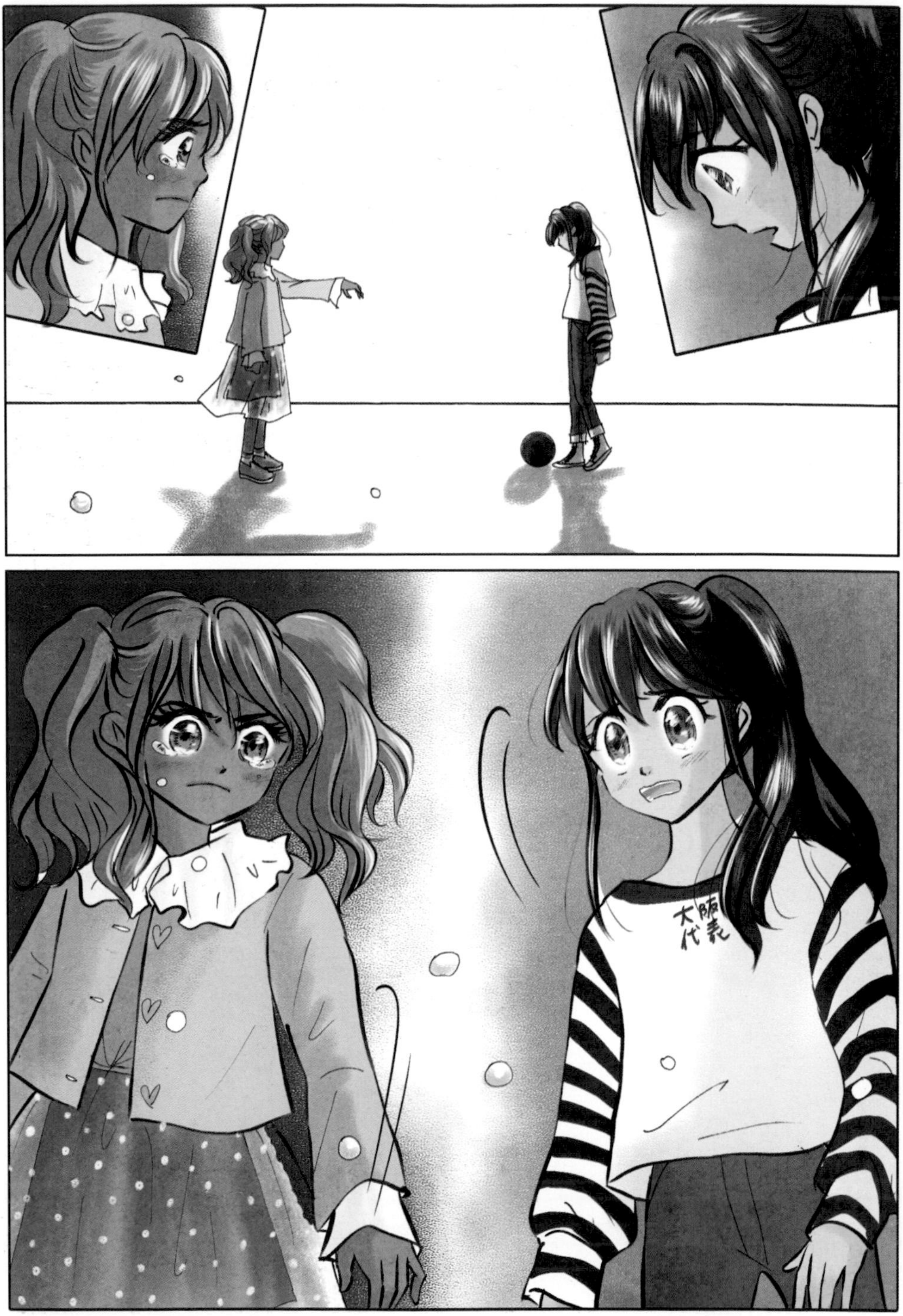
大阪代表

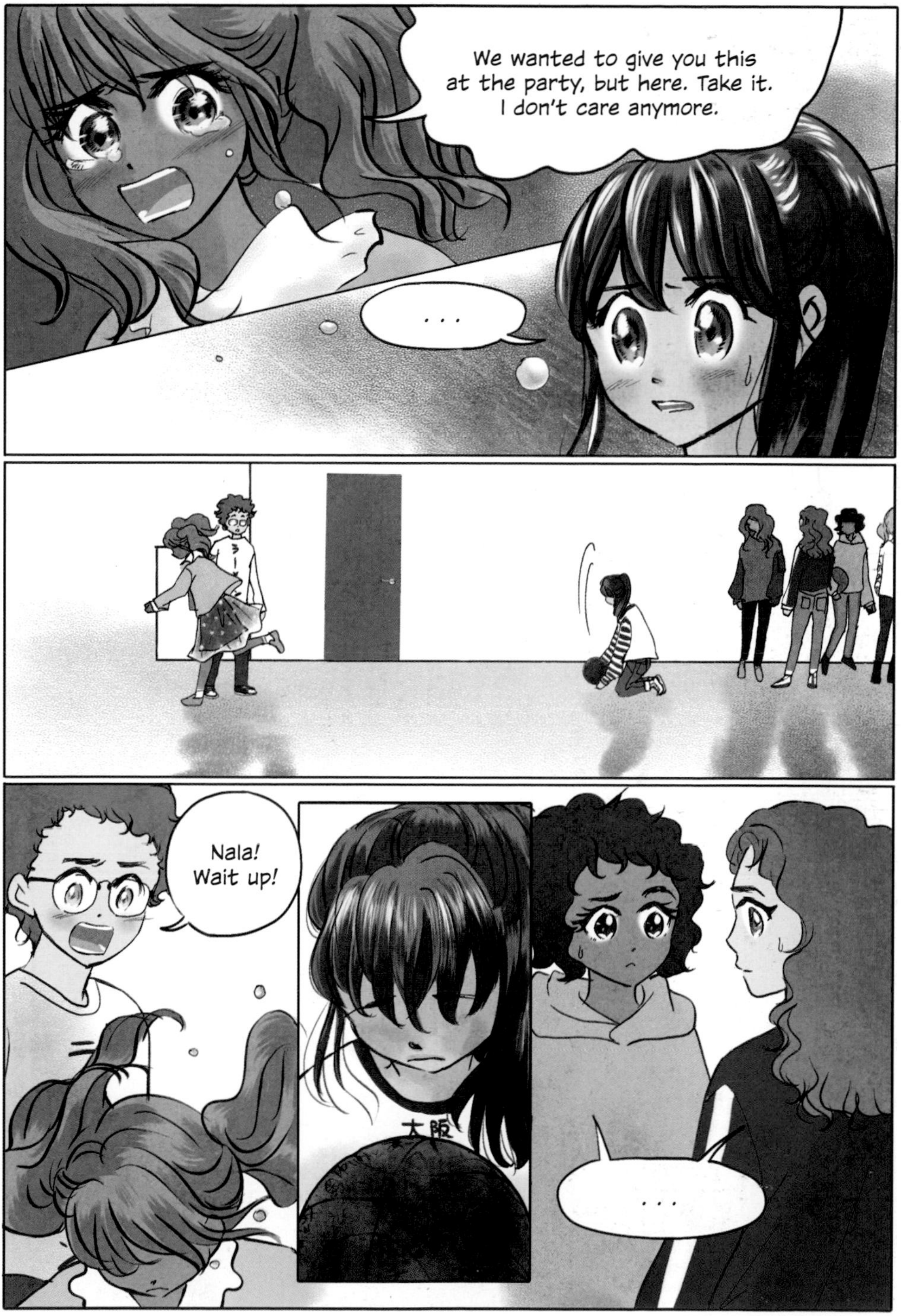
We wanted to give you this at the party, but here. Take it. I don't care anymore.
. . .
Nala! Wait up!
大阪
. . .

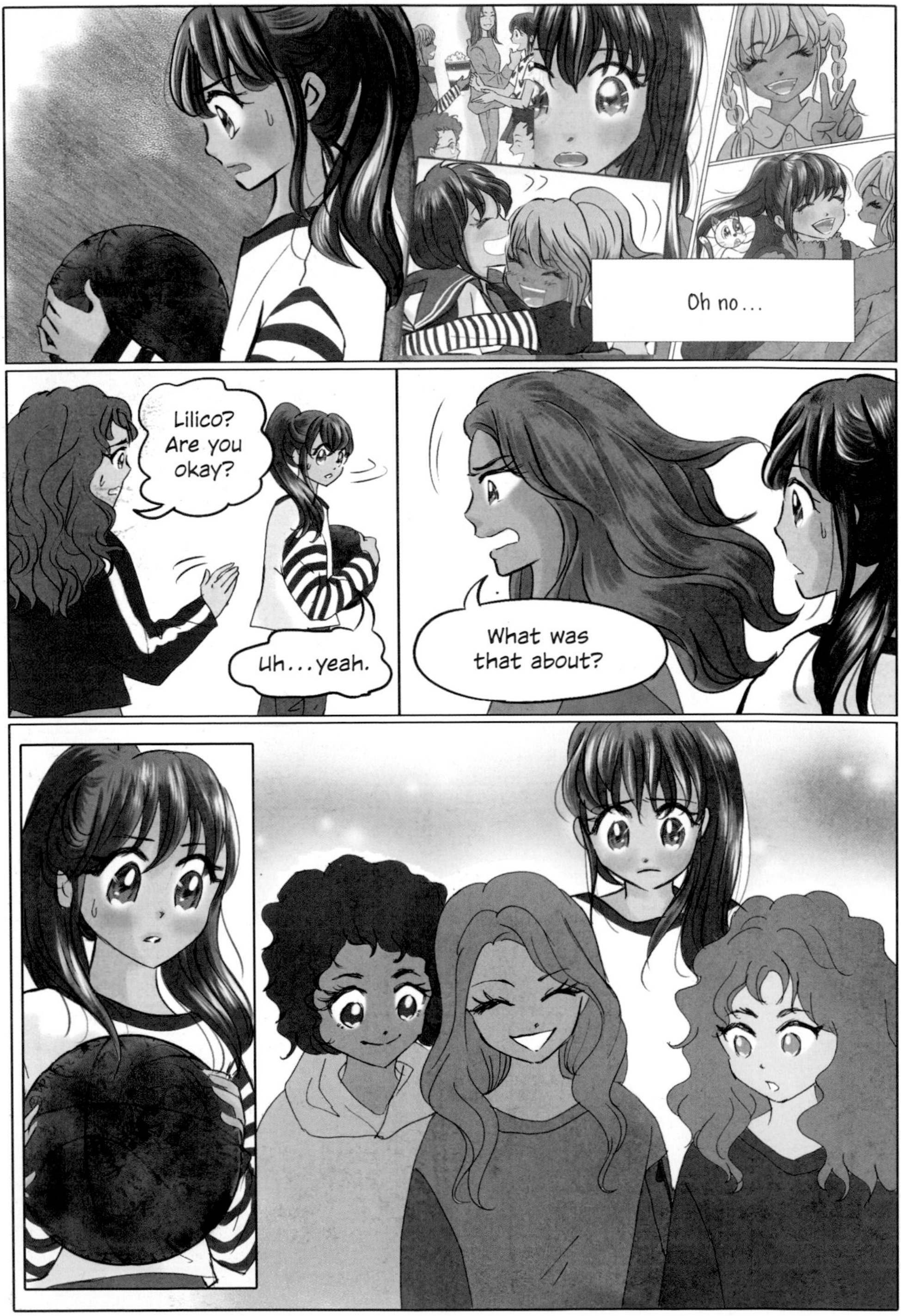

Oh no...
Lilico? Are you okay?
Uh...yeah.
What was that about?

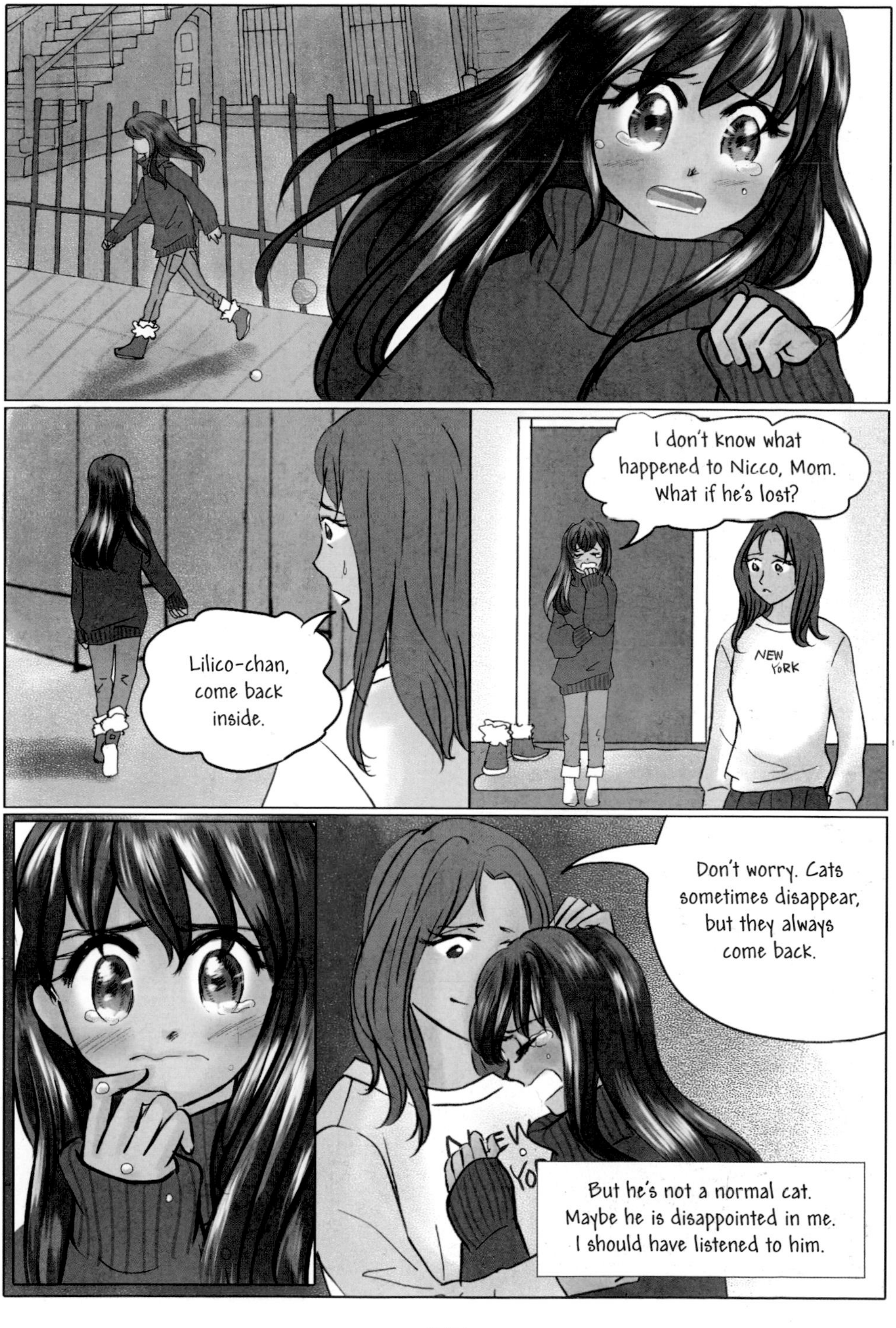
Lilico-chan, come back inside.
I don't know what happened to Nicco, Mom. What if he's lost?
NEW YORK
Don't worry. Cats sometimes disappear, but they always come back.
But he's not a normal cat. Maybe he is disappointed in me. I should have listened to him.

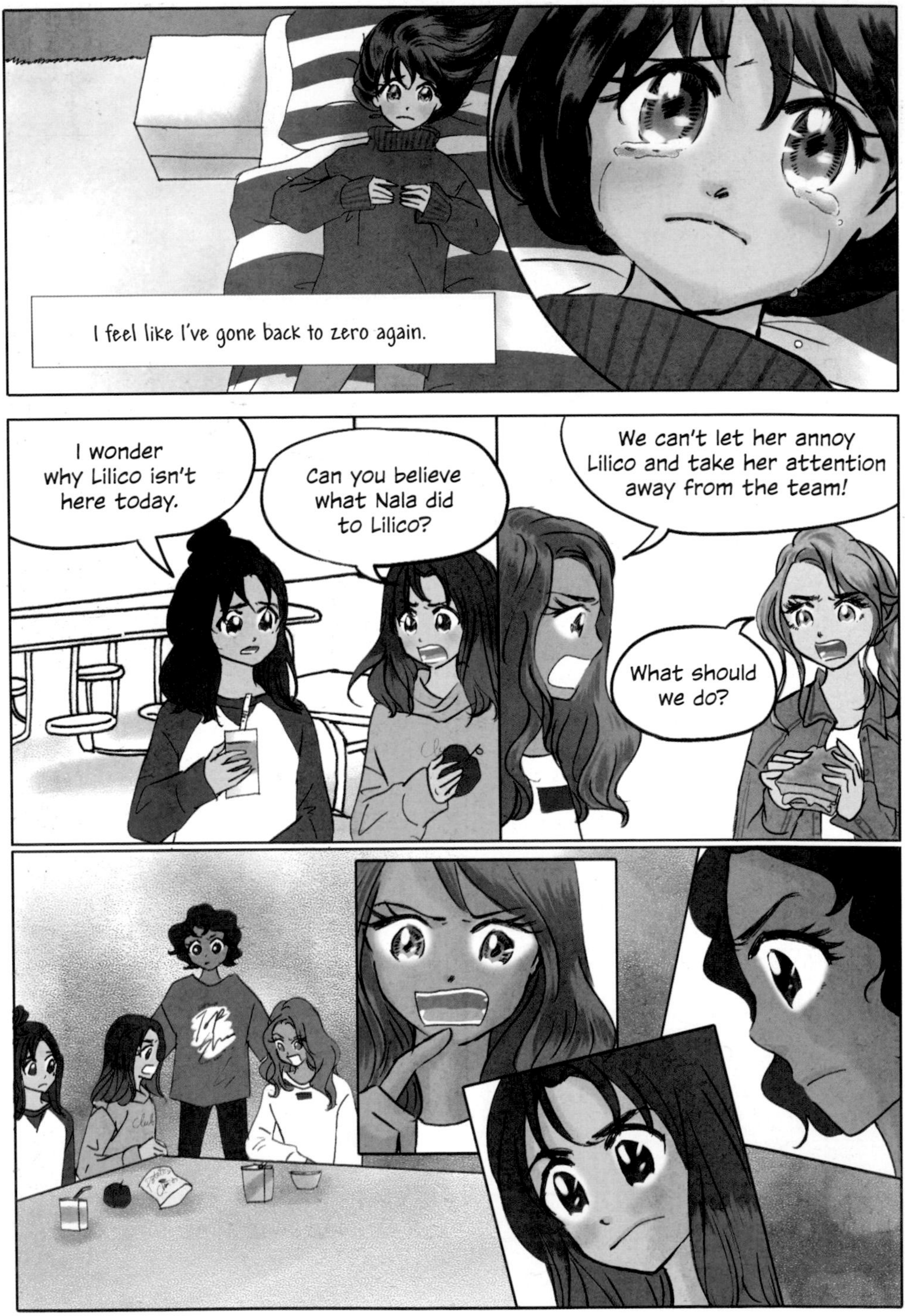
I feel like I've gone back to zero again.
I wonder why Lilico isn't here today.
Can you believe what Nala did to Lilico?
We can't let her annoy Lilico and take her attention away from the team!
What should we do?

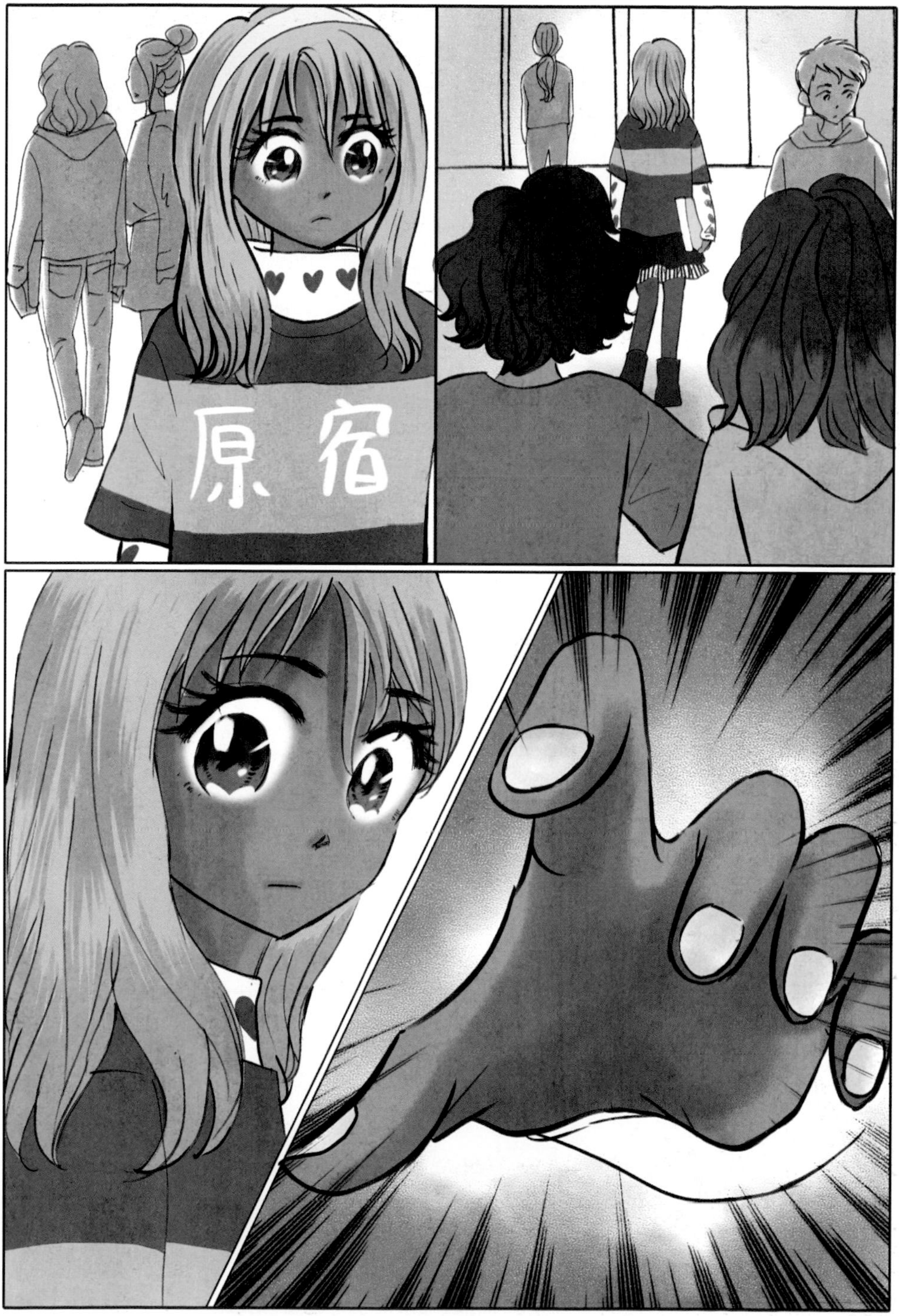
原宿

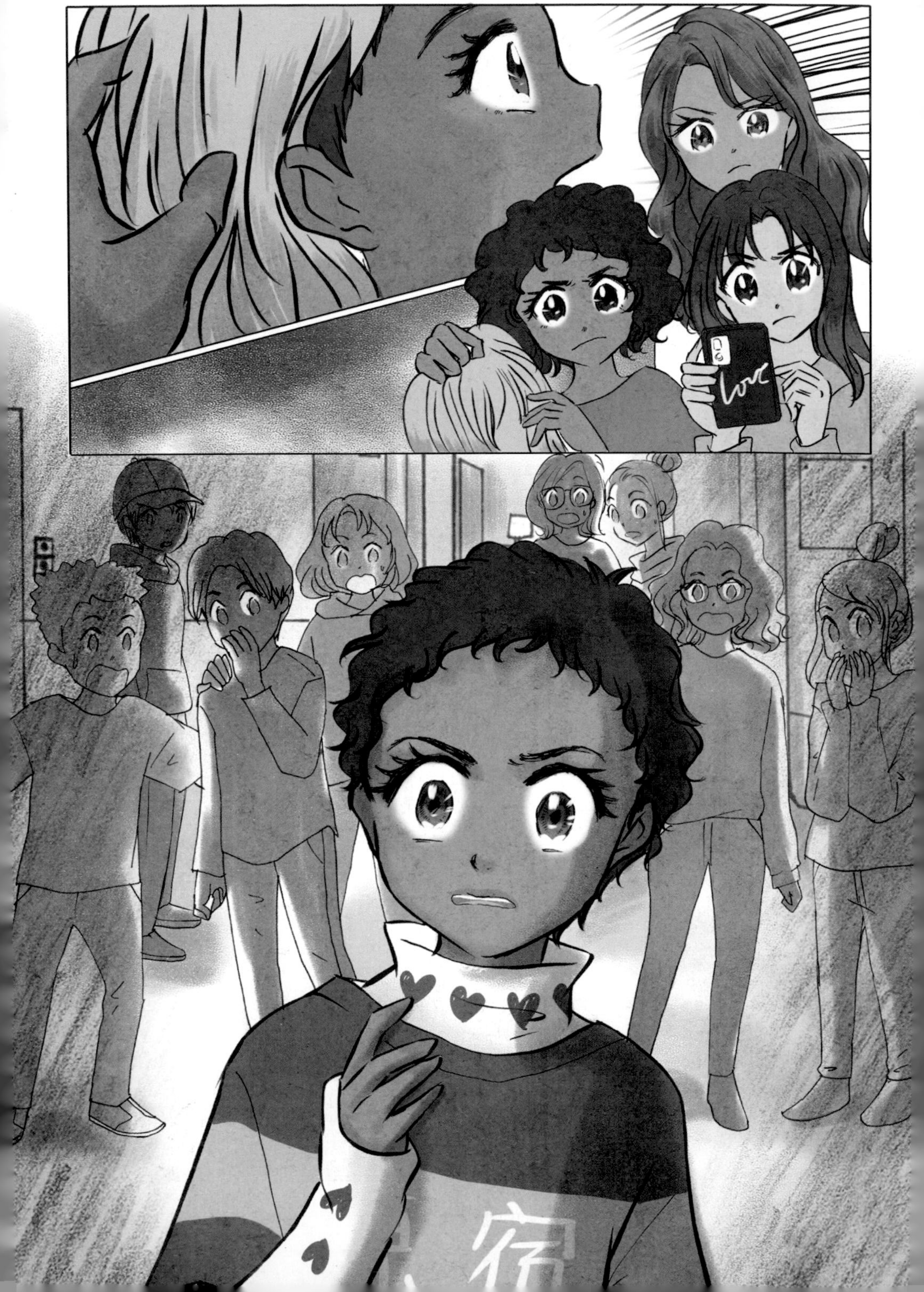
love

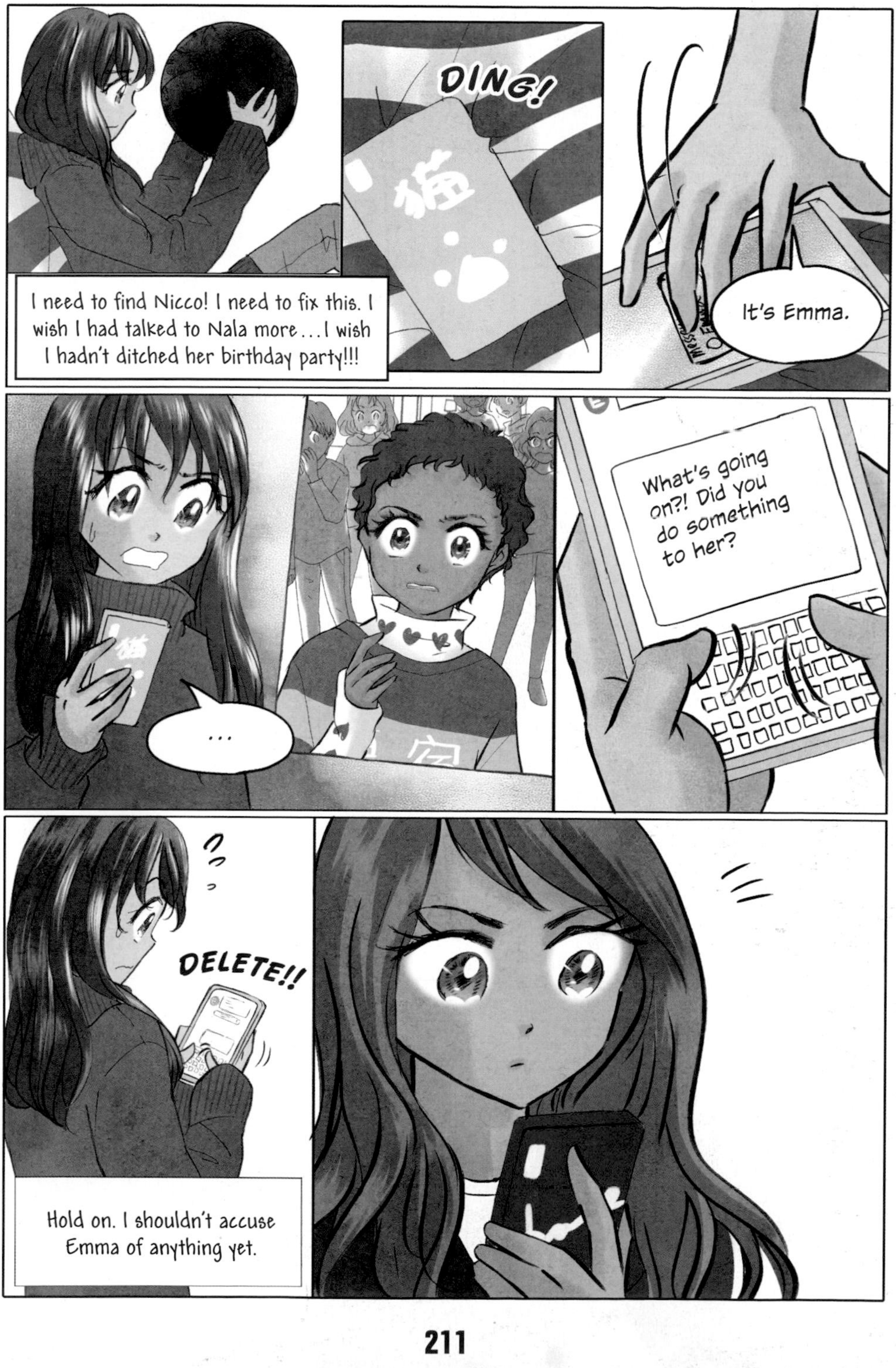
DING!
I need to find Nicco! I need to fix this. I wish I had talked to Nala more . . . I wish I hadn't ditched her birthday party!!!
It's Emma.
. . .
What's going on?! Did you do something to her?
DELETE!!
Hold on. I shouldn't accuse Emma of anything yet.

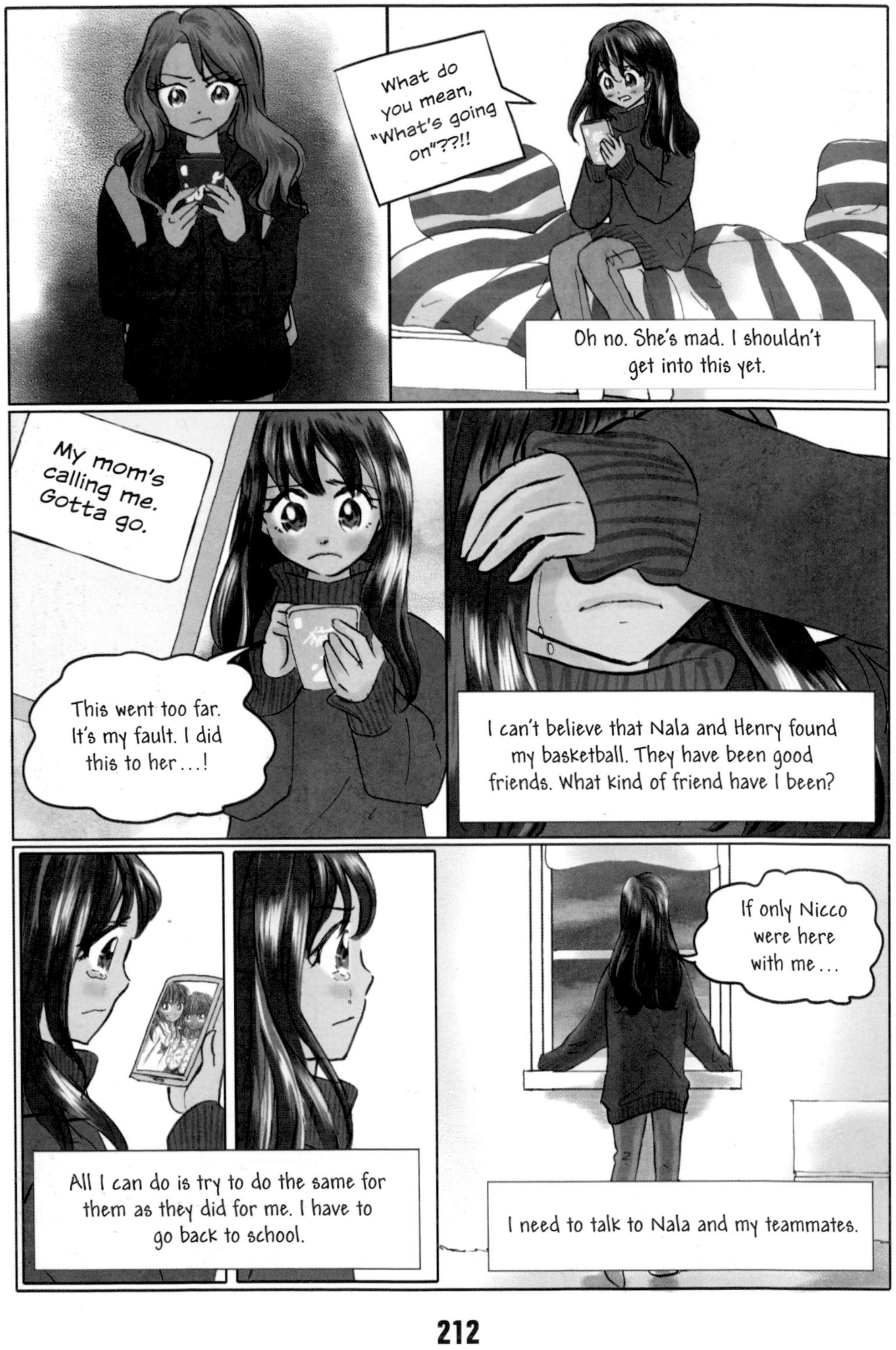
What do you mean, "What's going on"??!!
Oh no. She's mad. I shouldn't get into this yet.
My mom's calling me. Gotta go.
This went too far. It's my fault. I did this to her . . . !
I can't believe that Nala and Henry found my basketball. They have been good friends. What kind of friend have I been?
All I can do is try to do the same for them as they did for me. I have to go back to school.
If only Nicco were here with me . . .
I need to talk to Nala and my teammates.

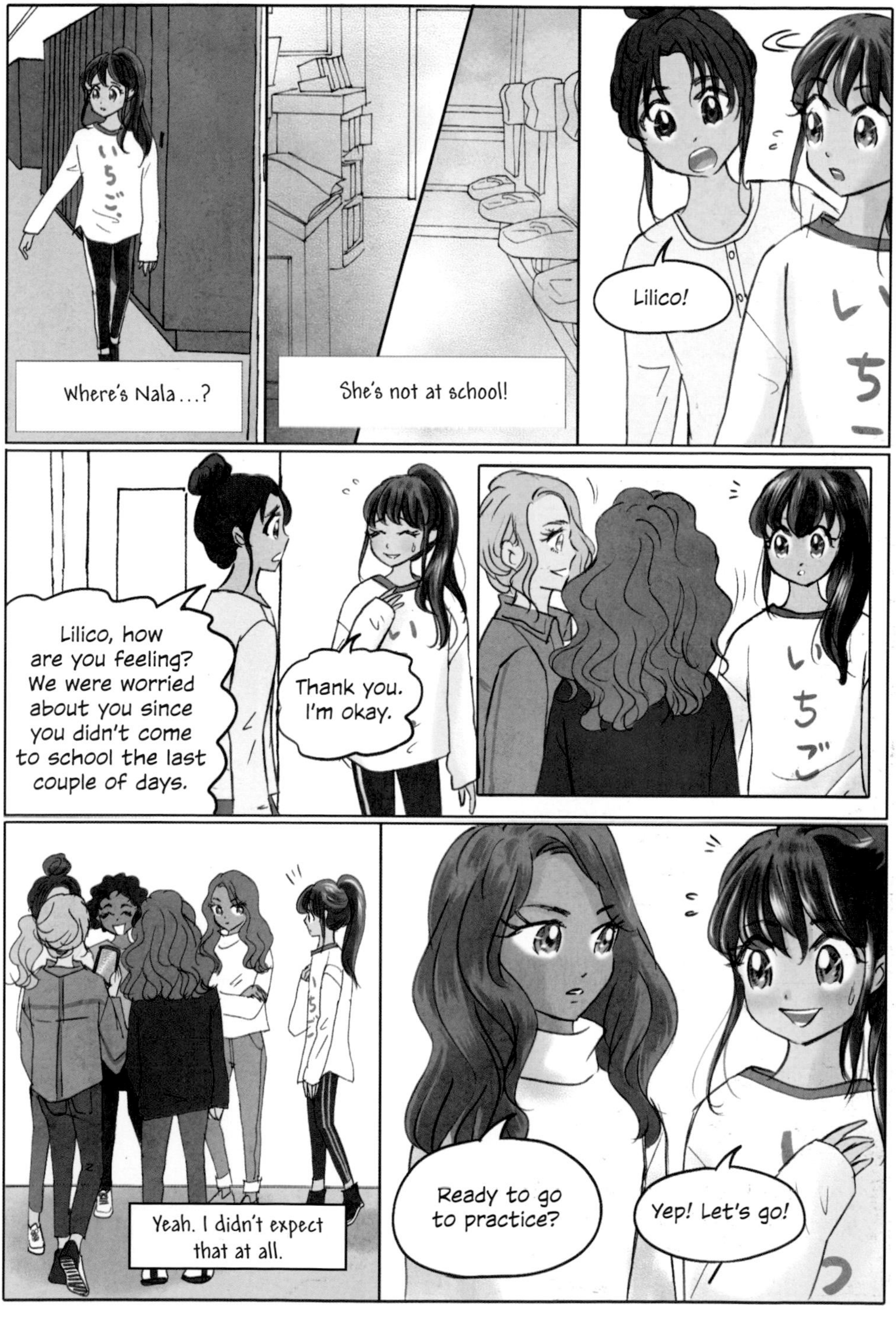
Where's Nala...?
She's not at school!
Lilico!
Lilico, how are you feeling? We were worried about you since you didn't come to school the last couple of days.
Thank you. I'm okay.
Yeah. I didn't expect that at all.
Ready to go to practice?
Yep! Let's go!

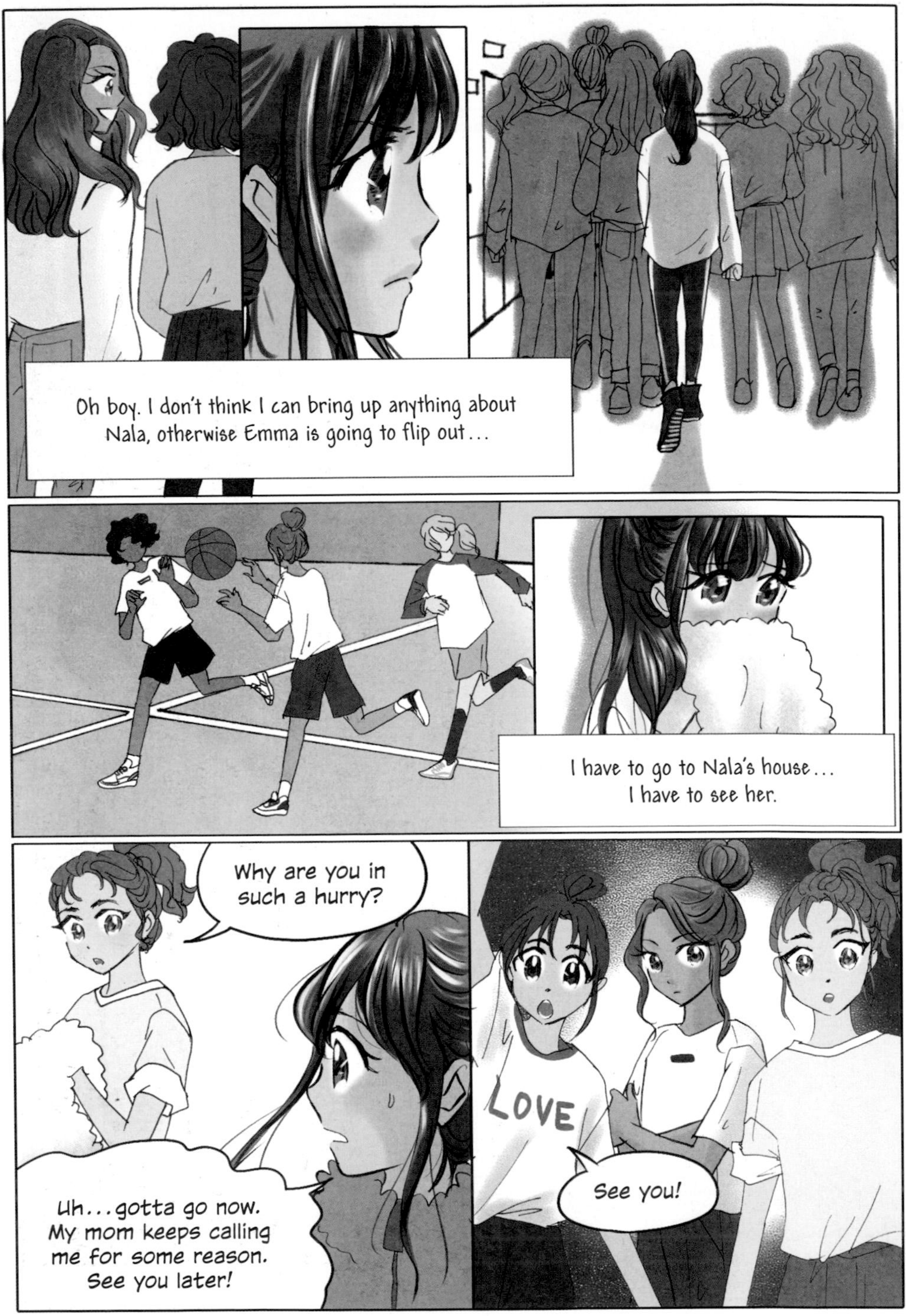
Oh boy. I don't think I can bring up anything about Nala, otherwise Emma is going to flip out...
I have to go to Nala's house... I have to see her.
Why are you in such a hurry?
Uh...gotta go now. My mom keeps calling me for some reason. See you later!
LOVE
See you!

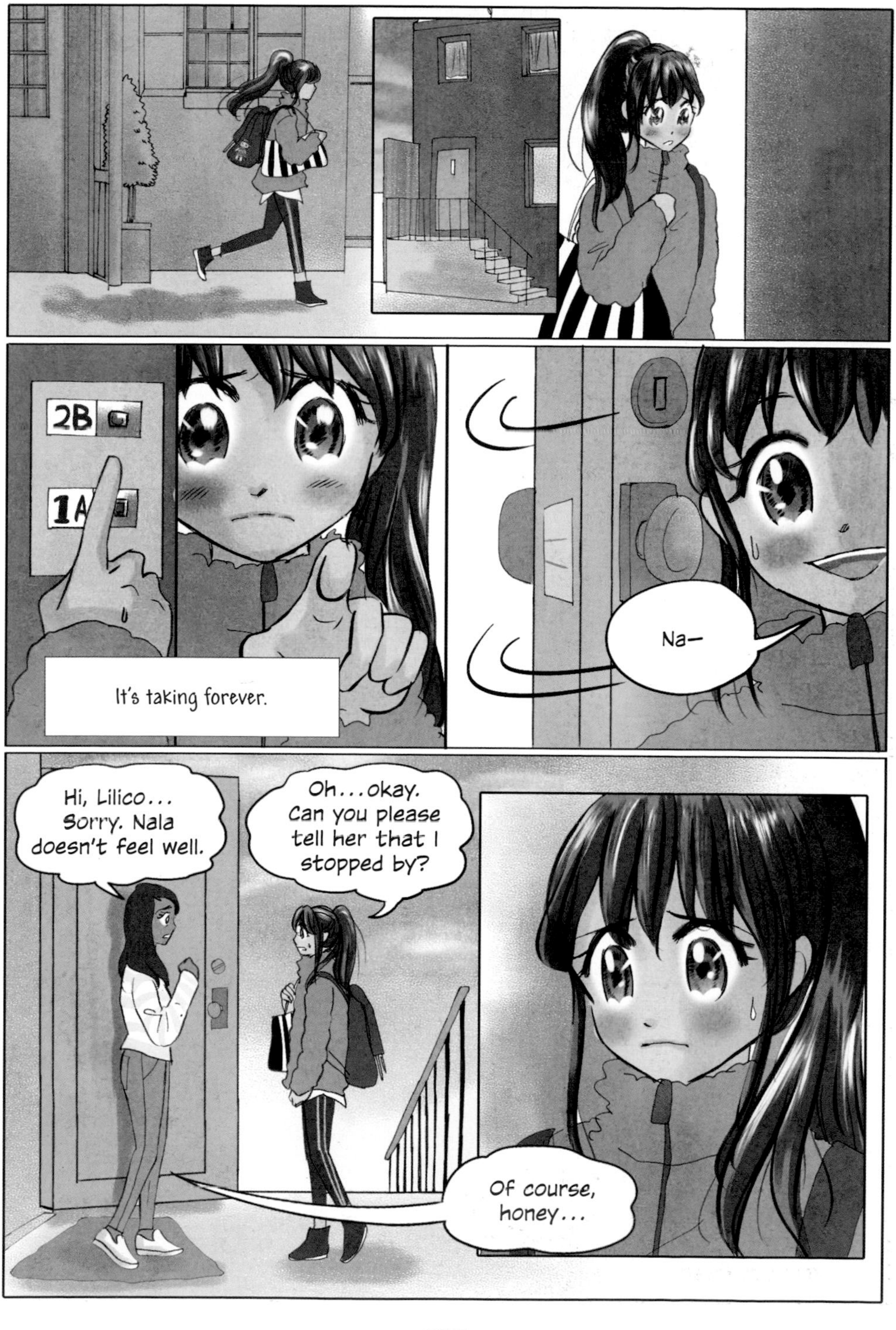
2B
1A
It's taking forever.
Na—
Hi, Lilico... Sorry. Nala doesn't feel well.
Oh...okay. Can you please tell her that I stopped by?
Of course, honey...

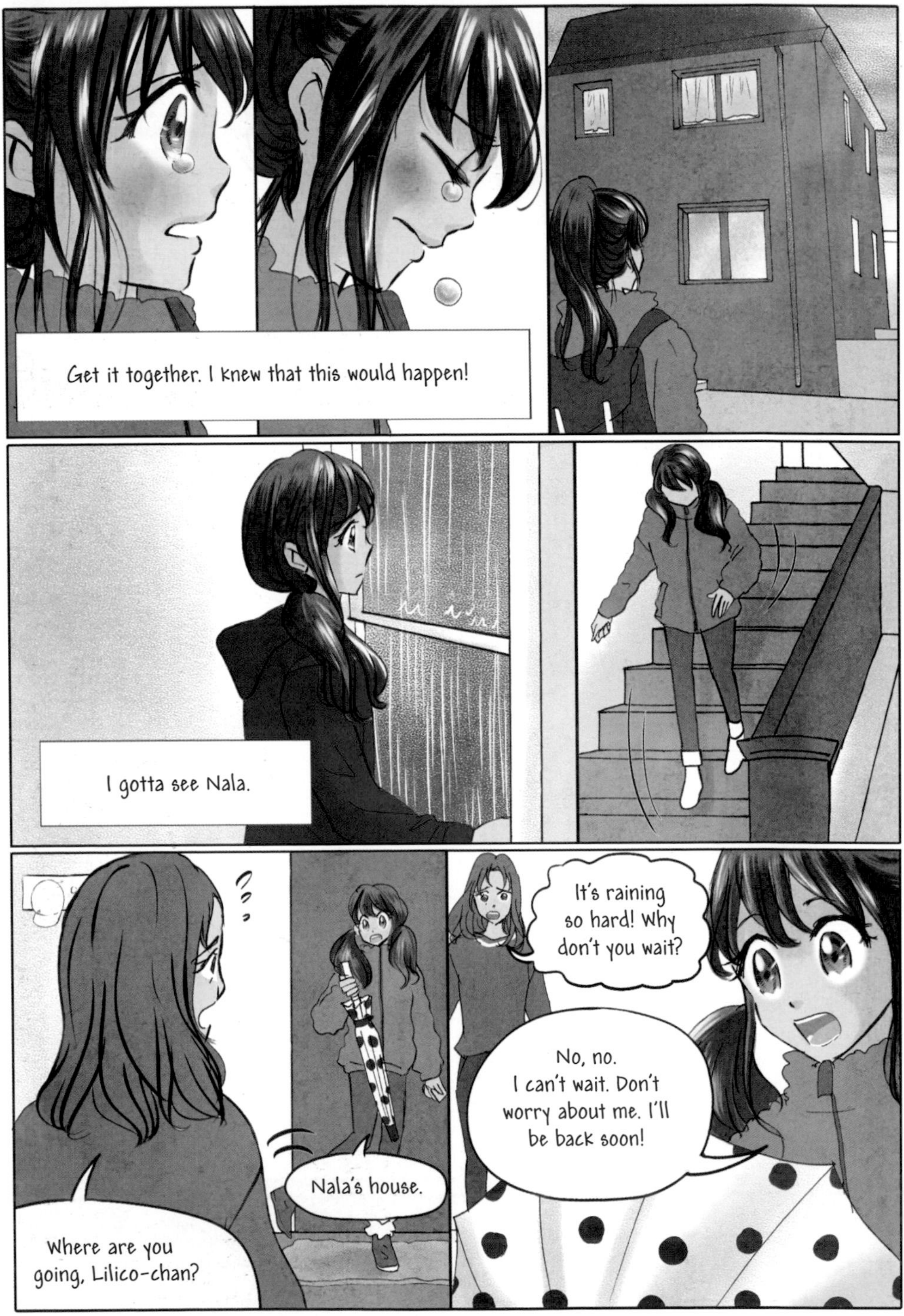
Get it together. I knew that this would happen!
I gotta see Nala.
Where are you going, Lilico-chan?
Nala's house.
It's raining so hard! Why don't you wait?
No, no. I can't wait. Don't worry about me. I'll be back soon!

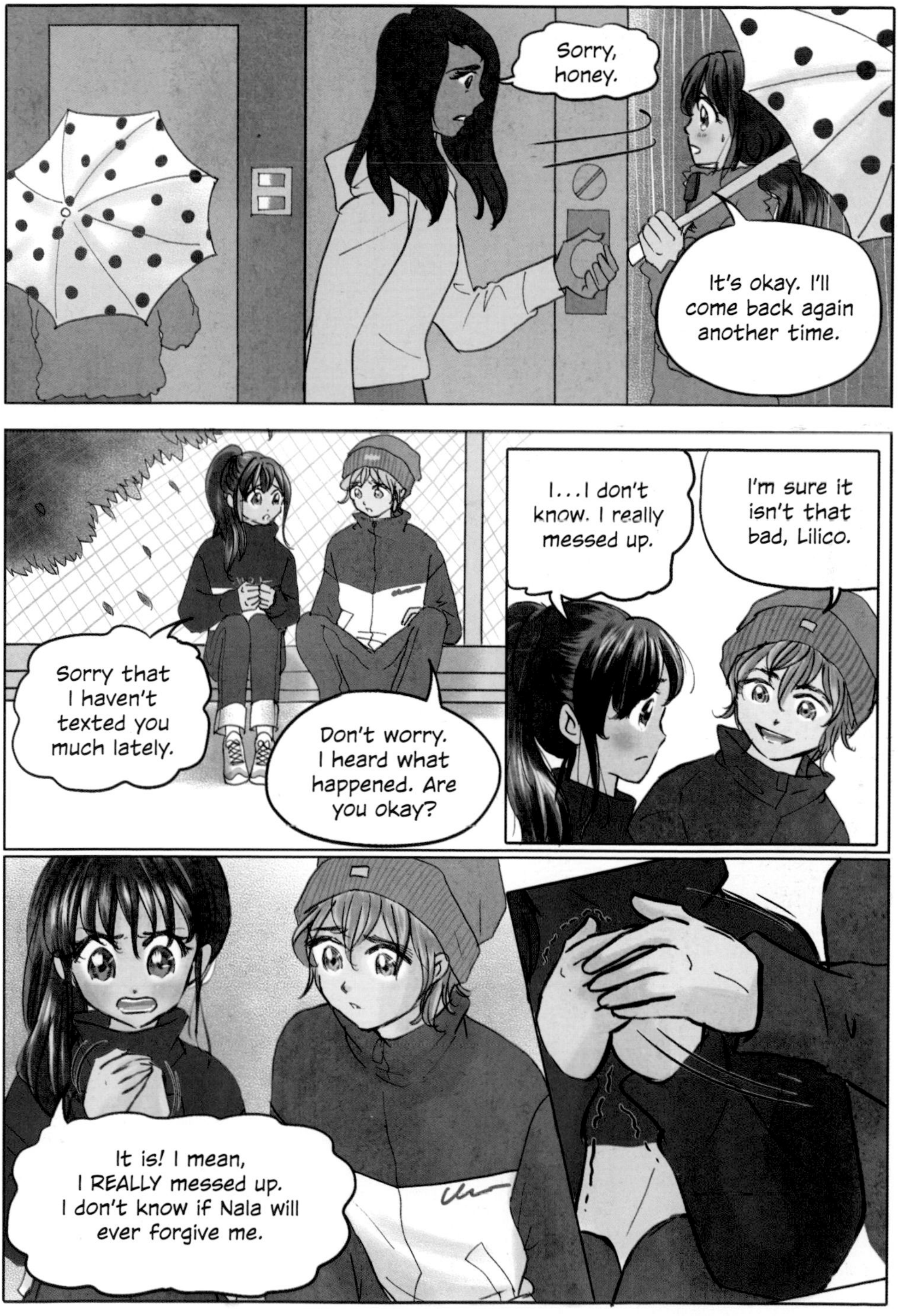
Sorry, honey.
It's okay. I'll come back again another time.
Sorry that I haven't texted you much lately.
Don't worry. I heard what happened. Are you okay?
I...I don't know. I really messed up.
I'm sure it isn't that bad, Lilico.
It is! I mean, I REALLY messed up. I don't know if Nala will ever forgive me.

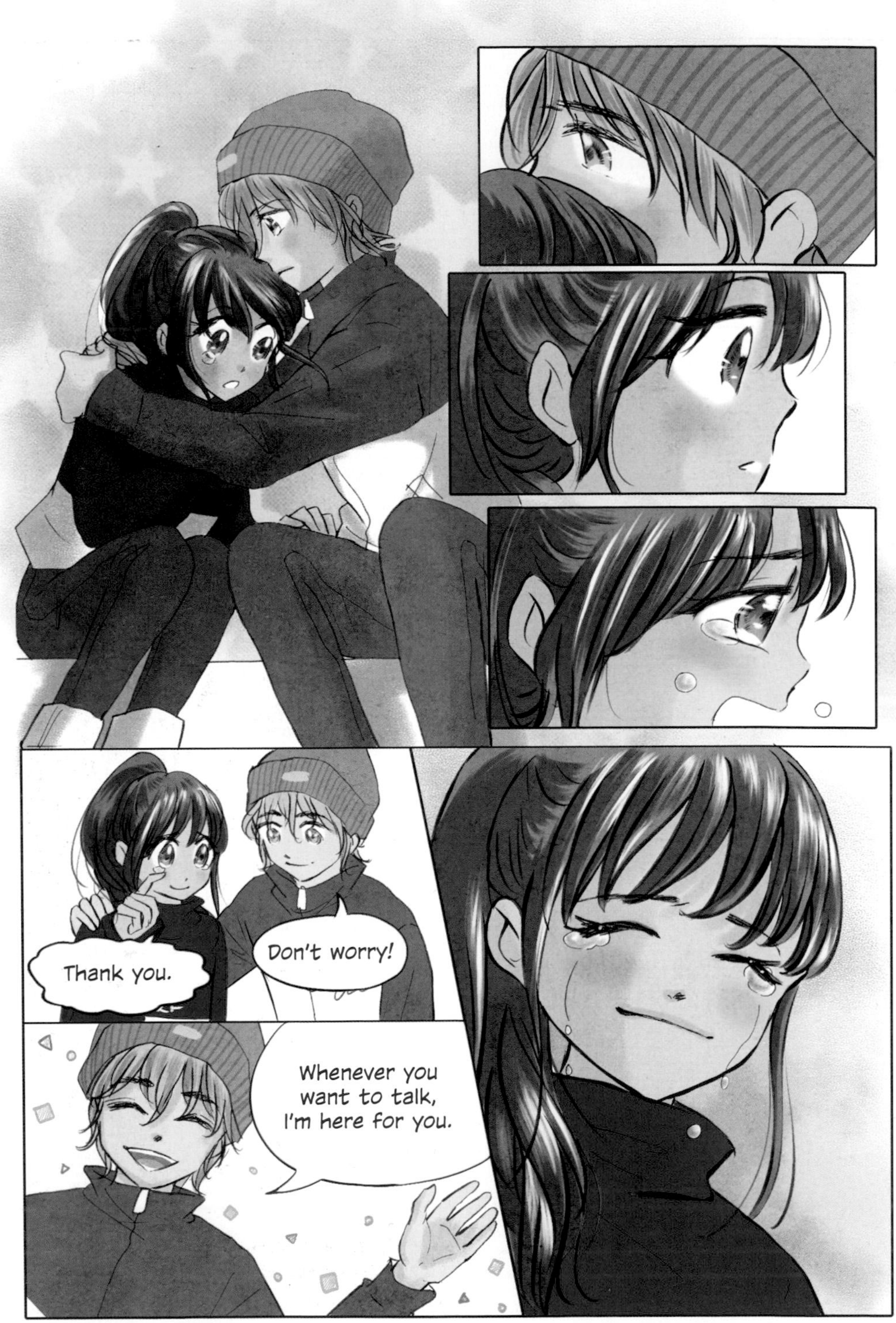
Thank you.
Don't worry!
Whenever you want to talk, I'm here for you.

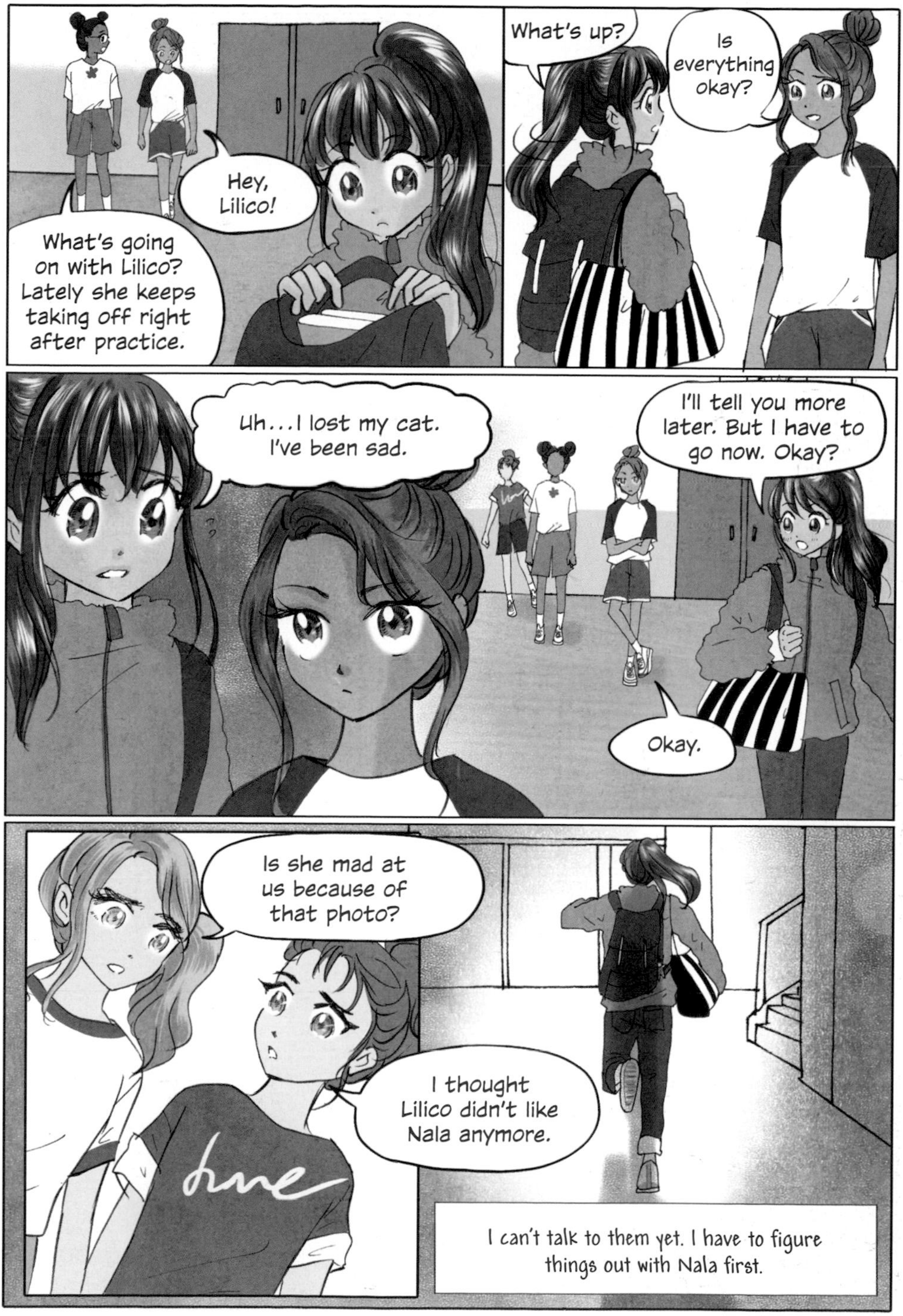
Hey, Lilico!
What's going on with Lilico? Lately she keeps taking off right after practice.
What's up?
Is everything okay?
Uh...I lost my cat. I've been sad.
I'll tell you more later. But I have to go now. Okay?
Okay.
Is she mad at us because of that photo?
I thought Lilico didn't like Nala anymore.
I can't talk to them yet. I have to figure things out with Nala first.

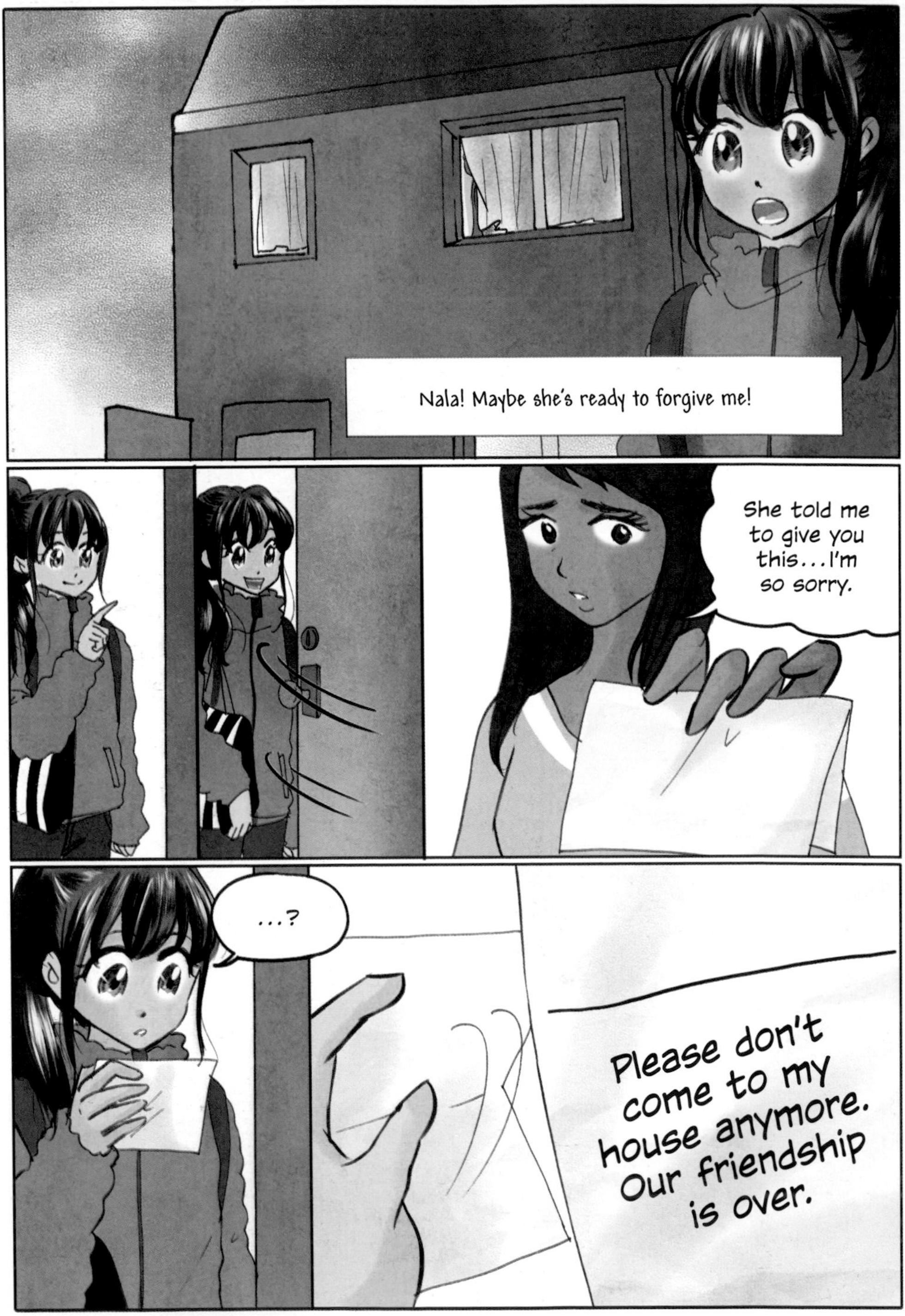

Nala! Maybe she's ready to forgive me!
She told me to give you this...I'm so sorry.
...?
Please don't come to my house anymore. Our friendship is over.

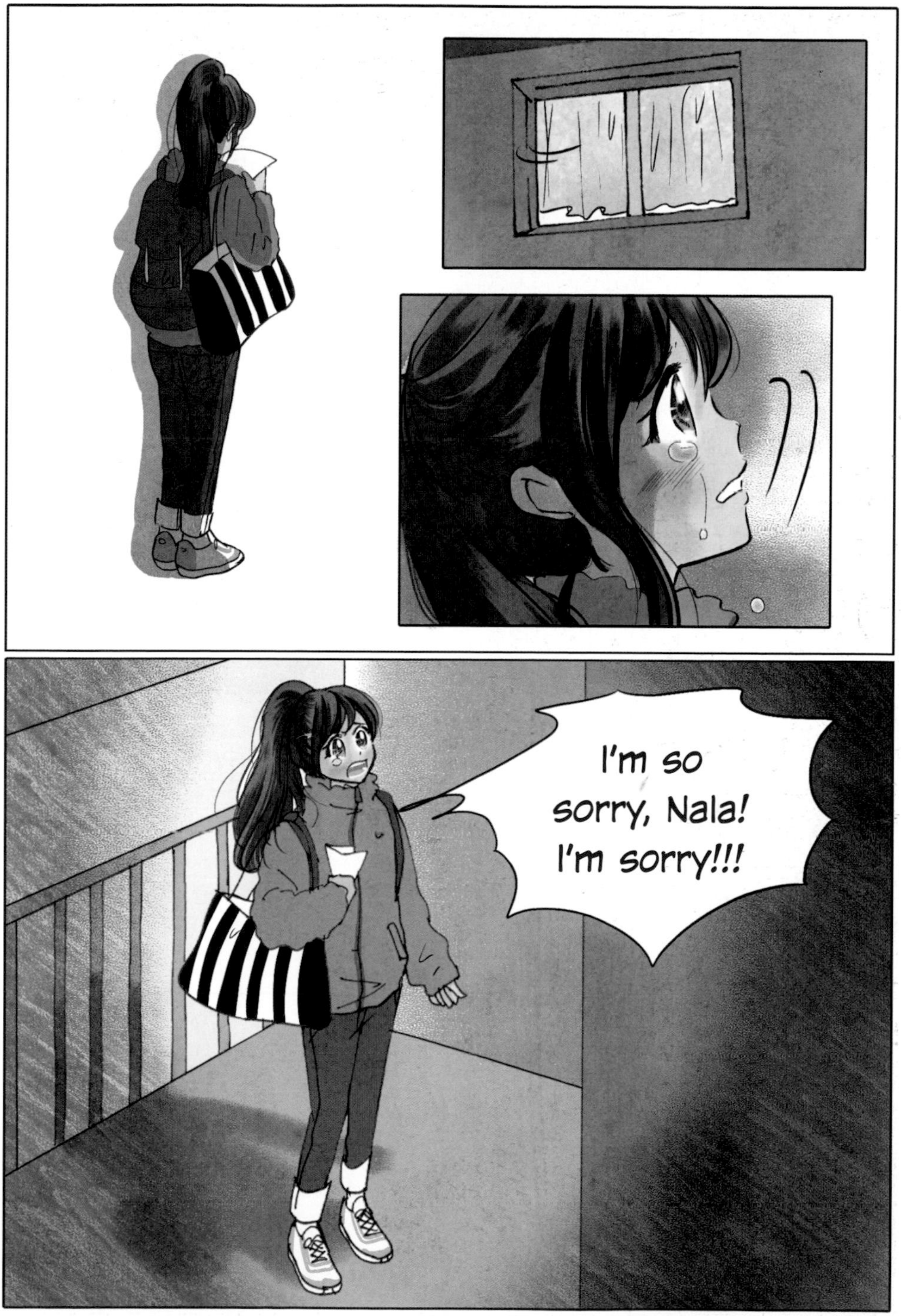
I'm so sorry, Nala! I'm sorry!!!

CHAPTER 8

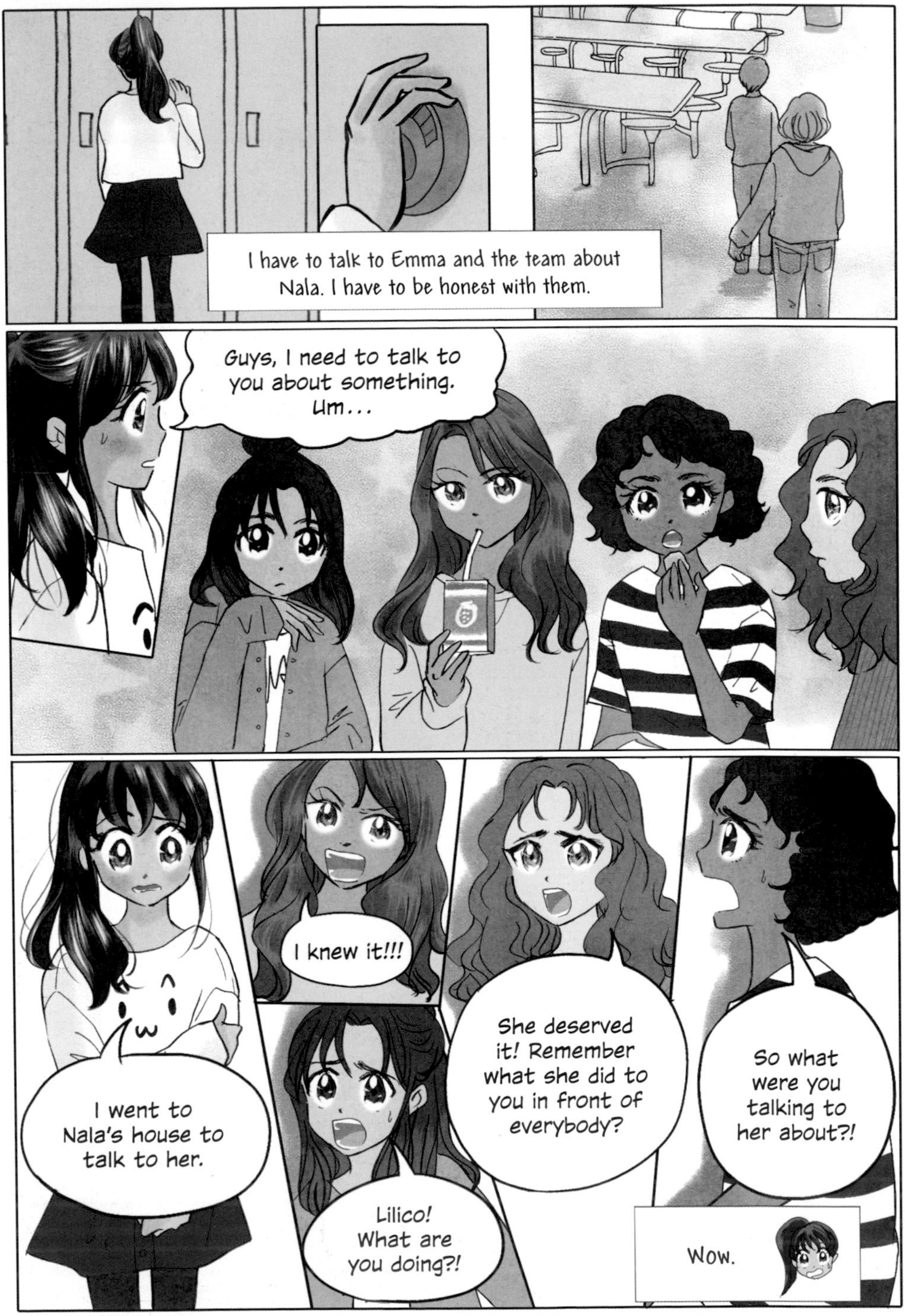
I have to talk to Emma and the team about Nala. I have to be honest with them.
Guys, I need to talk to you about something. Um...
I went to Nala's house to talk to her.
I knew it!!!
She deserved it! Remember what she did to you in front of everybody?
So what were you talking to her about?!
Lilico! What are you doing?!
Wow.

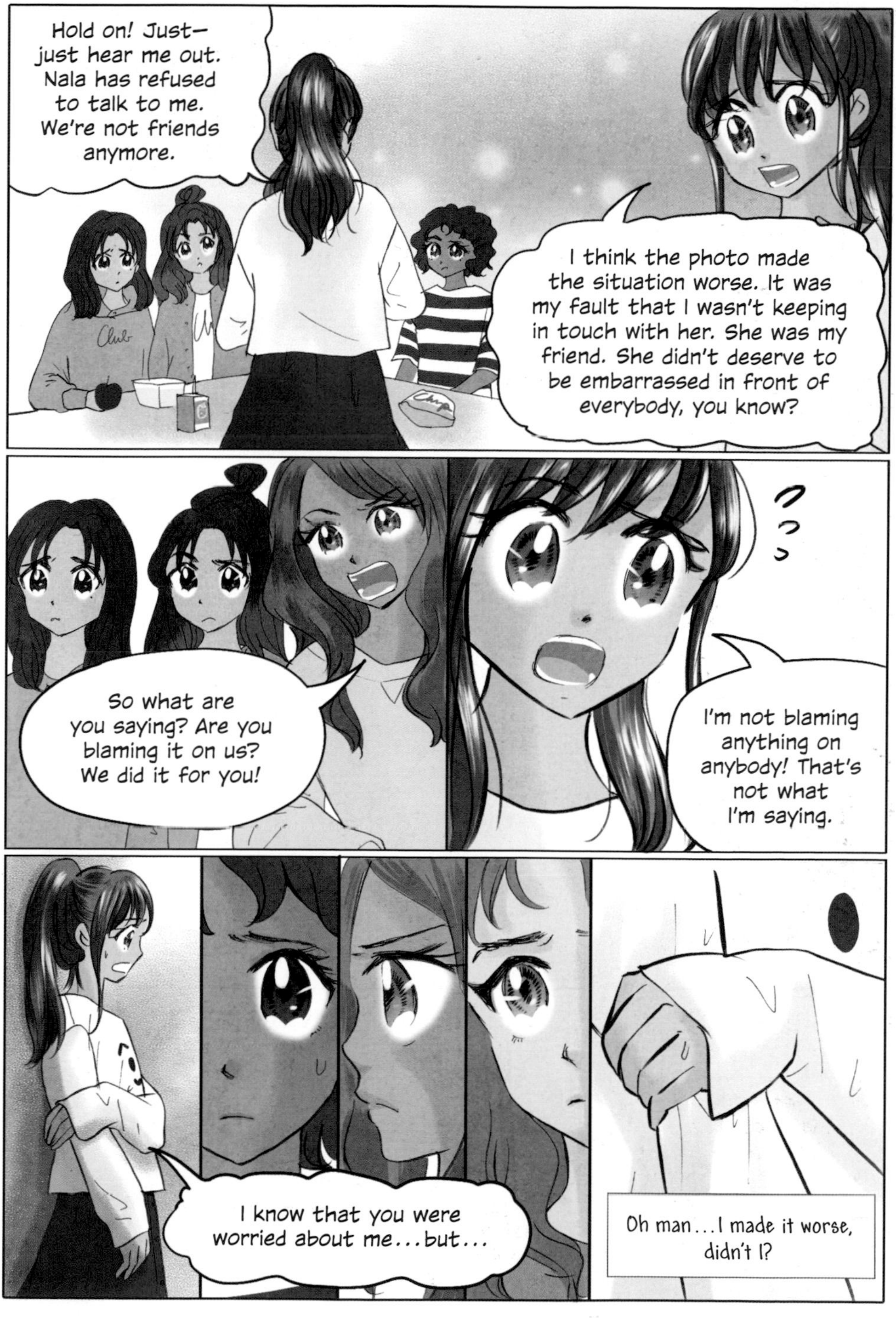
Hold on! Just—just hear me out. Nala has refused to talk to me. We're not friends anymore.
I think the photo made the situation worse. It was my fault that I wasn't keeping in touch with her. She was my friend. She didn't deserve to be embarrassed in front of everybody, you know?
So what are you saying? Are you blaming it on us? We did it for you!
I'm not blaming anything on anybody! That's not what I'm saying.
I know that you were worried about me...but...
Oh man...I made it worse, didn't I?

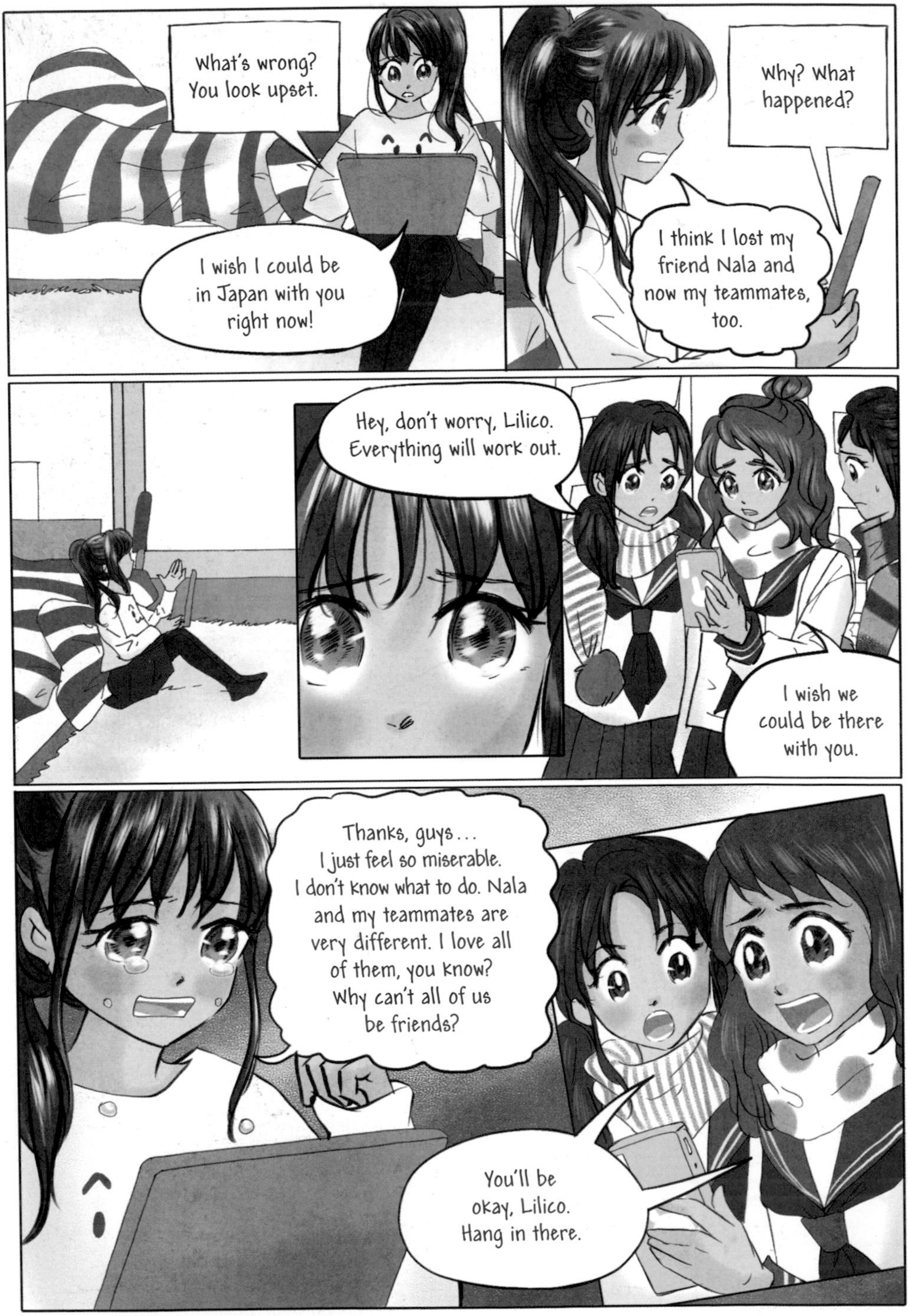
What's wrong? You look upset.
I wish I could be in Japan with you right now!
Why? What happened?
I think I lost my friend Nala and now my teammates, too.
Hey, don't worry, Lilico. Everything will work out.
I wish we could be there with you.
Thanks, guys... I just feel so miserable. I don't know what to do. Nala and my teammates are very different. I love all of them, you know? Why can't all of us be friends?
You'll be okay, Lilico. Hang in there.

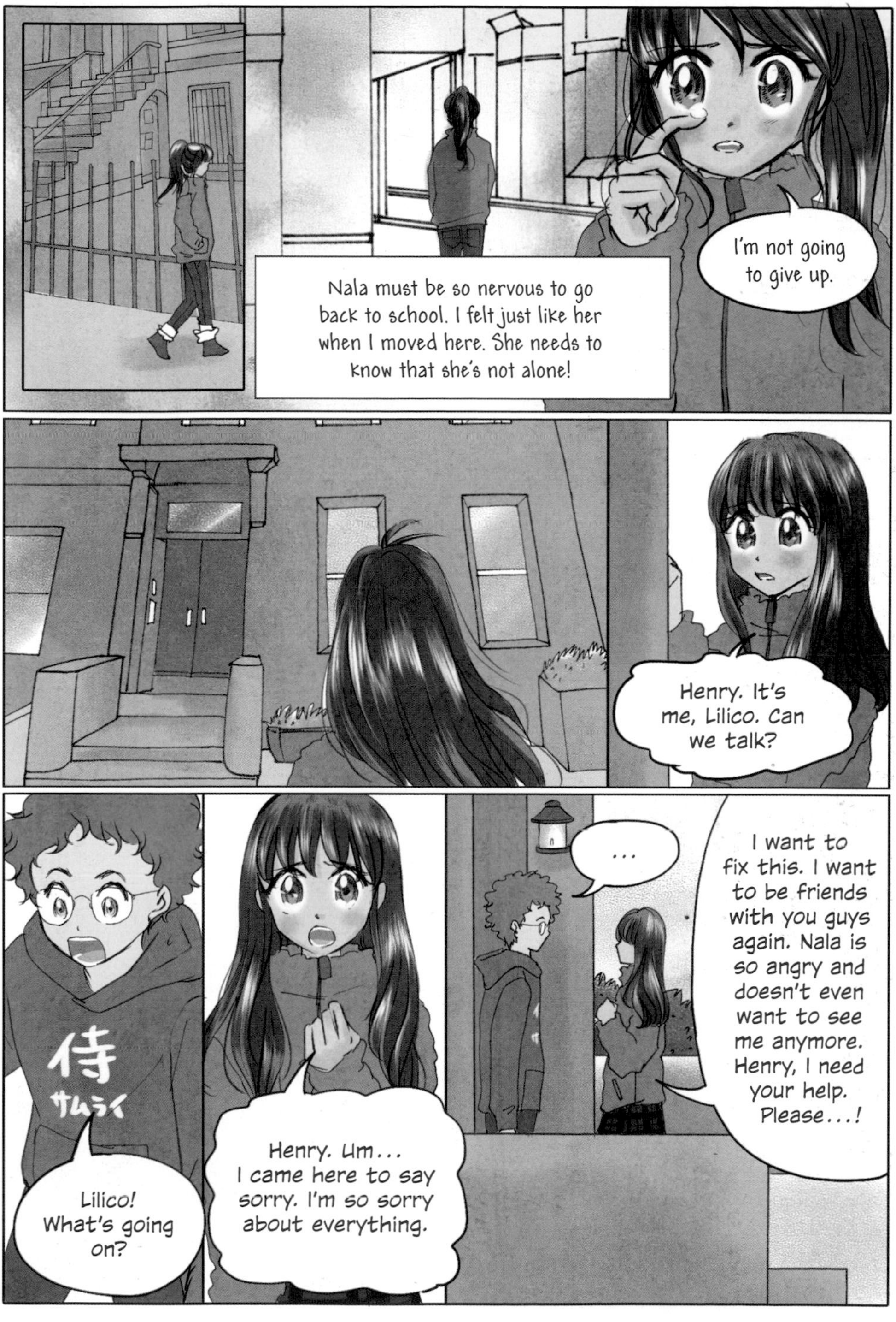
Nala must be so nervous to go back to school. I felt just like her when I moved here. She needs to know that she's not alone!
I'm not going to give up.
Henry. It's me, Lilico. Can we talk?
侍
サムライ
Lilico! What's going on?
Henry. Um... I came here to say sorry. I'm so sorry about everything.
...
I want to fix this. I want to be friends with you guys again. Nala is so angry and doesn't even want to see me anymore. Henry, I need your help. Please...!

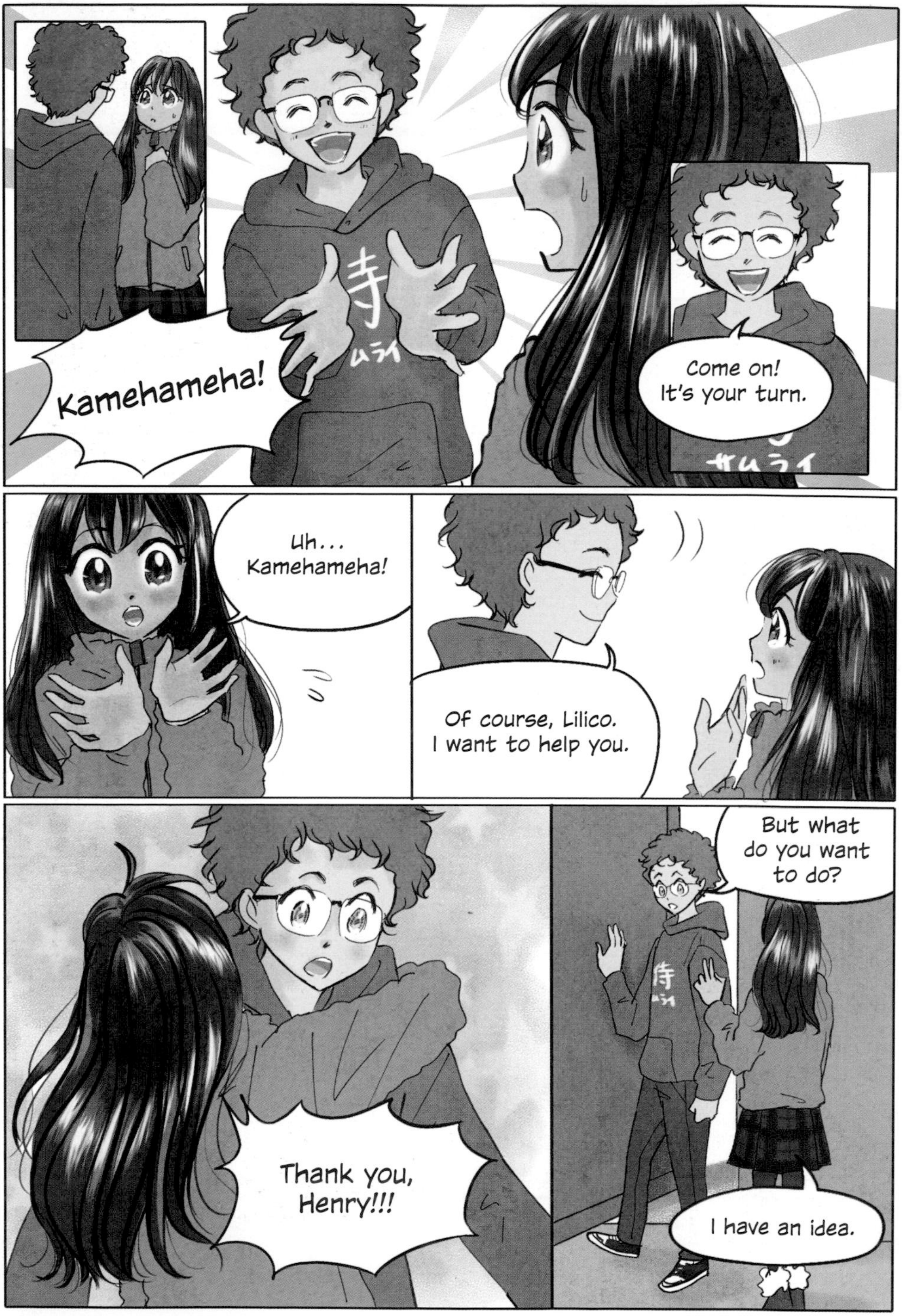
Kamehameha!
Come on! It's your turn.
Uh... Kamehameha!
Of course, Lilico. I want to help you.
Thank you, Henry!!!
But what do you want to do?
I have an idea.
サムライ

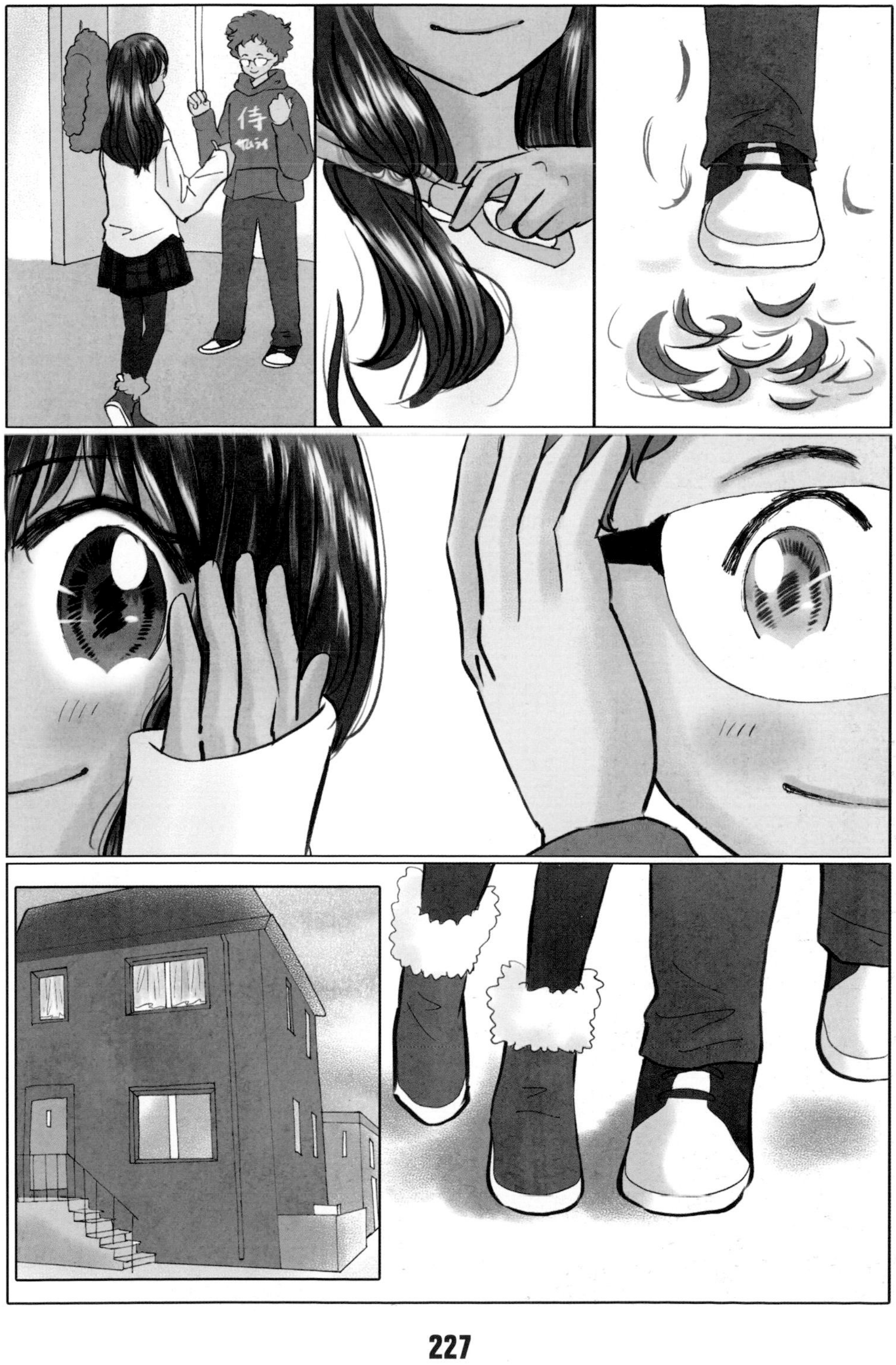
侍

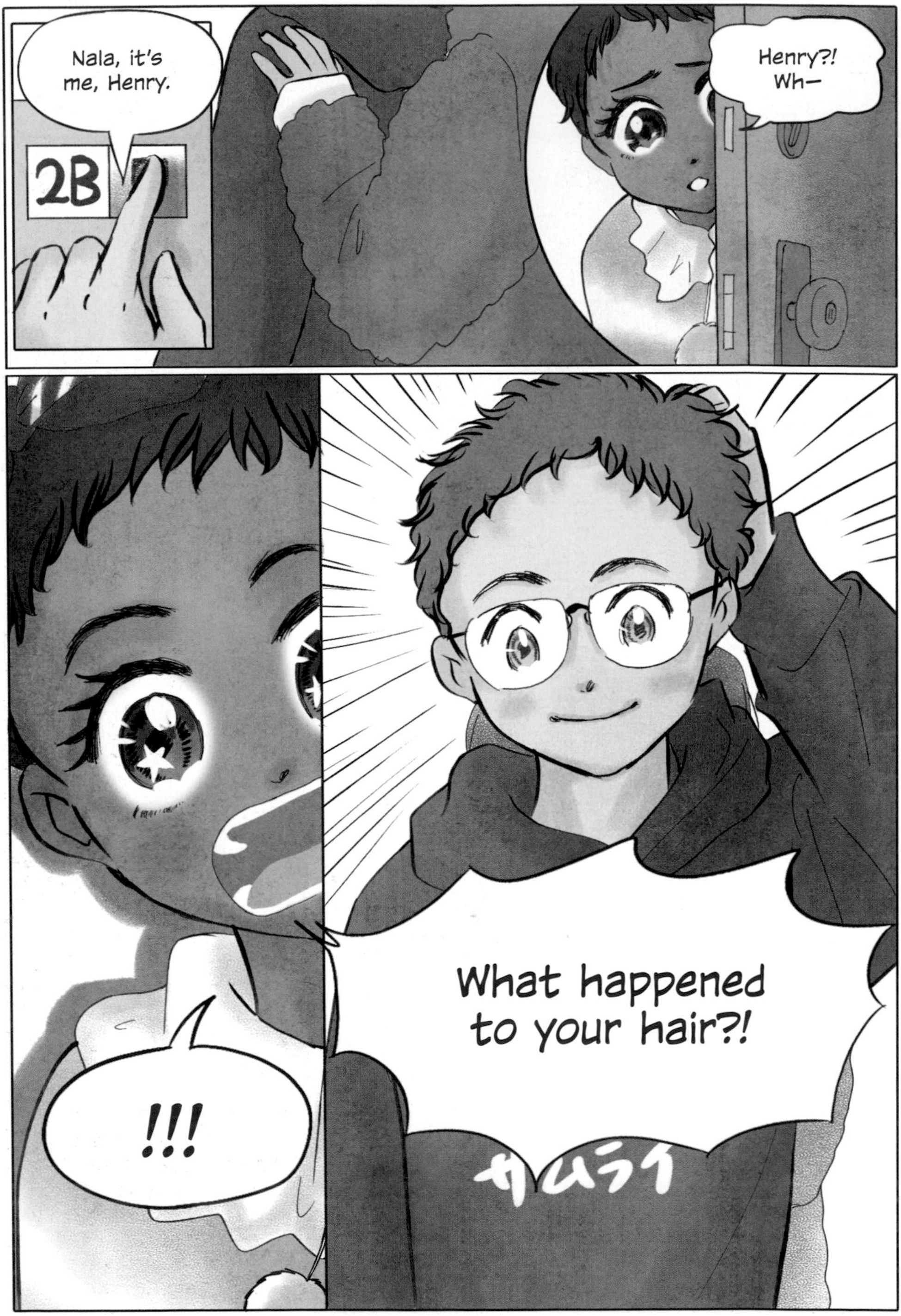
Nala, it's me, Henry.
2B
Henry?! Wh—
!!!
What happened to your hair?!
サムライ

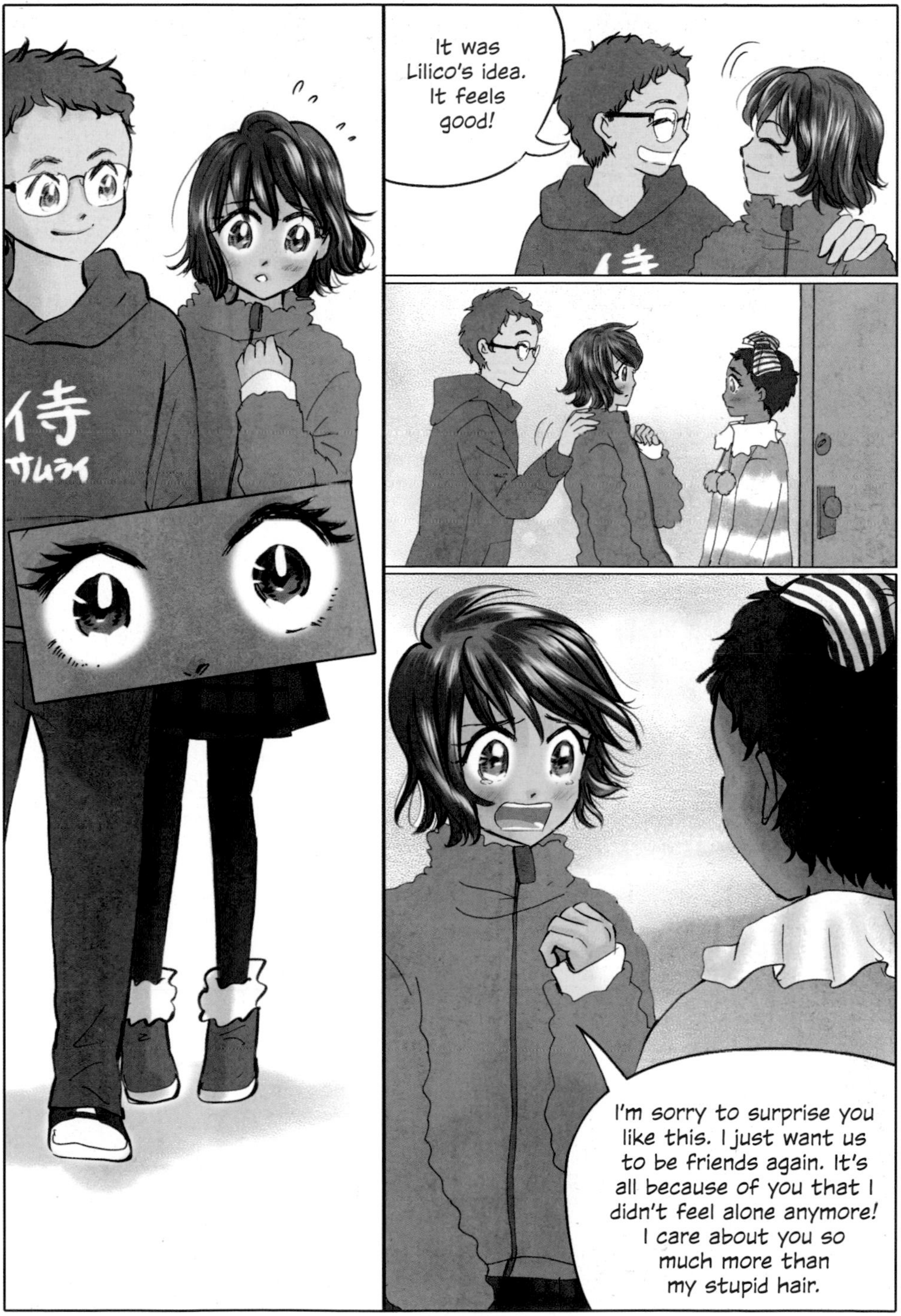
侍
サムライ
It was Lilico's idea. It feels good!
I'm sorry to surprise you like this. I just want us to be friends again. It's all because of you that I didn't feel alone anymore! I care about you so much more than my stupid hair.

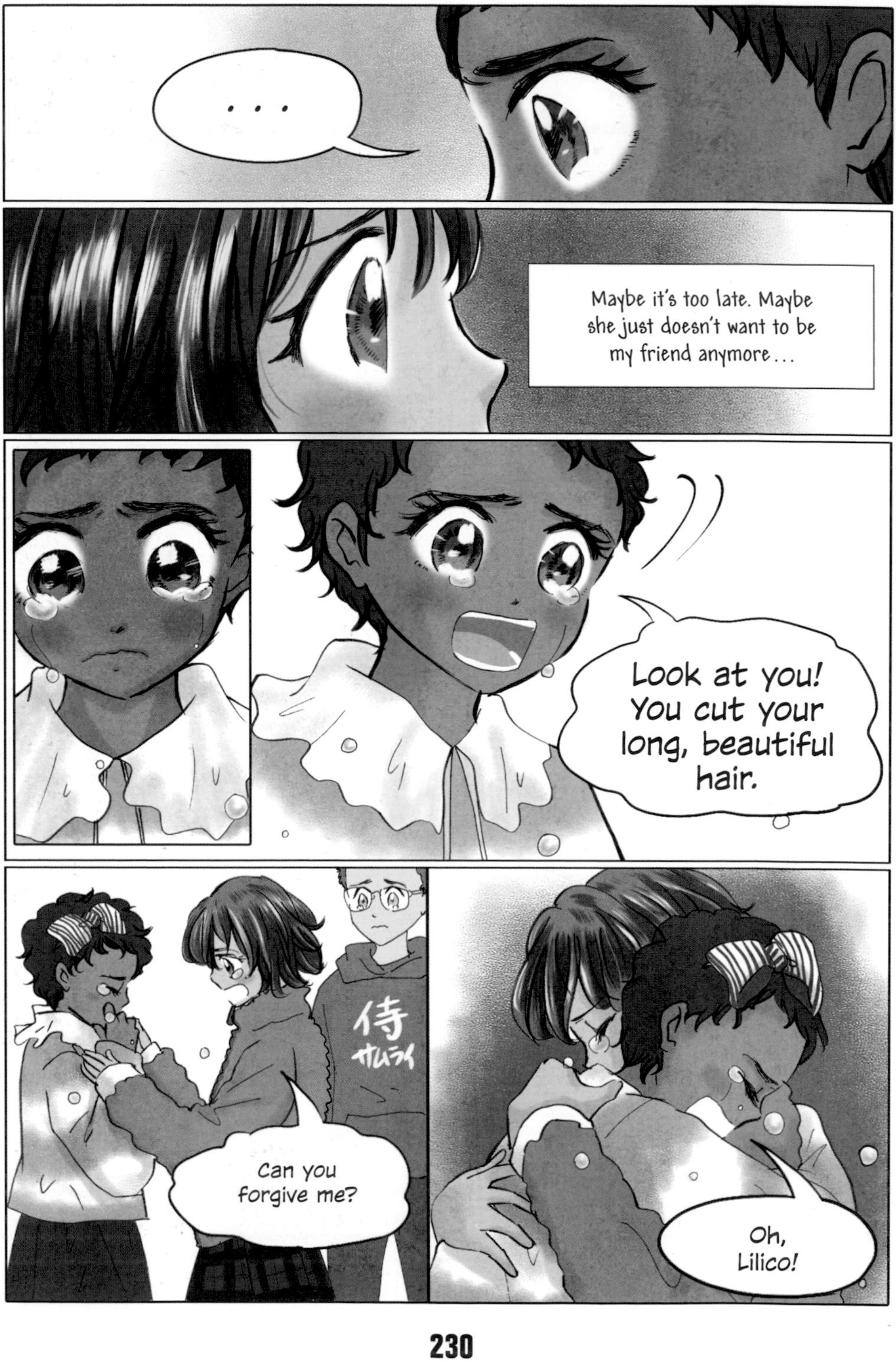
. . .
Maybe it's too late. Maybe she just doesn't want to be my friend anymore . . .
Look at you! You cut your long, beautiful hair.
侍
サムライ
Can you forgive me?
Oh, Lilico!

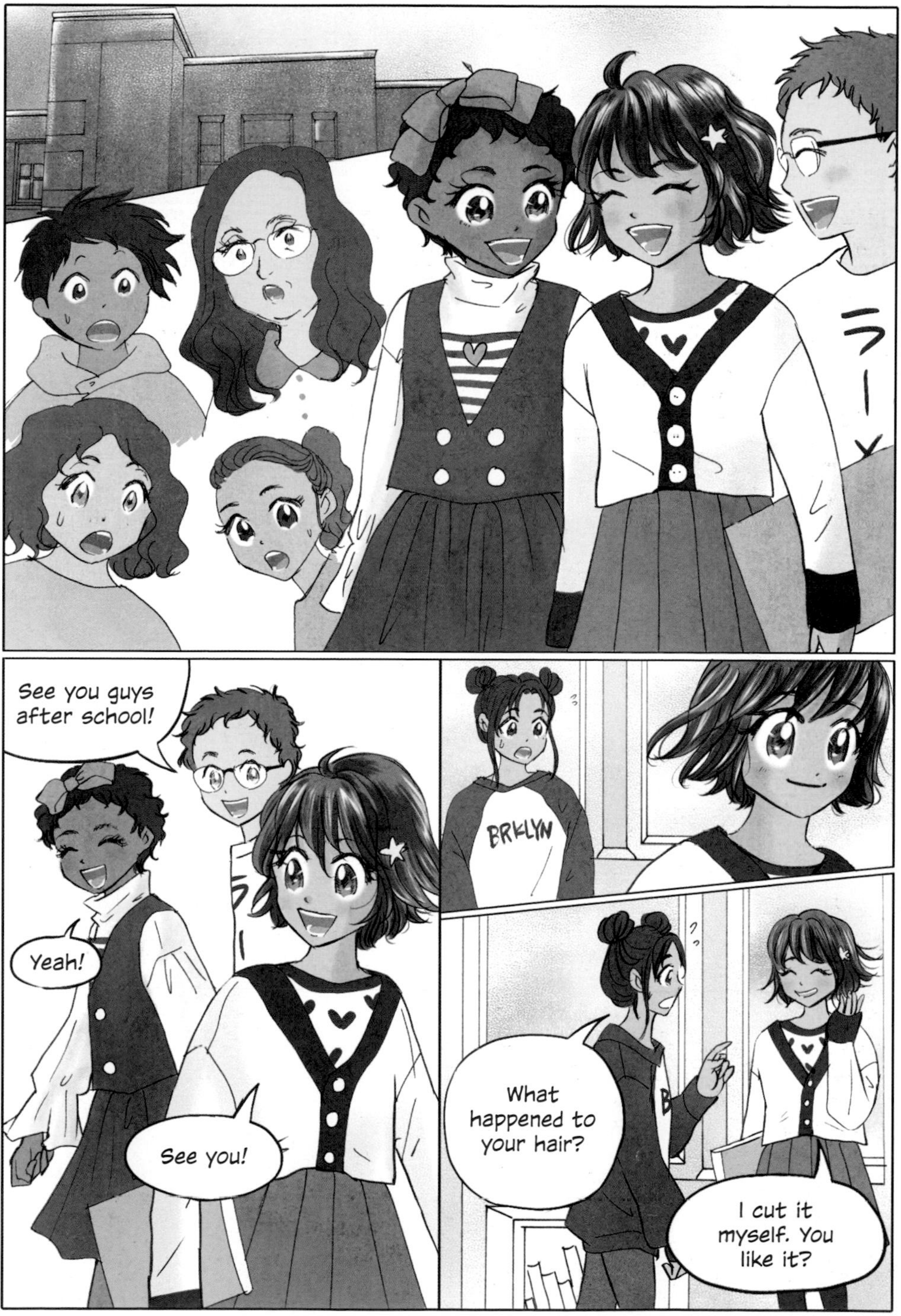
See you guys after school!
Yeah!
See you!
BRKLYN
What happened to your hair?
I cut it myself. You like it?

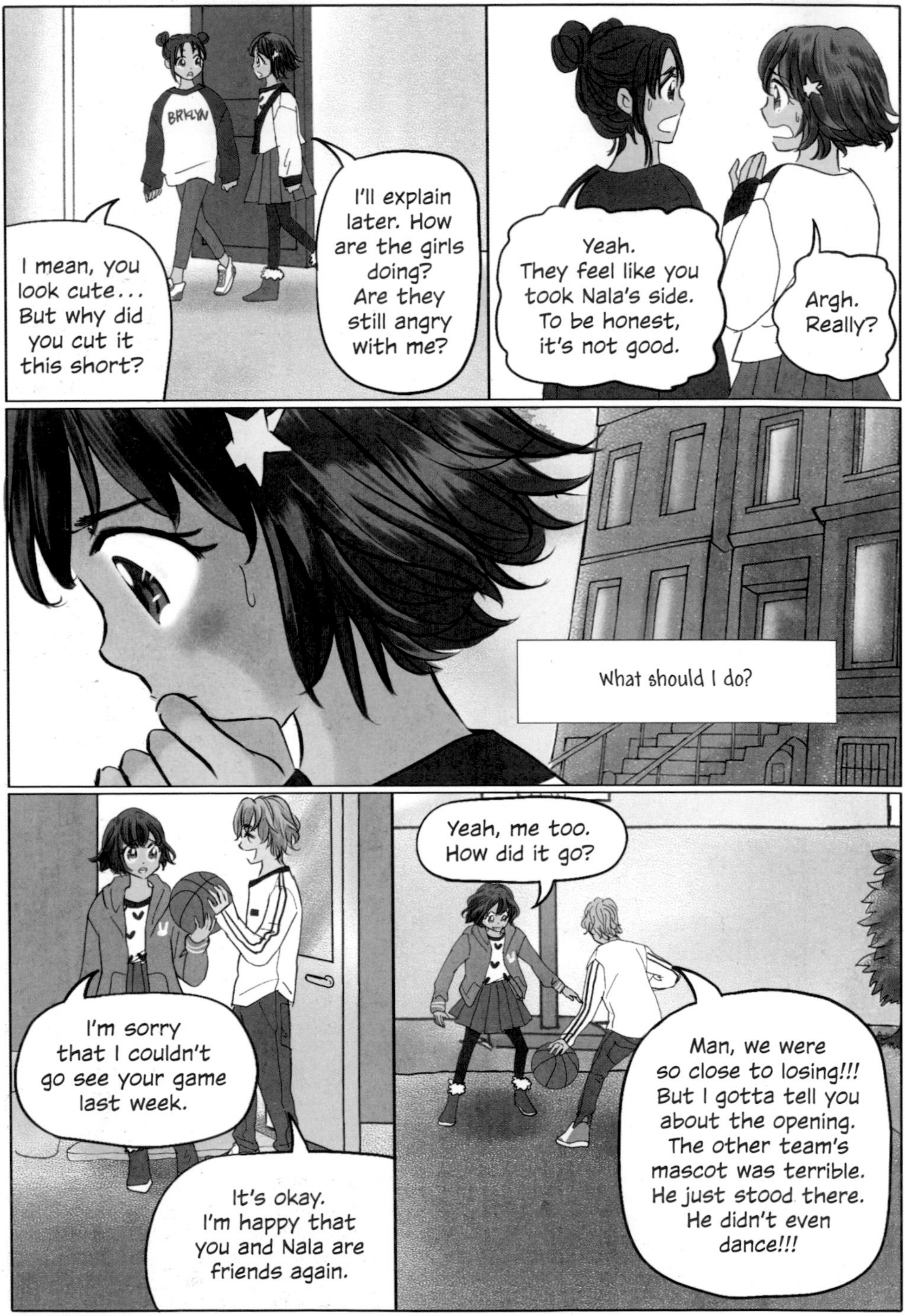
I mean, you look cute... But why did you cut it this short?
I'll explain later. How are the girls doing? Are they still angry with me?
BRKLYN
Yeah. They feel like you took Nala's side. To be honest, it's not good.
Argh. Really?
What should I do?
I'm sorry that I couldn't go see your game last week.
It's okay. I'm happy that you and Nala are friends again.
Yeah, me too. How did it go?
Man, we were so close to losing!!! But I gotta tell you about the opening. The other team's mascot was terrible. He just stood there. He didn't even dance!!!

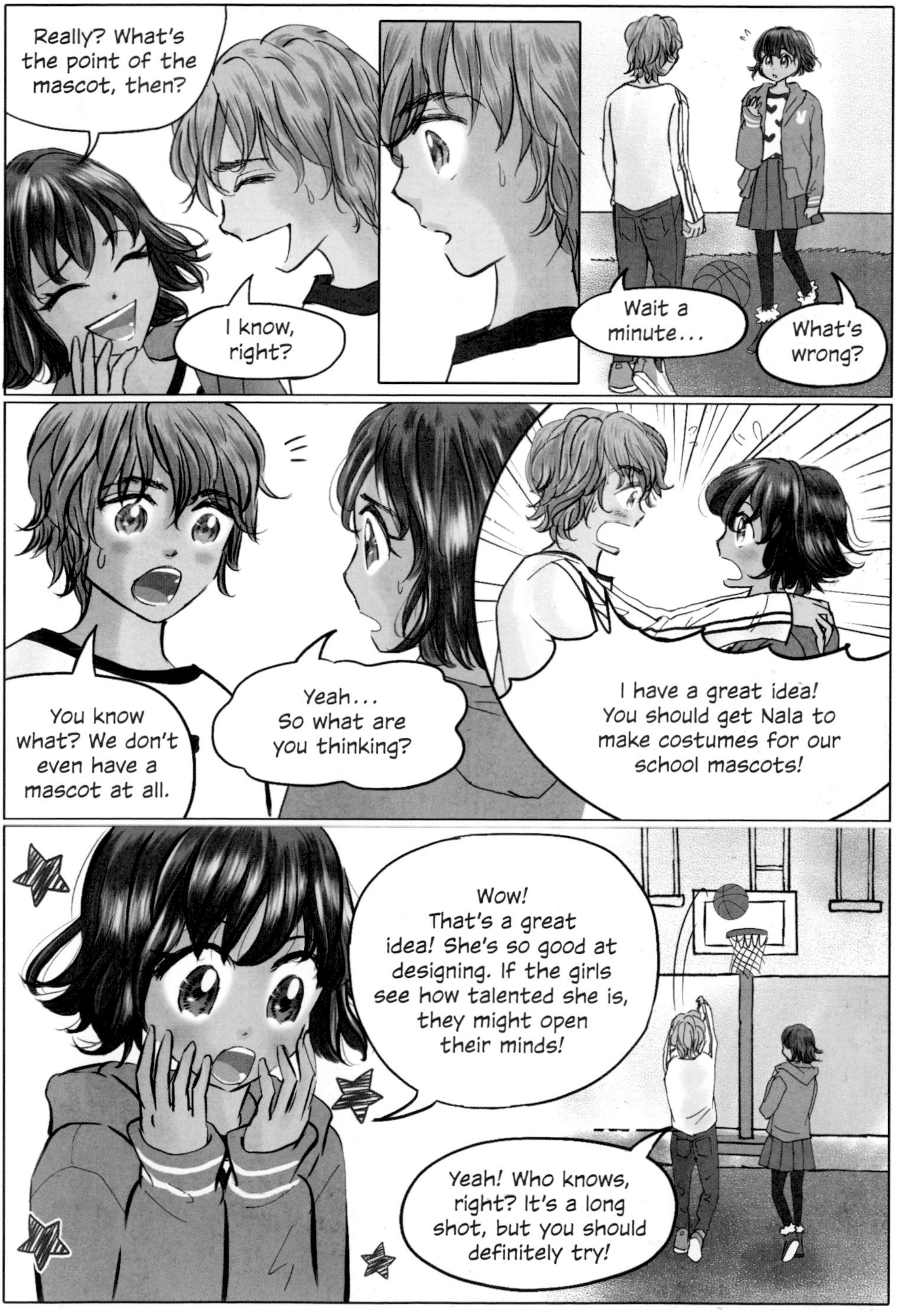
Really? What's the point of the mascot, then?
I know, right?
Wait a minute...
What's wrong?
You know what? We don't even have a mascot at all.
Yeah... So what are you thinking?
I have a great idea! You should get Nala to make costumes for our school mascots!
Wow! That's a great idea! She's so good at designing. If the girls see how talented she is, they might open their minds!
Yeah! Who knows, right? It's a long shot, but you should definitely try!

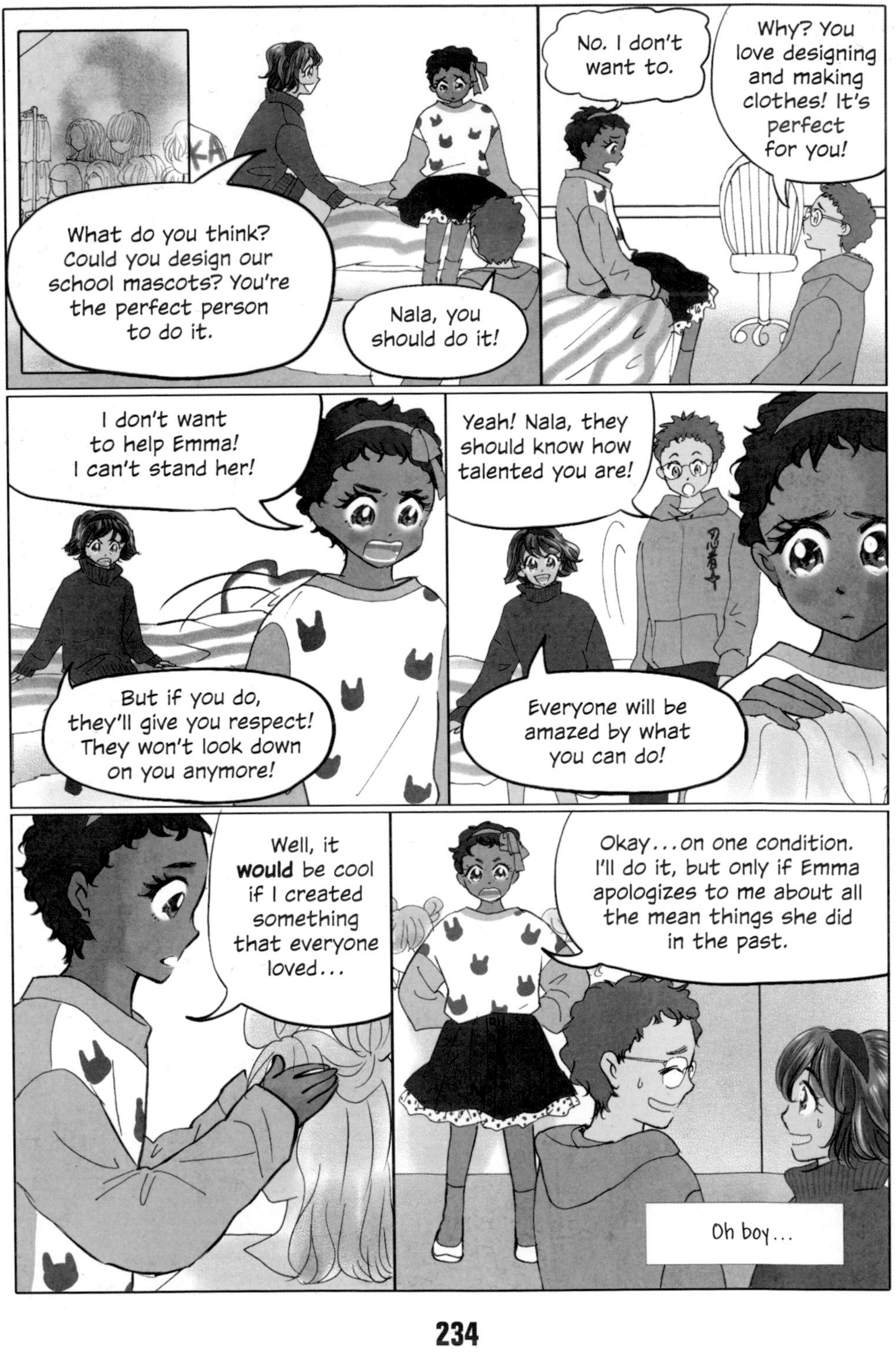
What do you think? Could you design our school mascots? You're the perfect person to do it.
Nala, you should do it!
No. I don't want to.
Why? You love designing and making clothes! It's perfect for you!
I don't want to help Emma! I can't stand her!
But if you do, they'll give you respect! They won't look down on you anymore!
Yeah! Nala, they should know how talented you are!
Everyone will be amazed by what you can do!
Well, it **would** be cool if I created something that everyone loved…
Okay…on one condition. I'll do it, but only if Emma apologizes to me about all the mean things she did in the past.
Oh boy…

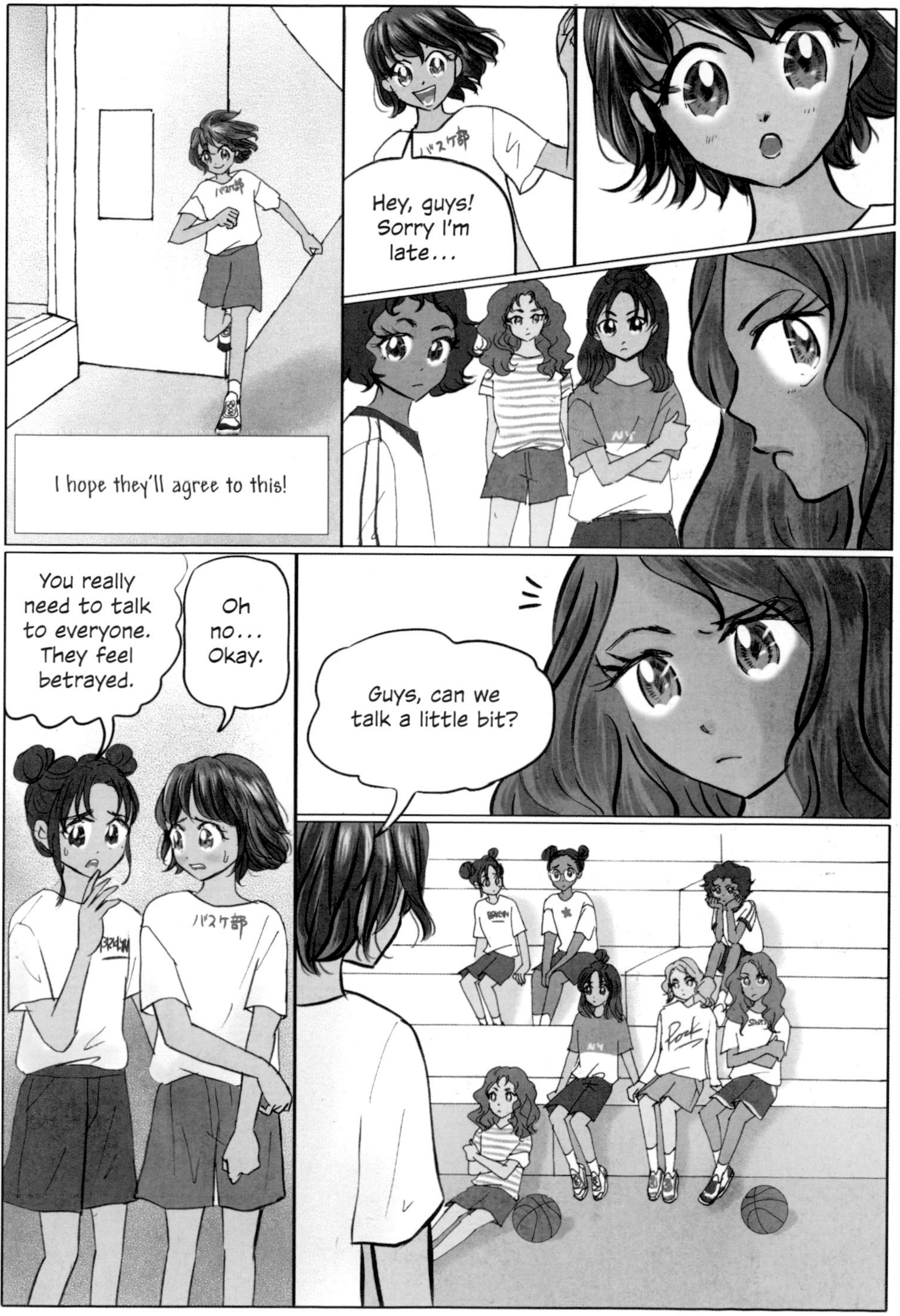
I hope they'll agree to this!
Hey, guys! Sorry I'm late...
You really need to talk to everyone. They feel betrayed.
Oh no... Okay.
Guys, can we talk a little bit?

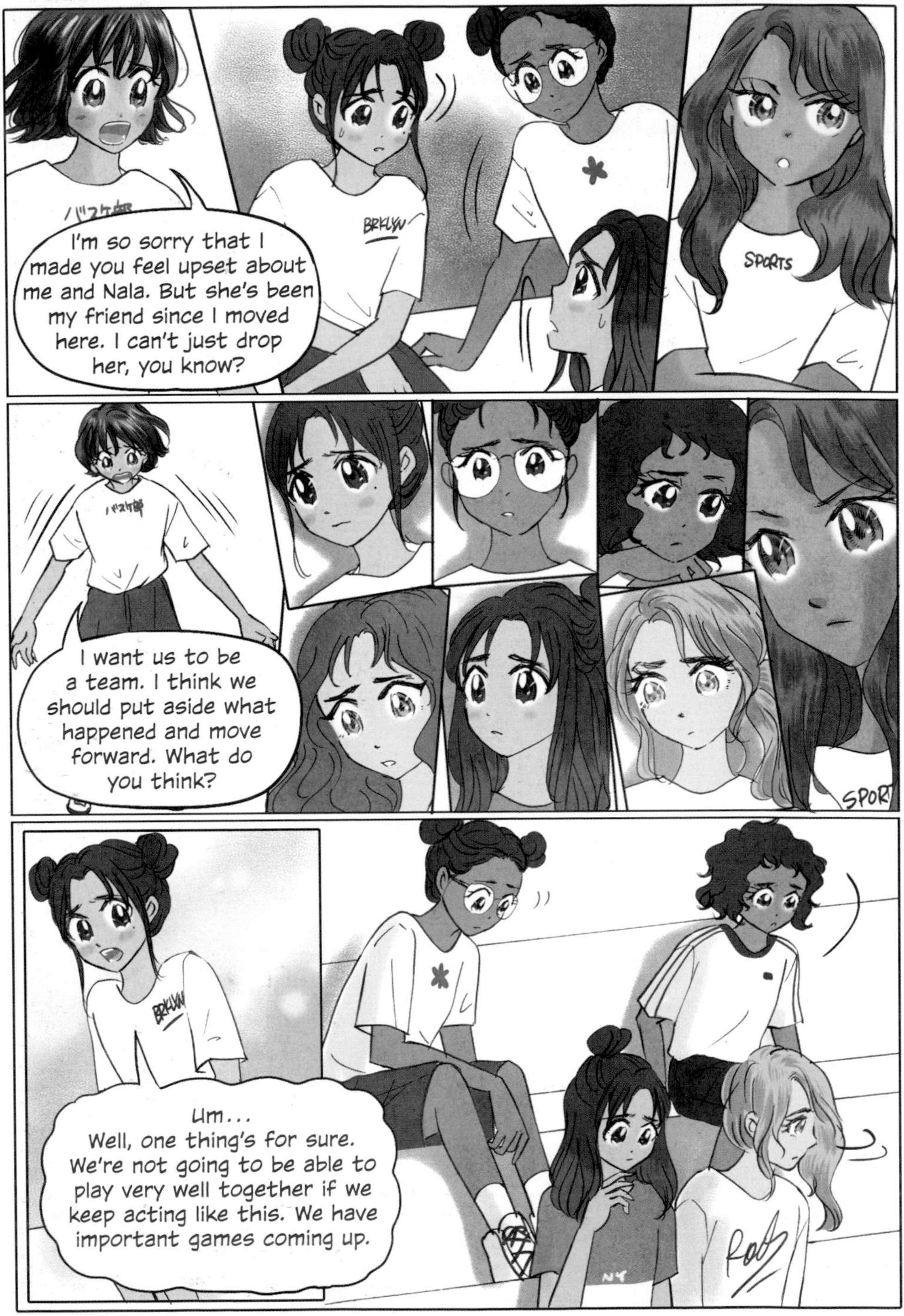
I'm so sorry that I made you feel upset about me and Nala. But she's been my friend since I moved here. I can't just drop her, you know?
I want us to be a team. I think we should put aside what happened and move forward. What do you think?
Um... Well, one thing's for sure. We're not going to be able to play very well together if we keep acting like this. We have important games coming up.

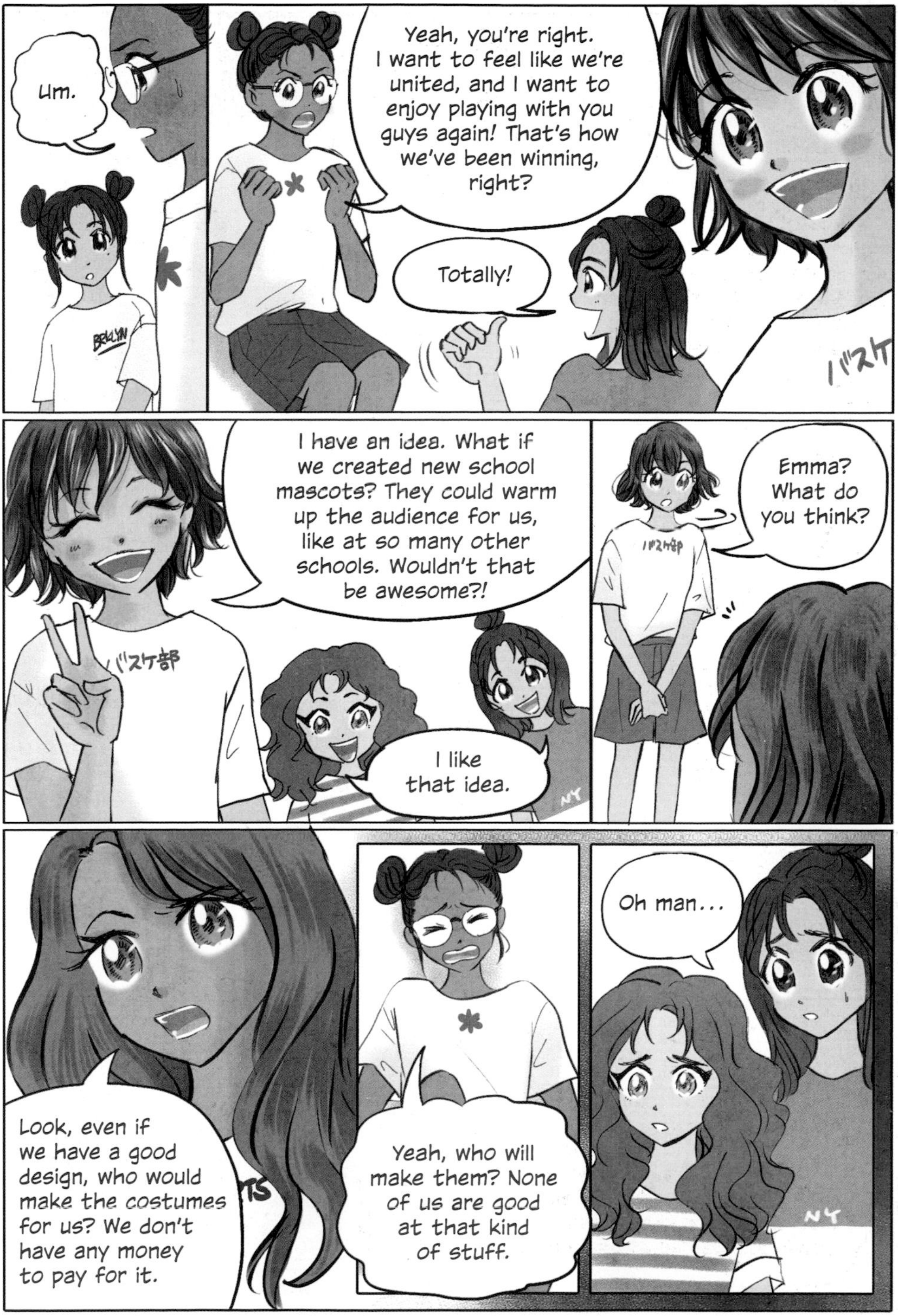
Um.
BRKLYN
Yeah, you're right. I want to feel like we're united, and I want to enjoy playing with you guys again! That's how we've been winning, right?
Totally!
バスケ
I have an idea. What if we created new school mascots? They could warm up the audience for us, like at so many other schools. Wouldn't that be awesome?!
バスケ部
I like that idea.
NY
Emma? What do you think?
バスケ部
Look, even if we have a good design, who would make the costumes for us? We don't have any money to pay for it.
Yeah, who will make them? None of us are good at that kind of stuff.
Oh man...
NY

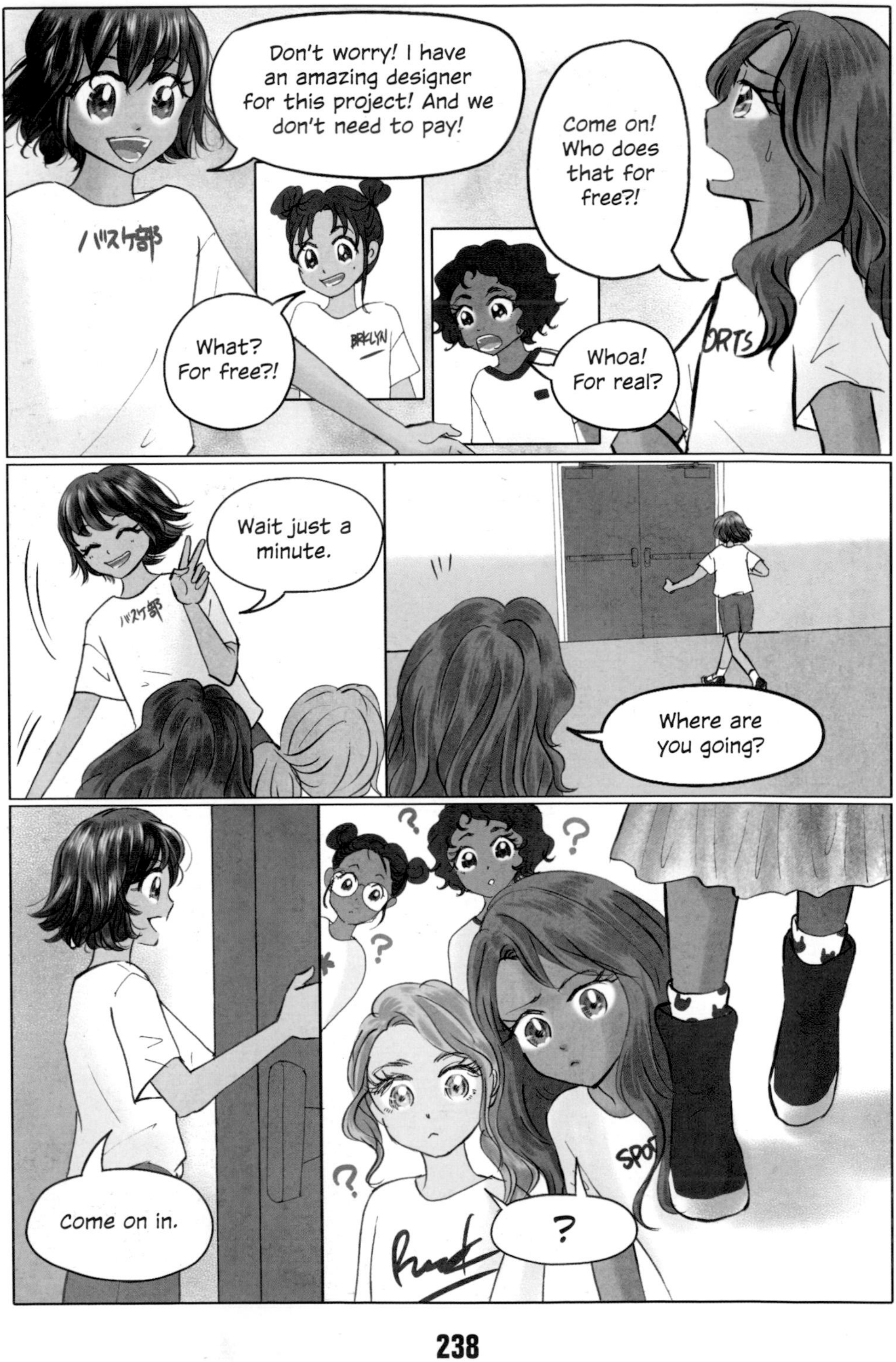
Don't worry! I have an amazing designer for this project! And we don't need to pay!
What? For free?!
Whoa! For real?
Come on! Who does that for free?!
Wait just a minute.
Where are you going?
Come on in.
?

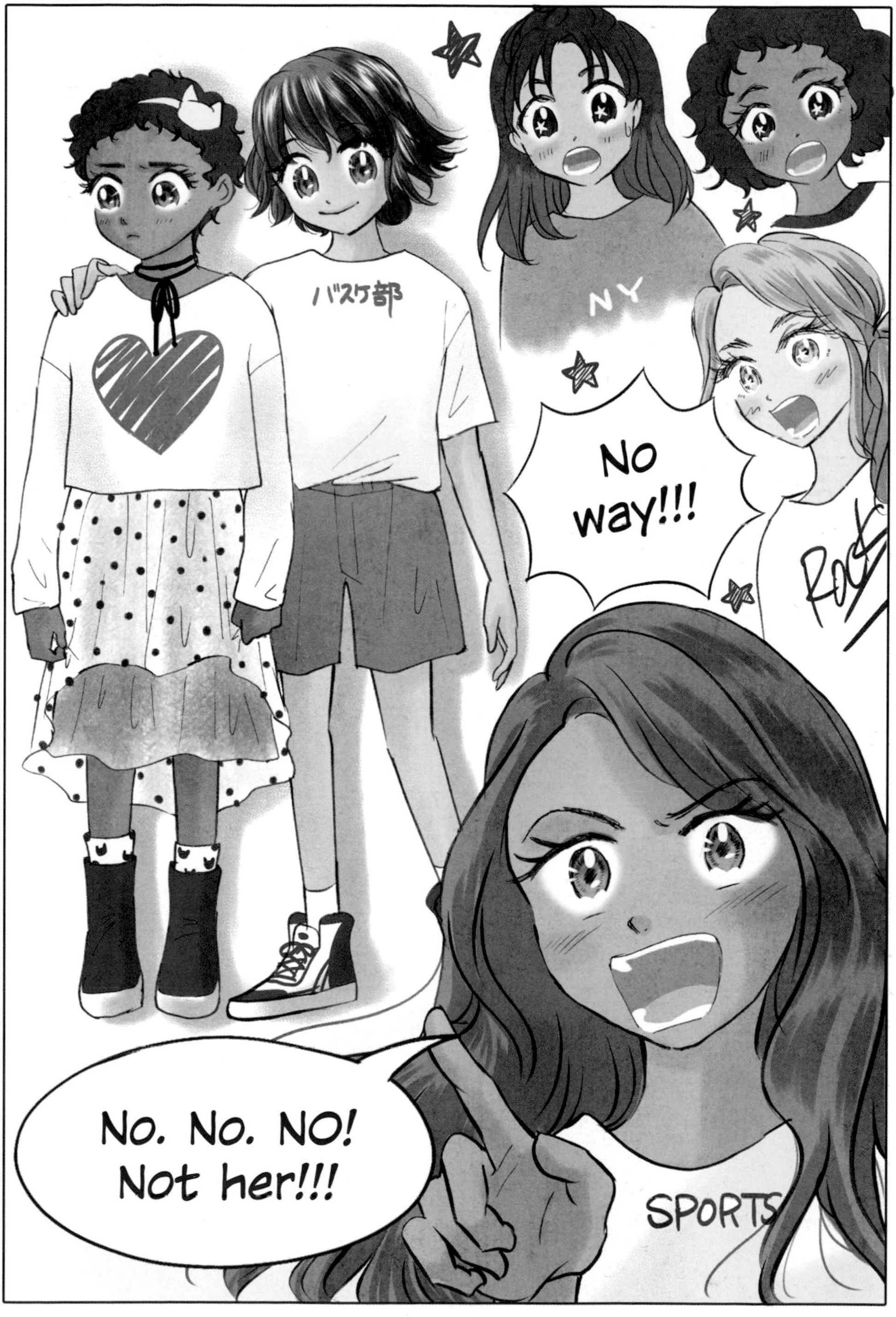
バスケ部
NY
No way!!!
ROC
No. No. NO! Not her!!!
SPORTS

CHAPTER 9

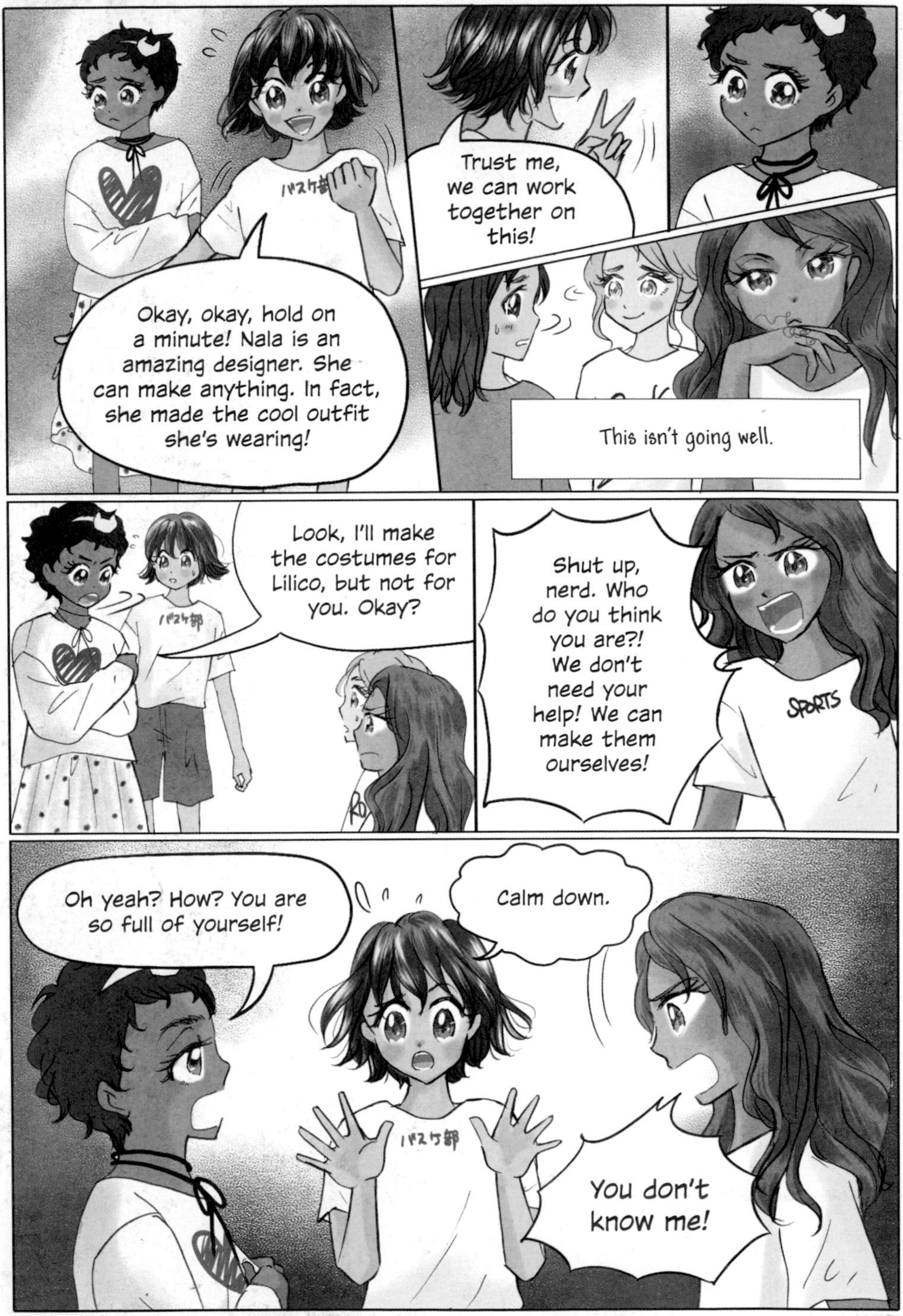
Okay, okay, hold on a minute! Nala is an amazing designer. She can make anything. In fact, she made the cool outfit she's wearing!
Trust me, we can work together on this!
This isn't going well.
Look, I'll make the costumes for Lilico, but not for you. Okay?
Shut up, nerd. Who do you think you are?! We don't need your help! We can make them ourselves!
Oh yeah? How? You are so full of yourself!
Calm down.
You don't know me!

Ha! Right! I've only known you since we were three!!!
Shut up!
SPORTS
What do we do?
Maybe we should stop them.
This is good! They are finally talking things out. At least, I think it's good…right?
SPORTS
You changed, Emma. I was always your friend. Then you started treating me like crap.
You don't understand how much you hurt me.

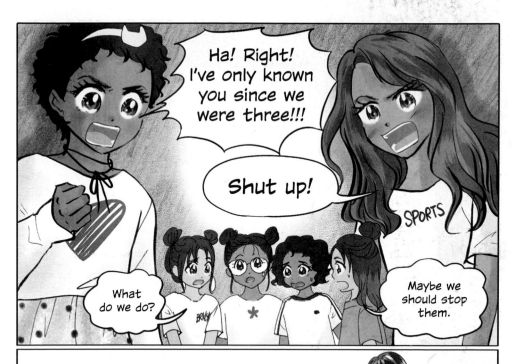

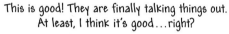

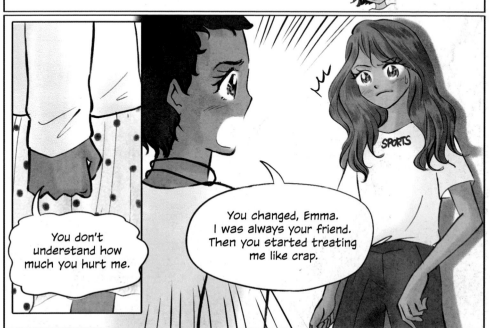

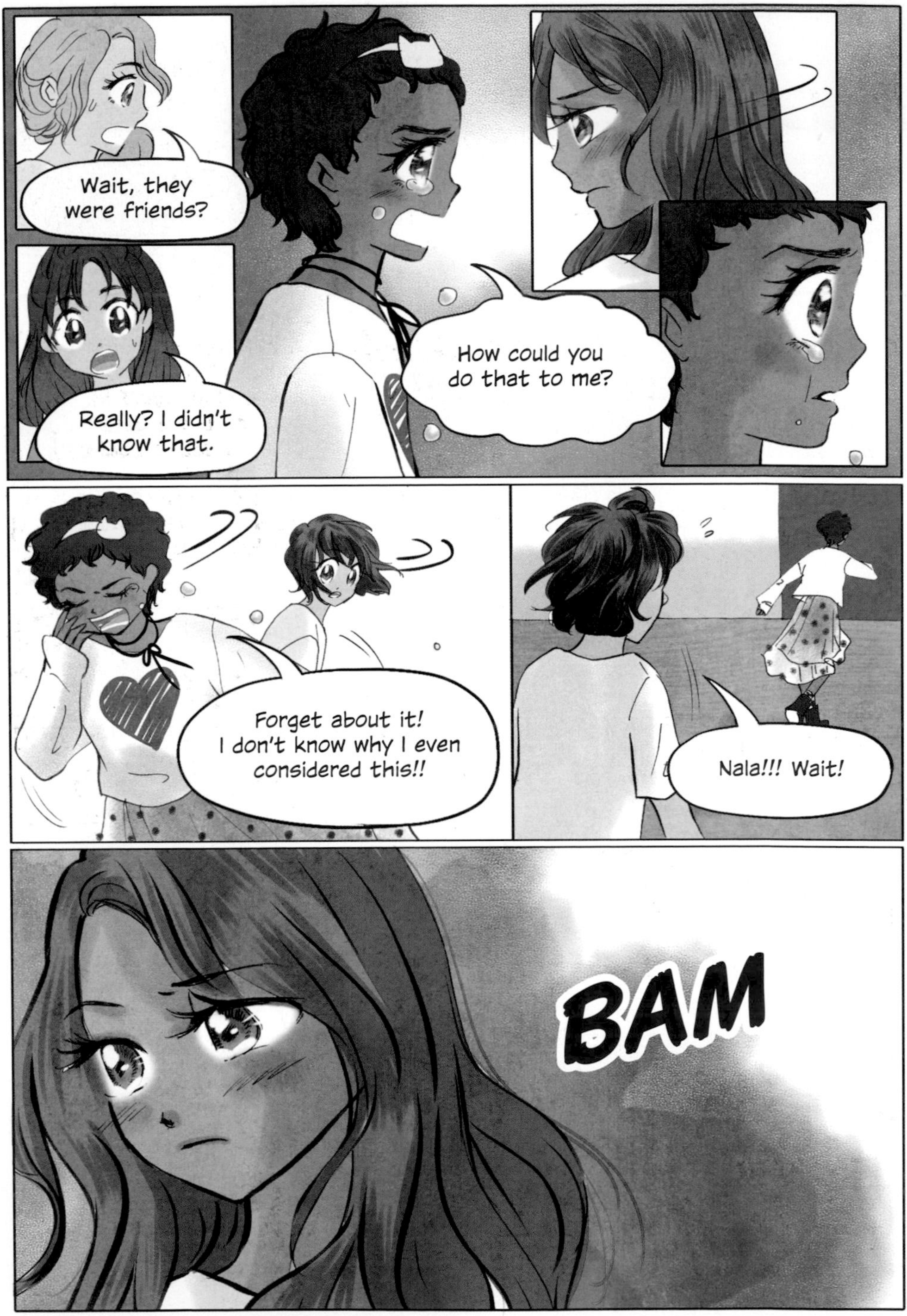
Wait, they were friends?
Really? I didn't know that.
How could you do that to me?
Forget about it! I don't know why I even considered this!!
Nala!!! Wait!
BAM

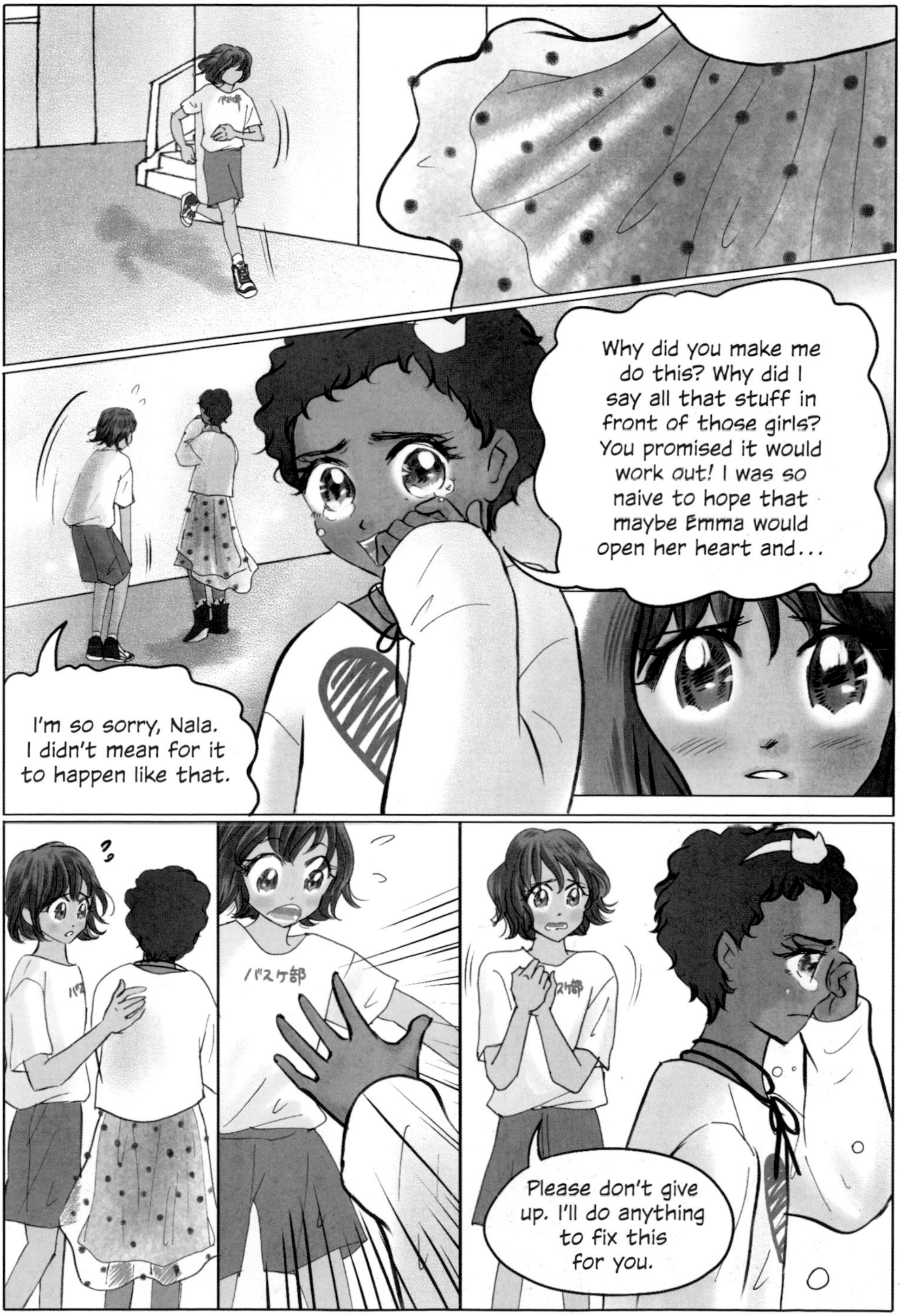

Why did you make me do this? Why did I say all that stuff in front of those girls? You promised it would work out! I was so naive to hope that maybe Emma would open her heart and...
I'm so sorry, Nala. I didn't mean for it to happen like that.
Please don't give up. I'll do anything to fix this for you.

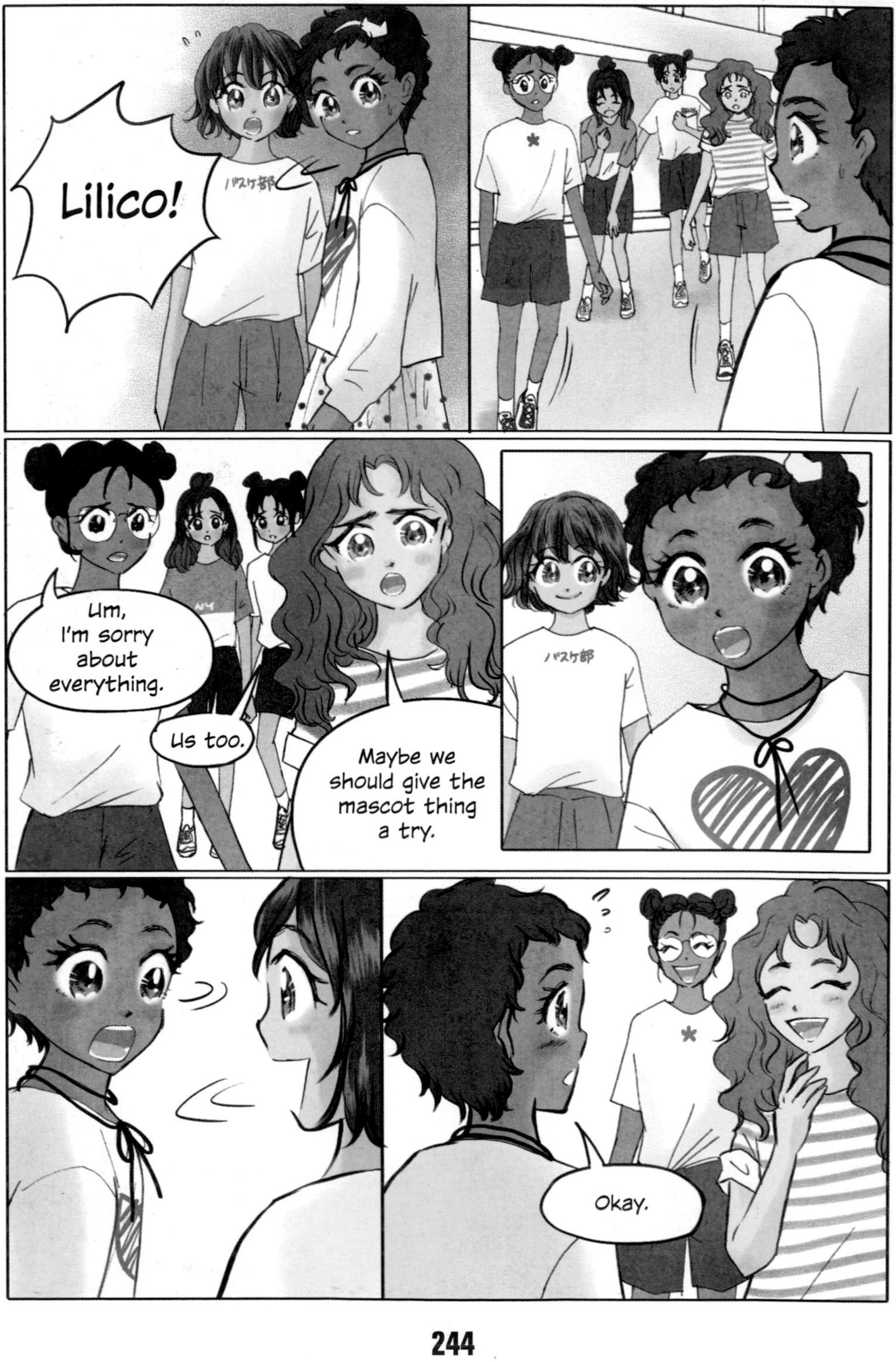
Lilico!
バスケ部
Um, I'm sorry about everything.
Us too.
Maybe we should give the mascot thing a try.
バスケ部
Okay.

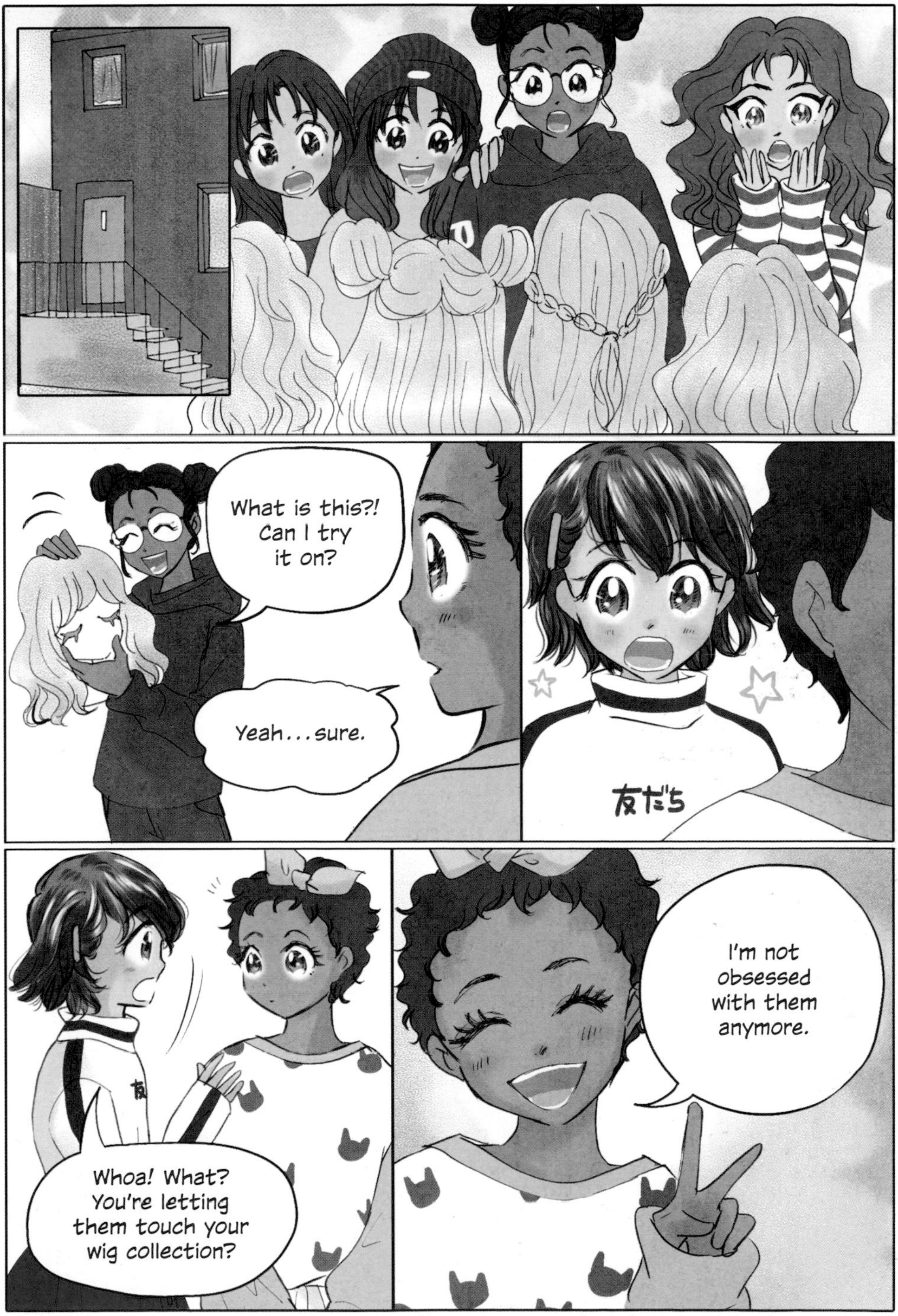
What is this?! Can I try it on?
Yeah...sure.
友だち
Whoa! What? You're letting them touch your wig collection?
I'm not obsessed with them anymore.

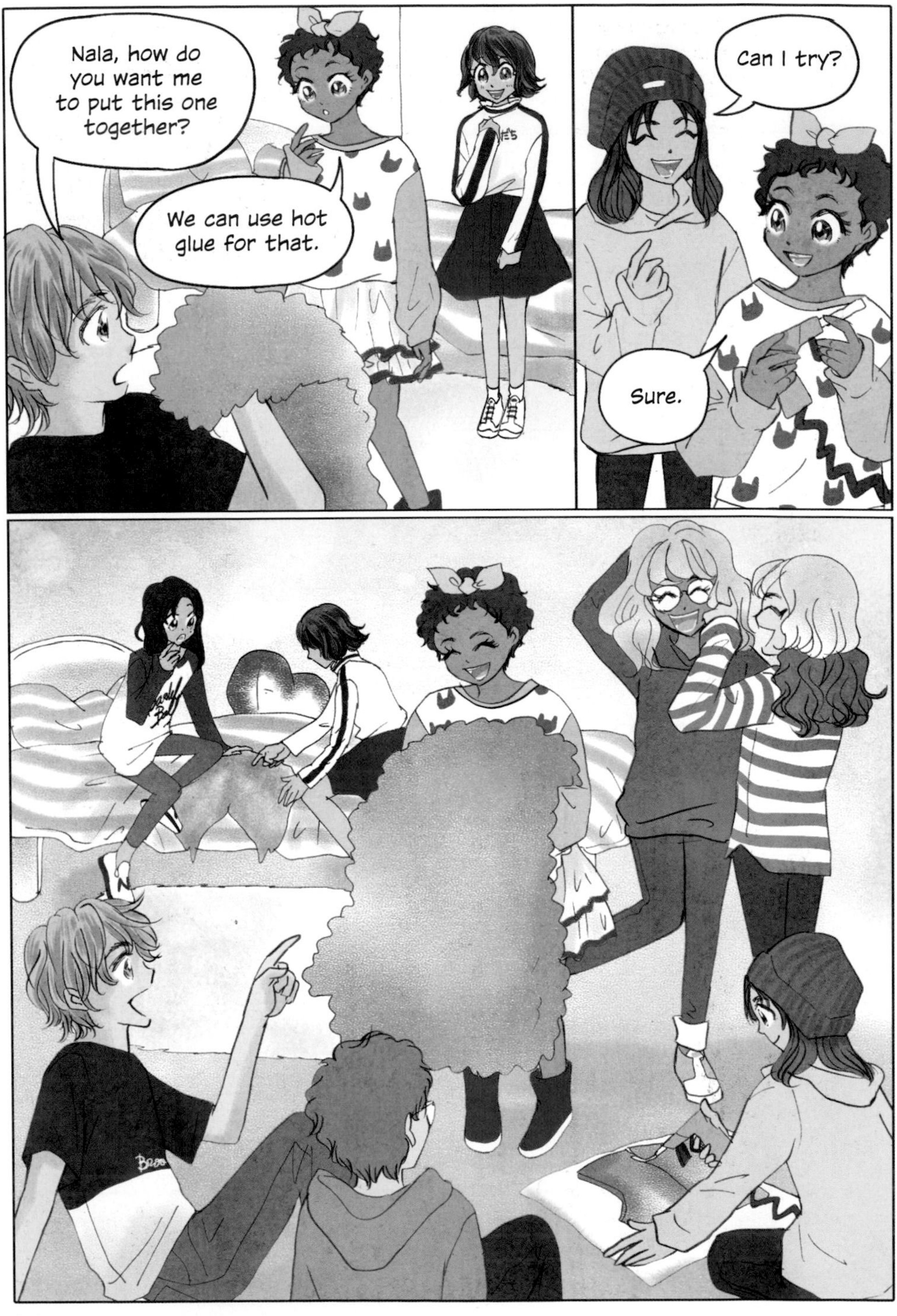
Nala, how do you want me to put this one together?
We can use hot glue for that.
Can I try?
Sure.

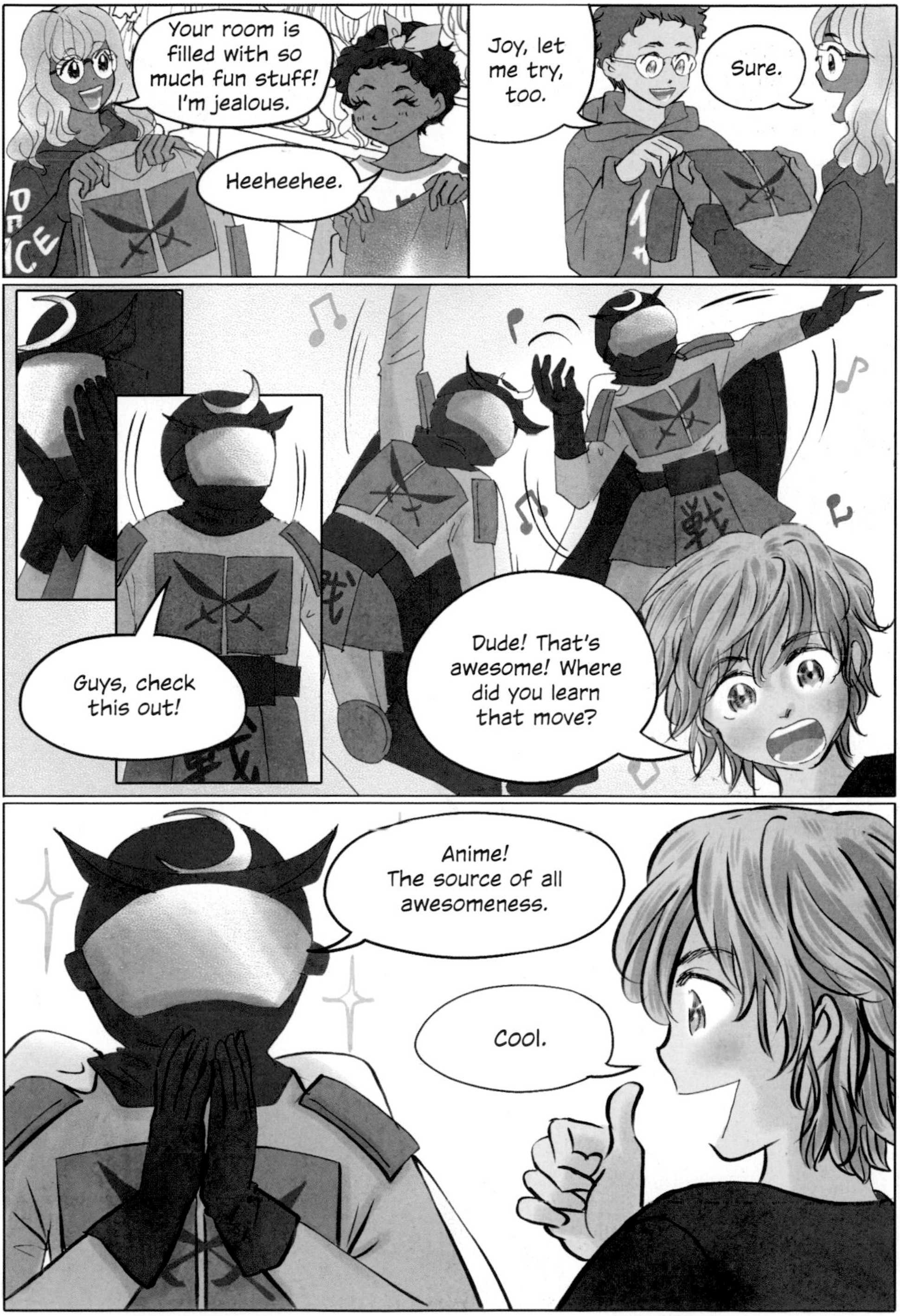
Your room is filled with so much fun stuff! I'm jealous.
Heeheehee.
Joy, let me try, too.
Sure.
Guys, check this out!
Dude! That's awesome! Where did you learn that move?
Anime! The source of all awesomeness.
Cool.

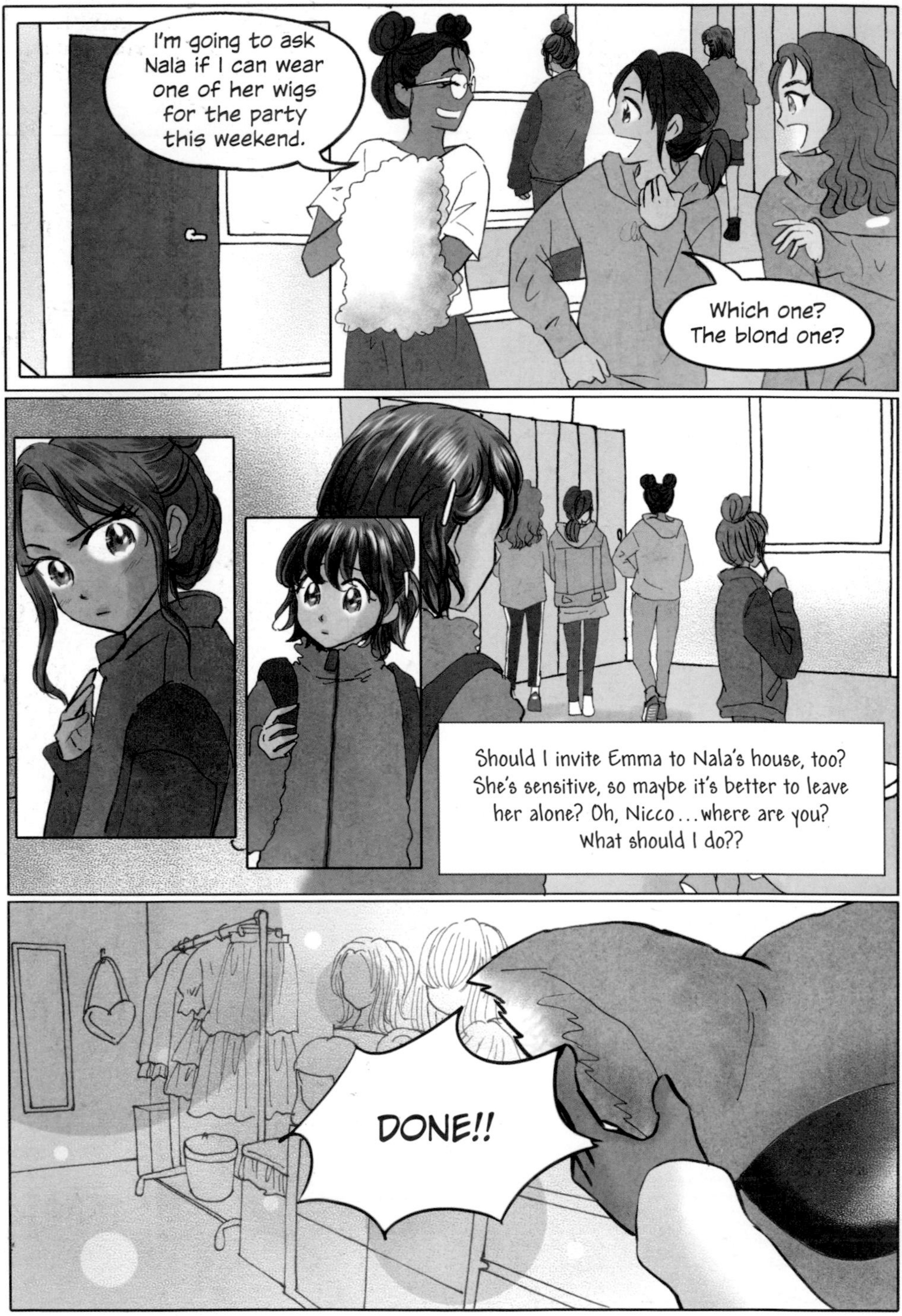
I'm going to ask Nala if I can wear one of her wigs for the party this weekend.
Which one? The blond one?
Should I invite Emma to Nala's house, too? She's sensitive, so maybe it's better to leave her alone? Oh, Nicco...where are you? What should I do??
DONE!!

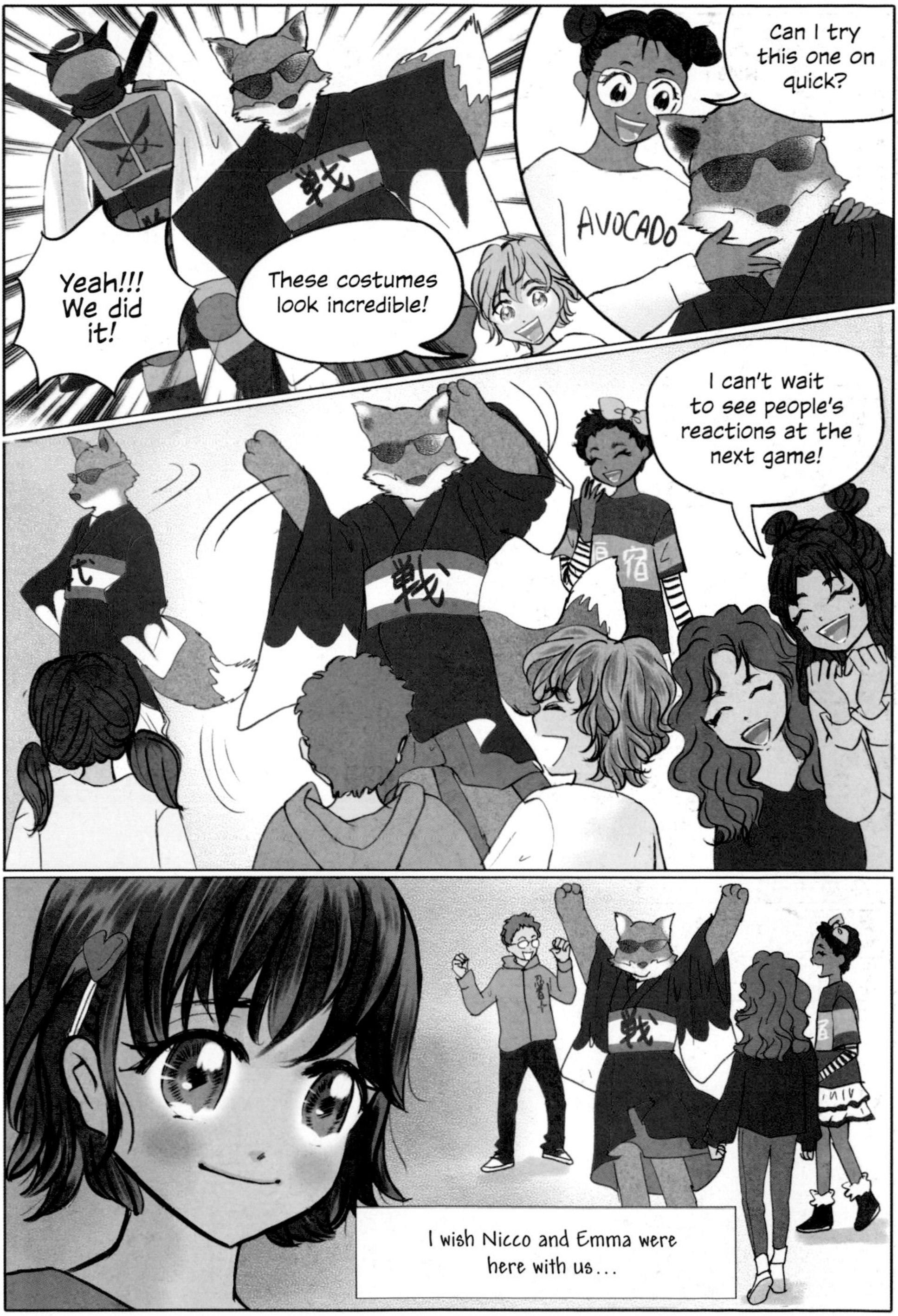
Yeah!!! We did it!
These costumes look incredible!
Can I try this one on quick?
AVOCADO
I can't wait to see people's reactions at the next game!
I wish Nicco and Emma were here with us...

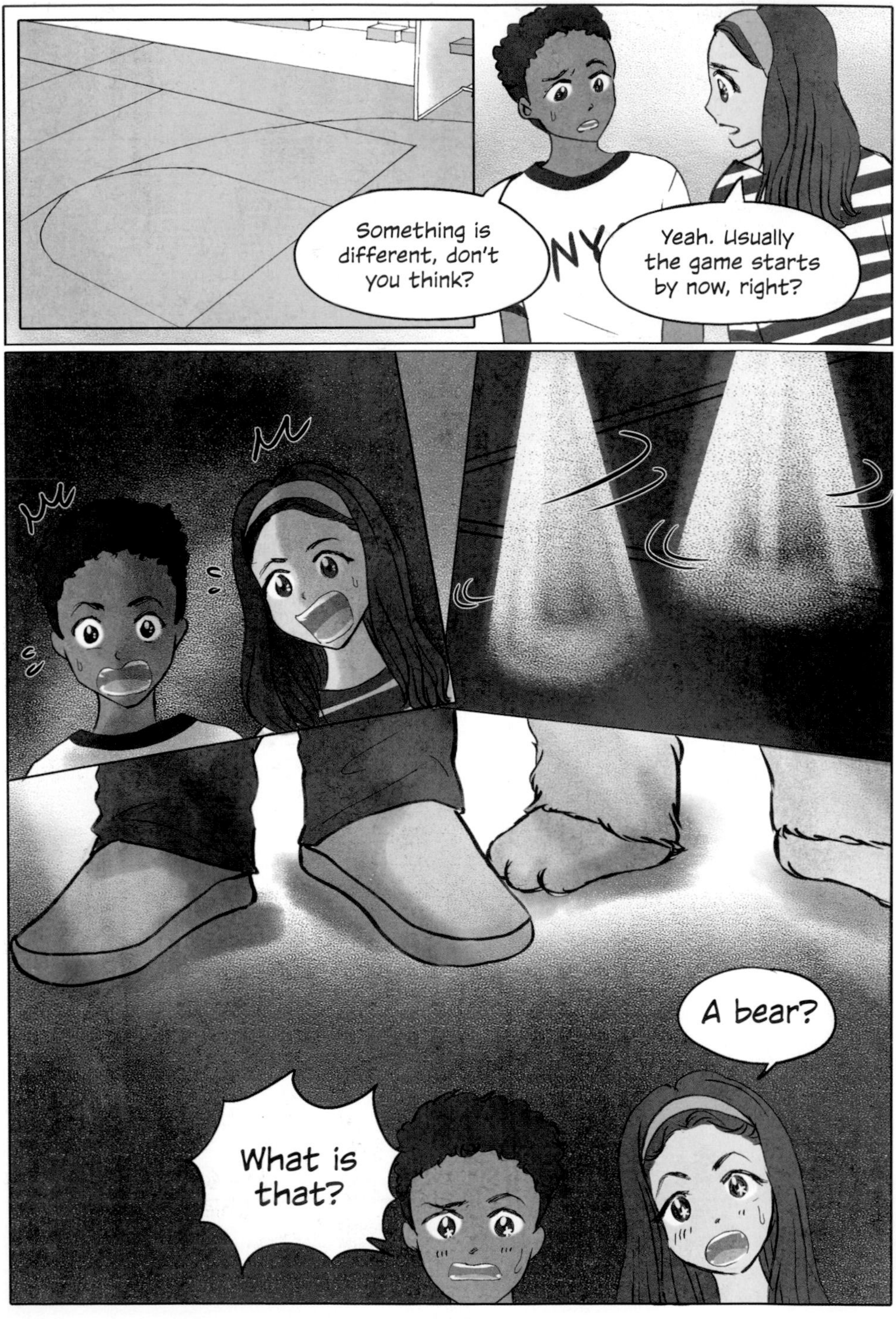
Something is different, don't you think?
Yeah. Usually the game starts by now, right?
A bear?
What is that?

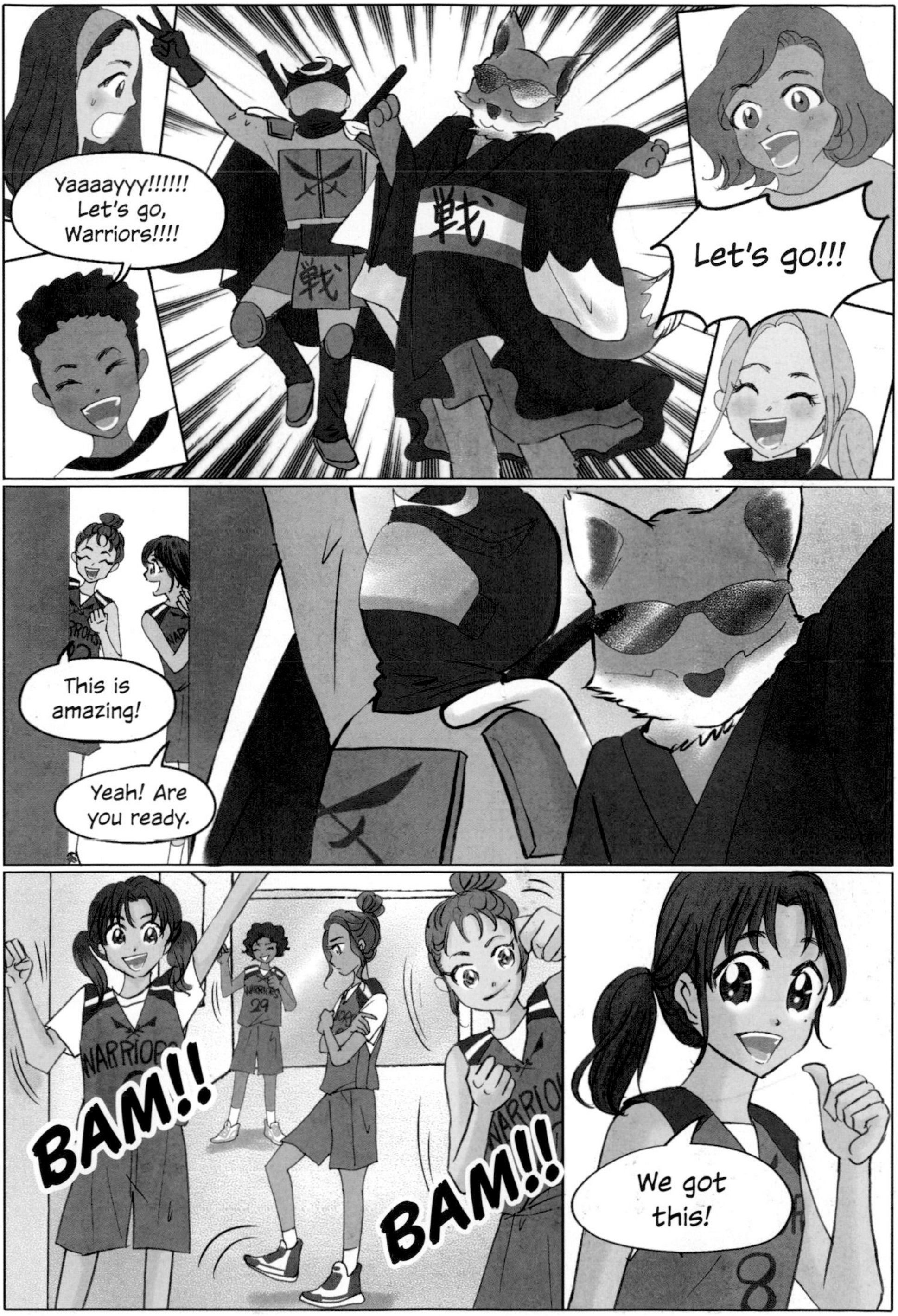
Yaaaayyy!!!!!! Let's go, Warriors!!!!
Let's go!!!
This is amazing!
Yeah! Are you ready.
BAM!!
BAM!!
We got this!

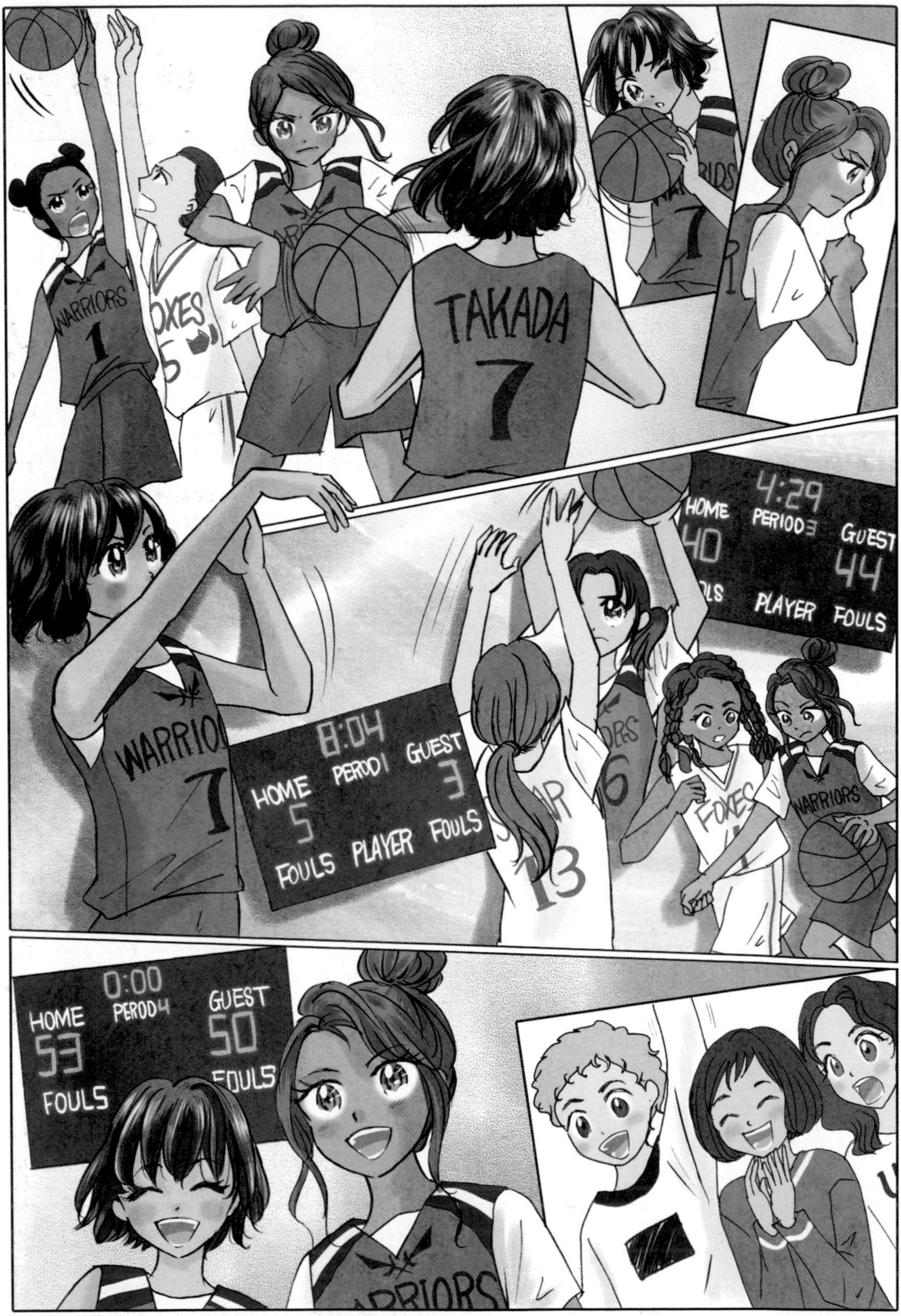
WARRIORS
1
TAKADA
7
8:04
HOME
PERODI
GUEST
5
3
FOULS
PLAYER
FOULS
4:29
HOME
PERIOD3
GUEST
40
44
PLAYER
FOULS
13
WARRIORS
0:00
HOME
PEROD4
GUEST
53
50
FOULS

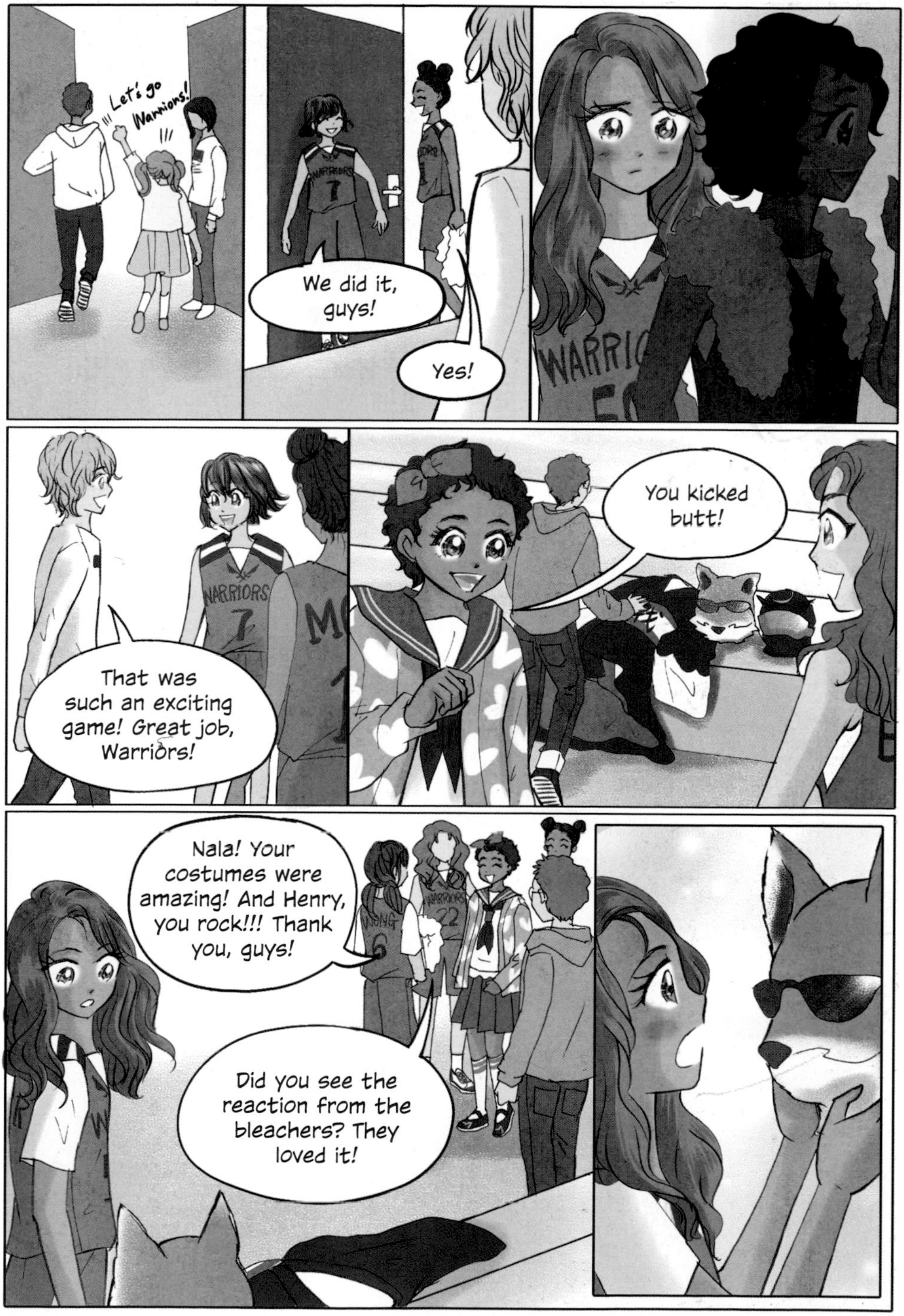
Let's go Warriors!
We did it, guys!
Yes!
That was such an exciting game! Great job, Warriors!
You kicked butt!
Nala! Your costumes were amazing! And Henry, you rock!!! Thank you, guys!
Did you see the reaction from the bleachers? They loved it!

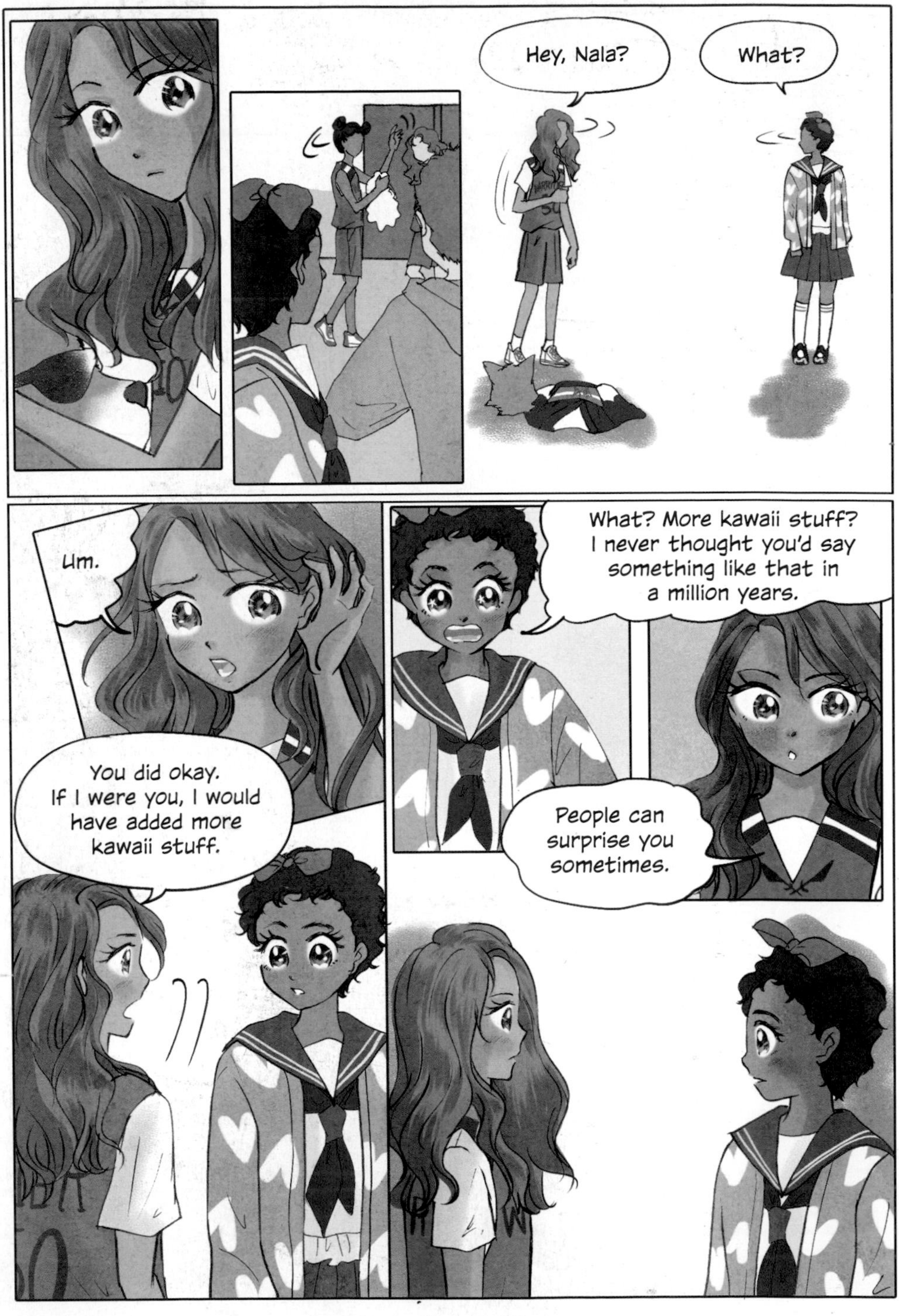
Hey, Nala?
What?
Um.
What? More kawaii stuff? I never thought you'd say something like that in a million years.
You did okay. If I were you, I would have added more kawaii stuff.
People can surprise you sometimes.

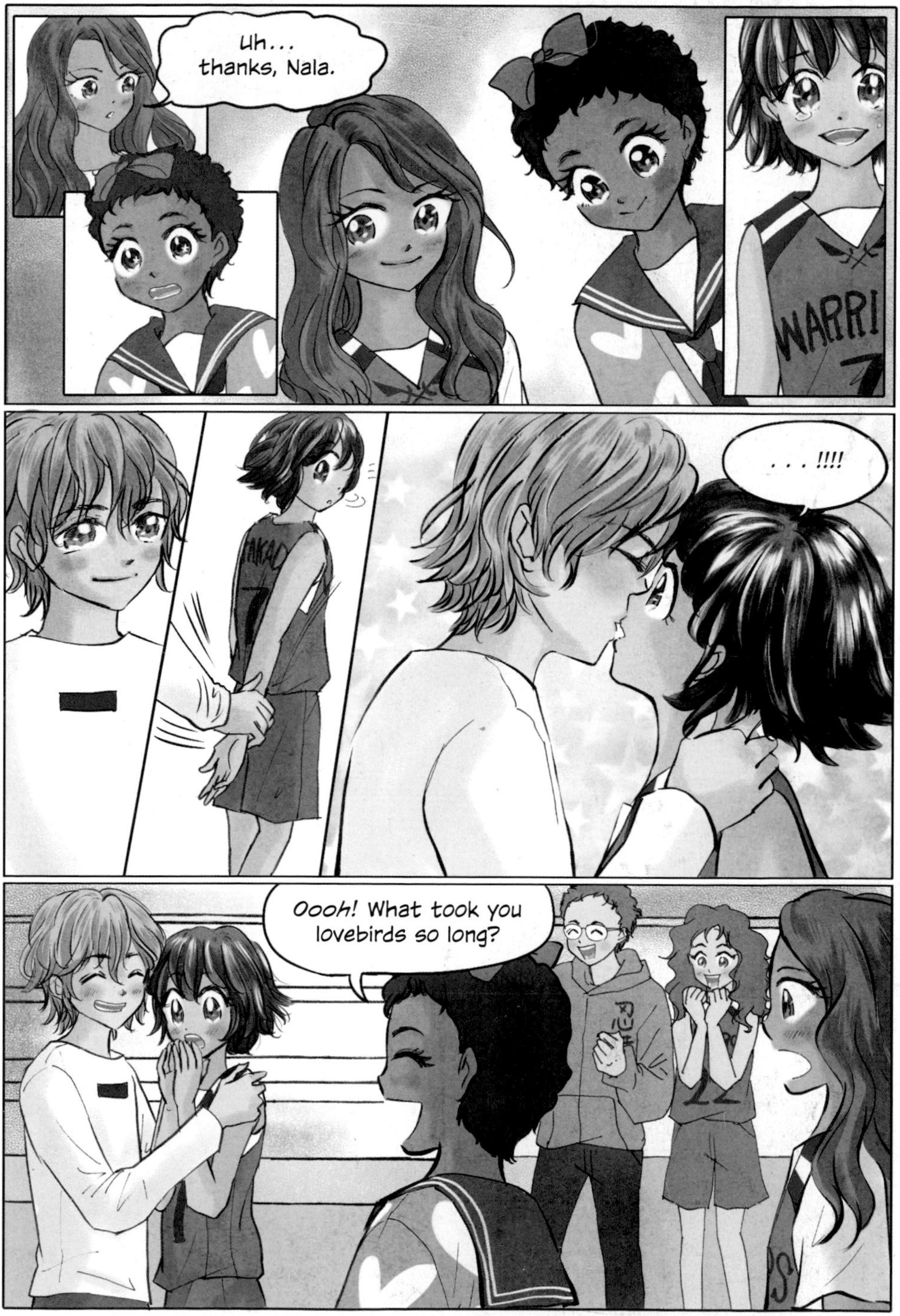
Uh...
thanks, Nala.
. . . !!!!
Oooh! What took you lovebirds so long?

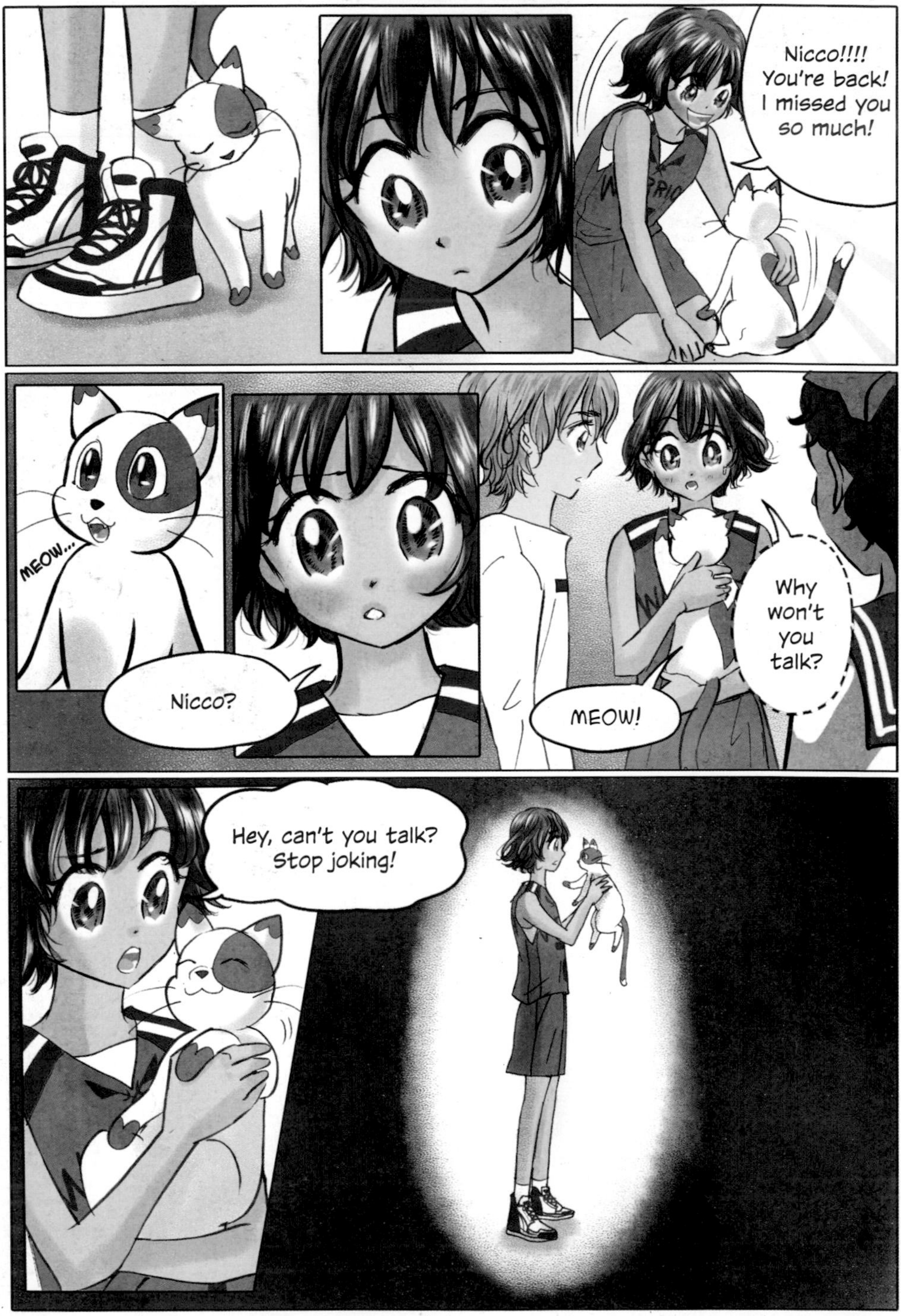
Nicco!!!! You're back! I missed you so much!
MEOW...
Nicco?
MEOW!
Why won't you talk?
Hey, can't you talk? Stop joking!

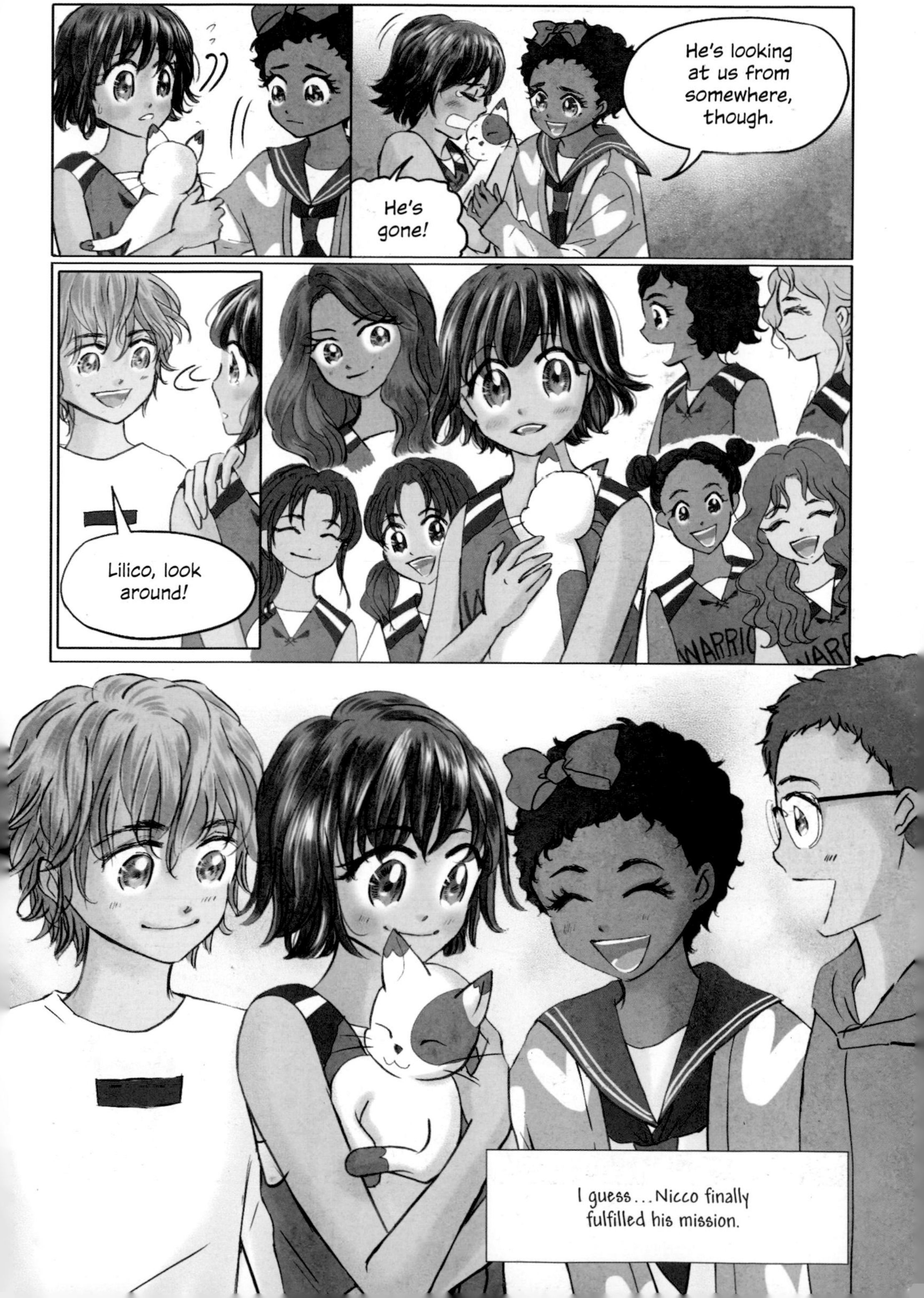
He's gone!
He's looking at us from somewhere, though.
Lilico, look around!
I guess . . . Nicco finally fulfilled his mission.

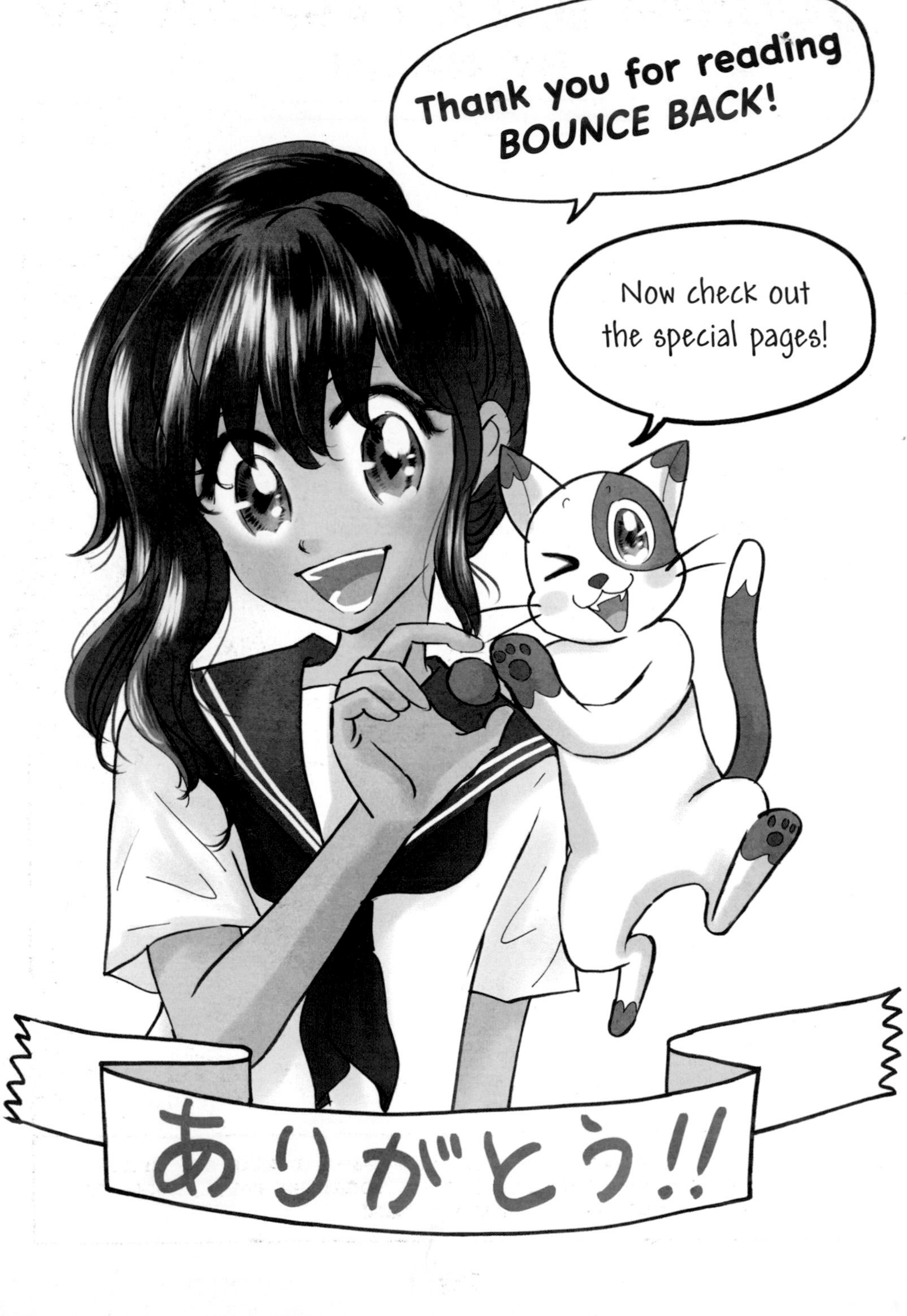
Thank you for reading BOUNCE BACK!
Now check out the special pages!
ありがとう!!

BOUNCE BACK FASHION DIY BY NALA!

LILICO: 13 Years Old
HEIGHT: 5'3"
HOMETOWN: Osaka, Japan
ZODIAC SIGN: Aries
FAVORITE FOOD: Tonkatsu!

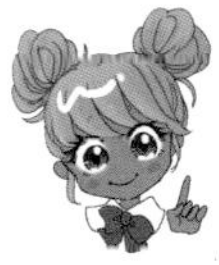

FASHION DIY: LILICO!

1. FIND A PLAIN T-SHIRT.
2. DRAW A KAWAII CHARACTER ON DIFFERENT FABRIC WITH A TEXTILE MARKER TO MAKE A PATCH.
3. CUT THAT PATCH AND SEW IT ON YOUR T-SHIRT!
4. NOW YOU HAVE YOUR OWN ONE-OF-KIND KAWAII T-SHIRT LIKE LILICO!

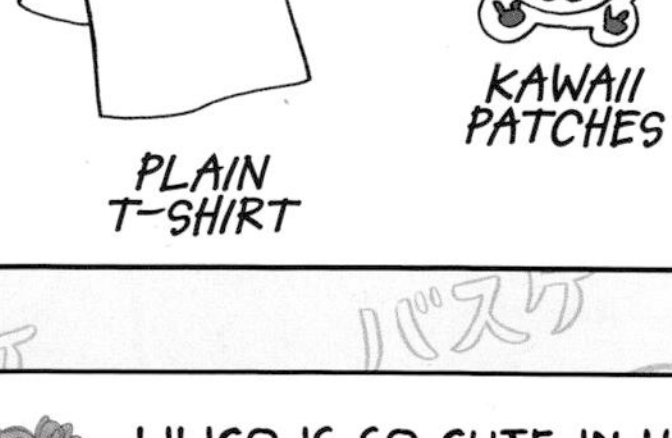
PLAIN T-SHIRT
KAWAII PATCHES

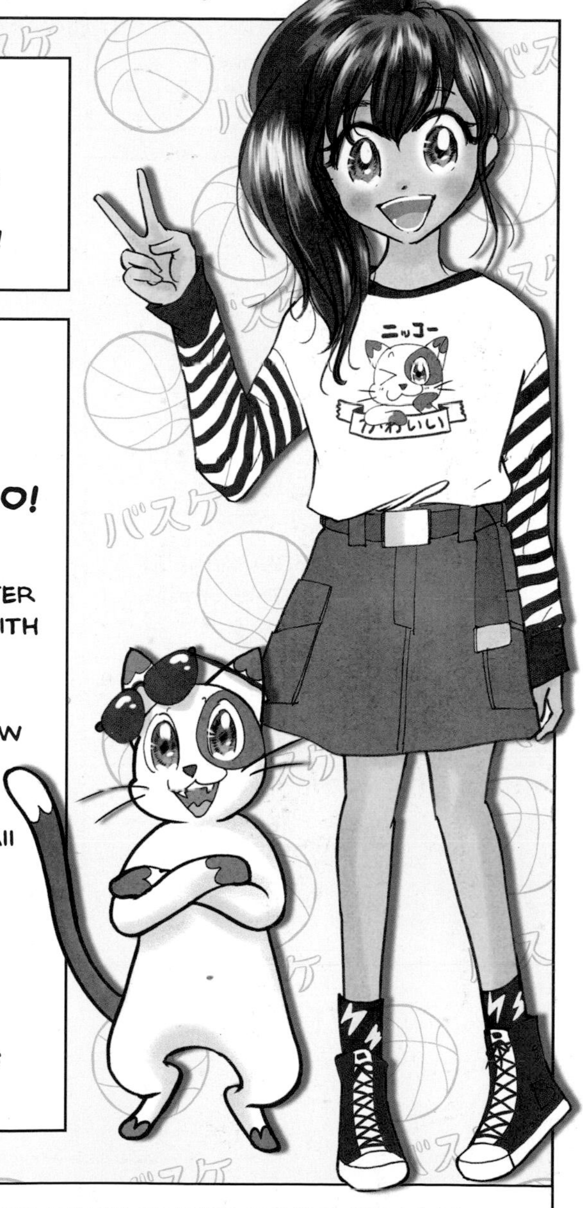
ニッコー
バスケ

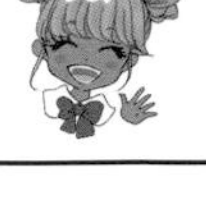

LILICO IS SO CUTE IN HER KAWAII GRAPHIC T-SHIRT! SHE LIKES MIXING KAWAII AND CASUAL STYLE TOGETHER. I'M PLANNING TO MAKE AN ORIGINAL T-SHIRT FOR HER!

EMMA: 13 Years Old
HEIGHT: 5'4"
HOMETOWN: Brooklyn, NY
ZODIAC SIGN: Leo
FAVORITE FOOD: cheese pizza. It has to be thin crust!

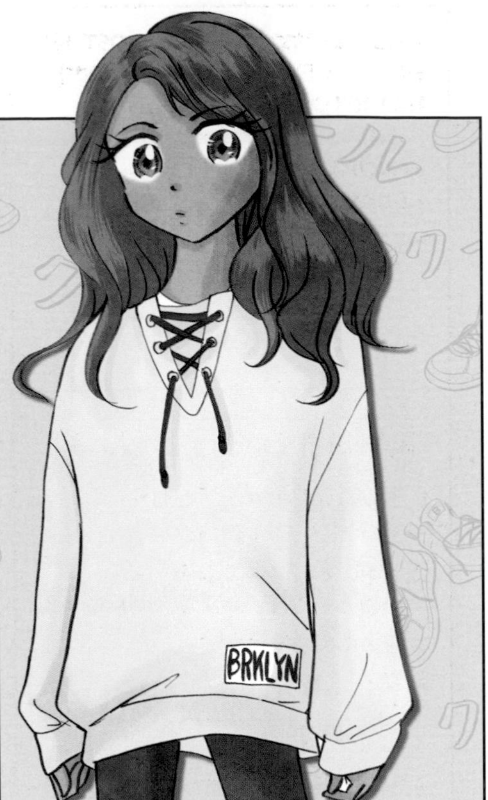
BRKLYN
クール

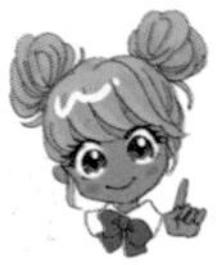

FASHION DIY: EMMA!

1. FIND YOUR PARENT'S, BIG BROTHER'S, OR BIG SISTER'S SWEATSHIRT OR HOODIE. THIS SHOULD BE AN "OVERSIZE" TOP!
2. IF YOU WANT TO MAKE IT KAWAII, ADD SOME SMALL PINS TO DECORATE IT.
3. WEAR IT WITH LEGGINGS AND CHUNKY SNEAKERS!

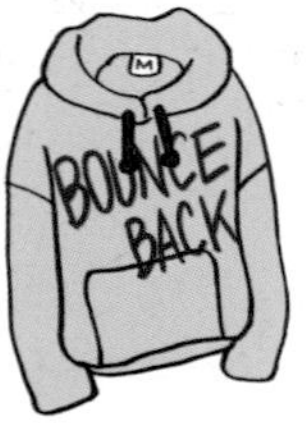
M
BOUNCE BACK

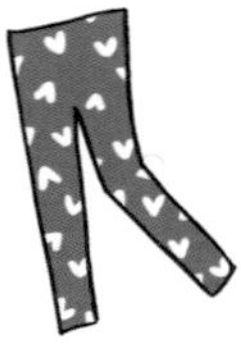

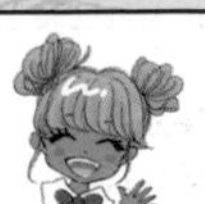

EMMA'S FAVORITE STYLE IS L.A. SPORTY. IF YOU WANT TO DRESS LIKE HER, THIS OVERSIZE TOP IS A MUST-HAVE ITEM!

NALA: 13 Years Old (ALMOST 14!)
HEIGHT: 5'0"(CLOSE TO 5'1")
HOMETOWN: Brooklyn, NY
ZODIAC SIGN: Libra
FAVORITE FOOD: Pocky, Hi-Chew, and pickles!!!

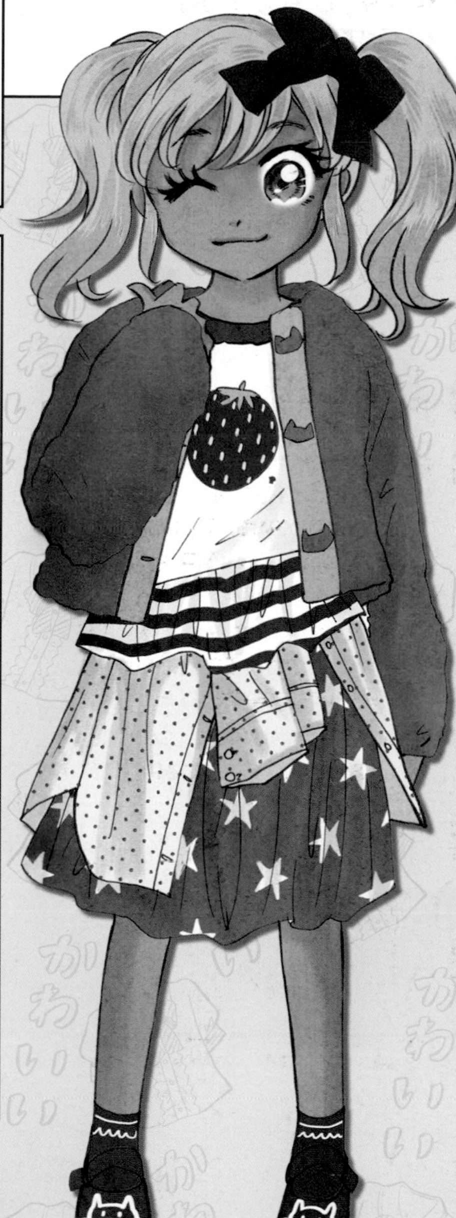

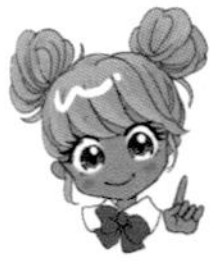

FASHION DIY: NALA!

1. START WITH A PLAIN BLOUSE OR SHIRT.
2. FIND SOME OLD HAIR ACCESSORIES YOU DON'T WEAR ANYMORE.
3. CUT OFF SOME BOWS OR POM-POMS AND ATTACH THEM WITH SAFETY PINS!
4. YOU CAN PUT THEM AROUND THE COLLAR OR POCKET!

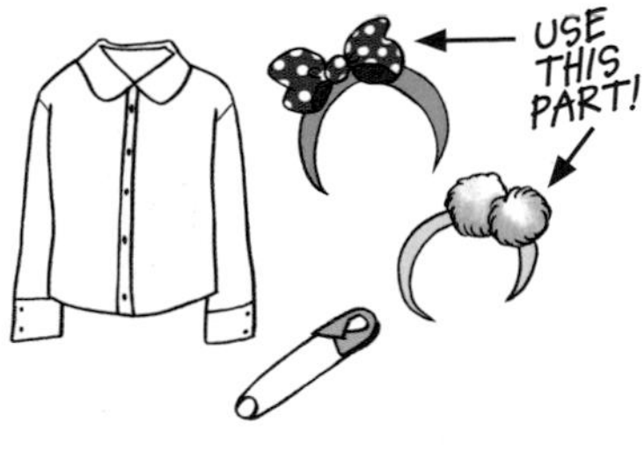
USE THIS PART!

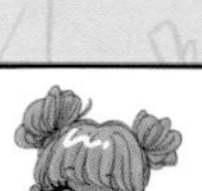

I ADORE HARAJUKU KAWAII FASHION! I ALWAYS NEED TO HAVE SOME PINK ITEMS SOMEWHERE IN MY OUTFIT. THAT'S MY RULE!

HOW TO DRAW NICCO!!

DRAW ME!

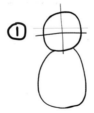

① DRAW
2 CIRCLES.

②  DRAW EARS AND EYES.
INSIDE OF HIS EYES, ADD
WHITE BUBBLES AND
A BLACK BUBBLE.

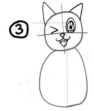

③ DRAW HIS NOSE
AND MOUTH. ADD
A TEETH LINE.

④ ADD LITTLE
CHEEKS.

⑤ ERASE CROSSED
LINES.

⑥ DRAW HIS ARMS.

⑦ THEN THE TOP
OF HIS LEGS.

⑧ FINISH THE REST
OF HIS LEGS.

⑨ ONCE YOU DRAW HIS
TAIL, IT'S DONE!

MISAKO'S DRAWING TOOLS!

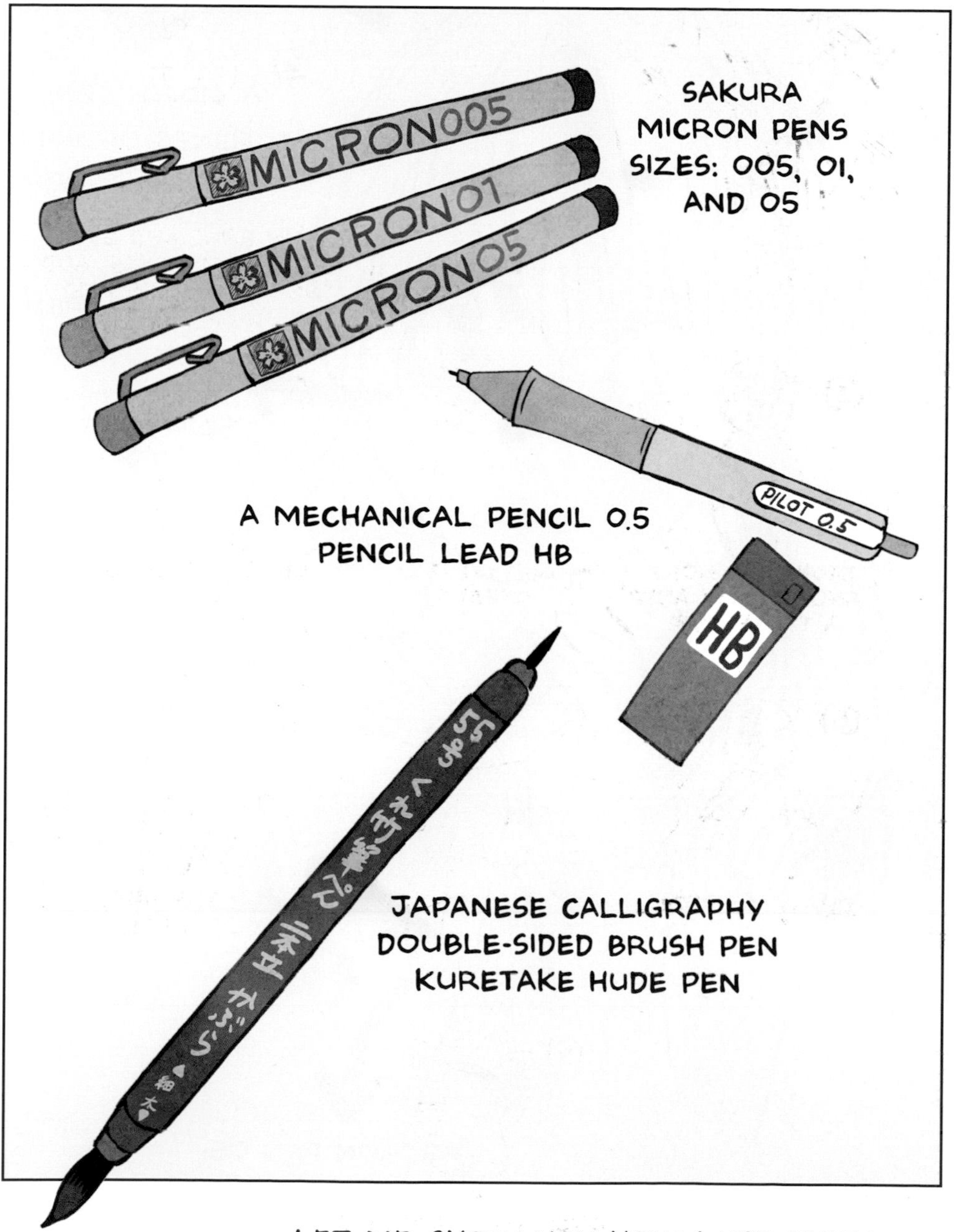
MICRON005
MICRON01
MICRON05
SAKURA MICRON PENS SIZES: 005, 01, AND 05
PILOT 0.5
HB
A MECHANICAL PENCIL 0.5
PENCIL LEAD HB
JAPANESE CALLIGRAPHY DOUBLE-SIDED BRUSH PEN KURETAKE HUDE PEN

LET ME SHOW YOU HOW I USE THEM...

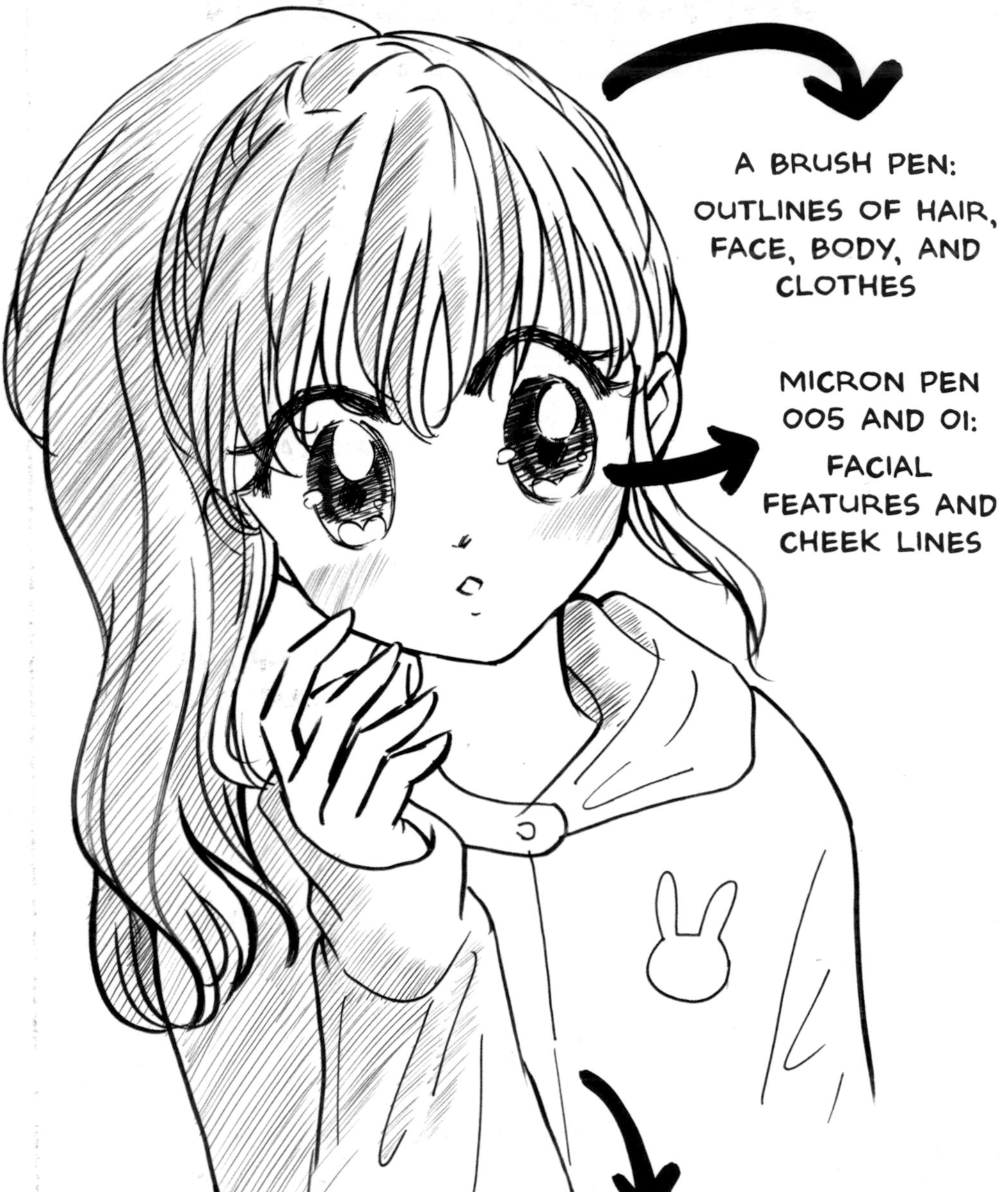
A BRUSH PEN:
OUTLINES OF HAIR, FACE, BODY, AND CLOTHES
MICRON PEN 005 AND 01:
FACIAL FEATURES AND CHEEK LINES
MICRON PEN 05:
FABRIC WRINKLES

JAPANESE LESSON WITH NICCO!

すごい
Su go i

SUgoi

IT MEANS
COOL AND AWESOME.

だいじょうぶ
Da i jo u bu

DAIjoubu

IT MEANS
I'M OKAY. IT'S OKAY.

ありがとう
A ri ga to u

ARIgatou

IT MEANS
THANK YOU.

ごめん
Go me nn

goMEnn

IT MEANS
I'M SORRY.

がんばって!
Ga nn ba tte

gannBAtte

IT MEANS
YOU CAN DO IT!

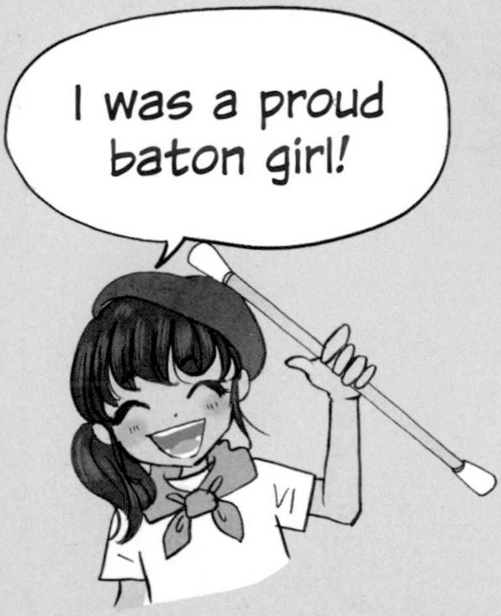
I was a proud baton girl!
VI

5TH GRADE

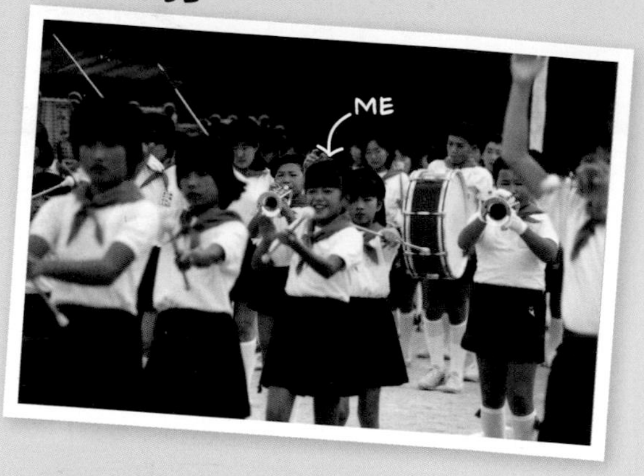
ME

6TH GRADE

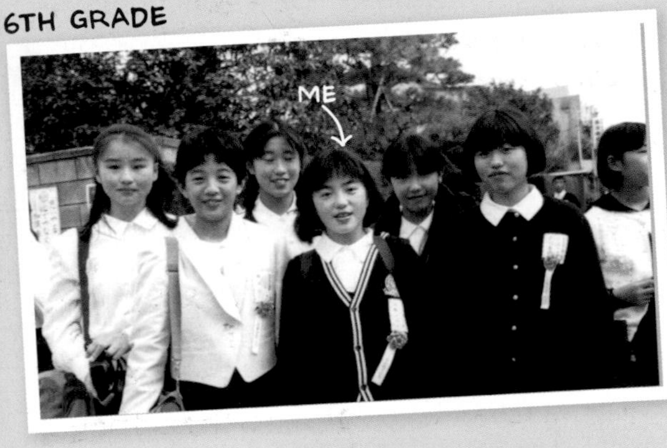
ME

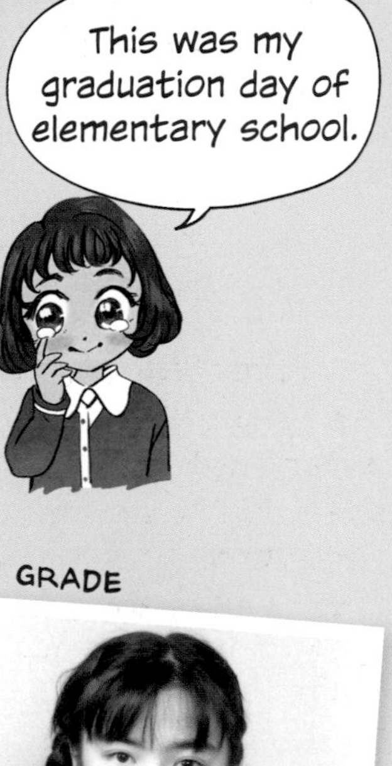
This was my graduation day of elementary school.

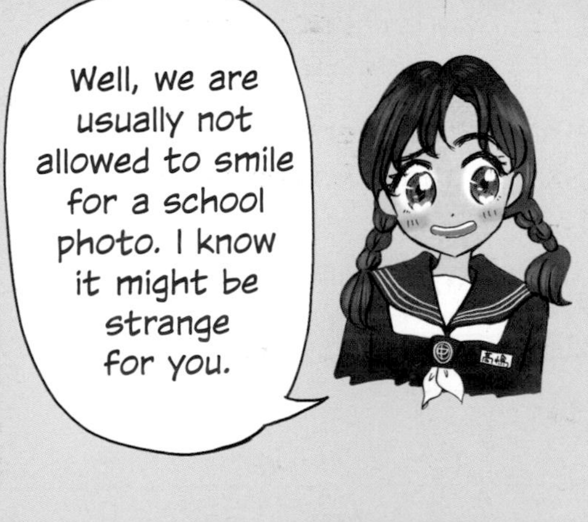
Well, we are usually not allowed to smile for a school photo. I know it might be strange for you.

9TH GRADE

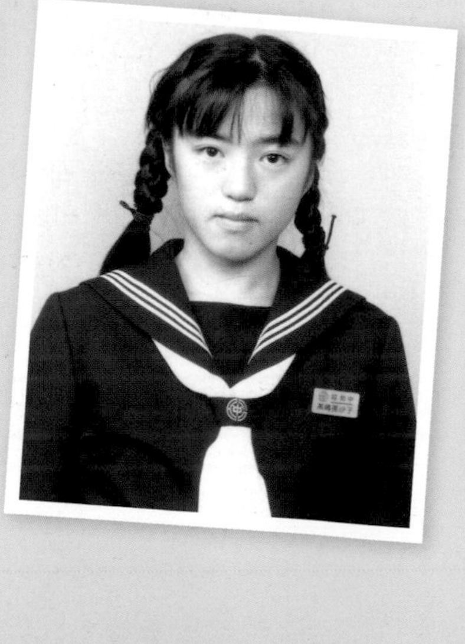

KONNICHIWA!

I'm a Japanese manga comic artist based in NYC.
Let me tell you, I'm still blown away by the fact
that I became an artist and live in America...
a country I'd dreamed of since I was just a kid in Japan!!!

I tried so many things and failed at so many things.
But I knew in my heart if I put my mind to it,
I could accomplish anything!

I started teaching manga at the Chapin School in NYC,
at museums and libraries, and with many private students.
After I got to know them better, they became my motivation.
Every kid has a story to tell. I want to make books that they
relate to. That's how the idea for *Bounce Back* was born!
I teamed up with my longtime friend/agent Janna Morishima.
We love the characters, the story, and most
importantly, my readers!

Besides making *Bounce Back*, I've been teaching
online manga lessons to kids who love kawaii manga
at my online community:

Learn Manga with Misako!

Find out more at www.misakorocks.com.

ARIGATO!

ACKNOWLEDGMENTS

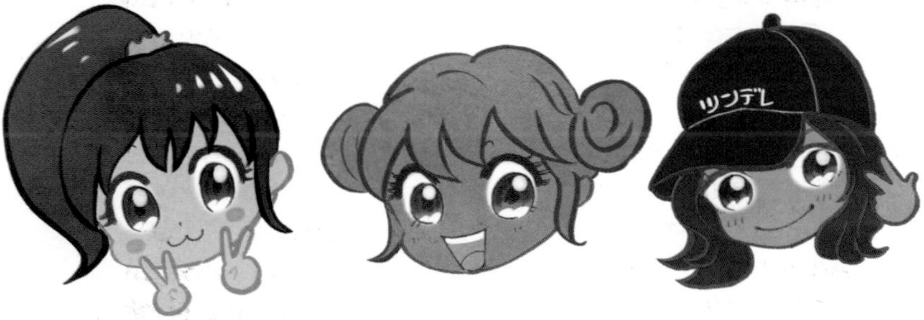
ツンデレ

SPECIAL THANKS TO . . .

Leyla Bayraktar as the model of Lilico
Luli Simonian as the model of Nala
Sofia
Mei

Feiwel & Friends, an imprint of Macmilan:
Jean Feiwel
Liz Szabla
Sharismar Rodriguez
Cindy De la Cruz
Foyinsi Adegbonmire
The marketing team

My agent/longtime friend, Janna Morishima

My husband, Christopher

MY BETA READERS:

Patricia Ackerson
Max Aibel
Leyla Bayraktar
Eve Craven
Lauren Cummings
Rebekah Fertel
Deborah Garza Garcia
Laura Gonzalez-Ortiz
Naomi Hairston
Adriana Griffin
Anna Leventon
Sofia Liu
Kaitlyn Loo
Léonie Malihot
Julieta Mariano

Sam Masson
Karo Miller
Ceci Murray
Nina Murray
Jamar Nicholas
Ava Osmond
Joe Pascullo
Yesha Patel
Michael Plociniak
Luli Simonian
Monica Shah
Laurie Taylor
Caydee Yarbrough
Kathy Yang

My members of Learn Manga with Misako

Misako Rocks! subscribers

My students at the Chapin School
My students at the Hewitt School
My private manga students

Staff of Anime NYC
Brooklyn Public librarians
Staff of Copic Marker
Staff of the Dalton School
Staff of Gochi Gang
Staff of NY Comic Con

New York Public librarians
Staff of Teen Bookfest
by the Bay
Librarians who I got
to know at TLA

All the librarians who invited me to their awesome schools

My family and friends in Japan

My readers!!!

BYE BYE!

THANK YOU FOR READING THIS FEIWEL & FRIENDS BOOK.
THE FRIENDS WHO MADE BOUNCE BACK POSSIBLE ARE:

Jean Feiwel, Publisher
Liz Szabla, Associate Publisher
Rich Deas, Senior Creative Director
Holly West, Senior Editor
Anna Roberto, Senior Editor
Kat Brzozowski, Senior Editor
Dawn Ryan, Executive Managing Editor
Kim Waymer, Senior Production Manager
Erin Siu, Associate Editor
Emily Settle, Associate Editor
Foyinsi Adegbonmire, Associate Editor
Rachel Diebel, Assistant Editor
Sharismar Rodriguez, Senior Art Director
Cindy De La Cruz, Associate Designer
Mandy Veloso, Senior Production Editor

Follow us on Facebook or visit us online at mackids.com.
Our books are friends for life.